WHITE
FIRE

Also by Douglas Preston and Lincoln Child

WHITE FIRE

DOUGLAS PRESTON
& LINCOLN CHILD

GRAND CENTRAL
PUBLISHING

NEW YORK   BOSTON

Grand Central Publishing
Hachette Book Group
237 Park Avenue
New York, NY 10017

HachetteBookGroup.com

Printed in the United States of America

BERRY

First Edition: November 2013

10 9 8 7 6 5 4 3 2 1

Grand Central Publishing is a division of Hachette Book Group, Inc.
The Grand Central Publishing name and logo is a trademark of Hachette Book Group, Inc.

The Hachette Speakers Bureau provides a wide range of authors for speaking events. To find out more, go to www.hachettespeakersbureau.com or call (866) 376-6591.

The publisher is not responsible for websites (or their content) that are not owned by the publisher.

Library of Congress Cataloging-in-Publication Data
Preston, Douglas J.
  White fire / Douglas Preston & Lincoln Child. — First edition.
    pages cm
  ISBN 978-1-4555-2583-6 (hardcover) — ISBN 978-1-4555-7623-4 (large print hardcover) — ISBN 978-1-61969-461-3 (audio download) — ISBN 978-1-4555-2585-0 (ebook)
  1. Pendergast, Aloysius (Fictitious character)—Fiction. I. Child, Lincoln, author. II. Title.
  PS3566.R3982W45 2013
  813'.54—dc23

               2013005680

ISBN 978-1-4555-5363-1 (international paperback)

Grateful acknowledgment to Conan Doyle Estate Ltd. for permission to use the Sherlock Holmes characters created by the late Sir Arthur Conan Doyle.

Lincoln Child dedicates this book to his daughter,
VERONICA

Douglas Preston dedicates this book to
DAVID MORRELL

WHITE
FIRE

PROLOGUE:
A TRUE STORY

August 30, 1889

The young doctor bid his wife good-bye on the Southsea platform, boarded the 4:15 express for London, and arrived three hours later at Victoria Station. Threading his way through the noise and bustle, he exited the station and flagged down a hansom cab.

"The Langham Hotel, if you please," he told the driver as he stepped up into the compartment, flushed with a feeling of anticipation.

He sat back in the worn leather seat as the cabbie started down Grosvenor Place. It was a fine late-summer evening, the rarest kind in London, with a dying light falling through the carriage-choked streets and sooty buildings, enchanting everything with a golden radiance. At half past seven the lamps were only just starting to be lit.

The doctor did not often get the chance to come up to London, and he looked out the window of the hansom cab with interest. As the driver turned right onto Piccadilly, he took in St. James's Palace and the Royal Academy, bathed in the afterglow of sunset. The crowds, noise, and stench of the city, so different from his home countryside, filled him with energy. Countless horseshoes rang out against the cobbles, and the sidewalks thronged with people from all walks of life: clerks, barristers, and swells rubbed shoulders with chimneysweeps, costermongers, and cat's-meat dealers.

At Piccadilly Circus, the cab took a sharp left onto Regent Street, passing Carnaby and the Oxford Circus before pulling up beneath the porte cochere of the Langham. It had been the first grand hotel erected in London, and it remained by far the most stylish. As he paid off the cabbie, the doctor glanced up at the ornate sandstone façade, with its French windows and balconies of wrought iron, its high gables and balustrades. He had a small interest in architecture, and he guessed the façade was a mixture of Beaux-Arts and North German Renaissance Revival.

As he entered the great portal, the sound of music reached him: a string quartet, hidden behind a screen of hothouse lilies, playing Schubert. He paused to take in the magnificent lobby, crowded with men seated in tall-backed chairs, reading freshly ironed copies of *The Times* and drinking port or sherry. Expensive cigar smoke hung in the air, mingling with the scent of flowers and ladies' perfume.

At the entrance to the dining room, he was met by a small, rather portly man in a broadcloth frock coat and dun-colored trousers, who approached him with brisk steps. "You must be Doyle," he said, taking his hand. He had a bright smile and a broad American accent. "I'm Joe Stoddart. So glad you could make it. Come in—the others just arrived."

The doctor followed Stoddart as the man made his way among linen-covered tables to a far corner of the room. The restaurant was even more opulent than the lobby, with wainscoting of olive-stained oak, a cream-colored frieze, and an ornate ceiling of raised plasterwork. Stoddart stopped beside a sumptuous table at which two men were already seated.

"Mr. William Gill, Mr. Oscar Wilde," Stoddart said. "Allow me to introduce Dr. A. Conan Doyle."

Gill—whom Doyle recognized as a well-known Irish MP—stood and bowed with good-humored gravitas. A heavy gold Albert watch chain swayed across his ample waistcoat. Wilde, who was in the midst of taking a glass of wine, dabbed at his rather full lips with a damask napkin and motioned Conan Doyle toward the empty chair beside him.

"Mr. Wilde was just entertaining us with the story of a tea party he attended this afternoon," Stoddart said as they took their seats.

"At Lady Featherstone's," Wilde said. "She was recently widowed. Poor dear—her hair has gone quite gold from grief."

"Oscar," Gill said with a laugh, "you really are wicked. Talking about a lady in such a manner."

Wilde waved his hand dismissively. "My lady would thank me. There is only one thing in the world worse than being talked about, and that is not being talked about." He spoke rapidly, in a low, mannered voice.

Doyle examined Wilde with a covert look. The man was striking. Almost gigantic in stature, he had unfashionably long hair parted in the middle and carelessly thrown back, his facial features heavy. His choice of clothing was of an eccentricity bordering on madness. He wore a suit of black velvet that fitted tightly to his large frame, the sleeves embroidered in flowery designs and puffed at the shoulders. Around his neck he had donned a narrow, three-rowed frill of the same brocaded material as the sleeves. He had the sartorial audacity to sport knee breeches, equally tight fitting, with stockings of black silk and slippers with grosgrain bows. A *boutonnière* of an immense white orchid drooped pendulously from his fawn-colored vest, looking as if it might dribble nectar at any moment. Heavy gold rings glittered on the fingers of his indolent hands. Despite the idiosyncrasy of his clothing, the expression on his face was mild, balancing the keen quality of his eager brown eyes. And for all this the man displayed a remarkable delicacy of feeling and tact. He spoke in a curious precision of statement, with a unique trick of small gestures to illustrate his meaning.

"You're most kind to be treating us out like this, Stoddart," Wilde was saying. "At the Langham, no less. I'd have been left to my own devices otherwise. It's not that I want for supper money, of course. It is only people who pay their bills who lack money, you see, and I never pay mine."

"I fear you'll find my motives are completely mercenary," Stoddart replied. "You might as well know that I'm over here to establish a British edition of *Lippincott's Monthly*."

"Philadelphia not large enough for you, then?" Gill asked.

Stoddart chuckled, then looked at Wilde and Doyle in turn. "It is my intention, before this meal is complete, to secure a new novel from each of you."

Hearing this, a current of excitement coursed through Doyle. In his telegram, Stoddart had been vague about the reasons for asking him to come to London for dinner, but the man was a well-known American publisher and this was exactly what Doyle had been hoping to hear. His medical practice had had a slower start than he would have liked. To fill the time, he'd taken to scribbling novels while waiting for patients. His last few had met with a small success. Stoddart was precisely the man he needed to further his progress. Doyle found him pleasant, even charming—for an American.

The dinner was proving delightful.

Gill was an amusing fellow, but Oscar Wilde was nothing short of remarkable. Doyle was captivated by the graceful wave of his hands; the languid expression that became quite animated when he delivered his peculiar anecdotes or amusing *bons mots*. It was almost magical, Doyle considered, that—thanks to modern technology—he'd been transported in a few short hours from a sleepy seacoast town to this elegant place, surrounded by an eminent editor, a member of Parliament, and the famous champion of aestheticism.

The dishes came thick and fast: potted shrimps, galantine of chicken, tripe fried in batter, *bisque de homard*. Red and yellow wine had appeared at the beginning of the evening, and the generous flow never ceased. It was astonishing how much money the Americans had; Stoddart was spending a fortune.

The timing was excellent. Doyle had just begun a new novel that Stoddart would surely like. His penultimate story, *Micah Clarke*, had been favorably reviewed, although his most recent novel, about a detective, based in part on his old university professor Joseph Bell, had been rather disappointingly received after appearing in *Beeton's Christmas Annual*...He forced himself back to the conversation at hand. Gill, the Irish MP, was questioning the veracity of the maxim that the good fortune of one's friends made one discontented.

Hearing this, a gleam appeared in Wilde's eyes. "The devil," he replied, "was once crossing the desert, and he came upon a spot where a number of fiends were tormenting a holy hermit. The man easily shook off their evil suggestions. The devil watched their failure and then stepped forward to give them a lesson. 'What you do is too crude,' said he. 'Permit me for one moment.' With that he whispered to the holy man, 'Your brother has just been made bishop of Alexandria.' A scowl of malignant jealousy at once clouded the serene face of the hermit. 'That,' said the devil to his imps, 'is the sort of thing which I should recommend.'"

Stoddart and Gill laughed heartily, then began to fall into an argument about politics. Wilde turned to Doyle. "You must tell me," he said. "Will you do a book for Stoddart?"

"I was rather thinking I would. The fact is, I've started work on a new novel already. I was thinking of calling it *A Tangled Skein*, or perhaps *The Sign of the Four*."

Wilde pressed his hands together in delight. "My dear fellow, that's wonderful news. I certainly hope it will be another Holmes story."

Doyle looked at him in surprise. "You mean to say you've read *A Study in Scarlet*?"

"I didn't read it, dear boy. I *devoured* it." Reaching into his vest, Wilde pulled out a copy of the Ward Lock & Co. edition of the book, with its vaguely Oriental lettering so in vogue. "I even looked through it again when I heard you would be dining with us this evening."

"You're very kind," Conan Doyle said, at a loss for a better reply. He found himself surprised and gratified that the prince of English decadence would enjoy a humble detective novel.

"I feel you have the makings of a great character in Holmes. But..." And here Wilde stopped.

"Yes?" Doyle said.

"What I found most remarkable was the *credibility* of the thing. The details of the police work, Holmes's inquiries, were enlightening. I have much to learn from you in this way. You see, between me and life there is a mist of words always. I throw probability out of the window for the sake of a phrase, and the chance of an epigram makes me desert truth. You don't share that failing. And yet...and yet I believe you could do more with this Holmes of yours."

"I would be much obliged if you'd explain," Doyle said.

Wilde took a sip of wine. "If he's to be a truly great detective, a great *persona*, he should be more eccentric. The world doesn't need another Sergeant Cuff or Inspector Dupin. No—make his humanity aspire to the greatness of his art." He paused a moment, thinking, idly stroking the orchid that drooped from his buttonhole. "In *Scarlet*, you call Watson 'extremely lazy.' In my opinion, you should allow the virtues of dissipation and idleness to be bestowed on your hero, not his errand boy. And make Holmes more reserved. Don't have *delight shining on his features*, or have him *barking with laughter*."

Doyle colored, recognizing the infelicitous phraseology.

"You must confer on him a vice," Wilde went on. "Virtuous people are so banal; I simply cannot bear them." He paused again. "Not just a vice, Doyle—give him a *weakness*. Let me think—ah, yes! I recall." He opened his copy of *A Study in Scarlet*, leafed quickly through the pages, found a passage, and began to quote Dr. Watson: "'I might have suspected him of being addicted to the use of some narcotic, had not the temperance and cleanliness of his whole life forbidden such a notion.'" He returned the book to his vest pocket. "There—you had the perfect weakness in your hands, but you let it go. Pluck it up again! Deliver Holmes into the clutches of some addiction. Opium, say. But no: opium is so dreadfully common these days, it's become quite overrun by the lower classes." Suddenly Wilde snapped his fingers. "I have it! Cocaine hydrochloride. There's a novel and elegant vice for you."

"Cocaine," Doyle repeated a little uncertainly. As a doctor, he had sometimes prescribed a seven percent solution to patients suffering from exhaustion or depression, but the idea of making Holmes an addict was, on the face of it, quite absurd. Although Doyle had asked for Wilde's opinion, he found himself slightly put out at actually receiving criticism from the man. Across the table, the good-humored argument between Stoddart and Gill continued.

The aesthete took another sip of wine and tossed his hair back.

"And what about you?" Doyle asked. "Will you do a book for Stoddart?"

"I shall. And it shall be under your influence—or rather, Holmes's influence—that I will proceed. Do you know, I've always believed there's no such thing as a moral or immoral book. Books are well written or badly written—that's all. But I find myself taken with the idea of writing a book about both art *and* morals. I'm planning to call it *The Picture of Dorian Gray*. And do you know, I believe it will be rather a ghastly story. Not a ghost story, exactly, but one in which the protagonist comes to a beastly end. The kind of story one wishes to read by daylight—not lamplight."

"Such a story doesn't seem to be exactly in your line."

Wilde looked at Doyle with something like amusement. "Indeed? Did you think that—as one who would happily sacrifice himself on the pyre of aestheticism—I do not recognize the face of horror when I stare into it? Let me tell you: the shudder of fear is as sensual as the shudder of pleasure, if not more so." He underscored this with another wave of his hand. "Besides, I was once told a story so dreadful, so distressing in its particulars and in the extent of its evil, that now I truly believe nothing I hear could ever frighten me again."

"How interesting," Doyle replied a little absently, still mulling over the criticism of Holmes.

Wilde regarded him, a small smile forming on his large, pale features. "Would you care to hear it? It is not for the faint of heart."

The way Wilde phrased this, it sounded like a challenge. "By all means."

"It was told to me during my lecture tour of America a few years back. On my way to San Francisco, I stopped at a rather squalid yet picturesque mining camp known as Roaring Fork. I gave my lecture at the bottom of their mine, and it was frightfully well received by the good gentlemen of the camp. After my lecture, one of the miners approached me, an elderly chap somewhat the worse—or, perhaps, the better—for drink. He took me aside, said he'd enjoyed my story so much that he had one of his own to share with me."

Wilde paused, wetting his thick, red lips with a delicate sip of wine. "Here, lean in a little closer, that's a good fellow, and I'll tell it you exactly as it was told to me..."

Ten minutes later, a diner at the restaurant in the Langham Hotel would have been surprised to note—amid the susurrus of genteel conversation and the tinkle of cutlery—a young man in the dress of a country doctor abruptly rise from his table, very pale. Knocking over his chair in his agitation, one hand to his forehead, the man staggered from the room, nearly upsetting a waiter's tray of delicacies. And as he vanished in the direction of the gentlemen's toilet area, his face displayed a perfect expression of revulsion and horror.

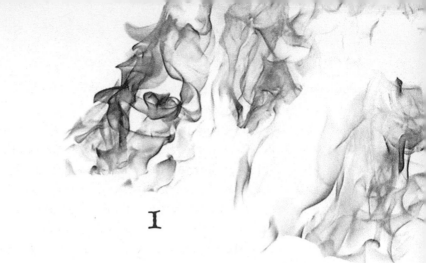

I

Present Day

Corrie Swanson stepped into the ladies' room for the third time to check how she looked. A lot had changed with her since she'd transferred to the John Jay College of Criminal Justice at the beginning of her sophomore year. John Jay was a buttoned-down place. She had resisted it for a while, but finally realized she needed to grow up and play the game of life instead of acting the rebel forever. Gone were the purple hair, the piercings, the black leather jacket, the dark eye shadow and other Goth accoutrements. There was nothing she could do about the Möbius strip tattoo on the nape of her neck, beyond combing her hair back and wearing high collars. But someday, she realized, that would have to go as well.

If she was going to play the game, she was going to play it well.

Unfortunately, her personal transformation had taken place too late for her advisor, a former NYPD cop who had gone back to school and turned professor. She got the feeling his first impression of her had been that of a perp, and nothing she'd done in the year since she'd first met him had erased that. Clearly, he had it in for her. He had already rejected her first proposal for the Rosewell thesis, which involved a trip to Chile to do a perimortem analysis on skeletal remains discovered in a mass grave of Communist peasants murdered by the

Pinochet regime back in the 1970s. Too far away, he said, too expensive for a research project, and besides it was old history. When Corrie replied that this was the point—these were old graves, requiring specialized forensic techniques—he said something about not involving herself in foreign political controversies, especially Communist ones.

Now she had another idea for her thesis, an even better one, and she was willing to do almost anything to see it happen.

Examining herself in the mirror, she rearranged a few strands of hair, touched up her conservative lipstick, adjusted her gray worsted suit jacket, and gave her nose a quick powdering. She hardly recognized herself; God, she might even be mistaken for a Young Republican. So much the better.

She exited the ladies' room and walked briskly down the hall, her conservative pumps clicking professionally against the hard linoleum. Her advisor's door was shut, as usual, and she gave it a brisk, self-confident rap. A voice inside said, "Come in."

She entered. The office was, as always, neat as a pin, the books and journals all lined up flush with the edges of the bookshelves, the comfortable, masculine leather furniture providing a cozy air. Professor Greg Carbone sat behind his large desk, its acreage of burnished mahogany unbroken by books, papers, family photographs, or knick-knacks.

"Good morning, Corrie," Carbone said, rising and buttoning his blue serge suit. "Please sit down."

"Thank you, Professor." She knew he liked to be called that. Woe to the student who called him Mister or, worse, Greg.

He settled back down as she did. Carbone was a strikingly handsome man with salt-and-pepper hair, wonderful teeth, trim and fit, a good dresser, articulate, soft-spoken, intelligent, and successful. Everything he did, he did well, and as a result he was an accomplished asshole indeed.

"Well, Corrie," Carbone began, "you are looking well today."

"Thank you, Dr. Carbone."

"I'm excited to hear about your new idea."

"Thanks." Corrie opened her briefcase (no backpacks at John Jay) and took out a manila file folder, placing it on her knee. "I'm sure you've been reading about the archaeological investigation going on down in City Hall Park. Next to the location of the old prison known as the Tombs."

"Tell me about it."

"The parks department has been excavating a small cemetery of executed criminals to make way for a new subway entrance."

"Ah yes, I did read about that," said Carbone.

"The cemetery was operational from 1858 to 1865. After 1865, all execution burials were moved to Hart Island and remain unavailable."

A slow nod from Carbone. He looked interested; she felt encouraged.

"I think this would make for a great opportunity to do an osteological study of those skeletons—to see if severe childhood malnourishment, which as you know leaves osteological markers, might correlate with later criminal behavior."

Another nod from Carbone.

"I've got it all outlined here." She laid a proposal on the table. "Hypotheses, methodology, control group, observations, and analysis."

Carbone laid a hand on the document, drew it toward himself, opened it, and began perusing.

"There are a number of reasons why this is a great opportunity," she went on. "First, the city has good records on most of these executed criminals—names, rap sheets, and trial records. Those who were orphans raised in the Five Points House of Industry—about half a dozen—also have some childhood records. They were all executed in the same way—hanging—so the cause of death is identical. And the cemetery was used for only seven years, so all the remains come from roughly the same time period."

She paused. Carbone was slowly turning over the pages, one after another, apparently reading. There was no way to tell what he was thinking; his face was a blank.

"I made a few inquiries, and it seems the parks department would be open to having a John Jay student examine the remains."

The slow turning of the pages paused. "You already contacted them?"

"Yes. Just a feeler—"

"A feeler...You contacted another city agency without seeking prior permission?"

Uh-oh. "Obviously I didn't want to bring you a project that might get shot down later by outside authorities. Um, was that wrong?"

A long silence, and then: "Did you not read your undergraduate handbook?"

Corrie was seized with apprehension. She had in fact read it—when she'd been admitted. But that was over a year ago. "Not recently."

"The handbook is quite clear. Undergraduate students are not to engage other city departments except through official channels. This is because we're a city institution, as you know, a senior college of the City University of New York." He said this mildly, almost kindly.

"I...Well, I'm sorry, I didn't recall that from the handbook." She swallowed, feeling a rising panic—and anger. This was such unbelievable bullshit. But she forced herself to keep her cool. "It was just a couple of phone calls, nothing official."

A nod. "I'm sure you didn't *deliberately* violate university regulations." He began turning the pages again, slowly, one after the other, not looking up at her. "But in any case I find other problems with this thesis proposal of yours."

"Yes?" Corrie felt sick.

"This idea that malnourishment leads to a life of crime...It's an old idea—and an unconvincing one."

"Well, it seems to me worth testing."

"Back then, almost everyone was malnourished. But not everyone became a criminal. And the idea is redolent of...how shall I put it?...of a certain philosophy that crime in general can be traced to unfortunate experiences in a person's childhood."

"But malnourishment—severe malnourishment—might cause neurological changes, actual damage. That isn't philosophy; that's science."

Carbone held up her proposal. "I can already predict the outcome: you'll discover that these executed criminals *were* malnourished as children. The *real* question is why, of all those hungry children, only a small percentage went on to commit capital crimes. And your research plan does not address that. I'm sorry, this won't fly. Not at all."

And, opening his fingers, he let her document drop gently to his desk.

2

The famous—some might say infamous—"Red Museum" at the John Jay College of Criminal Justice had started as a simple collection of old investigative files, physical evidence, prisoners' property, and memorabilia that, almost a hundred years ago, had been put into a display case in a hall at the old police academy. Since then, it had grown into one of the country's largest and best collections of criminal memorabilia. The crème de la crème of the collection was on display in a sleek new exhibition hall in the college's Skidmore, Owings & Merrill building on Tenth Avenue. The rest of the collection—vast rotting archives and moldering evidence from long-ago crimes—remained squirreled away in the hideous basement of the old police academy building on East Twentieth Street.

Early on at John Jay, Corrie had discovered this archive. It was pure gold—once she'd made friends with the archivist and figured out her way around the disorganized drawers and heaping shelves of stuff. She had been to the Red Museum archives many times in search of topics for papers and projects, most recently in her hunt for a topic for her Rosewell thesis. She had spent a great deal of time in the old unsolved-case files—those cold cases so ancient that all involved (including the possible perps) had definitely and positively died.

Corrie Swanson found herself in a creaking elevator, descending into the basement, one day after the meeting with her advisor. She was on a desperate mission to find a new thesis topic before it became too late to complete the approval process. It was mid-November already, and she was hoping to spend the winter break researching and writing up the thesis. She was on a partial scholarship, but Agent Pendergast had been making up the difference in tuition, and she was absolutely determined not to take one penny more from him than necessary. If her thesis won the Rosewell Prize, with its twenty-thousand-dollar grant, she wouldn't have to.

The elevator doors opened to a familiar smell: a mixture of dust and acidifying paper, underlain by an odor of rodent urine. She crossed the hall to a pair of dented metal doors, graced with a sign that said RED MUSEUM ARCHIVES, and pressed the bell. An unintelligible rasp came out of the antiquated speaker; she gave her name, and a buzzer sounded to let her in.

"Corrie Swanson? How good to see you again!" came the hoarse voice of the archivist, Willard Bloom, as he rose from a desk in a pool of light, guarding the recesses of the storage room stretching off into the blackness behind him. He presented a rather cadaverous figure, stick-thin, with longish gray hair, yet underneath was charming and grandfatherly. She didn't mind the fact that his eyes often wandered over various parts of her anatomy when he thought she wasn't paying attention.

Bloom came around with a veined hand extended, which she took. The hand was surprisingly hot, and it gave her a bit of a start.

"Come, sit down. Have some tea."

Some chairs had been set around the front of his desk, with a coffee table and, to the side, a battered cabinet with a hot plate, kettle, and teapot, an informal seating area in the midst of dust and darkness. Corrie flopped into a chair, setting her briefcase down with a thump next to her. "Ugh," she said.

Bloom raised his eyebrows in mute inquiry.

"It's Carbone. Once again he rejected my thesis idea. Now I have to start all over again."

"Carbone," Bloom said in his high-pitched voice, "is a well-known ass."

This piqued her interest. "You know him?"

"I know everyone who comes down here. Carbone! Always fussing about getting dust on his Ralph Lauren suits, wanting me to play step-n-fetchit. As a result, I can never find anything for him, poor man...You know the real reason he keeps rejecting your thesis ideas, right?"

"I figure it's because I'm a junior."

Bloom put a finger to his nose and gave her a knowing nod. "Exactly. And Carbone is old school, a stickler for protocol."

Corrie had been afraid of this. The Rosewell Prize for the year's outstanding thesis was hugely coveted at John Jay. Its winners were often senior valedictorians, who went on to highly successful law enforcement careers. As far as she knew, it had never been won by a junior—in fact, juniors were quietly discouraged from submitting theses. But there was no rule against it, and Corrie refused to be deterred by such bureaucratic baggage.

Bloom held up the pot with a yellow-toothed smile. "Tea?"

She looked at the revolting teapot, which did not appear to have been washed in a decade. "That's a teapot? I thought it was a murder weapon. You know, loaded with arsenic and ready to go."

"Always ready with a riposte. But surely you know most poisoners are women? If I were a murderer, I'd want to see my victim's blood." He poured out the tea. "So Carbone rejected your idea. Surprise, surprise. What's plan B?"

"That *was* my plan B. I was hoping you might be able to give me some fresh ideas."

Bloom sat back in his chair and sipped noisily from his cup. "Let's see. As I recall, you're majoring in forensic osteology, are you not? What, exactly, are you looking for?"

"I need to examine some human skeletons that show antemortem or perimortem damage. Got any case files that might point to something like that?"

"Hmm." His battered face screwed up in concentration.

"The problem is, it's hard to come by accessible human remains. Unless I go prehistoric. But that opens up a whole other can of worms with Native American sensitivities. And I want remains for which there are good written records. *Historic* remains."

Bloom sucked down another goodly portion of tea, a thoughtful expression on his face. "Bones. Ante- or perimortem damage. Historic. Good records. Accessible." He closed his eyes, the lids so dark and veiny they looked like he might have been punched. Corrie waited, listening to the ticking sounds in the archives, the faint sound of forced air, and a pattering noise she feared was probably rats.

The eyes sprang open again. "Just thought of something. Ever heard of the Baker Street Irregulars?"

"No."

"It's a very exclusive club of Sherlock Holmes devotees. They have a dinner in New York every year, and they publish all sorts of Holmesian scholarship, all the while pretending that Holmes was a real person. Well, one of these fellows died a few years back, and his widow, not knowing what else to do, shipped his entire collection of Sherlockiana to us. Perhaps she didn't know that Holmes was a *fictional* detective, and we only deal in *nonfiction* here. At any rate, I've been dipping into it now and then. Lot of rubbish, mostly. But there was a copy in there of Doyle's diary—just a photocopy, unfortunately—and it made entertaining reading for an old man stuck in a thankless job in a dusty archive."

"And what did you find, exactly?"

"There was something in there about a man-eating bear."

Corrie frowned. "A man-eating bear? I'm not sure—"

"Come with me."

Bloom went to a bank of switches and struck them all with the flat of his palm, turning the archives into a flickering sea of fluorescent light. Corrie fancied she could hear the rats scurrying and squealing away as the tubes blinked on, one aisle after another.

She followed the archivist as he made his way down the long rows between dusty shelving and wooden cabinets with yellowed, handwritten labels, finally reaching an area in the back where library tables were piled with cardboard boxes. Three large boxes sat together, labeled BSI. Bloom went to one box, rummaged through it, hauled out an expandable folder, blew off the dust, and began sorting through the papers.

"Here we are." He held up an old photocopy. "Doyle's diary. Properly, of course, the man should be referred to as 'Conan Doyle,' but that's such a mouthful, isn't it?" In the dim light, he flipped through the pages, then began to read aloud:

> …I was in London on literary business. Stoddart, the American, proved to be an excellent fellow, and had two others to dinner. They were Gill, a very entertaining Irish MP, and Oscar Wilde…

He paused, his voice dying into a mumble as he passed over some material, then rising again as he reached a passage he deemed important.

> …The highlight of the evening, if I may call it that, was Wilde's account of his lecture tour in America. Hard to believe, perhaps, but the famed champion of aestheticism attracted huge interest in America, especially in the West, where in one place a group of uncouth miners gave him a standing ovation…

Corrie began to fidget. She had so little time to waste. She cleared her throat. "I'm not sure Oscar Wilde and Sherlock Holmes are quite what I'm looking for," she said politely. But Bloom continued to read, holding up his finger for attention, his reedy voice riding over her objections.

> …Towards the close of the evening, Wilde, who had indulged a great deal in Stoddart's excellent claret, told me, sotto voce, a story of such singular horror, of such grotesque hideousness, that I had to excuse myself from the table. The story involved the killing and eating of eleven miners some years previous, purportedly by a monstrous "grizzled bear" in a mining camp

called Roaring Fork. The actual details are so abhorrent I cannot bring myself to commit them to paper at this time, although the impression left on my mind was indelible and one that will, unfortunately, follow me to the grave.

He paused, taking a breath. "And there you have it. Eleven corpses, eaten by a grizzly bear. In Roaring Fork, no less."

"Roaring Fork? You mean the glitzy ski resort in Colorado?"

"The very one. It started life as a silver boomtown."

"When was this?"

"Wilde was there in 1881. So this business with the man-eating bear probably took place in the 1870s."

She shook her head. "And how am I supposed to turn this into a thesis?"

"Nearly a dozen skeletons, eaten by a bear? Surely they will display exquisite perimortem damage—tooth and claw marks, gnawing, crunching, biting, scraping, worrying." Bloom spoke these words with a kind of relish.

"I'm studying forensic criminology, not forensic bearology."

"Ah, but you know from your studies that many, if not most, skeletal remains from murder victims show animal damage. You should see the files we have on that. It can be very difficult to tell the difference between animal marks and those left by the murderer. As far as I can recall, no one has done a comprehensive study of perimortem bone damage of this kind. It would be a most original contribution to forensic science."

Very true, Corrie thought, surprised at Bloom's insight. *And come to think of it, what a fabulous and original subject for a thesis.*

Bloom went on. "I have little doubt at least some of the poor miners were buried in the historic Roaring Fork cemetery."

"See, that's a problem. I can't go digging up some historic cemetery looking for bear victims."

A yellow smile appeared on Bloom's face. "My dear Corrie, the only reason I brought this up at all was because of the fascinating little article in the *Times* this very morning! Didn't you see it?"

"No."

"The original 'boot hill' of Roaring Fork is now a stack of coffins in a ski equipment warehouse. You see, they're relocating the cemetery on account of development." He looked at her and winked, his smile broadening.

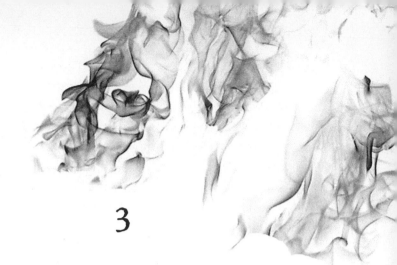

3

Along the Cote d'Azur in the South of France, on a bluff atop Cap Ferrat, a man in a black suit, surrounded by bougainvillea, rested on a stone balcony in the afternoon sun. It was warm for the time of year, and the sunlight gilded the lemon trees that crowded the balcony and descended the steep hill to the Mediterranean, ending in a strip of deserted white beach. Beyond could be seen a field of yachts at anchor, the rocky terminus of the cape topped by an ancient castle, behind which ran the blue horizon.

The man reclined in a chaise longue covered with silk damask, beside a small table on which sat a salver. His silvery eyes were half closed. Four items sat on the tray: a copy of Spenser's *Faerie Queene*; a small glass of pastis; a beaker of water; and a single unopened letter. The salver had been brought out two hours ago by a manservant, who now awaited further orders in the shade of the portico. The man who had rented the villa rarely received mail. A few letters bore the return address of one Miss Constance Greene in New York; the rest came from what appeared to be an exclusive boarding school in Switzerland.

As time passed, the manservant began to wonder whether the sickly gentleman who had hired him at excessively high wages might have suffered a heart attack—so motionless had he been these past few hours. But no—a languid hand now moved, reaching for the beaker of water. It poured a small measure into the glass of pastis, turning the yellow liquid a cloudy yellowish green. The man then raised the glass and took a long, slow drink before replacing it on the tray.

Stillness returned, and the shadows of afternoon grew longer. More time passed. The hand moved again, as if in slow motion, again raising the cut-crystal glass to pale lips, taking another long, lingering sip of the liqueur. He then picked up the book of poetry. More silence as the man appeared to read, turning the pages at long intervals, one after another. The afternoon light blazed its last glory on the façade of the villa. From below, the sounds of life filtered upward: a distant clash of voices raised in argument, the throbbing of a yacht as it moved in the bay, birds chattering among the trees, the faint sound of a piano playing Hanon.

And now the man in the black suit closed the book of poetry, laid it upon the salver, and turned his attention to the letter. Still moving as if underwater, he plucked it up and, with a long, polished nail, slit it open, unfolded it, and began to read.

Nov. 27

Dear Aloysius,

I'm mailing this to you c/o Proctor, in hopes he'll pass it along. I know you're still traveling and probably don't want to be bothered, but you've been gone almost a year and I figured maybe you were about ready to come home. Aren't you itching by now to end your leave of absence from the FBI and start solving murders again? And anyway, I just had to tell you about my thesis project. Believe it or not, I'm off to Roaring Fork, Colorado!

I got the most amazing idea for a thesis. I'll try to be brief because I know how impatient you are, but to explain I do have to go into a little history. In 1873, silver was discovered in the mountains over the Continental Divide from Leadville, Colorado. A mining camp sprang up in the valley, called Roaring Fork after the river flowing through it, and the surrounding mountains became dotted with claims. In May of 1876, a rogue grizzly bear killed and ate a miner at a remote claim in the mountains—and for the rest of the summer the bear totally terrorized the area. The town sent out a number of hunting teams to track and kill it, to no avail, as the mountains were extremely rugged and remote. By the time the rampage stopped, eleven miners had been mauled and horribly eaten. It was a big deal at the time, with a lot of local newspaper articles (that's how I learned these details), sheriff's reports, and such. But Roaring Fork was remote and the story died pretty quickly once the killings stopped.

The miners were buried in the Roaring Fork cemetery, and their fate was pretty much forgotten. The mines closed up, Roaring Fork dwindled in population, and in time it almost became a ghost town. Then, in 1946, it was bought up by investors and turned into a ski resort—and now of course it's one of the fanciest resorts in the world—average home price over four million!

So that's the history. This fall, the original Roaring Fork cemetery was dug up to make way for development. All the remains are now stacked in an old equipment shed high up on the ski slopes while everyone argues about what to do with them. A hundred and thirty coffins—of which eight are the remains of miners killed by the grizzly. (The other three were either lost or never recovered.)

Which brings me to my thesis topic:

A Comprehensive Analysis of Perimortem Trauma in the Skeletons of Eight Miners Killed by a Grizzly Bear, from a Historic Colorado Cemetery

There has never been a large-scale study of perimortem trauma on human bones inflicted by a large carnivore. Ever! You see, it isn't often that people are eaten by animals. Mine will be the first!!

My thesis advisor, Prof. Greg Carbone, rejected my two

earlier topics, and I'm glad the bastard did, if you'll excuse my language. He would have rejected this one, too, for reasons I won't bore you with, but I decided to take a page out of your book. I got my sweaty hands on Carbone's personnel file. I knew the man was too perfect to be real. Some years back, he'd been boning an undergraduate student in one of his classes—and then was dumb enough to flunk her when she broke it off. So she complained, not about the sex, but the bad grade. No laws were broken (the girl was twenty), but the scumbag gave her an F when she deserved an A. It was all hushed up, the girl got her A and had her tuition "refunded" for the year—a way of paying her off without calling it that, no doubt.

You can find anybody these days, so I tracked her down and gave her a call. Her name's Molly Denton and she's now a cop in Worcester, Mass.—a decorated lieutenant in the homicide department, no less. Boy, did she give me the lowdown on my advisor! So I went into the meeting with Carbone armed with a couple of nukes, just in case.

I wish you'd been there. It was beautiful. Before I even got into my new thesis idea, I mentioned all nice and polite that we had a mutual acquaintance: Molly Denton. And I gave him a big fat smirk, just to make sure he got the message. He went all pale. He couldn't wait to change the subject back to my thesis, wanted to hear about it, listened attentively, instantly agreed it was the most marvelous thesis proposal he'd heard in years, and promised he would personally shepherd it through the faculty committee. And then—this is the best part—he suggested I leave "as soon as possible" for Roaring Fork. The guy was butter in my hands.

Winter break just started, and so I'm off to Roaring Fork in two days! Wish me well. And if you feel like it, write me back c/o your pal Proctor, who will have my forwarding address as soon as I know it.

Love,
Corrie

P.S. I almost forgot to tell you one of the best things about my thesis idea. Believe it or not, I first learned about the grizzly bear killings from the diary of Arthur Conan Doyle! Doyle heard it himself from no less than Oscar Wilde at a dinner party in London in 1889. It seems Wilde was a collector of horrible stories, and he'd picked up this one on a lecture tour of the American West.

The manservant, standing in the shadows, watched his peculiar employer finish reading the letter. The long, white fingers seemed to droop, and the letter slid to the table, as if discarded. As the hand moved to pick up the glass of pastis, the evening breeze gently lofted the papers and wafted them over the railing of the balcony, over the tops of the lemon trees; then they went gliding off into blue space, fluttering and turning aimlessly until they had vanished from view, unseen, unnoticed, and completely disregarded by the pale man in the black suit, sitting on a lonely balcony high above the sea.

4

The Roaring Fork Police Department was located in a classic, Old West–style Victorian red-brick building, impossibly picturesque, that stood in a green park against a backdrop of magnificent snowy peaks. In front of it was a twelve-foot statue of Lady Justice, covered with snow, and—rather oddly—not wearing the traditional blindfold.

Corrie Swanson had loaded up with books about Roaring Fork and she had read all about this courthouse, which was noted for the number of famous defendants who had passed through its doors, from Hunter S. Thompson to serial killer Ted Bundy. Roaring Fork, she knew, was quite a resort. It had the most expensive real estate in the country. This proved to be annoying in the extreme, as she found herself forced to stay in a town called Basalt, eighteen winding miles down Route 82, in a crappy Cloud Nine Motel, with cardboard walls and an itchy bed, at the stunning price of $109 a night. It was the first day of December, and ski season was really ramping up. From her work-study jobs at John Jay—and money left over from the wad Agent Pendergast had pressed on her a year back, when he'd sent her away to stay with her father during a bad time—she had saved up almost four thousand dollars. But at a hundred and nine dollars a night, plus meals, plus the ridiculous thirty-nine bucks a day she was paying for a Rent-a-Junker, she was going to burn through that pretty fast.

In short, she had no time to waste.

The problem was, in her eagerness to get her thesis approved, she had told a little lie. Well, maybe it wasn't such a little lie. She had told Carbone and the faculty committee that she'd gotten permission to examine the remains: carte blanche access. The truth was, her several emails to the chief of the Roaring Fork Police Department, whom she determined had the power to grant her access, had gone unanswered, and her phone calls had not been returned. Not that anyone had been rude to her—it was just a sort of benign neglect.

By marching into the police station herself the day before, she'd finally finagled an appointment with Chief Stanley Morris. Now she entered the building and approached the front desk. To her surprise it was manned, not by a burly cop, but by a girl who looked to be even younger than Corrie herself. She was quite pretty, with a creamy complexion, dark eyes, and shoulder-length blond hair.

Corrie walked up to her, and the girl smiled.

"Are you, uh, a policeman?" Corrie asked.

The girl laughed and shook her head. "Not yet."

"What, then—the receptionist?"

The girl shook her head again. "I'm interning at the station over the winter vacation. Today just happens to be my day to man the reception desk." She paused. "I would like to get into law enforcement someday."

"That makes two of us. I'm a student at John Jay."

The girl's eyes widened. "No kidding!"

Corrie extended her hand. "Corrie Swanson."

The girl shook it. "Jenny Baker."

"I have an appointment with Chief Morris."

"Oh, yes." Jenny consulted an appointment book. "He's expecting you. Go right in."

"Thanks." This was a good beginning. Corrie tried to get her nervousness under control and not think about what would happen if the chief denied her access to the remains. At the very least, her thesis depended on it. And she had already spent a fortune getting here, nonrefundable airplane tickets and all.

The door to the chief's office was open, and as she entered the man rose from behind his desk and came around it, extending a hand. She was startled by his appearance: a small, rotund, cheerful-looking man with a beaming face, bald pate, and rumpled uniform. The office reflected the impression of informality, with its arrangement of old, comfortable leather furniture and a desk pleasantly disheveled with papers, books, and family photographs.

The chief ushered her over to a little sitting area in one corner, where an elderly secretary brought in a tray with paper coffee cups, sugar, and cream. Corrie, who had arrived the day before yesterday and was still feeling a bit jet-lagged, helped herself, refraining from her usual four teaspoons of sugar only to see Chief Morris put no less than five into his own cup.

"Well," Morris said, leaning back, "sounds like you've got a very interesting project going here."

"Thank you," Corrie said. "And thanks for meeting me on such short notice."

"I've always been fascinated with Roaring Fork's past. The grizzly bear killings are part of local lore, at least for those of us who know the history. So few do these days."

"This research project presents an almost perfect opportunity," Corrie said, launching into her carefully memorized talking points. "It's a real chance to advance the science of forensic criminology." She waxed enthusiastic as Chief Morris listened attentively, his chin resting pensively on one soft hand. Corrie touched on all the salient points: how her project would surely garner national press attention and reflect well on the Roaring Fork Police Department; how much John Jay—the nation's premier law enforcement college—would appreciate his cooperation; how she would of course work closely with him and follow whatever rules were laid down. She went into a revisionist version of her own story: how she'd wanted to be a cop all her life; how she'd won a scholarship to John Jay; how hard she'd worked—and then she concluded by enthusing over how much she admired his own position, how ideal it was having the opportunity to work in such an interesting and beautiful community. She laid it on as thick as she dared, and she could see, with satisfaction, that he was responding with nods, smiles, and various noises of approval.

When she was done, she gave as natural a laugh as she could muster, and said she'd been talking way too much and would love to hear his thoughts.

At this Chief Morris took another sip of coffee, cleared his throat, praised her for her hard work and enterprise, told her how much he appreciated her coming in, and —again—how interesting her project sounded. Yes, indeed. He would have to think about it, of course, and consult with the local coroner's office, and with the historical society, and a few others, to get their views, and then the town attorney should probably be brought into the loop... And he finished off his coffee and put his hands on the arm of his chair, looking as if he was getting ready to stand up and end the meeting.

A disaster. Corrie took a deep breath. "Can I be totally frank with you?"

"Why, yes." He settled back in his chair.

"It took me ages to scrape together the money for this project. I had to work two jobs in addition to my scholarship. Roaring Fork is one of the most expensive places in the country, and just being here is costing me a fortune. I'll go broke waiting for permission."

She paused, took a breath.

"Honestly, Chief Morris, if you consult with all those people, it's going to take a long time. Maybe weeks. Everyone's going to have a different opinion. And then, no matter what decision you make, someone will feel as if they were overridden. It could become controversial."

"Controversial," the chief echoed, alarm and distaste in his voice.

"May I make an alternative suggestion?"

The chief looked a bit surprised but not altogether put out by this. "Certainly."

"As I understand it, you have the full authority to give me permission. So..." She paused and then decided to just lay it out, completely unvarnished. "I'd be incredibly grateful if you'd please just give me permission right now, so I can do my research as quickly as possible. I only need a couple of days with the remains, plus the option to take away a few bones for further analysis. That's all. The quicker this happens, the better for everyone. The bones are just sitting there. I could get my work done with barely anyone noticing. Don't give people time to make objections. Please, Chief Morris—it's *so* important to me!"

This ended on more of a desperate note than she intended, but she could see that, once again, she had made an impression.

"Well, well," the chief said, with more throat clearings and hemmings and hawings. "I see your point. Hmmm. We don't want controversy."

He leaned over the edge of his chair, craned his neck toward the door. "Shirley? More coffee!"

The secretary came back in with two more paper cups. The chief proceeded once again to heap an astonishing amount of sugar into the cup, fussing with the spoon, the cream, stirring the cup endlessly while his brow remained furrowed. He finally laid down the plastic spoon and took a good long sip.

"I'm very much leaning toward your proposal," he said. "Very much. I'll tell you what. It's only noon. If you like I'll take you over now, show you the coffins. Of course you can't actually handle the remains, but you'll get an idea of what's there. And I'll have an answer for you tomorrow morning. How's that?"

"That would be great! Thank you!"

Chief Morris beamed. "And just between you and me, I think you can depend on that answer being positive."

And as they stood up, Corrie had to actually restrain herself from hugging the man.

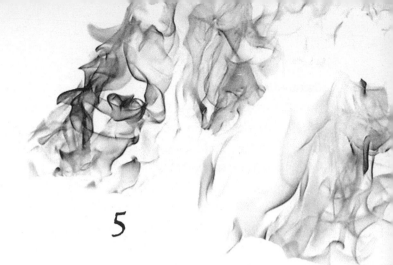

5

Corrie slid into the passenger seat of the squad car, next to the chief, who apparently eschewed a driver and drove himself about. Instead of the usual Crown Vic, the vehicle was a Jeep Cherokee, done up in the traditional cop-car two-tone, with the city symbol of Roaring Fork—an aspen leaf—painted on the side, surrounded by a six-pointed sheriff's star.

Corrie realized she had lucked out, big-time. The chief appeared to be a decent, well-meaning man, and although he seemed to lack spine he was both reasonable and intelligent.

"Have you been to Roaring Fork before?" Morris asked as he turned the key, the vehicle roaring to life.

"Never. Don't even ski."

"Good gracious. You need to learn. We're in the high season here—Christmas approaching and all—so you're seeing it at its finest."

The Jeep eased down East Main Street and the chief began pointing out some of the historic sights—City Hall, the historic Hotel Sebastian, various famous Victorian mansions. Everything was done up in festive lights and garlands of fir, the snow lying on the roofs, frosting the windows, and hanging on the boughs of the trees. It was like something out of a Currier & Ives print. They passed through a shopping district, the streets thicker with upscale boutiques than even the gold mile of Fifth Avenue. It was amazing, the sidewalks thronging with shoppers decked out in furs and diamonds or sleek ski outfits, packing shopping bags. The traffic moved at a glacial pace, and they found themselves creeping down the street sandwiched among stretch Hummers, Mercedes Geländewagens, Range Rovers, Porsche Cayennes—and snowmobiles.

"Sorry about the traffic," the chief said.

"Are you kidding? This is amazing," Corrie said, almost hanging out the window as she watched the parade of stores slide by: Ralph Lauren, Tiffany, Dior, Louis Vuitton, Prada, Gucci, Rolex, Fendi, Bulgari, Burberry, Brioni, the windows stuffed with expensive merchandise. They never seemed to end.

"The amount of money in this town is off the charts," said the chief. "And frankly, from a law enforcement point of view, that can be a problem. A lot of these people think the rules don't apply to them. But in the Roaring Fork Police Department, we treat everyone—and I mean *everyone*—the same."

"Good policy."

"It's the only policy in a town like this," he said, not without a touch of pomposity, "where just about everyone is a celebrity, a billionaire, or both."

"Must be a magnet for thieves," Corrie said, still staring at the expensive stores.

"Oh, no. The crime rate here is almost nil. We're so isolated, you see. There's only one road in—Route 82, which can be an obstacle course in the winter and is frequently closed due to snow—and our airport is only used by private jets. Then there's the cost of actually staying here—well beyond the means of any petty thief. We're too expensive for thieves!" He laughed merrily.

Tell me about it, Corrie thought.

They were now passing a few blocks of what looked like a recreation of a western boomtown: bars with swinging doors, assay offices, general goods stores, even a few apparent bordellos with gaudily painted windows. Everything was spotlessly neat and clean, from the gleaming cuspidors on the raised wooden sidewalks to the tall false fronts of the buildings.

"What's all that?" Corrie asked, pointing at a family getting their picture taken in front of the Ideal Saloon.

"That's Old Town," the chief replied. "What remains of the earliest part of Roaring Fork. For years, those buildings just sat around, decaying. Then, when the resort business picked up, there was a move to clear it all away. But somebody had the idea to restore the old ghost town, make it into a kind of museum for Roaring Fork's past."

Disneyland meets ski resort, Corrie thought, marveling at the anachronism of this scattering of old relics amid such a hotbed of conspicuous consumption.

As she stared at the well-maintained structures, a brace of snowmobiles roared past, throwing up billows of powder in their wakes.

"What's with all the snowmobiles?" she asked.

"Roaring Fork has an avid snowmobile culture," the chief told her. "The town's famous not only for its ski runs, but also for its snowmobile trails. There are miles and miles of them—mostly utilizing the maze of old mining roads that still exist in the mountains above the town."

They finally cleared the shopping district and, after a few turns, passed a little park full of snow-covered boulders.

"Centennial State Park," the chief explained. "Those rocks are part of the John Denver Sanctuary."

"John Denver?" Corrie shuddered.

"Every year, fans gather on the anniversary of his death. It's a really moving experience. What a genius he was—and what a loss."

"Yes, absolutely," Corrie said quickly. "I love his work. 'Rocky Mountain High'—my favorite song of all time."

"Still brings tears to my eyes."

"Right. Me, too."

They left the tight grid of downtown streets behind and continued up through a gorgeous stand of giant fir trees heavy with snow.

"Why was the cemetery dug up?" Corrie asked. She knew the answer, of course, but she wanted to see what fresh light the chief could shed on things.

"There's a very exclusive development up ahead called The

Heights—ten-million-dollar homes, big acreages, private access to the mountain, exclusive club. It's the most upscale development in town, and it carries a great deal of cachet. Old money and all that. Back in the late '70s, during the initial stage of its development, The Heights acquired 'Boot Hill'—the hill with the town's original cemetery—and got a variance to move it. That was in the days when you could still do that sort of thing. Anyway, a couple of years ago, they exercised that right so they could build a private spa and new clubhouse on that hill. There was an uproar, of course, and the town took them to court. But they had some pretty slick lawyers, and also that 1978 agreement, signed and sworn, with ironclad provisions in perpetuity. So they won, the cemetery ultimately got dug up, and here we are. For now, the remains are being stored in a warehouse up on the mountain. There's nothing left but buttons, boots, and bones."

"So where are they being moved to?"

"The development plans to rebury them in a nearby site as soon as spring comes."

"Is there still controversy?"

The chief waved his hand. "Once it was dug up, the furor died down. It wasn't about the remains, anyway—it was about preserving the historic cemetery. Once that was gone, people lost interest."

The fir trees gave way to a broad, attractive valley, glittering in the noontime light. At the near end stood a plain, hand-carved sign, of surprisingly modest dimensions, which read:

THE HEIGHTS

MEMBERS ONLY

PLEASE CHECK IN AT GUARD STATION

Behind was a massive wall of river stones set with wrought-iron gates, beside which stood a fairy-tale guard house with a pointed cedar-shake roof and shingled sides. The valley floor was dotted with gigantic mansions, hidden among the trees, and the walls of the valley rose up behind, rooflines peeking above the firs—many with stone chimneys trailing smoke. Beyond that rose the ski area, a braid of trails winding up to the peaks of several mountains, and a high ridge sporting yet more mansions, all framed against a brilliant blue Rocky Mountain sky sprinkled with clouds.

"We're going in?" Corrie asked.

"The warehouse is to one side of the development, on the edge of the slopes."

The chief was waved through by a security guard, and they headed along a winding, cobblestone drive, beautifully plowed and cleared. No, not cleared. The road was strangely free of ice and utterly dry, while the verges showed no signs of piled or plowed snow.

"Heated road?" asked Corrie as they passed what appeared to be the clubhouse.

"Not so uncommon around here. The ultimate in snow clearance—the flakes evaporate as soon as they touch down."

Climbing now, the road crossed a stone bridge over a frozen stream—which the chief labeled Silver Queen Creek—then passed through a service gate. Beyond, screened by a tall fence, up hard against a ski run, stood several large equipment sheds built of Pro-Panel on a leveled area of ground. Ten-foot icicles hung down their sides, glittering in the light.

The chief pulled up into a plowed area before the largest shed, parked, and got out. Corrie followed. It was a cold day but not desperately so, twenty or twenty-five perhaps, and windless. The great door to the shed had a smaller one set to the side of it, which Chief Morris unlocked. Corrie followed him into the dark space, and the smell hit her right away. And yet it was not an unpleasant odor, no scent of rot. Just rich earth.

The chief palmed a bank of switches and sodium lamps in the roof turned on, casting a yellow glow over all. If anything, it was colder inside the shed than outside, and she drew her coat more closely around her, shivering. In the front section of the shed, practically in the shadow of the large door, sat a line of six snowmobiles, almost all of identical make. Beyond, a row of old snowcats, some nearly antique looking, with huge treads and rounded cabs, blocked their view toward the back. They threaded their way among the cats and came to an open area. Here was the makeshift cemetery, laid out on tarps: neat rows of baby-blue plastic coffins of the kind used by medical examiners to remove remains from a crime scene.

They walked over to the nearest row, and Corrie looked at the first box. Taped to the lid was a large card of printed information. Corrie knelt to read it. The card indicated where the remains had been found in the cemetery, with a photo of the grave in situ; there was space to record whether or not there had been a tombstone and, if so, room for the information printed on it, along with another photo. Everything was numbered, cataloged, and arranged. Corrie felt relief: there would be no problems with documentation here.

"The tombstones are over there," said Chief Morris. He pointed to a far wall, against which was arrayed a motley collection of tombstones—a few fancy ones in slate or marble, but mostly boulders or slabs with lettering carved into them. They, too, had been cataloged and carded.

"We've got about a hundred and thirty human remains," said the chief. "And close to a hundred tombstones. The rest...we don't know who they are. They may have had wooden markers, or perhaps some tombstones were lost or stolen."

"Did any identify bear victims?"

"None. They're traditional—names, dates, and sometimes a phrase from the Bible or a standard religious epitaph. The cause of death isn't normally put on tombstones. And being eaten by a grizzly would not be something you'd want memorialized."

Corrie nodded. It didn't really matter—she had already put together a list of the victims from researching old local newspaper reports.

"Would it be possible to open one of these lids?" she asked.

"I don't see why not." The chief grasped a handle on the nearest box.

"Wait, I've got a list." Corrie fumbled in her briefcase and withdrew the folder. "Let's look for one of the victims."

"Fine."

They spent a few minutes wandering among the coffins, until

Corrie found one that matched a name on her list: Emmett Bowdree. "This one, please," she said.

Morris grabbed the handle and eased the lid off.

Inside were the remains of a rotten pine coffin that held a skeleton. The lid had disintegrated and was lying in pieces around and on top of the skeleton. Corrie stared at it eagerly. The bones of both arms and a leg lay to one side; the skull was crushed; the rib cage had been ripped open; and both femurs had been broken into pieces, crunched up by powerful jaws to obtain the marrow, no doubt. In her studies at John Jay, Corrie had examined many skeletons displaying perimortem violence, but nothing—*nothing*—quite like this.

"Jesus, the bear really did a number on him," murmured Morris.

"You're not kidding."

As she examined the bones, Corrie noticed something: some faint marks on the broken rib cage. She knelt, looking closer, trying to make them out. Christ, what she needed was a magnifying glass. Her eyes darted about, and—on the crushed femur—she noticed another, similar mark. She reached out to pick up the bone.

"Whoa, there, no touching!"

"I need to just examine this a little closer."

"No," said the chief. "Really, that's enough."

"Just give me a moment," Corrie pleaded.

"Sorry." He slid the lid back on. "You'll have plenty of time later."

Corrie rose, perplexed, not at all sure about what she'd seen. It might have been her imagination. Anyway, the marks surely must be antemortem: no mystery there. Roaring Fork was a rough place back in those days. Maybe the fellow had survived a knife fight. She shook her head.

"We'd better get going," the chief said.

They emerged into the brilliant light, the blaze off the glittering blanket of snow almost blinding. But try as she might, Corrie couldn't quite rid herself of the strangest feeling of disquiet.

6

The call came the following morning. Corrie was seated in the Roaring Fork Library, reading up on the history of the town. It was an excellent library, housed in a modern building designed in an updated Victorian style. The interior was gorgeous, with acres of polished oak, arched windows, thick carpeting, and an indirect lighting system that bathed everything in a warm glow.

The library's historical section was state of the art. The section librarian, Ted Roman, had been very helpful. He turned out to be a cute guy in his midtwenties, lithe and fit, who had recently graduated from the University of Utah and was taking a couple of years off to be a ski bum. She had told him about her research project and her meeting with Chief Morris. Ted had listened attentively, asked intelligent questions, and showed her how to use the history archives. To top it off, he had asked her out for a beer tomorrow night. And she'd accepted.

The library's albums of old newspapers, broadsheets, and public notices from the silver boom days had been beautifully digitized in searchable PDF form. She'd been able, in a matter of hours, to pull up dozens of articles on the history of Roaring Fork and on the grizzly killings, obituary notices, and all kinds of related memorabilia—far more than she'd obtained in New York.

The town had a fascinating history. In the summer of 1873, a doughty band of prospectors from Leadville braved the threat of Ute

Indians and crossed the Continental Divide, penetrating unexplored territory westward. There, they and others who followed made one of the biggest silver strikes in U.S. history. A silver rush ensued, with hordes of prospectors staking claims all through the mountains lining the Roaring Fork River. A town sprang up, along with stamp mills for crushing ore and a hastily built smelter for separating silver and gold from ore. Soon the hills were crawling with prospectors, dotted with mines and remote camps, while the town itself teemed with mining engineers, assayists, charcoal burners, sawmill workers, blacksmiths, saloonkeepers, merchants, teamsters, whores, laborers, piano players, faro dealers, con men, and thieves.

The first killing took place in the spring of 1876. At a remote claim high on Smuggler Mountain, a lone miner was killed and eaten. It took weeks for the man to be missed, and as a consequence his body wasn't discovered immediately, but the high mountain air kept it fresh enough to tell the gruesome tale. The body had been ripped open, obviously by a bear, then gutted, the limbs torn off. It appeared the bear had returned over the course of a week to continue feasting, with most of the bones stripped of their flesh, the tongue and liver eaten, the entrails and organs spread about and more or less consumed.

It was a pattern that would be repeated ten more times over the course of the summer.

From the beginning, Roaring Fork—and indeed much of Colorado Territory—had been plagued by aggressive grizzlies who were being driven to higher altitudes by settlements in the lower valleys. The grizzly bear—it was noted with relish in almost every newspaper report—was one of the few animals known to hunt and kill a human being for food.

During the course of that long summer, eleven miners and prospectors were killed and eaten by the rogue grizzly at a variety of remote claims. The animal had a large territory that, unfortunately, encompassed much of the upper range of the silver district. The killings caused widespread panic. But federal law required miners to "work a claim" in order to maintain rights to it, so even at the height of the terror most miners refused to abandon their sites.

Hunting posses were formed several times to chase the grizzly, but it was hard to track the animal in the absence of snow, amid the rocky upper reaches of the mountains above the tree line. Still, the real problem, it seemed to Corrie, was that the hunting posses were none too eager to find the bear. They seemed to spend more time organizing in the saloons and making speeches than actually out in the field tracking the bear.

The killings stopped in the fall of 1876, just before the first snow. Over time, people began to think the bear had moved on, died, or perhaps gone into hibernation. There was some apprehension the following spring, but when the killings did not resume...

Corrie felt her phone vibrate, plucked it out of her handbag, and saw it was a call from the police station. Glancing around and noting the library was empty—save for the ski bum librarian, sitting at his desk reading Jack Kerouac—she figured it was okay to answer.

But it wasn't the chief. It was his secretary. Before Corrie could even get through the usual niceties, the lady was talking fast and breathily. "The chief is so sorry, so very sorry, but it turns out he can't give you permission to examine the remains."

Corrie's mouth went dry. "What?" she croaked. "Wait a minute—"

"He's tied up all day in meetings so he asked me to call you. You see—"

"But he said—"

"It's just not going to be possible. He feels very sorry he can't help you."

"But *why?*" she managed to break in.

"I don't have the specifics, I'm sorry—"

"Can't I speak to him?"

"He's caught up in meetings all day and, um, for the rest of the week."

"For the rest of the *week?* But just yesterday he said—"

"I'm sorry, I told you I'm not privy to his reasons."

"Look," said Corrie, trying to control her voice without much success, "just a day ago he told me there wouldn't be any problems.

That he'd approve it. And now he changes his mind, refuses to say why, and...and then dumps on you the job of giving me the bum's rush! It isn't fair!"

Corrie got a final, frosty *I wish I could help you, but the decision is final*, followed by a decisive click. The line went dead.

Corrie sat down and, banging her palm on the table, cried: "Damn, damn, *damn!*"

Then she looked up. Ted was looking over at her, his eyes wide.

"Oh, no," Corrie said, covering her mouth. "I've disturbed the whole library."

He held up his hand with a smile. "As you can see, there's nobody here right now." He hesitated, then came around his desk and walked over. He spoke again, his voice having dropped to a whisper. "I think I understand what's going on here."

"You do? I'd wish you'd explain it to me, then."

Even though there was nobody around, he lowered his voice still further. "*Mrs. Kermode.*"

"Who?"

"Mrs. Betty Brown Kermode got to the chief of police."

"Who is Betty Brown Kermode?"

He rolled his eyes and looked around furtively. "Where to begin? First, she owns Town and Mount Real Estate, which is *the* real estate agency in town. She's the head of the Heights Neighborhood Association, and was the force behind getting the cemetery moved. She's basically one of those self-righteous people who run everything and everybody and brook no dissent. Fact is, she's the real power in this town."

"A woman like that's got influence over the chief of police?"

Ted laughed. "You met Morris, right? Nice guy. *Everyone* has influence over him. But especially her. I'm telling you, she's fearsome—even more so than that brother-in-law of hers, Montebello. I'm sure Morris had every intention of giving you permission—until he called Kermode."

"But why would she want to stop me? What harm would it do?"

"That," said Ted, "is what you're going to have to find out."

7

At nine the next morning, Corrie pulled her Rent-a-Junker up to the gates of The Heights. There the guard—not nearly as friendly as the last time she'd passed through, with the chief of police—spent a long, insolent amount of time checking her ID and calling to verify her appointment, all the while casting disdainful looks at her car.

Corrie was careful to remain polite, and at length she was driving along the road toward the clubhouse and development offices. A cluster of buildings on the valley floor soon came into view: picturesque, snowcapped and icicled, their stone chimneys smoking. Beyond, well up on the far side of the snow-blanketed valley, Corrie could see a massive dirt scar of ongoing construction—no doubt the new clubhouse and spa. She watched backhoes and loaders busily at work digging footings. She couldn't help but wonder why they needed a new clubhouse when the old one looked pretty amazing.

She parked in the visitor's lot and entered the clubhouse, where the secretary pointed her toward the offices of Town & Mount Real Estate.

The reception area of Town & Mount was sumptuous—all wood and stone, with Navajo rugs on the walls, a spectacular chandelier made of deer antlers, cowboy-style leather-and-wood furniture, and a stone fireplace in which a real log fire burned. Corrie took a seat and settled in to wait.

An hour later, she was finally ushered into the office of Mrs. Kermode, president of Town & Mount and director of the Heights Association. Corrie had dressed in her most corporate mode, a gray suit with a white blouse and low pumps. She was absolutely determined to keep her cool and win Mrs. Kermode over with flattery, charm, and persuasion.

The previous afternoon, she had done her damnedest to dig up dirt on Kermode, heeding the Pendergastian dictum that if you want something from somebody, always have something "ugly" to trade. But Kermode seemed to be a woman above reproach: a generous donor to local charities, an elder in the Presbyterian church, a volunteer at the local soup kitchen (it surprised Corrie that a town like Roaring Fork would even have a soup kitchen), and a businesswoman of acknowledged integrity. While she was not exactly loved, and was in fact heartily disliked by many, she was respected—and feared—by all.

Mrs. Kermode surprised Corrie. Far from being the dowdy woman conjured up by the name Betty Brown Kermode, she was an extremely well-put-together woman in her early sixties, slender and fit, with beautifully coiffed platinum hair and understated makeup. She was dressed in high cowboy style with a beaded Indian vest, white shirt, tight jeans, and cowboy boots. A Navajo squash blossom necklace completed the ensemble. The walls of her office were covered with photographs of her riding a stunning paint horse in the mountains and competing in an arena, charging through a herd of cows. A water cooler stood in one corner. Another corner of the office was dominated by a magnificent western saddle, tooled all over and trimmed in silver.

In an easy, friendly way, Mrs. Kermode came forward and shook Corrie's hand, inviting her to sit down. Corrie's irritation at being kept waiting for an hour began to dissipate in the warm welcome.

"Now, Corrie," she began, speaking with a pronounced Texas accent, "I want to thank you for coming in. It gives me a chance to explain to you, in person, why Chief Morris and I unfortunately can't grant your request."

"Well, I was hoping to explain—"

But Kermode was in a hurry and overrode Corrie's attempt to present her talking points. "Corrie, I'm going to be frank. The scientific examination of those mortal remains for a...college thesis is, in our view, disrespectful of the dead."

This was not what Corrie expected. "In what way?"

Kermode gave a poisonous little laugh. "My dear Miss Swanson, how can you ask such a question? Would you want some student pawing through your grandfather's remains?"

"Um, I would be fine with it."

"Come, now. Of course you wouldn't. At least where I come from, we treat our dead with respect. These are *sacred* human remains."

Corrie tried desperately to get back to her talking points. "But this is a unique opportunity for forensic science. This is going to help law enforcement—"

"A college thesis? Contribute to forensic science? Aren't you exaggerating the importance of this project just a *teensy* little bit now, Miss Swanson?"

Corrie took a deep breath. "Not at all. This could be a very important study and data collection of perimortem trauma caused by a large carnivore. When a skeleton of a murder victim is found, forensic pathologists have to distinguish animal tooth marks and other postmortem damage from the marks on the bones left by the perpetrator. It's a serious issue and this study—"

"So much Greek to me!" Mrs. Kermode gave a laugh and waved her hand, as if she understood nothing.

Corrie decided to shift tack. "It's important for me personally, Mrs. Kermode—but it could be important for Roaring Fork, as well. It's doing something constructive, something positive with these human remains. It would reflect well on the community and the chief—"

"It's just not respectful," said Kermode firmly. "It's not *Christian.*

There are many in this town who would find it deeply offensive. We are the guardians of those remains, and we take our responsibility seriously. I just can't under any circumstances allow it."

"But..." Corrie could feel her temper rising despite her best efforts to keep it down. "But...you dug them up to begin with."

A silence, and then Kermode spoke softly. "The decision was made long ago. Back in 1978, in fact. The town signed off on it. Here at The Heights we've been planning this new clubhouse and spa for almost a decade."

"Why do you need it when you've already got a beautiful clubhouse?"

"We'll need a larger one to serve Phase Three, as we open up West Mountain to a select number of custom home lots. Again, as I've repeatedly said to you, this has been in planning for years. We are responsible to our owners and investors."

Our owners and investors. "All I want to do is examine the bones—with the utmost respect—for valid and important scientific purposes. There's no disrespect in that, surely?"

Mrs. Kermode rose, a bright fake smile plastered on her face. "Miss Swanson, the decision has been made, it is final, and I am a very busy woman. It is now time for you to leave."

Corrie rose. She could feel that old, horrible, blood-boiling sensation inside her. "You dig up an entire cemetery so you can make money on a real estate development, you dump the bodies in plastic boxes and store them in a ski warehouse—and then you tell me *I'll* be disrespecting the dead by studying the bones? You're a hypocrite—plain and simple!"

Kermode's face grew pale. Corrie could see a vein in her powdered neck throbbing. Her voice became very low, almost masculine. "You little bitch," she said. "I'll give you five minutes to vacate the premises. If you ever—*ever*—come back, I'll have you arrested for trespassing. Now get out."

Corrie suddenly felt very calm. This was the end. It was over. But she wasn't going to let anyone call her a bitch. She stared back at Mrs. Kermode with narrowed eyes. "You call yourself an elder in the church? You're no Christian. You're a goddamn phony. A fake, grasping, deceitful *phony*."

On the way back to Basalt, it began to snow. As she crawled along at ten miles an hour in her car, windshield wipers slapping back and forth ineffectually, an idea came to her. Those anomalous marks she'd noticed on the bones...with a flash of insight, she realized there was possibly another way to skin this particular cat.

8

Lying on the bed of her room at the Cloud Nine Motel in Basalt, Colorado, Corrie made her decision. If those marks on the bones were what she thought they might be, her problems would be solved. There wouldn't be any choice: the remains would have to be examined. Even Kermode couldn't stop it. That would be her trump card.

But only if she could prove it.

And to do that, she needed access to the bones one more time. Five minutes, tops—just long enough to photograph them with the powerful macro lens on her camera.

But how?

Even before she asked herself the question, she knew the answer: she would have to break in.

All the arguments against such an action lined themselves up before her: that B&E was a felony; that it was ethically wrong; that if she got caught, her entire law enforcement career would be flushed down the toilet. On the other hand, it wouldn't be all that difficult. During their visit two days before, the chief hadn't turned off any alarm systems or other security devices; he'd simply unlocked a padlock on the door and they had walked in. The shed was isolated from the rest of the development, surrounded by a tall wooden fence and screened by trees. It was partly open to one of the ski slopes, but nobody would be skiing at night. The shed was marked on trail maps of the area, and they showed a service road leading to it from the equipment yard of the ski area itself, bypassing The Heights entirely.

As she weighed the pros and cons, she found herself asking the question: what would Pendergast do? He never let legal niceties stand in the way of truth and justice. Surely he would break in and get the information he needed. While it was too late to achieve justice for Emmett Bowdree, it was never too late for the truth.

The snow had stopped at midnight, leaving a brilliantly clear night sky with a three-quarter moon. It was extremely cold—according to the WeatherBug app on her iPad, it was five degrees. Outside, it felt a lot colder than that. The service road turned out to be snowmobile-only, covered with hard-packed snow but still walkable.

Leaving her car at the very base of the road, by a tall stand of trees and as inconspicuous as possible, Corrie labored uphill, her knapsack heavy with gear: the Canon with tripod and macro, a portable light and battery pack, loupes, flashlight, bolt cutter, ziplock bags, and her iPad loaded with textbooks and monographs on the subject of oste-ological trauma analysis. The thin mountain air left her gasping, the smoke of her condensing breath blossoming in the moonlight as she hiked, her feet squeaking in the layer of fluff atop the hard-packed snow. Below, the lights of the town spread out in a magical carpet; above, she could see the warehouse, illuminated by lights on poles and casting a yellow glow through the fir trees. It was two o'clock in the morning and all was quiet. The only activity was some headlights high on the mountain, where the grooming equipment was being op-erated.

Again and again, she had choreographed in her head the exact series of steps she'd need to take, rearranging and refining them to en-sure that she would spend as little time in the shed as possible. Five minutes, ten at most—and she'd be gone.

Approaching the shed, she did a careful recon to assure herself that she was alone. Then she stepped up to the fence gate and peered over it. To the left was the side door that she and the chief had used, illuminated in a pool of light, the snow well beaten down before it.

The door was securely padlocked. By habit, she carried a set of lock picks. In high school, she had practically memorized the underground manual known as the *MIT Guide to Lockpicking*, and she took great pride in her skills. The padlock was a ten-dollar, hardware-store variety—no problem there. But she would have to cross the lighted area in order to reach the door. And then she'd have to stand in the light while dealing with the lock. This was one of two elements of unavoidable danger in her plan.

She waited, listening, but all was quiet. The grooming machines were high up on the mountain and didn't look like they'd be passing by anytime soon.

Taking a deep breath, she vaulted the fence and darted across the lighted area. She had her set of lock picks ready. The lock itself was freezing, and her fingers quickly grew stupid in the cold. Nevertheless it took only twenty seconds for the padlock to spring open. She pulled the door ajar, ducked inside, and gently closed it behind her.

Inside the shed it was very cold. Fumbling a small LED light out of her backpack, she flicked it on and quickly moved past the rows of snowmobiles and antique snowcats to the rear of the structure. The coffins, laid out in neat rows, gleamed dully in her light. It only took a moment to find Emmett Bowdree's coffin. She removed the lid with care, trying to keep the noise to a minimum, then knelt, playing the light over the bones. Her heart was pounding in her chest, and her hands were shaking. Once again, a voice inside her pointed out that this was one of the dumbest things she'd ever done, and once again another voice responded that it was the only thing she could do.

Get a grip, she whispered to herself. *Focus.*

Following her mental script, Corrie pulled off her gloves again, laid her backpack on the ground, and unzipped it. She quickly inserted a loupe to her eye, tugged the gloves back on, pulled out the broken femur she'd noticed before, and peered at it under the light. The bone showed several long, parallel scrapes in the cortical surface. She examined them carefully for any sign of healing, bone remodeling or periosteal uplifting, but there was none. The longitudinal marks were clean, fresh, and showed no sign of an osseous reaction. That meant the scraping had occurred perimortem: at the time of death.

No bear could have made a mark like this. It had been done with a crude tool, perhaps the blade of a dull knife, and—clearly—it had been done to strip the flesh from the bones.

But could she be sure? Her field experience was so limited. Removing her gloves again, she fumbled out her iPad and called up one of her school e-textbooks, *Trauma Analysis*. She looked through the illustrations of antemortem, perimortem, and postmortem injuries, including some with scrapes similar to these, and compared the illustrations with the bone in her hand. They confirmed her initial impression. She tried to warm her frozen fingers by breathing on them, but that didn't work and so she pulled her gloves back on and beat her hands together as quietly as she could. That brought back a little sensation.

Now she had to photograph the damaged bone. Once again the gloves had to come off. She hauled out the portable light, battery pack, and small tripod from her backpack. Next came her digital camera, with the massive macro lens attachment that had cost her a fortune. She screwed the camera into the mount and set it up. Placing the bone on the floor, she arranged things as best she could in the dark, then flicked on the light.

This was the second danger point—the light would be visible from outside. But it was absolutely indispensable. She had arranged things so that it would be on for the shortest possible amount of time, without a red flag of turning it off and on—and so that right afterward she could pack up and leave.

God, it was bright, casting a glow over everything. She quickly positioned the camera and focused. She took a dozen photos as quickly as she could, moving the bone a little bit each time and adjusting the light for a raking effect. As she did this, she noticed, under the strong glare, something else on the bone: apparent tooth marks. She stopped just a moment to examine them with the loupe. They were indeed tooth marks, but not those of a grizzly: they were far too feeble, too close together, and with too flat a crown. She photographed them from several angles.

She hurriedly put the bone back in the coffin, and moved on to the next anomalous mark she'd noticed on her first visit—the broken skull. The cranium showed massive trauma, the skull and face literally crushed. The biggest and, it seemed, first blow had occurred to the right of the parietal bone, shattering the skull in a star pattern and separating it along the sutures. These, too, were clearly perimortem injuries, for the simple reason that survival was impossible after such a violent blow. The green-bone nature of the fractures indicated they had occurred when the bone was still fresh.

The anomaly here was a mark at the point of the blow. She examined the point of fracture. A bear could certainly shatter a skull with the strike of a paw, or crush it with its jaws and teeth. But this mark did not look like either teeth or claws. It was irregular, with multiple indents.

Under the loupe, her suspicions were confirmed. It had been made by a rough, heavy object—almost certainly a rock.

Working even more quickly now, she took a series of photographs of the skull fragments with her macro. This was proof enough. Or was it? She vacillated a moment, then on impulse took out a couple of zip-lock bags and slipped the fragment of femur and one of the damaged skull fragments into them. *That* was proof.

Done. She snapped off the light. Now she had incontrovertible evidence that Emmett Bowdree had not been killed and eaten by a bear. Instead, he had been killed and eaten by a human. In fact, judging from the extensive nature of the injuries, there might have been two or three, maybe more, who participated in the killing. They had first disabled him with a blow to the head, crushed his skull, smashed his bones, and literally ripped him apart with their bare hands. Then they had stripped the meat from the bones with a crude knife or piece of metal. Finally, they had eaten him raw—attested by the tooth marks and the absence of bone scorching and other evidence of cooking.

Horrible. Unbelievable. She had discovered a hundred-and-fifty-year-old murder. Which begged the next question: *Were the other ten miners killed in the same way, by humans?*

She glanced at her watch: eleven minutes. She felt a sudden shiver of fear: time to get the hell out. Quickly she began packing up her stuff, preparing to exit the shed.

Suddenly she thought she heard a noise. She flicked off the LED and listened. Silence. Then she heard it again: the faintest crunching sound of snow outside the door.

Jesus, someone was coming. Paralyzed with fear, her heart pounding, she continued to listen. A definite *crunch, crunch, crunch*. And then—across the warehouse, in a window high up in the eaves—she saw a beam of light flash quickly across the glass. More silence. And then the muffled sound of talk and the hiss of a two-way radio.

There were people outside. With a radio.

Heights security? Cops?

She zipped up her backpack with infinite care. The coffin lid was still off. Should she slide it back on? She began to move it back into place, but it made such a loud scraping noise that she stopped. She had to get it back on, though, so in one hasty movement she shoved it back in place.

Outside she could hear more activity: crunching, whispers. There were several people outside and they were trying, not very successfully, to be quiet.

She slid the knapsack over her shoulder and moved away from the coffins. Was there an exit door in the rear? She couldn't tell now—it was too dark—but she didn't recall seeing one. What she needed to do was find a secure hiding place and wait this out.

Tiptoeing across the floor, she headed for the rear of the warehouse, where the giant pieces of an old ski lift had been stored— pylons, chairs, and wheels. Even as she moved across the floor she heard the door open, and she ran the last few yards. Now hushed voices could be heard in the shed. More radio noise.

Reaching the stacks of old equipment, she burrowed her way in, getting down on her hands and knees and crawling as far back as she could, twisting and turning among the giant pieces of metal.

A sudden snapping noise, and then the fluorescent tubes came popping and clinking on, bathing the warehouse in brilliant light. Corrie crawled faster, throwing herself behind a huge coil of steel cable and balling herself up, hugging her backpack to her chest, making herself as small as possible. She waited, hardly daring to breathe. Maybe they thought the padlock had been accidentally left open. Maybe they hadn't noticed her car. Maybe they wouldn't find her...

Footsteps crossed the cement floor. And then Corrie heard a burst of whispering. Now she could distinguish individual voices and catch snatches of phrases. With a thrill of absolute horror she heard her own name spoken—in the Texas drawl of Kermode: querulous, inciting.

She buried her head in her gloved hands, reeling from the nightmare. She could feel her heart almost bursting with anxiety and dismay. Why had she done this? *Why?*

She heard a voice speak, loud and clear: the harsh twang of Kermode. "Corrie Swanson?"

It echoed dreadfully in the cavernous room.

"Corrie Swanson, we know you're in here. We *know* it. You're in a world of trouble. If you come out and show yourself now, that would be the smart thing to do. If you force these policemen to have to find you, that won't be smart. Do you understand?"

Corrie was choking with fear. More sounds: additional people were arriving. She couldn't move.

"All right," she heard the chief's unhappy voice say. "You, Joe, start in the back. Fred, stay by the door. Sterling, you poke around those cats and snowmobiles."

Still Corrie couldn't move. The game was up. She should show herself. But some crazy, desperate hope kept her hidden.

Burying her head deeper into her gloves, like a child hiding under the covers, she waited. She heard the tap of footsteps, the scrape and clank of equipment being moved, the hiss and crackle of radios. A few minutes passed. And then, almost directly above her, she heard, loudly: "Here she is!" And then, aimed at her: "This is the police. Stand up slowly and keep your hands in sight."

She simply could not move.

"Stand up slowly, hands in sight. *Now.*"

She managed to raise her head and saw a cop standing just a few feet away, service revolver drawn and pointed. Two other cops were just arriving.

Corrie rose stiffly, her hands out. The cop came over, grasped her wrist, spun her around, pulled her arms behind her, and slapped on a pair of handcuffs.

"You have the right to remain silent," she heard him say, as if from a great distance. "Anything you say may be used against you in court..."

Corrie couldn't believe this was happening to her.

"...You have the right to consult with an attorney, and to have that attorney present during questioning. If you are indigent, an attorney will be provided at no cost to you. Do you understand?"

She couldn't speak.

"Do you understand? Please speak or nod your answer."

Corrie managed to nod.

The cop said loudly: "I make note of the fact the prisoner has acknowledged understanding her rights."

Holding her by the arm, the cop led her out of the stacks of equipment and into the open. She blinked in the bright light. Another cop had unzipped her backpack and was looking through it. He soon extracted the two ziplock bags containing the bones.

Chief Morris watched him, looking exceedingly unhappy. Standing beside him and surrounded by several security officers of The Heights was Mrs. Kermode, dressed in a slim, zebra-striped winter outfit trimmed in fur—with a look on her face of malice triumphant.

"Well, well," she said, breathing steam like a dragon. "The girl studying law enforcement is actually a criminal. I had you pegged the moment I saw you. I knew you'd try something like this—and here you are, predictable as clockwork. Trespassing, vandalism, larceny, resisting arrest." She reached out and took a ziplock bag from the cop and waved it in Corrie's face. "And *grave robbing.*"

"That's enough," the chief said to Kermode. "Please give that evidence back to the officer and let's go." He took Corrie gently by the arm. "And you, young lady—I'm afraid you're under arrest."

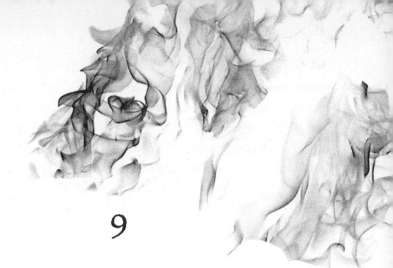

9

Five long days later, Corrie remained locked up in the Roaring Fork County Jail. Bail had been set at fifty thousand dollars, which she didn't have—not even the five-thousand-dollar surety—and the local bail bondsman declined to take her as a client because she was from out of state, with no assets to pledge and no relatives to vouch for her. She had been too ashamed to call her father, and anyway he sure didn't have the money. There was no one else in her life—except Pendergast. And even if she could reach him, she'd die before she took any more money from him—especially bond money.

Nevertheless, she'd had to write him a letter. She had no idea where he was or what he was doing. She hadn't heard from him in nearly a year. But he, or someone acting for him, had continued paying her tuition. And the day after her arrest, with the story plastered all over the front page of the *Roaring Fork Times*, she realized she had to write. Because if she didn't, and he heard about her arrest from someone else, saw those headlines... She owed it to him to tell him first.

So she had written a letter to his Dakota address, care of Proctor. In it she told the whole story, unvarnished. The only thing she left out was the bail situation. Writing everything down had really impressed on her what a brainless, overconfident, and self-destructive thing she had done. She concluded by telling him his obligation to her was over and that no reply was expected or wanted. He was no longer to concern himself with her. She would take care of herself from now on. Except that someday, as soon as she was able, she would pay him back for all the tuition he had wasted sending her to John Jay.

Writing that letter had been the hardest thing she had ever done. Pendergast had saved her life; plucked her out of Medicine Creek, Kansas; freed her from a drunken, abusive mother; paid for her to go to boarding school—and then financed her education at John Jay. And...for what?

But that was all over now.

The fact that the jail was relatively posh only made her feel worse. The cells had big, sunny windows looking out over the mountains, carpeted floors, and nice furniture. She was allowed out of her cell from eight in the morning until lockdown at 10:30 PM. During free time, the prisoners were allowed to hang around the dayroom and read, watch TV, and chat with the other inmates. There was even an adjacent workout room with an elliptical trainer, weights, and treadmills.

At that moment, Corrie was sitting in the dayroom, staring at the black-and-white checkered carpet. Doing nothing. For the past five days she had been so depressed that she couldn't seem to do anything—read, eat, or even sleep. She just sat there, all day, every day, staring into space, and then spent each night in her cell, lying on her back in her cot, staring into darkness.

"Corrine Swanson?"

She roused herself and looked up. A detention guard was standing in the door of the room, holding a clipboard.

"Here," she said.

"Your attorney has arrived for your appointment."

She'd forgotten. She hauled herself to her feet and followed the guard to a separate room. She felt as if the air around her were thick, granular. Her eyes wouldn't stop leaking water. But she wasn't crying, exactly; it seemed like a physiological reaction.

She went into a small conference room to find the public defender waiting at the table, briefcase open, manila folders spread out in a neat fan. His name was George Smith and she had already met with him a few times. He was a middle-aged, slight, sandy-haired, balding man with a perpetually apologetic look on his face. He was nice enough, and he meant well, but he wasn't exactly Perry Mason.

"Hello, Corrie," he said.

She eased down in a chair, saying nothing.

"I've had several meetings with the DA," Smith began, "and, well, I've made some progress on the plea deal."

Corrie nodded apathetically.

"Here's where we stand. You plead to breaking and entering, trespassing, and desecration of a human corpse, and they'll drop the petty larceny charge. You'll be looking at ten years, max."

"Ten years?"

"I know. It's not what I'd hoped. There's a lot of pressure being brought to bear to throw the book at you. I don't quite understand it, but it may have something to do with all the publicity this case has generated and the ongoing controversy about the cemetery. They're making an example of you."

"Ten *years?*" Corrie repeated.

"With good behavior, you could be out in eight."

"And if we go to trial?"

The lawyer's face clouded. "Out of the question. The evidence against you is overwhelming. There's a string of felonies here, starting with the B and E and going all the way to the desecration of a human corpse. That latter crime alone carries a sentence of up to thirty years in prison."

"You're kidding—thirty years?"

"It's a particularly nasty statute here in Colorado because of a long history of grave robbing." He paused. "Look, if you don't plead, the DA will be pissed and he could very well ask for that maximum sentence. He's threatened as much to me already."

Corrie stared at the scarred table.

"You've *got* to plead out, Corrie. It's your only choice."

"But...I can't believe it. Ten years, just for what I did? That's more than some murderers get."

A long silence. "I can always go back to the DA. The problem is, they've got you cold. You don't have anything to trade."

"But I *didn't* desecrate a human corpse."

"Well, according to the way those statutes are written, you did. You opened the coffin, you handled the bones, you photographed them, and you took two of them. That's what they'll argue, and I'd be hard-pressed to counter. It's not worth the risk. The jury pool here is drawn from the entire county, not just Roaring Fork, and there are a lot of conservative ranchers and farmers out there, religious folk, who would not look kindly on what you did."

"But I was just trying to prove that the marks on the bones..." She couldn't finish.

The attorney spread his thin hands, a pained look pinching his narrow face. "It's the best I can do."

"How long do I have to think about it?"

"Not long. They can withdraw the offer at any moment. If you could decide right now, that would be best."

"I've *got* to think about it."

"You have my number."

Corrie rose and shook his limp, sweaty hand, walked out. The guard, who had been waiting outside the door, led her back to the dayroom. She sat down and stared at the black-and-white carpet and thought about what her life would look like in ten years, after she got back out. Her eyes began leaking again, and she wiped at them furiously, to no avail.

10

Jenny Baker arrived at the Roaring Fork City Hall lugging Chief Stanley Morris's second briefcase in both hands. The chief carried two bulging briefcases to every meeting he attended, it seemed, so as to be prepared to answer any question that might come up. Jenny had tried to persuade him to get a tablet computer, but he was a confirmed Luddite and refused even to use the desktop computer in his office.

Jenny rather liked that, despite the inconvenience of having to lug around two briefcases. So far, the chief had proven a pleasant man to work for, rarely made demands, and was always agreeable. In the two weeks she had interned in the police station, she'd seen him flustered and worried but never angry. Now he walked alongside her, chatting about town business, as they entered the meeting room. Big town meetings were sometimes held in the Opera House, but this one—on December thirteenth, less than two weeks from Christmas—was not expected to be well attended.

She took a seat just behind the chief in the town-official seating area. They were early—the chief was always early—and she watched as the mayor came in, followed by the Planning Board, the town attorney, and other officials whose names she did not know. Hard on their heels came a contingent from The Heights, led by Mrs. Kermode, her coiffed, layered helmet of blond hair utterly perfect. She was followed by her brother-in-law, Henry Montebello, and several anonymous-looking men in suits.

The main item of the meeting—the agenda was routinely published in the paper—involved a proposal from The Heights regarding where the Boot Hill remains were to be reinterred. As the meeting opened, with the usual pledge of allegiance and the reading of minutes, Jenny's thoughts drifted to the woman she had met—Corrie—and what had happened to her. It sort of freaked her out. She had seemed so nice, so professional—and then to be caught breaking into a warehouse, desecrating a coffin, and stealing bones. You never could tell what some people were capable of doing. And a student at John Jay, too. Nothing like that had ever happened in The Heights, and the neighborhood was still up in arms about it. It was all her parents talked about at breakfast every morning, even now, ten days after the event.

As the preliminaries went on, Jenny was surprised to see just how many people were filing into the public seating area. It was already packed, and now the standing-room area in the back was filling up. Maybe the cemetery thing was going to erupt into controversy again. She hoped this wasn't going to make the meeting run late—she had a dinner date later that evening.

The meeting moved to the first item on the agenda. The attorney for The Heights rose and gave his presentation in a nasal drone. The Heights, he said, proposed to rebury the disinterred remains in a field they had purchased for just such a purpose on a hillside about five miles down Route 82. This surprised Jenny; she had always assumed the remains would be reburied within the town limits. Now she understood why so many people were there.

The attorney went through some legal gobbledygook about how this was all perfectly legal, reasonable, proper, preferable, and indeed, unavoidable for various reasons she didn't understand. As he continued, Jenny heard a slow rising of disapproving sounds, murmurings—even a few hisses—from the public area. She glanced in the direction of the noise. The proposal was, it seemed, not being greeted with favor.

Just as she was about to turn her attention back to the stage, she noted a striking figure in a black suit appear in the very rear of the public area. There was something about the man that gave her pause. Was it his sculpted, alabaster face? Or his hair, so blond it was almost white? Or his eyes of such pale gray-blue that, even across the room, he looked almost like an alien. Was he a celebrity? If not, Jenny decided, he should be.

Now a landscape designer was on his feet and giving his spiel, complete with slide show, images on the portable screen displaying a plat of the proposed burial area, followed by three-dimensional views of the future cemetery, with stone walls, a quaint wrought-iron archway leading in, cobbled paths among the graves. Next came slides of the actual site: a lovely green meadow partway up a mountain. It was pretty—but it wasn't in Roaring Fork.

As he spoke, the murmurings of disapproval, the restlessness, of the gathered public grew in suppressed intensity. Jenny recognized a reporter from the *Roaring Fork Times* sitting in the front row of the public area, and the look of anticipatory delight on his face signaled that he expected fireworks.

And now, at last, Mrs. Betty Brown Kermode rose to speak. At this, a hush fell. She was a commanding presence in town—even Jenny's father seemed intimidated by her—and those who had gathered to express their opinions were temporarily muted.

She began by mentioning the exceedingly unfortunate break-in of ten days earlier, the shocking violation of a corpse, and how this demonstrated the need to get those human remains back in the ground as soon as possible. She mentioned in passing the seriousness of the crime—so serious that the perpetrator had accepted a plea bargain that would result in ten years' incarceration.

The Heights, she went on, had been taking care of these remains with the utmost attention, deeply aware of their sacred duty to see that these rough miners, these pioneers of Roaring Fork, were given a burial site suitable to their sacrifice, their spirit, and their contribution to the opening of the American West. They had, she said, found the perfect resting place: on the slopes of the Catamount, with heartbreaking views of the Continental Divide. Surrounding the grave-yard, they had purchased over a hundred acres of open space, which would remain forever wild. This is what these Colorado pioneers de-served—not being jammed into some town lot, surrounded by the hustle and bustle of commerce, traffic, shopping, and sport.

It was an effective presentation. Even Jenny found herself agreeing with Mrs. Kermode. The grumbling was no longer audible when she returned to her seat.

Next to stand was Henry Montebello, who had married into Ker-mode's family and, as a result, gained instant power and respectability in the town. He was an older man, gaunt, reserved, and weathered looking. Jenny did not like him and was, in fact, afraid of him. He had a laconic mid-Atlantic accent that somehow caused every observation he made to sound cynical. Although he had been the master archi-tect for The Heights way back when, unlike Kermode he did not live within the development, but rather had his home and office in a large mansion on the other side of town.

He cleared his throat. No expense had been spared, he told the gathered crowd, in developing The Heights—and not that alone, but also in ensuring that it conformed, not only with the spirit and aes-thetic of Roaring Fork, but to the local ecology and environment, as well. He could say this, Montebello continued, because he had personally supervised the preparation of the site, the design of the mansions and clubhouse, and the construction of the development. He would, he said, oversee the creation of the new cemetery with the same close, hands-on attention he had given to The Heights. The implication seemed to be that the long-dead occupants of Boot Hill should be grateful to Montebello for his personal ministrations on their behalf. Montebello spoke with quiet dignity, and with aristo-cratic gravitas—and yet there was a steely undertone to his words, subtle but unmistakable, that seemed to dare anyone to challenge a single syllable of what he'd uttered. No one did, and he once again took his seat.

And now the mayor rose, thanked Mrs. Kermode and Mr. Mon-tebello, and called for public comment. A number of hands went up, and the mayor pointed at someone. But as that person rose to speak, the man in the black suit—who had somehow slipped all the way to the front—held up his hand for silence.

"You are out of turn, sir," said the mayor, sternly, rapping his gavel.

"That remains to be seen," came the reply. The voice was as smooth as honey, an unusual Deep South accent Jenny could not place, but something about it gave the mayor just enough pause to allow the man to continue.

"Mrs. Kermode," the man said, turning to her, "as you well know, permission from a qualified descendant is required to exhume human remains. In the case of historic burials, both Colorado and federal law state that a 'good-faith effort' must be made to locate such descendants before any remains can be exhumed. I assume that The Heights made such an effort?"

The mayor rapped his gavel. "I repeat, you are out of turn, sir!"

"I'm happy to answer the question," Mrs. Kermode said smoothly. "We did indeed make a diligent search for descendants. None could be found. These miners were mostly transients without families, who died a century and a half ago, leaving no issue. It's all in the public documentation."

"Very good," said the mayor. "Thank you, sir, for your opinion. We have many other people who wish to speak. Mr. Jackson?"

But the man went on. "That is strange," he said. "Because in just fifteen minutes of idle, ah, *surfing* on the Internet, I was able to locate a direct descendant of one of the miners."

A silence, and then the mayor spoke. "Just who are you, sir?"

"I'll get to that in a moment." The man raised a piece of paper. "I have here a letter from Captain Stacy Bowdree, USAF, just back from a tour in Afghanistan. When Captain Bowdree heard that you people had dug up her great-great-grandfather Emmett Bowdree, dumped his remains in a box, and stored them in a filthy equipment shed on a ski slope, she was exceedingly upset. In fact, she plans to press charges."

This was greeted by silence.

The man held up another piece of paper. "Colorado statute is very strict on the desecration of cemeteries and human remains. Allow me to read from Section Ninety-Seven of the Colorado Criminal Codes and Statutes: *Desecration of a Cemetery*." And he began to quote aloud.

(2) (a) Every person who shall knowingly and willfully dig up, except as otherwise provided by law with the permission of an authorized descendant, any corpse or remains of any human being, or cause through word, deed or action the same to happen, shall upon conviction be guilty of a Class A felony and shall be imprisoned for not more than thirty (30) years or fined not more than Fifty Thousand Dollars ($50,000.00), or both, in the discretion of the court.

Now the mayor rose in a fury, hammering his gavel. "This is not a court of law!" *Bang!* "I will not have these proceedings co-opted. If you, sir, have legal questions, take them up with the town attorney instead of wasting our time in a public meeting!"

But the man in the black suit would not be silenced. "Mayor, may I direct your attention to the language? *Or cause through word, deed or action the same to happen.* That seems to apply to *you* quite specifically, as well as to Mrs. Kermode and the chief of police. All three of you were responsible in *word, deed or action* for the illegal exhumation of Emmett Bowdree—were you not?"

"Enough! Security, remove this man from the premises!"

Even as two cops struggled to make their way to the man, he spoke again, his voice cutting the air like a razor. "*And are you not about to sentence someone to ten years in prison for violating this very statute that you, yourselves, have already so clearly violated?*"

Now the public was aroused, both pro and con. There were some murmurings and scattered shouts: "Is it true?" and "What goes?" along with "Get rid of him!" and "Who the hell is this guy?"

The two cops, pushing their way through the now-standing public crowd, reached the man. One took his arm.

"Don't give us any trouble, sir."

The man freed himself from the cop's grasp. "I would advise you not to touch me."

"Arrest him for disturbing the peace!" the mayor cried.

"*Let him speak!*" someone shouted.

"Sir," Jenny heard the cop say, "if you won't cooperate, we'll have to arrest you."

The man's response was drowned out by the hubbub. The mayor rapped his gavel repeatedly, calling for order.

"You're under arrest," said the cop. "Place your hands behind your back."

Instead of obeying the order, Jenny saw the man remove his wallet with a single, smooth motion and flip it open. There was a flash of gold, and the two officers froze.

The hubbub began to die down.

"In response to your earlier question," the man told the mayor in his dulcet southern voice, "I am Special Agent Pendergast of the Federal Bureau of Investigation."

Now the entire room went deathly silent. Jenny had never before seen the look she now saw on Mrs. Kermode's face: shock and fury. Henry Montebello's face betrayed nothing at all. Chief Morris, for his part, looked paralyzed. *Paralyzed* wasn't the word—he looked wilted. Slumped. As if he wanted to melt into his chair and disappear. The mayor looked merely undone.

"Emmett Bowdree," the man named Pendergast continued, "is just one of a hundred and thirty human remains that the four of you—Mrs. Kermode, the mayor, Mr. Montebello, and the chief of police who signed the actual order—are responsible for desecrating, according to Colorado statute. The criminal and civil liability is staggering."

Mrs. Kermode recovered first. "Is this how the FBI operates? You come in here, interrupt our public meeting, and make threats? Are you even a real agent? Come down here and present your credentials to the mayor in the proper fashion!"

"Gladly." The pale man slipped through the gate separating the public area from the official one and strolled down the aisle with a sort of insolent casualness. He arrived in front of the mayor and laid the shield down on the podium. The man examined it, his face reflecting growing consternation.

With a sudden, lithe movement, Agent Pendergast plucked the mayor's microphone out of its mount. Only then did Jenny realize that inviting the stranger to the front had probably not been the best idea. She could see the reporter from the *Roaring Fork Times* scribbling madly, a look of pure joy on his face.

Now the mayor spoke, raising his voice on account of having lost his amplification. "Agent Pendergast, are you here in an official capacity?"

"Not yet," came the answer.

"Then I move we adjourn this meeting so that our attorneys, the attorneys from The Heights, and you can address these issues in private." A bang of the gavel sealed this statement.

Agent Pendergast's black-clad arm snaked out, took the gavel, and moved it out of reach of the mayor's hand. "Enough of that uncivilized pounding."

This brought a laugh from the public section.

"I am not yet finished." Pendergast's voice, now amplified by the sound system, filled the hall. "Captain Bowdree wrote me that, since her great-great-grandfather's remains have been so rudely disinterred, and nothing can remedy the insult to his memory, she believes that they should at least be examined for cause of death—for historical purposes, of course. Therefore, she has given permission for a certain Ms. Corrine Swanson to examine those remains before they are reburied. In their *original* resting place, by the way."

"What?" Kermode rose in a fury. "Did that girl send you? Is *she* behind this?"

"She has no idea I'm even here," the man said smoothly. "However, it would seem that the most serious charge against her is now moot—but has instead redounded to the four of you. *You* are now the ones facing thirty years in prison—not on one count, but on one hundred and thirty." He paused. "Imagine if your sentences were to be served sequentially."

"These accusations are outrageous!" the mayor cried. "I hereby adjourn this meeting. Will security immediately clear the room!"

Chaos ensued. But Pendergast did nothing to prevent it, and the meeting room was finally cleared, leaving him alone with the town fathers, The Heights attorneys, Kermode, Montebello, Chief Morris, and a few other officials. Jenny waited in her seat beside the chief, breathless. What would happen now? For the first time, Kermode looked defeated—haggard, her platinum hair undone. The chief was bathed in sweat, the mayor pale.

"It looks like there's going to be quite a story in the *Roaring Fork Times* tomorrow," said Pendergast.

Everyone seemed to stagger at the thought. The mayor wiped his brow.

"In addition to that story," said Pendergast, "I'd like to see another one appear."

There was a long silence. Montebello was the first to speak. "And what might that be?"

"A story stating that you—" Agent Pendergast turned to Chief Morris— "have dropped all charges against Corrine Swanson and released her from jail."

He let that sink in.

"As I said before, the most serious charge is now moot. Ms. Swanson has permission to examine the remains of Emmett Bowdree. The other charges—trespassing and B and E—are less grave and could be dismissed with relative ease. Everything can, in fact, be chalked up to an unfortunate miscommunication between Chief Morris here and Ms. Swanson."

"This is blackmail," said Kermode.

Pendergast turned to her. "I might point out it wasn't actually a miscommunication. My understanding is that Chief Morris indicated she would have access to the remains. He then withdrew that assurance, due to your own gross interference. It was unfair. I am merely rectifying a wrong."

There was a pause while the others digested this. "And what," asked Kermode, "will you do for us in return? That is, if the chief releases this lady friend of yours."

"I'll persuade Captain Bowdree not to take her complaint *officially* to the FBI," Pendergast said smoothly.

"I see," said Kermode. "It all depends on this Captain Bowdree. Provided, of course, this person even exists."

"How unfortunate for you that Bowdree was an unusual name. It made my task so much easier. A phone call established that she was well aware of her Colorado roots and, in fact, quite proud of them. Mrs. Kermode, you claimed The Heights made a good-faith effort to locate descendants. That is clearly a falsehood. Naturally, this is something the FBI would have to look into."

Jenny noticed that under her makeup, Mrs. Kermode's face was very pale. "Let's get this straight. This Swanson girl—she's what, your girlfriend? A relative?"

"She's no relation to me." Agent Pendergast narrowed his silvery eyes and looked at Kermode in a most unsettling way. "I will, however, be remaining in Roaring Fork to take in the Christmas season—and to make sure you don't interfere with her again."

As Jenny watched, Pendergast turned to the chief. "I suggest you call the newspaper right away—I imagine their deadline is looming. I've already booked a room for Ms. Swanson at the Hotel Sebastian, and I hope that—for your sake—she does not spend another night in your jail."

11

It was a few minutes before midnight when the silver Porsche 911 Turbo S Cabriolet pulled up to the elegant front door of 3 Quaking Aspen Drive. It did not stop there, however, but continued on into the shadow of the four-car garage beyond.

The young man at the wheel put the vehicle into park. "Home," he said. "As you requested." He leaned over the gear lever to nuzzle the girl in the passenger seat.

"Stop it," she said, pushing him away.

The young man pretended to look hurt. "I'm a friend, aren't I?"

"Yes."

"Then bring on the benefits." Another attempt at nuzzling.

"What a dork." The girl got out of the car with a laugh. "Thanks for dinner."

"*And* the movie."

"And the movie." Jenny Baker slammed the door, then watched the car move off down the long, curving driveway until it reached the road leading to the gatehouse of The Heights, down in the valley half a mile away. For a lot of her girlfriends back at Hollywood High, losing one's virginity seemed like a badge of honor: the sooner the better. But Jenny didn't feel that way. Not on a first date, and certainly not with a dweeb like Kevin Traherne. Like so many of the male youth in

Roaring Fork, he seemed to think that his father's dough was the only excuse he needed to get into a girl's pants.

She stepped up to the closest garage door, punched a code into the panel, and waited for the door to ascend. Then she walked past the row of gleaming, expensive cars, pressed the button to close the garage, and opened the door to the house. The security alarm was, as usual, off—there were few burglaries in Roaring Fork, and never a one in The Heights…unless you counted Corrie Swanson's breaking into the warehouse, of course. Her thoughts returned to the town meeting earlier in the day, and to the intimidating FBI agent in the black suit who'd descended on it like an avenging angel. She felt sorry for the chief: he was a decent guy, but he had a real problem with letting other people—like that witch Kermode—walk all over him. Nevertheless, she was glad the agent—Pendergast was his name, she remembered—had gotten Corrie out of jail. She hoped to run into her again, ask her about John Jay, maybe…as long as the chief wasn't around.

Jenny walked through the mudroom, through the pantry, and into the expansive kitchen of the vacation home. Through glass doors she could see the Christmas tree, all decked out and blinking. Her parents and her younger sister, Sarah, would be upstairs asleep.

She snapped on a bank of lights. They illuminated the long granite countertops; the Wolf oven and dual Sub-Zero refrigerator and freezer units; the three doors leading, respectively, into the laundry, the second kitchen, and the dining room.

She suddenly realized there had been no patter of nails on the floor, no shaggy, friendly dog wagging his misshapen tail in greeting. "Rex?" she called out.

Nothing.

With a shrug, she got a glass from one of the cabinets, walked over to the fridge—decorated, as usual, with Sarah's stupid Nicki Minaj photos—poured herself a glass of milk, then took a seat at the table in the breakfast nook. There was a stack of books and magazines in the window seat, and she pushed a few aside—noting as she did so that Sarah had finally taken her advice and begun reading *Watership*

Down—and plucked out her copy of Schmalleger's *Criminal Justice Today*. As she did so, she noticed that one of the chairs of the kitchen table had been knocked over.

Sloppy.

She found her page in the book and began to read, sipping her milk as she did so. It drove her father—a high-profile Hollywood lawyer—crazy that she wanted to go into law enforcement. He tended to look down on cops and prosecutors as lower forms of life. But in point of fact he was partly responsible for her interest. All the cop action movie premieres she'd attended—produced or directed by her father's clients—had left her fascinated with the job from an early age. And starting next fall, she'd be studying the subject full-time, as a freshman at Northeastern University.

Finishing her milk, she closed the book again, put her glass in the sink, and walked out of the kitchen, heading for the stairs up to her room. Her father had the connections to keep her from getting summer jobs with the California police, but there was nothing he could do to prevent her winter break internship here in Roaring Fork. The very idea of it made him nuts.

Which, of course, was part of the fun.

The huge, rambling house was very still. She ascended the curving staircase to the second floor, the landing above dark and silent. As she climbed, she thought once again about the mysterious FBI agent. *FBI*, she thought. *Maybe I should look into an internship in Quantico next summer...*

At the top of the stairs, she stopped. Something was wrong. For a moment, she wasn't sure what it was. And then she realized: Sarah's door was wide open, faint light streaming out into the dim hall.

At sixteen, Sarah had reached the age where adolescent privacy was all-important. These days her door was closed at all times. Jenny sniffed the air, but there was no smell of weed. She smiled: her sister must have fallen asleep over a magazine or something. She'd take the opportunity to sneak in and rearrange her sister's stuff. That was sure to get a rise out of her.

Quietly, she crept down the hallway, approaching her sister's room on silent feet. She came up to the door frame, placed one hand upon it, then slowly leaned her head in.

At first, she could not quite process what she saw. Sarah lay on her bed, tied fast with wound wire, a dirty rag stuffed into her mouth, a billiard ball at its center—Jenny noticed a number, seven, engraved into its yellow-and-white surface—and secured behind her head with a bungee cord. In the faint blue light, Jenny saw that her sister's knees were bleeding profusely, staining the bedcovers black. As she gasped in horror and shock, Jenny saw Sarah's eyes staring back at her: wide, terrified, pleading.

Then Jenny registered something in her peripheral vision. She turned in mid-gasp to see a fearful apparition in the hall beside her: wearing black jeans and a tight-fitting jacket of dark leather. The figure was silent and utterly motionless. Its hands were gloved and gripped a baseball bat. Worst of all was the clown mask—white, huge red lips smiling maniacally, bright red circles on each cheek. Jenny stumbled backward, her legs going weak beneath her. Through the eyeholes on each side of the long pointed nose, she could see two dark eyes staring back at her, dreadful in their lack of expression, in awful counterpoint to the leering mask.

Jenny opened her mouth to scream, but the figure—springing into sudden, violent motion—reached forward and quickly stuffed an awful-smelling cloth over her mouth and nose. As her senses went black and she sank to the floor, she could just hear—as the darkness rushed over her—a faint, high-pitched keening coming through Sarah's gag...

Slowly, slowly, she regained her senses. Everything was fuzzy and vague. For a moment, she didn't know where she was. She was lying on something hard and smooth and that seemed to encircle her. Then, looking around in the darkness, she understood: she was in the tub of her private bathroom. What was she doing here? It felt as if she'd been asleep for hours. But no—the wall clock above her sink read ten minutes to one. She'd only been out for a couple of minutes. She tried to move—and realized she had been bound, hand and foot.

That was when the memory of what had happened came rushing back, falling upon her like a dead weight.

Instantly her heart accelerated, pounding hard in her chest. The rag was still in her mouth. She tried to spit it out, found she could not. The tight rope chafed at her wrists and ankles. Crime-scene photos she'd seen came into her mind, flashing quickly by in a terrible parade.

I'm going to be raped, she thought, shuddering at the recollection of that leering clown mask. But no—if rape was what he was after, he wouldn't have tied her up the way he did. This was a home invasion—and she'd walked right into the middle of it.

A home invasion.

Maybe he only wants money, she thought. *Maybe he only wants jewelry. He'll take what he can get, then leave, and then...*

But it was all so horribly stealthy—so diabolically calculating. First Sarah, now her...

...What about Mom and Dad?

At this thought, stark panic bubbled to the surface.

She struggled violently, jaw working, tongue pushing against the cloth wedged into her mouth. She tried to rise up, and an agonizing pain that almost caused her to faint lanced through her legs. She saw that her kneecaps had been beaten like her sister's, white edges of broken bone jutting up through torn, bloody flesh. She remembered the baseball bat clutched in one black-gloved hand, and she moaned in fresh panic, thrashing against the bottom of the tub despite the awful pain in her knees.

All of a sudden, sounds of fighting erupted from down the hall: her father yelling, her mother crying out in fear. Jenny listened in unspeakable horror. Furniture was overturned; there was the sound of breaking glass. Her mother's screams spiked in volume. A heavy thud. Abruptly, her father's shouts of anger and alarm changed to cries of pain. There was an ugly crack of what sounded like wood on bone, and his voice was abruptly cut off.

Jenny listened to the dreadful silence, whimpering under the gag, her heart beating even faster. And then, a moment later, came another sound: sobs, running feet. It was her mother, racing down the hall, trying to escape. Jenny heard her mother go into Sarah's room; heard her scream. And now a heavier tread came down the hall. It was not her father's.

Another cry of fear from her mother; the sound of feet pattering down the stairs. *She'll get away now,* Jenny thought, hope suddenly rising within her like white light. *She'll hit the alarm, she'll run out, call the neighbors, call the cops...*

The unfamiliar tread, faster now, went stomping down the steps.

Heart in her throat, Jenny listened as the sounds grew fainter. She heard her mother's step, running toward the kitchen and the master alarm panel. There was a cry as she was apparently cut off. The thunk of an overturned chair; the sound of glassware and dishes crashing to the floor. Jenny, struggling against her bonds, could hear it all, could follow the chase with dreadful articulation. She heard her mother's footsteps, running through the den, the living room, the library. A moment of silence. And then came a low, cautious sliding sound: it was her mother, quietly opening the door to the indoor pool. *She's going out the back,* Jenny thought. *Out the back, so she can get to the MacArthurs' house...*

All of a sudden there was a series of brutal crashes—her mother gave out a single, sharp scream—and then silence.

No...not quite silence. As Jenny listened, wide-eyed, whimpering, the blood rushing in her ears, she could make out the unfamiliar tread again. It was moving slowly now, deliberately. And it was getting closer. It was crossing the front hall. Now it was coming back up the stairs: she heard the squeak of the tread her father kept saying he'd get fixed.

Closer. Closer. The steps were coming down the hall. They were in her bedroom. And now a dark figure appeared in the doorway of her bath. It was silent, save for labored breathing. The clown mask leered down at her. There was no longer a baseball bat in one of the hands. It had been replaced by a plastic squeeze bottle, glowing pale gold in the faint light.

The figure stepped into the bathroom.

As it came closer, Jenny writhed in the tub, heedless of the pain in her knees. Now the invader was hovering over her. The hand holding the squeeze bottle came forward in her direction. As the figure began silently squeezing the liquid over her in long, arc-like jets, a powerful stench rose up: gasoline.

Jenny's struggles became frantic.

Painstakingly, Clown Mask sent the looping squirts of gasoline over and around her, missing nothing, dousing her clothes; her hair; the surrounding porcelain. Then—as her struggles grew ever more violent—the invader put down the bottle and took a step back. A hand reached into the pocket of the leather jacket, withdrew a safety match. Holding the match carefully by its end, the figure struck it against the rough surface of the bathroom wall. The head of the match flared into yellow life. It hovered over her, dangling, for an endless, agonizing second.

And then, with the parting of a thumb and index finger, it dropped.

...And Jenny's world dissolved into a roar of flame.

12

Corrie Swanson entered the dining room of the Hotel Sebastian and found herself dazzled by its elegance. It was done up in Gay Nineties style, with red velvet flocked wallpaper, polished-brass and cut-glass fixtures, a pressed-tin ceiling, and Victorian-era mahogany tables and chairs trimmed in silk and gold. A wall of windowpanes looked across the glittering Christmas lights of Main Street to the spruce-clad foothills, ski slopes, and mountain peaks beyond.

Even though it was close to midnight, the dining room was crowded, the convivial murmur of voices mingling with the clink of glassware and the bustle of waiters. The light was dim, and it took her a moment to spy the solitary figure of Pendergast, seated at an unobtrusive table by one of the windows.

She brushed off the maître d's pointed inquiries as to how he could help her—she was still dressed from jail—and made her way to Pendergast's table. He rose, extending his hand. She was startled by his appearance: he seemed to be even paler, leaner, more ascetic—the word *purified* seemed somehow to apply.

"Corrie, I am glad to see you." He took her hand in his, cool as marble, then held out her seat for her. She sat down.

She'd been rehearsing what she would say, but now it all came out in a confused rush. "I can't believe I'm free—how can I ever thank you? I was toast, I mean, I was up shit creek, you know they'd already forced me to accept ten years—I really thought my life was over—thank you, *thank you* for everything, for saving my ass, for rescuing me from my incredible, unbelievable *stupidity*, and I'm so sorry, really, *really* sorry—!"

A raised hand stopped the flow of words. "Will you have a drink? Wine, perhaps?"

"Um, I'm only twenty."

"Ah. Of course. I shall order a bottle for myself, then." He picked up a leather-bound wine list that was so massive, it could have been a murder weapon.

"This sure beats jail," said Corrie, looking around, drinking in the ambience, the aroma of food. It was hard to believe that, just a few hours ago, she'd been behind bars, her life utterly ruined. But once again Agent Pendergast had swooped in, like a guardian angel, and changed everything.

"It took them rather longer than I'd hoped to complete the paperwork," said Pendergast, perusing the list. "Fortunately, the Sebastian's dining room is open late. I think the Château Pichon-Longueville 2000 will do nicely—don't you?"

"I don't know jack about wine, sorry."

"You should learn. It is one of the true and ancient pleasures that make human existence tolerable."

"Um, I know this may not be the time...But I just have to ask you..." She found herself coloring. "*Why* did you rescue me like this? And why do you go to all this trouble for me? I mean, you got me out of Medicine Creek, you paid for my boarding school, you're helping pay my tuition at John Jay—why? I'm just a screwup."

He looked at her with an inscrutable gaze. "The Colorado rack of lamb for two would go well with the wine. I understand it's excellent."

She glanced at the menu. She was, it had to be admitted, starving. "Sounds good to me."

Pendergast waved over the waiter and placed the order.

"Anyway, getting back to what I was talking about...I would really like to know, once and for all, why you've helped me all these years. Especially when I keep, you know, effing up."

Again that impenetrable gaze met hers. "*Effing*? I see your penchant for charming euphemisms has not abated."

"You know what I mean."

The gaze seemed to go on forever, and then Pendergast said: "Someday, perhaps, you may make a good law enforcement officer or criminalist. That is why. No other reason."

She felt herself coloring again. She wasn't quite sure she liked the answer. Now she wished she hadn't asked the question.

Pendergast picked up the wine list again. "Remarkable how many bottles of excellent French wine in rare vintages have found their way into this small town in the middle of the mountains. I certainly hope they are drunk soon; the altitude here is most unhealthy for Bordeaux." He laid down the list. "And now, Corrie, please tell me in detail what you noticed about the bones of Mr. Emmett Bowdree."

She swallowed. Pendergast was so damn...*closed*. "I only had a few minutes to examine the bones. But I'm sure the guy was not killed by a grizzly bear."

"Your evidence?"

"I took some photographs, but they confiscated the memory chip. I can tell you what I saw—or at least *think* I saw."

"Excellent."

"First of all, the skull showed signs of having been bashed in by a rock. And the right femur had scrape marks made by some blunt tool, with no signs that I could see of an osseous reaction or infectious response."

A slow nod.

She went on with growing confidence. "It looked to me like there were faint human tooth marks in some of the cancellous bone. They were pretty feeble and blunt, not sharp like a bear's. I think the corpse was cannibalized."

In her zeal she'd raised her voice, and now she realized it had carried farther than she'd intended. The diners closest to them were staring at her.

"Oops," she said, looking down at her place setting.

"Have you told anyone of this?" Pendergast asked.

"Not yet."

"Very good. Keep it quiet. It will only create trouble."

"But I need access to more remains."

"I'm working on that. Of the other miners in question, I'm hoping we might find descendants in at least a few cases. And then, naturally, we'd have to get permission."

"Oh. Thanks, but, you know, I could really do those things my-self." She paused. "Um, how long do you plan to stay? A few days?"

"Such a lovely, self-indulgent, *rich* little town. I don't believe I've seen anything quite like it. And so charming at Christmastime."

"So you're going to stay...a long time?"

"Ah, here's the wine."

It had arrived, along with two big glasses. Corrie watched as Pendergast went through the whole routine of swirling the wine around in the glass, smelling it, tasting it, tasting it again.

"Corked, I'm afraid," he told the waiter. "Please bring another bottle. Make it an '01, to be on the safe side."

With profuse apologies, the waiter hurried off with the bottle and glass.

"Corked?" Corrie asked. "What's that?"

"It's a contaminant of wine, giving it a taste redolent of, some say, a wet dog."

The new bottle came out and Pendergast went through the routine again, this time nodding his approval. The waiter filled his glass, motioned the bottle toward Corrie. She shrugged and the man filled her glass as well.

Corrie sipped it. It tasted like wine to her—no more, no less. She said, "This is almost as good as the Mateus we all used to drink back in Medicine Creek."

"I see you still enjoy provoking me."

She took another sip. It was amazing, how quickly the memory of jail was fading. "Getting back to my release," she said. "How did you do it?"

"As it happens, I was already on my way back to New York when I received your second letter."

"You finally got sick of traveling the world?"

"It was your first letter, in part, that prompted my return."

"Oh? Why's that?"

Instead of answering, Pendergast peered into the dark ruby of his wineglass. "I was fortunate in locating Captain Bowdree so quickly. I explained everything to her frankly—how her ancestor had been rudely exhumed from his historic resting place to make way for a spa. I explained who you were, what your background was, how the chief promised you access and then withdrew it. I told her about your foolish break-in, how you got caught. And then I mentioned you were facing a ten-year prison sentence."

He sipped his wine. "The captain understood the situation immediately. She was most unwilling for you to be, as she put it, *fucked over* like that. She repeated that phrase several times with remarkable emphasis, and it led me to believe she may have had some experience in that line—perhaps in the military. At any rate, together we composed a rather effective letter, which on the one hand threatened to complain to the FBI and, on the other, gave you permission to study the remains of her ancestor."

"Oh," said Corrie. "And that's how you got me out?"

"There was a rather boisterous town meeting this afternoon, at which I discussed the captain's letter." Pendergast allowed himself the faintest of smiles. "My presentation was singularly effective. You'll read all about it in tomorrow's paper."

"Well, you saved my butt. I can't thank you enough. And please thank Captain Bowdree for me."

"I shall."

There was a sharp murmur in the dining room; a stir. Several patrons had begun looking toward the wall of windows, and some had stood up from their tables and were pointing. Corrie followed their gaze and saw a small, flickering yellow light on the side of a nearby ridge. As she watched, it rapidly grew in brightness and size. Now more restaurant patrons were standing, and some were walking toward the windows. The hubbub increased.

"Oh, my God, that's a house on fire!" Corrie said, standing up herself to get a better view.

"So it would seem."

The fire blossomed with shocking rapidity. It appeared to be a huge house and the flames engulfed it with increasing violence, leaping into the night air, sending up columns of sparks and smoke. A fire siren began to go off in the town somewhere, followed by another. And now the entire dining room was on its feet, eyes glued to the mountain. A sense of horror had fallen on the diners, a hush—and then a voice rang out.

"That's the Baker house, up in The Heights!"

13

Larry Chivers had seen many scenes of destruction in his career as a fire investigator, but he had never seen anything like this. The house had been gigantic—fifteen-thousand-plus square feet—and built with massive timbers, beams, log walls, and soaring, cedar-shake roofs. It had burned with a ferocity that left puddles of glass where the windows had been and even warped the steel I-beam stringers. The snow had completely vanished from within a five-hundred-yard perimeter of the house, and the ruin still radiated heat and plumes of foul steam.

Chivers, who ran a fire investigation consulting firm out of Grand Junction, had been called in at seven that morning. Most of his work was for insurance companies looking to prove arson so they didn't have to pay claims. But once in a while he got called in by the police to determine if a fire was an accident or a crime. This was one of those times.

It was a two-hour drive from Grand Junction, but he'd made it in ninety minutes, driving like hell in his Dodge pickup. Chivers liked traveling with the lightbar and siren going full blast, whipping past the poor speed-limit-bound schmucks on the interstate. Adding to the appeal of this case, the Roaring Fork Police Department paid well and didn't nickel-and-dime him to death like some of the other PDs he worked for.

But his exhilaration had been dampened by this scene of horror.

Even Morris, the chief of police, seemed undone by it: stammering, inarticulate, unable to take charge. Chivers did his best to shake the feeling. The fact is, these were rich Hollywood types who used this colossal house as a second home—second home!—only a few weeks out of the year. It was hard to gin up a lot of sympathy for people like that. No doubt the homeowner could build five more just like it and barely dent his wallet. The man who owned this house, a fellow named Jordan Baker, hadn't been heard from, and nobody had been able to reach him yet to inform him of the fire. He and his family were probably off at some posh resort. Or maybe they had a *third* home. It wouldn't surprise Chivers.

He began preparing himself for the walk-through, checking and organizing his equipment, testing his digital recorder, putting on latex gloves. One good thing about the chief's apparent paralysis was that the fire scene hadn't been trampled over and messed up by all the forensic specialists who were still gathering around, waiting to do their thing. Morris had pretty much kept everyone out, waiting for his arrival, and for that he was grateful. Although, as usual, there was considerable disturbance from firefighter activity—chopped-through floors and walls, shoveled and turned debris, everything soaked with water. The fire department had done a cursory structural integrity survey and had identified the areas that were unstable, taping them off.

Chivers shouldered his bag and nodded to Chief Morris. "Ready."

"Good," the chief said absently. "Fine. Rudy will take you through."

The fireman named Rudy lifted the tape for him, and he followed the man down the brick walkway and through where the front door had been. The fire scene stank heavily of burnt and soggy plastic, wood, and polyurethane. There was still some residual heat—despite the freezing temperature the house itself was still sending plumes of steam into the cold blue sky. While he was required to wear a hard hat, he did not wear a respirator: Chivers saw himself as an old-fashioned fire-scene investigator, tough, no-nonsense, who relied more on intuition and left the science to the lab rats. He was used to the stench—and he needed his nose to sniff out any residual accelerants.

Inside the door, in what had been the entryway, he paused. The second floor had collapsed into the first, creating a crazy mess. A staircase ended in the sky. Puddles of glass and metal lay in the low spots, along with heaps of fire-shattered porcelain.

He walked from the entryway into what had obviously been the kitchen, observing the burn patterns. The first order of business was to determine if this was arson—if a crime had been committed. And Chivers was already sure one had. Only accelerants could have caused a fire to burn so hot and fast. This was confirmed as he looked around the kitchen, where he could see faint pour patterns on the remains of the slate floor. He knelt, removed a portable hydrocarbon sniffer from his bag, and took some air samples, moving it about. Moderate.

Still kneeling, he jammed a knife into the burnt, flaking floor and pried up a couple of small pieces, placing them in nylon evidence bags.

The kitchen was a mess, everything fused, scorched, melted. A second-floor bathroom had fallen into the middle of it, with the remains of a porcelain-covered iron claw-foot tub and bits of the sink, toilet, tiled floor, and walls all heaped and scattered about.

Using the sniffer, he got a big positive hit from the remains of the second-floor bathroom. Moving forward on hands and knees, keeping the sniffer low to the ground, Chivers swept it about, looking for a source. The hydrocarbon signature appeared to increase as he approached the tub itself. He rose, peered inside. There was a lot of stuff in the tub—and at the bottom, a layer of thick, black muck in which debris was embedded.

He sampled the muck, giving it a little stir with a gloved finger. The sniffer went off the charts. And then Chivers stopped cold. Among the muck and debris he could see the fragments of bones poking up—and in the area he had stirred up, some teeth. Human teeth. He carefully probed with his gloved finger, exposing a small piece of a skull, a fragment of jaw, and the rim of an orbit.

Chivers steadied himself, lowered the sniffer. The needle shot up again.

He took out his digital recorder and began murmuring into it. The house had not been empty, after all. Clearly, a body had been placed in the bathtub and burned with accelerant. Putting aside the recorder, he removed another nylon evidence bag and took samples of the debris and muck, including a few small bone fragments. As he poked about in the black paste he saw the gleam of something—a lump of gold, no doubt once a piece of jewelry. He left that, but took samples from the grit and muck around it, including a charred phalange.

He stood up, breathing heavily, feeling a faint wave of nausea. This was a bit more than he was used to. But then again, this was clearly going to be a big case. A very big case. *Focus on that*, he told himself, taking another deep breath.

Chivers nodded to Rudy and continued to follow the fireman through the rest of the house, working the sniffer, taking samples, and speaking his observations into the handheld digital recorder. The charred corpse of what had once been a dog was fused to the stone floor at the back door of the house. Next to it lay two long, disordered piles of gritty ashes, which Chivers recognized as the much-burnt remains of two more victims, both adults judging by the length of the piles, lying side by side. More puddles of gold and silver.

Jesus. He took a sniffer reading but didn't come up with anything significant. Christ, no one had told him—and now he realized they probably didn't know—that the fire had claimed human victims.

Another couple of deep breaths, and Chivers moved on. And then, in what had been the living room, he came upon something else. Debris from the collapsed floor above lay in sodden heaps, and sitting in the center was a set of partly melted bedsprings. As he moved toward the twisted springs, he noted loops of baling wire affixed to them, as if something had been tied to the bed. Four loops—approximately where the ankles and hands would have been. And in one of those loops, he spied a fragment of a small, juvenile tibia.

Oh, Jesus and Mary. Chivers moved the sniffer to it, and again the needle pinned. It was all too clear what had happened. A kid had been wired to the bed, doused with accelerant, and set on fire.

"I need some air," he said abruptly, rising and staggering. "Air."

The fireman grabbed his arm. "Let me help you out, sir."

As Chivers exited the fire scene and reeled down the walkway, he saw—out of the corner of his eye—a pale man, dressed in black, no doubt the local coroner, standing beyond the edge of the crowd, staring at him. He made a huge effort to pull himself together.

"I'm all right, thanks," he said to the firefighter, shedding the embarrassing arm. He looked around, located Chief Morris at the makeshift command center, surrounded by the gathering forensic teams—photographers, hair and fiber, latent, ballistics, DNA. They were suiting up, preparing to go in.

Take it easy, he said to himself. But he could not take it easy. His legs felt like rubber, and it was hard to walk straight.

He approached the chief. Morris was sweating, despite the cold. "What did you find?" he asked, his voice quiet.

"It's a crime scene," said Chivers, trying to control the quaver in his voice. Faint lights were dancing in front of his eyes now. "Four victims. At least, four so far."

"Four? Oh, my God. So they were in there. The whole family..." The chief wiped his brow with a shaking hand.

Chivers swallowed. "One of the remains is of a...a juvenile who was...tied to a bed, doused with accelerant...and set on fire. Another was burned in...in..."

As Chivers tried to get out the words, the chief's face went slack. But Chivers barely noticed. His own world was getting darker and darker.

And then, as he was still trying to finish his sentence, Chivers folded to the ground, collapsing in a dead faint.

14

Corrie had risen before dawn, gathered her equipment, and headed up to Roaring Fork. Now, as noon approached, she was ensconced in the warehouse at The Heights and well into her work. The remains of Emmett Bowdree were carefully arranged on a plastic folding table Corrie had bought at Walmart, under a set of strong studio lights. She had her stereo zoom in place, hooked to her laptop, the screen displaying the view from the microscope. Her Nikon stood on its tripod. It was like a little piece of heaven, being able to work carefully and thoroughly, without being half scared out of her wits and worrying about detection at any moment.

The only problem was, she was freezing her ass off. It had been below zero when she began the long drive from Basalt—having refused the free room at the Hotel Sebastian, courtesy of Pendergast. She had skipped breakfast to save money, and now she was starving as well as cold. She'd set up a cheap electric heater at her feet, but it was rattling and humming and the stream of warm air seemed to dissipate within inches of its grille. It was doing a good job of warming her shins, but that was about it.

Still, not even the cold and hunger could dampen her growing excitement at what she was finding. Almost all the bones showed trauma in the form of scrape marks, blunt cuts, and gouges. None of the marks showed signs of an osseous reaction, inflammation, or granulation—which meant the damage had been inflicted at the actual time of death. The soft, cancellous or spongy bone tissue showed unmistakable tooth marks—not bear but human, judging from the radius of the bite and the tooth profile. There were, in fact, no bear tooth or claw marks at all.

Inside the broken femur and inside the skull, she had discovered additional scraping and gouging marks, indicating that the marrow and brains had been reamed out by a metal tool. Under the stereo zoom, these defleshing marks disclosed some very faint parallel lines, close together, and what looked like iron oxide deposits—which suggested the tool was iron and, quite possibly, a worn file.

The initial blow to the cranium had definitely been inflicted by a rock. Under the microscope, she had been able to extract a few tiny fragments of it, which a cursory examination showed to be quartz.

The rib cage had been split open—also with a rock—and pulled apart, as if to get at the heart. The bones showed little evidence of trauma inflicted by a sharp edge—such as an ax or knife—nor were there any injuries consistent with a gunshot wound. This puzzled her, as most miners of the time would no doubt have been armed with either a knife or a pistol.

The contemporary newspaper account of the discovery of Emmett Bowdree's body indicated that his bones had been found scattered on the ground a hundred yards beyond the door of a cabin; he had been "almost entirely eaten" by the so-called bear. The newspaper article, perhaps for reasons of delicacy, didn't go into much detail on exactly what had been eaten or how the bones were disarticulated, except to note that "pieces of the heart and other viscera were discovered at a distance from the body, partially consumed." The article made no mention of a fire or cooking, and her examination of the remains showed no evidence of heat.

Emmett Bowdree had been eaten raw.

As she worked, she began to see, in her mind's eye, the sequence of injuries that had been inflicted on the body of Bowdree. He had been set upon by a group—no single person could have pulled a human body apart with such an extremity of violence. They struck him on the back of the head with a rock, causing a severe depressed fracture. While it may not have killed him instantly, it almost certainly rendered him unconscious. They gave the body a savage beating that broke almost every bone, and then proceeded to chop and pound at the body's major articulations— there was evidence of disorganized, haphazard hacking with broken rocks, followed by separation via a strong lateral force. After breaking the joints, they pulled the arms and legs from the torso, separated the legs at the knees, broke open the skull and removed the brains, stripped the flesh from the bones, broke up the larger bones and reamed out the marrow, and removed most of the organs. The killers appeared to have only one tool, a worn-out file, which they supplemented with sharp pieces of quartz rock, their hands, and their teeth.

Corrie surmised that the killing started out as a product of fury and anger, then evolved into—essentially—a cannibal feast. She stepped back from the remains for a moment, thinking. Who was the gang who did this? Why? Again, it seemed exceedingly strange to her that a gang of murderers would be roaming the mountains in the 1870s without guns or knives. And why didn't they cook the meat? It was almost as if they were a tribe of Stone Age killers, merciless and savage.

Merciless and savage. As she warmed herself in front of the heater, rubbing her hands together, Corrie's mind wandered once again to the terrible fire that had taken place the evening before—and the death of the girl, Jenny Baker. It was beyond horrible, the entire family perishing in the fire like that. A maintenance worker had stopped by the warehouse an hour earlier and given her the news. No wonder she'd managed to breeze through The Heights security at ten that morning with barely a nod, left to her own devices without a minder.

The horror of it, and the face of Jenny Baker—so earnest and pretty—haunted her. *Focus on your work,* she told herself, straightening up and preparing to place another bone on the stage for examination.

What she really needed was to get her hands on more sets of remains for comparison. Pendergast had said he was going to help her track down more descendants. She paused for a moment in her work, trying to figure out what it was about this that annoyed her. The force of his personality was such that he dominated any situation he was in. But this was *her* project—and she wanted to do it on her own. She didn't want to have people back at John Jay, especially her advisor, dismissing her work because of the help of a big-time FBI agent. Even the smallest amount of assistance from him might contaminate her achievement, giving them an opening to dismiss it all.

Then Corrie shook this thought away as well. The guy had just saved her career and maybe even her life. To get so possessive, so proprietary, was churlish. Besides, Pendergast always shunned credit or publicity.

She pulled off her gloves to position a tibia on the stereo zoom stage, moving it around until the light raked over it at just the right angle. It showed the same signs as the other bones: fracture damage with plastic response, no evidence of healing, scrape marks, and the clearest set of tooth marks yet. The people who had done this were freaks. Or had they just been really, really angry?

Her hands just about froze, but she managed to get a set of photographs before she had to stop and warm herself again at the heater.

Of course, it was possible this was an isolated case. The other victims might have indeed been killed by a rogue grizzly. The news reports quoted witnesses who had seen the animal, and in one instance a miner had been found in the process of being eaten—or, at least, his bones gnawed upon. Corrie was sorely tempted to check one of the other coffins, but resisted the impulse. From now on, she was going to do everything absolutely and totally by the book.

Able to feel her hands once again, she straightened up. If the other remains did prove to be the work of a gang of killers, her thesis would have to change. She would have a hundred-and-fifty-year-old serial killing on her hands to document. And it would be very cool—and a huge boost to her nascent career—if she could actually manage to solve it.

15

Larry Chivers stood beside his truck, sealing the nylon evidence bags with a heat sealer and finishing up his notes and observations. He had recovered from his fainting spell, but not from his sense of furious embarrassment. Such a thing had never happened to him—ever. He imagined that everyone was looking at him, whispering about him.

With a grimace, he finished working on the final evidence bag, careful to make the seal complete. Already, he'd narrated the rest of his observations into the digital recorder while they were still fresh. He had to make absolutely sure he did everything just right. This was going to be a huge case—probably even national.

There was a sound behind him, and he turned to see Chief Morris approaching. The man looked utterly undone.

"Sorry about my reaction back there," Chivers muttered.

"I knew the family," the chief told him. "One of the girls worked as an intern in my office."

Chivers shook his head. "I'm sorry."

"I'd like to hear your reconstruction of the fire."

"I can give you my first impressions. The lab results may take a few days."

"Go ahead."

Chivers took a deep breath. "Point of origin of the fire, in my view, would be either the second-floor bath or the bedroom above the liv-

ing room. Both areas were doused heavily with accelerant—so much
so that the perp would have had to leave the house fairly quickly. Both
areas contained human remains."

"You mean, the Bakers…the victims…were burned with accelerant?"

"Two of them, yes."

"Alive?"

What a question. "That'll have to wait for the M.E. But I doubt it."

"Thank God."

"Two more victims were found by the back door—probably
where the perp made his exit. There was the body of a dog there, too."

"Rex," said the chief to himself, wiping his brow with a trembling
hand.

Chivers noted the same man in the black suit he'd seen before,
floating in the background, eyes on them. He frowned. Why was the
undertaker allowed inside the cordon?

"Motive?" asked the chief.

"Now I'm guessing," Chivers continued, "but from thirty years of
experience I'd say pretty definitely we're looking at a home invasion
and robbery, combined with possible sex crimes. The fact that the entire family was subdued and controlled suggests to me there might
have been more than one perp."

"This was no robbery," came a soft, drawling voice.

Chivers jerked his head around to find that the man in the black
suit had somehow managed to approach without being noticed and
was now standing behind them.

Chivers's scowl deepened. "I'm talking to the chief. Do you
mind?"

"Not at all. But if I may, I would like to offer a few observations for
the benefit of the investigation. A mere robber would not have gone
to the trouble to tie up his victims and then burn them alive."

"*Alive?*" the chief said. "How do you know?"

"The sadism and rage evident in the arc of this crime are palpable.
A sadist wishes to see his victims suffer. That is how he derives his
gratification. To tie someone to a bed, douse that person with gaso-

line, and light them on fire—where's the gratification in that, if the person is already dead?"

The chief's face went as gray as putty. His mouth moved but no sound came out.

"Bullshit," said Chivers fiercely. "This was a home invasion and robbery. I've seen it before. The perps break in, find a couple of pretty girls, have their way with them, load up on jewelry, and then burn down the place thinking they'll destroy the evidence—particularly the DNA inside the girls."

"Yet they didn't take the jewelry, as you yourself noted in your taped observations a few minutes ago, regarding some lumps of gold you discovered."

"Hold on, here. You were *listening* to me? Who the hell are you?" Chivers turned to the chief. "Is this guy official?"

The chief passed a sopping handkerchief across his brow. He looked indecisive and frightened. "Please. Enough."

The man in the black suit regarded him a moment with his silver eyes, and then shrugged nonchalantly. "I have no official role here. I am merely a bystander offering his impressions. I shall leave you gentlemen to your work."

With that he turned and began to leave. Then he paused to speak over his shoulder. "I should mention, however: there may well be...*more*."

And with that he walked off, slipping under the tape and disappearing into the crowd of rubberneckers.

16

Horace P. Fine III stopped, swiveled on his instep, and looked Corrie up and down, as if he had just thought of something.

"Do you have any experience house-sitting?" he asked.

"Yes, absolutely," Corrie replied immediately. It was sort of true: she'd watched their trailer home overnight more than once when her mother went on an all-night bender. And then there was the time she'd stayed at her father's apartment six months before, when he'd gone to that job fair in Pittsburgh.

"Never anyplace this big, though," she added, looking around.

Fine looked at her suspiciously—but then again, maybe it was just the way his face was put together. It seemed that every syllable she'd uttered had been greeted by distrust.

"Well, I don't have time to check your references," he replied. "The person I'd arranged to take the position backed out at the last minute, and I'm overdue in New York." His eyes narrowed slightly. "But I'll be keeping an eye on you. Come on, I'll show you to your rooms."

Corrie, following the man down the long, echoing first-floor hallway, wondered just how Horace P. Fine planned to keep an eye on her from two thousand miles away.

At first it had seemed almost like a miracle. She'd learned of the opening by coincidence: a conversation, overheard at a coffee shop, about a house that needed looking after. A few phone calls led her to the mansion's owner. It would be an ideal situation—in Roaring Fork no less. No more driving eighteen miles each way to her fleabag motel room. She could even move in that very day. Now she'd be earning money instead of spending it—and doing so in style.

But when she'd dropped by the mansion to meet with the owner, her enthusiasm dimmed. Although the house was technically in Roaring Fork, it was way up in the foothills, completely isolated, at the end of a narrow, winding, mile-long private road. It was huge, to be sure, but of a dreary postmodern design of glass, steel, and slate that was more reminiscent of an upscale dentist's office than a home. Unlike most of the big houses she'd seen, which were perched on hillsides offering fantastic views, this house was built in a declivity, practically a bowl in the mountains, surrounded on three sides by tall fir trees that seemed to throw the place into perpetual gloom. On the fourth side was a deep, icy ravine that ended in a rockfall of snow-covered boulders. Ironically, most of the vast plate-glass windows of the house overlooked this "feature." The decor was so aggressively contemporary as to be almost prison-like in austerity, all chrome and glass and marble—not a straight edge to be found anywhere save the doorways—and the walls were covered with grinning masks, hairy weavings, and other creepy-looking African art. And the place was cold, too—almost as cold as the ski warehouse where she did her work. Corrie had kept her coat on during the entire walk-through.

"This leads down to the second basement," Fine said, pausing to point at a closed door. "The older furnace is down there. It heats the eastern quarter of the house."

Heats. Yeah, right. "Second basement?" Corrie asked aloud.

"It's the only part of the original house that still exists. When they demolished the lodge, the developer retained the basement for retrofitting into the new house."

"There was a lodge here?"

Fine scoffed. "It was called Ravens Ravine Lodge, but it was just an old log cabin. A photographer used it for a home base when he went out into the mountains to take pictures. Adams, the name was. They tell me he was famous."

Adams. Ansel Adams? Corrie could just picture it. There had probably been a cozy, rustic little cabin here once, nestled in among the pines—until it got razed for this monstrosity. She wasn't surprised that Fine was not familiar with Adams—only a Philistine, or his soon-to-be ex-wife, could have bought all this freaky art.

Horace Fine himself was almost as cold as the house. He ran a hedge fund back in Manhattan. Or maybe it was the U.S. branch of some foreign investment bank; Corrie hadn't really been listening when he told her. Hedge, branch—it was all so much shrubbery to her. Luckily, he seemed not to have heard of her or her recent stay in the local jail. He'd made it quite clear that he detested Roaring Fork; he hated the house; and he loathed the woman who had forced him to buy it and who was now making its disposal as difficult as she possibly could. "The virago" was the way he had named her to Corrie over the last twenty minutes. All he wanted to do was get someone in the house and get the hell back to New York, the sooner the better.

He led the way down the corridor. The house was as strangely laid out as it was ugly. It seemed to be made up of a single endless hallway, which veered at an angle now and then to conform with the topography. All the important rooms were on the left, facing the ravine. Everything else—the bathrooms, closets, utility rooms—was on the right, like carbuncles on a limb. From what she could tell, the second floor featured a similar layout.

"What's in here?" she asked, stopping before a partially open door on the right. There were no overhead lights on inside, but the room was nevertheless lit up with a ghostly gleam from dozens of points of green, red, and amber.

Fine stopped again. "That's the tech space. You might as well see it, too."

He opened the door wide and snapped on the light. Corrie looked around at a dizzying array of panels, screens, and instrumentation.

"This is a 'smart' house, of course," Fine said. "Everything's automated, and you can monitor it all from here: the generator status, the power grid, the security layout, the surveillance system. Cost a fortune, but it ultimately saved me a lot in insurance charges. And it's all networked and Internet-accessible, too. I can run the whole system from my computers in New York."

So that's what he meant by keeping an eye on me, Corrie thought. "How does the surveillance system work?"

Fine pointed to a large flat panel, with a small all-in-one computer to one side and a device below that looked like a DVD player on steroids. "There are a total of twenty-four cameras." He pressed a button and the flat panel sprang to life, showing a picture of the living room. There was a number in the upper left-hand corner of the image, and time and date stamps running along the bottom. "These twenty-four buttons, here, are each dedicated to one of the cameras." He pressed the button marked DRIVEWAY and the image changed, showing a picture of, what else, the driveway, with her Rent-a-Junker front and center.

"Can you manipulate the cameras?" Corrie asked.

"No. But any motion picked up by the sensors activates the camera and is recorded on a hard disk. There—take a look." Fine pointed to the screen, where a deer was now passing across the driveway. As it moved, it became surrounded by a small cloud of black squares—almost like the framing windows of a digital camera—that followed the animal. At the same time, a large red *M* inside a circle appeared on the screen.

"*M* for 'movement,'" Fine said.

The deer had moved off the screen, but the red letter remained. "Why is the *M* still showing?" Corrie asked.

"Because when one of the cameras detects movement, a recording of that video feed is saved to the hard disk, starting a minute before movement begins and continuing one minute past when it stops. Then—if there's no more movement—the *M* goes away."

Movement. "And you can monitor all this over the Internet?" Corrie asked. She didn't like the idea of being the subject of a long-distance voyeur.

"No. That part of the smart system was never connected to the Internet. We stopped the work on the security system when we decided to sell the house. Let the new owner pick up the cost. But it works just fine from in here." Fine pointed to another button. "You can also split the screen by repeatedly pressing this button." For the first time, Fine seemed engaged. He demonstrated, and the image split in two: the left half of the monitor showing the original image of the driveway, with the right showing a view looking over the ravine. Repeated pressings of the button split the screen into four, then nine, then sixteen increasingly smaller images, each from a different camera.

Corrie's curiosity was quickly waning. "And how do I operate the security alarm?" she asked.

"That was never installed, either. That's why I need someone to keep an eye on the place."

He snapped off the light and led the way out of the room, down the hallway, and through a door at its end. Suddenly the house became different. Gone was the expensive artwork, the ultramodern furniture, the gleaming professional-grade appliances. Ahead lay a short, narrow hall with two doors on each side, ending in another door leading into a small bathroom with cheap fixtures. The floor was of linoleum, and the pasteboard walls were devoid of pictures. All the surfaces were painted dead white.

"The maid's quarters," Fine said proudly. "Where you'll be staying."

Corrie stepped forward, peering into the open doors. The two on the left opened into bedrooms of almost monastic size and asceticism. One of the doors on the right led into a kitchen with a dorm-style refrigerator and a cheap stove; the other room appeared to be a minuscule den. It was barely a cut above her motel room in Basalt.

"As I said, I'm leaving almost immediately," Fine said. "Come back to the den and I'll give you the key. Any questions?"

"Where's the thermostat?" Corrie asked, hugging herself to keep from shivering.

"Down here." Fine stepped out of the maid's quarters and went back down the hall, turning in to the sitting room. There was a thermostat on the wall, all right—covered in a clear plastic box with a lock on it.

"Fifty degrees," Fine said.

Corrie looked at him. "I'm sorry?"

"Fifty degrees. That's what I've set the house at and that's where it's going to stay. I'm not going to spend a penny more on this god-damn house than I have to. Let the virago pay the utilities if she wants to. And that's another thing—keep electricity use to a minimum. Just a couple of lights, as absolutely necessary." A thought seemed to strike the man. "And by the way, the thermostat settings and the kilowatt usage *have* been wired into the Internet. I'll be able to monitor them from my iPhone."

Corrie looked at the locked thermostat with a sinking heart. *Great. So now I'm going to be freezing my rear off by night as well as by day.* She began to understand why the original applicant had decided against the job.

Fine was glancing at her with a look that meant the interview was over. That left just one question.

"How much does the house-sitting job pay?" she asked.

Fine's eyes widened in surprise. "Pay? You're getting to stay, free, in a big, beautiful house, right here in Roaring Fork—and you expect a *salary*? You're lucky I'm not charging you rent."

And he led the way back toward the den.

17

Arnaz Johnson, hairdresser to the stars, had seen a lot of unusual people in his day hanging out at the famous Big Pine Lodge on the very top of Roaring Fork Mountain—movie starlets decked out as if for the Oscars; billionaires squiring about their trophy girlfriends in minks and sables; wannabe Indians in ten-thousand-dollar designer buckskins; pseudo-cowboys in Stetson hats, boots, and spurs. Arnaz called it the Parade of the Narcissists. Very few of them could even ski. The Parade was the reason Arnaz bought a season pass and took the gondola to the lodge once or twice a week: that, and the atmosphere of this most famous ski lodge in the West, with its timbered walls hung with antique Navajo rugs, the massive wrought-iron chandeliers, the roaring fireplace so large you could barbecue a bull in it. Not to mention the walls of glass that looked out over a three-hundred-sixty-degree ocean of mountains, currently gray and brooding under a darkening sky.

But Arnaz had never seen anyone quite like the gentleman who sat at a small table by himself before the vast window, a silver flask of some unknown beverage in front of him, gazing out in the direction of snowbound Smuggler's Cirque, with its complex of ancient, long-abandoned mining structures huddled like acolytes around the vast rickety wooden building that housed the famous Ireland Pump

Engine: a magnificent example of nineteenth-century engineering, once the largest pump in the world, now just a rusted hulk.

Arnaz had been observing the ghostly man with fascination for upward of thirty minutes, during which time the man had not moved so much as a pinkie. Arnaz was a fashionista, and he knew his clothes. The man wore a black vicuña overcoat of the finest quality, cut, and style, but of a make that Arnaz did not recognize. The coat was un-buttoned, revealing a bespoke tailored black suit of an English cut, a Zegna tie, and a gorgeous cream-colored silk scarf, loosely draped. To top off the ensemble—literally—the man wore an incongruous, sable-colored trilby hat of 1960s vintage on his pale, skull-like head. Even though it was warm in the great room of the lodge, the man looked as cold as ice.

He wasn't an actor; Arnaz, a movie buff, knew he had never seen him on the silver screen, even in a bit part. He surely wasn't a banker, hedge fund manager, CEO, lawyer, or other business or financial wiz-ard; that getup would be entirely unacceptable in such a crowd. He wasn't a poseur, either; the man wore his clothes casually, noncha-lantly, as if he'd been born in them. And he was far too elegant to be in the dot-com business. So what the heck was he?

A gangster.

Now, that made sense. He was a criminal. A very, very successful criminal. Russian, perhaps—he did have a slightly foreign look about him, in those pale eyes and high cheekbones. A Russian oligarch. But no... where were his women? The Russian billionaires that came to Roaring Fork—and there were quite a few—always went about with a passel of spangled, buxom whores.

Arnaz was stumped.

Pendergast heard himself being addressed and turned, slowly, to see Chief Stanley Morris approaching him from across the vast room.

"May I?"

Pendergast opened his hand in a slow invitation to sit.

"Thank you. I heard you were up here."

"And how did you hear that?"

"Well... You're not exactly inconspicuous, Agent Pendergast."

A silence. And then Pendergast removed a small silver cup from his overcoat, and placed it on the table. "Sherry? This is a rather indifferent Amontillado, but nevertheless palatable."

"Ah, no thanks." The chief looked restless, shifting his soft body in the chair once, twice. "Look, I realize I messed up with your, um, protégée, Miss Swanson, and I'm sorry. I daresay I had it coming there at the town meeting. You don't know what it's like being chief of police in a town like this, where they're always pulling you in five different directions at once."

"I am indeed sorry to say this, but I fear your microscopic problems do not interest me." Pendergast poured himself a small tot of sherry and tossed it back in one feral motion.

"Listen," said the chief, shifting about again, "I came to ask your help. We've got this horrific quadruple murder, a one-acre crime scene of unbelievable complexity. All my forensic people are arguing with each other and that fire expert, they're paralyzed, they've never seen anything like this before..." His voice cracked, then trailed off. "Look, the girl—Jenny, the older daughter—was my intern. She was a *good* kid..." He managed to pull himself together. "I need help. Informally. Advice, that's all I'm asking. Nothing official. I looked into your background—very impressive."

The pale hand snaked out again, poured another tot; it was tossed off in turn. There was silence. Finally, Pendergast spoke. "I came here to rescue my protégée—your term, not mine—from your incompetency. My goal—my *only* goal—is to see Miss Swanson finish her work without further meddling from Mrs. Kermode or anyone else. And then I shall leave this perverse town and fly home to New York with all possible alacrity."

"Yet you were up at the scene of the fire this morning. You showed your badge to get inside the tape."

Pendergast waved away these words as one might brush off a fly.

"You were there. Why?"

"I saw the fire. I was ever so faintly intrigued."

"You said there would be more. Why did you say that?"

Another casual wave-off.

"Damn it! *What made you say that?*"

No answer.

The chief rose. "You said there would be more murders. I looked into your background and I realized that you, of all people, would know. I'm telling you, if there are more—and you refuse to help—then those murders will be on your head. I swear to God."

This was answered by a shrug.

"Don't you shrug at me, you son of a bitch!" the chief shouted, losing his temper at last. "You saw what they did to that family. How can you just sit there, drinking your sherry?" He gripped the side of the table and leaned forward. "I have just one thing to say to you, Pendergast—fuck you, and thanks for nothing!"

At this, the smallest hint of a smile crossed the thin lips. "Now, that is more like it."

"More like what?" Morris roared.

"An old friend of mine in the NYPD has a colorful expression that is appropriate for this situation. What was it again? Ah, yes." Pendergast glanced up at the chief. "I will help you, but only on the condition that you—as I believe he would put it—*grow a pair.*"

18

Chief Stanley Morris stared at the ruined house. The residual heat from the previous day's fire was now gone and a light snow had fallen the night before, covering the scene of horror with a soft white blanket. Plastic tarps had been spread over the main areas of evidence, and now his men were carefully removing them and shaking off the snow in preparation for the walk-through. It was eight o'clock in the morning, sunny, and fifteen degrees above zero. At least there was no wind.

Nothing like this had ever happened to Morris, on either a personal or a professional level, and he steeled himself for the ordeal that lay ahead. He'd hardly slept the night before, and when he finally did a dreadful nightmare had immediately awakened him again. He felt like hell and still hadn't been able to fully process the depravity and horror of the crime.

He took a deep breath and looked around. To his left stood Chivers, the fire specialist; to his right, the figure of Pendergast, in his vicuña overcoat, incongruously pulled over an electric-blue down jacket. Puffy mittens and a hideous wool hat completed the picture. The man was so pallid he looked like he'd already been stricken by hypothermia. And yet his eyes were very much alive, moving restlessly about the scene.

Morris cleared his throat and made an effort to project the image of a chief of police firmly in control. "Ready, gentlemen?"

"You bet," said Chivers, with a distinct lack of enthusiasm. He was clearly unhappy about the presence of the FBI agent. *Tough shit*, thought Morris. He was getting fed up with the disagreements, turf squabbles, and departmental infighting this case was generating.

Pendergast inclined his head.

The chief ducked under the tape, the others following. The fresh snow covered everything save where the tarps had been laid down, and those areas were now large dark squares in an otherwise white landscape. The M.E. had not yet removed the human remains. Forensic flags of various colors dotted the ruins, giving the scene an incongruously festive air. The stench of smoke, burnt electrical wiring, rubber, and plastic still hung heavy and foul.

Now Pendergast took the lead, moving lightly despite the bulky clothing. He darted forward, knelt, and with a small brush whisked away a patch of snow, examining the burnt slate floor. He did this at several apparently random spots as they continued moving through. At one point a glass tube made an appearance from under his coat, into which he put some microscopic sample with tweezers.

Chivers hung back, saying nothing, a frown of displeasure gathering on his thick face.

They finally reached the gruesome bathtub. Morris could hardly look at it. But Pendergast went right over and knelt beside it, bowing over it almost as if he were praying. Removing one glove, he poked around with his white fingers and the pair of long tweezers, putting more samples into tubes. At last he rose and they continued making their way through the ruined house.

They came to the burnt mattress with its loops of wire and bone fragments. Here Pendergast stopped again, gazing at it for the longest time. Morris began to shiver as the inactivity, cold, and a clammy sick feeling all began to penetrate. The agent removed a document from his coat and opened it, revealing a detailed plat of the house—where had he gotten that?—which he consulted at length before folding it up and putting it away. Then he knelt and examined with a magnifying glass the charred remains of the skeleton tied to the mattress, really just bone fragments, and various other things as well. Morris could feel the cold creeping deeper into his clothing. Chivers was becoming restless, moving back and forth and sometimes slapping his gloves together in an effort to keep warm—broadcasting through his body language that he considered this a waste of time.

Pendergast finally straightened up. "Shall we move on?"

"Great idea," said Chivers.

They continued through the burnt landscape: the ghostly standing sticks covered with hoarfrost, the scorched walls, the heaps of frozen ashes, the glistering puddles of glass and metal. Now the corpse of the dog could be seen to one side, along with the two parallel, crumbled piles of ash and bone representing Jenny Baker's mother and father.

Morris had to look away. It was too much.

Pendergast knelt and examined everything with the utmost care, taking more samples, maintaining his silence. He seemed particularly interested in the charcoaled fragments of the dog, carefully probing with his long-stemmed tweezers and a tool that looked like a dental pick. They moved into the ruins of the garage, where the burnt and fused hulks of three cars rested. The FBI agent gave them a cursory look.

And then they were done. Beyond the perimeter tape, Pendergast turned. His eyes startled Morris—they glittered so sharply in the bright winter sun.

"It is as I feared," he said.

Morris waited for more but was greeted only with silence.

"Well," said Chivers loudly, "this just reinforces what I reported to you earlier, Stanley. All the evidence points toward a botched robbery with at least two perps, maybe more. With a possible sex-crime component."

"Agent Pendergast?" Morris finally said.

"I'm sorry to say that an accurate reconstruction of the sequence of the crime may be impossible. So much information was taken by the fire. But I am able to salvage a few salient details, if you wish to hear them."

"I do. Please."

"There was a single perpetrator. He entered through an unlocked back door. Three members of the family were at home, all upstairs and probably sleeping. The perpetrator immediately killed the dog who came to investigate. Then he—or she—ascended the front staircase to the second floor, surprised a juvenile female in her bedroom, incapacitated and gagged her before she could make significant noise, and wired her to the bed, still alive. He may have been on his way to the parents' room when the second juvenile female arrived home."

He turned to Morris. "This would be your intern, Jenny. She came in through the garage and went upstairs. There she was ambushed by the perpetrator, incapacitated, gagged, and placed in the bathtub. This was accomplished with utmost efficiency, but nevertheless this second assault appears to have awakened the parents. There was a short fight, which began upstairs and ended downstairs. I suspect one of the parents was killed there, on the spot, while the other was dragged down later. They may have been beaten."

"How can you know all this?" said Chivers. "This is sheer speculation!"

Pendergast went on, ignoring this outburst. "The perpetrator returned upstairs, doused both juvenile victims with gasoline, and set them on fire. He then made a—by necessity—rapid exit from the premises, dragging the other parent down the stairs and spreading additional accelerant on his way out. He left on foot—not by car. A pity the snowy woods around the house were trampled by neighbors and firefighters."

"No way," said Chivers, shaking his head. "No way can you draw all those conclusions from the information we have—and the conclusions you've drawn, well, with all due respect, most of them are wrong."

"I must say I share Mr. Chivers's, ah, skepticism as to how you can learn all this from a mere walk-through," said Morris.

Pendergast replied in the tone of someone explaining to a child. "It's the only logical sequence that fits the facts. And the facts are these: When Jenny Baker returned home, the perpetrator was already in the house. She came in through the garage—the boyfriend confirmed that—and if the parents had already been killed she would have seen their bodies at the back door. She didn't see the dog's body because it was behind a counter that once existed, here." He pulled out the plat.

"But how do you know he was already upstairs when Jenny arrived home?"

"Because Jenny was ambushed upstairs."

"She could have been attacked in the garage and forced upstairs."

"If she was the first victim, and was attacked in the garage, the dog would be alive and would have barked, awakening the parents. No—the very first victim was the dog, killed at the back door, probably with a blow to the head by something like a baseball bat."

"A *bat?*" Chivers said in disbelief. "How do you know he didn't use a knife? Or gun?"

"The neighbors heard no shots. Have you ever tried to kill a German shepherd with a knife? And finally, the dog's burnt cranium showed green-bone fracture patterns." He paused. "One needn't be Sherlock Holmes to analyze a few simple details like these, Mr. Chivers."

Chivers fell silent.

"Therefore, when Jenny arrived home, the perpetrator was already upstairs and had already incapacitated the sister, as he would not have been able to subdue two at once."

"Unless there were two perps," said Chivers.

"Go on," Morris told Pendergast.

"Using the bat or some other method, he immediately subdued Jenny."

"Which is exactly why there must have been two perps!" said Chivers. "It was a robbery gone bad. They broke into the house, but things spiraled out of control before they could commence the robbery. Happens all the time."

"No. The sequence was well planned and the perpetrator had everything under control at all times. The psychological hallmarks of the crime—the savagery of it—suggests a lone perpetrator who had a motive other than robbery."

Chivers rolled his eyes at Morris.

"And as for your theory about a burglary gone wrong, the perpetrator was well aware there were at least three people at home. An organized burglar doesn't break into an occupied house."

"Unless there are a couple of girls they might want to..." Chivers swallowed, glanced at the chief.

"The girls were not molested. If he intended to rape the girls he would have removed the threat of the parents by killing them first. And a rape fits neither the time line nor the sequence. I might point out that the elapsed time between the boyfriend dropping Jenny off and the fire appearing on the mountain was ten minutes or less."

"And how do you know one of the parents was killed downstairs and the other dragged down later?"

"That is, admittedly, an assumption. But it is the only one that matches the evidence. We are dealing with a lone killer, and it seems unlikely he would have fought both parents, downstairs, simultaneously. This arranging of the parents is another staged element of the attack—a grisly detail, intended to sow additional fear and unrest."

Chivers shook his head in disgust and disbelief.

"So." The chief could hardly bring himself to ask the question he knew he had to. "What makes you think there might be more killings like this?"

"This was a crime of hatred, sadism, and brutality, committed by a person who, while probably insane, was still in possession of his faculties. Fire is often the weapon of choice for the insane."

"A revenge killing?"

"Doubtful. The Baker family was not well known in Roaring Fork. You yourself told me they appear to have no enemies in town and only spend a couple of weeks here a year. So if not revenge, what is the motive? Hard to say definitively, but it may not be one directed at this family specifically—but rather, *at what this family represents.*"

A silence. "And what does this family represent?" Morris asked.

"Perhaps what this entire town represents."

"Which is?"

Pendergast paused, and then said: "Money."

19

Corrie entered the history section of the Roaring Fork Library. The beautiful, wood-paneled space was once again empty save for Ted Roman, who was reading a book at his desk. He looked up as Corrie entered, his lean face lighting up.

"Well, well!" he said, rising. "Roaring Fork's most infamous girl returns in triumph!"

"Jeez. What kind of a welcome is that?"

"A sincere one. I mean it. You and that FBI agent really nailed Kermode. God, it was one of the best things I've ever seen in this town."

"You were at the town meeting?"

"Sure as hell was. It's about time someone took down that...well, I hope you won't be offended if I use the word, but here goes: that *bitch*."

"No offense here."

"And not only did the man in black cut Kermode off at the knees, but he took on that cozy little triumvirate, her, the police chief, and the mayor. Your friend just about had the three of them soiling their drawers—Montebello, too!" He almost cackled with glee, and his laugh was so infectious Corrie had to join in.

"I have to admit, it was satisfying to hear the story," Corrie said. "Especially after spending ten days in jail because of them."

"I knew as soon as I read you'd been arrested that it was bullshit..." Ted tried to smooth down the cowlick that projected from his forehead. "So. What are you working on today?"

"I want to find out all I can about the life of Emmett Bowdree—and his death."

"The miner you've been analyzing? Let's see what we can find."

"Is the library always this empty?" she asked as they walked over to the computer area.

"Yeah. Crazy, huh? The prettiest library in the West and nobody comes. It's the people in this town—they're too busy parading down Main Street in their minks and diamonds." He aped a movie star, sashaying as if on a fashion runway, making faces.

Corrie laughed. Ted had a funny way about him.

He sat down at a computer terminal and logged on. He began various searches, explaining what he was doing while she peered over his shoulder.

"Okay," he said, "I've got some decent hits on your Mr. Bowdree." She heard a printer fire up behind her. "You take a look at the list and tell me what you want to see."

He fetched the printed sheets and she scanned them quickly, pleased—in fact, almost intimidated—by the number of references. It seemed that there was quite a lot on Emmett Bowdree: mentions in newspaper articles, employment and assay records, mining documents and claims, and other miscellanea.

"Say..." Ted began, then stopped.

"What?"

"Um, you know, considering how you stood me up for that beer last time..."

"Sorry. I was busy getting myself arrested."

He laughed. "Well, you still owe me one. Tonight?"

Corrie looked at him, suddenly blushing and awkward and hopeful. "I'd love to," she heard herself say.

20

The chief had held press conferences before, usually when some bad-boy celebrity got in trouble. But this was different—and worse. As he observed the audience from the wings, he felt a rising apprehension. These people were seething, demanding answers. Because the old police station building only had a small conference room, they were back in the City Hall meeting room—site of his recent humiliation—and the reminder was not a pleasant one.

On the other hand, he had Pendergast on his side. The man who had started out as his nemesis was now—he might as well admit it—his crutch. Chivers was furious, and half his own department was in revolt, but Morris didn't care. The man was brilliant, even if he was a bit strange, and he was damn grateful to have him in his corner. But Pendergast wasn't going to be able to help him with this crowd. This was something he had to do on his own. He had to go in there looking like the Man in Charge.

He glanced at his watch. Five minutes to two—the hubbub of voices was like an ominous growl. *Grow a pair.* Fair enough: he would try his best.

Reviewing his notes one last time, he stepped out on stage, walking briskly to the podium. As the sound of voices dropped, he took another moment to observe the audience. The room was packed, standing-room only, and it looked like more were outside. The press gallery, too, was crammed. His eye easily picked out the black blot of Pendergast, sitting anonymously in the public area in front. And in the reserved section, he could see the ranks of officials, the mayor, fire chief, senior members of his department, the M.E., Chivers, and the town attorney. Conspicuously absent was Mrs. Kermode. Thank God.

He leaned over, tapped the microphone. "Ladies and gentlemen." The room fell silent.

"For those who may not know me," he said, "I'm Chief Stanley Morris of the Roaring Fork Police Department. I'm going to read a statement, and then I will take questions from the press and the public."

He squared his papers and began to read, keeping his voice stern and neutral. It was a short statement that confined itself to the indisputable facts: the time of the fire, the number and identity of the victims, the determination it was a homicide, the status of the investigation. No speculation. He ended with an appeal for all persons to come forward with any information they might have, no matter how trivial. He of course did not mention Pendergast's suggestion that there might be more such events; that would be far too incendiary. Besides, there was no evidence for it—as Chivers had said, it was mere speculation.

He looked up. "Questions?"

An immediate tumult from the press gallery. Morris had already decided whom he was going to call on and in what order, and he now pointed to his number one journalist, an old pal from the *Roaring Fork Times*.

"Chief Morris, thank you for your statement. Do you have any suspects?"

"We have some important leads we're following up," Morris replied. "I can't say more than that." *Because we don't have shit*, he thought grimly.

"Any idea if the perp is local?"

"We don't know," said Morris. "We've gotten guest lists from all the hotels and rentals, we've got lift ticket sales, and we've enlisted the help of the National Center for the Analysis of Violent Crime, which is currently searching their databases for previous arson convictions."

"Any possible motive?"

"Nothing concrete. We're looking into various possibilities."

"Such as?"

"Burglary, revenge, perverted kicks."

"Wasn't it true that one of the victims worked in your office?"

God, he had hoped to avoid that line of questioning. "Jenny Baker was an intern in my office, working over her winter break." He swallowed, tried to go on despite the sudden fuzziness in his voice. "She was a wonderful girl who had aspirations to a career in law enforcement. It was...a devastating loss."

"There's a rumor that one of the victims was tied to a bed and doused with gasoline," another reporter interjected.

Son of a bitch. Did Chivers leak that? "That is true," said the chief, after a hesitation.

This caused a sensation.

"And another victim was found burned to death in a bathtub?"

"Yes," said the chief, without elaborating.

More uproar. This was getting ugly.

"Were the girls molested?"

The press would ask anything; they had no shame. "The M.E. hasn't concluded his examination. But it may not be possible to know, given the state of the remains."

"Was anything taken?"

"We don't know."

"Were they burned alive?"

Rising furor.

"It'll be at least a week before most of the evidence has been analyzed. All right—please—enough questions from the press—we'll move on to the public." The chief dearly hoped this would be easier.

The entire section was on its feet, hands waving. Not a good sign. He pointed to someone he didn't know, a meek-looking elderly woman, but a person in front of her misunderstood—deliberately or not—and immediately responded in a booming voice. Christ, it was Sonja Marie Dutoit, the semi-retired actress, infamous in Roaring Fork for her obnoxious behavior in shops and restaurants and for her face, which had been lifted and Botoxed so many times it bore a perpetual grin.

"Thank you for choosing me," she said in a smoke-cured voice. "I'm sure I speak for everyone when I say how shocked and horrified I am about this crime."

"Yes, indeed," said Morris. "Your question, please?"

"It's been thirty-six hours since this terrible, horrible, frightening fire. We all saw it. And judging from what you just said, you haven't made much progress—if any."

Chief Morris said, calmly, "Do you have a question, Ms. Dutoit?"

"I certainly do. Why haven't you caught the killer yet? This isn't New York City: we've only got two thousand people in this town. There's only one road in and out. So what's the problem?"

"As I said, we've brought tremendous resources to bear, bringing in specialists from as far away as Grand Junction, as well as the involvement of the NCAVC. Now, I'm sure other people have questions—"

"I'm not done," Dutoit went on. "When's the next house going to get burned down?"

This led to a susurrus of muttering. Some people were rolling their eyes in reaction to Dutoit's questions; others were beginning to look ever so slightly nervous.

"There's not a shred of evidence that we're dealing with a serial arsonist," the chief said, eager to cut off this avenue of speculation.

But Dutoit, it seemed, was not yet through. "Which one of us is going to wake up in flames in their own bed tonight? *And what in the name of God are you doing about it?*"

21

It was hard to believe the Mineshaft Tavern was part of Roaring Fork, with the sawdust on the floor, the basement rock walls hung with rusty old mining tools, the smell of beer and Texas barbecue, the scruffy working-class clientele—and above all, the talentless stoner at the mike strumming some tune of his own composition, his face contorted with excessive pathos.

As she walked in, Corrie was pleasantly surprised. This was much more her kind of place than the restaurant of the Hotel Sebastian.

She found Ted at "his" table in the back, just where he'd said he would be, with an imperial pint in front of him. He stood up—she liked that—and helped her into her seat before sitting down again.

"What'd you like?"

"What are you drinking?"

"Maroon Bells Stout, made right down the road. Fantastic stuff."

The waiter came over and she ordered a pint, hoping she wouldn't get carded. That would be embarrassing. But there were no problems.

"I didn't know a place like this could exist in Roaring Fork," said Corrie.

"There are still plenty of real people in this town—ski lift attendants, waiters, dishwashers, handymen...*librarians*." He winked. "We need our cheap, low-down places of entertainment."

Her beer arrived, and they clinked glasses. Corrie took a sip. "Wow. Good."

"Better than Guinness. Cheaper, too."

"So who's the guy on stage?" Corrie kept her voice neutral in case he was a friend of Ted's.

Ted snickered. "Open-mike night. Don't know him, poor fellow. Let's hope he hasn't quit his day job." He picked up his menu. "Hungry?"

She thought for a moment: could she spare the money? But the menu wasn't too expensive. If she didn't eat, she might get drunk and do something stupid. She smiled, nodded.

"So," said Ted. "How are things going in the charnel house up on the mountain?"

"Good." Corrie contemplated telling him about what she'd discovered but decided against it. She didn't know Ted well enough. "The remains of Emmett Bowdree have a lot to say. I hope to get permission to work on a few more skeletons soon."

"I'm glad it's working out for you. I love to think of Kermode getting her knickers in a twist while you're up there doing your thing."

"I don't know," Corrie said. "She's got worse things to worry about now. You know—the fire."

"I'll say. Jesus, how awful was that?" He paused. "You know, I grew up there. In The Heights."

"Really?" Corrie couldn't hide her surprise. "I never would have guessed that."

"Thank you, I'll take that as a compliment. My dad was a television producer—sitcoms and the like. He palled around with a lot of Hollywood people. My mother slept with most of them." He shook his head, sipped his beer. "I had a kind of messed-up childhood."

"Sorry to hear that." In no way was Corrie ready to talk to Ted about her own childhood, however.

"No big deal. They got divorced and my dad raised me. With all the sitcom residuals, he never had to work again. When I came back from college I got my butt out of The Heights and found an apartment in town, down on East Cowper. It's tiny, but I feel better about breathing its air."

"Does he still live up there in The Heights?"

"Nah, he sold the house a few years back, died of cancer last year—only sixty years old, too."

"I'm really sorry."

He waved his hand. "I know. But I was glad to get rid of the connection to The Heights. It really frosts me the way they handled that Boot Hill thing—digging up one of the most historic cemeteries in Colorado to build a spa for rich assholes."

"Yeah. Pretty ugly."

Then Ted shrugged, laughed lightly. "Well, stuff happens. What are you going to do? If I hated the place so much, I wouldn't still be here—right?"

Corrie nodded. "So what did you major in at the University of Utah?"

"Sustainability studies. I wasn't much of a student—I wasted too much time skiing and snowmobiling. I love snowmobiling almost as much as I do skiing. Oh, and mountain climbing, too."

"Mountain climbing?"

"Yeah. I've climbed forty-one Fourteeners."

"What's a Fourteener?"

Ted chuckled. "Man, you really are an eastern girl. Colorado has fifty-five mountains over fourteen thousand feet—we call them Fourteeners. To climb them all is the holy grail of mountaineering in the U.S.—at least, in the lower forty-eight."

"Impressive."

Their food arrived: shepherd's pie for Corrie, a burger for Ted, with another pint for him. Corrie declined a refill, thinking about the scary mountain road up to her dentist's-office-on-the-hill.

"So what about you?" Ted asked. "I'm curious about how you know the man in black."

"Pendergast? He's my…" *God, how to put it?* "He's sort of my guardian."

"Yeah? Like your godfather or something?"

"Something like that. I helped him on a case a few years ago, and ever since he's kind of taken an interest in me."

"He's one cool dude—no kidding. Is he really an FBI agent?"

"One of the best."

A new singer took over the mike—much better than the previous one—and they listened for a while, talking and finishing their meal. Ted tried to pay but Corrie was ready for him and insisted on splitting the check.

As they got up to leave, Ted said, his voice dropping low: "Want to see my tiny apartment?"

Corrie hesitated. She was tempted—very tempted. Ted looked like he was all sinew and muscle, lean and hard, and yet charming and goofy, with the nicest brown eyes. But she had never quite been able to feel good about a relationship if she slept with the guy on the first date.

"Not tonight, thanks. I've got to get home, get my sleep," she said, but added a smile to let him know it wasn't absolute.

"No problem. We'll have to do this again—soon."

"I'd like that."

As she drove away from the restaurant, heading toward the dark woods and thinking about crawling into a freezing bed, Corrie started to regret her decision not to "see" Ted's tiny apartment.

22

In his suite of rooms on the top floor of the Hotel Sebastian, Agent Pendergast laid aside the book he was reading, drained the small cup of espresso that sat on the side table, and then—standing up—walked over to the picture window on the far side of the sitting room. The suite was perfectly silent: Pendergast disliked the clamor of anonymous neighbors and had reserved the rooms on both sides of his own to ensure he would remain undisturbed. He stood at the window, absolutely still, looking down over East Main Street and the light snow that was falling onto the sidewalks, buildings, and passersby, softening the evening scene and bestowing a muted, dream-like quality on the millions of Christmas lights stretching many blocks. He remained there for perhaps ten minutes, gazing out into the night. Then, turning away again, he walked over to the desk, where a FedEx envelope lay, unopened. It was from his factotum in New York, Proctor, addressed to him in care of the Hotel Sebastian.

Pendergast picked up the envelope, slit it open with a smooth motion, and let the contents slip onto the desk. Several sealed envelopes of various sizes fell out, along with an oversize card—embossed and engraved—and a brief note in Proctor's handwriting. The note said merely that Pendergast's ward, Constance Greene, had left for Dharamsala, India, where she planned to spend two weeks visiting the nineteenth rinpoche. The fancy card was an invitation to the wedding of Lieutenant Vincent D'Agosta and Captain Laura Hayward, which was scheduled for May twenty-ninth of the following spring.

Pendergast's gaze moved to the sealed envelopes. He glanced over them for a moment without touching any. Then he picked up an airmail envelope and turned it over thoughtfully in his hands. Leaving the others, he walked back to his sitting room chair, sat down, and opened the letter. A single sheet of thin paper lay inside, a letter in a childish hand, written in the old-fashioned German script known as Sütterlin. He began to read.

December 6
  École Mère-Église
  St. Moritz, Switzerland
  Dear Father,
  It seems a long time since you last visited. I have been counting the days. They number one hundred and twelve. I hope you will again soon come.
  I am treated well. The food here is very good. On Saturday suppers we have Linzer Torte for desert. Have you ever eaten Linzer Torte? It is good.
  A lot of the teachers here speak German but I try always to use my English. They say my English is getting better. The teachers are very nice except for Madame Montaine who always smells of rose water. I like History and Science but not Mathematiks. I am not good at Mathematiks.
  In the autumn I enjoyed walking on the hill sides after classes but now there is too much snow. They tell me that over the Christmas holidays I will be taught how to ski. I think I will like that.
  Thank you for your letter. Please send me another. I hope we shall meet again soon.
  Love,
  Your son,
  Tristram

Pendergast read the letter a second time. Then, very slowly, he refolded it and placed it back into its envelope. Turning off the reading lamp, he sat in the dark, lost in thought, book forgotten, as the minutes ticked by. Finally he stirred again, pulled a cell phone from his suit pocket, and dialed a number with a northern Virginia area code.

"Central Monitoring," came the crisp, accentless voice.

"This is S. A. Pendergast. Please transfer me to South American Operations, Desk 14-C."

"Very good." There was a brief silence, a click, and then another voice came on the line. "Agent Wilkins."

"Pendergast speaking."

The voice stiffened slightly. "Yes, sir."

"What's the status of Wildfire?"

"Stable but negative. No hits."

"Your monitoring efforts?"

"All listening posts are active. We're monitoring national and local police reports and news media twenty-four seven, and we're electronically combing the daily NSA feeds as well. In addition, we continue to interface with CIA field agents in Brazil and the surrounding countries in search of any . . . anomalous activity."

"You have my updated location?"

"In Colorado? Yes."

"Very good, Agent Wilkins. As always, please inform me immediately if the status of Wildfire changes."

"We'll do that, sir."

Pendergast ended the call. Picking up the house phone, he ordered another espresso from room service. Then he used his cell phone to make another call: this one to a suburb of Cleveland called River Pointe.

The call was answered on the second ring. There was no voice; just the sound of a connection being made.

"Mime?" Pendergast said into the silence.

For a moment, nothing. Then a high, thin voice wheezed: "Is that my main man? My main Secret Agent Man?"

"I'd like an update, please, Mime."

"All quiet on the Western Front."

"Nothing?"

"Not a peep."

"One moment." Pendergast paused as a room service attendant brought in the espresso. He tipped the man, then waited until he was once again alone. "And you're confident that you've cast your net widely, and finely, enough to spot the... target if he surfaces?"

"Secret Agent Man, I've got a series of AI algorithms and heuristic search patterns online that would make you stain your government-issue BVDs. I'm monitoring all official, and a goodly amount of un-official, web traffic in and out of the target area. You can't imagine the bandwidth I'm burning through. Why, I've had to siphon off server farms from at least half a dozen—"

"I can't imagine. Nor do I want to."

"Anyway, the objective's totally offline, no Facebook updates for this dude. But if the guy's as sick as you say, then the moment he surfaces—hoo, boy!" A sudden silence. "Um, oops. I keep forgetting Alban's your son."

"Just keep up the monitoring operations, please, Mime. And let me know the instant you note anything."

"You got it." The phone went dead.

And Pendergast sat in the darkened room, unmoving, for a long time.

23

Corrie parked her Rent-a-Junker Ford Focus in the sprawling driveway of 1 Ravens Ravine Road—aka, the Fine mansion—and got out. It was almost midnight, and a huge pale moon, hanging low in the sky, turned the pine trees blue against a creamy bed of white snow, striped with shadows. A light snow was falling, and here, in this bowl-like vale at the edge of a ravine, she felt like she was inside some child's overturned snow globe. Ahead, the row of six garage doors stood against the cement drive like big gray teeth. She killed the engine—for some obscure reason, Fine didn't want her to use the garage—and got out of the car. She walked up to the closest door, plucked off her glove, punched in the code. Then, as it rose on its metal rails, she turned suddenly, with a sharp intake of breath.

There, in the shadow of the side of the garage, was a shape. At first, Corrie couldn't make out what it was. But as the light from the garage door motor provided a faint illumination, she made out a small dog, shivering in the darkness.

"Well!" Corrie said, kneeling beside it. "What are you doing out here?"

The dog came over, whining, and licked her hand. It was a mutt, looking like a cross between a small hound dog and a spaniel, with droopy ears, big sad brown eyes, and brown and white splotches of fur. It was not wearing a collar.

"You can't stay out here," she said. "Come on in."

The dog followed her eagerly into the garage. Walking up to a bank of buttons, she pressed the one for the bay she'd entered. The garage was empty—a ludicrous expanse of concrete. Outside, she could hear the moaning of the wind as it shook the trees. Why on earth couldn't she park in here?

She glanced down at the dog, which was looking up at her and wagging its tail, a desperately hopeful look in its eyes. Screw Mr. Fine—the pooch would stay.

Corrie waited until the garage door had closed completely before unlocking the door and stepping into the house. Inside, it was almost as cold as outdoors. She walked through a laundry room with machines big enough to service a battalion, past a pantry larger than her father's entire apartment, and then into the hallway that ran the length of the mansion. She continued on, dog at her heels, along the corridor as it bent once, then twice, following the contours of the ravine, past room after huge room filled with uncomfortable-looking avant-garde furniture. The corridor itself was filled with that African statuary, all big bellies and long angry faces and carven eyes that seemed to follow her as she passed by. The tall picture windows of the various rooms to her left had no curtains, and the bright moonlight threw skeletal shadows against the pallid walls.

The night before—her first night in the place—Corrie had checked out both the second floor and the basement, familiarizing herself with the rest of the layout. The upstairs consisted of a huge master bedroom, with dual bathrooms and walk-in closets, six other unfurnished bedrooms, and numerous guest bathrooms. In the main basement was a gym, a two-lane bowling alley, a mechanical room, a swimming flume—empty—and several storage areas. It seemed obscene that any house should be this big—or this empty.

She finally reached the end of the hallway and the door leading into her own small suite of rooms. She entered, closed the door behind her, and switched on the small space heater in the room she'd chosen as her own. Pulling a couple of bowls from the cabinet, she set out water and an improvised dinner of crackers and cereal for the dog—tomorrow, if she couldn't find the owner, she'd pick up some kibble.

She watched the little brown-and-white animal as it ate ravenously. The poor thing was starving. While a mutt, it was an endearing one, with a big shock of unruly hair that fell over its eyes. It reminded her of Jack Corbett, a kid she'd known in seventh grade back in Medicine Creek. His hair had flopped down over his face in just the same way.

"Your name is Jack," she said to the dog, while it looked up at her, wagging its tail.

She thought for a moment about fixing a cup of herbal tea for herself, but she felt too tired to make the effort and instead washed up, changed quickly into her nightwear, then slipped between the chilly sheets. She heard the tick of claws as the dog came in and settled down on the floor at the foot of the bed.

Gradually, her body heat and the little space heater—cranked to maximum—blunted the worst of the cold. She decided against doing any reading, preferring to use the electricity for heat instead of light. She'd gradually increase the amount of juice she used, and see if Fine complained.

Her thoughts drifted back to the date she'd had with Ted. He was earnest, and funny, and nice, if a bit goofy—but then, ski bums were supposed to be goofy. Handsome and goofy and carefree. He was no lightweight, though—he had principles. Idealistic, too. She admired his independence in leaving his parents' grand house for a small apartment downtown.

She turned in the bed, slowly becoming drowsy. He was hot, and on top of it a nice guy, but she wanted to get to know him just a little better before...

...Somewhere, from the distant spaces of the house overhead, came a loud bump.

She sat up in bed, instantly wide awake. What the hell was that?

She remained motionless. The only light in the room came from the bright orange coils of the space heater. As she sat, listening intently, she could hear, faintly, the mournful call of the wind as it coursed through the narrow valley.

There was nothing else. It must have been a dead branch, broken loose by the wind and knocked against the roof.

Slowly, she settled back down into the bed. Now that she was aware of the wind, she listened to its faint muttering and groaning as she lay in the darkness. As the minutes passed, drowsiness began to return. Her thoughts drifted toward her plans for the next day. Her analysis of the Bowdree skeleton was just about complete, and if she was going to make any progress on her theory she'd need to get permission to examine some of the other remains. Of course, Pendergast had offered to do just that, and she knew enough of his meddling ways to believe that he would—

Meddling. Now, why had she used that word?

And come to think of it, why did the mere thought of Pendergast—for the first time ever, since she'd known him—cause an upwelling of annoyance? After all, the man had rescued her from a ten-year prison sentence. He'd saved her career. He'd paid for her education, basically put her life on track.

If she was honest with herself, she had to admit it had nothing to do with Pendergast—and everything with herself. This cache of skeletons was a big project, and an incredible opportunity. She was wary at the thought of anyone else stepping in and stealing some of the limelight. And Pendergast—unintentionally—was capable of doing just that. If even a whiff got out that he'd helped her, everyone would assume that he'd done the real work and discount her own contribution.

Her mother had taken great relish in pointing out, again and again, what a loser she was. Her classmates back in Medicine Creek had called her a freak, a waste of space. She'd never realized, until now, just how much it meant to her to accomplish something important...

There it was: another sound. But this was no bump of a tree branch hitting the roof. This was a low scratching sound, coming from some spot not all that far away from her own bedroom: soft, even stealthy.

Corrie listened. Maybe it was the wind again, rubbing a pine branch back and forth against the house. But if it was the wind, it sounded awfully regular.

She pushed back the covers, got out of bed, and—heedless of the cold—stood in her darkened bedroom, listening.

Scratch. Scratch. Scratch. Scratch. Scratch.

At her feet, Jack whined.

She stepped out into the little hallway, turned on the light, opened the door into the mansion proper, and paused again to listen. The sound seemed to have stopped. No: there it was again. It seemed to be coming from the ravine side of the house, maybe the living room.

Corrie walked quickly down the corridor, shadow-striped and echoing, and ducked into the security room. The various devices were on, humming and clicking, but the central flat panel was off. She turned it on. An image swam into view: camera one, the default, showing the front drive, currently empty.

She pushed the button that toggled the screen into a checker-board of smaller images, looking at the feeds from various cameras. Two, four, nine, sixteen...and there, in the window of camera nine, she saw it: a red *M*, with a circle around it.

M for "movement."

Quickly she pressed the button dedicated to camera nine. Now its image filled the screen: it was the view out the back door, leading from the kitchen onto the vast deck overlooking the ravine. The *M* was much bigger now. But there was no movement, nothing she could see. She squinted at the pixelated image. Nothing.

What the hell had Fine said? When a camera registered move-ment, it recorded the video feed to hard disk: one minute prior to detecting the movement, and continuing for another minute after the movement ceased.

So what movement had triggered camera nine?

It couldn't be the wind, shaking the tree limbs: there were no trees in view. Even as Corrie watched, the *M* disappeared from the screen. Now she saw only the back of the house, with the date and time stamps imprinted across the bottom of the feed.

She toggled it back to the checkerboard of cameras and looked at the computer, hoping to get a playback of camera nine. The machine was turned on, but when she moved the mouse a window popped open, demanding a password.

Shit. Now she cursed herself for not asking more questions.

Something red flashed in her peripheral vision. Quickly she turned back to the screen. There it was, in camera eight: something large and dark, creeping around the side of the house. Black rectangles hovered around it, tracking its progress. The *M* was once again flashing on the screen.

Maybe she should call 911. But she'd left her mobile in her car, and the cheap bastard Fine had of course disconnected the house phones.

Corrie looked closer, heart starting to pound. That section of the back deck was in shadow, the moonlight obscured by the house, and she couldn't make out exactly what she was seeing. Was it an animal? A coyote, maybe? No: it was too big to be a coyote. Something about the stealthy, deliberate way in which it moved sent a thrill of fear coursing through her.

Now it was off the screen. No alerts came up on the other images. But Corrie was not reassured. Whatever she'd seen, it had been coming around the side of the house. Her side of the house.

She turned suddenly. What was that noise? The squeaking of a mouse? Or—maybe, just maybe—the soft protesting squeal of a window, being gingerly tried?

Heart in her mouth, she ran out of the security room and across the corridor into the den. The tall windows yawned dark before her.

"Get the fuck away from here!" she yelled at them. "I've got a gun—and I'm not afraid to use it! Any closer, and I'm calling the cops!"

Nothing. Utter silence.

Corrie stood in the darkness, breathing hard. Still nothing.

At length she returned to the security room. The video feeds were quiet; no movement registered on any of them.

She stayed before the monitor, eyes glued to the various feeds, for fifteen minutes. Then she went through the entire house, dog at her heels, checking all the doors and windows to make sure they were locked. Finally she returned to her bedroom, lay down in the dark, and gathered the covers around her. But she did not fall asleep.

24

The following morning was, if possible, even colder than it had been the day before. But for the time being, as she bustled around the ski shed, Corrie barely noticed. After a breakfast spent convincing herself she'd been imagining things the night before, she bundled up and went outside—only to find out there were very real, very human footprints in the snow all around the house. Someone apparently had been wandering around out there for a long time, perhaps hours.

It scared the hell out of her, but she couldn't follow the confused welter of tracks or figure out where they'd come from.

Getting into her car and checking her cell phone, she played back a message from Pendergast announcing that he'd arranged the necessary permissions for her to examine three more skeletons from among the coffins in the shed. She drove down to the Hotel Sebastian to collect the necessary paperwork and thank Pendergast—only to learn that he was out, but had left everything for her at the front desk.

She almost forgot the cold as she tracked down the first of the three skeletons—Asa Cobb—carefully removed the remains from the rude coffin, and placed them on the examination table. Arranging her tools, she took a deep breath, then began a methodical analysis of the bones.

It was as she suspected. Many of the bones displayed damage from a tool: scrapes, gouges, cuts. Again, there were tooth marks: clearly human, not bear. And again, there was no sign of pot polishing, burning, or cooking of any kind—this man, too, had been eaten raw. Nor were there signs of bullet or knife wounds—death had been caused by a massive blow to the head with a rock, followed by the same brutal beating and dismemberment evidenced by the bones of Bowdree. The old brown bones told a graphic, violent tale of a man who was set upon, torn to pieces, and consumed raw.

She straightened up. There was no longer any doubt: these miners had fallen victim to a gang of serial killers.

"Is it as you expected?" came the honeyed drawl from behind her.

Corrie whirled around, heart suddenly pounding like mad in her chest. There was Pendergast, dressed in a black overcoat, a silk scarf around his neck. His face and hair were almost as white as the snow that clung to his shoes. The guy had the damnedest ability to sneak up on a person.

"I see you got my message," Pendergast said. "I had tried calling you last night, as well, but you didn't pick up your phone."

"Sorry." As her heart returned to normal, she felt herself flushing. "I was on a date."

One eyebrow went up. "Indeed? May I inquire as to whom with?"

"Ted Roman. A librarian here in Roaring Fork. Grew up in town. Nice guy, ex–ski bum, snowmobile addict. Good researcher, too. He's helped me quite a bit."

Pendergast nodded, then turned—significantly—toward the examination table.

"I've only had a chance to examine one of the skeletons," she said, "but it seems to have all the earmarks of the Bowdree killing."

"So it's your opinion we're dealing with, how shall we call it, a *group* engaged in serial killing."

"Exactly. I would think at least three or four, possibly more."

"Interesting." Pendergast picked up one of the bones and turned it over in his hands, giving it a perfunctory examination. "Two murderers working together is uncommon, but not unheard of. Three or more, however, acting in concert, is a *rara avis* indeed." He put the bone back on the table. "Technically, three separate killings are necessary to establish a serial killer."

"Eleven miners died. Isn't that enough to qualify?"

"Almost assuredly. I shall look forward to receiving your detailed reports on the other two miners, as well."

Corrie nodded.

Hands in his pockets, Pendergast looked around the equipment shed before finally returning his pale gaze to her. "When was the last time you read *The Hound of the Baskervilles?*"

This question was so unexpected, Corrie was certain she'd misheard. "What?"

"*The Hound of the Baskervilles.* When did you last read it?"

"The Sherlock Holmes story? Ninth grade. Maybe eighth. Why?"

"Do you recall the initial letter you sent me regarding your thesis? In a postscript, you made reference to a meeting between Arthur Conan Doyle and Oscar Wilde. During that meeting, Wilde told Conan Doyle a rather dreadful story he'd heard on his American lecture tour."

"Right." Corrie stole a glance at the table. She was eager to get back to work.

"Would you find it interesting to know that one of the stops Oscar Wilde made on his lecture tour was right here in Roaring Fork?"

"I know all about that. It was in Doyle's diary. One of the Roaring Fork miners told Wilde the story of the man-eating grizzly, and Wilde passed on the story to Doyle. That's what gave me the idea for my thesis in the first place."

"Excellent. My question to you is this: Do you believe Wilde's story might have inspired Doyle to write *The Hound of the Baskervilles?*"

Corrie hopped from one cold foot to the other. "It's possible. Likely, even. But I'm not sure I see the relevance."

"Just this: if you were to take a look through *The Hound*, there's a chance you might come across some clues as to what actually happened."

"What actually happened? But...I'm sure Wilde heard the false story and told it to Doyle. Neither one could possibly have known the truth—that these miners weren't killed by a bear."

"Are you sure?"

"Doyle wrote about the 'grizzled bear' in his diary. He didn't mention a cannibalistic gang."

"Consider for a moment: what if Wilde heard the *real* story and told it to Doyle? And what if Doyle found it too disturbing to put in his diary? What if Doyle instead concealed some of that information in *The Hound*?"

Corrie had to stop herself from scoffing. Was it possible Pendergast was serious? "I'm sorry, but that's pretty far-fetched. Are you really suggesting that a Sherlock Holmes story could possibly shed light on my project?"

Pendergast did not reply. He simply stood there in his black overcoat, returning her gaze.

She shivered. "Look, I hope you don't mind, but I'd really like to get back to my examination, if it's okay with you."

Still Pendergast said nothing; he merely regarded her with those pale eyes of his. For some reason, Corrie got the distinct feeling that she had just failed some kind of test. But she couldn't help that; the answer lay not in fictional stories but right here, in the bones themselves.

After a long moment, Pendergast gave the slightest of bows. "Of course, Miss Swanson," he said coolly. Then he turned and left the equipment shed as silently as he had come.

Corrie watched until she heard the faint clunk of the door shutting. Then—with a mixture of eagerness and relief—she returned to the earthly remains of Asa Cobb.

25

Chief Stanley Morris had shut his office door and given his secretary orders not to disturb him for any reason whatsoever while he updated his corkboard case-line. It was how the chief managed complex cases: reducing everything to color-coded three-by-five cards, each with a single fact, a piece of evidence, a photograph, or a witness. These he would organize chronologically, pin to a corkboard, and then—with string—connect the cards, looking for patterns, clues, and relationships.

It was a standard approach and it had worked well for him before. But as he surveyed the chaos on his desk, the corkboard overflowing with a rainbow of cards, the strings going in every direction, he began to wonder if he needed a different system. He felt himself growing more frustrated by the minute.

The phone buzzed and he picked it up. "For heaven's sake, Shirley, I asked not to be disturbed!"

"Sorry, Chief," said the voice, "but there's someone here you really must see—"

"I don't care if it's the pope. I'm busy!"

"It's Captain Stacy Bowdree."

It took a minute for the ramifications of this to sink in. Then he felt himself go cold. *This is all I need.* "Oh. Jesus ... All right, send her in."

Before he could even prepare himself, the door opened and a striking woman strode in. Captain Bowdree had short auburn hair, a handsome face, and a pair of intense, dark brown eyes. She was all of six feet tall and somewhere in her midthirties.

He rose and held out his hand. "Chief Stanley Morris. This is quite a surprise."

"Stacy Bowdree." She gave his hand a firm shake. Even though she was dressed in casual clothes—jeans, a white shirt, and a leather vest—her bearing was unmistakably military. He offered her a seat, and she took it.

"First," said the chief, "I want to apologize for the problems with the exhumation of your, ah, ancestor. I know how upsetting it must be. We here at the Roaring Fork PD believed the developers had done a thorough search, and I was dismayed, *truly* dismayed, when your letter was brought to my attention—"

Bowdree flashed the chief a warm smile and waved her hand. "Don't worry about it. I'm not upset. Truly."

"Well, thank you for your understanding. I...We'll make it right, I promise you." The chief realized he was almost babbling.

"It's not a problem," she said. "Here's the thing. I've decided to take the remains back for reburial in our old family plot in Kentucky once the research is complete. That's why I'm here. So you see, given the circumstances there's no longer any reason to rebury Emmett in the original location, as I originally requested."

"Well, I'd be lying if I said I wasn't relieved. It makes things simpler."

"Say...is that coffee I smell?"

"Would you like a cup?"

"Thank you. Black, no sugar."

The chief buzzed Shirley and put in the order, with a second for himself. There was a brief, awkward silence. "So..." he said. "How long have you been in town?"

"Not long, a few days. I wanted to get the lay of the land, so to speak, before making my presence known. I realize my letter made quite a stir, and I didn't want to freak everyone out by storming into town like the Lone Ranger. You're the first person, in fact, that I've introduced myself to."

"Let me then welcome you most warmly to Roaring Fork." The chief felt hugely relieved by all she was saying—and also by her friendly, easygoing manner. "We're glad to have you. Where are you staying?"

"I was in Woody Creek, but I'm looking for a place in town. Having a little trouble finding something I can afford."

"I'm afraid we're in the high season. I wish I could give you some advice, but I think the town is pretty much full up." He recalled the tumultuous, acrimonious press conference and wondered if things would stay that way.

The coffee arrived and Bowdree accepted it eagerly, took a sip. "Not your usual police station coffee, I must say."

"I'm a bit of a coffee aficionado. We've got a coffee roaster in town who does a mean French roast."

She took another big sip, then another. "I don't want to keep you—I can see you're busy. I just wanted to drop in to introduce myself and tell you about my plans for the remains." She set down the cup. "And I also wondered if you could help me. Where exactly are the remains now, and how do I get there? I wanted to see them and meet the woman who's doing the research."

The chief explained, drawing her a little map of The Heights. "I'll call Heights security," he said. "Tell them you're coming."

"Thanks." Captain Bowdree rose, once again impressing the chief with her stature. She was a damn fine-looking woman, supple and strong. "You've been really helpful."

Morris rose again hastily and took her hand. "If there's anything I can do, anything at all, please let me know."

He watched her leave, feeling like the week from hell might finally be ending on a positive note. But then his gaze drifted to the corkboard, and the chaos of cards and strings on his desk, and the old feeling of dread returned. The week from hell, he realized, was far from over.

26

Corrie heard the clang of the ski shed door and paused in her work, wondering if Pendergast had returned. But instead of a dark-suited figure, a tall woman strode into view wearing fleece winter warm-ups and a big knitted woolen hat with dangling pom-poms.

"Corrie Swanson?" she said as she approached.

"That's me."

"Stacy Bowdree. I'd shake your hand, but I've got these coffees." She handed Corrie a tall Starbucks cup. "Venti skinny latte with four shots, extra sugar. I had to guess."

"Wow. You guessed right." Corrie accepted the cup gratefully. "I had no idea you were coming to Roaring Fork. This is quite a surprise."

"Well, here I am."

"God, Stacy—can I call you that?—do I *owe* you. You saved my butt with that letter. I was looking at ten years in prison, I can't thank you enough—"

"Don't embarrass me!" Bowdree laughed, uncovered her own coffee, and took a generous swig. "If you want to thank someone, you can thank your friend Pendergast. He explained the whole situation to me, and what they'd done to you. I was only too happy to help." She looked around. "Look at all these coffins. Which one's Great-Great-Granddad Emmett?"

"Right over here." Corrie led her to the man's remains, spread out on an adjacent table. If she'd known the woman was coming, she could have tried to put them in some modicum of order. She hoped Emmett's descendant would understand.

Corrie sipped her coffee a little nervously as Bowdree walked over, reached out, and gently picked up a piece of skull. "Jeez, that bear really did a number on him."

Corrie started to say something, then stopped herself. Pendergast, with excellent reason, had advised her against telling any-one—anyone—of the real cause of death until she had finished her work.

"I think this work is fascinating," said Bowdree, gently putting down the piece of skull. "So you really want to be a cop?"

Corrie laughed. She liked Bowdree immediately. "Well, I think I'd like to become an FBI agent, actually, with a specialty in forensic an-thropology. Not a lab rat, but a field agent with special skills."

"That's great. I've sort of been thinking about law enforcement myself...I mean, it's logical after a career in the military."

"Are you out, then? No longer a captain?"

She smiled. "I'll always be a captain, but yes, I've been dis-charged." She paused. "Well, I'd better get a move on. I've got to find a cheaper place to stay if I'm going to hang around here much longer—the hotel I'm in now is bankrupting me."

Corrie smiled. "I know the feeling."

"I just wanted to introduce myself and tell you that I think what you're doing here is great." Bowdree turned to go.

"Just a minute."

Bowdree turned back.

"Want to grab a coffee at Starbucks later?" She gestured with her cup. "I'd like to return the favor—if you don't mind it being on the late side. I plan to make a long day of it—assuming I don't freeze first."

Bowdree's face brightened. "That would be great. How does nine o'clock sound?"

"See you then."

27

Mrs. Betty B. Kermode sipped a cup of Earl Grey tea and looked from the picture window of her living room over the Silver Queen Valley. Her house on the top of the ridge—the best lot in the entire development of The Heights—commanded a spectacular view, with the surrounding mountains rising up and up toward the Continental Divide and the towering peaks of Mount Elbert and Mount Massive, the highest and second highest peaks in Colorado, which were mere shadows at this hour of the night. The house itself was quite modest—despite what people assumed, she was not by nature a showy woman—one of the smallest in the development, in fact. It was more traditional than the others, as well, built in stone and cedar on a relatively intimate scale: none of this ultra-contemporary, postmodern style for her.

The window also afforded an excellent view of the equipment shed. It had been from this same window that, not quite two weeks before, Mrs. Kermode had seen the telltale light go on in the shed, very late at night. She immediately knew who was inside and had taken action.

The cup rattled in its saucer as she put it down and she poured herself another. It was difficult to make a decent cup of tea at eight thousand five hundred feet, where water boiled at one hundred ninety-six degrees, and she could never get used to the insipid flavor, no matter what kind of mineral water she used, how long she steeped it, or how many bags she put in. She pursed her lips tightly as she added milk and a touch of honey, stirred, and sipped. Mrs. Kermode was a lifelong teetotaler—not for religious reasons, but because her father had been an abusive alcoholic and she associated drinking with ugliness and, even worse, a lack of control. Mrs. Kermode had made control the centerpiece of her life.

And now she was angry, quietly but furiously angry, at the humiliating disruption of her control by that girl and her FBI friend. Nothing like that had ever happened to her, and she would never forget, let alone forgive, it.

She took another swallow of tea. The Heights was the most sought-after enclave in Roaring Fork. In a town filled with vulgar new money, it was one of the oldest developments. It represented taste, Brahmin stability, and a whiff of aristocratic superiority. She and her partners had never allowed it to grow shabby, as other 1970s-era ski developments tended to do. The new spa and club-house would be a vital part of keeping the development fresh, and the opening of Phase III—thirty-five two-acre lots, priced at $7.3 million and up—promised to bring a stupendous financial windfall to the original investors. If only this cemetery business could be resolved. The *New York Times* article had been an annoyance, but it was nothing compared with the bull-in-a-china-shop antics of Corrie Swanson.

That bitch. It was her fault. And she would pay.

Kermode finished her cup, put it down, took a deep breath, then picked up the phone. It was late in New York City, but Daniel Stafford was a night owl and this was usually the best time to reach him.

He picked up on the second ring, his smooth patrician voice coming down the line. "Hello, Betty. How's the skiing?"

A wave of irritation. He knew perfectly well she didn't ski. "They tell me it's excellent, Daniel. But I'm not calling to bandy civilities."

"Pity."

"We've got a problem."

"The fire? It's only a problem if they don't catch the fellow—which they will. Trust me, by the time Phase Three comes online he'll be heading to the electric chair."

"The fire isn't what I'm calling about. It's that girl. And the meddling FBI agent. I hear he's managed to dig up three more descendants who've given permission to look at their ancestors' bones."

"And the problem?"

"What do you mean, *and the problem*? It's bad enough that this Captain Bowdree has shown up in person—at least she wants to bury her ancestor's bones somewhere else. Daniel, what if those other descendants demand reburial in the original cemetery? We're five million dollars into construction!"

"Now, now, Betty, calm down. Please. That's never going to happen. If any so-called descendants take legal action—which they haven't yet—our attorneys will tie them up in knots for years. We've got the money and legal power to keep a case like this going forever."

"It's not just that. I'm worried about where it could lead—if you know what I mean."

"That girl's just looking at the bones, and when she's done, it ends. It isn't going to lead where you're worried it might lead. How could it? And if it does, trust me, we'll take care of it. Your problem, Betty, is that you're like your mother: you worry too much and you cherish your anger. Mix yourself a martini and let it go."

"You're disgusting."

"Thank you." A chuckle. "I'll tell you what. To ease your mind, I'll get my people to dig into their background, find some dirt. The girl, the FBI agent... anyone else?"

"Captain Bowdree. Just in case."

"Fine. Remember, I'm only doing this to keep our powder dry. We probably won't have to use it."

"Thank you, Daniel."

"Anything for you, my dear cousin Betty."

28

They sat in comfortable chairs in the all-but-empty Starbucks. Corrie cradled her cup, grateful for the warmth. Across the small table, Stacy Bowdree stared into her own coffee. She seemed quieter, less effusive, than she had that morning.

"So why did you leave the air force?" Corrie asked.

"At first I wanted to make a career of it. After 9/11. I was in college, both my parents were dead, and I was looking for direction, so I transferred to the academy. I was really gung-ho, totally idealistic. But two tours in Iraq, and then two more in Afghanistan, cured me of that. I realized I wasn't cut out to be a lifer. It's still a man's game, no matter what they say, especially in the air force."

"Four tours? Wow."

Bowdree shrugged. "Not uncommon. They need a lot of people on the ground over there."

"What did you do?"

"On the last tour, I was the commanding officer of the 382nd Expeditionary EOD Bunker. Explosive Ordnance Disposal. We were stationed at FOB Gardez, Paktia Province."

"You defused bombs?"

"Sometimes. Most of the time, we'd clear areas of the base or take munitions to the range and get rid of them. Basically, any time they wanted to put a shovel in the ground, we had to clear the area first. Once in a while, we had to go beyond the wire and clear IEDs."

"You mean, with those big bomb suits?"

"Yeah, like in that film *The Hurt Locker.* Although mostly we used robots. Anyway, that's all in the past. I got my discharge a few months ago. I've sort of been drifting, wondering what to do with my life—and then Pendergast's bit of news came along."

"And so you're here in Roaring Fork."

"Yes, and you're probably wondering why."

"Well, I am, a little." Corrie laughed, still a little nervous. She had been afraid to ask the question.

"When you're done with him, I'm taking Great-Great-Granddad back to Kentucky and I'm going to bury him in the family plot."

Corrie nodded. "That's cool."

"My parents are gone, I don't have any brothers or sisters. I've been getting interested in my family's past. The Bowdrees go back a long way. We've got Colorado pioneers like Emmett, we've got military officers going back to the Revolution, and then there's my favorite, Captain Thomas Bowdree Hicks, who fought for the South in the Army of Northern Virginia—a real war hero and a captain, just like me." Her face glowed with pride.

"I think it's great."

"I'm glad you think so. Because I'm not here to rush your work along. I don't have any burning agenda—I just want to reconnect with my past, with my roots, to make a personal journey of sorts, and in the end bring my ancestor back to Kentucky. Maybe by then I'll have a better idea of what to do next."

Corrie simply nodded.

Bowdree finished her coffee. "What a bizarre thing, getting eaten by a bear."

Corrie hesitated. She'd been thinking about it all afternoon, and had decided she really couldn't in good conscience keep back the truth. "Um, I think there's something you should know about your ancestor."

Bowdree looked up.

"This has to remain confidential—at least until I've finished my work."

"It will."

"Emmett Bowdree wasn't killed and eaten by a grizzly bear."

"No?"

"Nor were the other remains—at least the ones I've looked at." She took a deep breath. "They were murdered. By a gang of serial killers, it seems. Murdered and..." She couldn't quite say it.

"Murdered and...?"

"Eaten."

"You've got to be kidding me."

Corrie shook her head.

"And nobody knows this?"

"Only Pendergast."

"What are you going to do about it?"

Corrie paused. "Well, I'd like to stay here and solve the crime."

Bowdree whistled. "Good God. Any idea of who? Or why?"

"Not yet."

A long silence ensued. "You need any help?"

"No. Well, maybe. I've got a whole lot of old newspapers to comb through—I guess I could use a hand with that. But I need to do all the forensic analysis on my own. It's my first real thesis and... well, I want it to be my own work. Pendergast thinks I'm crazy and wants me to finish up and go back to New York with what I've got, but I'm not ready for that yet."

Bowdree gave a big smile. "I get it totally. You're just like me. I like doing things on my own."

Corrie sipped her drink. "Any luck finding a place to stay?"

"Nada. I've never seen such a gold-plated town."

"Why don't you stay with me? I'm house-sitting an empty mansion on Ravens Ravine Road, just me and a stray dog, and to be honest the place is creeping me out. I'd love to have someone keep me company." *Especially ex-military.* She'd been thinking about those footprints all afternoon, thinking how much better she'd feel with a roommate. "All you'll have to do is avoid a few security cameras—

the nonresident owner is a bit of a busybody. But I'd love to have you."

"Are you serious? Really?" Bowdree's smile widened. "That would be fantastic! Thank you so much."

Corrie drained her drink and stood up. "If you're ready, you can follow me up there now."

"I was born ready." And with that, Bowdree grabbed her gear and followed Corrie out into the freezing night.

29

At five minutes to four in the morning, London time, Roger Kleefisch stepped into the large sitting room of his town house on Marylebone High Street and surveyed the dim surroundings with satisfaction. Everything was in its precise position: the velvet-lined easy chairs on each side of the fireplace; the bearskin hearth rug on the floor; the long row of reference works on the polished mantelpiece, a letter jammed into the wood directly below them by a jackknife; the scientific charts on the wall; the bench of chemicals heavily scarred with acid; the letters *V.R.* tattooed into the far wall with bullet holes—simulated bullet holes, of course. There was even a worn violin sitting in a corner—Kleefisch had been trying to learn how to play, but of course even discordant scrapings would have been sufficient. As he looked around, a smile formed on his face. Perfect—as close as he could possibly make it to the descriptions in the stories themselves. The only thing he'd left out had been the solution of cocaine hydrochloride and hypodermic needle.

He pressed a button beside the door, and the lights came up—gas, of course, specially installed at great expense. He walked thoughtfully over to a large mahogany bookcase and peered through the glass doors. Everything within was devoted to a single subject—*the* subject. The top three shelves were taken up with various copies of The Canon—of course he wasn't able to purchase the very first editions, even on his barrister's salary, but he nevertheless had some extremely choice copies, especially the 1917 George Bell edition of *His Last Bow*, with dust wrapper intact, and the 1894 George Newnes printing of *The Memoirs of Sherlock Holmes*, the spine still quite bright, with just the smallest amount of wear and foxing. The lower shelves of the bookcase were taken up by various volumes of scholarship and back issues of the *Baker Street Journal*. This last was a periodical issued by the Baker Street Irregulars, a group devoted to the study and perpetuation of Sherlockiana. Kleefisch had himself published several articles in the *Journal*, one of which—an exceedingly detailed work devoted to Holmes's study of poisons—had prompted the Irregulars to offer him a membership in the organization and present him with an "Irregular Shilling." One did not apply for membership in the Irregulars; one had to be asked. And becoming an Investiture was, without doubt, the proudest achievement of Kleefisch's life.

Opening the cabinet doors, he hunted around the lower shelves for a periodical he wanted to re-read, located it, closed the doors again, then walked over to the closest armchair and sat down with a sigh of contentment. The gaslights threw a warm, mellow light over everything. Even this town house, in the Lisson Grove section, had been chosen for its proximity to Baker Street. If it had not been for the infrequent sound of traffic from beyond the bow window, Kleefisch could almost have imagined himself back in 1880s London.

The phone rang, an antique "Coffin" dating to 1879, of wood and hard rubber with a receiver shaped like an oversize drawer handle. The smile fading from his face, he glanced at his watch and picked up the receiver. "Hallo."

"Roger Kleefisch?" The voice was American—southern, Kleefisch noticed—coming in from a long distance, it seemed. He vaguely recognized it.

"Speaking."

"This is Pendergast. Aloysius Pendergast."

"Pendergast." Kleefisch repeated the name, as if tasting it.

"Do you remember me?"

"Yes. Yes, of course." He had known Pendergast at Oxford, when he had been studying law and Pendergast had been reading philosophy at the Graduate Centre of Balliol College. Pendergast had been a rather strange fellow—reserved and exceedingly private—and yet a kind of intellectual bond had formed between them that Kleefisch still remembered with fondness. Pendergast, he recalled, had seemed to be nursing some private sorrow, but Kleefisch's tactful attempts to draw him out on the subject had met with no success.

"I apologize for the lateness of the call. But I remembered your keeping, shall we say, unusual hours and hoped that the habit had not deserted you."

Kleefisch laughed. "True, I rarely go to bed before five in the morning. When I'm not in court, I prefer to sleep while the rabble are out and about. To what do I owe this call?"

"I understand you are a member of the Baker Street Irregulars."

"I have that honor, yes."

"In that case, perhaps you can assist me."

Kleefisch settled back in the chair. "Why? Are you working on some academic project regarding Sherlock Holmes?"

"No. I am a special agent with the FBI, and I'm investigating a series of murders."

There was a brief silence while Kleefisch digested this. "In that case, I can't imagine what possible service I could be to you."

"Let me summarize as briefly as I can. An arsonist has burned down a house and its inhabitants at the ski resort of Roaring Fork, Colorado. Do you know of Roaring Fork?"

Naturally, Kleefisch had heard of Roaring Fork.

"In the late nineteenth century, Roaring Fork was a mining community. Interestingly, it is one of the places where Oscar Wilde stopped on his lecture tour of America. While he was there, he was told a rather colorful tale by one of the miners. The tale centered on a man-eating grizzly bear."

"Please continue," Kleefisch said, wondering just where this strange story was going.

"Wilde told this story, in turn, to Conan Doyle during their 1889 dinner at the Langham Hotel. It seemed to have had a powerful effect on Conan Doyle—powerful, unpleasant, and lasting."

Kleefisch said nothing. He knew, of course, about the legendary dinner. He would have to take another look at the Conan Doyle diary entry about that.

"I believe that what Conan Doyle heard so affected him that he wove it—suitably fictionalized, of course—into his work, as an attempt at catharsis. I'm speaking in particular about *The Hound of the Baskervilles.*"

"Interesting," Kleefisch said. To the best of his knowledge, this was a new line of critical thinking. If it proved promising, it might even lead to a scholarly monograph for the Irregulars. To be written by himself, of course: of late he had been searching for a new subject on which to focus. "But I confess I still don't see how I can be of help. And I certainly don't understand what all this has to do with the arson case you're investigating."

"On the latter point, I'd prefer to keep my own counsel. On the former point, I am becoming increasingly convinced that Conan Doyle knew more than he let on."

"You mean, more than he alluded to in *The Hound of the Baskervilles?*"

"Precisely."

Kleefisch sat up. This was more than interesting—this was downright exciting. His mind began to race. "How do you mean?"

"Just that Conan Doyle might have written more about this man-eating bear, somewhere else—perhaps in his letters or unpublished works. Which is why I'm consulting you."

"You know, Pendergast, there might actually be something in your speculations."

"Pray explain."

"Late in life, Conan Doyle supposedly wrote one last Holmes story. Nothing about it is known—not its subject, not even its name. The story goes that Conan Doyle submitted it for publication, but it was returned to him because its subject was too strong for the general public. What happened to it then is unknown. Most suspect it was destroyed. Ever since, this lost Holmes story has been the stuff of legends, endlessly speculated upon by members of the Irregulars."

There was silence on the other end of the line.

"To tell you the truth, Pendergast, I'd rather suspected it of being just another Holmesian tall tale. They are legion, you know. Or, perhaps, a shaggy dog story perpetuated by Ellery Queen. But given what you've said, I find myself wondering if the story might actually exist, after all. And if it does, that it might..." His voice trailed off.

"That it might tell the rest of the story that always haunted Conan Doyle," Pendergast finished for him.

"Exactly."

"Do you have any idea how one might go about searching for such a story?"

"Not off the top of my head. But as an Irregular, and a Holmes scholar, there are various resources at my disposal. This could be an extraordinary new avenue of research." Kleefisch's brain was working even faster now. To uncover a lost Sherlock Holmes story, after all these years...

"What's your address in London?" Pendergast asked.

"Five-Seventy-Two, Marylebone High Street."

"I hope you don't mind if I call on you in the near future?"

"How near?"

"Two days, perhaps. As soon as I can break away from this arson investigation. I'll be staying at the Connaught Hotel."

"Excellent. It will be a pleasure to see you again. In the meantime, I'll make some initial inquiries, and we'll be able to—"

"Yes," Pendergast interrupted. His voice had changed abruptly; a sudden urgency had come into it. "Yes, thank you, I'll do my best to see you then. But now, Kleefisch, I have to go; you'll excuse me, please."

"Is something wrong?"

"There appears to be another house on fire." And with that, Pendergast abruptly hung up and the line went dead.

30

Even with liberal goosing of the siren and repeated yelling through the squad car's external megaphone, Chief Morris couldn't get closer than a block to the station, so thick was the press of cars, media, and people. And it wasn't even eight o'clock in the morning. With this second arson, the story had gone national—no surprise, given the identity of the victims—and the crime feeders were all there, along with the network news shows, CNN, and God only knew who else.

The chief now regretted he'd driven himself; he had no one to run interference, and his only option was to get out of the car and scrimmage his way through these jokers. They had surrounded his squad car, cameras rolling, microphones waving at him like clubs. He'd spent all night at the scene of the fire, which had started at eight in the evening, and he was now filthy, stinking of smoke, exhausted, coughing, and hardly able to think. What a state to face the cameras.

The chief's car was jostled and rocked by the unruly crowd of reporters. They were calling out questions, hollering at him, jockeying with each other for position. He realized he'd better think of something to say.

He took a deep breath, collected himself, and forced open the door. The reaction was instant, the crowd pushing forward, the cameras and mikes swinging dangerously, one even knocking his hat off. He stood up, dusted off his hat, replaced it, and held up his hands. "All right. All right! Please. I can't make a statement if you keep this up. Give me some room, *please!*"

The crowd backed off a little. The chief looked around, acutely aware that his image was going to be broadcast on every nightly news show in the country.

"I will make a brief statement. There will be no questions afterward." He took a breath. "I've just come from the crime scene. I can assure you we are doing everything humanly possible to solve these vicious crimes and bring the perpetrators to justice. We have the finest forensic and crime-scene investigators in the state on this case. All our resources and those of the surrounding communities have been brought to bear. On top of that, we have brought in as a consultant one of the FBI's top agents specializing in serial killings and deviant psychology, as it appears we may be dealing with a serial arsonist."

He cleared his throat. "Now to the crime itself. The scene is of course still being analyzed. Two bodies have been recovered. They have been tentatively identified as the actress Sonja Dutoit and her child. Our thoughts and prayers are with the victims, their families, and all of you who have been touched by this horrible event. This is a huge tragedy for our town and, truthfully, I can't find the words to express the depth of my shock and sorrow..." He found himself temporarily unable to continue, but quickly mastered the constriction in his throat and wrapped things up. "We will have more information for you at a press conference later today. That is all I have to say for the moment. Thank you."

He barreled forward, ignoring the shouted questions and the forest of microphones, and within five minutes managed to stagger into his office. There was Pendergast, sitting in the outer office, dressed in his usual impeccable style, sipping tea. The television was on.

Pendergast rose. "Allow me to congratulate you on a most effective appearance."

"What?" Morris turned to Shirley. "I was on the tube already?"

"It was live, Chief," she said. "And you handled it very well. You looked like a hero, with that determined voice...and those streaks of soot on your face."

"Soot? On my face?" Damn, he should have washed up.

"A Hollywood makeup artist couldn't have done a finer job," said Pendergast. "That, combined with the disheveled uniform, the windswept hair, and the evident emotion, made for a singular impression."

The chief threw himself down in a chair. "I couldn't care less what they think. My God, I've never seen anything like this. Agent Pendergast, if you heard what I said on television, then you know I just elevated you to official consulting status."

Pendergast inclined his head.

"So I hope to God in heaven you will accept. I need your help more than ever. How about it?"

The man responded by removing a slim envelope from his suit and dangling it in front of Morris by his fingertips. "I'm afraid I beat you to it. I'm not just consulting—now I'm official."

31

As Corrie entered the empty library, it seemed less cheerful than before, more foreboding. Maybe it was because an atmosphere of doom seemed to have descended on the town—or perhaps it was simply due to the dark storm clouds that were gathering over the mountains, promising snow.

Stacy Bowdree, following her into the history section, whistled softly. "Does this town have money, or what?"

"Yeah, but nobody ever comes in here."

"Too busy shopping."

She saw Ted, at his desk across the room, rising from his book to greet them. He was wearing a tight T-shirt and looking exceptionally good, and Corrie felt her heart flutter unexpectedly. She took a breath and introduced Stacy.

"What's on the program today, ladies?" Ted asked, giving Stacy an appreciative once-over. Corrie had to admit Stacy was striking and that any man would enjoy looking at her, but his attentive eye still concerned her.

"Murder and mayhem," Corrie said. "We want all the articles you've got on murders, hangings, robberies, vigilantism, shootings, feuds—in short, everything bad—for the period of the grizzly killings."

At this Ted laughed. "Just about every issue of the old *Roaring Fork*

Courier is going to have some kind of crime story. It was a hot town in those days—a real place, unlike now. What issues do you want to start with?"

"The first grizzly killing was in May 1876, so let's start with, say, April first, 1876, and go six months out from that."

"Very good," Ted replied.

Corrie noticed that his eyes were still straying regularly to Stacy—and not just to her face. But the captain seemed oblivious—or perhaps she was just used to it from her years in the military.

"The old newspapers are all digitized. I'll set you up at some terminals and show you what to do." He paused. "Sure is crazy in town today."

"Yeah," said Corrie. The truth was, aside from all the traffic she hadn't paid much attention.

"It's like *Jaws*."

"What do you mean?"

"What was the name of that town—Amity? You know, the tourists leaving in droves. Well, that's what's happening here. Haven't you noticed? All of a sudden the ski slopes are deserted, the hotels are emptying out. Even the second-homers are making preparations to leave. In a day or two, the only people who'll still be here are the press. It's nuts." He typed away at two side-by-side terminals, then straightened. "Okay, they're all set up for you." He showed them how to work the equipment. He paused. "So, Stacy, when did you get here?"

"Four days ago. But I've been lying low, didn't want to cause a ruckus."

"Four days. The day before the first fire?"

"I guess it must have been. I heard about it the following morning."

"I hope you enjoy our little town. It's a fun place—if you're rich." He laughed, winked, and, to Corrie's relief, went back to his desk. Was she jealous? She didn't have a lock on him—she'd even declined his offer to see his apartment.

They divided up the searching by date, Corrie taking the first three months while Stacy took the next three. Silence descended, broken only by the soft rapping of keys.

And then Stacy whistled softly. "Listen to this."

THEY WANTED THE SAME GIRL
And They Fought a Duel by Lantern Light on Her Account
BOTH MEN LITERALLY CUT TO RIBBONS

Two Ohio swains meet at midnight and, by the aid of a lantern, proceed to hack each other with swords and pocket knives until both are unconscious. One of the rivals, rousing himself, runs his adversary through with his sword, causing a fatal injury. The lady, Miss Williams, is prostrate with grief over the terrible affray.

"That's pretty bizarre," said Corrie, hoping that Stacy wasn't going to read aloud every silly story she came across. It was only with a degree of soul searching that she'd accepted Stacy's offer of assistance.

"I like that. *Prostrate with grief.* I'll bet she just soaked her bloomers over the *affray.*"

The crudity of the comment shocked Corrie. But maybe that was the way women talked in the military.

As Corrie paged through the headlines, she realized Ted was right: Roaring Fork, at least in the summer of 1876, was a bloody town. There was practically a murder a week, along with daily stabbings and shootings. There were stagecoach robberies on Independence Pass, mining claim disputes, the frequent murder of prostitutes, stealing of horses, and vigilante hangings. The town was overrun with card sharps, shysters, thieves, and murderers. There was also a huge economic divide. Some few struck it rich and built palatial mansions on Main Street, while most lived in teeming boardinghouses, four or five to a room, and tent encampments overrun with filth, rats, and mosquitoes. A casual and pervasive racism infected everything. One end of town, called "China Camp," was populated with so-called coolies who were horribly discriminated against. There was also a "Negro Town."

And the newspaper noted a squalid camp in a nearby canyon that was occupied by "assorted drunken, miserable specimens of the Red Race, the sad remnants of the Utes of yore."

In 1876, law had barely come to Roaring Fork. Most "justice" was administered by shadowy vigilantes. If a drunken shooting or knifing occurred in a saloon the night before, the perpetrator would often be found the next morning hanging from a large cottonwood tree at the far end of town. The corpses were left up for days to greet newcomers. In a busy week there might be two, three, or even four bodies hanging on the tree, with "the maggots dropping out of them," as one reporter wrote with relish. The papers were full of colorful and outrageous stories: of a feud between two families that ended with the complete extermination of all but one man; of an obese horse thief whose weight was such that his hanging decapitated him; of a man who went berserk from what the newspaper called a "Brain Storm," thought he was Jesus, barricaded himself in a whorehouse, and proceeded to kill most of the ladies in order to rid the town of sin.

Work in the mines was dreadful, the miners descending before daybreak and coming up after sunset, six days a week, only seeing the light of day on Sundays. Accidents, cave-ins, and explosions were common. But it was even worse in the stamp mills and the smelter. There, in a large industrial operation, the silver ore was pulverized by gigantic metal "stamps" weighing many tons. These literally smashed the ore, pounding day and night, producing a ceaseless din that shook the entire town. The resulting grit was dumped into immense iron tanks with mechanical agitators and grinding plates to further reduce it to a mush-like paste; then mercury, salt, and copper sulfate were added. The resulting witches' brew was cooked and stirred for days, heated by enormous coal-fired boilers that belched smoke. Because the town was in a valley surrounded by mountains, the coal smoke created a choking, London-style fog that blocked the sun for days on end. Those who worked in the mill and smelter had it worse than the miners, as they were often scalded to death by burst steam pipes and boilers, suffocated by noxious fumes, or horribly maimed by heavy equipment. There were no safety laws, no regulation of hours or pay, and no unions. If a man was crippled by machinery, he was immediately dismissed without even an extra day's wage, cast off to fend for himself. The worst and most dangerous jobs were given to the Chinese "coolies," whose frequent deaths were reported in the back of the paper in the same offhand tone one might use to describe the death of a dog.

Corrie found herself becoming increasingly indignant as she read about the injustice, the exploitation, and the casual cruelty in pursuit of profit perpetrated by the mining companies. What surprised her most, however, was to learn that it was the Staffords—one of the most respected philanthropist families in New York City, famous for the Stafford Museum of Art and the wealthy Stafford Fund—who had initially established their fortune during the Colorado silver boom as the financiers behind the mill and smelter in Roaring Fork. The Stafford family, she knew, had done a lot of good with their money over the years—which made the unsavory origin of their fortune all the more surprising.

"What a place," said Stacy, interrupting Corrie's train of thought. "I had no idea Roaring Fork was such a hellhole. And now look at it: the richest town in America!"

Corrie shook her head. "Ironic, isn't it?"

"So much violence and misery."

"True," said Corrie, adding in a low voice: "though I'm not finding anything that might point to a gang of cannibalistic serial killers."

"Me neither."

"But the clues are there, somewhere. They *have* to be. We just have to find them."

Stacy shrugged. "You think it might be those Ute Indians up in the canyon? They had a good motive: their land was stolen by the miners."

Corrie considered this. Around that time, she'd read, the White River and Uncompahgre Utes had been fighting back against the whites who were pushing them westward through the Rocky Mountains. The conflict culminated in the White River War of 1879, when the Utes were finally expelled from Colorado. It was possible that some Indians in the conflict had worked their way southward and taken revenge on the miners of Roaring Fork.

"I thought of that," she said at length. "But the miners weren't scalped—scalping leaves distinctive markings. And I learned that the Utes had a huge taboo against cannibalism."

"So did whites. And maybe they didn't scalp them so as to conceal their identity."

"Possible. But the killings were high-quality. What I mean is," Corrie hastily added, "they were not sloppy and disorganized. It can't be easy to ambush a wily, hardened Colorado miner guarding his claim. I don't think a sad camp of Utes could have perpetrated these killings."

"What about the Chinese? I can't believe how terribly they were treated—it was as if they were considered subhuman."

"I thought about that, too. But if the motive was revenge, why *eat* them?"

"Maybe they just faked the eating thing, to make it look like a bear."

Corrie shook her head. "My analysis shows they really did consume the flesh—raw. And another question: why did they suddenly stop? What goal had they accomplished, if any?"

"That's a really good question. But it's one o'clock, and I don't know about you, but I'm so hungry I could eat a couple of miners myself."

"Let's get lunch."

As they got up to leave, Ted came over. "Say, Corrie," he began. "I meant to ask you. How about dinner tonight? Won't be any problems getting a reservation." He ran his fingers through his curly brown hair and looked at her, smiling.

"I'd love to," she said, gratified that Ted, despite his attention to Stacy, still was interested. "But I'm supposed to have dinner with Pendergast."

"Oh. Well. Some other time, then." He smiled, but Corrie noticed he wasn't quite able to fully conceal a look of hurt. It reminded her of a puppy dog, and she felt a stab of guilt. Nevertheless, he turned gamely toward Stacy and gave her a wink. "Good to meet you."

As they bundled up in their coats and walked out into the winter air, Corrie wondered where another date with Ted might lead. The fact was, it seemed like a long time since she'd had a boyfriend, and her bed in the mansion up Ravens Ravine was so very, very cold.

32

It was like a persistent nightmare, which terrifies you one night, then returns the next in an even more malevolent form. At least, so it seemed to Chief Morris as he walked through what was left of the Dutoit house. The smoldering ruins stood on the shoulder of a hill, with sweeping views of the town below and the surrounding ring of snowy mountains. He could hardly bear it: walking along the same corridors of plastic tape; smelling the same stench of burnt wood, plastic, and rubber; seeing the charred walls and melted puddles of glass, the scorched beds and heat-shattered toilets and sinks. And then there were the little things that had weirdly survived: a drinking glass, a bottle of perfume, a sodden teddy bear, and a poster of the movie *Marching Band*, Dutoit's most famous film, still pinned to a gutted wall.

It had taken most of the night to extinguish the fire and beat it down to this damp, steaming pile. The forensic specialists and the M.E. had gone in at dawn, and had identified the victims as best they could. They hadn't been burned quite as badly as the Baker family—which only added to the horror. At least, the chief thought, he didn't have to deal with Chivers this time, who had already been through the crime scene and was now off preparing his report—a report that Chief Morris was doubtful of. Chivers was clearly in over his head.

He was, however, grateful for Pendergast's presence. The man was strangely reassuring to the chief, despite his eccentricities—and despite the fact that everyone else was put out by his presence. Pendergast wandered ahead of Morris, dressed in his inappropriate formal black coat and white silk scarf, with that same strange hat on his head, silent as the grave. The sun was obscured by heavy winter clouds, and the temperature outside the ruin was hovering in the low teens. Inside, though, the residual heat and plumes of steam created a humid, stinking microclimate.

They finally reached the first victim, which the M.E. had tentatively identified as Dutoit herself. The remains looked more or less like an oversize, blackened fetus nestled in a pile of springs, metal plates, screws, carpet tacks, and burnt layers of cotton batting, with bits of melted plastic and wire here and there. The skull was whole, the jaws gaping in a frozen scream, the arms burned to the bone, the finger bones clenched, the body curled in upon itself by the heat.

Pendergast halted and spent a long time just looking at the victim. He did not pull out test tubes and tweezers and take samples. All he did was look. Then, slowly, he circled the hideous thing. A hand lens came out, and he used it to peer at traces of melted plastic and other, obscure points of interest. While he was doing this, the wind shifted and the chief got a noseful of roasted meat, causing an instant gagging sensation. God, he wished Pendergast would hurry it up.

Finally the FBI agent rose and they continued their perambulation of the gigantic ruin, heading inexorably toward the second victim—the young girl. This was even worse. The chief had deliberately skipped breakfast in preparation, and there was nothing in his stomach to lose, but nevertheless he could feel the dry heaves coming on.

The victim, Dutoit's daughter, Sallie, had been ten years old. She went to school with the chief's own daughter. The two children had not been friends—Sallie had been a withdrawn child, and no wonder, with a mother like that. Now, as they approached the corpse, the chief ventured a glance. The girl's body was in a sitting position, burned only on one side. She had been handcuffed to the pipes under a sink.

He felt the first dry heave, which came like a hiccup, then another, and quickly looked away.

Again, Pendergast spent what seemed a lifetime examining the remains. The chief didn't even begin to understand how he could do it. Another heave came, and he tried to think of something else—*anything* else—to get himself under control.

"It's so perplexing," Morris said, more to distract himself than for any other reason. "I just don't understand."

"In what way?"

"How . . . well, how the perp selects his victims. I mean, what do the victims have in common? It all seems so random."

Pendergast rose. "The crime scene is indeed challenging. You are correct that the victims are random. However, the *attacks* are not."

"How so?"

"The killer did not choose victims. He—or she, as the etiology of the attacks does not yet indicate gender—chose houses."

The chief frowned. "Houses?"

"Yes. Both houses share one trait: they are spectacularly visible from town. The next house will no doubt be equally conspicuous."

"You mean, they were selected for show? In God's name, why?"

"To send a message, perhaps." Pendergast turned away. "Now back to the matter at hand. This crime scene is primarily interesting for the light it sheds on the mind of the killer." Pendergast spoke slowly as he peered around. "The perpetrator would appear to meet the Millon definition of a sadistic personality of the 'explosive' subtype. He seeks extreme measures of control; he takes pleasure—perhaps sexual pleasure—in the intense suffering of others. This disorder presents violently in an individual who would otherwise seem normal. In other words, the person we seek might appear to be an ordinary, productive member of the community."

"How can you know that?"

"It is based on my reconstruction of the crime."

"Which is?"

Pendergast looked around the ruins again before letting his eyes settle on the chief. "First, the perpetrator entered through an upstairs window."

The chief refrained from asking how Pendergast could determine this, especially since there was no second floor left.

"We know this because the house doors were massive and the locks were all engaged. To be expected, given the fear recently generated by the first fire and, perhaps, by the relative isolation of the structure. In addition, the first-floor windows are of massive, multilight construction, glazed with expensive, high-R-value triple-paned glass with anodized aluminum cladding over oak. The ones I examined were all locked, and we can assume the rest were shut and locked as well, given the low temperatures and, as I said, the fear generated by the first attack. Such a window is extremely hard to break, and any attempt would be noisy and time consuming. It would alarm the house. Someone would have called nine-one-one or hit a panic button, with which this house was equipped. But the two victims were caught unawares—upstairs, probably while sleeping. The upstairs windows were less robust, double-paned, and furthermore not all locked—as is evident from this one, here." Pendergast pointed at a tracery of ash and metal at his feet. "Thus, I conclude that the killer came and left by an upstairs window. The two victims were subdued, then brought downstairs for the, ah, *denouement.*"

The chief found it hard to concentrate on what Pendergast was saying. The wind had shifted again, and he was breathing assiduously through his mouth.

"This tells us not only the killer's state of mind, but also some of his physical characteristics. He or she is certainly an athletic individual, perhaps with some rock climbing or other strenuous field experience."

"Rock climbing experience?"

"My dear Chief, it follows directly from the fact there is no evidence of a ladder or rope."

Chief Morris swallowed. "And the, ah, 'explosive' sadism?"

"The woman, Dutoit, was duct-taped to the downstairs sofa. The tape was wrapped all the way around the sofa—quite a job—rendering her immobile. She appears to have been doused with gasoline and burned alive. Most significantly, this occurred without the victim being gagged."

"Which means?"

"The perpetrator wanted to talk to her, to hear her plead for her life, and then, after the fire began... to hear her scream."

"Oh, dear Lord." Morris remembered Dutoit's strident voice at the press conference. He felt another dry heave.

"But the sadism evident here—" Pendergast made a gentle gesture in the direction of the remains of the dead girl— "is even more extreme."

Morris didn't want to know more, but Pendergast went on. "This girl was not doused with gasoline. That would have been too quick for our perpetrator. Instead, he started a fire to the right of her, there, and let it burn toward her. Now, if you will examine the pipes that the victim was handcuffed to, you will notice that they are bent. She was pulling on them with all her might in an effort to escape."

"I see." But the chief didn't even make a pretense of looking.

"But note the *direction* in which they are bent."

"Tell me," said Chief Morris, covering his face, no longer able to take it.

"They are bent in the direction of the fire."

A silence fell. "I'm sorry," the chief said. "I don't understand."

"Whatever she was trying to get away from—it was even worse than the fire."

33

The last time Corrie was in the old Victorian police station, she'd been in handcuffs. The memory was fresh enough that she felt a twinge upon entering. But Iris, the lady at the reception desk, was almost too nice and happily directed her to Pendergast's temporary office in the basement.

She descended the stuffy staircase, walked past a dim, rumbling furnace, and came to a narrow corridor. The office at the end had no name on it, just a number; she knocked and Pendergast's voice invited her in.

The special agent stood behind an ancient metal desk covered by racks of test tubes, along with a chemistry setup of unknown function that was bubbling away. The office had no windows, and the air was stifling.

"Is this what they gave you?" Corrie asked. "It's a dungeon!"

"It is what I requested. I did not wish to be disturbed, and this office is in a location where that is assured. No one comes to bother me here—no one."

"It's hot as Hades in here."

"It's no worse than a New Orleans spring. As you know, I am averse to cold."

"Shall we go to dinner?"

"So as not to blight our meal with talk of corpses and cannibalism, perhaps we could spend a few moments catching up with your research first. Please sit down."

"Sure thing, but can we please keep it short? *I'm* averse to heatstroke." She took a seat and Pendergast did likewise.

"How are you progressing?"

"Great. I've finished examining four sets of remains, and they tell the same story: all victims of a gang of cannibalistic serial killers."

Pendergast inclined his head.

"It's unbelievable, really. But there's no question. I did find something interesting in the last skeleton I looked at. The guy with the weird name, Isham Tyng. He was one of the first to be killed, and his bones do show extensive signs of perimortem damage from a large, powerful animal, no doubt a grizzly bear—along with the usual signs of beating, dismemberment, and cannibalism performed by human beings. I looked up the newspaper accounts of the killing, and in this case a bear was scared off the remains by the arrival of Tyng's partners. No doubt the bear was scavenging the victim *after* he'd been killed by the cannibal gang. But this sighting is clearly what cemented the idea in everyone's mind that the killer was a grizzly. A reasonable assumption—but also, sheer coincidence."

"Excellent. The story is now complete. I assume you don't need to examine any more remains?"

"No, four is plenty. I've got all the data I need."

"Very good," murmured Pendergast. "And when will you be returning to New York?"

Corrie took a deep breath. "I'm not going back yet."

"And why is that?"

"I've ... decided to expand the scope of my thesis."

She waited, but Pendergast did not react.

"Because, I'm sorry, but the fact is the story *isn't* complete. Now that we know these miners were murdered..." She hesitated. "Well, I'm going to do my damnedest to *solve* the murders."

Another dead silence. Pendergast's silver eyes narrowed ever so slightly.

"Look, it's a fascinating case. Why not pursue it to its end? Why were these miners killed? Who did it? And why did the killings stop so abruptly? There are tons of questions, and I want to find the answers. This is my chance to turn a good thesis into a really great one."

"If you survive," said Pendergast.

"I don't think I'm in any danger. In fact, since the fires I've been ignored. And nobody knows about my most important discovery—everyone still believes a grizzly did it."

"Nevertheless, I am uneasy."

"Why? I mean, if you're worried about where I'm house-sitting, it's miles away from the houses that were burned. And I've got a new roommate—Captain Bowdree, as it happens. You couldn't ask for better protection than that. Let me tell you something: she's got a .45 and, believe me, she knows how to use it." She didn't mention the footsteps she'd found circling the mansion.

"I have no doubt. But the fact is, I must leave Roaring Fork for several days, perhaps longer, and as a result I'll be unable to give you the benefit of my protection. I fear that your looking into this case may awaken the proverbial sleeping dog. And there is an ugly dog sleeping in this rich little town, of that I am sure."

"Surely you don't believe the arson attacks are somehow linked to the miner killings? They were a hundred and fifty years ago."

"I don't *believe* anything—yet. But I sense deep, strong water. I'm not in favor of your remaining in Roaring Fork any longer than necessary. I advise you to leave on the first plane out."

Corrie stared at him "I'm twenty, and this is *my* life. Not yours. I'm really thankful for all your help, but...you're not my father. I'm staying."

"I will discourage it by withdrawing my financial support."

"Fine!" Corrie's pent-up anger came bursting out. "You've been interfering with my thesis from the beginning. You can't help interfering—it's the way you are—but I don't appreciate it. Can't you see how important this is to me? I'm getting tired of you telling me what to do."

Something flashed across Pendergast's face—something that, had she not been so angry, she would have recognized as dangerous. "My only concern in the matter is your safety. And I must add that the risks you face are greatly augmented by your unfortunate tendency toward impetuousness and imprudence."

"If you say so. But I'm done talking. And I'm staying in Roaring Fork whether you like it or not."

As Pendergast began to speak again, she got up so abruptly she knocked over her chair and left the room without waiting to hear him out.

34

It was one of the most prominent Victorian mansions on the main drag. Ted, who was a fountain of information on Roaring Fork, had told Corrie its story. The house had been built by Harold Griswell, known as the Silver King of Roaring Fork, who made a fortune and was then bankrupted by the Panic of 1893. He committed suicide by leaping into the main shaft of the Matchless Mine, leaving behind a young widow—a former saloon dancer named Rosie Ann. Rosie Ann spent the next three decades hiring and firing lawyers and bringing countless lawsuits, trying tirelessly to recover the repossessed mines and properties; eventually, when all her legal options ran out, she boarded over the windows of the Griswell Mansion and became a recluse, refusing even to shop for basic provisions and subsisting on the kindness of neighbors, who took it upon themselves to leave food at her door. In 1955, the neighbors complained of a bad smell coming from the house. When the police entered, they found an incredible scene: the entire house was packed floor-to-ceiling with tottering stacks of documents and other bric-a-brac, much of it amassed during the woman's endless lawsuits. There were bundles of newspapers, canvas bags full of ore samples, theater bills, broadsheets, ledgers, assay reports, mining certificates, depositions, trial transcripts, payroll records, bank statements, maps, mine surveys, and the like. They had found Rosie Ann's wizened body buried under a ton of paper; an entire wall of documents, undermined by gnawing mice, had toppled over and pinned her to the floor. Rosie Ann Griswell had starved to death.

She died intestate with no heirs, and the town acquired the building. The hoarded documents proved a historical treasure trove of unruly proportions. Over half a century later, the sorting and cataloging process was still going on, fitfully, whenever the impecunious Roaring Fork Historical Society could scrape together a grant.

Ted had warned Corrie about the state of the collection, which was very unlike the sleek, digitized newspaper archive that he ran. But after combing through the papers for evidence of a cannibalistic gang of killers and coming up empty-handed, Corrie decided to look into the Griswell Archive.

The archivist, it seemed, came in only two days a week. Ted had warned Corrie that he was an unqualified asshole. When Corrie arrived that gray December morning, with a few flakes drifting down from a zinc sky, she found the archivist in the mansion's parlor, sitting behind a desk, messing around with his iPad. While the parlor was free of paper, she could see, through the open doors leading off it, floor-to-ceiling metal shelves and filing cabinets packed with stuff.

The archivist rose and held out his hand. "Wynn Marple," he said. He was a prematurely balding, ponytailed man in his late thirties, with an incipient potbelly but retaining the confident, winking air of an aging Lothario.

She introduced herself and explained her mission—that she was looking for information on the year 1876, the grizzly killings, and also on crime and possible gang activity in Roaring Fork.

Marple responded at length, quickly segueing to what was evidently his favorite subject: himself. Corrie learned that he, Marple, had once been on the Olympic Ski Team that trained in Roaring Fork, which is why he had fallen in love with the town; that he was still a rad skier and a hot dude off piste as well; and that there was no way he could allow her into the archives without the proper paperwork and approvals, not to mention a much more specific and narrower scope of work.

"You see," he said, "fishing expeditions aren't permitted. A lot of these documents are private and of a confidential, controversial, or—" and here came another wink— "scandalous nature."

This speech was accompanied by several lickings of the lips and rovings of the eyes over Corrie's body.

She took a deep breath and reminded herself not to be her own worst enemy for once. A lot of guys just couldn't help being jerks. And she needed these archives. If the answer to the killings wasn't here, then it had probably been lost to history.

"You were an Olympic skier?" she asked, larding her voice with phony admiration.

That produced another gust of braggadocio, including the information that he would have won a bronze but for the course conditions, the temperature, the judges... Corrie stopped listening but kept nodding and smiling.

"That's really cool," she said when she realized he was finished. "I've never met an Olympic athlete before."

Wynn Marple had a lot more to say on that point. After five or ten minutes, Corrie, in desperation, had agreed to a date with Wynn for Saturday night—and, in return, gained complete and unrestricted access to the archive.

Wynn tagged along after her as she made her way into the elegant yet decayed rooms, packed with paper. Adding to her woes, the papers had only been roughly sorted chronologically, with no effort made to arrange them by subject.

With the now-eager Wynn fetching files, Corrie sat down at a long baize-covered table and began to sort through them. They were all mixed up and confused, full of extraneous and misfiled material, and it became obvious that whoever had done the filing was either negligent or an idiot. As she sorted through one bundle after another, the smell of decaying paper and old wax filled the room.

The minutes turned into hours. The room was overheated, the light was dim, and her eyes started to itch. Even Wynn finally got tired of talking about himself. The papers were dry, and dust seemed to float off the pages with every shuffle. There were reams of impenetrable legal documents, filings, depositions, notices and interrogatories, trial transcripts, hearings, grand jury proceedings, commingled with plats, surveys, assay results, mining partnership agreements, payrolls, inventories, work orders, worthless stock certificates, invoices, and completely irrelevant posters and broadsides. Once in a while the tide of documents yielded a colorful playbill announcing the arrival of a busty burlesque queen or slapstick comedy troupe.

Infrequently, Corrie would turn up a document of faint interest—a criminal complaint, the transcript of a murder trial, WANTED posters, police records pertaining to undesirables and transients who were suspected of or charged with crimes. But there was nothing that stood out, no gang of crazies, no one with a motive to murder and consume eleven miners.

The name of Stafford turned up regularly, especially with respect to the smelting and refining personnel records. Those records were particularly odious, with ledger pages that listed killed workers like so much damaged equipment, next to sums paid to their widows or orphans, never amounting to more than five dollars, with the majority of the sums listed as $0.00 along with the notation "no payment/worker error." There were records of workers crippled, poisoned, or injured on the job who were then summarily dismissed with no compensation or recourse whatsoever.

"What a bunch of scumbags," Corrie muttered to herself, handing over another batch of papers to Wynn.

At one point a handbill turned up that stopped Corrie.

THE AESTHETIC THEORY

A lecture by
Mr. Oscar Wilde of London, England
The practical application of the principles of the aesthetic theory, with observations upon the fine arts, personal adornment, and house decoration

To Be Given at The Grand Gallery of the
Sally Goodin Mine
Sunday Afternoon, June 2$^\text{d}$
At Half-Past Two O'Clock
Tickets Seventy-Five Cents

Corrie almost had to laugh at the odd quaintness of it. This had to be the lecture where Wilde heard the story of the grizzly killings. And clipped to the handbill was a sheaf of news items, letters, and notes about the lecture appearance. It seemed ludicrous that the rough miners of Roaring Fork would have had any interest whatsoever in the aesthetic theory, let alone personal adornment or house decoration. But by all accounts the lecture had been a great success, resulting in a standing ovation. Perhaps it was the figure Wilde cut, with his outré dress and foppish mannerisms, or his preternatural wit. The poor miners of Roaring Fork had precious little entertainment beyond whoring and drinking.

She quickly leafed through the attached documents and came across an amusing handwritten note, apparently a letter by a miner to his wife back east. It was entirely without punctuation.

My Deere Wife Sun Day there was a Lektior by Mister Oscor Wild of London After the Lektior which was veery well Reseeved Mister Wild enjoyt talking to the Miners and Roufh Necks he was veery gray sheous while I was wating to speek to him that old drunk cogger Swinton button holt him pulld him asite and told him a storey that turnt the pore Man as Pail as a Gost I thot he wud drop and fent . . .

Wynn, reading over her shoulder, made a snorting laugh. "Illiterate bastard." He tapped the lecture handbill. "You know, I'll bet this is worth money."

"I'm sure it is," she said, hesitating, and then clipping it all back together. As charming as the miner's letter was, it was too far afield to merit inclusion in her thesis.

She shuffled the papers aside and moved on to the next file. She noted that when Wynn carried the bundle back to the shelf, he slipped out the handbill and tucked it in another place. The guy was probably going to sell it on eBay or something.

She told herself what he did was none of her business. The next big bundle arrived, and then the next. Most of the papers dealt with milling and refining, and this time almost everything related to the Stafford family, which, by all indications, became more oppressive as their wealth and power increased. They seemed to have survived the silver panic of 1893 nicely, and even used the opportunity to pick up mines and claims at pennies on the dollar. There were plenty of faded maps of the mining districts, as well, with each mine, shaft, and tunnel carefully marked and identified. Strangely, though, there were precious few records of the smelting operations.

And then a document stopped her cold. It was a postcard dated 1933, from a family member named Howland Stafford to a woman named Dora Tiffany Kermode. It opened *Dear Cousin.*

Kermode. Cousin.

"Jesus!" Corrie blurted out. "That bitch Kermode is *related* to the family who squeezed this town dry."

"Who are you talking about?" Wynn asked.

She slapped the document with the back of her hand. "Betty Kermode. That horrible woman who runs The Heights. She's related to the Staffords—you know, the ones who owned the smelter back in Roaring Fork's mining days. Unbelievable."

It was only then that Corrie realized her mistake. Wynn Marple was drawing himself up. He spoke in a reproving, almost schoolmarmish tone. "Mrs. Kermode is one of the finest, most *gracious* people in this entire town."

Corrie hastily backtracked. "I'm sorry. I was just...I mean, she's responsible for putting me in jail...I didn't realize she was a friend of yours."

Her stammered apology seemed to work. "Well, I can appreciate how you might be upset with her for that, but I can vouch for her, I really can. She's *good people.*" Another wink.

Bully for you. In five hours, Corrie hadn't found anything, and now she was saddled with going on a date with this buffoon for nothing. She hoped it could be made short and in a place where Ted would never, ever see them. Or maybe she could beg off sick at the last moment. That's what she'd do.

She glanced at her watch. There was no way she was going to find what she needed in this hellhole of paper. For the first time, she began to feel that maybe she was overreaching. Perhaps Pendergast was right. She had enough for an excellent thesis already.

She got up. "Look, this isn't working. I'd better be going."

Wynn followed her to the front parlor. "I'm sorry you weren't more successful. But at least…" He winked again. "It resulted in our getting together."

She would definitely have to call in sick.

She swallowed. "Thanks for your help, Wynn."

He leaned toward her, way too close. "My pleasure."

She suddenly paused. What was that she felt on her ass? His hand. She took a half step back and turned, but the hand followed like an octopus's sucker, this time giving her butt cheek a little squeeze.

"Do you *mind?*" she said acidly, brushing it away.

"Well…we *do* have a date coming up."

"And that *justifies* you *groping* my *ass?*"

Wynn looked confused. "But…I was just being friendly. I figured you'd like it. I mean, it isn't every day you get to go out with an Olympic skier, and I figured…?"

It was the final leering wink that did it. Corrie rounded on him. "Olympic skier? When was the last time you looked at yourself in the mirror? Here's what you'll see—a balding, potbellied, mouth-breathing loser. I wouldn't go on a date with you if you were the last man alive."

With that she turned, grabbed her coat, and left, the cold air hitting her like a wall as she stepped outside.

Wynn Marple sat down at his desk. Both his hands were trembling and his breath was coming shallow and fast. He could hardly believe how that bitch had treated him, after all the help he'd given her. One of those feminazi types, objecting to a little innocent, friendly pat.

Wynn was so furious, so outraged, he felt the blood pounding in his head like a tom-tom. It took a few minutes, but then finally he was able to pick up the phone and dial.

35

Betty Brown Stafford Kermode, sitting in the living room of her house at the top of The Heights, a piñon fire roaring in the fireplace, hung up the princess phone. She sat very still for some minutes, staring out the picture window at the mountains, considering the problem. Her brother-in-law, Henry Montebello, sat in a wing chair on the opposite side of the fire. He was dressed in a three-piece suit, a hand-knotted bow tie of dark paisley setting off a crisp white shirt. He was examining his nails with an air of patrician boredom. A weak winter sun filtered in.

Kermode considered the problem for another minute. And then she picked up the phone again and dialed Daniel Stafford.

"Hello again, my dear," came the dry, sardonic voice. Kermode did not particularly enjoy talking to her cousin Daniel, but "liking" and "caring" did not figure in the bonds that held the Stafford family together. Those bonds were made of money, and all family relation-ships were defined by it. As Daniel was not only the head of the Stafford Family Trusts, with assets of two billion dollars, but also one of two managing partners of the family investment company, with as-sets under management of sixteen billion dollars, she considered him close to her. Very close. It never occurred to her to wonder whether she actually liked the man or not.

"Am I on speakerphone?" Stafford asked.

"Henry is here with me," Kermode replied. She paused. "We have a problem."

"If you're referring to the new fire, thank heaven it didn't occur in The Heights. This is wonderful, in fact—the impact on The Heights is now much diluted. What we need is a third fire even farther afield." A dry chuckle followed.

"That's not amusing. In any case, I'm not calling about that. I'm calling because that girl—Corrie Swanson—made the connection between the Kermodes and the Staffords."

"That's not exactly a state secret."

"Daniel, she got into the Griswell Archive and hit a trove of documents related to the mines, mills, and smelter operations going way back. *All* the way back."

A silence. And then she heard her cousin swear genteelly on the other end of the line. "Anything, ah, *more* than that?" His voice was suddenly less flippant.

"No. At least, not yet."

More silence. "How good a researcher is she?"

"She's like a damn terrier, sinks her sharp little teeth in and never lets go. She doesn't seem to have made the connection yet, but if she keeps digging, she will."

Another long silence. "I was under the impression that the germane documents had been removed."

"A mighty effort was made, but the archives are a complete mess. Anything might have slipped through."

"I see. Well now, this *is* a problem."

"Did you dig up any dirt on her and the others, as you promised?"

"I did. This fellow Pendergast has a checkered history, but he's untouchable. Bowdree's something of a war hero, with a raft of citations and medals, which makes her a tricky target. Except that she got a medical discharge from the air force."

"Was she wounded?" Kermode asked. "She looked healthy enough to me."

"She spent a couple of months at the U.S. military hospital in

Landstuhl, Germany. Her actual medical records are sealed, and the air force protects those files like the dickens."

"And the girl, Swanson?"

"She's a little hellion. Grew up in a trailer park in a dreadful little town in Kansas. Parents were low, *low* working-class, split up after she was born. Mother's a raging alcoholic, father a ne'er-do-well, once accused of robbing a bank. She herself has a juvenile record as long as your arm. The only reason she got as far as she did is because this Pendergast fellow took her under his wing and financed her schooling. No doubt there's a quid pro quo there. The problem is, as long as Pendergast is around she'll be hard to get at."

"The chief of police tells me he left for London last night."

"That's lucky news. You'd better act fast."

"And do what, exactly?"

"You're perfectly capable, my dear, of taking care of this problem before that FBI agent returns. I might just remind you what is at stake here. So don't play games. Hit hard. And if you decide to hire out, only hire the best. Whatever you do, I don't want to know about it."

"What a coward you are."

"Thank you. I'm quite willing to concede that you're the one in this family with the high testosterone, dear cousin."

Kermode pressed the SPEAKERPHONE button with an angry jab, ending the phone call.

Montebello had remained silent throughout the conversation, his attention seemingly focused on his well-manicured nails. Now, however, he looked up. "Leave this to me," he said. "I know just the person for the job."

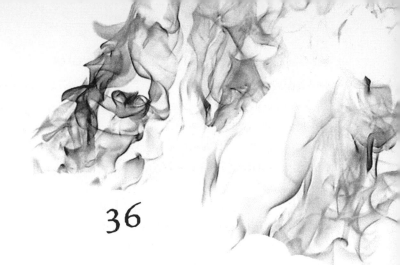

36

Espelette, the upscale brasserie off the lobby of the Connaught Hotel, was a cream-and-white confection of tall windows and crisp linen tablecloths. The climatic change from Roaring Fork was most welcome. London had so far been blessed with a mild winter, and mellow afternoon sunlight flooded the gently curving space. Special Agent Pendergast, seated at a large table overlooking Mount Street, rose to his feet as Roger Kleefisch entered the restaurant. The figure was, Pendergast noted, a trifle stouter, his face seamed and leathery. Kleefisch had been practically bald even as a student at Oxford, so the shiny pate was no surprise. The man still walked with a brisk step, moving with his body thrust forward, nose cutting the air with the anxious curiosity of a bloodhound on a scent. It was these qualities—as much as the man's credentials as a Baker Street Irregular—that had given Pendergast confidence in his choice of partner for this particular adventure.

"Pendergast!" Kleefisch said, extending his hand with a broad smile. "You look exactly the same. Well, almost the same."

"My dear Kleefisch," Pendergast replied, shaking the proffered hand. They had both fallen easily into the Oxbridge convention of referring to each other by their last names.

"Look at you: back at Oxford, I'd always assumed you'd been in

mourning. But I see that was a misapprehension. Black suits you."
Kleefisch sat down. "Can you believe this weather? I don't think Mayfair has ever looked so beautiful."

"Indeed," said Pendergast. "And I noted this morning, with no little satisfaction, that the temperature in Roaring Fork had dropped below zero."

"How dreadful." Kleefisch shivered.

A waiter approached the table, laid out menus before them, and withdrew.

"I'm so glad you were able to catch the morning flight," Kleefisch said, rubbing his hands as he looked over the menu. "The 'chic and shock' afternoon tea here is especially delightful. And they serve the best Kir Royale in London."

"It is good to be back in civilization. Roaring Fork, for all its money—or perhaps because of it—is a boorish, uncouth town."

"You mentioned something about a fire." The smile faded from Kleefisch's face. "The arsonist you spoke of struck again?"

Pendergast nodded.

"Oh, dear... On a brighter note, I think you'll be pleased with a discovery I've made. I'm hopeful your trip across the pond won't prove entirely in vain."

The waiter returned. Pendergast ordered a glass of Laurent-Perrier champagne and a ginger scone with clotted cream, and Kleefisch a variety of finger sandwiches. The Irregular watched the waiter move away, then reached into his fat lawyer's briefcase, withdrew a slender book, and slid it across the table.

Pendergast picked it up. It was by Ellery Queen, and was titled *Queen's Quorum: A History of the Detective Crime Short Story As Revealed in the 106 Most Important Books Published in This Field Since 1845.*

"*Queen's Quorum,*" Pendergast murmured, gazing over the cover. "I recall you mentioning Ellery Queen in our phone conversation."

"You've heard of him, of course."

"Yes. Them, to be more accurate."

"Precisely. Two cousins, working under a pseudonym. Perhaps

the preeminent anthologizers of detective stories. Not to mention being authors in their own right." Kleefisch tapped the volume in Pendergast's hands. "And this book is probably the most famous critical work on crime fiction—a collection, and study, of the greatest works in the genre. That's a first edition, by the way. But here's the odd thing: despite its title, *Queen's Quorum* has 107 entries—not 106. Have a look at *this*." And taking the book back, he opened it, turned to the contents page, and indicated an entry with his finger:

74. Anthony Wynne – *Sinner Go Secretly* – 1927
75. Susan Glaspell – *A Jury of Her Peers* – 1927
76. Dorothy L. Sayers – *Lord Peter Views the Body* – 1928
77. G.D.H. & M. Cole – *Superintendent Wilson's Holiday* – 1928
78. W. Somerset Maugham – *Ashenden* – 1928
78A. Arthur Conan Doyle – *The Adventure of* (?) – 1928 (?)
79. Percival Wilde – *Rogues in Clover* – 1929

"Do you see that?" Kleefisch said with something like triumph in his voice. "*Queen's Quorum* number seventy-eight A. Title uncertain. Date of composition uncertain. Even the existence uncertain: hence the A. And no entry in the main text—just a mention in the contents. But clearly, Queen had—most likely due to his preeminence in the field—heard enough about its rarity, secondhand, to believe it worth inclusion in his book. Or then again, maybe not. Because when the book was later revised in 1967, bringing the list up to one hundred twenty-five books, *seventy-eight A was left out.*"

"And you think this is our missing Holmes story."

Kleefisch nodded.

Their tea arrived. "Uniquely, Conan Doyle has a prior entry in the book," Kleefisch said, taking a bite of a smoked salmon and wasabi cream sandwich. "*The Adventures of Sherlock Holmes. Queen's Quorum number sixteen.*"

"Then it would seem that the obvious next step should be to determine just what Ellery Queen knew about this Holmes story, and where he—they—learned it from."

"Unfortunately, no. Believe me, the Irregulars have been down that path countless times. As you might imagine, *Queen's Quorum* seventy-eight A is one of the seminal bugbears of our organization. A special title has been created and is waiting to be conferred on the member who tracks down that story. The two cousins have been dead for decades and left behind no shred of evidence regarding either why seventy-eight A was in the first edition of *Queen's Quorum* or why it was later removed."

Pendergast took a sip of champagne. "This is encouraging."

"Indeed." Kleefisch put the book aside. "Long ago, the Irregulars amassed a large number of letters from Conan Doyle's later life. To date, we have not allowed outside scholars to examine the letters—we wish to mine them for our own scholarly publications in the *Journal* and elsewhere. However, the late-in-life letters have for the most part been ignored, since they deal with that time in Conan Doyle's life when he was heavily involved in spiritualism, writing such nonfiction works as *The Coming of the Fairies* and *The Edge of the Unknown* while Holmes was set aside."

Kleefisch picked up another finger sandwich, this one of teriyaki chicken and grilled aubergine. He took a bite, then another, closing his eyes as he chewed. He wiped his fingers daintily on a linen napkin, and then—with a mischievous twinkle in his eye—he reached into the pocket of his jacket and pulled out two worn, faded letters.

"I am hereby swearing you to secrecy," he told Pendergast. "I have, ah, temporarily borrowed these. You wouldn't want to see me blackballed."

"You have my assurance of silence."

"Very good. In that case, I don't mind telling you that both of these letters were written by Conan Doyle in 1929—the year before his death. Each is addressed to a Mr. Robert Creighton, a novelist and fellow spiritualist that Conan Doyle befriended in his last years." Kleefisch unfolded one. "This first letter mentions, in passing: 'I expect any day to receive news of the Aspern Hall business, which has been pressing on my mind rather severely of late.'" He refolded the letter, returned it to his pocket, and turned to the other. "The second letter mentions, also in passing: 'Have learned bad news about Aspern Hall. I am now in a quandary about how to proceed—or whether I should proceed at all. And yet I cannot rest easy until I've seen the matter through.'"

Kleefisch put the letter away. "Now, all the Irregulars who've read these letters—and there have not been many—assumed that Conan Doyle was involved in some sort of real estate speculation. But I spent all of yesterday morning going over the rolls of both England and Scotland... and there is no record of any Aspern Hall on the register. *It does not exist.*"

"So you're suggesting that Aspern Hall is not a place—but a story title?"

Kleefisch smiled. "Maybe—just maybe—it's the title of Conan Doyle's rejected tale: 'The Adventure of Aspern Hall.'"

"Where could the story be?"

"We know where it isn't. It's not in his house. After being bedridden for months with angina pectoris, Conan Doyle died in July 1930 at Windlesham, his home in Crowborough. In the years since, countless Irregulars and other Holmes scholars have traveled down to East Sussex and explored every inch of that house. Partial manuscripts, letters, other documents were found—but no missing Holmes story. That's why I can't help but fear that..." Kleefisch hesitated. "That the story's been destroyed."

Pendergast shook his head. "Recall what Conan Doyle said in that second letter: that he was in a quandary about how to proceed; that he couldn't rest until he'd *seen the matter through.* That doesn't sound like a man who would later destroy the story."

Kleefisch listened, nodding slowly.

"The same cathartic urge that prompted Conan Doyle to write the story in the first place would have prompted him to preserve it. If I had any doubts before, that entry in *Queen's Quorum* has silenced them. That story is out there—somewhere. And it may just contain the information I seek."

"Which is?" Kleefisch asked keenly.

"I can't speak of it yet. But I promise you that if we find the story—you'll be the one to publish."

"Excellent!" He brought his hands together.

"And so the game—to coin a phrase—is afoot." With that, Pendergast drained his glass of champagne and signaled the waiter for another.

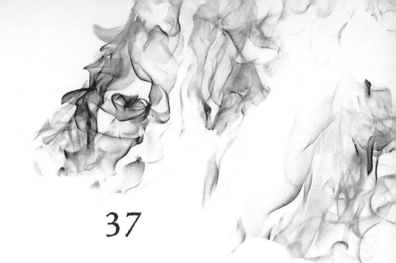

37

Stacy was proving to be a big-time sleeper, often not rising until ten or eleven, Corrie thought as she dragged herself out of bed in the dark and eyed with envy the form through the open door, sleeping in the other bedroom. She remembered being like that before figuring out what she wanted to do with her life.

Instead of making coffee in her tiny kitchen, Corrie decided to drive into town and splurge on a Starbucks. She hated the freezing house, and even with Stacy Bowdree in residence she spent as little time there as she could.

She glanced at the outdoor thermometer: two degrees below zero. The temperature just kept dropping. She bundled up in a hat, gloves, and down coat, and made her way out to the driveway where her car was parked. As she dusted it off—a very light snow had fallen the night before—she once again regretted her outburst at Wynn Marple. It had been stupid to burn that bridge. But it was vintage Corrie, with her temper and her long-standing inability to suffer jerks. That behavior might have worked in Medicine Creek, when she was still a rebellious high-school student. But there was no excusing it anymore—not here, and not now. She simply *had* to stop lashing out at people—especially when she knew all too well that it was counterproductive to her own best interests.

She started the car and eased down the steep driveway to Ravens

Ravine Road. The sky was gray, and the snow had started falling yet again. The weather report said a lot more was on the way—which in a ski resort like Roaring Fork was greeted as a farmer greets rain, with celebration and chatter. Corrie for her part was sick to death of it. Maybe it really was time to cash in her chips and get out of town.

She drove slowly, as there were often patches of ice on the hairpin road going down the canyon and her rental car, with its crappy tires, had lousy traction.

So what now? She had at most a day or two more of work on the skeletons—crossing the T's forensically, so to speak. Then that would be that. Even though it seemed unlikely, she would see if Ted had any more ideas about where she might find clues to the identity of the killers—tactfully, since of course he didn't know the truth about how the miners had really died. He'd asked her out again, for dinner tomorrow; she made a mental note to talk to him about it then.

Six days before Christmas. Her father had been begging her to come to Pennsylvania and spend it with him. He would even send her the money for airfare. Perhaps it was a sign. Perhaps...

A loud noise, a shuddering *BANG!*, caused her to jam on the brakes and scream involuntarily. The car screeched and slid, but didn't quite go off the road, instead coming to a stop sideways.

"What the *hell*?" Corrie gripped the steering wheel. What had happened? Something had shattered her windshield, turning it into an opaque web of cracks.

And then she saw the small, perfectly round hole at their center.

With another scream she ducked down, scrunching herself below the door frame. All was silent as her mind raced a mile a minute. That was a bullet hole. Someone had tried to shoot her. Kill her.

Shit, shit, shit...

She had to get out of there. Taking a deep breath and tensing, she swung herself back up, punched at the sagging window with her gloved hand, ripped a hole big enough to see through, then grabbed the wheel again and jammed on the gas. The Focus skidded around and she managed to get it under control, expecting more shots at any moment. In her panic she accelerated too fast; the car hit a patch of ice and slid again, heading for the guardrail above the ravine. The car ricocheted off it, slid back onto the road with a screech of rubber, and turned around another hundred eighty degrees. Corrie was shaken but—after a brief, panicked moment—realized she was unhurt.

"*Shit!*" she screamed again. The shooter was still out there, might even be coming down the road after her. The car had stalled and the passenger side was all bashed up, but it didn't seem to be a total wreck; she turned the key and the engine came to life. She eased the Focus back around, forcing herself to do a careful three-point turn, and drove down the road. The car still ran, but it made a nasty noise—a fender seemed to be scraping one of the tires.

Slowly, carefully, hands trembling on the steering wheel, she guided the vehicle down the mountain and into town, heading straight for the police department.

After Corrie had filled out an incident report, the sergeant behind the desk promptly showed her into the chief's office. Apparently, she was now a person of importance. She found Chief Morris behind his desk, which was heaped with three-by-five cards, photographs, string, pins, and glue. On the wall behind him was an incomprehensible chart that was no doubt related to the arson killings.

The chief looked like death warmed over. His cheeks hung like slabs of suet on his face, his eyes were sunken coals, his hair was unkempt. At the same time, there was a severe cast to his eye that hadn't been there before. That, at least, was an improvement.

He took the report and gestured for her to sit. A few minutes went by while he read it, then read it again. And then he laid it on the table. "Is there any reason you can think of that someone might be unhappy with you?" he asked.

At this Corrie, shaken as she was, had to laugh. "Yeah. Like just about everyone in The Heights. The mayor. Kermode. Montebello. Not to mention you."

The chief managed a wan smile. "We're going to open an investigation, of course. But...listen, I hope you won't think I'm trying to brush this off if I tell you we've been looking for a poacher up in that area for several weeks now. He's been killing and butchering deer, no doubt selling the meat. One of his wild shots went through the window of a house just last week. So what happened to you might—*might*—have been a stray shot from his poaching activity. This happened early in the morning, which is when the deer—and our poacher—are active. Again, I'm not saying that's what happened. I'm just mentioning it as a possibility...to ease your mind more than anything."

"Thanks," said Corrie.

They rose, and the chief held out his hand. "I'm afraid I'll have to impound your car as evidence—do a ballistics analysis and see if we can recover the round."

"You're welcome to it."

"I'll have one of my officers drive you where you need to go."

"No, thanks, I'm just going around the corner for a Starbucks."

As Corrie sat sipping her coffee, she wondered if it really had been a poacher. It was true she had annoyed a lot of people early on, but that had blown over, especially with the start of the arson killings. Shooting at her car—that would be attempted murder. What kind of threat was she to merit that? Problem was, the chief was so overwhelmed—as was everyone else in the police department—that she had little faith he would be able to conduct an effective investigation. If the shooting was meant to intimidate her, it wasn't going to work. She might be frightened—but there was no way she'd be frightened out of town. If anything, it would make her want to stay longer.

Then again...it might be the poacher. Or it could be some other random crazy. It could even be the serial arsonist, switching M.O.'s. Her thoughts turned to Stacy up in the ravine, probably still asleep. She was eventually going to come into town, and she might also be in danger, get shot at, too.

She pulled out her cell phone and dialed Stacy. A sleepy voice answered. As soon as Corrie started telling her the story, she woke up fast.

"Somebody shot up your car? I'm going looking for the mother."

"Wait. Don't do that. That's crazy. Let the police handle it."

"His tracks will be out there, in the snow. I'll follow the fucker back to whatever spider hole he crawled out of."

"No, *please*." It took Corrie ten minutes to persuade Stacy not to do it. As Corrie was about to hang up, Stacy said: "I hope he shoots at *my* car. I've got a couple of Black Talon rounds just itching to explore his inner psyche."

Next, she called Rent-a-Junker. The agent went on and on about how the chief of police himself had just called, how awful being shot at must've been, was she all right, did she need a doctor...And would an upgrade—a Ford Explorer?—be acceptable, at no extra charge, of course?

Corrie smiled as she hung up. The chief seemed to be acquiring, at long last, a bit of backbone.

38

Roger Kleefisch sprawled in one of the two velvet-lined armchairs in the sitting room of his London town house, feet on the bearskin rug, his entire frame drinking in the welcome warmth from the crackling fire on the grate. Agent Pendergast sat in the other chair, motionless, his eyes gazing into the flames. When Kleefisch had let him in, the FBI agent had glanced around at the room, raising his eyebrows but making no other comment. And yet, somehow, Kleefisch felt that he approved.

He rarely let anyone into his sitting room, and he couldn't help but feel a little like Sherlock Holmes himself, here at home, partner in detection at his side. The thought managed to lift his spirits a little. Although, were he to be honest with himself, he should probably be assuming the role of Watson. After all, Pendergast was the professional detective here.

At last, Pendergast shifted, placed his whisky-and-soda on a side table. "So, Kleefisch. What have you uncovered so far?"

It was the question Kleefisch had been dreading. He swallowed, took a deep breath, and spoke. "Nothing, I'm afraid."

The pale eyes gazed at him intently. "Indeed?"

"I've tried everything over these last twenty-four hours," he replied. "I've looked back through old correspondence, read and re-read Conan Doyle's diary. I've examined every book, every treatise on the man's last years that I could find. I've even tried picking the brains—circumspectly—of several of our most brilliant Investitures. I've found nothing, not even a trace of evidence. And I must say, despite my initial enthusiasm, it doesn't come as a surprise. All this ground had been covered so thoroughly by Irregulars in the past. I was a fool to think there might be something new."

Pendergast did not speak. With the firelight flickering over his gaunt features, his head bowed, an expression of intense thought on his face, surrounded by Victorian trappings, he suddenly looked so much like Holmes himself that Kleefisch was taken aback.

"I'm truly sorry, Pendergast," Kleefisch said, averting his gaze to the bearskin rug. "I was so hopeful." He paused. "I fear you're on a wild goose chase—one that I may have encouraged. I apologize for that."

After a moment, Pendergast stirred. "On the contrary. You've already done a great deal. You confirmed my suspicions about the missing Holmes story. You showed me the evidence in *Queen's Quorum*. You made the connection, in Conan Doyle's letters, to Aspern Hall. Almost despite yourself, you've convinced me not only that 'The Adventure of Aspern Hall' existed—but that it still exists. I must locate it."

"For an Irregular like me, a Holmes scholar, that would be the coup of a lifetime. But again I have to ask—why is it so important to you?"

Pendergast hesitated a moment. "I have certain ideas, conjectures, that this story might confirm—or not."

"Conjectures about what?"

A small smile curled Pendergast's lip. "You—a Holmes scholar—encouraging an investigator to indulge in vulgar speculation? My dear Kleefisch!"

As this Kleefisch colored.

"While I normally despise those who claim a sixth sense," Pendergast said, "in this case I *feel* that the lost story is at the center of all mysteries here—past and present."

"In that case," Kleefisch finally said, "I'm sorry I've come up empty."

"Fear not," Pendergast replied. "I haven't."

Kleefisch raised his eyebrows.

Pendergast went on. "I proceeded on the assumption that the more I could learn about Conan Doyle's final years, the closer I'd come to finding the lost story. I focused my efforts on the circle of spiritualists he belonged to in the years before he died. I learned that this group frequently met at a small cottage named Covington Grange, on the edge of Hampstead Heath. The cottage was owned by a spiritualist by the name of Mary Wilkes. Conan Doyle had a small room at Covington Grange where he would sometimes write essays on spirituality, which he would read to the group of an evening."

"Fascinating," Kleefisch said.

"Allow me to pose this question: is it not likely that, while writing his late texts on spiritualism at Covington Grange, he also wrote his final Sherlock Holmes story, 'The Adventure of Aspern Hall'?"

Kleefisch felt a quickening of excitement. It made sense. And this was an avenue that had never, to his knowledge, been explored by a fellow Irregular.

"Given its incendiary nature, isn't it also possible that the author might not have hidden it somewhere in that little room he used for writing, or somewhere else in the Grange?"

"Might he not indeed!" Kleefisch rose from his chair. "My God. No wonder the manuscript was never found at Windlesham! So what's next, then?"

"What's next? I should have thought that obvious. Covington Grange is next."

39

Teacup in hand, Dorothea Pembroke stepped back into her tidy alcove at the Blackpool headquarters of the National Trust for Places of Historic Interest or Natural Beauty. It was past ten forty-five, and Miss Pembroke was almost as serious about her elevenses as she was about her position, about which she was very serious indeed. A cloth napkin, placed daintily upon the desktop; a cup of Harrisons & Crosfield jasmine tea, one lump; and a wheatmeal biscuit dipped twice—not once, not three times—into the cup before being nibbled.

In many ways, Ms. Pembroke felt, she *was* the National Trust. There were more important jobs than hers in the nonprofit association, of course, but nobody could boast a finer pedigree. Her grandfather, Sir Erskine Pembroke, had been master of Chiddingham Place, one of the more impressive stately homes in Cornwall. But his company had failed, and when the family realized they couldn't maintain either the taxes or the upkeep of the mansion, they entered into talks with the National Trust. The building's foundations and general fabric were restored, its gardens expanded, and ultimately Chiddingham Place was opened to visitors, while the family stayed on in modest rooms on the top floor. A few years later, her father had taken a position with the National Trust, as a development manager. As soon as she was out of school, Miss Pembroke had joined the Trust herself, rising over the past thirty-two years to the position of deputy administrator.

All in all, a most satisfactory rise.

As she put away the teacup and was folding the napkin, she became aware that a man was standing in the doorway. She was much too well bred to show surprise, but she paused just a moment before giving the napkin a final fold and placing it away in her desk. He was a rather striking-looking man—tall and pale, with white-blond hair and eyes the color of glacial ice, dressed in a well-cut black suit—but she did not recognize him, and visitors were usually announced.

"Forgive me," he said in an American accent—southern—accompanied by a charming smile. "I don't mean to intrude, Ms. Pembroke. But the secretary in your outer office was away from her desk, and, well, we *did* have an appointment."

Dorothea Pembroke opened her book and glanced at the current day's page. Yes, indeed: she did have an eleven fifteen appointment with a Mr. Pendergast. She recalled that he had particularly asked to see her, as opposed to an administrator—most unusual. Still, he had not been announced, and she did not hold with such informality. But the man had a winning way about him, and she was prepared to overlook this breach of propriety.

"May I sit down?" he asked, with another smile.

Miss Pembroke nodded toward an empty seat before her desk. "What, may I inquire, do you wish to speak with me about?"

"I wish to visit one of your properties."

"Visit?" she said, allowing the faintest tinge of disapproval to color her voice. "We have volunteers out in front who can assist you with that." Really, it was too much, her being bothered with such a trivial request.

"I do apologize," the man replied. "I don't wish to take up your valuable time. I spoke about the matter with Visitor Services, and they referred me to you."

"I see." That did put another spin on things. And, really, the man had the most courtly manners. Even his accent spoke of breeding—not one of those harsh, barbarous American drawls. "Before we get started, we have a little regulation here. We require visitor identification, if you please."

The man smiled again. He had beautifully white teeth. He reached into his black suit and removed a leather wallet, which he laid open upon the table, exposing a brilliance of gold on top with a photo ID card below. Miss Pembroke was startled.

"Oh! Goodness! The Federal Bureau of Investigation? Is this...a criminal matter?"

The man gave a most winning smile. "Oh, no, don't be the slightest bit alarmed. This is a personal matter, nothing official. I would have shown you my passport, but it's in the hotel safe."

Miss Pembroke allowed her fluttering heart to subside. She had never been involved in a criminal matter and looked on such a possibility with abhorrence.

"Well, then, Mr. Pendergast, that is reassuring, and I am at your service. Please tell me the property you'd like to visit?"

"A cottage named Covington Grange."

"Covington Grange. Covington Grange." Miss Pembroke was not familiar with the name. But then again, the Trust had hundreds of properties in its care—including many of England's greatest estates—and she could not be expected to remember all of them.

"Half a moment." She turned to her computer, moused through a few menus, and entered the name into the waiting field. Several photos and a long textual entry appeared on the screen. As she read the entry, she realized she did have a faint recollection of the site. No wonder the people at Visitor Services recommended the man speak to an administrator.

She turned back. "Covington Grange," she said again. "Formerly owned by Leticia Wilkes, who died in 1980, leaving it to the government."

The man named Pendergast nodded.

"I'm very sorry to tell you, Mr. Pendergast, that a visit to Covington Grange is out of the question."

At this news, a look of devastation crossed the man's face. He struggled to master himself. "The visit needn't be a long one, Ms. Pembroke."

"I'm sorry, it's quite impossible. According to the file, the cottage has been shut up for decades, closed to the public while the Trust decides what to do with it."

Poor man—he looked so desolated that even Dorothea Pembroke's hard and ever so correct heart began to soften. "It's suffered serious damage from the elements," she said, by way of explanation. "It is unsafe and requires extensive conservation before we could ever allow anyone inside. And at present, our funds—as you might imagine—are limited. There are numerous other properties, more important properties, that also need attention. And, to be frank, it is of marginal historical interest."

Mr. Pendergast looked down, clasping and unclasping his hands. Finally, he spoke. "I thank you for taking the time to explain the situation. It makes perfect sense. It's just—" And here, Mr. Pendergast looked up again, meeting her gaze— "It's just that I am Leticia Wilkes's last remaining descendant."

Miss Pembroke looked at him in surprise.

"She was my grandmother. Of the family line, only I remain. My mother died of cancer last year, and my father was killed in a train accident the year before. My . . . sister was killed just three weeks ago, in a robbery gone bad. So, you see . . ." Mr. Pendergast paused a moment to collect himself. "You see, Covington Grange is all I have left. It is where I spent my summers as a boy, before my mother took us to America. It contains all the happy memories I have of my lost family."

"Oh, I see." This was a heartbreaking story indeed.

"I just wanted to see the place one last time, just once, before the contents go to wrack and ruin. And . . . in particular, there's an old family photo album I remember paging through as a boy, put up in a cupboard, which I'd like to take—if that's all right with you. I have nothing, *nothing*, of the family. We left everything behind when we went to America."

Miss Pembroke listened to this tragic story, pity welling up in her heart. After a moment she cleared her throat. Pity was one thing, *duty* quite another.

"As I've said, I'm very sorry," she said. "But for all the reasons I've told you, it's simply out of the question. And in any case all the contents belong to the Trust, even the photographs, which might hold historic interest."

"But they're just rotting away! It's been over thirty years and nothing's been done!" Pendergast's voice had taken on a wheedling tone. "Just ten minutes inside? Five? Nobody would have to know besides you and me."

This insinuation—that she might be privy to an underhanded scheme unbeknownst to the Trust—broke the spell. "That is out of the question. I am surprised you would make such an overture."

"And that's your final word?"

Miss Pembroke gave a curt nod.

"I see." The man's air changed. The forlorn expression, the faint tremor in the voice, vanished. He sat back in his chair and regarded her with quite a different expression than before. There was suddenly something in the expression—something Miss Pembroke could not quite put a finger on—that was ever so faintly alarming.

"This is of such importance to me," said the man, "that I will go to unreasonable lengths to achieve it."

"I'm not sure what that means, but my mind is made up," she said with absolute firmness.

"I greatly fear that your recalcitrance leaves me no choice." And, reaching into his pocket, the FBI agent pulled out a quire of papers and held them up.

"What is this?" she demanded.

"I have information here that might prove of interest to you." The man's tone of voice had changed, as well. "I understand your family used to reside at Chiddingham Place?"

"Not that it can be of any interest to you, but they still do."

"Yes. On the fourth floor. The material I think you'll find to be particularly interesting concerns your grandfather." He placed the papers on her desk with a courtly motion. "I have here information—*incontrovertible* information—that during the final months of his business, just before he went bankrupt, he borrowed against the value of the stocks of his own shareholders in a desperate attempt to keep the company alive. To do so, he not only committed serious financial fraud, but he also lied to the bank, claiming the securities as his own." He paused. "His criminal actions left many of his shareholders penniless, among whom were a number of widows and pensioners who, subsequently, died in abject penury. I fear the story makes highly unpleasant reading."

He paused.

"I'm sure, Ms. Pembroke, you would not wish the good name of your grandfather—and of the Pembroke family by extension—to be sullied." The man paused to display his white teeth. "So wouldn't it be in your best interests to give me temporary access to Covington Grange? A small thing. I think it would work out best for everyone—don't you?"

It was that final, cold smile—those small, even, perfect teeth—that did it. Miss Dorothea Pembroke went rigid. Then, slowly, she rose from her chair. Just as slowly, she picked up the papers the man Pendergast had left on her desk. And then, with a disdainful motion, she tossed them at his feet.

"You have the effrontery to come into my office and attempt to blackmail me?" Her voice remained remarkably calm, surprising her. "I have never in my life been subjected to such appalling behavior. You, sir, are nothing more than a confidence man. I wouldn't be surprised if that story you told me was as false as I suspect that badge is."

"True or false, the information I have on your grandfather is rock-solid. Give me what I want or I hand it over to the police. Think of your family."

"My duty is to my office and the truth. No less, no more. If you wish to destroy my family's name, if you wish to drag us through the muck, if you wish to take what little financial security we have—so be it. I shall live with that. What I shall *not* live with is a breach of my responsibility. And so I say to you, Mr. Pendergast—" she extended her arm, pointing a steady finger at the exit, her voice quiet yet unyielding— "leave this building at once, or I shall have you bodily ejected. Good day."

Standing on the front steps of the National Trust for Places of Historic Interest or Natural Beauty, Agent Pendergast glanced around for a moment, the look of exasperation slowly giving away to a very different expression: admiration. True courage sometimes revealed itself in the most unlikely places. Few could have resisted such a thorough assault; Miss Pembroke, who was, after all, just doing her job, was one in a thousand. His thin lips twitched in a smile. Then he tossed the papers into a nearby trash can. And—as he descended the steps, heading for the station and the train back to London—he quoted under his breath: "'To Sherlock Holmes she is always *the* woman. I have seldom heard him mention her under any other name. In his eyes she eclipses and predominates the whole of her sex...'"

40

Mockey Jones was smashed again and glad of it. Jones often thought of himself in the third person, and the little voice in his head was telling him that here was Mockey Jones, titubating down East Main Street, feeling no pain (or cold), with five expensive martinis and an eighty-dollar steak in his gut, his loins recently exercised, with a wallet full of cash and credit cards, no job, no work, and no worries.

Mockey Jones was one of the one percenters—actually one of the one-tenth of one-tenth of one percenters—and, while he hadn't actually earned a dime of his money, it didn't matter because money was money and it was better to have it than not have it, and better to have a lot of it than only some. And Mockey Jones had a lot of it.

Mockey Jones was forty-nine and had left three wives and as many children scattered in his wake—he gave a little bow as he proceeded down the street in homage to them—but now he was unattached and totally irresponsible, with nothing to do but ski, eat, drink, screw, and yell at his investment advisors. Mockey Jones was very happy to live in Roaring Fork. It was his kind of town. People didn't mind who you were or what you did as long as you were rich. And not just millionaire rich—that was bullshit. The country was lousy with cheap middle-class millionaires. Such people were despised in Roaring Fork. No—you had to be a billionaire, or at least a centimillionaire, to fit into the right circle of people. Jones was himself in the centi category, but while that was an embarrassment he had gotten used to, the two hundred million he had inherited from his jerk-off father—another bow to the memory—was adequate for his needs.

He stopped, looked around. Christ, he should have pissed back at the restaurant. This damn town had no public restrooms. And where the hell had he left his car? Didn't matter—he wasn't stupid enough to get behind the wheel in his condition. No way would there ever be the headline in the *Roaring Fork Times*: MOCKEY JONES ARRESTED FOR DUI. He would call one of the late-night drunk limo services, of which there were several, kept busy squiring home those like Mockey who had "dined too well." He pulled out his cell phone, but it slipped out of his gloved hands and landed in a snowbank; with an extravagant curse he bent down, picked it up, brushed it off, and hit the appropriate speed dial. In a moment he had arranged for the ride. Those martinis back at Brierly's Steak House had sure tasted good, and he was looking forward to another when he got home.

Standing at the curb, swaying slightly, waiting for the limo, Mockey Jones became vaguely aware of something rapidly intruding on his right field of vision. Something yellowish—and glowing unnaturally. He turned and saw, in the Mountain Laurel neighborhood on the eastern hillside just at the end of town, not even a quarter mile away, a large house literally exploding in flames. Even as he watched, he could feel the heat of it on his cheek, see the flames leaping ever higher into the air, the sparks rising like stars into the dark sky...And—oh, dear God—was that someone in an upstairs window, silhouetted by fire? Even as he watched, the window exploded and the body came tumbling out like a flaming comet, writhing, with a hideous scream that cut like a knife through the midnight air, echoing and re-echoing off the mountains as if it would never end, even after the burning body had disappeared below the fir trees. Almost immediately, within seconds it seemed, sirens were going off; there were police cars and fire trucks and bystanders in the streets; and—moments later—television vans with dishes on their roofs careening about. Last of all came the choppers, plastered with call signs, sweeping in low over the trees.

And then, with that hideous scream still echoing in his confused and petrified brain, Mockey Jones felt something first warm, then cool, between his legs. A moment later he realized he'd pissed his pants.

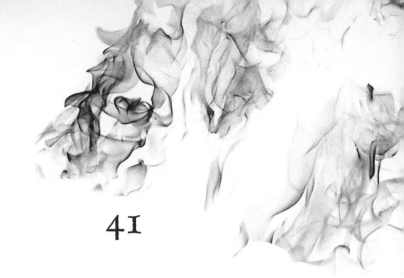

41

Corrie Swanson eased the rented Explorer into the driveway, and looked up at the cold, dark house. Not a light was on, even though Stacy's car was in the driveway. Where was she? For some reason, Corrie found herself worrying about Stacy, feeling oddly protective toward her, when in fact she had hoped the opposite would happen—that Stacy would make her feel safe.

Stacy had probably gone to bed, even though she seemed to be a late-to-bed, later-to-rise person. Or maybe a date had picked her up in his car and they were still out.

Corrie got out of the car, locked it, and went into the house. The kitchen light had been turned off. That settled it: Stacy was asleep.

A helicopter flew low overhead, then another. During her drive up the canyon, there had been a lot of chopper activity, accompanied by the faint sound of sirens coming from the town. She hoped it wasn't another house burning down.

Her date with Ted hadn't quite ended as she'd hoped. She wasn't sure why, but at the last minute she'd turned down his request to come back with her and warm her cold bed. She'd been tempted, exceedingly tempted, and she could still feel her lips tingling from his long kisses. Jesus, why had she said no?

It had been a wonderful evening. They'd eaten at a fancy restaurant in an old stone building that had been beautifully renovated, cozy and romantic, with candles and low lighting. The food had been excellent. Corrie, feeling famished, had consumed a gigantic porterhouse steak, rare, accompanied by a pint of ale, scalloped potatoes (her favorite), a romaine salad, and finished off with a brownie sundae that was positively obscene. They had talked and talked, especially about that jackass, Marple, and about Kermode. Ted had been fascinated—and shocked—to learn that Kermode was related to the infamous Stafford family. Having grown up in The Heights, he had known Kermode a long time and come to loathe her, but to learn she was part of the heartless family that had exploited and squeezed the town during the mining days really set him off. In turn, he told her an interesting fact: the Stafford family had originally owned the land The Heights had been built on—and their holding company still owned the development rights to the Phase III portion, slated to launch as soon as the new spa and clubhouse opened.

Putting away these thoughts, Corrie stepped out of the kitchen and into the central corridor. Something made her uneasy—there was a foreign feeling she couldn't quite pinpoint, a strange smell. She walked through the house and headed to their rooms to check on Stacy.

Her bed was empty.

"Stacy?"

No answer.

Suddenly she remembered the dog. "Jack?"

There hadn't been any barking, leaping, crazy little mutt to greet her. Now she was starting to freak out. She went down the little hall, calling the dog's name.

Still nothing.

She headed back into the main portion of the house. Maybe he was hiding somewhere, or had gotten lost. *"Jack?"*

Pausing to listen, she heard a muffled whine and a scratching sound. It came from the grand living room—a room that had been shut up and which she'd been strictly forbidden to enter. She went to the closed set of pocket doors. "Jack?"

Another whine and bark, accompanied by more scratching.

She felt her heart pounding. Something was very, very wrong.

She placed her hand on the doors, found them unlocked, and slowly pulled them apart. Immediately, Jack rushed out from the darkness beyond, crouching and whining and licking her, tail clamped between his legs.

"Who put you in here, Jack?"

She looked about the dark room. It seemed quiet, empty—and then she saw a dark outline of a figure on the sofa.

"Hey!" she cried in surprise.

Jack cowered behind her, whining.

The figure moved a little, very slowly.

"Who are you and what are you doing here?" Corrie demanded. This was stupid. She should get out, now.

"Oh," came a thick voice out of the blackness. "It's you."

"Stacy?"

No answer.

"Good God, are you all right?"

"Fine, no problem," came the slurred voice again.

Corrie turned on the lights. And there was Stacy, slumped on the sofa, a fifth of Jim Beam half empty in front of her. She was still bundled up in her winter clothes—scarf, hat, and all. A small puddle of water lay at her feet, and watery tracks led to the sofa.

"Oh, no. Stacy!"

Stacy waved her arm, before letting it fall to the sofa. "Sorry."

"What have you been doing? Were you outside?"

"Out for a walk. Looking for that mother who shot up your car."

"But I *told* you not to do that. You could have frozen to death out there!" Corrie noticed that Stacy was packing, a .45 holstered to her hip. Jesus, she would have to get that gun away.

"Don't worry about me."

"I do worry about you. I'm *totally* worried about you!"

"Come on, siddown, have a drink. Relax."

Corrie sat but ignored the offer of a drink. "Stacy, what's going on?"

At this Stacy hung her head. "I dunno. Nothing. My life sucks."

Corrie took her hand. No wonder the dog had been freaked out.

"I'm sorry. I feel the same way myself sometimes. You want to talk about it?"

"My military career—shot. No family. No friends. Nothing. There's nothing in my life but a box of old bones to haul back to Kentucky. And for what purpose? What a fucked-up idea that was."

"But your military career. You're a captain. All those medals and citations—you can do anything..."

"My life's fucked. I was discharged."

"You mean...you didn't resign?"

Stacy shook her head. "Medical discharge."

"Wounded?"

"PTSD."

A silence. "Oh, Jesus. I'm sorry, I really am."

There was a long pause. Then Stacy spoke again. "You have *no* idea. I get these rages—no reason. Screaming like a fucking maniac. Or hyperventilation: total panic attack. Christ, it's awful. And there's no warning. I feel so *down* sometimes, I can't get out of bed, sleep fourteen hours a day. And then I start doing this shit—drinking. Can't get a job. The medical discharge...they see that on a job application, it's like, oh, we can't hire her, she's fucking mental. They've all got yellow ribbons on their cars, but when it comes to hiring a vet with posttraumatic stress disorder? Outta here, bitch."

She reached out to take up the bottle. Corrie intercepted her and gently grasped it at the same time. "Don't you think you've had enough?"

Stacy jerked the bottle out of her hand, went to take a swig, and then, all of a sudden, threw it across the room, shattering it against the far wall. "Fuck, yeah. Enough."

"Let me help you get to bed." She took Stacy's arm. Stacy rose unsteadily to her feet while Corrie supported her. God, she stank of bourbon. Corrie felt so sorry for her. She wondered if she could slip the .45 out of its holster unnoticed, but decided that might not be a good idea, might set Stacy off. Just get her into bed and then deal with the gun.

"They catch the fuck shot your car?" Stacy slurred.

"No. They think it might have been a poacher."

"Poacher, my ass." She stumbled and Corrie helped right her. "Couldn't find the bastard's tracks. Too much fresh snow."

"Let's not worry about that now."

"I *am* worrying!" She clapped her hand to the sidearm and yanked it out, waving it about. "I'm gonna smoke that fucker!"

"You know you shouldn't handle a firearm when you've been drinking," Corrie said quietly and firmly, controlling her disquiet.

"Yeah. Right. Sorry." Stacy ejected the magazine, which she fumbled and dropped to the floor, scattering bullets. "You'd better take it."

She held it out, butt-first, and Corrie took it.

"Careful, there's still one in the chamber. Lemme eject it for you."

"I'll do it." Corrie racked the round out of the chamber, letting it fall to the floor.

"Hey. You know what you're doing, girl!"

"I'd better, since I'm studying law enforcement."

"Fuck, yeah, you're gonna make a good cop someday. You will. I *like* you, Corrie."

"Thanks." She helped Stacy along the hallway toward their rooms. Corrie could hear more choppers overhead, and, through a window, a spotlight from one of them trained on the ground, moving this way and that. Something was happening.

She finally got Stacy tucked under the covers, putting a plastic wastebasket next to the bed in case she puked. Stacy fell asleep instantly.

Corrie went back to the living room and started cleaning up, Jack trailing her. Stacy's drunkenness had freaked out the poor dog. It had freaked her out, as well. As she was straightening up she heard yet another chopper flying overhead. She went to the plate-glass windows and peered into the darkness. She could just see, over the ridge in the direction of town, an intense yellow glow.

42

Just when things couldn't possibly get worse, they did, thought Chief Morris as he looked at the two wrecked cars blocking Highway 82 and the furious, desperate traffic jam piling up behind. The medevac chopper was just lifting off, rotor wash blowing snow everywhere, as if there weren't enough of it in the air already, carrying away the two victims to the advanced trauma unit at Grand Junction, where at least one of them, shot through the head, was probably going to die. What really infuriated the chief was that no one had been hurt in the accident; instead, it had generated a road-rage incident in which the driver of a BMW X5 had pulled a gun and shot the two occupants of the Geländewagen that had rear-ended him. He could hear the perp now, handcuffed in the back of his cruiser while waiting for the snowcat to arrive, yelling at the top of his lungs about "self-defense" and "standing my ground." So if the victim died—and most people with a .38 round through the skull did—that would mean nine murders in little more than a week. All in a town that hadn't seen a murder in years.

What a nightmare—with no end in sight.

Four days before Christmas, and the snow was now falling heavily, with a prediction of twenty-four to thirty inches over the next three days, with accompanying high winds toward the tail end of the storm. Highway 82—the only way out of town—was gridlocked because of the accident; the snowplows couldn't operate; the blizzard was quickly getting ahead of them; and in an hour or less the road would have to be closed and all these people sitting furiously in their cars, yelling and honking and screeching like maniacs, would have to be rescued.

McMaster Field had seen nonstop flights out as all the Gulf-streams and other private jets and planes fled the town, but it, too, would soon be closing. And when that happened, Roaring Fork would be bottled up, no way in or out except by snowcat.

He glanced in the rearview mirror, back in the direction of town. The third arson attack had been the worst of all. Not in terms of numbers of deaths, but in terms of the psychological effect it had on Roaring Fork. The burnt house stood just at the edge of town, on the first rise of the hill: a grand old Victorian belonging to Maurice Girault, the celebrity fund manager and New York socialite, number five on the Forbes list, a dashing older fellow with an ego as big as Mount Everest. The victims were himself and his fresh young wife, who looked as if she couldn't be a day over eighteen—and who had precipitated herself out an upper-story window while afire.

The entire town had seen it—and been traumatized. And this snarl of traffic, this road-rage shooting, this classic example of a FUBAR situation, was the result.

His thoughts returned, unwillingly, to Pendergast's now-prophetic words. *The next house will no doubt be equally conspicuous.* And his conclusion: *To send a message.*

But what message?

He returned his gaze to the mess. His idling squad car, with the shooter in the back, had its lights and sirens going—all for show. Idiots fleeing town had blocked both sides of the highway as well as the breakdown lanes, and high banks of snow on either side prevented cars from turning around—creating total gridlock. Even the chief was locked in; despite all his efforts to prevent cars from coming up behind and blocking him, they had.

At least they had managed to temporarily block the way out of town, preventing any more vehicles from adding to the mess. And, thank God, the RFPD had three snowcats, all of which were on their way. Even as he sat in his car, the wipers ineffectually swiping the snow back and forth, he heard the first one approaching. Immediately he grabbed his radio, directing the officer in the cat to get the perp out of there first. An angry crowd had started to gather around his squad car, yelling at the shooter, cursing and threatening him, offering to string him up on the nearest tree, while the perp, for his part, was yelling back, taunting them. It was amazing, just like the days of the vigilantes. The veneer of civilization was thin indeed.

And on top of everything else, Pendergast had vanished, split, gone off to London at the worst possible moment. Chivers, the fire investigator, was now openly at war with the police department, and his own investigators were demoralized, angry, and disagreeing with each other.

Now the second snowcat had arrived, delivering a CSI team and a couple of detectives to document the accident and crime scene and to interview witnesses. The snow was beginning to fall more heavily, big fat flakes coming down fast. Getting out of his squad car, the chief walked back to the cat and climbed aboard, along with some of his other men who needed to get back to town and work the new arson attack. A number of desperate motorists wanted a ride back to town as well, and the chief allowed a few of them—a couple with a baby—to get on board, causing a ruckus among those left behind.

As the vehicle headed back to town through the deep snow on the side of the highway, the chief turned his thoughts again, for the thousandth time, to the central mystery of the arson attacks: what was the message? Was he completely insane? But if that was the case, how could the crimes be so carefully planned and executed?

As they entered the town, the chief was struck—after the chaos down on the highway—by the eerie emptiness of it. It had practically returned to ghost-town status, the streets hung with Christmas decorations and the shop windows stuffed with glittering, expensive merchandise adding a Twilight Zone element. It felt like the day after Armageddon.

The chief wondered if Roaring Fork would ever be the same.

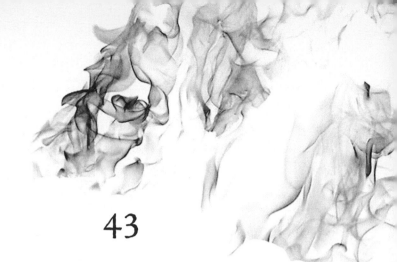

43

Later that afternoon, on her way back from the ski warehouse, Corrie decided to stop in town and warm up with a cup of hot chocolate while catching up on email. It was dark, the snow was falling, and she knew she should be getting home, but she did not want to face that horrible, cold mansion after spending most of the day freezing in the warehouse, which she had begun to refer to in her head as the "Siberian torture chamber."

The snow had lightened a bit as she parked her new Ford Explorer on the street. Since the arson attack of last evening, there was parking everywhere, when before you practically had to give up your firstborn to find a space. Despite the closing of the highway and the airport earlier in the day, an awful lot of people had managed to get out of town. She strolled into Ozymandias, one of the few ordinary, unpretentious cafés in town, with free Wi-Fi and a relaxed wait staff who didn't look down their noses at her.

The place was almost empty, but a friendly waitress came over and added a bit of cheer to Corrie's dreary mood. She ordered a hot chocolate and took out her iPad. There were quite a few emails, including one from her advisor asking for another update on her work, fishing for inside details on what was really going on in Roaring Fork, and complaining that she wasn't keeping him informed. It was true, she had been cagey in her reports; she didn't want him interfering or trying to shut her down, and she figured the less information he had to latch on to, the better. Once her thesis was completed and turned in, it would blow the committee away; her advisor would have no choice but to join in the general accolade; it would win the Rosewell Prize... or, at least, she hoped that's how it would happen. So to satisfy Carbone she composed a vague, ambiguous reply to his email, dressing it up as a report but saying essentially nothing, implying her work was getting off to a slow start and that she had little real information as yet. She hit the SEND button, hoping that would hold him for another few days.

Her hot chocolate arrived and she sipped it as she browsed through the last of the emails. Nothing from Pendergast—not that she'd expected it; he wasn't, apparently, an emailer. Email complete, she checked the *New York Times*, the *Huff Post*, and a few other sites. The *Times* had a front-page story on the arson attacks, which she read with interest. The story had gone national after the second attack, but this third one elevated it to one of those horrific, sensationalistic stories that captured the attention of the country. Ironic: now it was big news, just as the storm was about to hit and no reporters could get in to cover it.

Chocolate finished, she figured she really had better get home. Pulling her scarf tight, she exited the café and was surprised to see, walking down the far side of the street, just passing under a streetlamp, a couple she recognized as Stacy and Ted. She stared. While they weren't exactly walking hand in hand, they seemed pretty friendly, talking and chatting together. As she watched, they disappeared into a restaurant.

Corrie experienced a sudden sick feeling. Earlier, Stacy had claimed she was going to spend the day back at the Fine house, on account of her hangover. But the hangover didn't seem so bad that she couldn't go to dinner with Ted. Were the two of them cheating on her behind her back? It seemed unthinkable—and yet, suddenly, quite possible. Maybe this was some sort of payback on Ted's part for her refusal to sleep with him the previous night. Was he taking up with Stacy on the rebound?

...And what about Stacy? Maybe she was messed up enough to do something like that. After all, she sure hadn't turned out to be the supremely confident air force captain that Corrie had initially thought, but rather a confused and lonely woman. She hated the idea that all this had changed her feelings toward Stacy, but she couldn't help but think of her now as a different person. She wondered what the PTSD meant and how it might manifest itself. And then there was the odd fact that Stacy had arrived in town several days before revealing herself to anyone. What had she been doing during that time? Had she really just been "getting a feel" for the place?

Corrie got into her car and started the engine. There was still some residual heat so it warmed up fast, which made her grateful. She drove out of town and headed up Ravens Ravine Road, taking the switchbacks very slow, the snow building up on her wipers. It was falling so thickly now that anyone waiting with a gun wouldn't even see her car on the road, let alone have a shot. So much the better. She thought ahead to her crappy meal of beans and rice—all she could afford—and another evening of freezing her ass in the house. The hell with it, she was going to pick the thermostat lock, turn up the heat, and let the owner howl. Ridiculous that a multimillionaire was so concerned about a few extra dollars.

The mansion emerged from the falling snow, dark and gloomy. Stacy's car was gone, as expected. Corrie hoped she wouldn't drink in the restaurant and try to drive home in this weather afterward.

She parked in the driveway. Her car would be plowed in the next morning, as it had been several times before, requiring her to shovel it out. All because the owner wouldn't let her use the garage. No wonder he was locked in a horrible divorce.

As she got out of the car, freezing already, it abruptly occurred to her that Pendergast was right. It was time to get out of Roaring Fork. Her basic research was complete, and it was all too clear she wasn't going to solve the hundred-fifty-year-old serial killings. She'd exhausted all avenues without coming up with so much as a clue. As soon as the highway was opened, she'd split.

Decision made.

She stuck her key into the door of the house and opened it, expecting the usual flurry of barks and yips to greet her—only to be met with silence.

She felt a welling of apprehension. It was like last night all over again. "Jack?" she called out.

No answer. Had Stacy brought the dog into town with her, in case he was lonely? But she hadn't shown much interest in Jack and professed to prefer cats.

"Jack? Here, *Jack!*"

Not even a whimper. Corrie tried once again to control her pounding heart. She flicked on all the lights—screw the electric bill—and called again and again. Making her way down the hall to her wing of the house, she found her bedroom door shut but unlocked. She pushed it open. "Jack?"

The room was dark. There was a form at the foot of the bed, and a very dark area around it. She turned on the lights, and saw Jack's body—minus the head—lying on top of the rug, surrounded by a huge crimson stain.

She didn't scream. She couldn't scream. She simply stared.

And then she saw the head, propped up on the dresser, eyes open and staring, a cascade of congealing blood dripping down the fake wood front. Stuck between the jaws was a piece of paper. In an almost dream-like state, disconnected, as if it was happening to someone else, Corrie managed to pick up a letter opener, pry open the jaws, take out the paper, and read the message.

Swanson: Get out of town today or you're dead. A bullet through that sweet little head of yours.

Corrie stared. It was like some sick take on *The Godfather*...And what made it totally ridiculous was that, even if she wanted to get out of town, she couldn't.

The note snapped her out of her fog. Amid a sick wash of fear and disgust, she also felt a groundswell of rage so powerful it frightened her: fury at the crude attempt at intimidation, fury for what had been done to poor, innocent Jack.

Leave? No way. She was staying right here.

44

Hampstead Heath, Roger Kleefisch remarked to himself, had changed sadly since the days when Keats used to traverse it on his way from Clerkenwell to the cottage of Cowden Clarke, there to read his poetry and chat about literature; or since Walter Hartright, drawing teacher, had crossed it late at night, deep in thought, only to encounter the ghostly Woman in White on a distant byroad. These days it was hemmed in on all sides by Greater London, NW3, with bus stops and Underground stations dotted along its borders where once only groves of trees had stood.

Now, however, it was almost midnight; the weather had turned chilly, and the heath was relatively deserted. They had already left Parliament Hill and its marvelous panorama of the City and Canary Wharf behind and were making their way northwest. Hills, ponds, and clumps of woodlands were visible as mere shadows beneath the pale moon.

"I brought a dark lantern along," Kleefisch said, more to keep up his spirits than to be informative. He brandished the device, which he'd kept hidden beneath his heavy ulster. "It seemed appropriate to the occasion, somehow."

Pendergast glanced toward it. "Anachronistic, but potentially useful."

Earlier, from the comfort of his lodgings, planning this little escapade had filled Kleefisch with excitement. When Pendergast had been unable to secure permission to enter Covington Grange, he had declared he would do so anyway, extralegally. Kleefisch had enthusiastically volunteered to help. But now that they were actually executing the plan, he felt more than a little trepidation. It was one thing to write scholarly essays on Professor Moriarty, the "Napoleon of crime," or on Colonel Sebastian Moran, the "second most dangerous man in London." It was quite another thing, he realized, to be actually out on the heath, with breaking and entering on the agenda.

"There's the Hampstead Heath constabulary, you know," he said.

"Indeed," came the response. "What's their complement?"

"Maybe a dozen or so. Some use police dogs."

To this there was no response.

They skirted South Meadow and passed into the heavy woods of the Dueling Ground. To the north, Kleefisch could make out the lights of Highgate.

"Then there's the National Trust groundskeepers to consider," he added. "There's always the chance one of them might be loitering about."

"In that case, I would suggest keeping that lantern well concealed."

They slowed as their objective came into sight over the lip of a small hill. Covington Grange was sited just at the far edge of the Dueling Ground, surrounded on three sides by woods. Stone Bridge and Wood Pond lay to the right. To the north, a green lawn ran away in the direction of sprawling Kenwood House. Beyond, late-night traffic hushed along Hampstead Lane.

Pendergast looked about him, then nodded to Kleefisch and made his way forward, keeping to the edge of the wood.

The Grange itself was an archaeological enigma, as if its builder could not decide which school, or even which era, he wished it to belong to. The low façade was half-timbered and Tudor, but a small addition to one side was a bizarre bit of neo-Romanesque. The long sloping wooden roof, bristling with exposed eaves, presaged the Craftsman era by a good half century. A greenhouse clung to the far side, its glass panels now cracked and covered with vines. The entire structure was enclosed by a hurricane fence, sagging and weathered, which appeared to have been erected as a security measure decades ago and long since forgotten.

Following Pendergast's lead, Kleefisch crept up to the front of the building, where a narrow gate in the fencing was held in place with a padlock. Beside it, a weather-beaten sign read: PROPERTY OF H. M. GOV'T. NO TRESPASSING.

"Shall we, Roger?" Pendergast asked, as calmly as if he were inviting Kleefisch in for cucumber sandwiches at the Ritz.

Kleefisch glanced uneasily around, clutched the dark lantern more closely to him. "But the lock—" he began. Even as he spoke, there was a faint clicking noise and the padlock sprang open in Pendergast's hand.

They stepped quickly past the gate, and Pendergast closed it behind them. Clouds had drifted over the moon; it was now very dark. Kleefisch waited in the forecourt while Pendergast made a quick reconnoiter. He was aware of a variety of sounds: distant laughter; a faint staccato honk from the motorway; and—or so he imagined—the nervous beating of his own heart.

Pendergast returned, then gestured them toward the front door. This, too, yielded almost immediately to the FBI agent's touch. The two passed inside, Pendergast shut the door, and Kleefisch found himself in utter darkness. He was aware of several additional things now: the smell of mildew and sawdust; the pattering of small feet; the low squeaking of disturbed vermin.

A voice came out of the darkness. "To aid us in our search, let us review again what we know. For over a decade, from about 1917 to 1929, Conan Doyle came here frequently, as a guest of Mary Wilkes, to further his study of spiritualism and to read his writings on the subject to like-minded friends. He died in 1930, bound for—in his words—'the greatest and most glorious adventure of all.' Mary Wilkes herself died in 1934. Her daughter, Leticia Wilkes, lived here—joined in the early years by her niece and nephew—until her own death in 1980, at which time she left the property to the government. It has not been lived in—indeed, it has apparently remained untouched—ever since."

Kleefisch could add little to this, so he said nothing.

A small glow of red appeared. Pendergast was holding up a flashlight, a filter fixed to its end. The faint beam swept here and there, revealing a hallway leading back into what was obviously a furnished and, at one time, well-lived-in house, circa 1980. There were piles of books set along the wall in disorganized ranks, and various tiny gnomes and glass figurines sat on a brace of side tables, heavy with dust. The far end of the hallway gave onto a kitchen: to the left and right were openings leading to a parlor and dining room, respectively. The first floor seemed to be covered in shag carpet of a detestable orange color.

Pendergast sniffed the air. "The odor of wood rot and decay is strong. My friend at the National Trust was correct: this house is in a state of dangerous decrepitude and may be structurally unsound. We must proceed with caution."

They moved into the parlor, pausing in the doorway while Pendergast swept his muted light around the room. It was a scene of confusion. An upright piano stood in one corner, sheet music spilling from its music stand and overturned bench onto the floor; several card tables, furry with mold, held abandoned jigsaw puzzles and half-finished games of Monopoly and Chinese checkers. Magazines were spread haphazardly across the chairs and sofas.

"It would appear Leticia Wilkes allowed her charges to run wild," Pendergast said with a disapproving sniff.

The rest of the first floor was the same. Toys, bric-a-brac, discarded jackets, swimming trunks, and slippers—and everywhere that same odious orange carpet, lit a dreadful crimson by Pendergast's hooded light. No wonder the National Trust had let the place fall to wrack and ruin, Kleefisch thought to himself. He could imagine some poor functionary, poking his head into the place for a minute, taking an exploratory glance around, and then closing the door again, despairing of renovation. He stared at the paisley-papered walls, at the worn and stained furniture, looking for some ghostly evidence of the enchanted cottage in which, once upon a time, Conan Doyle had worked and entertained. He was unable to find any.

The basement yielded nothing more than empty storage rooms, a cold furnace, and dead beetles. Pendergast led the way up the dangerously creaking stairs to the second floor. Six doors led off the central hallway. The first was a linen closet, its contents ravaged by time and moths. The second was a common bathroom. The next three doors opened onto bedrooms. One, in somewhat decent order, had apparently been that of Leticia herself. The others had obviously been used by her niece and nephew, as attested to by the Dion and Frankie Valli posters in the first room and the numerous issues of the *Sun*, all opened to page three, in the other.

That left just the single, closed door at the far end of the hall. Kleefisch's heart sank. Only now did he realize how much he'd allowed himself to hope that, at long last, the missing Holmes story might actually be found. But he'd been a fool to believe he would succeed where so many of his fellows had already failed. And especially in this mess, which would take a week to search properly.

Pendergast grasped the knob, opened the final door—and as quickly as Kleefisch's heart had sunk, it leapt anew.

The room that lay beyond was as different from the rest of the house as day was from night. It was like a time capsule from a period that had vanished well over a hundred years before. The room was a study, sparsely but tastefully furnished. After the dreadful clutter of the rest of the house, it was to Kleefisch like a breath of fresh air. He stared, excitement overcoming his apprehension, as Pendergast moved his light around. There was a writing desk and a comfortable chair. Sporting prints and daguerreotypes hung on the walls in simple frames; nearby stood a bookcase, nearly empty. There was a single diamond-pane window, high up. Ornamental hangings, of austere design but nevertheless tasteful, were placed along the walls.

"I believe we might risk a little more light," Pendergast murmured. "Your lantern, please."

Kleefisch brought the lantern forward, grasped its sliding panel, and slid it open a crack. Immediately, the room leapt into sharper focus. He noticed with admiration the beautiful wood floor, composed of polished parquet, laid out in an old-fashioned design. A small square carpet, of the kind once known as a drugget, lay in the middle of the room. Against a far wall, between the hangings, was a chaise longue that appeared to have also served in the capacity of a daybed.

"Do you think—?" Kleefisch asked, turning to Pendergast, almost afraid to ask the question.

As if in answer, Pendergast pointed to one of the daguerreotypes on the wall beside them.

Kleefisch took a closer look. He realized, with some surprise, that it was not a daguerreotype after all, but a regular photograph, apparently from early in the twentieth century. It showed a young girl amid a pastoral, sylvan scene, chin supported by one hand, gazing out at the camera with a look of bemused seriousness. In the foreground before her, four small creatures with slender limbs and large butterfly wings danced, cavorted, or played tunes on wooden reeds. There was no obvious evidence of trickery or manipulation of the image: the sprites seemed to be an integral part of the photograph.

"The Cottingley Fairies," Kleefisch whispered.

"Indeed," Pendergast replied. "As you well know, Conan Doyle firmly believed in the existence of fairies and in the veracity of these pictures. He even devoted a book to the subject: *The Coming of the Fairies*. Two Yorkshire girls, Elsie Wright and her cousin Frances Griffiths, claimed to see fairies and to have photographed them. These are some of their photographs."

Kleefisch stepped back. He felt his heart accelerate. There could no longer be any doubt: this had been Conan Doyle's study away from home. And the Wilkes family had preserved it with loving care, even while allowing the rest of the house to go to wrack and ruin.

If the missing story was anywhere to be found, it would be in this room.

With sudden energy, Pendergast stepped forward, ignoring the fearful creaking of the floorboards, his flashlight arrowing here and there. He opened the desk and made an exhaustive search of its contents, removing drawers and tapping on the sides and back. Next he moved to the bookshelf, removing the few dusty tomes and looking carefully through each, going so far as to peer down the hinges of each spine. Then he took the pictures from the wall one at a time, looked behind each, and felt gently along the paper backings for anything that might be hidden within the frames. Next, he approached each of the decorative hangings in turn, feeling carefully along their lengths.

He paused, his silvery eyes roaming the room. Taking a switchblade from one pocket, he stepped over to the chaise longue, made a small, surgical incision where the fabric met the wooden framing, inserted his light into it, and then his fingers, making a painstaking examination of the interior—obviously to no avail. Next, he applied himself to the walls, holding one ear to the plaster while knocking gently with his knuckles. In such a fashion, he circled the room with agonizing thoroughness: once, twice.

As he watched this careful search, done by an expert, Kleefisch felt the familiar sinking feeling return once again.

His eyes fell to the floor—and to the small rug that lay at its center. Something was familiar about it: very familiar. And then, quite abruptly, he realized what it was.

"Pendergast," he said, his voice little better than a croak.

The FBI agent turned to look at him.

Kleefisch pointed at the carpet. "'It was a small, square drugget in the center of the room,'" he quoted. "'Surrounded by a broad expanse of wood-flooring in square blocks, highly polished.'"

"I fear my knowledge of The Canon is not as nuanced as yours. What is that from? 'The Musgrave Ritual'? 'The Resident Patient'?"

Kleefisch shook his head. "'The Second Stain.'"

For a moment, Pendergast returned his gaze. Then, suddenly, his eyes glittered in comprehension. "Could it be so simple?"

"Why not recycle a good thing?"

In a moment, Pendergast was kneeling upon the floor. Pushing away the carpet, he began applying his fingertips as well as the blade of his knife to the floorboards, pushing here, probing gently there. Within a minute, there was the squeak of a long-disused hinge and one of the parquet squares flipped up, exposing a small, dark cavity beneath.

Pendergast gently reached into the hole. Kleefisch looked on, hardly daring to draw breath, as the agent withdrew his hand. When he did, it was clutching a rolled series of foolscap sheets, brittle, dusty, and yellowed with age, tied up with a ribbon. Rising to his feet, Pendergast undid the ribbon—which fell apart in his hands—and unrolled the quire, brushing off the topmost sheet with care.

Both men crowded around as Pendergast held his light up to the words scrawled in longhand across the top of the page:

The Adventure of Aspern Hall

Nothing more needed to be said. Quickly and silently, Pendergast closed the little trapdoor and pushed the rug back into place with his foot; then they stepped out of the room and made for the head of the stairs.

Suddenly there was a dreadful crash. A monumental billow of dust rose up to surround Kleefisch, blotting out his lantern and plunging the hallway into darkness. He waved the dust away, coughing and spluttering. As his vision cleared, he saw Pendergast, his head, shoulders, and outstretched arms down at the level of Kleefisch's feet. The floor had given way beneath him and he had saved himself from falling through at just the last minute.

"The manuscript, man!" Pendergast gasped, straining with the effort of holding himself in place. "Take the manuscript!"

Kleefisch knelt and plucked the manuscript carefully from Pendergast's hand. Snugging it into a pocket of his ulster, he grabbed Pendergast's collar and—with a great effort—managed to pull him back up onto the second-floor landing. Pendergast regained his breath, stood up and, with a grimace, dusted himself off. They maneuvered their way around the hole and had begun creeping down the stairs when a slurred voice sounded from outside:

"Oi! Who's that, then?"

The two froze.

"The groundskeeper," Kleefisch whispered.

Pendergast gestured for Kleefisch to shutter his lantern. Then, raising his hooded light to reveal his face, he put a finger to his lips and pointed to the front door.

They moved forward at a snail's pace.

"Who's there!" came the voice again.

Silently, Pendergast drew a large handgun out of his jacket, turned it butt-first.

"What are you doing?" Kleefisch said in alarm as he grasped Pendergast's hand.

"The man's intoxicated," came the whispered reply. "I should be able to, ah, render him harmless with little effort."

"Violence?" Kleefisch said. "Good Lord, not upon one of Her Majesty's own!"

"Do you have a better suggestion?"

"Make a dash for it."

"A dash?"

"You said it yourself—the man's drunk. We'll rush out of the gate and run south into the wood."

Pendergast looked dubious but put away the weapon nevertheless. He led the way across the carpeting to the front door, opened it a crack, and peered out. Hearing nothing further, he motioned Kleefisch to follow him down the narrow walkway to the hurricane fence. Just as he opened the gate, the moon emerged from behind the clouds and a shout of triumph came from a nearby stand of hemlock:

"You, there! Don't go no further!"

Pendergast burst through the gate and took off at high speed, Kleefisch at his heels. There was the shattering blast of a shotgun, but neither paused in their headlong run.

"You've been hit!" Kleefisch gasped as he struggled to keep up. He could see droplets of blackish red liquid fly up from Pendergast's shoulder with every stride the man took.

"A few superficial pellet strikes, I suspect; nothing more. I'll remove them with a tweezers back at the Connaught. What of the manuscript? Is it undamaged?"

"Yes, yes. It's fine!"

Kleefisch had not run like this since his Oxford days. Nevertheless, the thought of the drunken groundskeeper and his weapon brought vigor to his limbs, and he continued to follow Pendergast, past Springett's Wood to the Vale of Health, and from there—*Deo Gratias!*—to East Heath Road, a taxi, and freedom.

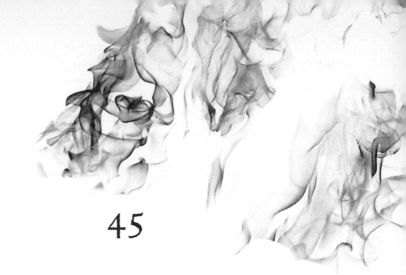

45

It was still snowing when Corrie awoke in her room at the Hotel Sebastian, after a night full of restless, fragmentary nightmares. She got up and looked out the window. The town lay under a blanket of white and the snowplows were working overtime, rumbling and scraping along the downtown streets, along with front-end loaders and dump trucks removing the piles of snow and trucking them out of town.

She glanced at her watch: eight o'clock.

Last night had been awful. The police had come up immediately, to their credit, with the chief himself leading the way. They took away Jack's corpse and the note, asked questions, collected evidence, and promised to investigate. The problem was, they were clearly overwhelmed by the serial arsonist. The chief looked like he was on the verge of a nervous breakdown, and his men were so sleep-deprived they could have been extras in a zombie flick. There was no way they were going to be able to conduct a thorough investigation on this, any more than they were on the shooting at her car—the target of which she was no longer in any doubt.

And so Corrie had driven back into town and booked a room at the Hotel Sebastian. Including the stint in the jail, she'd been in Roaring Fork for three weeks now, and she'd been burning through her four thousand dollars with depressing speed. Lodgings at the Sebastian would take up a good portion of the money she had left, but she was so frightened by the murder of her dog that there was no way she could spend the night in that mansion—or any night, ever again.

She had called Stacy, telling her what had happened and warning her it was too dangerous to return to the Fine house. Stacy said she would make arrangements to spend the night in town—Corrie had a horrible feeling it might have been at Ted's place—and they'd agreed to meet that morning at nine in the hotel's breakfast room. In one hour. It was a conversation she was not looking forward to.

Adding to her woes, the police had contacted the owner of the mansion, and he had then called Corrie on her cell, waking her up at six, screeching and hollering, saying it was all her fault, that she had broken every house rule, turning up the heat and letting in squatters. As he got more and more worked up, he called her a criminal, speculated that she might be a drug addict, and threatened to sue her and her dyke friend if they went back into the house.

Corrie had let the man vent, and then given the bastard a royal licking of her own, telling him what a despicable human being he was, that she hoped his wife took every penny he had, and concluding with a speculation on the relationship between the failure of his marriage and the inadequate size of his dick. The man had become inarticulate with rage, which gave Corrie a certain satisfaction as she hung up at the start of yet another foulmouthed rant. The satisfaction was short-lived once she considered the problem of where she was going to stay. She couldn't even go back to Basalt, because of the closed road, and one more night in the Hotel Sebastian—or any hotel in town, for that matter—would bankrupt her. What was she going to do?

The one thing she did know was that she was not leaving Roaring Fork. Was she afraid of the bastards who'd shot at her, who'd killed her dog? Of course she was. But nobody was going to drive her out of town. How could she live with herself if she allowed that to happen? And what kind of law enforcement officer would she be if she backed down in the face of these threats? No: one way or another, she was going to stay right here and help catch the people responsible.

★ ★ ★

Stacy Bowdree was already seated with a big mug of coffee in front of her when Corrie entered the breakfast room. Stacy looked awful, with dark circles under her eyes, her auburn hair unkempt. Corrie took a seat and picked up the menu. Three dollars for an orange juice, ten for bacon and eggs, eighteen for eggs Benedict. She put the menu down: she couldn't even afford a cup of coffee. When the waitress came over she ordered a glass of tap water. Stacy, on the other hand, ordered the Belgian waffles with a double side of bacon and a fried egg. And then pushed her coffee mug forward. "Go ahead," she said.

With a grunt of thanks, Corrie took a sip, then a big drink. God, she needed caffeine. She drained the mug, pushed it back. She didn't quite know where to start.

Luckily, Stacy started it for her. "We need to talk, Corrie. About this scumbag threatening your life."

Okay. If you want to start there, fine. "It makes me sick what they did to Jack."

Stacy laid a hand on hers. "Which is why this is no joke. The people who did this are bad, *bad* people, and they aren't fooling around. They see you as a huge threat. Do you have any idea why?"

"I can only assume I dug up a hornet's nest somewhere in my research. Came close to something somebody wants to keep hushed up. I wish I knew what."

"Maybe it's the Heights Association and that bitch Kermode," said Stacy. "She looks like she's capable of anything."

"I don't think so. All that's been resolved, the new location of the cemetery has been approved, they're busy tracking down various descendants and getting permission—and most important, you're not insisting any more on having your ancestor reburied in the original Boot Hill."

"Well then, do you think it might be the arsonist?"

"Not the same M.O. at all. The key is for me to figure out what information I have, or almost got, that spooked them so badly. Once I know that, maybe I'll be able to identify them. But I don't really think they're going to kill me—or they would've done it already."

"Corrie, don't be naive. Anyone who would decapitate a dog is totally capable of killing a person. Which is why, from now on, I'm not leaving your side. Not me or..." Stacy patted the place where she carried her .45.

Corrie looked away.

"What's wrong?" Stacy said, looking at her anxiously.

Now Corrie saw no reason to hold back. "I saw you with Ted last night. The least you could do was tell me you were going to date him. Friends don't do that to friends." She sat back.

Stacy sat back herself. An unreadable expression crossed her face. "Date him?"

"Well, yeah."

"*Date* him? Jesus Christ, how the hell could you even think such a thing?" Stacy had raised her voice.

"Well, what was I supposed to think, seeing you two go into that restaurant—"

"You know why we went into that restaurant? Because Ted asked me to dinner to talk about *you*."

Corrie looked at her, astonished. "Me?"

"Yes, you! He's totally smitten with you, says he might be in love with you, and he's worried he's doing something wrong, thinking that he rubbed you the wrong way. He wanted to ask me about it—we spent the whole damn evening talking about you and nothing else. Do you think I enjoyed getting out of bed and driving into town, with a pounding head, to listen to some man spend the night talking about another *woman*?"

"I'm sorry, Stacy. I guess I was jumping to conclusions."

"You're goddamn right!" Suddenly, Stacy was on her feet, her face a mixture of reproach and betrayal. "It's the same old bullshit! Here, I befriend you, protect you, look after your best interests at the expense of my own—and what's my reward? Fucking accusations of two-timing with your boyfriend!"

Stacy's sudden upwelling of anger was scaring Corrie. The few other diners in the room were turning their heads. "Look, Stacy," Corrie said in a calming voice. "I'm really, really sorry. I guess I'm kind of insecure about my relationships with guys, and you being so attractive and all, I just—"

But Stacy didn't let her finish. With a final, blazing glance, she turned on her heel and stalked out of the restaurant—leaving her breakfast unfinished and unpaid for.

46

The familiar, silken voice invited her in. Corrie took a deep breath. He'd agreed to see her; that was a good first step. She'd been telling herself that he hadn't contacted her since leaving Roaring Fork only because he was too busy; she'd fervently hoped that was the case. The last thing she wanted to do, she now realized, was allow her relationship with Pendergast to be damaged by her own impetuousness and shortsightedness.

And now he was back just as abruptly as he had left.

That afternoon, the basement was, if possible, even stuffier than the last time Corrie had visited Pendergast's temporary office. He sat behind the old metal desk, which was now swept clear of the chemistry apparatus that had cluttered it before. A thin manila file was the only thing that lay on the scarred surface. It must have been eighty-five degrees in the room, and yet the special agent still had his suit jacket on.

"Corrie. Please take a seat."

Obediently, Corrie sat. "How did you get back into town? I thought the road was closed."

"The chief kindly sent one of his men in a snowcat to pick me up in Basalt. He was, it seems, rather anxious to have me back. And in any case there is talk of the road being reopened—temporarily, at any rate."

"How was your trip?"

"Fruitful."

Corrie shifted uncomfortably at the small talk and decided to get to the point right away. "Look. I wanted to apologize for the way I acted the other day. It was immature, and I'm embarrassed. The fact is, I'm incredibly grateful for all you've done for me. It's just that...you sort of overshadow everything you get involved in. I don't want my professors at John Jay saying, *Oh, her friend Pendergast did it all for her.*" She paused. "No doubt I'm overreacting, this being my first big research project and all."

Pendergast looked at her a moment. Then he simply nodded his understanding. "And how did things go while I was gone?"

"Pretty well," said Corrie, avoiding his direct gaze. "I'm just finishing up my research."

"Nothing untoward happened, I hope?"

"There was another awful fire, right up on the hill behind town, and a road-rage killing out on Highway 82—but I suppose the chief must've told you all about that."

"I meant untoward, directed at you."

"Oh, no," Corrie lied. "I couldn't make any headway solving the crimes, so I've decided to drop that. I did stumble over a few interesting tidbits in my research, but nothing that shed light on the killings."

"Such as?"

"Well, let's see...I learned that Mrs. Kermode is related to the Stafford family, which owned the old smelter back during the silver boom and is still the force behind the development of The Heights."

A brief pause. "Anything else?"

"Oh, yes, something that might intrigue you—given your interest in Doyle and Wilde."

Pendergast inclined his head, encouraging her to continue.

"While digging through some old files at the Griswell Archive, I came across a funny letter about a codger who buttonholed Wilde after his lecture and, it seems, told him a story that almost made him faint. I would bet you anything it was the man-eating grizzly tale."

Pendergast went very still for a moment. Then he asked: "Did the letter mention the old fellow's name?"

Corrie thought back. "Only a surname. Swinton."

Another silence, and then Pendergast said: "You must be low on funds."

"No, no, doing fine," she lied again. Damn it, she was going to have to get a temporary job somewhere. And find another place to live. But no way was she going to take any more money from Pendergast after all he'd done for her already. "Really, there's no reason for you to worry about me."

Pendergast didn't respond, and it was hard to read his expression. Did he believe her? Had he heard anything from the chief about the shot through her windshield or the dead dog? Impossible to tell. Neither had been covered in the local paper—everything was still about the serial arsonist.

"You haven't told me anything about your trip," she said, changing the subject.

"I accomplished what I set out to do," he said, his thin fingers tapping the manila folder. "I found a lost Sherlock Holmes story, the last ever written by Conan Doyle and unpublished to this day. It is most interesting. I recommend it to you."

"When I have time," she said, "I'll be glad to read it."

Another pause. Pendergast's long fingers edged the file toward her. "I should read this now, if I were you."

"Thanks, but the fact is I've still got a lot on my plate, finishing things up and all." Why did Pendergast keep pushing this Doyle business? First *The Hound of the Baskervilles*, and now this.

The pale hand reached out, took the edge of the folder, and opened it. "There can be no delay, Corrie."

She looked up and saw his eyes, glittering in that peculiar way she knew so well. She hesitated. And then, with a sigh of acquiescence, she took out the sheaves of paper within and began to read.

47

The Adventure of Aspern Hall

Of the many cases of Sherlock Holmes for which I've had the privilege to act as his Boswell, there is one I have always hesitated to put to paper. It is not because the adventure itself presented any singularly grim or *outré* elements—no more so than Holmes's other investigations. Rather, I believe it due to the ominous, indeed baneful air that clung to every aspect of the case; an air that chilled and almost blighted my soul; and that even today has the power to vex my sleep. There are some experiences in life one might wish never to have had; for me, this was one. However, I will now commit the story to print, and leave it to others to judge whether or not my reluctance has merit.

It took place in March of '90, at the beginning of a drear and comfortless spring following hard on the heels of one of the coldest winters in living memory. At the time I was resident in Holmes's Baker Street lodgings. It was a dark evening, made more oppressive by a fog that hung in the narrow streets and turned the gaslights to mere pinpricks of yellow. I was lounging in an armchair before the fire, and Holmes—who had been striding restlessly about the room—had now placed himself before the bow window. He was describing to me a chemical experiment he had undertaken that afternoon: how the application of manganese dioxide as a catalyst accelerated the decomposition of potassium chlorate into potassium chloride and, much more importantly, oxygen.

As he spoke, I silently rejoiced at his enthusiasm. Bad weather had kept us very much shut in for weeks; no "little problems" had arisen to command his attention; and he had begun to exhibit the signs of *ennui* that all too frequently led him to indulge his habit of cocaine hydrochloride.

Just at that moment, I heard a knock at the front door.

"Are you expecting company, Holmes?" I asked.

His only reply was a curt shake of the head. Moving first to the decanter on the sideboard, then to the gasogene beside it, he mixed himself a brandy and soda, then sprawled into an armchair.

"Perhaps Mrs. Hudson is entertaining," I said, reaching for the pipe-rack.

But low voices on the stairs, followed by footfalls in the passage, put the lie to this assumption. A moment later there came a light rap on the door.

"Come in," cried Holmes.

The door opened and Mrs. Hudson appeared. "There's a young lady to see you, sir," she said. "I told her it was late, and that she should make an appointment for tomorrow, but she said it was most urgent."

"By all means, show her in," Holmes replied, rising once again to his feet.

A moment later, a young woman was in our sitting room. She was wearing a long travelling coat of fashionable cut, along with a veiled hat.

"Pray have a seat," Holmes said, ushering her towards the most comfortable chair with his usual courtesy.

The woman thanked him, undid her coat and removed her hat, and sat down. She was possessed of a pleasing figure and a refined carriage, and a decided air of self-possession. The only blemish of which I was aware was that her features seemed rather severe, but that may have been the result of the anxiety that was present in her face. As was my custom, I tried to apply Holmes's methods of observation to this stranger, but was unable to notice anything of particular value, aside from the Wellington travelling boots she wore.

I became aware that Holmes was regarding me with some amusement. "Other than the fact that our guest comes from Northumberland," he told me, "that she is a devoted horsewoman, that she arrived here by hansom cab rather than the Underground—and that she is engaged to be married—I can deduce little myself."

"I have heard of your famed methods, Mr. Holmes," said the young woman before I could answer. "And I expected something like this. Allow me, please, to deduce your deductions."

Holmes gave a slight nod, an expression of surprise registering on his face.

The woman held up her hand. "First, you noted my engagement ring but saw no wedding band."

An affirmative incline of the head.

She kept her hand raised. "And you perhaps remarked on the half-moon callus along the outer edge of my right wrist, precisely where the reins cross when held by someone of good seat, with riding crop in hand."

"A most handsome callus," said Holmes.

"As for the hansom cab, that should be obvious enough. You saw it pull to the kerb. For my part, I saw you standing in the window."

At this, I had to laugh. "It looks as if you've met your match, Holmes."

"As for Northumberland, I would guess you noted a trace of accent in my speech?"

"Your accent is not precisely of Northumberland," Holmes told her, "but rather contains a suggestion of Tyne and Wear, perhaps of the Sunderland area, with an overlay of Staffordshire."

At this the lady evinced surprise. "My mother's people were from Sunderland, and my father's from Staffordshire. I wasn't aware I had retained a hint of either accent."

"Our modes of speech are bred in the bone, madam. We cannot escape them any more than we can the colour of our eyes."

"In that case, how did you know I came from Northumberland?"

Holmes pointed at the woman's footwear. "Because of your Wellingtons.

I would surmise you began your journey in snow. We have not had rain in the last four days; Northumberland is the coldest county in England; and it is the only one presently with snow still on the ground."

"And how would you know there is snow in Northumberland?" I asked Holmes.

Holmes gestured at a nearby copy of *The Times*, a pained expression on his face. "Now, madam, do me the kindness of telling us your name and how we may be of assistance."

"My name is Victoria Selkirk," the woman said. "And my impending marriage is, in large part, why I am here."

"Do go on," Holmes said, relapsing into his seat.

"Please forgive my calling on you without prior notice," Miss Selkirk said. "But the fact is I don't know who else to turn to."

Holmes took a sip of his brandy and waited for the young lady to continue.

"My fiancé's estate, Aspern Hall, is situated a few miles outside Hexham. My mother and I have taken a cottage on the grounds in preparation for the wedding. Over the last few months, the region has been plagued by a ferocious wolf."

"A wolf?" I remarked in surprise.

Miss Selkirk nodded. "To date it has killed two men."

"But wolves are extinct in Britain," I said.

"Not necessarily, Watson," Holmes told me. "Some believe they still exist in the most remote and inaccessible locales." He turned back to Miss Selkirk. "Tell me about these killings."

"They were savage, as would be expected of a wild beast." She hesitated. "And—increasingly—the creature seems to be developing a taste for its victims."

"A man-eating wolf?" I said. "Extraordinary."

"Perhaps," Holmes replied. "Yet it is not beyond the bounds of possibility. Consider the example of the man-eating lions of Tsavo. When other game is scarce—and you will recall the severity of last winter—carnivores will adapt in order to survive." He glanced at Miss Selkirk. "Have there been eyewitnesses?"

"Yes. Two."

"And what did they report having seen?"

"A huge wolf, retreating into the forest."

"What was the distance from which these observations were made?"

"Both were made across a blanket bog...I would say several hundred yards."

Holmes inclined his head. "By day or by night?"

"By night. With a moon."

"And were there any particular distinguishing characteristics of this wolf, besides its great size?"

"Yes. Its head was covered in white fur."

"White fur," Holmes repeated. He put his fingertips together and fell silent for a moment. Then he roused himself and addressed the young woman again. "And how, exactly, can we be of help?"

"My fiancé, Edwin, is the heir to the Aspern estate. The Aspern family is the most prominent in that vicinity. Given the fear that has gripped the countryside, he feels it necessary to take onto himself the task of destroying this beast before it kills yet again. He has been going out into the forest at night, often alone. Even though he is armed, I'm terrified for his safety and fear that some misfortune may befall him."

"I see. Miss Selkirk—" Holmes continued, now a little severely— "I fear that I am unable to assist you. What you need are the services of a game hunter, not a consulting detective."

The anxiety on Miss Selkirk's features deepened. "But I had heard of your successful close with that dreadful business at Baskerville Hall. That is why I came to you."

"That business, my dear woman, was the work of a man, not a beast."

"But..." Miss Selkirk hesitated. Her air of self-possession grew more tenuous. "My fiancé is most determined. He feels it an obligation because of his station in life. And his father, Sir Percival, hasn't seen fit to prevent him. Please, Mr. Holmes. There is no one else who can help me."

Holmes took a sip of his brandy; he sighed, rose, took a turn round the room, then sat down again. "You mentioned the wolf was seen retreating into a forest," he said. "May I assume you are speaking of Kielder Forest?"

Miss Selkirk nodded. "Aspern Hall abuts it."

"Did you know, Watson," Holmes said, turning to me, "that Northumberland's Kielder Forest is the largest remaining wooded area in England?"

"I did not," I replied.

"And that it is famed, in part, for housing the country's last large remaining population of the Eurasian red squirrel?"

Glancing over at Holmes, I saw that his look of cold disinterestedness had been replaced with one both sharp and keen. I of course knew of his great interest in *Sciurus vulgaris*. He was perhaps the world's foremost expert on the creature's behaviour and taxonomy, and had published several monographs on the subject. I also sensed in him an unusual admiration for this woman.

"In a population bed that large, there may well be opportunities to observe variances heretofore undiscovered," Holmes said, more to himself than to us. Then he glanced at our guest. "Do you have rooms in town?" he asked.

"I arranged to stay with relatives in Islington."

"Miss Selkirk," he replied, "I am inclined to take up this investigation—almost in spite of the case rather than because of it." He looked at me, and then—significantly—at the hat stand, upon which hung both my bowler and his cloth cap with its long ear-flaps.

"I'm your man," I replied instantly.

"In that case," Holmes told Miss Selkirk, "we will meet you tomorrow morning at Paddington Station, where—unless I am much mistaken—there is an 8:20 express departing for Northumberland."

And he saw the young woman to the door.

The following morning, as planned, we met Victoria Selkirk at Paddington Station and prepared to set off for Hexham. Holmes, normally a late riser, appeared to have regained his dubiousness concerning the case. He was restless and uncommunicative, and as the train puffed out it was left to me to make conversation with the young Miss Selkirk. To pass the time, I asked her about Aspern Hall and its tenants, both older and younger.

The Hall, she explained, had been rebuilt from the remains of an ancient priory, originally constructed around 1450 and partially razed during Henry VIII's dissolution of the monasteries. Its current owner, Sir Percival Aspern, had been a hatter by trade. In his youth he had patented a revolutionary method for making green felt.

Holmes paused in his perusal of the passing scenery. "Green felt, you say?"

Miss Selkirk nodded. "Beyond its use for gaming tables, the colour was most fashionable in millinery shops during the '50s. Sir Percival made his fortune with it."

Holmes waved a hand, as if swatting away an insect, and returned his attention to the compartment window.

Sir Percival's specialty hats, Miss Selkirk informed me, now held a royal warrant from Queen Victoria and formed the basis for his knighthood. His son Edwin—her fiancé—had gone into the army quite early, having held a commission in the light dragoons. He was now in temporary residence at the Hall, considering whether or not to make the military a lifelong career.

Although Miss Selkirk was the most tactful of her sex, I nevertheless sensed that, whilst Edwin's father wished him to take up the family trade, Edwin himself was of two minds on the subject.

As our journey lengthened, the rich grasses and hedgerows of the Home Counties began giving way to wilder vistas: moorlands, bogs, and skeletal trees, punctuated at intervals by rocky outcroppings and escarpments. At length we arrived at Hexham, an attractive country-town, consisting of a cluster of cottages fashioned of thatch and stone, huddled along a single High Street. A wagonette was waiting for us at the station, a dour-looking servant at the reins. Without a word, he loaded our valises and grips, then returned to his perch and directed his horses away from the station, along a rutted country lane in the direction of the Hall.

The road made its way down a gentle declivity, into an increasingly damp and dreary landscape. The snow—which Holmes had remarked on the day before—could still be seen in patches here and there. The sun, which had at last made its appearance during our train journey, once again slipped behind clouds, bestowing the vista round us with a sense of oppressive gloom.

After we had gone perhaps five miles, Holmes—who had not spoken since we alighted from the train—aroused himself. "What, pray, is that?" he enquired, pointing off in the distance with his walking-stick.

Looking in the indicated direction, I saw what appeared to be a low fen, or marsh, bordered on its fringe by swamp grass. Beyond it, in the late-afternoon mist, I could just make out an unbroken line of black.

"The bog I spoke of earlier," Miss Selkirk replied.

"And beyond it is the verge of Kielder Forest?"

"Yes."

"And am I to infer, from what you mentioned, that the wolf attacks occurred between the one and the other?"

"Yes, that is so."

Holmes nodded, as if satisfying himself on some point, but did not speak further.

The country lane ambled on, making a long, lazy bend in order to avoid the bog, and at length we could make out Aspern Hall in the distance. It was an old manor-house of a most unusual design, with unmatched wings and dependencies set seemingly at cross-angles to each other, and I attributed this architectural eccentricity to the fact that the manse had risen from the ruins of an ancient abbey. As we drew closer, I could make out additional details. The façade was rusticated and much dappled by lichen, and wisps of smoke rose from a profusion of brick chimneys. Sedge and stunted oaks surrounded the main structure as well as the various cottages and outbuildings. Perhaps it was the chill in the spring air, or the proximity of the bog and the dark forest, yet I could not help but form the distinct notion that the house had absorbed into itself the bleakness and foreboding of the very landscape in which it was situated.

The coachman pulled the wagonette up beneath the mansion's porte-cochère. He removed Miss Selkirk's travelling bag, then started for ours, when Holmes stopped him, asking him to wait instead. Following Miss Selkirk, we stepped inside and found ourselves in a long gallery, furnished in rather austere taste. A man, clearly the squire of Aspern Hall himself, was waiting for us in the entrance to what appeared to be a salon. He was gaunt and tall, some fifty-odd years of age, with fair thinning hair and a deep-lined face. He wore a black frock-coat, and held a newspaper in one hand and a dog-whip in the other. Evidently he had heard the wagonette draw up. Putting the newspaper and dog-whip aside, he approached.

"Sir Percival Aspern, I presume?" Holmes said.

"I am, sir; but I fear you have the advantage of me."

Holmes gave a short bow. "I am Sherlock Holmes, and this is my friend and associate, Doctor Watson."

"I see." Sir Percival turned to our female companion. "So this is the reason you went into town, Miss Selkirk?"

Miss Selkirk nodded. "Indeed it is, Sir Percival. If you'll excuse me, I must see to my mother." She departed the gallery rather abruptly, leaving us with the squire.

"I have heard of you, Mr. Holmes," Sir Percival said, "but I fear that you have made a long journey to no purpose. Your methods, brilliant as I understand them to be, will have little application against a beast such as the one that plagues us."

"That remains to be seen," Holmes said shortly.

"Well, come in and have a brandy, won't you?" And Sir Percival led us into the salon, where a butler poured out our refreshment.

"It would appear," Holmes said once we were seated round the fire, "that you do not share your future daughter-in-law's concern for the safety of your son."

"I do not," Sir Percival replied. "He's lately returned from India, and knows what he's about."

"And yet, by all reports, this beast has already killed two men," I said.

"I have hunted with my son in the past, and can vouch for his skill as both tracker and marksman. The fact is, Mr.—Watson, was it?—Edwin takes his responsibilities as heir to Aspern Hall very seriously. And I might say that his courage and initiative have not gone unnoticed in the district."

"May we speak with him?" Holmes asked.

"Certainly—when he returns. He is out in the forest at present, hunting the beast." He paused. "If I were a younger man, I would be at his side."

This excuse seemed to me to betray a streak of cowardice, and I shot a covert glance at Holmes. However, his attention remained fixed on Sir Percival.

"Still, womanish fears or not, the fair sex must be humoured," the man went on. "I am certainly willing to give you free run of the place, Mr. Holmes, and offer you all the assistance you might need, including lodgings, if you so wish."

The invitation, generous as it was, was offered with a certain ill-grace.

"That won't be necessary," Holmes said. "We passed an inn back in Hexham—The Plough, I believe—which we will make our base of operations."

As he was speaking, Sir Percival spilt brandy on his shirtfront. He set the glass aside with a mild execration.

"I understand, sir, that you are in the hat-making trade," Holmes said.

"In years past, yes. Others look after the business for me now."

"I've always been fascinated by the process of making felt. Purely a scientific curiosity, you understand: chemistry is a hobby of mine."

"I see." Our host dabbed absently at his damp shirtfront.

"The basic problem, as I understand it, is in softening the stiff animal hairs to render them sufficiently pliable for shaping felt."

I glanced again at Holmes, wondering where in the devil this particular tack could be leading.

"I recall reading," Holmes continued, "that the Turks of old solved this problem by the application of camel urine."

"We have come a long way from those primitive methods," Sir Percival replied.

Miss Selkirk entered the salon. She looked in our direction, smiled a trifle wanly, and took a seat. She was evidently much worried about her fiancé, and seemed to be at pains to maintain her self-command.

"No doubt your own process is much more modern," Holmes said. "I should be curious to hear its application."

"I wish I could satisfy you on that score, Mr. Holmes, but it remains a trade secret."

"I see." Holmes shrugged. "Well, it is of no great consequence."

At this point there was a commotion in the hall. A moment later, a young man in full hunting dress appeared in the doorway. This was clearly Sir Percival's son, and—with his determined features, his military bearing, and the heavy rifle slung over one shoulder—he cut a fine figure indeed. Immediately, Miss Selkirk rose and, with a cry of relief, flew to him.

"Oh, Edwin," she said. "Edwin, I beg of you—let this time be the last."

"Vicky," the young man said, gently but firmly, "the beast must be found and destroyed. We cannot allow another outrage to occur."

Sir Percival rose as well and introduced Holmes and myself. My friend, however, interrupted these civilities with some impatience in order to question the new arrival.

"I take it," he said, "that this afternoon's foray was unsuccessful."

"It was," Edwin Aspern replied with a rueful smile.

"And where, may I ask, did you undertake your stalk?"

"In the western woods, beyond the bog."

"But was nothing discovered? Tracks? Scat? Perhaps a den?"

Young Aspern shook his head. "I saw no sign."

"This is a very devious, clever wolf," Sir Percival said. "Even dogs are hopeless to track it."

"A deep business," Holmes murmured. "A deep business indeed."

Holmes declined an invitation to supper, and after a brief survey of the grounds we rode the wagonette back into Hexham, where we took rooms at The Plough. After breakfast the following morning, we made application to the local police force, which, it turned out, comprised a single individual, one Constable Frazier. We found the constable at his desk, employed in jotting industriously into a small notebook. From my earlier adventures with Holmes, I had not formed a particularly high opinion of local constabulary. And at first sight, Constable Frazier—with his dark olive dustcoat and leather leg-gings—seemed to bear out my suspicions. He had heard of Holmes, however, and as he began to respond to the enquiries of my friend, I realized that we had before us—if not necessarily a personage of superior intellect—at the least a dedicated and competent officer with, it seemed, a laudable doggedness of approach.

The wolf's first victim, he explained, had been an odd, vaguely sinister individual, a shabbily-dressed and wild-haired man of advanced years. He had shown up abruptly in Hexham some weeks before his death, skulking about and frightening women and children with inarticulate ravings. He did not stay at the inn, seemingly being without ready funds, and after a day or two the constable was called in by concerned citizens to learn the nameless man's busi-ness. After a search, the constable discovered the man staying in an abandoned wood-cutter's hut within the borders of Kielder Forest. The man refused to answer the constable's enquiries or to explain himself in any way.

"Inarticulate ravings?" Holmes repeated. "If you could be more precise?"

"He spoke to himself a great deal, gesturing frantically, quite a lot of nonsense, really. Something about all the wrongs that had been done him. Amongst other rot."

"Rot, you say. Such as?"

"Mere fragments. How he had been betrayed. Persecuted. How cold he was. How he would go to law and get a judgement."

"Anything else?" Holmes pressed.

"No," replied the constable. "Oh yes—one other very odd thing. He often mentioned carrots."

"Carrots?"

Constable Frazier nodded.

"Was he hungry? Did he mention any other foods?"

"No. Just carrots."

"And you say he mentioned carrots not once, but many times?"

"The word seemed to come up again and again. But as I said, Mr. Holmes, it was all a jumble. None of it meant anything."

This line of questioning struck me as a useless diversion. To dwell on the ravings of a madman seemed folly, and I could see no connection to his tragic end at the jaws of a wolf. I sensed that Constable Frazier felt as I did, for he took to looking at Holmes with a certain speculative expression.

"Tell me more about the man's appearance," Holmes said. "Everything that you can remember. Pray spare no details."

"He was singularly unkempt, his clothes mere rags, his hair uncombed. His eyes were bloodshot, and his teeth black."

"Black, you say?" Holmes interrupted with sudden eagerness. "You mean, black as in unsound? Decayed?"

"No. It was more a dark, uniform grey that in dim light almost looked black. And he seemed to be in a state of continual intoxication, though where he got the money for liquor I haven't the faintest idea."

"How do you know he was intoxicated?"

"The usual symptoms of dipsomania: slurred speech, shaking hands, unsteady gait."

"Did you come across any liquor bottles in the wood-cutter's hut?"

"No."

"When you spoke with him, did you smell spirits on his breath?"

"No. But I've had to deal with enough drunkards in my time to know the signs, Mr. Holmes. The matter is absolutely beyond question."

"Very well. Pray continue."

The constable took up again the thread of his narrative with evident relief. "Well, opinion in town was strong against him, so strong that I was about to run him off, when that wolf did the job for me. The morning after I questioned him, he was found on the edge of the forest, his body dreadfully torn and mangled, with tooth marks on the arms and legs."

"I see," said Holmes. "And the second victim?"

At this point, I confess I nearly objected to the line of enquiry. Holmes had questioned the constable closely on trivial matters, but was leaving the main points unbroached. Who, for example, had found the body? But I held my tongue, and Constable Frazier continued.

"That took place two weeks later," the constable said. "The victim was a visiting naturalist up from Oxford to study the red fox."

"Found in the same location as the first?"

"Not far away. Somewhat nearer the bog."

"And how do you know both killings were done by the same animal?"

"It was the look of the wounds, sir. If anything, the second attack was even more vicious. This time, the man was...partially eaten."

"How did the town react to this second killing?"

"There was a lot of talk. Talk—and fear. Sir Percival took an interest in the case. And his son, who was recently returned from the Indian campaign, began roaming the woods at night, armed with a rifle, intent on shooting the beast. I opened an investigation of my own."

"After the second killing, you mean."

"Beg pardon, Mr. Holmes, but there didn't seem to be any purpose to one before. You understand: good riddance to that ancient ruffian. But this time, the victim was a respectable citizen—and we clearly had a man-eater on our hands. If the wolf had killed twice, he would kill again...if he could."

"Did you interview the eyewitnesses?"

"Yes."

"And did their stories agree?"

The constable nodded. "After the second killing, they saw the beast skulking back into the forest, a fearsome creature."

"Seen from how far away?"

"At a distance, at night, but with a moon. Close enough to note the fur on its head having gone snow white."

Holmes thought for a moment. "What did the doctor who presided over the inquests have to say?"

"As I said, amongst other things he noted the fact that, whilst both victims were severely mauled, the second had been partially eaten."

"Yet the first merely had a few tentative bite marks." Holmes turned to me. "Do you know, Watson, that that is the usual pattern by which beasts become man-eaters? So it was with the Tsavo lions, as we spoke of previously."

I nodded. "Perhaps this wolf's hunting range is deep within the forest, and it has been driven closer to civilization because of the long, cold winter."

Holmes turned back to the constable. "And have you made any further observations?"

"Lack of observations is more like it, I'm afraid, Mr. Holmes."

"Pray explain."

"Well, it's strange." Constable Frazier's face assumed a look of perplexity. "My family farm is at the edge of the forest, and I've had opportunity to go out looking for traces of the animal half a dozen times, at least. You'd think a beast that large would be easy to track. But I only found a few tracks, just after the second killing. I'm no tracker, but I could swear there was something unusual in that beast's movements."

"Unusual?" Holmes asked. "In what way?"

"In the paucity of sign. It's as if the beast were a ghost, coming and going invisibly. That's why I've been out of an evening, searching for fresh track."

At this, Holmes leaned forwards in his chair. "Permit me to advise you right now, Constable, I want you to put a stop to that immediately. There are to be no more nocturnal ramblings in the forest."

The constable frowned. "But I have certain obligations, Mr. Holmes. Besides, the person in true danger is young Master Aspern. He is out half the night, every night, looking for the creature."

"Listen to me," Holmes said severely. "That is utter nonsense. Aspern is in no danger. But you, Constable, I warn you—look to yourself."

This brusque dismissal, and the notion that Miss Selkirk's fears for her fiancé were unfounded, amazed me. But Holmes said nothing more, and had no further questions—save to again warn the constable to stay out of the woods—and, for the time being at any rate, our interview had ended.

It being Sunday, we were forced to confine our investigations to interviews with various inhabitants of Hexham. Holmes first tracked down the two eyewitnesses, but they had little to add to what Mr. Frazier had already told us: they had both seen a large wolf, remarkably large in fact, loping off in the direction of the bog, the fur on the top of its head a brilliant white in the moonlight. Neither had investigated further, but instead had the good sense to return to their homes with all speed.

We then repaired to The Plough, where Holmes contented himself with asking the customers their opinion of the wolf and the killings. Everyone we spoke to was on edge about the situation. Some, as they lifted their pints, made brave statements about taking on the hunt themselves one day or another. The majority were content to let young Master Aspern track down the beast on his own and expressed much admiration for his courage.

There were only two dissenting opinions. One was a local grocer, who was of the firm belief that the killings were the result of a pack of feral dogs that lived deep within Kielder Forest. The other was the publican himself, who told us that the second victim—the unfortunate Oxford naturalist—had stated point-blank that the beast which committed these outrages was no wolf.

"No wolf?" Holmes said sharply. "And to what erudition, pray tell, do we owe this unequivocal statement?"

"Can't rightly say, sir. The man simply stated that, in his opinion, wolves were extinct in England."

"That's hardly what I would call an empirical argument," I said.

Holmes looked at the publican with a keen expression. "And what particular beast, then, did the good naturalist substitute for the wolf of Kielder Forest?"

"I couldn't tell you that, sir. He didn't offer anything else." And the man went back to polishing his glassware.

Save for the interview with the constable, it proved on the whole to be a day of rather fruitless enquiry. Holmes was uncommunicative over dinner, and he retired early, with a dissatisfied expression on his face.

Early the following morning, however, barely past dawn, I was awakened by a cacophony of voices from beneath my window. Glancing at my watch, I saw it was just past six. I dressed quickly and went downstairs. A cluster of people had gathered in the High Street, and were all talking and gesturing animatedly. Holmes was already there, and when he saw me emerge from the inn he quickly approached.

"We must hurry," he said. "There has been another wolf sighting."

"Where?"

"In just the same spot, between the bog and the edge of the forest. Come, Watson—it is imperative we be the first on the scene. Do you have your Webley's No. 2 on your person?"

I patted my right waistcoat pocket.

"Then let us be off with all speed. That pistol may not bring down a wolf, but at least it will drive him away."

Securing the same wagonette and ill-tempered driver we had employed before, we quickly left Hexham at a canter, Holmes urging the man on in strident tones. As we headed out into the desolate moorlands, my friend explained that he had already spoken to the eyewitness who had caused this fresh disturbance: an elderly woman, an apothecary's wife, who was out walking the road in search of herbs and medicinal flowers. She could add nothing of substance to the other two eyewitnesses, save to corroborate their observations about the beast's great size and the shock of white fur atop of its head.

"Do you fear—?" I began.

"I fear the worst."

Reaching the spot, Holmes ordered the driver to wait and—without wasting a second—jumped from the wagonette and began making his way through the sedge- and bramble-covered landscape. The bog lay to our left; the dark line of Kielder Forest to our right. The vegetation was damp with a chill morning dew, and there were still patches of snow on the ground. Before we had gone a hundred yards, my shoes and trousers were soaked through. Holmes was far ahead of me already, bounding on like one possessed. Even as I watched, he stopped at the top of a small hillock with a cry of dismay, and abruptly knelt. As I made my way to him, my pistol at the ready, I was able to discern what he had discovered. A body lay amidst the swamp grass, not two hundred yards from the edge of the forest. A military rifle, apparently a Martini-Henry Mk IV, lay beside it. All too well I recognized the dustcoat and leather leggings, now torn and shredded in a most violent fashion. It was Constable Frazier—or, more precisely, what was left of him, poor fellow.

"Watson," Holmes said in an imperious tone, "touch nothing. However, I would appreciate, via visual observation only, your medical opinion of this man's condition."

"He's obviously been savaged," I said, examining the lifeless body. "By some large and vicious creature."

"A wolf?"

"That would seem most likely."

Holmes questioned me closely. "Do you see any specific and identifiable marks? Of fangs, perhaps, or claw marks?"

"It's difficult to say. The ferocity of the attack, the ruined condition of the body, render specific observation difficult."

"And are any pieces of the body—missing?"

I took another look. Despite my medical background, I found this a most disagreeable undertaking. I had seen, more than once, native tribesmen of India who had been mauled by tigers, but nothing in my experience came close to the savagery under which Constable Frazier had fallen.

"Yes," I said at length. "Yes, I believe some few."

"Consistent with the description of the second victim? The naturalist?"

"No. No, I'd say this attack was more extensive in that regard."

Holmes nodded slowly. "You see, Watson. It is again as it was with the man-eating lions of Tsavo. With each victim, they grow more brazen—and more partial to their newfound diet."

With this, he removed a magnifying glass from his pocket. "The rifle has not been fired," he announced as he examined the Martini-Henry. "Apparently, the beast snuck up and struck our man from behind."

After a brief inspection of the corpse, he began moving about in an ever-increasing circle, until—with another cry—he bent low, then started slowly forwards, eyes to the ground, in the direction of a distant farmhouse surrounded by two enclosed fields: the residence, I assumed, of the unfortunate constable. At some point, Holmes stopped, turned round, and then—still employing the magnifying glass—returned to the body and moved slowly past it, until he had reached the very edge of the blanket bog.

"Wolf tracks," he said. "Without doubt. They lead from the forest, to a spot near that farmhouse, and thence to the site where the attack took place. No doubt it emerged from the woods, stalked its victim, and killed him on open ground." He applied his glass once more to the swamp grass along the verge of the marsh. "The tracks go directly into the bog, here."

Now Holmes undertook a circuit of the bog: a laborious activity, involving several halts, backtracks, and exceedingly close inspections of various points of interest. I stayed by the body, touching nothing as Holmes had instructed, watching him from a distance. The process took over an hour, by which time I was drenched to the skin and shivering uncontrollably. A small group of curious onlookers were by now standing back along the roadside, and the local doctor and the magistrate had come up—the latter being the titular authority, with the demise of Constable Frazier—just as Holmes completed his investigation. He said not a word of his discoveries, but simply stood there amongst the marsh grass, deep in thought, as the doctor, the magistrate, and myself wrapped up the body and carried it to the wagonette. As the vehicle rolled off in the direction of town, I made my way back out to where Holmes remained standing, quite still, apparently oblivious to his soaked trousers and waterlogged boots.

"Did you remark anything of further interest?" I asked him.

After a moment, he glanced at me. Instead of answering, he pulled a briar pipe from his pocket, lit it, and replied with a question of his own. "Don't you find it rather curious, Watson?"

"The entire affair is mysterious," I replied, "at least insofar as that blasted elusive wolf is concerned."

"I am not referring to the wolf. I am referring to the affectionate relationship between Sir Percival and his son."

This *non sequitur* stopped me in my tracks. "I'm afraid I don't see what you're driving at, Holmes. From my perspective, the relationship seems anything but affectionate—at least, with regard to the father's callous unconcern for his son's life and safety."

Holmes puffed at his pipe. "Yes," he replied enigmatically. "And *that* is the mystery."

Being now rather closer to Aspern Hall than to Hexham, and having had our transportation commandeered by the magistrate, we made our way down the road to the Hall, arriving there in just under an hour. We were met by Sir Percival and his son, who had just finished breakfasting. The news of the latest attack had not yet reached them, and almost immediately the estate was thrown into an uproar. Young Edwin stated his intention of setting out directly to track the beast, but Holmes counselled him against it: in the wake of this latest attack, the animal had no doubt retreated to his lair.

Next, Holmes asked Sir Percival if he could have the use of his brougham; it was his intention to ride into Hexham without delay and catch the first train to London.

Sir Percival expressed astonishment but gave his consent. Whilst the coach was being called for, Holmes glanced in my direction and suggested we take a stroll round the garden.

"I think you should ride into Hexham with me, Watson," he said. "Gather up your things from The Plough and then return here to Aspern Hall for the night."

"What on earth for?" I ejaculated.

"Unless I am much mistaken, I will be returning from London perhaps as soon as tomorrow," he said. "And when I do, I shall bring with me the confirmation I seek as to the riddle of this vicious beast."

"Why, Holmes!"

"But until then, Watson, your life remains at grave risk. You must promise me that you will not leave the Hall until I return—not even for a turn about the grounds."

"I say, Holmes—"

"I insist upon it. In this matter I shall not give way. Do not leave the main house—especially after dark."

Although this request seemed eccentric in the last degree—especially given the fact that Holmes believed the much more aggressive Edwin Aspern to be in no danger—I relented. "I must say, old man, that I don't see how you can be so certain of solving the case," I told him. "The wolf is here in Hexham—not in London. Unless you are planning to return with a brace of heavy-calibre rifles, I confess that in this matter I see nothing."

"Quite the contrary—you see everything," Holmes retorted. "You must be bolder in drawing your inferences, Watson." But just at that moment there was a clatter of horseshoes on the gravel drive and the brougham drew up.

I spent a dreary day at Aspern Hall. A wind came up, followed by rain: light at first, then rather heavier. There was little to do, so I occupied the hours with reading a day-old copy of *The Times*, jotting in my diary, and glancing through the books in Sir Percival's extensive library. I saw nobody but servants until dinner. During that meal, Edwin declared his intent of going out again that very evening in search of the wolf. Miss Selkirk, who was by now naturally even more concerned for her fiancé's well-being, protested violently. There was an ugly scene. Edwin, though not unmoved by Miss Selkirk's objections, remained determined. Sir Percival, for his part, was clearly proud of his son's courage and—when confronted by his daughter-in-law-to-be—defended himself with talk of the family honour and the high approval of the countryside. After Edwin had left, I took it upon myself to stay with Miss Selkirk and try to draw her into conversation. It was a difficult business, given her state of mind, and I was heartily glad when—at around half past eleven—I heard Edwin's footsteps echoing in the Hall. He had again been unsuccessful in the hunt, but at least he was safely returned.

It was very late the following afternoon when Sherlock Holmes reappeared. He had wired ahead to have Sir Percival's brougham meet him at the Hexham station, and he arrived at the Hall in high spirits. Holmes had brought the magistrate and the town doctor with him, and he wasted no time in assembling the family and servants of the Hall.

When all were settled, Holmes announced that he had solved the case. This caused no end of consternation and questioning, and Edwin demanded to know what he meant by "solving" the case when everyone knew the culprit was a wolf. Holmes refused to be sounded further on the matter. Despite the late hour, he explained, he would return to his rooms at The Plough, where he had certain critical notes on the case, in order to put his conclusions into order. He had made use of the carriage ride to confer with the magistrate and the doctor, and had only come out to the Hall in order to bring me back to town with him to assist with the final details. Tomorrow, he declared, he would make his conclusions public.

Towards the end of this little speech, a coachman came in to make known that the rear axle of Sir Percival's carriage had broken and could not be repaired until morning. There was no way that Holmes—or the magistrate or town doctor, for that matter—could return to Hexham until the following day. There was nothing for it; they would all have to spend the night at Aspern Hall.

Holmes was dreadfully put out by this development. During almost the entire dinner that followed he said not a word, a peevish expression on his face, morosely pushing the food on his plate idly about with his fork, one elbow lodged on the damask tablecloth in support of his narrow chin. Just as dessert was served, he announced his intention of walking back to Hexham.

"But that's out of the question," said Sir Percival in astonishment. "It's over ten miles."

"I shan't be taking the road," Holmes replied. "It's far too indirect. I shall make my way from Aspern Hall to Hexham in a direct line, as the crow flies."

"But that will take you right past the blanket bog," Miss Selkirk said. "Where..." She fell silent.

"I will accompany you, then," Edwin Aspern spoke up.

"You shall do nothing of the sort. The wolf's most recent attack occurred just the night before last, and I doubt its hunger will have returned so soon. No; I shall undertake the trip on my own. Watson, once I reach Hexham I will leave word for the wagonette to come for you and the others in the morning."

And so the matter was settled—or so I thought. Shortly after the men had passed into the library for brandy and cigars, however, Holmes took me aside.

"Look here," he told me *sotto voce.* "As soon as you are able to effect it successfully, you will contrive to sneak out of the house, making sure your departure is undetected. That point is most vital, Watson—you *must* leave undetected. Remember that, for the time being, you remain in grave danger."

Despite my surprise, I assured Holmes that I was his man.

"You are to make your way unobserved to the vicinity of that small hillock where we found Constable Frazier. Find a suitable hiding spot from which no approach can reveal your position—not the bog, not the forest, not the road. Be sure to be in position no later than ten o'clock. And there you are to wait for me to pass by."

I nodded my understanding.

"When I come into sight, however, under no circumstances are you to call out, or stand, or in any manner betray your presence."

"Then what am I to do, Holmes?"

"Depend upon it—when it comes time to act, you shall know. Now: do you still have your pistol about you?"

I patted my waistcoat pocket, where my Webley had been in residence ever since we had arrived at the Hall the previous day.

My friend nodded his satisfaction. "Excellent. Keep it close at hand."

"And you, Holmes?"

"I myself will spend some time here before I take my leave, engaging young Aspern in conversation, billiards, or whatever proves necessary to distract him. It is vital that he not indulge his penchant for wolf-hunting, tonight of all nights."

Accordingly, I bided my time, waiting until the gentlemen were engrossed in a game of whist. Then, retiring to my room, I retrieved my cap and travelling coat, and—making sure I was observed by neither family nor servants—I left the house by way of the French doors of the morning room, slipped across the lawn, and from there out onto the Hexham road. The rain had stopped, but the moon remained partially obscured by clouds. Heavy tendrils of mist lay across the bleak landscape.

I followed the muddy lane as it curved leisurely to the northeast, anticipating in its course the expanse of bog that lay ahead. It was a chill night, and here and there patches of snow could still be seen amidst the brambles and swamp grass. After several miles, at the bend where the road reached its northernmost point and angled eastwards towards town, I struck off south through the low undergrowth in the direction of the bog itself. The moon had by now emerged from behind the clouds and I could just make out the bog ahead, shimmering with a kind of ghastly glow. Beyond it, and barely discernible in the darkness, was the black border of Kielder Forest.

Reaching the hillock at last, I glanced round, then set about following Holmes's instructions: to find a blind in which I could remain unseen from all directions. It took some doing, but at last I found a depression on the eastwards side of the hillock, partially surrounded by gorse and furze, which afforded excellent opportunities for concealment, whilst at the same time commanding a view of all approaches. And here I settled down to wait.

Over the next hour I held a most gloomy vigil. My limbs grew stiff from inactivity, and my travelling coat did little to keep out the damp and chill. From time to time, I examined the various approaches; on other occasions, from sheer force of nervous habit, I checked the state of my weapon.

It was past eleven o'clock when I at last heard the sound of footsteps, coming through the marsh grass from the direction of Aspern Hall. Carefully, I peered out from my place of concealment. It was Holmes, unmistakable in his cloth cap and long coat, his thin frame emerging out of the mists with its characteristic loping stride. He was walking along the very edge of the blanket bog, headed in my direction. Slipping the Webley out of my waistcoat pocket, I steeled myself for whatever action might now transpire.

I waited, motionless, as Holmes continued his approach, hands in his pockets, heading for Hexham with perfect equanimity, as if out for nothing more than an evening's stroll. Suddenly, from the direction of the forest, I saw another form appear. It was large and dark, almost black, and as I watched in horror it bounded directly towards Holmes on all fours. From his position on the far side of the hillock, my friend would not yet be able to catch sight of the creature. I tightened my grip on the Webley: it was beyond any doubt that here was the fearsome wolf itself, and that it was intent on bringing down a fourth victim.

I watched it draw near, ready with my pistol should the beast get too close to Holmes. But then—when the animal was some hundred yards from my friend, and just as it came into view of Holmes himself—the most peculiar thing happened. The beast stopped short, creeping forwards with savage menace.

"Good evening, Sir Percival," Holmes said matter-of-factly.

The beast greeted this sally with a vicious bark. I was by now out of my blind and approaching the wolf from the rear. The wolf abruptly reared up on its hind legs. Drawing closer, whilst trying my best to conceal the sound of my approach, I saw to my astonishment that the creature was, in fact, human: Sir Percival, dressed in what appeared to be a heavy bearskin coat. The soles of his leather boots had been fitted out with makeshift claws, and wolf pads dangled by large buttons from his gloves. One hand appeared holding a pistol; the other a large, claw-like implement with a heavy handle and long, wicked tines. His fair, thinning hair shone a pale, unnatural white in the light of the rising moon. I found myself almost paralysed by this bizarre and wholly unexpected turn of events.

Sir Percival laughed again—a maniacal laugh. "Good evening, Mister Holmes," he said. "You shall make an excellent repast." And with a raving torrent of words that I could not begin to follow or understand, he cocked his pistol and raised it at Holmes.

This extremity broke my paralysis. "Stand down, Sir Percival," I cried from his flank, my own weapon raised. "I have you in my sights."

Caught off guard, Sir Percival wheeled towards me, aiming in my direction. As he did so, I squeezed off a shot, catching him in the arm. With a cry of pain, the man clutched at his shoulder, then fell to his knees. In a moment, Holmes was at his side. He relieved Sir Percival of his weapon and the grotesque device—no doubt, I realized, used to simulate the lacerations of a wolf's claws—then turned to me.

"I should be glad, Watson, if you could head into town as quickly as you can," he said calmly. "Return with a dog-cart and several able-bodied men. I shall remain here with Sir Percival."

The rest of the particulars can be summed up in short order. After Sir Percival was taken up by the authorities and remanded to the police-court, we returned to Aspern Hall. Holmes spoke briefly, in turn, with the magistrate; young Edwin Aspern; and Miss Selkirk, and then insisted on our returning to London by the very next train.

"I must confess, Holmes," I told him as our carriage made its way along the road back towards Hexham just as dawn was breaking, "that whilst I have often been in the dark in past cases, this is your most singular surprise yet. Without doubt it will prove your *coup-de-maître*. How on earth did you know that a human, not a wolf, was behind these outrages—and how in particular did you know it was Sir Percival, if in fact you knew that at all?"

"My dear Watson, you do me a disservice," Holmes replied. "Naturally I knew it was Sir Percival."

"Then pray explain yourself."

"Several clues presented themselves, for anyone with the discernment to sift the important from the mere coincident. To begin with, we have the madman—the first victim. When there is more than one killing to reckon with, Watson, you must always pay particular attention to the *first*. Frequently the motive, and therefore the entire case, rests upon that particular crime."

"Yes, but the first victim was nothing but a mindless vagrant."

"He might have been so in recent years, but he was not always thus. Recall, Watson, that in his ravings, a single word stood out again and again: *carrot*."

I recalled this, and Holmes's fascination with it, all too well. How it could have any significance seemed to defy credibility. "Go on," I said.

"Carroting, you must understand, was a process by which animal fur is bathed in a solution of mercury nitrate, in order to render the hairs more supple, thus producing a superior *felt.*" At this last word, he threw a significant glance in my direction.

"Felt," I repeated. "You mean, for the making of hats?"

"Precisely. The solution is of an orange colour, hence the term *carroting.* However, this process had rather severe side effects on those who worked with it, which is why its use today is much reduced. When mercury vapours are inhaled over a long enough period of time—particularly, for our purposes, in the close quarters of a hat-making operation—toxic and irreversible effects almost inevitably follow. One develops tremors of the hands; blackened teeth; slurred speech. In severe cases, dementia or outright insanity can occur. Hence the term *mad as a hatter.*" Holmes waved a hand. "I know all this, of course, due to my long-abiding interest in chemistry."

"But what does all this have to do with Sir Percival?" I asked.

"Let us proceed in a linear fashion, if you please. You will recall that Constable Frazier believed our vagabond to be a drunkard, citing as evidence the man's slurred speech and impaired movement. And yet he detected no smell of alcohol on the man's breath. I immediately assumed that the real cause of the man's affliction was not drunkenness, but rather the effects of mercury poisoning. His mention of 'carrots' explained how this poisoning had come about: as an occupational hazard of making felt, from working as a hatter. I naturally realized that there could be no coincidence between Sir Percival's former occupation and the sudden arrival of this curious fellow upon the scene. No: this man had clearly once been in business with Sir Percival. Recall, if you will, two things. First, how this man had raved about betrayal, about getting a judgement from a court of law. Second, how Sir Percival made his fortune by a unique felt-making process—a process, you may recollect, he refused to discuss with me when I broached the topic at Aspern Hall."

The carriage continued its jostling way towards Hexham, and Holmes went on. "Remarking on these facts, I began to consider the possibility that this man, now sadly reduced, had once been Sir Percival's business partner—and, perhaps, the true author of that revolutionary felt-making process. Now, years later, he had returned to square accounts with his former partner, to expose and ruin him. In other words, this whole matter began as a mere business dispute; one that Sir Percival solved in a traditional manner—by murder. It seemed to me highly likely that when this fellow appeared in Hexham, Sir Percival had promised him amends, and had agreed to meet with him in a lonely spot at the edge of the bog. There, Sir Percival murdered his former partner, and—to keep any suspicion from ever redounding upon him—tore the body cruelly, even going so far as to leave some tentative bite marks, so as to make it appear the work of a large and savage beast, most likely a wolf."

"And in so doing, he seemed to have been entirely successful," I said. "Why, then, kill again?"

"The second person killed, you will recall, was a naturalist from Oxford. He was heard in the local inn debunking the rumours of a wolf, declaring that no wolves still survived in England. By killing this man, Sir Percival accomplished several goals. He silenced the man's insistence on the extinction of the English wolf—the very last thing Sir Percival would want was attention returning to the initial killing. Also, by this time he had of course heard the rumours in Hexham about a wolf being the culprit in his partner's murder. In case he was spotted, he had now had the opportunity to fit out a large bear coat, complete with wolf-paw gloves and boots that he—with his hatter's skill—could make entirely convincing. He used this disguise to run to and from the second murder scene on all fours. I believe, Watson, he was actually *hoping* for a witness this time, in order to inflame the rumours of a man-eating wolf. In this, at least, he was fortunate."

"Yes, I can see a cruel logic in such a course of action," I said. "But what, then, of the constable?"

"Constable Frazier was, if not the world's most accomplished investigator, a man of great doggedness and persistence. No doubt Sir Percival perceived him to be a threat. Recall how the constable hinted at certain suspicions about the wolf's behaviour. Those suspicions, I would hazard, had to do with why the wolf tracks entered the bog *but never came out again.* The constable would have remarked on this after the second murder, if not before. I myself found this curious phenomenon to be the case after the constable's own death, when I made a circuit of the bog. Wolf tracks entered the region from the east; only human tracks emerged from the west. Sir Percival, you see, would have entered the bog on all fours, as a wolf; he would have used the concealing vegetation to come out from the bog as merely himself, should anyone encounter him. The constable must have mentioned his suspicions to Sir Percival—remember, Watson, his remarking he'd been to the Hall just the day before, to warn young Aspern to cease his hunting of the wolf—and in so doing, signed his own death warrant."

Hearing these revelations, presented in Holmes's complacent tone, was nothing less than astounding. I could only shake my head.

"What clinched the case for me was Sir Percival's cavalier, indeed encouraging, attitude towards his son's hunting of the beast. He seemed to evince total unconcern for young Edwin's well-being. Why? At this point in the game, the answer was obvious to me: he knew his son was in no danger from the wolf, *because the wolf was himself.* Then, of course, there was the manner in which Sir Percival spilt his brandy."

"What of it?"

"He was making great pains to hide his trembling hands. That incipient palsy demonstrated to my satisfaction that he himself was well on the road to madness brought on by mercury poisoning, and that he would soon be reduced to the same pitiable state as his former partner."

By this time we had arrived at the Hexham station; we descended with our valises and mounted the platform, just in time for the 8:20 to Paddington.

"Armed with these suspicions," Holmes went on, "I went to London. It did not take me long to uncover the facts I was looking for: that, many years before, Sir Percival did indeed have a business partner. At the time, he accused Sir Percival of stealing a valuable patent, claiming it as his own. He was adjudged a lunatic, however, and was committed to an asylum—through the offices of Sir Percival himself. This poor unfortunate was released just days before the initial appearance of the raving madman in Kielder Forest.

"I returned from London, secure in the knowledge that, not only was there no man-eating wolf, but Sir Percival himself was the murderer of three men.

The only question remaining was how to catch him up. I couldn't very well reveal the truth—that there was no wolf. No; I had to find a reason to manoeuvre Sir Percival into making me his next target, and to arrange it, so to speak, on home ground. Hence my dramatic announcement of having solved the case—and my nocturnal shortcut across the open countryside, between the bog and the forest edge, site of the previous killings. Unless I had made a mistake in my calculations, I felt certain Sir Percival would take the opportunity to make me his fourth victim."

"But you undertook that walk only because Sir Percival's carriage broke an axle," I said. "How could you have anticipated such an eventuality?"

"I did not anticipate it, Watson. I precipitated it."

"You mean—?" I stopped.

"Yes. I fear I committed an act of sabotage against Sir Percival's brougham. Perhaps I should send down a cheque for its repair."

A faint whistle echoed out across the morning sky. A moment later, the express came into view. Within minutes we were boarding. "I confess myself astonished," I said as we entered our compartment. "You are like the artist that outdoes his best work. There remains only one particular I do not understand."

"In that case, my dear Watson, pray unburden yourself."

"It is one thing, Holmes, to make a killing look like the work of an animal; quite another to actually devour portions of a body. Why did Sir Percival continue to do so—and, in fact, to an increasing extent?"

"The answer is quite simple," Holmes replied. "It would seem Sir Percival, in his growing madness, had begun acquiring a taste for his, ah, *prey.*"

The subject of the Hexham Wolf did not come up again until perhaps half a year later, when I came across a notice in *The Times* stating that the new owner of Aspern Hall and his fiancée were to be married in St. Paul's the following month. It appeared that—in local opinion, at least—the atrocities of the father were more than compensated for by the son's military success, and by the courage he had displayed in his hunt for the would-be wolf. As for myself, I would have wished to have spent more time, had the circumstances been more pleasant, in the company of one of the handsomest young ladies of my acquaintance: Miss Victoria Selkirk.

On the lone occasion Holmes himself later referred to the case, he merely expressed a passing regret that the excursion had not furnished him with an opportunity to further his study of *Sciurus vulgaris*—the Eurasian red squirrel.

48

Corrie finished the story and looked up to find Pendergast's silvery eyes upon her. She realized she had been holding her breath, and exhaled. "Holy crap," she said.

"One could say that."

"This story...I can hardly get my head around it." A thought struck her. "But how did you know it was key?"

"I didn't. Not at first. But consider: Doyle was a medical man. Before starting his private practice, he had been the doctor on a whaling ship and ship's surgeon on a voyage along the West African coast. Those are among the most difficult postings a medical man could experience. He had surely seen a great deal of unpleasantness, to put it mildly, on these voyages. A story that would send him fleeing from the dining table had to be far more repugnant than a mere man-eating grizzly."

"But the lost story? What led you to that in particular?"

"Doyle was so unsettled by the story he heard from Wilde that he did what many authors do to exorcise their demons: he incorporated it into his fiction. Almost immediately after the meeting in the Langham Hotel he wrote *The Hound of the Baskervilles*, which of course has a few parallels to Wilde's actual story. But *Hound*, while a marvelous story in its own right, was a mere ghost of the truth. Not much exorcism to be had there. One can surmise that Wilde's story continued to work on his mind for a long time. I began to wonder whether, in later years, Doyle finally felt compelled to write something closer to the bone, with much more of the truth in it, as a kind of catharsis. I made some inquiries. An English acquaintance of mine, an expert in Sherlockiana, confirmed to me a rumor of a missing Holmes story, which we surmised was titled 'The Adventure of Aspern Hall.' I put two and two together—and went to London."

"But how did you know it was *that* story?"

"By all accounts the Aspern Hall story was soundly rejected. Never published. Consider that: a fresh Sherlock Holmes story, from the master himself, the first one in ages—and it is rejected? One might surmise it contained something unusually objectionable to Victorian taste."

Corrie wrinkled her nose in chagrin. "You make it sound so simple."

"Most detection is simple. If I teach you nothing else, I hope you'll learn that."

She colored. "And I was so dismissive of this lead for so long. What an idiot I am. I'm sorry about that, really."

Pendergast waved a hand. "Let us focus on the matter before us. The famed *Hound of the Baskervilles* merely touched on the grizzly story. But this tale: this *incorporates* far more of what Doyle heard from Wilde, who had in turn heard it from this fellow you found, Swinton. A commendable discovery, that."

"An accident."

"An accident is only a puzzle piece that hasn't yet found its place in the picture. A good detective collects all 'accidents,' no matter how insignificant."

"But we need to figure out what connection the story has to the real killings," said Corrie. "Okay: you have a bunch of cannibalistic murderers who are behaving somewhat like this guy Percival. They're killing and eating miners up on the mountain, trying to disguise what they're doing as grizzly killings."

"No. If I may interrupt: the identification of the killings with a man-eating grizzly was originally made by chance, as you've probably learned for yourself. A grizzly bear passed by and masticated the remains of one of the early victims, and that clinched matters to the town's satisfaction. Later random sightings of grizzlies seem to confirm the connection. It is all about how human beings construct a narrative out of random events, baseless assumptions, and simple-minded prejudices. In my opinion, the gang of killers you mention *did not* set out to disguise their work as the result of a man-eating grizzly."

"All right, so the gang wasn't trying to disguise their killings. But still, the story doesn't explain *why* they're killing. What's the motivation? Sir Percival has a motivation: he kills his partner to cover up the fact that he cheated him and stuck him in an insane asylum. I can't see how that has anything to do with what prompted the killers in the Colorado mountains."

"It doesn't." Pendergast looked at Corrie a long time. "Not directly, at any rate. You're not focusing on the salient points. One should ask, first: why did Sir Percival *eat* portions of his victims?"

Corrie thought back to the story. "At first, to make it look like a wolf. And then later, because he was going crazy and thought he was developing a taste for it."

"Ah! And *why* was he going crazy?"

"Because he was suffering from mercury poisoning as a result of making felt." Corrie hesitated. "But what does hat making have to do with silver mining? I can't see it."

"On the contrary, Corrie—you see everything. *You must be bolder in drawing your inferences.*" Pendergast's eyes gleamed as he quoted the line.

Corrie frowned. What possible connection could there be? She wished Pendergast would just tell her, rather than pulling the Socratic method on her. "Can we dispense with the teachable moment? If it's obvious, why can't you just tell me?"

"This is not an intellectual game we are playing. This is deadly serious—particularly for you. I am surprised that you have not already been threatened."

He paused. In the silence, Corrie thought of the shot at her car, the dead dog, the note. She should tell him—clearly he would find out sooner or later. What if she confided in Pendergast? But that would only result in him putting more pressure on her to leave Roaring Fork.

"My first instinct," Pendergast went on, almost as if reading her thoughts, "was to spirit you away from town immediately, even if it meant commandeering one of the chief's snowcats. But I know you well enough to realize that would be futile."

"Thank you."

"The next best thing, therefore, is to get you thinking properly about this case—what it means, why you are in extreme danger, and from where. This is not, as you put it, a *teachable moment*."

The seriousness of his tone hit her hard. She swallowed. "Okay. Sorry. You've got my attention."

"Let's return to the question you just asked, which I will rephrase in more precise terms: what does nineteenth-century English hat making have in common with nineteenth-century silver refining?"

It came to her in a flash. It *was* obvious. "Both processes use mercury."

"*Precisely.*"

All of a sudden, everything started to fall into place. "According to the story, mercury nitrate was used to soften fur for the making of felt for hats. Carroting, they called it."

"Go on."

"And mercury was also used in smelting, to separate silver and gold from crushed ore."

"Excellent."

Now Corrie's mind was racing. "So the gang of killers was a group of miners who must've worked in the smelter. And gone crazy, in turn, from mercury poisoning."

Pendergast nodded.

"The smelter fired the crazy workers and hired fresh ones. Perhaps a few of those who were fired banded together. Without work, totally nuts, unemployable, they took to the hills, angry and vengeful, where they went progressively crazier. And, of course...they needed to eat."

Another slow nod from Pendergast.

"So they preyed on isolated miners up at their claims, killing and eating them. And like the man-eating lions of Tsavo—and Sir Percival—they began to develop a taste for it."

This was followed by a long silence. *What else?* Corrie asked herself. Where did the present danger come from? "All this happened a hundred and fifty years ago," she finally said. "I don't see how this affects us now. Why am I in danger?"

"You have not put the last, crucial piece into place. Think of the 'accidental' information you told me you'd recently uncovered."

"Give me a hint."

"Very well, then: who owned the smelter?"

"The Stafford family."

"Go on."

"But the history of labor abuses and the use of mercury at the smelter are already well known. It's a matter of historical record. It would be stupid for them to take steps to cover that up now."

"Corrie." Pendergast shook his head. "Where *was* the smelter?"

"Um, well, it was somewhere in the area where The Heights is now. I mean, that's how the family came to own all that land to turn into the development."

"And...?"

"And what? The smelter's long gone. It was shut in the 1890s and they tore down the ruins decades ago. There's nothing left of...*Oh, my God.*" She clasped one hand to her mouth.

Pendergast remained silent, waiting.

Corrie stared at him. Now she understood. "Mercury. That's what's left of it. *The ground beneath the development is contaminated with mercury.*"

Pendergast folded his hands and sat back in his chair. "Now you are starting to think like a true detective. And I hope you will live long enough to become that detective. I fear for you: you have always been, and still remain, far too rash. But despite that shortcoming, even you must see what is at stake here—and the grave danger you have placed yourself in by continuing this most unwise investigation. I would not have revealed any of this to you—not the lost Holmes story, not the Stafford family connection, not the poisonous groundwater—were it not, given your, ah, impetuous nature, necessary to convince you to leave this ugly place, as directly as I can make arrangements."

49

A. X. L. Pendergast surveyed the town of Leadville with tightly pursed lips. A sign announced its altitude, 10,150 feet, and stated it was the HIGHEST INCORPORATED TOWN IN THE UNITED STATES. It stood in stark contrast with Roaring Fork, across the Continental Divide. Its downtown strip was a single street bordered by Victorian buildings in various states of shabbiness and disrepair, with frozen heaps of snow along the verges. Beyond, forests of fir trees swept up to immense mountain peaks in almost all directions. The excessive Christmas decorations draped over every cornice, lamppost, streetlight, and parapet lent a sort of desperate air to the forlornness of the town, especially two days before Christmas. And yet despite the early-morning hour and the bitter cold, Pendergast was aware of a certain relief simply to be away from the oppressive wealth, entitlement, and smugness that hung like a miasma over Roaring Fork. Leadville, while impoverished, was a real place with real people—although it was nevertheless inconceivable why anyone would want to live in this white Gehenna, this algid Siberian wasteland, this desert of frost buried in the mountains, far from the delights of civilization.

He had had the devil of a time tracking down any progeny of the aged Swinton, first name unknown, who had buttonholed Oscar Wilde after the Roaring Fork lecture and told him the fateful story. With the help of Mime, he had finally identified one remaining descendant: a certain Kyle Swinton, born in Leadville thirty-one years previously. He was an only child whose parents had been killed in a car accident around the time he dropped out of Leadville High. After that, his digital trail had vanished. Even Mime, Pendergast's shadowy and reclusive computer genius and information gatherer, had been unable to track the man beyond establishing the crucial fact that there was no record of his death. Kyle Swinton, it seemed, was still alive, somewhere within the borders of the United States; that was all Pendergast knew.

As soon as the snow had stopped in Roaring Fork—or rather paused, as the main event was still to come—the road had been cleared and Pendergast had made his way to Leadville to see if he could pick up a trace of the man. Weighed down by a sweater vest, heavy black suit, down vest, overcoat, two scarves, thick gloves and boots, and a woolen hat under his trilby, he exited his vehicle and made his way into what appeared to be the only five-and-dime drugstore in the town. He glanced around the store and selected the oldest employee: the pharmacist manning the prescription counter.

Unwrapping his scarves so he could speak, Pendergast said, "I am trying to trace the whereabouts of a man named Kyle Swinton, who attended Leadville High School in the late '90s."

The pharmacist looked Pendergast up and down. "Kyle Swinton? What do you want with him?"

"I'm an attorney, and it's about an inheritance."

"Inheritance? His family didn't have two nickels to rub together."

"There was a great-uncle."

"Oh. Well, good for him, I suppose. Kyle, he doesn't come into town very often. Maybe not till spring."

This was excellent. "If you could direct me to his house, I should be grateful."

"Sure, but he's snowed in. Lives off the grid. You won't get up there except on a snowmobile. And..." The man hesitated.

"Yes?"

"He's one of those survivalist types. He's holed up in Elbert Canyon waiting for, I don't know, the end of civilization maybe."

"Indeed?"

"He's got a bunker up there, stockpiles of food—and a big-time arsenal, or so they say. So if you go up there, you'd better be damn careful or he's liable to blow a hole in you."

Pendergast was silent for a moment. "Where, pray tell, may I rent a snowmobile?"

"There's a couple of places, it's a big sport in these parts." He gave Pendergast another once-over, doubtfully. "You know how to operate one?"

"Naturally."

The druggist gave Pendergast the information and drew a map, showing him how to get to Kyle Swinton's place up in Elbert Canyon.

Pendergast exited the pharmacy and strolled down Harrison Avenue, as if shopping, despite the five-degree weather, the piles of snow, and the sidewalks so icy that even the salt froze to them. Finally he went into a gun-and-ammo store that also doubled as a pawnshop.

A man with a tattoo of an octopus on the shaved dome of his head strolled over. "What can I do for you?"

"I would like to buy a small box of the Cor-Bon .45 ACP."

The man placed the box on the counter.

"Does a Mr. Kyle Swinton shop here?"

"Sure does, good customer. Crazy fucker, though."

Pendergast considered for a moment the kind of person a man like this might think of as crazy.

"I understand he has quite a collection of firearms."

"Spends every last penny on guns and ammo."

"In that case, there must be quite a variety of ammo he buys from you."

"Hell, yes. That's why we got all these rounds here. He's got a collection of heavy-caliber handguns you wouldn't believe."

"Revolvers?"

"Oh, yeah. Revolvers, pistols, all loads. Probably got a hundred K worth of firearms up there."

Pendergast pursed his lips. "Come to think of it, I'd like to also purchase a box of the .44 S&W Special, one of the .44 Remington Magnum, and another of .357 S&W Magnum."

The man placed the boxes on the counter. "Else?"

"That will suffice, thank you very much."

The man rang the purchase up.

"No bag, I'll put them in my pockets." Everything disappeared into his coat.

Business had not been good at the nearest snowmobile rental place. Pendergast was able to overcome their initial difficulty about renting him a machine for the day, despite his wildly inappropriate dress, southern accent, and lack of even minimal familiarity with its operation. They put a helmet and visor on his head and gave him a quick lesson in how to ride it, took him out for a five-minute practice spin, had him sign multiple disclaimers, and wished him luck. In so doing, Pendergast learned more about Kyle Swinton. He appeared to be known to all Leadville as a "crazy fucker." His parents had been alcoholics who finally went through the guardrail at Stockton Creek, drunk as skunks, and rolled a thousand feet down the ravine. Kyle had lived off the land ever since, hunting, fishing, and panning for gold when he needed ready cash to buy ammunition.

As Pendergast was leaving, the rental shop manager added: "Don't go rushing up to the cabin, now, Kyle's liable to get excited. Approach real nice and slow, and keep your hands in sight and a friendly smile on your face."

50

The ride to Swinton's cabin was exceedingly unpleasant. The snowmobile was a coarse, deafening, stinking contraption, prone to jackrabbit starts and sudden stops, with none of the refinement of a high-performance motorcycle, and as Pendergast maneuvered it up the winding white road it threw up a steady wake of snow that plastered his expensive coat, building up layers. Pendergast soon looked like a helmeted snowman.

He followed the advice he'd been given and slowed down as soon as he saw the cabin, half buried in snow, with a trickle of smoke curling from a stovepipe on top. Sure enough, as he came within a hundred yards a man appeared on the porch, small and ferret-like, with a gap between his two front teeth visible even at this distance. He was holding a pump-action shotgun.

Pendergast halted the snowmobile, which jerked to a stop. Plates of snow broke off and fell from his coat. He fumbled awkwardly with the helmet and finally managed to raise the visor with his bulky gloves.

"Greetings, Kyle!"

The response was a conspicuous racking of the pump. "State your business, sir."

"I'm here to see you. I've heard a lot about your outfit up here. I'm a fellow survivalist and I'm touring the country looking at what other people are doing, for an article in *Survivalist* magazine."

"Where'd you hear about me?"

"Word gets around. You know how it is."

A hesitation. "So you're a journalist?"

"I'm a survivalist first, journalist second." A cold gust of wind swirled the snow about Pendergast's legs. "Mr. Swinton, do you think you might extend me the courtesy of your hospitality so that we could continue this conversation in the confines of your home?"

Swinton wavered. The word *hospitality* had not gone unnoticed. Pendergast pressed his advantage. "I wonder if keeping a man freezing in the cold at gunpoint is the kind of hospitality one should accord a kindred spirit."

Swinton squinted at him. "At least you're a white man," he said, putting down the gun. "All right, come on in. But see that you broom yourself off at the door; I don't want no snow tracked in my house." He waited as Pendergast struggled through the deep snow to the porch. A broken broom stood next to the door and Pendergast swept himself as clean as he could while Swinton watched, frowning.

He followed Swinton in the cabin. It was surprisingly large, extending into a warren of rooms in the back. The gleam of gunmetal could be seen everywhere: racks of assault rifles, AK-47s and M16s illegally altered to fire on full-auto; a set of Uzis and TAR-21 bullpup assault rifles; another set of Chinese Norinco QBZ-97 rifles and carbines, again altered for fully automatic action. A nearby case contained a huge array of revolvers and pistols, just as the man in Leadville had said. Beyond, in one of the rooms, Pendergast glimpsed a collection of RPGs, including a pair of Russian RPG-29s—all quite illegal.

Other than the walls being completely covered with weaponry, the cabin was surprisingly cozy, with a fire burning in a woodstove with an open door. All the furniture was handmade of peeled logs and branches, draped with cowhides. And everything was neat as a pin.

"Shed that coat and seat yourself, I'll get the coffee."

Pendergast removed the coat and draped it over a chair, straightened his suit, and sat down. Swinton fetched some mugs and a coffeepot off the woodstove and poured two cups. Without asking he heaped in a tablespoon of Cremora and two of sugar before handing it to Pendergast.

The agent took the mug and made a show of drinking. It tasted as if it had been boiling on the stove for days.

He found Swinton looking at him curiously. "What's with the black suit? Somebody die? You come up here by snowmobile in that getup?"

"It was functional."

"You sure as hell don't look like a survivalist to me."

"What do I look like?"

"Some pussy professor from Jew York City. Or with that accent, maybe Jew Orleans. So what're you packing?"

Pendergast removed his .45 Colt and laid it on the table. Swinton picked it up, immediately impressed. "Les Baer, huh? Nice. You know how to fire that?"

"I try," said Pendergast. "This is quite a collection you have. Do *you* know how to fire all those weapons?"

Swinton took offense, as Pendergast knew he would. "You think I hang shit like that on my wall if I don't know how to fire it?"

"Anyone can pull the trigger on a weapon," Pendergast said, sipping his coffee.

"I fire almost every weapon I own at least once a week."

Pendergast pointed to the handgun cabinet. "What about that Super Blackhawk?"

"That's a fine weapon. Updated Old West." He got up, took it down from the rack.

"May I see it?"

He handed it to Pendergast. He hefted it, sighted, then opened the barrel and dumped out the ammo.

"What you doing?"

Pendergast picked up one of the rounds, inserted it back in the barrel, gave it a spin, then laid the revolver down.

"You think you're tough, right? Let's play a little game."

"What the hell? What game?"

"Put the gun to your head and pull the trigger. And I'll give you a thousand dollars."

Swinton stared at him. "Are you stupid or something? I can see the fucking round isn't even in firing position."

"Then you've just won a thousand dollars. If you pick the gun up and pull the trigger."

Swinton picked the gun up, put it to his head, and pulled the trigger. There was a click. He laid it down.

Without a word, Pendergast reached into his suit-coat pocket, pulled out a brick of one-hundred-dollar bills, and peeled off ten of them. Swinton took the money. "You're crazy, you know that?"

"Yes, I am crazy."

"Now it's your own damn turn." Swinton picked up the revolver, spun the barrel, laid it down.

"What will you give me?"

"I don't got no money, and I ain't giving you back the thousand."

"Then perhaps you'll answer a question instead. Any question I choose to ask. Absolute truth."

Swinton shrugged. "Sure."

Pendergast removed another thousand and put it on the table. Then he picked up the gun, placed it at his temple, and pulled the trigger. Another click.

"And now for the question."

"Shoot."

"Your great-great-grandfather was a miner in Roaring Fork during the silver boom days. He knew quite a bit about a series of killings, allegedly done by a man-eating grizzly bear, but in actuality done by a group of crazy miners."

He paused. Swinton had risen from his chair. "You're no damn magazine writer! Who are you?"

"I am the one who is asking you a question. Presuming that you're a man of honor, I will receive an answer. If you wish to know who I really am, that must await the next round of the game. Provided, of course, you have the fortitude to continue."

Swinton said nothing.

"Your ancestor knew more than most people about those killings. In fact, I think he knew the truth—the entire truth." Pendergast paused. "My question is: What *is* the truth?"

Swinton shifted in his chair. The expression on his face went through several rapid changes. He exposed his ferrety teeth several times, his lips twitching. This went on for a while, then at last he cleared his throat. "Why do you want to know?"

"Private curiosity."

"Who are you gonna tell?"

"Nobody."

Swinton stared hungrily at the thousand dollars sitting on the table. "You swear to that? It's been a secret in my family for a long, long time."

Pendergast nodded.

Another pause. "It started with the Committee of Seven," Swinton said at last. "My great-great-granddaddy, August Swinton, was one of them. At least, that's what was passed down." A tinge of pride edged into his voice. "As you said, those were no grizzly killings. They was done by four crazy bastards, former smelter workers, who were living wild in the mountains and had turned cannibal. A man named Shadrach Cropsey went up to track the bear and discovered it wasn't a bear at all, but these fellers living in an abandoned mine. He figured out where they were holed up and then pulled together this Committee of Seven."

"And then what happened?"

"That's a second question."

"So it is." Pendergast smiled. "Time for another round?" He picked up the revolver, spun the cylinder, and laid it down.

Swinton shook his head. "I can still see the round, and it ain't in the firing chamber. Another thousand bucks?"

Pendergast nodded.

Swinton picked up the gun and pulled the trigger again, put it down, held out his hand. "This is the dumbest damn game I ever saw."

Pendergast handed him a thousand dollars. Then he picked up the gun, spun the barrel, and without looking at it put it to his head and pulled the trigger. *Click.*

"You really are one crazy motherfucker."

"There appear to be a great many like me in this area," Pendergast replied. "And now for my question: What did Shadrach Cropsey and this Committee of Seven do then?"

"Back in those days, they handled problems the right way—they did it themselves. Fuck the law and all its bullshit. They went up there and smoked those cannibals. The way I heard it, old Shadrach got his ass killed in the fight. After that, there weren't no more 'grizzly' killings."

"And the place where they killed the miners?"

"Another question, friend."

Pendergast spun the barrel, placed it on the table. Swinton eyed it nervously. "I can't see the round."

"Then it is either in the firing chamber or in the opposite chamber, hidden by the frame. Which means there is a fifty–fifty chance you will live."

"I ain't playing."

"You just said you would. I didn't imagine you were a coward, Mr. Swinton." He reached in his pocket and pulled out the brick of hundreds. This time he peeled off twenty. "We'll double the stakes. You will receive two thousand—if you pull the trigger."

Swinton was sweating heavily. "I ain't gonna play."

"You mean, you pass on your turn? I won't insist."

"That's what I mean. I pass."

"But I do not pass on my turn."

"Go ahead. Be my fucking guest."

Pendergast spun the barrel, held the revolver up, pulled the trigger. *Click.* He put it down.

"My final question: Where did they kill the miners?"

"I don't know. But I do have the letter."

"What letter?"

"The one that got passed down to me. It sort of explains things." He rose from his creaking chair and shuffled off into the dim recesses of the cabin. He returned a moment later with a dusty old piece of yellow paper sandwiched in Mylar. He eased himself back down and handed the letter to Pendergast.

It was a handwritten note, undated, with no salutation or signature. It read:

mete at the Ideal 11 oclock Sharp to Night they are Holt Up in the closed Christmas Mine up on smugglers wall there are 4 of them bring your best Guns and lantern burn this Letter afore you set out

Pendergast lowered the letter. Swinton held out his hand, and Pendergast returned it. Swinton's brow was still beaded with sweat, but the look on his face was pure relief. "I can't believe you played that game without ever looking at the cylinder. That's just crazy-ass dangerous."

Pendergast dressed again in his coat, scarves, and hat, and then took up the revolver. He opened the cylinder and let the .44 magnum round drop into his hand. "There was never any danger. I brought this round with me and substituted it for one of yours after I unloaded the gun." He held it up. "It's been doctored."

Swinton rose. "Mother*fucker*!" He came at Pendergast, drawing his carry, but in a flash Pendergast had shoved the round back in and rotated it into firing position, pointing the Blackhawk at Swinton.

"Or maybe I *didn't* doctor it."

Swinton froze.

"You'll never know." Pendergast picked up his own Les Baer, and—while covering Swinton with it—removed the round from the Blackhawk and put it in his coat pocket. "And now I will answer your earlier question: I'm not a magazine writer. I'm a federal agent. And there's one thing I promise you: if you lied to me, I'll know it, sooner rather than later—and in that case, none of your weapons will save you."

51

That same day, at three o'clock in the afternoon, Corrie lounged in the room she had acquired at the Hotel Sebastian, wearing a terry-cloth bathrobe supplied by the hotel, first admiring the view, and then checking out the mini-bar (which she couldn't afford, but enjoyed rummaging through anyway) before moving into the marble bathroom. She turned on the shower, adjusted the water, and slipped out of the bathrobe, stepping in.

As she luxuriated in the hot shower, she considered that things were looking up. She felt badly about what happened at breakfast the day before, but even that paled in comparison with Pendergast's revelations. The Doyle story, the mercury-crazed miners—and the Stafford family connection—it was truly remarkable. *And* truly frightening. Pendergast was right: she had placed herself in grave danger.

Roaring Fork had now pretty much resumed the ghost-town status it once held, except it was all dressed up for Christmas with nowhere to go. Totally surreal. Even the press seemed to have packed up their cameras and microphones. The Hotel Sebastian had lost most of its guests and staff, but the restaurant was still going strong—stronger than ever, as those remaining in town, it seemed, all wanted to eat out. Corrie had managed to drive a hard bargain with the hotel manager, snagging room and breakfast free of charge in return for six hours of kitchen work every day. And although her arrangement with the hotel came with only one meal a day, Corrie had plenty of experience with all-you-can-eat deals and was confident she could scarf down enough food in one sitting to last twenty-four hours.

She got out of the shower, toweled off, and combed her hair. As she was drying it, she heard a knock at the door. Quickly donning the bathrobe again, she went to the door and peeked through the eyehole.

Pendergast.

She opened the door, but the agent hesitated. "I'd be glad to re-turn later—"

"Don't be silly. Sit down, I'll only be a moment." She went back into the bathroom, finished blowing out her hair, wrapped the bathrobe a little tighter, and came back out, seating herself on the sofa.

Pendergast did not look well. His usual alabaster face was mottled with red and his hair looked like it had been in a wind tunnel.

"How did it go?" Corrie asked. She knew he had gone to Leadville to see if he could trace a Swinton descendant.

Instead of answering the question, he said, "I am delighted to find you safely ensconced in the hotel. As for the cost, I'd be happy to help—"

"Not necessary, thank you," Corrie said quickly. "I managed to fi-nagle free room and board in return for a few hours of kitchen work."

"How enterprising of you." He paused, his face growing more se-rious. "I regret that you felt it necessary to deceive me. I understand from the chief that your car was shot at and your dog killed."

Corrie colored deeply. "I didn't want you to worry. I'm sorry. I was going to tell you eventually."

"You didn't want me to take you away from Roaring Fork."

"That, too. And I wanted to find the bastard who killed my dog."

"You must not attempt to find out who killed your dog. I hope you now understand you're dealing with dangerous and highly moti-vated people. This is far bigger than a dead dog—and you're intelli-gent enough to realize that."

"Of course. I understand that clearly."

"There's a development worth two hundred million dollars at stake—but this isn't just about money. It will lead to heavy criminal indictments against those involved, some of whom happen to belong to one of the wealthiest and most powerful clans in this country, beginning with your Mrs. Kermode and quite likely ending with members of the Stafford family as well. Perhaps now you can understand why they will not hesitate to kill you."

"But I want them brought to justice—"

"And they will be. But not by you, and not while you're here. When you're safely back in New York, I will bring in the Bureau and all will be exposed. So you see, there's nothing left for you to do here except pack your bags and return to New York—as soon as the weather permits."

Corrie thought about the coming storm. It would close the road again. She supposed she could start writing things up, get an outline of her thesis nailed down, before she had to leave.

"All right," she said.

"In the meantime, I want you to stay within the confines of the hotel. I've spoken to the chief of security here, an excellent woman, and you'll be safe. You may be stuck here for a few days, however. The weather forecast is dire."

"Fine with me. So...are you going to tell me about your trip to Leadville?"

"I am not."

"Why?"

"Because the knowledge would only put you in more unnecessary danger. Please allow me to handle this from now on."

Despite his kindly tone, Corrie felt irritated. She'd agreed to what he asked. She was going back to New York as soon as the weather cleared. Why couldn't he take her into his confidence? "If you insist," she said.

Pendergast rose. "I would invite you to dine with me, but I have to confer with the chief. They have made little progress on the arsonist case."

He left. Corrie thought for a moment, and then went over to the mini-bar. She was starving and had no money for food. Her breakfast deal didn't begin until the next morning. The can of Pringles was eight dollars.

Screw it, she thought as she tore off the lid.

52

Three o'clock in the morning, December twenty-fourth. After flitting like a specter past the worn shopfronts and dark windows of Old Town, Pendergast took just seconds to break into the Ideal Saloon, picking the picturesque but ineffectual nineteenth-century lock.

He stepped into the dim space of the bar-*cum*-museum, its interior illuminated only by several strips of emergency fluorescent lighting, which cast garish shadows about the room. The saloon consisted of a large, central room, with circular tables, chairs, and a plank floor. A long bar ran the entire length of the far end. The walls consisted of wainscoting of vertical beadboard, gleaming with varnish and darkened by time, below flocked velvet wallpaper in a flowery Victorian pattern. The wall was decorated with sconces of copper and cut glass. Behind the bar and to the right, a staircase led up to what had been a small whorehouse. And farther off to the right, in an alcove partly under the staircase, stood some gaming tables. Velvet ropes just inside two swinging doors created a viewing area, preventing visitors from proceeding into the restored saloon.

Moving without noise, Pendergast ducked under the ropes and took a long, thoughtful turn about the room. A whisky bottle and some shot glasses stood on the bar, and several tables were also arrayed with bottles and glasses. Behind the bar stood a large mirrored case of antique liquor bottles filled with colored water.

He moved through the bar and into the gaming area. A poker table stood in one corner, covered with green felt, with hands of five-card stud laid out: four aces against a straight flush. A blackjack table, also artfully arranged with cards, stood beside a splendid antique roulette wheel with ivory, red jasper, and ebony inlay.

Pendergast glided past the gaming area to a door under the stairs. He tried to open it, found it locked, and swiftly picked the lock.

It opened into a small, dusty room, which remained unrestored, with cracked plaster walls and peeling wallpaper, some old chairs, and a broken table. Graffiti, some bearing dates from the 1930s, when Roaring Fork was still a ghost town, were scratched into the wall. A pile of broken whisky bottles lay in one corner. At the back of this room stood a door that led, Pendergast knew, to a rear exit.

He took off his coat and scarf and carefully draped them over one of the chairs, and looked around, slowly and carefully, as if committing everything to memory. He stood, quite still, for a long time, and then finally he stirred. Choosing a vacant spot on the floor, he lay down on the dirty boards and folded his hands over his chest, like a corpse in a coffin. Slowly, very slowly, he closed his eyes. In the silence, he focused on the sounds of the snowstorm: the muffled wind shaking and moaning about the exterior walls, the creaking of the wood, the rattling of the tin roof. The air smelled of dust, dry rot, and mildew. He allowed his respiration and pulse to slow and his mind to relax.

It was in this back room, he felt certain, that the Committee of Seven would have met up. But before he went down that avenue, there was another place he wished to visit first—a visit that would take place entirely within his mind.

Pendergast had once spent time in a remote Tibetan monastery, studying an esoteric meditative discipline known as Chongg Ran. It was one of the least known of the Tibetan mind techniques. The teachings were never put down in writing, and they could only be transmitted directly teacher-to-pupil.

Pendergast had taken the heart of Chongg Ran and combined it with several other mental disciplines, including the concept of a memory palace as described in a sixteenth-century Italian manuscript by Giordano Bruno titled *Ars Memoria*, Art of Memory. The result was a unique and highly complex form of mental visualization. With training, careful preparation, and a fanatical degree of intellectual discipline, the exercise allowed him to take a complex problem with many thousands of facts and surmises, and mentally stitch them together into a coherent narrative, which could then be processed, analyzed—and, especially, *experienced*. Pendergast used the technique to help solve elusive problems; to visualize places, via the force of his intellect, that could not be reached physically—far distant places, or even places in the past. The technique was extremely draining, however, and he employed it sparingly.

He lay for many minutes, as still as a corpse, first arranging a hugely complex set of facts into careful order, then tuning his senses to the surrounding environment while simultaneously shutting down the voice in his mind, turning off that incessant running commentary all people carry in their heads. The voice had been especially voluble of late, and it took a great deal of effort to silence it; Pendergast was forced to move his meditative stance from the Third Level to the Fourth Level, doing complex equations in his head, playing four hands of bridge simultaneously. At last, the voice was silenced, and he then began the ancient steps of Chongg Ran itself. First, he blocked every sound, every sensation, one after another: the creaking of the building, the rustling of the wind, the scent of dust, the hard floor beneath him, the seeming infinitude of his own corporal awareness—until at length he arrived at the state of *stong pa nyid*: the condition of Pure Emptiness. For a moment, there was only nonexistence; even time itself seemed to fall away.

But then—slowly, very slowly—something began to materialize out of the nothingness. At first it was as miniaturized, as delicate, as beautiful as a Fabergé egg. With that same lack of hurry, it grew larger and clearer. Eyes still shut, Pendergast allowed it to take on form and definition around him. And then, at last, he opened his eyes to find himself within a brightly lit space: a splendid and elegant dining room, refulgent with light and crystal, the clinking of glasses, and the murmur of genteel conversation.

To the smell of cigar smoke and the learned discourse of a string quartet, Pendergast took in the opulent room. His eyes traveled over the tables, finally stopping at one in a far corner. Seated at it were four gentlemen. Two of the men were laughing together over some witticism or other—one wearing a broadcloth frock coat, the other in evening dress. Pendergast, however, was more interested in the other two diners. One was dressed flamboyantly: white kid gloves, a vest and cutaway coat of black velvet, a large frilled necktie, silk knee breeches and stockings, slippers adorned with grosgrain bows. An orchid drooped in his buttonhole. He was in deep descant, speaking animatedly, one hand pressed against his breast, the other pointing heavenward, index finger extended in a travesty of John the Baptist. The man beside him, who seemed to be hanging on his companion's every word, presented an entirely different appearance, a contrast so strong as to almost be comical. He was a stocky fellow in a somber, sensible English suit, with big mustaches and an awkward bearing.

They were Oscar Wilde and Arthur Conan Doyle.

Slowly, in his mind, Pendergast approached the table, listening intently, as the conversation—or, more frequently, monologue—became audible.

"Indeed?" Wilde was saying, in a remarkably deep and sonorous voice. "Did you think that—as one who would happily sacrifice himself on the pyre of aestheticism—I do not recognize the face of horror when I stare into it?"

There was no empty seat. Pendergast turned, motioned to a waiter, indicated the table. Immediately, the man brought up a fifth chair, placing it between Conan Doyle and the man Pendergast realized must be Joseph Stoddart.

"I was once told a story so dreadful, so distressing in its particulars and in the extent of its evil, that now I truly believe nothing I hear could ever frighten me again."

"How interesting."

"Would you care to hear it? It is not for the faint of heart."

As he listened to the conversation taking place beside him, Pendergast reached forward, poured himself a glass of wine, found it excellent.

"It was told to me during my lecture tour of America a few years back. On my way to San Francisco, I stopped at a rather squalid yet picturesque mining camp known as Roaring Fork." Wilde pressed his hand to Doyle's knee for emphasis. "After my lecture, one of the miners approached me, an elderly chap somewhat the worse—or, perhaps, the better—for drink. He took me aside, said he'd enjoyed my story so much that he had one of his own to share with me." He paused for a sip of burgundy. "Here, lean in a little closer, that's a good fellow, and I'll tell it you exactly as it was told to me."

Doyle leaned in, as requested. Pendergast leaned in, as well.

"I tried to escape him, but he would have none of it, presuming to approach me in a most familiar way, breathing fumes of the local *ubriacant*. My first impulse was to push past, but there was something about the look in his eye that stopped me. I confess I was also intrigued—in an anthropological fashion, Doyle, don't you know—by this leathern specimen, this uncouth bard, this bibulous miner, and I found myself curious as to what he considered a 'good story.' And so I listened, and rather attentively, as his American drawl was nigh indecipherable. He spoke of events that had occurred some years earlier, not long after the silver strikes that established Roaring Fork. Over the course of one summer, a grizzled bear—or so it was believed—had taken to roaming the mountains above the town, attacking, killing...*and* eating...lone miners working their claims."

Doyle nodded vigorously, his face concentrated with the utmost interest.

"Naturally, the town fell into a state of perfect terror. But the killings went on, as there were many lone men upon the mountain. The bear was merciless, ambuscading the miners outside their cabins, killing and savagely dismembering them—and then feasting upon their flesh." Wilde paused. "I should have liked to have known whether the, ah, *consumption* commenced while consciousness was still present. Can you imagine what it would be like to be devoured alive by a savage beast? To watch it tear your flesh off, then chew and swallow, with evident satisfaction? That is a contemplation never even considered by Huysmans in his *À Rebours*. How sadly lacking the aesthete was, in hindsight!"

Wilde glanced over to see what effect his words were having on the country doctor. Doyle had grasped his glass of claret and taken a deep draught. Listening, Pendergast took a sip of his own glass, then signaled a waiter to bring him a menu.

"Many a fellow tried to track the grizzled bear," Wilde continued, "but none was successful—save for one miner, a man who had learned the fine art of tracking while living among Indians. He conceived a notion that the killings were not the work of a bear."

"Not the work of a bear, sir?"

"Not the work of a bear, sir. And so, waiting until the next killing, this chap—his name was Cropsey—went a-tracking, and soon discovered that the perpetrators of this outrage were a group of men."

At this, Doyle leaned back rather abruptly. "I beg your pardon, Mr. Wilde. Do you mean to say that these men were...cannibals?"

"Indeed I do. American cannibals."

Doyle shook his head. "Monstrous. Monstrous."

"Quite so," Wilde said. "They have none of the good manners of your English cannibals."

Doyle stared at his fellow guest in shock. "This is no matter for levity, Wilde."

"Perhaps not. We shall see. In any case, our Cropsey tracked these cannibals to their lair, an abandoned mine shaft somewhere on the mountain, at a place called Smuggler's Wall. There was no constabulary in the town, of course, and so this fellow organized a small group of local vigilantes. They cognominated themselves the Committee of Seven. They would scale the mountain in the dark of night, surprise the cannibals, and administer the rough justice of the American West." Wilde toyed with his *boutonnière*. "The very next night, at midnight, this group gathered at the local saloon to discuss strategy and no doubt fortify themselves for the coming ordeal. They then departed by a back door, heavily armed, and equipped with lanterns, rope, and a torch. This, my dear Doyle, is where the story turns...well, not to put too fine a point on it, rather ghastly. Do steady yourself, there's a good chap."

The waiter brought over a menu, and Pendergast turned his attention to it. Three or four minutes later, he was jarred from his perusal by Doyle's sudden violent rise from the table—knocking his chair over in his agitation—and subsequent flight from the dining room, his face a mixture of shock and disgust.

"Why, whatever's the matter?" Stoddart said, frowning, as Doyle disappeared in the direction of the gentlemen's lounge.

"I suspect it must be the prawns," Wilde replied, and he dabbed primly at his mouth with a napkin...

...As slowly as it had come, the voice began to fade from Pendergast's mind. The sumptuous interior of the Langham Hotel began to waver, as if dissolving into mist and darkness. Slowly, slowly, a new scene materialized—a very different scene. It was the smoke-filled, whisky-redolent back room of a busy saloon, the sounds of gambling, drinking, and argument penetrating the thin wooden walls. A back room, in fact, remarkably similar to the one in which Pendergast was—in the Roaring Fork of the present—currently situated. After a brief exchange of determined voices, a group of seven men rose from a large table: men carrying lanterns and guns. Following their leader, one Shadrach Cropsey, they made their way out the back door of the little room and into the night.

Pendergast followed them, his incorporeal presence hovering in the cool night air like a ghost.

53

The group of miners walked down the dirt main street of town, casually and without hurry, until they reached the far end, where settlement ceased and the forests mounted upward into the mountains. It was a moonless night. The scent of wood fires was in the air, and in the nearby corrals, horses were moving restlessly about. Silently, the group lit their lanterns and proceeded along a rough mining road, which made its way by switchbacks up, and then farther up, passing beneath the dark fir trees.

The night was cool and the sky was pricked with stars. A lone wolf howled somewhere in the great bowl of mountains, quickly answered by another. As the men gained altitude, the fir trees grew smaller, shorter, twisted into grotesque shapes by incessant winds and deep snows. Gradually the trees thinned out into matted thickets of krummholz, and then the cart path broached the tree line.

In his mind, Pendergast followed the group.

The line of yellow lanterns advanced up the barren, rock-strewn slopes approaching Smuggler's Cirque. They were now entering a recently abandoned mining zone, and around the men appeared ghostly tailings, like pyramids, spilling down the sides of the ridge, the gaping holes of the mines above, punctuated by rickety ore chutes, trestles, sluice boxes, and flumes.

Looming in the darkness to the right was an immense wooden

structure, set into the flat declivity at the base of Smuggler's Cirque: the main entrance to the famed Sally Goodin Mine, still in operation now, in the early fall of 1876. The building housed the machines and pulley works used to raise and lower the cages and buckets; it also enclosed the two-hundred-ton Ireland Pump Engine, capable of pumping over a thousand gallons per minute, used to dewater the mine complex.

Now all the lanterns went out but one: a red-glass lamp that cast a bloody gleam in the murky night. The cart path divided into many winding tracks cut into the hillsides rising above the cirque. Their objective lay above, the highest of the abandoned tunnels high on the slope known as Smuggler's Wall, situated at an altitude close to thirteen thousand feet. A single track led in that direction, carved by hand out of the scree, switchbacking sharply as it climbed. It came over a ridge and skirted a small glacial tarn, the water black and still, its shore dotted with rusted pumping machinery and old flume gates.

Still the group of seven men climbed upward. Now the dark, square hole of the Christmas Mine became visible in the faint starlight against the upper scree slope. A trestle ran from the hole, and below it stood a tailings pile of lighter color. A jumble of wrecked machinery was strewn about the slope below.

The group paused, and Pendergast heard a low murmur of voices. And then they silently divided. One man made his way up, hiding among boulders above the entrance. A second took up a covered position among the scree just below the entrance.

Lookouts in place, the rest—four men led by Cropsey, now holding the lantern himself—entered the abandoned tunnel. Pendergast followed. The shutter on the red lamp was adjusted to produce only the faintest glow. Arms at the ready, the men walked single-file along the iron rails leading into the tunnel, making no noise. One carried a torch of pitch, ready to be lit.

As they proceeded, a smell came toward them, a smell that became ever more awful in the hot, moist, stifling atmosphere.

The Christmas Mine tunnel opened into a crosscut: a horizontal tunnel driven at right angles to the main tunnel. The group paused before the crosscut and readied their weapons. The torch was lowered, a match was struck, and the pitch set afire. In that moment, the men rounded the corner, weapons aimed down the tunnel. The smell was now almost overwhelming.

Silence. The flickering flames disclosed something in the darkness at the end of the tunnel. The group cautiously moved forward. It was an irregular, lumpy shape. When they drew close, the men saw that it was a heap of soft things: rotting burlap, old gunnysacks, leaves and pine needles, chunks of moss. Mingled into the material were pieces of gnawed bone, broken skulls, and strips of what looked like dried rawhide.

Skin. Hairless skin.

All around the heap lay a broad ring of human feces.

One of the men spoke hoarsely. "What... *is this?*"

The question was initially answered with silence. Finally, one of the others replied. "It's an animal den."

"It ain't *animal*," said Cropsey.

"God Almighty."

"Where are they?"

Now their voices were rising, echoing, as fear and uncertainty began to set in.

"The bastards must be out. Killing."

The torch sputtered and burned as their voices rose, discussing what to do. The guns were put away. There was disagreement, conflict.

Suddenly Cropsey held up his hand. The others fell silent, listening. There were sounds of shuffling, along with guttural, animalistic breathing. The noises stopped. Quickly the man carrying the torch doused it in a puddle of water, while Cropsey shut the lantern down. But now all was deathly silent: it seemed likely the killers had seen the light or heard their voices—and knew they were here.

"Give us some light, for Jesus's sake," whispered one of the men, his voice tight with anxiety.

Cropsey opened the lantern a fraction. The others were crouching, rifles and pistols at the ready. The dim glow barely penetrated the gloom.

"*More* light," someone said.

The lantern now threw light to the edge of the cross tunnel. All was silent. They waited, but nothing came around the corner. Nor were there sounds of flight.

"We go get 'em," Cropsey announced. "Afore they get away."

No one moved. Finally Cropsey himself began stalking forward. The others followed. He crept to the crosscut. The rest waited behind. Holding up the lantern, he paused, crouched, then suddenly swung around the corner, wielding the rifle like a pistol in one hand, the lantern in the other. "*Now!*"

It happened with incredible speed. A flash of something darting forward; a gargling scream; and then Cropsey spun around, dropping his rifle and writhing in agony. A naked, filthy man was astride his back, tearing at his throat, more like a beast than a human being. None of the other four could fire; the combatants were too close together. Cropsey screamed again, staggering about, trying to shake off the man who tore at him with nails and teeth, ripping away anything he could reach: ears, lips, nose; there was a sudden spurt of arterial blood from the neck and Cropsey went down, the monster still on top of him, the lantern falling to the ground and shattering.

Simultaneously, as with a single mind, the other four began to shoot, aiming wildly into the darkness. From the muzzle flashes more figures could be seen, bellowing like bulls, running toward them from around the corner of the crosscut, a melee amid the wild eruption of gunfire. The two lookouts came charging down the tunnel, aroused by the din, and joined in with their own weapons. The guns roared again and again, the flashes of light blooming within clouds of ugly gray smoke—and then all went silent. For a moment, there was only darkness. Then came the sound of a match, scraping against rock; another lantern was lit—and its feeble light illuminated a splay of corpses, the four cannibals now just ruined bodies scattered about the tunnel, taken apart by heavy-caliber bullets, lying like so much ropy waste atop the sundered carcass of Shadrach Cropsey.

It was over.

Fifteen minutes later, Pendergast opened his eyes. The room was cool and quiet. He rose, brushed off his black suit, bundled himself up, and let himself out the back door of the saloon. The storm was in full blast, the fury of it thundering down Main Street and shaking the Christmas decorations like so many cobwebs. Bundling his coat around himself, wrapping his scarf tighter, and lowering his head against the wind, he made his way through the storm-shaken town back to his hotel.

54

At eleven o'clock that morning—Christmas Eve day—after buttering two hundred pieces of toast, washing twice that number of dishes, and mopping the kitchen from wall to wall—Corrie went back to her room, bundled up in her coat, and ventured out into the storm. The idea that Kermode or her thugs might be out in this weather, waiting for her, seemed far-fetched; nevertheless, she felt an electric tickle of fear. She consoled herself with the thought that she was on her way to the safest place in town—the police station.

She had decided to confront Pendergast. Not so much confront him, exactly, but rather to make another pitch about why he should share with her the information he'd apparently gotten on his trip to Leadville. The way she saw things, it was unfair of him to withhold it. She had, after all, discovered the Swinton connection and shared the name with him. If he'd found information about the old killings, the least he could do would be to let her include it in her thesis.

The wind and flying snow came buffeting down the street as she turned onto Main. She leaned into it, holding her cap. The business district of Roaring Fork was relatively compact, but even so it proved a damn long journey in a blizzard.

The police station loomed up through the blowing snow, its windows glowing with yellow light, perversely inviting. All were apparently at work despite the storm. She walked up the steps, stomped off the snow in the vestibule, shook out her woolen hat and scarf, and went in.

"Is Special Agent Pendergast in?" she asked Iris, the lady at the reception desk, with whom she had gotten friendly over the past ten days.

"Oh, dear," she sighed. "He doesn't sign in and out, and he keeps the oddest hours. I just can't keep track." She shook her head. "Feel free to check his office."

Corrie went down into the basement, grateful for once for the heat. His door was closed. She knocked; no answer.

Where could he be, in a storm like this? Not at the Hotel Sebastian, where he hadn't been answering his phone.

She turned the handle, but it was locked.

She paused for a moment, thoughtfully, still grasping the handle. Then she went back upstairs.

"Find him?" Iris asked.

"No luck," said Corrie. She hesitated. "Listen, I think I left something important in his office. Do you have a key?"

Iris considered this. "Well, I do, but I don't think I can let you in. What did you leave?"

"My cell phone."

"Oh." Iris thought some more. "I suppose I *could* let you in, so long as I stay with you."

"That would be great."

She followed Iris back down the stairs. In a moment the woman had opened the door and turned on the light. The room was hot and stuffy. Corrie looked around. The desk was covered with papers that had been carefully arranged. She scanned the surface with her eyes but it was all too neat, too squared away, to expose much information.

"I don't see it," said Iris, looking about.

"He might have put it away in a drawer."

"I don't think you should be opening up any drawers, Corrie."

"Right. Of course not."

She looked frantically around the desk, this way and that. "It's got to be here somewhere," she said.

And then Corrie caught a glimpse of something interesting. A page torn out of a small notebook, covered with Pendergast's distinctive copperplate handwriting, its top part sticking out of a sheaf of documents. Three underlined words jumped out: *Swinton* and *Christmas Mine*.

"Is it over here?" Corrie bent over the desk, as if looking behind a lamp, while "accidentally" pushing the notebooks with her elbow, exposing a few more lines of the torn page, on which Pendergast had printed:

mete at the Ideal 11 oclock Sharp to Night they are Holt Up in the closed Christmas Mine up on smugglers wall there are 4 of

"*Really*, Corrie, it's time to go," Iris said firmly, with a frown on her lips at noticing Corrie reading something on the desk.

"Okay. I'm sorry. Now, where *did* I leave that darn phone?"

Back at the hotel, Corrie quickly wrote out the lines from memory, then stared at them thoughtfully. It seemed obvious Pendergast had copied a note or old document that mentioned the place where the attack on the cannibals would take place: the Christmas Mine. In the Griswell Mansion, she had seen a number of maps of the mining district, with each mine and tunnel marked and identified. It would be simple to find the location, and maybe even the layout, of this Christmas Mine.

This was interesting. This changed everything. She'd suspected the mercury-crazed miners had been hiding in some abandoned mine. If they were killed in a tunnel or shaft, their remains could still be there somewhere.

The Christmas Mine . . . if she recovered a few bone and hair samples from the remains, she could have them tested for mercury poisoning. Such a test was cheap and easy; you could even send away for a home kit. And if the tests were positive, it would be the final feather in her cap. She would have definitely solved the old murders and established a most unusual motivation.

She thought about her promise to Pendergast—to stay in the hotel, to abandon any attempt to find the person who'd shot at her and decapitated her dog. Well, she *had* abandoned the attempt. Pendergast shouldn't have withheld information from her—especially information of such crucial importance to her thesis.

She glanced out the window. The blizzard was still going strong. Since it was getting on toward Christmas Eve, everything was closed, and the town was almost completely deserted. Right now would be a perfect time to pay a little visit to the archives in the Griswell Mansion.

Corrie paused for a moment, then pocketed her small set of lock picks. The Griswell place would most likely have a period lock—no challenge at all.

Once again she bundled up and ventured out into the storm. Encouragingly, nobody except the snowplows was out and about as she made her way through the deserted streets. Some of the Christmas decorations, evergreen garlands and ribbons, had blown loose in the wind and were flapping and swinging forlornly from lampposts and street banners. Strings of bulbs had also come loose and were sputtering erratically. She couldn't see the outline of the mountains, but she could still hear, muffled by the snow, the hum and rumble of the lifts, which had been kept running despite all that had happened and the almost complete absence of skiers. Perhaps skiing was such an ingrained part of Roaring Fork culture that the lifts and snow-grooming equipment simply never stopped operating.

As she turned the corner of East Haddam, she suddenly had the impression someone was behind her. She spun around and peered into the murk, but could see nothing except swirling snow. She hesitated. It might have been a passerby, or perhaps her imagination. Still, Pendergast's warning echoed in her mind.

There was one way to check. She retraced her steps—still quite visible in the snow. And indeed: there were additional footprints. The footprints had apparently been tracing hers, but they had suddenly veered away and gone off into a private alley—at just about the point where she had spun around.

Corrie suddenly found her heart beating hard. Okay, someone *was* following her. Maybe. Was it the thug who'd been trying to drive her out of town? Of course it might also be coincidence, paired with her justified sense of paranoia.

"Screw this," she said out loud, turned back, and hurried down the street. Another corner and she found herself in front of the Griswell Mansion. The lock, as she figured, was old. It would be a simple matter to get inside.

But was the place alarmed?

A gust of wind buffeted her as she peered inside the door panes for signs of an alarm system. She couldn't see anything obvious like infrared sensors or motion detectors mounted in the corners; nor was the building posted with an alarm warning. The place had an air about it of neglect and penny pinching. Maybe no one felt the piles of paper inside had any value or needed to be protected.

Even if the place *was* alarmed, and she set it off, were the police really going to respond? Right now they had bigger fish to fry. And in a storm like this, with high winds, falling branches, and ice, alarms were probably going off all over town.

Looking around, she removed her gloves and quickly picked the lock. She slipped inside, shut the door, took a deep breath. No alarm, no blinking lights, nothing. Just the shudder of the wind and snow outside.

She rubbed her hands together to warm them. This was going to be a piece of cake.

55

Half an hour later, hunched over a pile of papers in a dim back room, Corrie had found what she needed. An old map showed her the location and layout of the Christmas Mine. According to the information she had dug up, the mine was a bust, one of the first to become played out and be abandoned, way back in 1875, and as far as she could tell never again reopened. That was probably why the crazed miners had used it as a home base.

She took another, more careful, look at the map. While the mine was high up on Smuggler's Wall, at nearly thirteen thousand feet in altitude, it was readily accessible by the web of old mining roads on the mountain, now used by four-wheelers in the summer and snowmobilers in the winter. The mine stood above a well-known complex of old structures situated in a natural bowl known as Smuggler's Cirque, which was a popular tourist destination in the summertime. One of the buildings, by far the tallest, was famous for holding the remains of the Ireland Pump Engine, supposedly the largest pump in the world when it was constructed, which had been used to dewater the mines as the shafts were dug below the water table.

The Christmas Mine would surely be sealed—all the old mines and tunnels in Roaring Fork, Corrie had learned, had been bricked up or, in some cases, plated with iron. The mine might be difficult or even impossible to break into, especially considering the snow. But it was worth a try. She had every reason to believe the remains of the cannibals would still be there, perhaps secreted away someplace by the vigilantes who killed them.

As she looked over the papers, maps, and diagrams, she realized that—quite subconsciously—a plan had already formed in her mind. She'd go up to the mine, locate the bodies, and take her samples. And she'd do it now—while the routes out of town were still impassable, and before Pendergast could force her to return to New York.

But how to get up there, way up the side of a mountain in a furious storm? Even as she posed the question, she realized the answer. There were snowmobiles up at the ski shed. She would simply go up to The Heights, borrow a snowmobile...and pay a quick visit to the old Christmas Mine.

And now really was the perfect time: Christmas Eve day, when ninety percent of the town had left and everyone else was hunkered down at home. Even if somebody *was* tailing her, they'd never follow her to the mine—not in weather like this. Just a brief reconnaissance up to the mountain and back...and then she'd hole up in the hotel until she could make arrangements to leave town.

It occurred to her that it wasn't just Kermode's thugs she should be aware of, but the weather as well. If anybody else would be crazy going out in this storm, then wasn't she acting a little crazy, too? She told herself she'd take it one step at a time. If the storm got too bad, or if she felt she was getting into a situation she couldn't handle, she'd abandon the recon and head back.

Pocketing the old map of the mine and another map of the overall mining district showing all the connecting tunnels, she made her way back to the Hotel Sebastian, keeping an eye out for the suspected stalker but seeing no sign. In her room she began to prepare for the task ahead. She packed her backpack with a small water bottle, sampling bags, headlamp with extra batteries, extra gloves and socks, matches, canteen, Mars Bars and Reese's Pieces, her lock-picking tools, a knife, Mace (which she carried everywhere), and her cell phone. She took another look at the Christmas Mine map she'd liberated from the archives, noting with satisfaction that the underground courses of the tunnels were clearly delineated.

The hotel concierge was able to provide—most useful of all—a snowmobile route map of the surrounding mountains. She also managed to "borrow" from hotel maintenance a claw hammer, bolt cutter, and wrecking bar.

She bundled up, loaded her car, and headed down Main Street in the storm, windshield wipers slapping. The snow was lightening a bit, the wind dropping. The snowplows were still out in force—snow clearing was amazingly efficient in this town—but even so the storm had gotten ahead of the clearing and there were three to four inches of snow on most of the roads. Nevertheless, the Ford Explorer handled well. As she approached The Heights, she rehearsed what she would say to the guard on duty; but when she actually arrived at the gate she found it open and the guardhouse empty. And why not? The workers would want to be home on Christmas Eve—and who in their right mind would be out in this storm anyway?

The heated road beyond was not bad, even though the snow was overwhelming the ability of the heating system to keep up. She almost got stuck a few times. But she shifted into 4L and managed to keep going. At least on the way out it would be mostly downhill.

The clubhouse came into view through the blowing snow, its lights on, the big plate-glass windows casting an inviting yellow glow. But the parking lot was empty, and Corrie pulled up close to the side of the building, got out of the car. In a storm like this, she doubted anyone would be inside. Nevertheless, she didn't want any prying eyes observing her taking one of the snowmobiles from the ski shed. After stamping and brushing the snow off herself, she walked around to the front and tried the door.

Locked.

She peered in the little row of panes to the right of the door. Inside, the place was lit up and festooned with decorations. A gas fire burned merrily in a fireplace. But nobody could be seen.

Just to be safe, she walked around the rest of the building, staring through windows, the wind, though abating, still crying in her ears. It was the work of five slow, careful minutes to satisfy herself that there was no one home.

She headed back to the side of the building, ready to continue up toward the ski shed. As she walked across the parking lot, she noticed that the snow had almost ceased. The unpaved road leading to the shed would still be passable. She got into the Explorer, started the engine. Everything was going her way. She'd have her pick of snowmobiles to choose from...and she still had the key to the shed padlock.

But then, as she was pulling around the circular driveway to the clubhouse and back toward the main, heated road, she noticed a second set of tire tracks in the snow, lying on top of hers.

56

Coincidence? It was certainly possible. Corrie told herself that the tracks might be from someone in the development—after all, there were dozens of houses up there. Perhaps it was just some resident, hurrying home before the storm got worse. On the other hand, she'd been followed earlier, back in town. And why had the car pulled in to the parking lot? She felt a surge of apprehension and looked around, but there were no other vehicles in sight. She glanced at her watch: two o'clock. Three hours of daylight left.

The Explorer fishtailed up the road, Corrie gunning its engine. She skidded around the last bend and pulled the car up to the fence surrounding the shed. The snow had slacked off even further, but looking up she could see thick gray clouds that promised more on the way.

Keeping the car running, she double-checked her backpack—all was there, in good order. She didn't have a snowmobile suit, but had put on practically all her layers of winter clothes, along with two pairs of gloves, a balaclava, and heavy Sorel snow boots.

She got out of the car and hefted the heavy backpack, slinging it over one shoulder. It was strangely still. Everything was bathed in a cold, gray light; the air was frosty, her breath condensing. It smelled like evergreens. The tree boughs were laden with snow and drooping, the roofline of the shed piled deep, the rows of icicles dull and cold in the half light.

She unlocked the padlock with her key and entered the shed, turning on the light. The snowmobiles were all there, neatly lined up, keys in the ignitions, helmets hung on a nearby pegboard. She walked down the line, looking them over, checking the gas gauges. While she had never driven a snowmobile, as a teenager back in Kansas she had spent a fair amount of time on dirt bikes, and the snowmobiles seemed to work the same way, with the throttle on the right handlebar and the brake on the left. It looked straightforward enough. She picked out the cleanest-looking one, made sure it had a full tank of gas, selected a helmet, and stowed her backpack in the under-seat storage compartment.

Stepping over to the main door of the shed, she unlocked it from the inside and slid it open with difficulty. Snow piled up against the door avalanched inside. Starting the snowmobile, she sat on the seat and looked over the controls, throttle, brakes, and shift, then turned the lights on and off a few times.

Despite the fear and anxiety that gnawed at her, she couldn't help but feel a sense of excitement welling up. She should be looking at this as a sort of adventure. If someone was following her, would they follow her up the mountain? It seemed unlikely.

She put on the helmet and gave the machine a little gas, edging it cautiously through the doorway. Once outside she tried to shut the shed door, but the snow that had fallen inside prevented it from sliding.

It occurred to her that she was, in fact, stealing a snowmobile, which was probably a felony. But with the holiday, the snowstorm, and the police occupied with the arsonist, the chances of getting caught seemed nil. According to the map, the Christmas Mine entrance was about three miles away, up old mining roads that were now established snowmobile trails. If she proceeded cautiously, she could be there in, say, ten to fifteen minutes. Of course, a lot of things could go wrong. Maybe she wouldn't be able to break into the tunnel, or would find it caved in; perhaps the remains would have been buried or hidden. Or—God forbid—she might find Pendergast there ahead of her. After all, she'd indirectly learned the location from him.

But at least she'd feel she'd done her best. Regardless, she could be up and back in less than an hour.

She took a long look at her maps, trying to memorize the route, then tucked them into the glove box below the small windshield. She eased the machine farther into the snow, where it began to sink alarmingly. With a little more gas, however, it rode higher and more securely. Gingerly goosing the throttle, she accelerated up the service road that, according to her map, joined the network of snowmobile trails into the mountains, eventually leading to the old mining road that would take her to Smuggler's Cirque and the mine entrance above.

Pretty soon she had the feel of the controls and was moving at a good clip, twenty miles per hour, the machine throwing up a wake of snow behind. It was unexpectedly exhilarating, flashing through the spruce trees, the frosty air rushing by, magnificent mountain peaks all around. She was plenty warm in her many layers.

As she attained the ridge, she came to the main snowmobile trail, conveniently marked with a sign. The heavy snow had obliterated any snowmobile tracks that might have been there, but the road cut itself was clearly visible as it went up Maroon Ridge, marked by tall posts with Day-Glo orange cards.

She continued on. As the altitude increased, the trees became smaller and stunted, some mere lumps of snow—and then, quite suddenly, she emerged above the tree line. She stopped to check her map—all good. The views were outstanding: Roaring Fork itself was spread out in the valley below, a miniature village, doll-like, cloaked in white. To her left, the ski area rose into the mountains in ribbons of white trails. The lifts were still running, but only the most hard-core skiers seemed to be out. Behind her stood the awe-inspiring peaks of the Continental Divide, fourteen thousand feet high.

According to the map, she was already halfway to the area of old mining buildings in the cirque.

She suddenly heard a distant buzzing sound coming up from below and halted to listen better. It was a snowmobile engine. Looking back down the route she had come up, she caught a glimpse of a black dot coming around one of the hairpin turns of the trail before vanishing into the trees.

She felt a wave of panic. Someone *was* following her. Or could it be just another snowmobiler? No—coincidence was one thing, but this was the third time that day she'd had the feeling she was being followed. It *had* to be the stalker—Kermode's hired thug, she was certain, the person who had menaced her, killed her dog. At the thought a fresh surge of fear swept over her. This wasn't an adventure. This was sheer foolhardiness: she'd placed herself in a vulnerable position, alone on the mountain, far from help.

She immediately took out her cell phone. No service.

The sound of the engine grew rapidly. She didn't have much time.

Her mind raced. She couldn't turn around and go back—there was only one trail down, unless she went straight down the almost vertical ridge. She couldn't pull off the trail and hide—the machine made such obvious tracks. And the snow was too deep for her to abandon the snowmobile and go on foot.

It began to sink in that she had put herself in real trouble. The best thing, she decided, would be to continue on up to the mine, break in if she could, and get away from the stalker in there. She had a map of the Christmas Mine and he surely did not.

Even as she started up the trail again, she saw the snowmobile come around the final bend before the tree line, accelerating toward her.

Goosing the throttle, she tore up the trail, notching the snowmobile up to thirty miles an hour, then thirty-five, then forty. The machine practically flew, an almost sheer cliff to one side of the trail, on the other a steep wall of snow. In another five minutes the trail came over the lip of a hanging valley and she found herself in the old mining complex, nestled in the broad hollow marked on the map as Smuggler's Cirque: surrounded by high ridges, with derelict mining buildings scattered about, their sagging rooflines mantled with snow, some mere piles of broken boards. She paused briefly to orient herself with the map. The Christmas Mine was higher still, on a steep slope halfway up the mountainside, directly above the old buildings. Smuggler's Wall. Map in hand, she squinted upward in the gray light, locating the entrance. The official snowmobile trail ended here, but the map showed an old mining road, still extant, that led up to the mine. As she looked at the steep wall of the cirque she made out the road cut, switchbacking up in a series of terrifying hairpin turns, with heavy drifts of snow lying across it.

Again, she could hear the snowmobile closing in behind her.

Stuffing away the map, she gunned the engine, riding past the old buildings and heading for the far side of the bowl, where the slope climbed upward again. She was surprised to see fresh snowmobile tracks among the buildings, somewhat snowed over but clearly made earlier in the day.

She reached the base of the road cut. This was going to be scary. But even as she contemplated the almost vertical wall above her, the sound of the pursuing snowmobile grew louder and she turned to see it coming over the rim of the cirque, not half a mile away.

Revving the throttle, she started up the trail, keeping as much to the inside edge as she could, blasting through drifts and fins of snow. The first hairpin turn was so steep and narrow, it just about stopped her heart. As she crawled around it, decelerating sharply, she almost became stuck in a drift and her efforts to get loose sent snow cascading down in a plume, the snowmobile tipping. She gunned it hard, spewing snow, and just managed to get back on the track. She paused, breathing hard, terrified by the yawning white space below her. It occurred to her that the avalanche danger on this steep slope must be high. She could see her pursuer was now riding through the old mining complex, following in her tracks. He was close enough for her to see the rifle slung over his shoulder.

She realized she had allowed herself to become cornered on the mountain. The road ended at the mine, and there was nothing but vertical cliffs above. And a killer below.

She made it past another half a dozen terrifying turns, driving recklessly through the deep snow, not letting the machine stop and settle. She finally reached the entrance to the Christmas Mine, marked by a rickety trestle and a square opening of massive, rotten timbers. She pulled the snowmobile right up to the opening, tore off her helmet, pulled up the seat, and hauled out her backpack. As soon as the engine was off she could hear the roar of the other snowmobile, much closer.

The door was set back into the tunnel about ten feet, which meant it was not drifted up with snow. The entrance had a rusted door set into a plate of riveted steel, deeply pitted by age, fixed with a heavy, ancient padlock.

The engine sound got louder. Corrie began to panic. She stripped off her gloves, grabbed her lock-pick tools, and tried to insert a bump key, but it was immediately apparent the lock was frozen with rust and unpickable. Even as she fumbled around she could hear the approaching roar of the snowmobile.

She grabbed the bolt cutters from her pack, but they were not heavy enough for the jaws to fit over the thick bar of the lock. They did, however, fit partway across the hasp. She jammed the jaws of the cutter over the hasp and drew down hard, the jaws closing with much effort. Taking the hammer, she gave the partially cut hasp a tremendous blow, then another, bending it enough for her to cut it the rest of the way through. Even so, everything was so solid with rust she had to pound the pieces with the hammer to shake them loose.

She threw herself against the iron door but it hardly budged, letting out a great screech of protesting metal.

The approaching snowmobile engine gave a sudden roar; she saw a flurry of snow; and then it appeared at the mouth of the mine, driven by a man in a black helmet and puffy snowsuit. He rose from the machine, undoing his helmet and unshipping his rifle at the same time.

With an involuntary cry she threw herself against the door, almost dislocating her shoulder in the process, and with a loud *scree* it budged open just enough for her to squeeze through. Grabbing her backpack she rammed herself through the opening, then turned and threw herself back against the iron, thrusting the door shut again—just as there came a deafening boom from the rifle, with a round clanging off the door and ricocheting into the mine, sending up sparks as it splintered on the rocks behind her.

A second push shut the door completely. Bracing against it, Corrie fumbled out her headlamp, pulled it on over her balaclava, and turned it on. A pair of rounds smacked into the door with a deafening noise, but it was made of thick iron and they left only dents. And now she felt a person slam into the door on the other side, pushing it open a few inches. Once more, she threw herself against it hard, slamming it shut again, and then she yanked the wrecking bar out of her pack and wedged it under the door edge, giving it a blow with a hammer, then another blow, until it held, even as she felt the man on the other side shouldering the door, trying to force it open.

He pounded furiously on the door, the bar sliding back just a little. It would hold only so long. She cast about. Broken rocks lay every-where, along with old pieces of iron and ancient equipment.

Wham! The man was now throwing himself against the door, jar-ring the wrecking bar loose.

She hammered it back into place and began piling rocks and iron against the door. Down the tracks she could see an old ore cart, and with great difficulty she got it moving, levering it off the tracks so that it tipped over against the door. She rolled some larger rocks in place. Now the door would hold—at least for a while. She sagged against the rock wall, panting hard, trying to recover her breath and figure out what to do next.

More shots were fired against the door, producing a series of deaf-ening clangs in the enclosed space and causing her to jump. Grabbing her pack, she turned and retreated down the tunnel. For the first time she could see the space she was in. The air was cold, but not so cold as outside, and it smelled of mold and iron. The tunnel ran straight ahead through solid rock, supported every ten feet or so by heavy wooden timbers. A set of ore tracks led into darkness.

She started down the tunnel at a jog. The sounds of the stalker try-ing to break in echoed down the passageway. Corrie came to a cross tunnel, turned in to it, and then, at a cul-de-sac, finally had to stop to rest. And think.

She had bought some time, but eventually the man would man-age to wedge open the door. The old map she had indicated that a section of the Christmas Mine connected to other, lower mines, form-ing a maze of tunnels and shafts—assuming they were all still passable. If she could reach them, find her way out...but what good would that do? The snow outside was several feet deep, impossible to walk through. There was only one way off the mountain—via snowmobile.

And nobody knew she was up here. She hadn't told anyone. *My God*, she thought, *what a mess I've gotten myself into*.

At that moment she heard a shriek of metal, then another. She looked around the corner of the passage, back toward the distant door, and saw a wedge of light. Another screech and the wedge grew wider.

The man was prying open the door. She made out a shoulder, a cruel-looking face—and an arm with a handgun.

She ran as the shot was fired.

57

The shots came screaming past her, sparking off the stone floor of the main tunnel ahead, the ricocheting fragments whining away like bees. She ran in terror, leaping the old car rails, expecting any moment to feel a round slam into her back and knock her to the ground. The tunnel ended in another cross tunnel, a wall of rock. Another fusillade of shots came booming down the tunnel, smacking the timbers above her with a burst of splinters and dust, flashing against the rock face before her.

She skidded around the corner and kept running. She desperately tried to remember the layout of tunnels she'd seen on the map, but her mind had shut down in panic. The shots had temporarily stopped after she turned the corner, and now she saw another, much narrower tunnel going off to the right, sloping steeply downward in a series of crude steps like a gigantic stone staircase. She flew down them, two steps at a time, to find herself in a lower tunnel, a trickle of water flowing along its bottom. It was warmer here, maybe even above freezing, and she was sweating in her bulky winter outfit.

"You can't escape," came a yell from behind. "It's all dead ends in here!"

Bullshit, she told herself with a bravado she didn't feel, *I've got a map.*

Another pair of shots came, but they struck to the rear and she felt the spray of rock pepper her jacket. She looked around. Another tunnel branched off to the left—also headed downward at an even steeper angle, the steps slick with water, with a rotting rope strung along as a kind of banister.

She took it, running at a reckless speed. Partway down she slipped and grasped frantically for the rope, which came apart like dust in her hands. She pitched forward, breaking her fall with her shoulder and rolling hard downhill, finally crashing into the bottom and sprawling on the wet stone. Her bulky winter clothes and woolen hat cushioned the fall—but not by much.

She staggered to her feet, her limbs aching, a burning cut on her forehead. She was in a broad, low seam, barely five feet high, with pillars of rock holding up the ceiling. It extended in two dimensions as far as the beam of her headlamp could penetrate. She ran at a crouch, zigzagging past the pillars, briefly shining the light ahead to see where she was going, and then turning it off again and running onward into the dark. She did this two more times, and then on the third time, while the light was off, she took a sharp right angle, slowing down and moving as silently as she could.

The flashlight beam of her pursuer lanced through the darkness behind her, wobbling as he ran, probing this way and that. She moved behind a pillar and pressed herself against it, waiting. He was now off course and heading past her. In a moment she could see him slow down and look around, a pistol in his right hand. Clearly, he realized he had lost her.

She slipped from behind the pillar and went back the way they had come, then veered off into a new passage, creeping ahead in the dark, not daring to turn on the headlight but rather feeling her way with her hands. She blinked, wiped her eyes—blood was running freely from the cut on her forehead. After a while she saw a flicker of light behind her and realized he, too, had turned around and was coming back. She hurried faster now, pulling the headlamp off her head and holding it down low, just flicking the beam on for a second to see ahead so she could move faster.

Bad move: a pair of shots boomed out and then she heard him

running, his light beam flashing around, illuminating her. Another shot. But the idiot was firing while running, which only worked on TV, and she took the opportunity to sprint like mad.

She almost didn't see it in time—a vertical shaft yawning directly ahead. She stopped so fast that she slid on her side like a base runner. Even so, one leg went over the edge. She scrambled and clawed her way back from the gaping chasm with an involuntary yelp of fear. An iron catwalk crossed the chasm, but it looked rotten as hell. An iron ladder went down into the blackness—also corroded.

It was either one or the other.

She chose the ladder, grasped the rung, and swung around, her foot finding a rung below, then another. The thing groaned and shook under her weight. A stale draft of still-warmer air came up from below. No going back now: she started down as fast as she could, the entire ladder shuddering and swaying. There was a loud snapping sound, then a second, as bolts holding the ladder to the stone broke free, and the ladder jerked violently down. She clung to it, tensing for a horrible, fatal fall—but with a screech of metal it came to an uneasy stop.

A light shone down from above, along with the gleam of a gun. Grabbing the edges of the ladder with her gloves, and taking her feet from the rungs and pressing them against the vertical sides of the ladder, she slid down—faster, faster, the rust coming off in a stream, until she hit the bottom hard, tumbling away, just as the shots came, gouging holes into the stone floor where she had just been.

Damn, she'd done something to her ankle.

Did he have the guts to descend the precarious ladder? Right at its base was a pile of rotting canvas and a stack of old planking. Limping over, she half dragged, half hauled the canvas underneath the ladder. The material was dry as dust and practically falling apart in her hands. The ladder was shaking now, groaning—her pursuer was descending.

Which meant he wouldn't be able to fire his weapon.

She shoved the heap of canvas against the base of the ladder and piled on the planks, pulled out her lighter, and lit the makeshift pyre. It was so desiccated, it went up like a bomb.

"Burn in hell!" she screamed as she dragged herself down the tunnel, trying to ignore the pain in her ankle. God, it felt like it was broken. Limping, the pain excruciating, she continued along another tunnel and then another, taking turns at random, now completely lost. Clearly, though, she was well out of the Christmas Mine and deep into the labyrinths of the Sally Goodin or one of the other, lower mines that honeycombed the mountain. She could hear sounds from behind, which seemed to indicate her pursuer had somehow gotten past the fire, or perhaps he'd just waited until it burned out.

Ahead, her headlight disclosed a cave-in, a bunch of jagged boulders strewn about on the floor of the tunnel, with some crossed beams lying atop. A narrow path, however, could be seen twisting through the rubble. Cold air streamed down from above. She climbed painfully over the piles of rock and broken timbers, then looked up. A crack disclosed a piece of dark, gray sky—but that was all. There was no way out, no way to reach it.

She continued picking her way through the rubble and came at last to a flat area on the far side. Suddenly, she heard a buzzing noise. She stopped, shone her light ahead, then gave a little cry and shrank back. Nestled among the fallen boulders, blocking the way, was a huge, ropy mass of hibernating rattlesnakes. They were half asleep in the cold air, but the twisted clump still moved in a kind of horrible slow motion, pulsing, rotating, almost like a single entity. Some were awake enough to be rattling in warning.

She shone the light around and saw that other rattlers were coiled up into the various small spaces between the rocks. They were everywhere—seemingly hundreds of them. Even—she realized with a sickening sensation—behind her.

Suddenly the boom of the gun sounded, and she felt one hand jerk in response to an impact. Instinctively, she leapt over the mass of snakes, scrambling among the boulders, the pain in her ankle even more excruciating. Another shot followed, then another, and she took refuge behind a large boulder—right next to a fat, sleeping rattler. There were some stones nearby—this was an opportunity she couldn't pass up. She picked up a heavy stone in her right hand—

something was wrong with her left hand but she'd worry about that later—and jumped onto the large boulder, letting the rock fly with great violence at the main mass of snakes.

The rock smacked into the bolus of reptiles, and the reaction was immediate and terrifying—an eruption of buzzing that filled the tunnel with a sound like a thousand bees, accompanied by an explosive writhing of movement. The lazy mass of snakes suddenly turned into a whirlwind, coiling, striking, sliding off in all directions—several coming straight at her.

She scrambled backward. Another shot struck the rocks around her, ricocheting about, and she fell in between two boulders. The buzzing filled the cave like a vast humming dynamo. She got up and ran, dragging her injured ankle. Half a dozen snakes struck at her and she jumped away. Two got hung up by their fangs on the thick fabric of her snow pants. With a scream she whacked them off, fairly dancing among the striking snakes, as another pair of shots whined among the rocks. A few moments later she was beyond the furious mass, limping away, until she could stand it no longer and finally collapsed in pain. She lay there, gasping, the tears running down her face. Her ankle was certainly broken. And then there was her hand: even in the dark she could see that her glove was soaked with warm liquid. She removed it gingerly, held her hand up to the light, and was amazed by what she saw: her pinkie finger was dangling by a mere thread of skin, blood welling out.

"Fuck!"

She shook off the useless finger, almost passing out from a combination of dizziness and disgust. Unwrapping her scarf, she cut a strip of it off with a knife and wrapped it around her hand and the stump of the finger, tightening it to stem the flow of blood.

My finger. Jesus. In a dream, almost in shock from disbelief, she pulled the glove back over the wadded scarf as best she could to hold it in place. As she did so, she heard a shout from behind, then a scream, and the wild firing of the gun. But this time the shots were not directed at her. A rattling noise filled the tunnel with an unholy sound of reptilian fury. More shots and yells.

She had to keep going—eventually he would get through the snakes, unless by great good luck he was bitten. She hauled herself to her feet, fighting the dizziness and, now, a growing nausea. Christ, she needed a crutch, but there was nothing at hand. Limping badly, she continued along the tunnel, which descended steadily for some distance, passing several crosscuts. In time she came to a small side alcove, blocked up with rocks that formed a makeshift wall, now half collapsed. A place to hide? She dragged herself to it, pulled out some more stones, and looked in.

The beam of light fell upon a horde of rats, which erupted in excitement and went scurrying every which way with a chorus of squeals—exposing the remains of several bodies.

She stared with something like stupefaction. There were four in all, laid out in a row of skeletons—or rather, partial mummies, as they still had dried flesh on their bones, rotten clothes, old boots, and hair. Their dried-up heads were tilted back, their jaws wide open as if screaming, exposing mummified mouths full of black, rotten teeth.

As she crawled in to look more closely, she could see all the signs. They had been shot—she could see numerous holes in their skulls, many other bones broken by what looked like bullet impacts. A firing-squad attack far in excess of what would have been necessary to kill them—a display of violent, homicidal fury.

The four mercury-crazed miners. They'd been killed somewhere in this tunnel system, probably the Christmas Mine, and their bodies dragged down here and hidden.

Near the corpses lay a long, heavy stick—a cudgel, really, perhaps carried by one of the killers. It would do for an improvised crutch.

As quickly as she could without compromising the integrity of the evidence, Corrie took off her knapsack, removed the specimen bags, and laid them out. Removing the glove from her good hand and dropping to her knees, she crawled from body to body, taking from each a sample of hair, a fragment of papery dried flesh, and a small bone. She sealed them in the bags and put them back in her backpack. She photographed the bodies with her cell phone, then put the pack back on.

With a gasp of pain, she managed to get to her feet, leaning on the cudgel. Now she had to figure out where she was and find her way out—without getting shot in the process.

As if on cue, she could hear, way back near the cave-in, additional firing. She almost imagined she could hear the buzzing of the rattlers, a soft hiss in the distance: pleasant, like the ocean.

She made her way farther down the tunnel, gasping with pain, trying to find some distinctive landmark that she could in turn locate on the map, and thus orient herself toward an exit. And to her great relief, ten minutes of slow wandering brought her to a junction of tunnels—three horizontal ones and a vertical shaft coming together. She collapsed, took out the map, and scrutinized it.

And there it was.

Thank God. A break, at last. According to the map, she was now in the Sally Goodin Mine, not far from a lower exit. A dewatering tunnel, containing a large pipe, lay a few hundred yards from where she was, and it led directly to the Ireland Pump Engine, in the cirque below the Christmas Mine. Folding up the map, she tucked it away and took the indicated tunnel.

Sure enough: after a few more minutes of excruciating travel she finally came to a low stream of water that covered the rock floor, and then to the opening of an ancient pipe, nearly three feet in diameter, that ran along one side of the tunnel. She stooped and crawled into its mouth, grateful to be off her feet, and began making her way down its length.

It was dark and close, and her bulky suit kept catching and tearing on rusted areas of the pipe. But the going was relatively clear, with no cave-ins or narrowings. Within ten minutes she could feel the flow of air growing colder and fresher, and she fancied she could smell snow. In another few minutes she made out the dimmest of lights ahead, and soon she emerged, first through a shunt, and then a partially open wooden door, into a dark, dingy space, thick with rusted pipes and giant valves. It was now very cold, and a dim gray light filtered in through gaps and cracks in the wooden ceiling. She figured she must be somewhere in the depths of the old Ireland Pump building.

Giving a sob of relief, she looked around and saw an old staircase leading upward. As she limped toward it, she saw, out of the corner of her eye, a dark, moving shape. A human shape—coming at her fast.

He's gotten through the snakes. Somehow he's gotten through the snakes and flanked me...

One arm wrapped around her waist; another around her neck, covering her mouth, stifling her scream and pulling her head back. Then a face appeared, in the dimness—a face that was just recognizable.

...Ted.

"You!" Ted cried, suddenly loosening his grip and uncovering her mouth. "It's *you*! What on earth are you doing here—?"

"Oh, my God," she gasped, "Ted! There's a man. Back there...he tried to kill me..." She gasped, unable to continue, as he held her.

"You're bleeding!" he exclaimed.

She started to sob. "Thank God, Ted, thank God you're here. He's got a gun..."

Ted's grip tightened again as he held her up. "He's fucked if he comes here," he said quietly, in a dark voice.

She sobbed, gasped. "I'm so glad to see you...My finger's been shot off...I need to get to a hospital..."

He continued to hold her. "I'm going to take care of you."

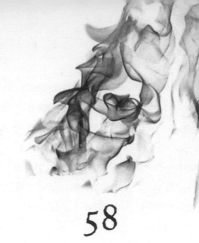

58

At half past two o'clock in the afternoon, a man wearing an enormous greatcoat, bundled up in gloves, silk scarf, and a trilby hat, carrying a bottle of champagne, rang the doorbell of the large Italianate mansion at 16 Mountain Trail Road. A maid, dressed in a starched black uniform with a white apron and cap, answered the door.

"May I help—?" she began, but the man came striding in with a cheery Christmas greeting, overriding her voice. He handed her his hat, scarf, and coat, revealing himself to be dressed in a severe black suit.

"The storm seems to be letting up!" he said to no one in particular, his voice loud in the echoing marble foyer. "My goodness, it's cold out there!"

"The family is at Christmas Eve dinner—" the maid began again, but the man in black didn't seem to hear as he strode across the foyer and past the great curving staircase into the long hall leading to the dining room, the maid hurrying after him, burdened with his outerwear. "Your name, please, sir?"

But the man paid no attention.

"I'm supposed to announce you—"

She could hardly keep up with him. He arrived at the great double doors to the dining room, grasped the handles, and threw them open, to reveal the entire family, a dozen or more, seated around an elegant table gleaming with silver and crystal, the remains of a suckling pig on a giant platter in the center. The pig had been reduced to a rib cage surrounded by greasy gobbets and bones, the only thing remaining intact being its head, with its crispy curled ears and the requisite baked apple in its mouth.

Everyone at the table stared at the man in surprise.

"I tried to—" the maid began, but the gentleman in black interrupted her as he held up the bottle of champagne.

"A bottle of Perrier-Jouët Fleur de Champagne and a Merry Christmas to each and every one of you!" he announced.

A shocked silence. And then Henry Montebello, sitting at the head of the table, rose. "What is the meaning of this interruption?" His eyes narrowed. "You—you're that FBI agent."

"Indeed I am. Aloysius Pendergast, at your service! I'm making the rounds of all my friends, bringing season's greetings and gifts of cheer!" He sat down in the only empty chair at the table.

"Excuse me," Montebello said coldly. "That chair is reserved for Mrs. Kermode, who should be here momentarily."

"Well, Mrs. Kermode's not here yet, and I am." The man plunked the champagne down on the table. "Shall we open it?"

Montebello's patrician features hardened. "I don't know who you think you are, sir, bursting into a private family dinner like this. But I must ask you to leave this house at once."

The agent paused, swaying slightly in the chair, a hurt expression gathering on his face. "If you're not going to open the champagne, fine, but don't send me away without a little glass of *something*." He reached over the table and picked up a half-full bottle of wine, examining the label. "Hmmm. A 2000 Castle's Leap Cabernet."

"What are you doing?" Montebello snapped. "Put that down and leave at once, or I shall call the police!"

Ignoring this, the man plucked a nearby glass off the table, poured a measure of the wine, and made a huge production of swirling it about, sticking his nose in the glass, sipping, noisily drawing in air, puffing his cheeks, sipping again. He put the glass down. "Some good berry notes, but no body and a short finish. Dull, I'm afraid; very dull. What sort of wine is this to serve at a Christmas Eve dinner? Are we but barbarians, Squire Montebello? Philistines?"

"Lottie, call nine-one-one. Report a home invasion."

"Ah, but I was invited in," said Pendergast. He turned to the maid. "Wasn't I, dear?"

"But I just opened the door—"

"And what is more," Montebello said, his voice crackling with fury as the rest of the family looked on with blank consternation, "you are *drunk!*"

In that moment, as if on cue, a cook entered from the kitchen, flanked by attendants, carrying a huge flambé, the flames leaping up from the silver server.

"Cherries jubilee!" Pendergast cried, jumping to his feet. "How marvelous!" He surged forward. "It's too heavy for you—let me help. That fire could be dangerous—especially here, in Roaring Fork!"

The cook, alarmed at the drunken man coming at her, took a step backward, but she was too slow. The FBI agent seized the great flaming platter; there was a sudden moment of imbalance; and then it overturned, the platter, cherries, ice cream, and burning brandy all crashing to the table and splattering over the remains of the pig.

"Fire! Fire!" Pendergast cried, aghast as the flames leapt up, his face a mixture of dismay and panic. "This is dreadful! Run! Everyone outside!"

A chorus of cries and shrieks went up around the table as everyone scrambled backward, knocking over chairs, spilling wine.

"Out, quickly!" shouted Pendergast. "Pull the alarm! The house is burning down! We'll be burned alive *just like the others!*"

The sound of terror in his voice was infectious. There was instant pandemonium. A smoke alarm went off, which only increased the mindless panic to get out, to get away at all costs from the fire. In mere seconds the diners, cook, and wait staff had all cleared the room, some pushing others away in their panic, and stampeded down the hall and across the foyer. One after another, they burst out the front door and into the night. The man in black was left alone in the house.

With sudden calm, he reached out, picked up an enormous gravy boat, and poured it over the alcohol flames, which were largely sputtering out anyway due to the melting ice cream and juices of the roasted carcass. A dash of wine from the bottle of inferior Cabernet completed the fire suppression. And then, with great aplomb and rapid efficiency of movement, he strode through the dining room, into the living room, and through it to a series of formally decorated rooms in the back, where Henry Montebello maintained his home legal office. There, Pendergast went straight to a cluster of filing cabinets. Perusing the labels on the front of each, he chose one, jimmied it open with a swift, sure motion, flipped through the papers, removed a fat accordion file, shut the cabinet, and carried the file back through the house to the front hall, plucking his bottle of champagne from the dining table in the process. In the front hall, he retrieved his greatcoat, scarf, hat, and gloves from where the maid had dumped them on the floor in her panic, secreted the file in the bulk of his coat, and stepped outside.

"Ladies and gentlemen," he announced, "the fire is out. It's safe to return now."

He strode off into the snowy afternoon, to his waiting car, and drove away.

59

Corrie felt Ted's powerful arms around her, holding her tight. The tightness of it made her feel safe. Relief flooded through her. She relaxed and took the pressure off her broken ankle as he continued to hold her up. "I'm going to take care of you," he said again, a little louder.

"I can't believe you're here," she sobbed. "That guy in the mine—he's a goon, hired by Kermode to run me out of town. He's the one who killed my dog, shot up my car...and now he's trying to kill me."

"Kermode," Ted said, his voice taking on an edge. "Figures. That bitch. I'm going to take care of her as well. Oh, God, will I take care of *that* bitch."

She was a little taken aback by his vehemence. "It's okay," she said. "God, I'm so light-headed. I think I need to lie down."

He didn't seem to have heard. The arms tightened even more.

"Ted, help me sit down..." She twisted a little because he was gripping her so hard it was beginning to hurt.

"Fucking bitch," he said, louder.

"Forget Kermode...Please, Ted—you're hurting me."

"Not talking about Kermode," he said. "Talking about you."

Corrie was sure she hadn't heard right. She was so dizzy. His arms tightened even more, to the point where she could hardly breathe. "Ted...That hurts. Please!"

"Is that all you've got to say for yourself, *bitch?*"

His voice was different now. Rough, hoarse.

"Ted...*what?*"

"*What, Ted, what?*" He mimicked her in a high, squeaky voice. "What a piece of work you are."

"What are you talking about?"

He squeezed so hard she cried out. "You like that? 'Cause you *know* what I'm talking about. Don't play the innocent little girl."

She struggled, but had almost no strength left. It was like a nightmare. Maybe it *was* a nightmare—maybe all of this was. "What are you saying?"

"What are you *say*-ing?" he mimicked.

She twisted, trying to break free, and he roughly spun her around, his face almost touching hers. The red, sweaty, misshapen, furious look that disfigured his face frightened her terribly. Both his eyes were bloodshot and leaking water. "Look at you," he said, lowering his voice, his lips warped with anger. "Leading me on, always teasing, first promising and then saying no, making a fool of me."

He gave her a sudden, violent squeeze with his powerful arms and she felt a rib crack under the pressure, pain lancing through her chest. She screamed, gasped, tried to speak, but he squeezed her again, forcing the air from her lungs. "The cocktease stops right here, *right now.*" Spittle splattered her face. His lips, covered with a white film, were now brushing hers, his strangely foul breath washing over her like fumes from a rotting carcass.

She tried to breathe but couldn't. The combined pain of her ankle, her hand, and now her ribs was so excruciating she was unable to think straight. Fear and shock sent her heart, already racing from the pursuit through the mines, into overdrive. She had never seen a face so twisted and so terrifying. He was completely mad.

*Mad. Mad...*She didn't want to think of the ramifications of that—she would not, *could* not, follow that thought to its natural conclusion.

"Please—" she managed to gasp.

"Isn't this perfect? You just running into my arms like this. It's karma. It saves me all the usual kinds of preparation. The universe wants to teach you a lesson, and I'll be the teacher."

With that he threw her to the ground. She fell sprawling, with a cry of pain. He followed up with a kick to her injured ribs. The pain was unbearable and she cried out again, gasping for air. She felt the world swirling around, a strange ethereal floating sensation, pain and fright and disbelief overpowering all rational thought. A mist passed before her eyes, and consciousness shut down.

A long, dark time seemed to pass before another searing lance of pain brought her back to herself. She was still in the dingy room. Mere moments must have ticked by. Ted stood over her, his face still grotesquely distorted, eyes watering, lips covered with a sticky bloom of white. He reached down, seized her leg, spun her around, and began dragging her over the rough floorboards. She tried to scream but couldn't. Her head banged roughly against the floor and once again she felt herself on the verge of passing out.

He dragged her from the back room into the main section of the structure. The vast pump rose above her, a monstrous juggernaut of giant pipes and cylinders. The tall building creaked in the wind. He pulled her alongside a horizontal pipe, yanked off her gloves, took notice of her damaged hand—lips curling into a malevolent smile at the sight—then lifted the other arm and roughly cuffed her wrist to the pipe.

She lay there, gasping, swimming in and out of consciousness.

"Look at you now," he said, and spat on her.

As she struggled weakly to sit up, gasping in pain, part of her mind seemed to sense that this was happening, not to her, but to somebody else, and that she was watching from someplace far, far away. But there was another part of her mind—cold and relentless—that kept telling her exactly the opposite. This was real. Not only that—Ted was going to kill her.

Having shackled her to the pipe, Ted stepped back, crossed his arms, and surveyed his handiwork. The dark mist that hovered around her seemed to clear slightly, and she grew more aware of her surroundings. Old pieces of lumber littered the floor. A couple of kerosene lanterns were hung nearby, casting a feeble yellow light. In one corner was a cot with a sleeping bag on it, a box of handcuffs, a couple of balaclavas, and several large cans of kerosene. A table held several hunting knives, coils of rope, duct tape, a glass-stoppered vial with some clear liquid within, wadded piles of wool socks and heavy sweaters, all black. There was a gun, too, that looked to Corrie like a 9mm Beretta. Why would Ted have a handgun? Pegs on the walls held a dark leather coat and—perversely—assorted clown masks.

This seemed to be a hideout of some sort. A lair—*Ted's* lair. But why should he need one? And what were all these things for?

An old woodstove was burning to one side, the light shining between the cracks in the cast iron, throwing out heat. And now she noticed an odor in the air—a vile odor.

Ted pulled up a chair, turned it around, and straddled it, balancing his arms on the chair back. "So here we are," he said.

Something was terribly wrong with him. And yet the furious, violent, half-demented Ted of the last few minutes had changed. Now he was calm, mocking. Corrie swallowed, unable to take all this in. Maybe if she talked to him, she could learn what was troubling him, bring him back from whatever dark place he was in. But when she tried, all that came out was a pathetic garble of sound.

"When you first arrived in town, I thought maybe you were different from the others around here," he said. His voice had changed again, as if his rage had buried itself deep in ice. It was remote, cold, detached, like someone speaking to himself—or, perhaps, to a corpse. "Roaring Fork. Back when I was young, it used to be a real town. Now the ultra-high-net-worth bastards have taken over, the assholes with their social-climbing bimbos, the movie stars and CEOs and Masters of the Universe. Raping the mountains, clear-cutting the forests. Oh, they talk a good line about the environment! About going organic, about reducing their carbon footprints by buying offsets for their Gulfstream jets, about how 'green' their ten-thousand-square-foot mansions are. Mother*fuckers*. That's just sick. They're parasites on our society. Roaring Fork is where they all gather, flattering each other, grooming each other of their lice like fucking chimpanzees. And they treat the rest of us—the real folk, the native-born residents—as scum fit only to sweep their palaces and stroke their egos. There's only one cure for all that: fire. This place should burn. It *needs* to burn. And it *is* burning." He grinned, another fleshy, demonic distortion, frighteningly close to the face he'd shown her before.

Kerosene. Handcuffs. Rope. *It needs to burn.* Now, through the fog in her head, Corrie understood: Ted was the arsonist. A huge shudder of fear coursed through her, and she struggled against the cuffs despite the pain that racked her body.

But then, as soon as she started to struggle, she stopped again. He cared for her—she knew he did. Somehow, she had to reach him.

"Ted," she croaked, managing to speak. "Ted. You know I'm not one of them."

"*Oh, yes you are!*" he screamed, leaning toward her, the white scum flying off his lips in droplets. As quickly as it had come, the icy, methodical veneer fell away, replaced by a mad, bestial rage. "You faked it for a while, but no—you're just like them! You're here for the same reasons they are: *money.*"

His eyes were so bloodshot, they were almost red. His hands were trembling with rage. His whole body was trembling. And his voice was so strange, so different. Looking at him was like looking into the maw of hell. It was so awful, so inhuman an expression, Corrie had to avert her eyes.

"But I don't have any money," she said.

"Exactly! Why are you here? To find some rich asshole. *I* wasn't rich enough for you! That's why you *played* with me. Leading me on the way you did."

"No, no, that wasn't it at all..."

"*Shut* the *fuck* up!" he screamed at a larynx-shredding volume, so loud that Corrie felt her eardrums tremble at the pressure.

And then, just as abruptly as it had left, the icy control returned. The fluctuation—from homicidal, brutish, barely controlled rants to a

cold and calculating distance—was unbearable. "You should be grateful," he said, turning away, sounding for a minute like the Ted of old.
"I have conferred wisdom onto you. Now you understand. The others—the others that I've taught—they learned nothing."

Then, suddenly, he spun back, staring at her with a hideous, speculative grin. "You ever read Robert Frost?"

Corrie couldn't bring herself to speak.

He began to recite:

> *Some say the world will end in fire;*
> *Some say in ice.*
> *From what I've tasted of desire*
> *I hold with those who favor fire.*

He reached out, grasped a long, dry stick of old lumber from the
many that littered the floor, and used the end of it to toggle the latch
on the woodstove door open. The flames inside threw a flickering
yellow light about the room. He shoved the stick into the fire and
waited.

"Ted, *please*." Corrie took a deep breath. "You don't have to do
this."

He began to whistle a tuneless melody.

"We're friends. I didn't reject you." She sobbed a moment, gathered her wits as best she could. "I just didn't want to rush things, that's
all…"

"Good. That's very good. I haven't rejected you, either. And—I
won't rush things. We'll just let nature take its course."

He withdrew the stick, the end burning brightly now, dropping
sparks. His eyes, reflecting the dancing light of the fire, rolled slowly
toward her, their bloodshot whites shockingly large. And Corrie,
looking from him to the burning brand and back again, realized what
was about to happen.

"Oh, my God!" she said, voice rising into a shriek. "Please don't.
Ted!"

He took a step toward her, waving the burning stick before her face. Another step closer. Corrie could feel the heat of the flaming brand. "No," was all she could manage.

For a minute, he just stared at her, the stick sparking and glowing in his hand. And when he spoke, his voice was so quiet, so controlled, it nearly drove her mad.

"It's time to burn," he said simply.

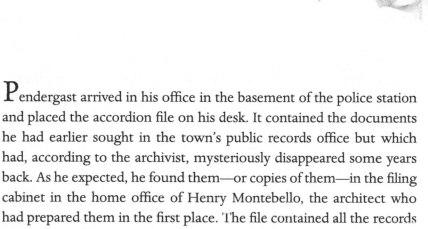

60

Pendergast arrived in his office in the basement of the police station and placed the accordion file on his desk. It contained the documents he had earlier sought in the town's public records office but which had, according to the archivist, mysteriously disappeared some years back. As he expected, he found them—or copies of them—in the filing cabinet in the home office of Henry Montebello, the architect who had prepared them in the first place. The file contained all the records relating to the original development of The Heights—documents that, by law, were supposed to be a matter of public record: plats, surveys, permit applications, subdivision maps, and terrain management plans.

Delving into the accordion file, Pendergast removed several manila folders and laid them out in rows, their tabs lined up. He knew exactly what he was looking for. The first documents he perused involved the original survey of the land, done in the mid-1970s, with corresponding photographs. They included a detailed topographic survey of the terrain, along with a sheaf of photos depicting exactly how the valley and ridges looked before the development began.

It was most revealing.

The original valley had been much narrower and tighter, almost a ravine. Along its length, carved into a benchland a hundred feet above the stream known as Silver Queen Creek, stood the remains of an extensive ore-processing complex first built by the Staffords in the 1870s—the fountainhead of much of their wealth. The first building to be erected housed the "sampler" operation, to test the richness of the ore as it came from the mine; next came a much larger "concentrator" building, containing three steam-powered stamp mills, which crushed the ore and concentrated the silver tenfold; and finally, the smelter it-self. All three operations generated tailings, or waste piles of rock, and those tailings were clearly visible on the survey as enormous piles and heaps of rubble and grit. The tailings from all of the operations con-tained toxic minerals and compounds that leached out into the water table. But it was the last set of tailings—from the smelter—that were truly deadly.

The Stafford smelter in Roaring Fork used the Washoe amalgama-tion process. In the smelter, the crushed, concentrated ore was further ground up into a paste, and various chemicals were added...including sixty pounds of mercury for each ton of ore concentrate processed. The mercury dissolved the silver—amalgamated with it—and the re-sulting heavy paste settled to the bottom of the vat, with the waste slurry coming off the top to be dumped. The silver was recovered by heating the amalgam in a retort and driving off the mercury, which was recaptured through condensation, leaving behind crude silver.

The process was not efficient. About two percent of the mercury was lost in each run. That mercury had to end up somewhere, and that somewhere was in the vast tailings dumped into the valley. Pen-dergast did a quick mental calculation: a two percent loss equaled about a pound of mercury for each ton of concentrate processed. The smelter processed a hundred tons of concentrate a day. By inference, that meant a hundred pounds of mercury had been dumped into the environment on a daily basis—over the nearly two decades during which the smelter operated. Mercury was an exceedingly toxic, perni-cious substance, which over time could cause severe and permanent brain damage in people who were exposed to it—especially in chil-dren and, to an even greater extent, to the unborn.

It all added up to one thing: The Heights—or at least, the portion of the development that had been erected in the valley—was essentially sitting atop a large Superfund site, with a toxic aquifer underneath.

As he replaced the initial documents, everything came together in Pendergast's mind. He understood everything with great clarity—everything—including the arson attacks.

Moving more rapidly now, Pendergast glanced through documents relating to the early development itself. The terrain management plan called for using the vast tailing piles to fill the narrow ravine and create the broad, attractive valley floor that existed today. The clubhouse was built just downstream from where the old smelter had been, and a dozen large homes were situated within the valley. Henry Montebello, the master architect, had been in charge of it all: the demolishment of the smelter ruins, the terrain alterations, the spreading of tailings into a nice broad, level area for the lower development and the clubhouse. And his sister-in-law, Mrs. Kermode, had also been an integral player.

Interesting, Pendergast thought, that Montebello's mansion was on the far side of town, and that Kermode's own home was built high up on the ridge, far from the zone of contamination. They, and the other members of the Stafford family who were behind the development of The Heights, must have known about the mercury. It occurred to him that the real reason they were building a new clubhouse and spa—which had seemed the very essence of needless indulgence—and situating it on the old Boot Hill cemetery was, in fact, to get it out of the area of contamination.

Pendergast moved from one manila folder to the next, paging through documents relating to the original subdivisions and association planning. The lots were large—minimum two-acre zoning—and as a result there was no community water system: each property had its own well. Those houses situated in the valley floor, as well as the original clubhouse, would have obtained their water from wells sunk directly into the mercury-contaminated aquifer.

And, indeed, here was a file of the well permits. Pendergast looked through it. Each well required the testing of water quality—standard procedure. And every single well had passed: no mercury contamination noted.

Without question, falsified results.

Now came the sales contracts for the first houses built in The Heights. Pendergast selected those dozen properties in the contaminated zone in the valley for special scrutiny. He examined the names of the purchasers. Most appeared to be older, wealthy individuals in retirement. These houses had changed hands a number of times, especially as real estate values skyrocketed in the 1990s.

But Pendergast did recognize the name of one set of purchasers: a "Sarah and Arthur Roman, husband and wife." No doubt the future parents of Ted Roman. The date of purchase: 1982.

The Roman house was built directly on the site of the smelter, in the zone of greatest contamination. Pendergast thought back to what Corrie had told him about Ted. Assuming he was her age, or even a few years older, there was little doubt that Ted Roman had been exposed to toxic mercury in his mother's womb, and raised in a toxic house, drinking toxic water, taking toxic showers...

Pendergast put the records aside, a thoughtful expression on his face. After a moment, he picked up the phone and called Corrie's cell phone. It went directly over to her voice mail.

He then called the Hotel Sebastian and, after speaking to several people, learned that she had left the hotel shortly after her work shift ended at eleven. In her car, destination unknown. However, she had asked the concierge for a snowmobile map of the mountains surrounding Roaring Fork.

With somewhat more alacrity, Pendergast dialed the town library. No answer. He looked up the head librarian's home number. When she answered, she explained to him that December twenty-fourth was normally a half day at the library, but she had decided not to open at all because of the storm. In response to his next question, she replied that Ted had, in fact, told her he was going to take advantage of the free day by engaging in one of his favorite activities: snowmobiling in the mountains.

Again, Pendergast hung up the phone. He called Stacy Bowdree's cell, and it, too, went over to voice mail.

A furrow appeared on his pale brow. As he was hanging up, he noticed something he normally would have seen immediately had he not been preoccupied: the papers on his desk were disarranged.

He stared at the papers, his near-photographic mind reconstructing how he had left them. One sheet—the sheet on which he'd copied the message of the Committee of Seven—had been pulled partway out and the papers surrounding it displaced:

mete at the Ideal 11 oclock Sharp to Night they are Holt Up in the closed Christmas Mine up on smugglers wall

Pendergast quickly left his office and went upstairs, where Iris was still dutifully manning the desk.

"Has anyone been in my office?" he asked pleasantly.

"Oh, yes," the secretary said. "I brought Corrie down there for a few minutes, early this afternoon. She was looking for her cell phone."

61

The vile, rotting odor in the air seemed to intensify as Ted waved the burning stick about. The flames licking at its end began to die back into coals, and he pushed it back into the stove.

"Love is the Fire of Life; it either consumes or purifies," he quoted as he slowly twirled the stick among the flames, as if roasting a marshmallow. There was something awful—after his fierce and passionate ranting—about the calm deliberation with which he now moved. "Let us prepare for the purification." He pulled the stick from the stove and passed it again before Corrie's face, with a strangely delicate gesture, gingerly, tentative now—and yet it hovered so close that, although she twisted away, it singed her hair.

Corrie tried to gain control of her galloping panic. She had to reach him, talk him out of this. Her mouth was dry, and it was hard to articulate words through her haze of pain and fear. "Ted, I liked you. I mean I *like* you. I really do." She swallowed. "Look, let me go and I'll forget all about this. We'll go out. Have a beer. Just like before."

"Right. Sure. You'd say anything now." Ted began to laugh, a crazy, quiet laugh.

She pulled against the cuff, but it was tight around her wrist, securely fastened to the pipe. "You won't get in trouble. I won't tell anyone. We'll forget all about this."

Ted did not reply. He pulled the burning brand away, inspec closely, as one would a tool prior to putting it to use.

"We had good times, Ted, and we can have more. You don't have to do this. I'm not like those others, I'm just a poor student, I have to wash dishes at the Hotel Sebastian just to pay for my room!" She sobbed, caught herself. "Please don't hurt me."

"You need to calm down, Corrie, and accept your fate. It will be by fire—purifying fire. It will cleanse you of your sins. You should thank me, Corrie. I'm giving you a chance to atone for what you did. You'll suffer, and for that I'm sorry—but it's for the best."

The horror of it, the certainty that Ted was telling the truth, closed her throat.

He stepped back, looked around. "I used to play in all these tunnels as a kid." His voice was different now—it was sorrowful, like one about to perform a necessary but distasteful service. "I knew every inch of these mine buildings up here. I know all this like the back of my hand. This is my childhood, right here. This is where it began, and this is where it will end. That door you came out of? That was the entrance to my playground. Those mines—they were a *magical* playground."

His tone became freighted with nostalgia, and Corrie had a momentary hope. But then, with terrible rapidity, his demeanor changed utterly. "And *look what they did!*" This came out as a scream. "Look! This was a nice town once. Friendly. Everyone mingled. Now it's a fucking tourist trap for billionaires...billionaires and all their toadies, bootlickers, lackeys. People like you! *You...!*" His voice echoed in the dim space, temporarily drowning out the sound of the storm, the wind, the groaning timbers.

Corrie began to realize, with a kind of awful finality, that nothing she could say would have any effect.

As quickly as it had come, the fit passed again. Ted fell abruptly silent. A tear welled up in one eye, trickled slowly down his cheek. He picked up the gun from the table and snugged it into his waistband. Without looking at her, he turned sharply on his heel and strode away, out of her vision, into a dark area behind the pump engine. Now all she could see was the burning end of his stick, dancing and floating in the darkness, slowly dwindling, until it, too, disappeared.

She waited. All was silent. Had he left? She could hardly believe it. Hope came rushing back. Where had he gone? She looked around, straining to see in the darkness. Nothing.

But no—it was too good to be true. He hadn't really left. He had to be around somewhere.

And then she smelled a faint whiff of smoke. From the woodstove? No. She strained, peering this way and that into the darkness, the pain in her hand, ribs, and ankle suddenly forgotten. There was more smoke—and then, abruptly, a whole lot more. And now she could see a reddish glow from the far side of the pump engine.

"Ted!"

A gout of flame suddenly appeared out of the blackness, and then another, snaking up the far wall, spreading wildly.

Ted had set the old building on fire.

Corrie cried out, struggled afresh with the handcuffs. The flames mounted upward with terrible speed, great clouds of acrid smoke roiling up. A roar grew in intensity, until it was so ferocious it was a vibration in the air itself. She felt the sudden heat on her face.

It had all happened in mere seconds.

"No! *No!*" she screamed. And then, through her wild cries, she saw Ted's tall figure framed in the doorway to the dingy room from which she'd first emerged. She could see the open door to the Sally Goodin Mine, the dewatering tunnel running away into darkness. He was standing absolutely still, staring at the fire, waiting; and as it grew brighter and stronger she could see the expression on his face: one of pure, unmitigated excitement.

Corrie squeezed her eyes closed for a moment, prayed—prayed for the first time in her life—for a quick and merciful end.

And then, as the flames began to lick up all around, consuming the wooden building on all sides, bringing with them unbearable heat, Ted turned and vanished into the mountain.

The flames roared all around Corrie, so loudly that she couldn't even hear her own screams.

62

At three o'clock in the afternoon, Mike Kloster had pulled his VMC 1500 snowcat with its eight-way hydraulic grooming blade out of the equipment shed, getting it ready for the night ahead. Twenty inches of snow had fallen over the last forty-eight hours, and at least another eight were on the way. This was going to be a long night—and it was Christmas Eve, no less.

Turning up the heat in the cab, he let the machine warm up while he pulled over the tow frame and began bolting it on to the rear. As he bent over the hitch, he sensed a presence behind him. Straightening up again, he turned to see a bizarre figure approaching, bundled up in a black coat and trilby hat, wearing heavy boots. He looked almost clown-like.

He was about to make a wisecrack when his gaze fell on the man's face. It was as cold and pale as the surrounding landscape, with eyes like chips of ice, and the words died in Kloster's throat.

"Um, this is a restricted area—" he began, but the man was already removing something from his coat, a worn alligator wallet, which fell open to reveal a badge.

"Agent Pendergast. FBI."

Kloster stared at the badge. FBI? For real? But before he could even answer, the man went on.

"Your name, if you please?"

"Kloster. Mike Kloster."

"Mr. Kloster, unbolt that device immediately and get in the cab. You are going to take me up the mountain."

"Well, I've got to, you know, get some kind of authorization be-fore—"

"You will do as I instruct, or you will be charged with impeding a federal officer."

The tone of voice was so absolute, and so convincing, that Mike Kloster decided he would do exactly as this man said. "Yes, sir." He unhitched the tow frame and climbed into the cab, sliding behind the wheel. The man got into the passenger side, his movements remark-ably agile given the ungainly dress.

"Um, where are we going?"

"To the Christmas Mine."

"Where's that?"

"It is above the old Smuggler's Cirque mine complex where the Ireland Pump building is situated."

"Oh. Sure. I know where that is."

"Then proceed, if you please. Quickly."

Kloster engaged the gears, raised the front groomer blade, and started up the slopes. He thought of radioing his boss to tell him what was going on, but decided against it. The guy was a pain in the ass and he might just put up a fuss. Better to tell him after the fact. His pas-senger was FBI, after all, and what better excuse was there?

As they climbed, curiosity began to get the better of Kloster. "So, what's this all about?" he asked in a friendly way.

The pale-faced man did not answer. He didn't appear to have heard.

The VMC had an awesome sound system, and Kloster had his iPod all docked and ready to go. He reached out to turn it on.

"No," said the man.

Kloster snatched back his hand as if it had been bitten.

"Make this machine go faster, please."

"Well, we're not supposed to take it over three thousand rpms—"

"I'll thank you to do as I say."

"Yes, sir."

He throttled up, the groomer crawling a little faster up the mountain. The snow had started again and now the wind was blowing as well. The flakes were of the tiny, BB-pellet variety—from long experience, Kloster knew every variety of snowflake there was—and they bounced and ticked noisily off the windscreen. Kloster put on the wipers and flicked the lights to high. The cluster of beams stabbed into the grayness, the pellets of snow flashing through. At three thirty it was already starting to get dark.

"How long?" the man asked.

"Fifteen minutes, maybe twenty, to the mine buildings. I don't think this machine'll get any higher than that—the slopes are too steep above Smuggler's Cirque. The avalanche danger is pretty extreme, too. They're gonna be setting off avalanche charges all Christmas Day, I bet, with this new snow."

He realized he was babbling—this man sure made him nervous—but again the agent didn't even acknowledge having heard.

At the top of the ski slope, Kloster took the service road that led to the top of the ridge, where it joined the network of snowmobile trails. Arriving at the trails, he was surprised to see fresh snowmobile tracks. Whoever it was, they were hard-core, venturing out on a day like this. He continued on, wondering just what the heck his passenger was after...

And then, above the dark spruce trees, he saw something. A glow, up on the mountain. Instinctively he slowed, staring.

The FBI agent saw it, too. "What is that?" he asked sharply.

"I don't know." Kloster squinted upward. He could make out, beyond and above the trees, the upper part of Smuggler's Cirque. The steep slopes and peaks were bathed in a flickering yellow glow. "Looks like a fire."

The pale man leaned forward, gripping the dashboard, his eyes so bright and hard they unnerved Kloster. "Where?"

"Damn, I'd say it's in that old mine complex."

Even as they watched, the glow grew in intensity, and now Kloster could see dark smoke billowing upward into the snowstorm.

"Fast. *Now.*"

"Right, sure." Kloster really gunned it this time, the VMC churning across the snow at top speed—only twenty miles an hour, but plenty fast for an unwieldy groomer.

"Faster."

"It's pegged, sorry."

Even as he made the last turn before the tree line, he could see that the fire in the cirque was big. Huge, in fact. Flames were shooting up at least a hundred feet, sending up towering pillars of sparks and black smoke, as thick as a volcanic eruption. It had to be the Ireland Pump Engine building itself—nothing else up there was big enough to produce that kind of inferno. Even so, it couldn't be a natural fire—nothing natural could spread so fast and so fiercely. It occurred to Kloster that this must be the work of the arsonist, and he felt a stab of fear, which was not reassured by the strange intensity of the man next to him. He kept the pedal to the metal.

The last stubby trees slid past them and they were now on the bare ridge. The snow was shallower here, due to wind scouring, and Kloster was able to eke out a few more miles per hour. God, it was like a firestorm up there, mushroom clouds of smoke and flame pummeling the sky, and he fancied he could even hear the sound of it above the roar of the diesel engines.

They crossed the last part of the ridge and headed up the lip to the hanging valley above. The snow grew deeper again and the VMC churned its way forward. They cleared the lip and, instinctually, Kloster stopped. It was indeed the Ireland building, and it had burned so fast, so furiously, that all that remained was a burning skeleton of timbers—which even as they watched collapsed with a thunderous cracking noise, sending up a colossal cascade of sparks. It left the Ireland Pump itself standing alone, naked, the paint peeling and smoking. The fire began to die as quickly as it had exploded: when the building collapsed, huge piles of snow had fallen from the roof into the burning rubble, sending up volatile plumes of steam.

Kloster stared, stunned by the violence of the scene, the utter suddenness of the building's immolation.

"Move closer," the man ordered.

He eased the groomer forward. The wooden frame had been consumed with remarkable speed, and the cascade of snow from the collapsing roof and the continuing blizzard were damping down what remained of the fire. None of the other buildings had burned—their snow-laden roofs were protecting them from the incredible shower of sparks that rained downward all around them like the detritus of countless fireworks.

Kloster eased the cat among the old mining structures. "This is as far as I'd better go," he said. But instead of the argument he expected, the pale man simply opened the door and got out. Kloster watched, first in amazement, and then horror, as the man walked toward the smoking, fire-licked remains of the structure and circled it slowly, like a panther, close—way too close.

Pendergast stared into the hellish scene. The air around him was alive with falling sparks mingled with snowflakes, which dusted his hat and coat, hissing out in the dampness. The engine and all its pipework had survived intact, but the building was utterly gone. Plumes of smoke and steam billowed up from hundreds of little pockets of heat, and timbers lay scattered about, hissing and smoking, with tongues of fire flickering here and there. There was an acrid stench, along with the whiff of something else: singed hair and burnt meat. All that could be heard now was the low hiss of steam, the crackle and pop of isolated fires, and the sound of the wind moaning through the ruins. He made a circuit around the perimeter of the fire. There was enough light from the many dying fires to see everything.

At a certain point he paused abruptly.

Now, moving ever so slowly, he stepped deeper into the fire zone, raising the scarf to cover his mouth against the acrid smoke. Winding his way among pipes and valves, his feet crunching on the cracked cement floor littered with nails and glass, he approached the thing that had stopped him in his tracks. It resembled a long, black log, and it, too, was hissing and smoking. As he got closer he confirmed it was the remains of a human body, which had been handcuffed to a set of pipes.

Even though the arm had burned off, and the body had dropped to the floor, a carbonized hand remained in the cuffs, the fingers curled up like the legs of a dead spider, blackened bones sticking out from where the wrist should have been.

Pendergast sank to his knees. It was an involuntary motion, as if all the strength was suddenly drained from his body, forcing him down against his will. His head fell forward and his hands clasped together. A sound came from his mouth—low, barely audible, but undeniably the by-product of a grief beyond words.

63

Pendergast did not linger long over the charred body. He rose, a tall figure among the smoking ruins, his cold gaze surveying the burnt remains of the pump building. For a moment, he remained as immobile as a statue, only his two pale eyes exploring the scene, pausing here and there to take in some invisible detail.

A minute passed. And then his eyes turned back to the corpse. He reached into his coat, slid out his custom Les Baer 1911 Colt, ejected the magazine, checked it, slid it back into place, and racked a round into the chamber. The firearm remained in his right hand.

Now he began to move forward, a small flashlight appearing in his other hand. The heat of the fire had melted much of the snow in the immediate vicinity of the area, leaving puddles of water and even, here and there, exposed brown grass, now quickly being reblanketed with snow. He made a circuit of the ruined building, peering through the falling snow, stepping over the innumerable piles of charred and smoking debris. Darkness was falling, and the snow thickened on his shoulders and hat, making him appear like a wandering ghost.

At the far side of the devastation, where the flanks of the mountainside began to rise up, he paused to examine a small, scorched wooden door, which covered what appeared to be a tunnel entrance. After a moment he knelt and examined the handle, the nearby ground, and then the door itself. He grasped the handle and tested the door, finding it locked from the inside—padlocked, apparently.

Pendergast rose and—with a sudden explosion of movement—stove in the door with a massive kick. He grasped the broken pieces and ripped them out by main force with his hands, throwing them aside. As quickly as it had come, the furious violence passed. He knelt, shining the light inside. The beam revealed an empty dewatering tunnel running straight into the mountain.

He turned the light to the ground. There were fresh scuffs and various confused marks in the dust, both coming and going. A moment of stasis...and then he was suddenly in motion, trotting alongside the pipe as smoothly as a cat, his coat billowing behind him, the Colt in his hand gleaming faintly in the dimness.

The pipe ended in a low stream of water that interrupted the tracks. Moving forward, Pendergast came to an intersection; continued on; reached another, and then—trying to think like his quarry—took a right, where the tunnel abruptly changed slope and ascended steeply to a higher level.

The tunnel continued for a quarter mile, deep into the mountain, until it struck what had once been a complex mineral seam, perhaps a dozen feet wide. This seam almost immediately divided the tunnel into a warren of shafts, crawl spaces, and alcoves, the spaces that remained after the ancient mining operation had cleared out every vein and pocket of a complex ore body that had once threaded this way and that through the heart of the mountain.

Pendergast paused. He understood that his quarry would have anticipated pursuit, and as a result had led his presumed pursuer to this very place: this maze of tunnels, where he, with his undoubtedly superior knowledge of the mine complex, would have the advantage. Pendergast sensed it was very likely his presence had already been noted. The prudent course of action would be to retreat and return with additional manpower.

But that would not do. Not at all. His quarry might use such a delay to escape. And besides, it would deprive Pendergast of what he needed to do so very badly that he could taste the bile of it in his mouth.

He doused the light and listened. His preternaturally acute sense of hearing picked up many sounds—the steady drip of water, the faint movement of air, the occasional *tick-tick* of settling rock and wooden cribbing.

But there was no light, no telltale sound or scent. And yet he sensed, he *knew*, that his quarry—Ted Roman—was near and well aware of his presence.

He turned the light back on and examined the surrounding area. Much of the rock in this section of the mine was rotten, shot through with cracks and seams, and extra cribbing had been placed to hold it up. He stepped over to a vertical member, removed a knife from his pocket, and pushed it into the wood. It sank into the cribbing like butter, all the way to the hilt. He pulled it out and pried away at the wood, pulling off big, dusty pieces.

The wood was thoroughly weakened by dry rot. It might not be hard to bring it down . . . but that would lead to unpredictable consequences.

He ceased moving and paused, frozen in place, listening. He heard a faint sound, the tiny drop of a pebble. It was impossible, in the echoing spaces, to tell whence it came. It almost seemed to him deliberate, a tease. He waited. Another ping of rock against rock. And now he knew for certain that Ted Roman was playing with him.

A fatal mistake.

With the light on, acting as if he had heard nothing, unsuspecting, Pendergast chose a tunnel at random and passed down it. After a few steps he halted to discard his bulky coat, gloves, and hat, and stuff them into an out-of-the-way alcove. It was much warmer here, deep in the mine—and the coat was too constricting for the work that lay ahead of him.

The tunnel twisted and turned, dipped and rose, dividing and redividing. Many small tunnels, stopes, and shafts branched off in odd directions. Old mining equipment, pulleys, cages, cables, buckets, carts, and rotting ropes were strewn about in various stages of decay. At several points, vertical shafts sank down into darkness. Pendergast examined each one of these carefully, shining his light on the descending walls and testing the depths with a dropped pebble.

At one shaft, he lingered somewhat longer. It took two seconds for the pebble to hit bottom; a quick mental calculation indicated the distance would be twenty meters, or about sixty feet. Sufficient. He examined the rock making up the wall of the shaft and found it rough, solid, with enough adequate footholds: suitable for the purpose he had in mind.

Now, making a detour around the shaft, he stumbled and fell hard, the flashlight dropping to the ground with a clatter and going out. With a curse, Pendergast lit a match and tried to edge around the shaft, but the match went out, burning his fingers, and he dropped it with another muttered deprecation. He got up and tried to light another match. It sputtered to life and he took several steps, but he was moving too fast now and the light went out again, right at the edge of the deep pit; he slipped and, in the process, swept a loose rock off the edge, giving a loud cry as he himself went over. His powerful fingers grasped a fissure just below the edge of the shaft, and he swung his body down so that he was dangling into the dark void, out of sight of the tunnel above. He abruptly cut off his cry when the rock he had dislodged crashed into the bottom.

Silence. Dangling, he found a purchase for his toes, his knees well flexed, giving him the leverage he needed. He waited, clinging to the edge of the shaft, listening intently.

Soon he could hear Roman cautiously making his way down the tunnel. The beam of a flashlight flickered over the lip of the shaft as the sound of movement paused. Then, ever so slowly, he heard the man advance toward the pit. Pendergast's muscles tensed as he sensed the man creeping toward the edge he hid beneath. A moment later, Roman's face appeared, bloodshot eyes wild, flashlight in one hand, handgun in the other.

Uncoiling like a snake, Pendergast leapt up and grabbed Roman's wrist, yanking him forward and pulling him toward the void. With a scream of surprise and dismay, Roman reared back, his gun and flashlight skittering off across the rocky ground as he used both hands to fend off the attack and counteract the pull. He was immensely strong and quick, surprisingly so, and he managed to correct the sudden imbalance and dig in his heels, striking at Pendergast's forearm with a bear-like roar of rage. But Pendergast was up and over the edge in a flash, Roman scrabbling backward. Pendergast raised his own gun to fire, but it was now black and Roman, anticipating the shot, threw himself sideways. The bullet ricocheted harmlessly off the rock floor, but the flash of the discharge betrayed Roman's position. Pendergast fired again, but now the muzzle flash revealed nothing: Roman had vanished.

Pendergast dug into his suit and pulled out his backup light: a handheld LED. Roman had apparently launched himself into a narrow, low-ceilinged seam that angled down steeply from the main tunnel. Dropping to his knees, Pendergast crawled into the seam and followed. Ahead, he could hear Roman in panicked flight, scrabbling along the low passage, gasping in fear. He, too, it seemed, had a second light: Pendergast could make out a jerky glow in the darkness of the seam ahead.

Relentlessly, Pendergast pursued his quarry. But as hard as he pushed, Roman stayed well ahead. The young man was in peak physical condition and had the advantage of knowing the tunnels, their fantastic complexity only adding to his edge. Pendergast was doing little more than moving blind, following the sound, the light, and—occasionally—the tracks.

Now Pendergast entered an area of large tunnels, cracks, and yawning, vertical chimneys. Still he pursued with monomaniacal intensity. Roman, Pendergast knew, had lost his weapon and was in a state of panic; Pendergast retained his weapon and his wits. To heighten Roman's terror and keep him off balance, now and then Pendergast would fire a round in the direction of the fleeing man, the bullet cracking and zinging as it tore through the tunnels ahead. There was little chance he would hit Roman, but that was not his intention: the deafening roar of the gun, and the terrifying ricochet of the rounds, was having the desired psychological effect.

Roman seemed to be going somewhere, and it soon became clear—as the air in the tunnels grew steadily fresher and colder—that he was heading outside. Into the storm...where Pendergast, having jettisoned his outerwear, would be at an additional disadvantage. Ted Roman might be beside himself with fear—but he was still able to think ahead and strategize.

A few minutes later, Pendergast's suspicions were confirmed: he rounded a corner and saw, directly ahead, a rusty steel wall with a door in it, open, swinging in the wind, the sound of the storm filling the entranceway. Rushing to the door, Pendergast shone his flashlight out into the murk. All was black; night had settled. The dim light disclosed a mine entrance, broken trestle, and the plunging slope of the cirque, falling away at a fifty-degree angle. The beam did not penetrate far, but nevertheless he could make out Roman's footprints in the deep snow, floundering off into the storm. Farther below, through the murk, he could see a cluster of glowing pinpoints—the smoldering remains of the pump building—and the lights of the idling snowcat nearby.

He turned off his light. He could just see the faint, bobbing glow of Roman's flashlight, descending the steep slope, about a hundred yards to one side. The man was moving slowly. Pendergast raised his weapon. It would be an exceptionally difficult shot, due to the high winds and the added complication of altitude. Nevertheless, Pendergast took a careful bead on the wavering light, mentally compensating for windage and drop. Very slowly, he squeezed the trigger. The firearm kicked with the shot, the report loud against the mountainside, the rolling echoes coming back from several directions.

A miss.

The figure kept moving, faster now, floundering downhill, getting ever farther out of range. Pendergast, without winter clothing, had no hope of catching him.

Ignoring the snow that stung his face and the vicious wind that penetrated his suit, Pendergast took another bead and fired, missing again. The chance for a hit was becoming nil. But then—as he took aim a third time—he heard something: a muffled *crack*, followed by a low-frequency rumble.

Above and ahead of Pendergast, the heavy snow surface was fracturing into large plates, the plates detaching and sliding downward, slowly at first, then faster and faster, breaking up and tumbling into chaos. It was an avalanche, triggered by the noise of his shots and, no doubt, Roman's own floundering about. With a growing roar the churning front of snow blasted past the mine entrance. The air was suddenly opaque, full of roiling, violent snow, and the gust of its passing knocked Pendergast backward as it thundered by him.

Within thirty seconds the roar had subsided. It had been a small slide. The slope before Pendergast was now swept clean of deep snow, the residual, trickling streams of it sliding down the mountain in rills. All was silent save for the cry of the wind.

Pendergast glanced downward to where Roman's bobbing flashlight had been. There was nothing now but a deep expanse of snow rubble. There were no signs of movement; no calls for help—nothing.

For a moment, Pendergast just stared down into the darkness. For the briefest of moments—as the blood rage that had taken possession of him still pulsed through his veins—he grimly contemplated the justice of the situation. But even as he stared, his fury ebbed. It was as if the avalanche had scoured his mind clear. He paused to consider what, subconsciously, he'd already understood until the sight of Corrie's burnt corpse swept all logic from his mind: that Ted Roman was as much a victim as Corrie herself. The true evil lay elsewhere.

With a muffled cry, he sprang from the mine entrance into the snow and struggled down the slope, coatless, sliding and floundering to where the avalanche had piled up along the top of the cirque. It took a few minutes to get there, and by the time he reached the spot he was half frozen.

"Roman!" he cried. "Ted Roman!"

No reply but the wind.

Now Pendergast jammed one ear into the snow to listen. Just barely, he could hear a strange, muffled, horrifying sound, almost like a cow bawling: *Мииииииии тииииии, тиии тиии.*

It seemed to be coming from the edge of the snow rubble. Moving toward it in the bitter cold, Pendergast began to dig frantically, with his bare hands. But the snow was compacted by the pressure of the avalanche, his hands inadequate to the task. Without jacket or hat, the cold had penetrated to his skin, and he weakened, his hands numbing to uselessness.

Where was Roman? He listened again, placing his ear against the hard-packed snow, trying to warm his hands.

Muuu...muuu...

It was rapidly growing fainter. The man was suffocating.

He dug and dug, and then paused to listen again. Nothing. And now he saw, out of the corner of his eye, a light coming up the slope. Ignoring it, he kept digging. A moment later a pair of strong hands grasped him and gently pulled him away. It was Kloster, the snowcat operator, with a shovel and a long rod in his hands.

"Hey," he said. "Hey, easy. You're going to kill yourself."

"There's a man down there," Pendergast gasped. "Buried."

"I saw it. You go down to the cat before you freeze to death. There's nothing you can do. I'll take care of it." The man began probing with the rod across the rubble of the avalanche, sliding it into the snow, working fast and expertly. He had done this kind of thing before. Pendergast did not go to the cat but stood nearby, watching and shivering. After a few moments Kloster paused, probing more gingerly in a tighter area, and then he began to dig with the shovel. He worked with energy and efficiency, and within minutes had exposed part of Roman's body. A few more minutes of extremely rapid work uncovered the face.

Pendergast approached as the man's light played over it. The snow was soaked with blood all around the head, the skull partly depressed, the mouth open as if in a scream but completely stoppered with snow, the eyes wide open and crazy.

"He's gone," said Kloster. He put an arm on Pendergast to steady him. "Listen, I'm going to take you back to the cat now so you can warm yourself up—otherwise, you're going to be following him."

Pendergast nodded wordlessly and allowed himself to be helped through the deep snow to the cab of the idling machine.

64

Half a mile away, on the lower, eastern slope of the cirque, a metal door opened at the entrance to a mine tunnel. Moments later a figure came staggering out, dragging one leg, leaning on a stick and coughing violently. The figure paused in the mine opening, swayed, leaned against a bracing timber, then doubled over with another coughing fit. Slowly, the figure slid down, unable to support itself, and ended up in the snow, propped against the vertical timber.

It was her. Just as he'd expected. He knew she had to come out sometime—and what a perfect target she made. She wasn't going anywhere, and he had all the time in the world to set up his shot.

The sniper, crouched in the doorway of an old mining shack, unshouldered his Winchester 94, worked the lever to insert a round into the chamber, then braced the weapon against his shoulder, sighting through the scope. While it was dark, there was still just enough ambient light in the sky to place the crosshairs on her dark, slumped form. The girl looked like she was in pretty bad shape already: hair singed, face and clothes black with smoke. He believed at least one of his earlier shots had hit home. As he'd pursued her through the tunnels, he had seen copious drops of blood. He wasn't sure where she'd been hit, but a .30-30 expanding round was no joke, wherever it connected.

The sniper did not understand why she was up here, why the

snowcat had raced by on its way up the mountain, or why the pump building had burned. He didn't need to know. Whatever crazy shit she was involved in was none of his business. Montebello had given him an assignment and paid him well to do it—extremely well, in fact. His instructions had been simple: scare the girl named Corrie Swanson out of town. If she didn't leave, kill her. The architect hadn't told him anything more, and he didn't want to know anything more.

The shot through the car window hadn't done it. Decapitating the mutt hadn't done it—although he recalled the scene with a certain fondness. He was proud of the tableau he'd arranged, the note in the dead dog's mouth—and he was disappointed and surprised it hadn't scared her off. She had proven to be one feisty bitch. But she didn't look so feisty now, slumped against the timber, half dead.

The moment had come. He'd been following her almost continuously now for thirty-six hours, waiting for an opportunity. As an expert hunter, he knew the value of patience. He had not had a good shot either in town or at the hotel. But when she had gone to The Heights, stolen a snowmobile, and taken it up the mountain on whatever insane errand she was on, the opportunity was placed in his hands, like a gift. He had borrowed another snowmobile and followed her. True, she had proven unusually resourceful—that business with the rattlesnakes back in the tunnel had seriously put him out. But he had found another way out of the mine and—when he discovered her snowmobile was still there—decided to stick around: He positioned himself a little way down the mountain, in the darkness of a mining shack, a blind that commanded an excellent view of most of the old adits and tunnel entrances up on the cirque. If she was still inside the mountain, he'd reasoned, she would eventually come out one of those. Or, perhaps, from the Christmas Mine, where she'd left her snowmobile. In any case, she'd have to pass by him on the way down.

And now, here she was. And in a good location, away from the activity around and above, where the pump building had burned and where the snowcat was parked. Someone had fired shots, which, it seemed, had in turn triggered an avalanche. From his hiding place, through the magnification of the scope, he watched the frantic digging and the discovery of the body. Something crazy-big was going down—drugs, he figured. But it had nothing to do with him, and the sooner he killed the target and got his ass out of there, the better.

Easing out his breath, finger on the trigger, he aimed at the slumped girl. The crosshairs steadied, his finger tightened. Finally, the time had come. He'd take her out, climb on his snowmobile parked behind the shack, and go collect his pay. One shot, one kill...

Suddenly the rifle was knocked brutally from behind, and it went off, discharging the round into the snow.

"What the—?" The sniper grasped the rifle, tried to rise, and as he did so felt something cold and hard pressed against his temple. The muzzle of a pistol.

"So much as blink, motherfucker, and I'll make a snow angel with your brains."

A woman's voice—full of authority and seriousness.

A hand reached out, seized his rifle by the barrel. "Let go."

He let go the rifle and she flung it out into the deep snow.

"All your other weapons—toss them into the snow. *Now.*"

He hesitated. He still had a handgun and knife, and if he forced her to search him there might be an opportunity...

The blow against the side of his head was so hard it knocked him to the ground. He lay dazed on the wooden floor for a moment, wondering why the heck he was lying here and who this woman was standing over him. Then it all started to come back as she bent over him, searched him roughly, removed the knife and pistol, and threw them far out into the snow as well.

"Who...who the fuck are you?" he asked.

The answer came with another stunning blow to his face from the butt of her gun, leaving the inside of his lips torn and bloody and his mouth full of broken fragments of teeth.

"My name," she said crisply, "is Captain Stacy Bowdree, USAF, and I am the very worst thing that's happened to you in your entire shitty life."

65

Corrie Swanson saw the tall, handsome figure of Stacy Bowdree emerge out of the swirling snow, leading a man with his hands tied together and his shaggy head bowed. She dimly wondered if it was all a dream. Of course it was a dream. Stacy would never be up here.

As Stacy stopped before her, Corrie managed to say, "Hello, dream."

Stacy looked aghast. "My God. What happened to you?"

Corrie tried to think back on all that had happened, and couldn't quite bring it into focus. The more she tried to remember, the stranger everything became. "Are you for real?"

"You're damn right!" Stacy bent forward, examined Corrie closely, her blue eyes full of concern. "What are you doing with these handcuffs fastened to your wrist? And your hair is burned. Jesus, were you in that fire?"

Corrie tried to form the words. "A man...tried to kill me in the tunnels...but the rattlesnakes..."

"Yeah. This is him." Stacy shoved the man facedown into the snow before Corrie and put her booted foot on his neck. Corrie noticed the .45 in Stacy's hand. She tried to focus on the man lying on the ground but her eyes were swimming.

"This is the guy hired to kill you," Stacy went on. "I caught him just as he was about to pull the trigger. He won't tell me his name, so I'm calling him Dirtbag."

"How? How...?" It all seemed so confusing.

"Listen. We've got to get you to a hospital and Dirtbag to the po-lice chief. There's a snowcat about half a mile away, near the burnt pump building."

Pump building. "Burn...He tried to burn me alive."

"Who? Dirtbag here?"

"No...Ted. I had my bump key...picked the cuffs...just in time..."

"You're not making much sense," Stacy said. "Let me help you up. Can you walk?"

"Ankle's broken. Lost...a finger."

"Shit. Let's take a look at you."

She could feel Stacy examining her, gently touching her ankle, asking questions and probing for injuries. She felt comforted. A few minutes later Stacy's face came back in focus, close to her own. "Okay, you've got a few second-degree burns. And you're right: your ankle's broken and a little finger's gone. That's bad enough, but luckily it seems to be all. Thank God you were bundled up in winter clothes, otherwise you'd be a lot more burned than you are."

Corrie nodded. She couldn't quite understand what Stacy was say-ing. But was it really Stacy, and not some vision? "You disappeared..."

"Sorry about that. When I cooled off I realized those assholes had hired some thug to drive you out of town, and so I shadowed you for a while and pretty soon saw Dirtbag, here, skulking after you like a dog sniffing for shit. So I followed him. In the end, I stole a snowmobile back there in the equipment shed—just as the two of you did—followed your tracks up here just in time to see Dirtbag vanish into the mine entrance. I lost you in the mines but figured he had, as well, and I managed to backtrack in time."

Corrie nodded. Nothing was making any sense to her. People had been trying to kill her—that much she knew. But Stacy had saved her. That's all she needed to know. Her head was spinning and she couldn't even seem to hold it up. Black clouds gathered in front of her eyes.

"Okay," Stacy continued, "you stay here, I'll take Dirtbag to the cat and then we'll drive back to get you." She felt Stacy's hand on her shoulder, giving it a squeeze. "Hang in there just a minute more, girl. You're dinged up, but you're going to be okay. Trust me, I know. I've seen…" She paused. "Much worse." She turned away.

"No." Corrie sobbed, reaching out for Stacy. "Don't go."

"Have to." She gently put Corrie's hand to her side. "I can't keep Dirtbag under control and help you, too. It's better if you don't walk. Give me ten minutes, tops."

It seemed a lot shorter than ten minutes. Corrie heard the roar of a diesel, then saw a cluster of moving headlamps stabbing through the murk, approaching fast, pulling up to the mine entrance in a swirling cloud of snow. A strange, pale figure emerged—Pendergast?—and she felt herself suddenly in his arms, lifted bodily as if she were a child again, her head cradled against his chest. She felt his shoulders began to convulse, faintly, regularly, almost as if he was weeping. But that was, of course, impossible, as Pendergast would never cry.

EPILOGUE

The brilliant winter sun streamed in the window and lay in stripes across Corrie's bed at the Roaring Fork Hospital. She had been given the best room in the hospital, a corner single on a high floor, the large window overlooking most of the town and the mountains beyond, everything wreathed in a magical blanket of white. This was the view Corrie had awoken to after the operation on her hand, and the sight had cheered her considerably. That was three days ago, and she was set to be discharged in two more. The break in her foot had not been serious, but she had lost her little finger. Some of the burns she'd suffered might scar, but only slightly, and only, they had told her, on her chin.

Pendergast sat in a chair on one side of the bed and Stacy sat in another. The foot of the bed was covered in presents. Chief Morris had been in to pay his respects—he'd been a regular visitor since her operation—and after inquiring about how Corrie was feeling and thanking Pendergast profusely for his help in the investigation, he'd added his own gift (a CD of John Denver's greatest hits) to the pile.

"Well," said Stacy, "are we going to open them, or what?"

"Corrie shall go first," said Pendergast, handing her a slim envelope. "To mark the completion of her research."

Corrie tore it open, puzzled. A computer printout emerged, covered with columns of crabbed figures, graphs, and tables. She unfolded it. It was a report from an FBI forensic lab in Quantico—an analysis of mercury contamination in twelve samples of human re-mains—the crazed miners she'd found in the tunnels.

"My God," Corrie said. "The numbers are off the charts."

"The final detail you require for your thesis. I have little doubt you will be the first junior in the history of John Jay to win the Rosewell Prize."

"Thank you," Corrie said, and then hesitated. "Um, I owe you an apology. *Another* apology. A really big one this time. I messed up, well and truly. You've helped me so much, and I just never really appreci-ated it the way I should have. I was an ungrateful—" she almost said a bad word but amended it on the fly— "girl. I should have listened to you and never gone up there alone. What a stupid thing to do."

Pendergast inclined his head. "We can go into that some other time."

Corrie turned to Stacy. "I owe a big apology to you, too. I'm really ashamed that I suspected you and Ted. You saved my life. I really don't have the words to thank you . . ." She felt her throat close up with emo-tion.

Stacy smiled, squeezed her hand. "Don't be hard on yourself, Cor-rie. You're a true pal. And Ted . . . Jesus, I can hardly believe he was the arsonist. It gives me nightmares."

"On one level," Pendergast said, "Roman wasn't responsible for what he did. It was the mercury in his brain, which had been poison-ing his neurons since he was in his mother's womb. He was no more a criminal than were those miners who went mad working in the smelter and ultimately became cannibals. They are all victims. The true criminals are certain others, a family whose malevolent deeds go back a century and a half. And now that the FBI is on it, that family will pay. Perhaps not as brutally as Mrs. Kermode did, but they will pay nonetheless."

Corrie shuddered. Until Pendergast had told her, she hadn't any idea that, the whole time she'd been shackled to the pump, Mrs. Ker-mode had been in the building as well, out of sight, handcuffed to the far side of the engine—probably unconscious after being beaten up by Ted. *Oh, God, will I take care of that bitch*, he'd said . . .

"I was in such a hurry to escape the flames, I never even saw her," Corrie said. "I'm not sure anyone deserves to be burned alive like that."

The expression on Pendergast's face indicated he might disagree.

"But there's no way Ted could have known that Kermode and the Staffords were responsible for his own madness—was there?" Corrie asked.

Pendergast shook his head. "No. Her end at his hands was poetic justice, nothing more."

"I hope the rest of them rot in prison," said Stacy.

After a silence, Corrie asked, "And you really thought Kermode's burnt body was mine?"

"There was no question in my mind," Pendergast replied. "If I'd been thinking more clearly, I might have realized that Kermode was potentially Ted's next victim. She represented everything he despised. That entire *auto-da-fé* up on the mountain was arranged for her, not for you. You just fell into his lap, so to speak. But I do have a question, Corrie: how did you undo the handcuffs?"

"Aw, they were crappy old handcuffs. And I'd tucked my picks into the space between the inner and outer glove when I was trying to pick the lock into the mine—because, as you of all people know, you have to use several tools simultaneously."

Pendergast nodded. "Impressive."

"It took me a while to remember I even had the tools, I was so terrified. Ted was...I've never seen anything like it in my life. The way he shifted from screaming rage to cold, calculated precision...God, it was almost more frightening than the fire itself."

"A common effect of mercury-induced madness. And that perhaps explains the mystery of the bent pipes in the second fire—"

Stacy said hastily, "Um, let's open the rest of the presents and stop talking about this."

"I'm sorry I don't have anything for anyone," said Corrie.

"You were otherwise engaged," said Pendergast. "And while I'm on the subject, given what also happened to you in Kraus's Kaverns back in Medicine Creek, in the future I would advise you to avoid underground labyrinths, especially when they are tenanted by homicidal maniacs." He paused. "Incidentally, I'm very sorry about your finger."

"I suppose I'll get used to it. It's almost colorful, like wearing an eye patch or something."

Pendergast took up a small package and examined it. There was no card, just his name written on it. "This is from you, Captain?"

"Sure is."

Pendergast removed the paper, revealing a velvet box. He opened it. Inside, a Purple Heart rested on satin.

He stared at it for a long time. Finally he said: "How can I accept this?"

"Because I've got three more and I want you to have it. You deserve a medal—you saved my life."

"Captain Bowdree—"

"I mean it. I was lost, confused, drinking myself into oblivion every evening, until you called out of the blue. You got me here, explained about my ancestor, gave me purpose. And most of all...you respected me."

Pendergast hesitated. He held up the medal. "I will treasure this."

"Merry Christmas—three days late."

"And now you must open yours."

Stacy took up a small envelope. She opened it and extracted an official-looking document. She read it, her brow furrowing. "Oh, my God."

"It's nothing, really," said Pendergast. "Just an appointment for an interview. The rest is up to you. But with my recommendation, and your military record, I feel confident you will pass muster. The FBI needs agents like you, Captain. I've rarely seen a finer candidate. Corrie here may rival you, one day—all she lacks is a certain seasoning of judgment."

"Thank you." It looked for a moment like Bowdree might hug Pendergast, but then she seemed to decide the gesture might not be welcome. Corrie smiled inwardly; this entire ceremony, with its attendant displays of affection and emotion, seemed to be making him a little uncomfortable.

There were two more presents for Corrie. She opened the first, to find within the wrapping a well-worn textbook: *Techniques for Crime Scene Analysis and Investigation: Third Edition.*

"I know this book," she said. "But I already have a copy—a much later edition, which we use at John Jay."

"I'm aware of that," Pendergast said.

She opened it, suddenly understanding. Inside, the text was heavily annotated with marginalia: comments, glosses, questions, insights into the topic being discussed. The handwriting was precise, and she recognized it immediately.

"This...this was your copy?"

Pendergast nodded.

"My God." She touched the cover, caressing it almost reverentially. "What a treasure trove. Maybe by reading this I'll be able to think like you someday."

"I had considered other, more frivolous gifts, but this one seemed—given your evident interest in a law enforcement career—perhaps the most useful."

There was one gift left. Corrie reached for it, carefully removed the expensive-looking wrapping paper.

"It's from Constance," Pendergast explained. "She just returned from India a few days ago, and asked me to give you this."

Inside was an antique Waterman fountain pen with a filigreed overlay of gold, and a small volume in ribbed leather, with cream-colored, deckle-edged pages. It was beautifully handmade. A small note fell out, which she picked up and read.

Dear Miss Swanson,

I have read with interest some of your online "blogs" (hateful word). I thought that perhaps you might find indulging in a more permanent and private expression of your observations to be a useful occupation. I myself have kept a diary for many years. It has always been a source to me of interest, consolation, and personal insight. It is my hope this slight volume will help confer those same benefits on you.

Constance Greene

Corrie looked at the presents scattered around her. Then she glanced at Stacy, seated on the edge of the bed, and Pendergast, relaxing in his chair, one leg thrown lightly over the other. All of a sudden, to her great surprise, she burst into tears.

"Corrie!" Stacy said, leaping to her feet. "What's wrong? Are you in pain?"

"No," Corrie said through her tears. "I'm not in pain. I'm just happy—so happy. I've never had a happier Christmas."

"Three days late," Pendergast murmured, with a twitch of his facial features that might have indicated a smile.

"And there's nobody on earth I'd rather share it with than you two." Corrie furiously brushed away the tears and, embarrassed, turned to look out the window, where the morning sun was gilding Roaring Fork, the low flanks of the mountains, and—farther up—the bowl-like shape of Smuggler's Cirque and the small, dark smudge against the snow where a fire had almost ended her life.

She tapped the journal. "I already know what my first entry will be," she said.

Acknowledgments

We'd like to thank the following for their support and assistance: Mitch Hoffman, Eric Simonoff, Jamie Raab, Lindsey Rose, Claudia Rülke, Nadine Waddell, Jon Lellenberg, Saul Cohen, and the Estate of Sir Arthur Conan Doyle.

We salute the most excellent work of the Baker Street Irregulars.

And we apologize in advance for any liberties taken with Kielder Forest, *Queen's Quorum*, Hampstead Heath, and any other places or entities mentioned in *White Fire*.

About the Authors

DOUGLAS PRESTON and **LINCOLN CHILD** are coauthors of many bestselling novels, including *Relic*, which was made into a number one box office hit movie, as well as *The Cabinet of Curiosities, Still Life with Crows, Brimstone, The Book of the Dead, Fever Dream*, and *Gideon's Sword*. Preston's bestselling nonfiction book, *The Monster of Florence*, is being made into a motion picture starring George Clooney. His interests include horses, scuba diving, skiing, and exploring the Maine coast in an old lobster boat. Lincoln Child is a former book editor who has published four bestselling novels of his own. He is passionate about motorcycles, exotic parrots, and nineteenth-century English literature. Readers can sign up for *The Pendergast File*, a monthly "strangely entertaining note" from the authors, at their website, www.prestonchild.com. The authors welcome visitors to their alarmingly active Facebook page, where they post regularly.

The Assassination of
ROBERT F.
KENNEDY

WILLIAM W. TURNER
JONN G. CHRISTIAN

Random House New York

The Assassination of
ROBERT F. KENNEDY

A Searching Look at the Conspiracy and Cover-up 1968-1978

Library of Congress Cataloging in Publication Data
Christian, Jonn
The assassination of Robert F. Kennedy.
1. Kennedy, Robert F., 1925-1968—Assassina-
tion. I. Turner, William W., joint author.
II. Title.
E840.8.K4C5   364.1'524   77-90234
ISBN 0-394-40273-1

Manufactured in the United States of America
9 8 7 6 5 4 3 2
First Edition

This book is respectfully and affectionately dedicated to William W. Harper, one of the world's premier criminalists, and a man whose personal and professional sacrifices should one day be acknowledged by a grateful American public

Acknowledgments

IT WOULD TAKE A BOOK IN ITSELF TO NAME EVERYONE TO WHOM WE became indebted over the years as *The Assassination of Robert F. Kennedy* evolved from an investigative project to a finished volume. But we would especially like to thank Vincent T. Bugliosi, Robert J. Joling and Allard K. Lowenstein, eminent lawyers all, whose forensic skills and determined probing are chronicled herein. Also Jocelyn Brando, Robert Vaughn, Dianne Hull and Paul Le Mat, Hollywood citizen-actors whose moral support and encouragement were indispensable over the long haul.

The tedious task of transforming our investigative file into a manuscript was aided immeasurably by John A. "Jack" Thomas, a young man willing to open his mind and dedicate himself to the project, and English-born Lorraine Y. S. Cradock, who undertook more responsibility than most native citizens might have in turbulent times. We are also grateful to Fremont Bodine "Peter" Hitchcock, a friend whose unfortunate and premature death kept him from knowing that his contribution has borne fruit, and to the late Sara Jane Churchill De Witt, her son Jack and her daughter Mrs. Bill (Bettie) Anderson for their unlimited understanding and encouragement; and to Ms. Jackie Henken, a young woman concerned and caring enough to get involved in the most important of ways. And it would hardly be an exaggeration to say there would be no book without the commitment and forbearance of our families, who proved through often hectic phases of this project that love is indeed boundless.

Nor can a book see the light of print without a publisher, for which we are appreciative of Random House and its editorial director Jason Epstein for their vision and resolve in taking it on. We are likewise indebted to our working editor Susan Bolotin for her inexhaustible patience in nurturing it through the production process. To say that *The Assassination of Robert F. Kennedy* is not the easiest book they have been involved with is to say that the sun rises in the east, and we suspect, now that the tribulations are over, that they do care.

Contents

Introduction

AS <u>HELTER SKELTER</u> SO LUCIDLY DEPICTED THE PROSECUTION'S USE
of direct and circumstantial evidence against the Manson Family,
and *The Godfather* provided a clear window to the inside machina-
tions of organized crime, *The Assassination of Robert F. Kennedy*
stands as a unique study on the subject of contemporary political
murder in America. It might well be classified by historians as the
Helter Skelter–Godfather of assassination books.

The story at hand concerns itself with what I consider to be
the single most important issue of our time: the assassinations of
our finest leaders over the past decade and a half. The central
theme here is the conspiracy and cover-up surrounding the assassination of Senator Robert Kennedy, with evidential tributaries leading in the direction of the murders of President John F. Kennedy
and Dr. Martin Luther King, Jr., as well as the attempt on the
life of Governor George C. Wallace. The implications are staggering.

This thoroughly researched and meticulously documented book
is the end result of its authors' relentless pursuit of the actual facts
in these cases, which in my opinion has produced the most impressive investigative file ever privately assembled. In effect, it is a
formidable grand jury presentation in book form. And the information presented herein surely warrants the immediate re-examination
of the entire assassination issue at the highest levels of the United
States government.

I wholly concur with the authors of this book that we, the
American public, deserve resolution of the disturbing unanswered
questions in these murders at the earliest moment, or we face the
distinct possibility that further attempts on the lives of more political

leaders could occur at any time. I'm convinced that most thinking Americans sense this too; and I'm certain that the readers of this book will soon join the swelling numbers of us demanding that justice be done, for the future of our nation is truly the responsibility of each of us.

DR. ROBERT J. JOLING

Dr. Joling is a former president of the American Academy of Forensic Sciences (1975-76); Vice President, International Association of Forensic Sciences. Member: British Academy of Forensic Sciences; the American Bar Association; Association of Trial Lawyers of America; American College of Legal Medicine; American Arbitration Association. Graduate, Juris Doctoris, Marquette University Law School, 1951. Admissions to Practice: Supreme Court of the United States; United States Tax Court; District Courts of Arizona and Wisconsin; Wisconsin Supreme Court. He is a law partner in Joling & Rizzo, Kenosha, Wisconsin.

Prologue

CALIFORNIA WAS MAKE-OR-BREAK FOR SENATOR ROBERT F. KEN-
nedy in his quest for the 1968 Democratic presidential nomination.
On May 28 he lost the Oregon primary to Senator Eugene
McCarthy, and a setback the following week in the nation's most
populous state would probably ruin his chances. On the other hand,
a victory would gain him 174 delegate votes and much-needed
momentum for the showdown at the national convention in Chicago.
It would virtually eliminate McCarthy, leaving only Hubert H.
Humphrey in his way. A symbol of the old politics with the albatross
of Lyndon Johnson's escalated war in Vietnam hanging from his
neck, the Vice President was not a good bet to withstand the tides
of renewal surging through the party. Most observers thought that
RFK would ride the tide past Humphrey and defeat the Republicans'
likely candidate, Richard M. Nixon.

Kennedy came to California for a home-stretch drive so frenetic
that on election eve he was on the brink of collapse. He had to
cancel a San Diego appearance that night, but the next morning he
was back on his feet, buoyed by a just-completed poll showing him
safely ahead of McCarthy. After a day of last-minute campaigning,
he went to the Malibu home of movie director John Frankenheimer
for a quiet supper party that included Roman Polanski and his
fated wife Sharon Tate. After supper Frankenheimer drove him to
the Ambassador Hotel, where he would watch the election returns
on television in the Royal Suite.

By midnight he was ready to claim victory. He checked himself
in a full-length mirror before leading his entourage down a service
elevator to the Embassy Room on the ground floor. The ballroom

was jammed with campaign workers and supporters, and a thunderous cheer went up as the candidate came into view. Speaking into a bundle of microphones on the small stage, he gave a brief speech. "Mayor Yorty has just sent me a message that we have been here too long already," he cracked, drawing laughs from the audience (Sam Yorty was a right-wing Democrat who had supported Nixon against RFK's brother in the 1960 election). RFK wound up by flashing the V sign and exhorting, "On to Chicago! Let's win there!"

Kennedy intended to meet with the press in their headquarters in the adjacent Colonial Room. Ordinarily, he would have crossed the ballroom floor and exited through the main door, but the crush of people was so great that a last-minute decision was made to route him through a service pantry. A maître d' gripped his right wrist tightly and led him through the gold curtain behind the stage and into the pantry. His progress was slow as he greeted admiring kitchen workers.

Suddenly a gunman sprang at him, snarling, "Kennedy, you son of a bitch!" He fired two rapid shots. Kennedy reeled backwards, flinging his right arm in front of his face for protection. People grabbed for the gunman.

Kennedy landed on his back, his arms splayed outward as in a crucifixion, a halo of blood widening around his head. Within inches of his right hand was a clip-on bow tie he had apparently snatched from someone close-by as he sagged from the impact of three bullets in his body and head.

Up in San Francisco we—the authors of this book—were stunned by the news. William Turner had run for the U.S. Congress in the same Democratic primary, with Jonn Christian as his campaign manager. As the chief plank in our platform we had advocated the establishment of a joint Senate-House committee to reinvestigate the 1963 assassination of President John F. Kennedy. Now the final line of our campaign brochure seemed horrifyingly prescient: "To do less not only is indecent but might cost us the life of a future President of John Kennedy's instincts."

Robert Kennedy died slightly more than a day later. When the plane carrying his body back to New York landed at Kennedy International Airport, NBC television correspondent Sander Vanocur, who had covered the RFK campaign, came down the ramp to face his own network's cameras. Forcing back tears, he reported that during the flight Edward Kennedy had remonstrated bitterly about the "faceless men" who had been charged with the slayings of his brothers and Dr. Martin Luther King, Jr. First Lee Harvey Oswald, then James Earl Ray, and now Sirhan Sirhan. Always faceless men with no apparent motive. "There has to be more to it," Ted Kennedy had told Vanocur.

But Ted Kennedy's words, uttered in a private moment and never to be repeated by him in public, were lost in the rush as the campaign instantly went into reverse. What had begun as a great national groundswell of revulsion against the war, so strong that it swept an incumbent President out of the running, became a nightmare of reaction and irrelevancy. There were pious outcries in Congress for tougher gun laws, breast-beating in the media about how America's violent society had spawned another deranged assassin, and demands for a law-and-order crackdown.

It was almost anticlimactic when Hubert Humphrey finagled the Democratic nomination at the violence-wracked convention and tried to pull the shattered party together. He was no match for Richard Nixon, who cynically called himself the "peace with honor" candidate and boasted of a "secret plan" for ending the conflict (which would drag on for four more years). So the nation had another "accidental President" catapulted to power by a "lone nut" assassin.

The conclusion that Sirhan Sirhan had acted alone and unaided was duly arrived at by the Los Angeles Police Department, which had primary investigative jurisdiction. The FBI, which conducted a parallel inquiry under the civil rights laws, concurred. And most of the American people accepted the theory, since the case seemed as open and shut as the shooting of Oswald by Jack Ruby in front of millions of television viewers.

Committed though we were to reopening the John Kennedy case, we did not immediately dispute the official verdict. We had no way of knowing, in the days that followed RFK's death, what we were later to learn about the case.

Scarcely a month after the assassination, through a curious set of circumstances, we came upon a self-ordained evangelist who told about a chance encounter with Sirhan the day before the shooting.

It was a bizarre story, and it set us off on our own investigation that has continued to this day. What we discovered led us to disbelieve the preacher's story, then search for what was behind it. For he in fact had told it not merely to us but to the Los Angeles police, filing his report only hours after the shooting.

Our efforts came to a climax in the summer of 1975 when a little-noticed trial shed stark new light on a crime that altered the course of American history.

The Assassination of
ROBERT F.
KENNEDY

1

The Evangelist and the Cowboy

IT HAD BEGUN AS A SOMEWHAT ROUTINE CIVIL TRIAL, ONE OF hundreds each year in Los Angeles Superior Court that drone on to uneventful verdicts. It opened on July 2, 1975, in Department 32, Judge Jack A. Crickard presiding. The plaintiff was Jerry Owen, a hallelujah evangelist who bills himself as "The Walking Bible" because of a professed ability to quote all 31,173 verses of the Holy Book, punctuation marks and all.

The primary defendant was television station KCOP, an independent channel in the City of Angels. In 1969 Jerry Owen had contracted with KCOP for air time each Sunday for a year for a religious program called *The Walking Bible*, but after three broadcasts the station abruptly canceled the program. In 1970, after months of bitter wrangling, Owen filed a breach-of-contract and defamation-of-character suit against KCOP seeking $1.4 million in damages. In response to an interrogatory question posed in 1974, Owen stated that he had been libelously accused by then-president of KCOP John Hopkins of being "a thief, burned down six churches, was a convict, undesirable, a crook, a fraud, etc., [a] no good, sent to prison for arson, and not a minister of the Gospel, was involved in [Senator Robert F.] Kennedy's death."*

A secondary defendant was Ohrbach's department store, a fixture on the Wilshire Boulevard "Miracle Mile." On June 17, 1969, in the midst of his short-lived television series, Owen was arrested in the store for shoplifting three shirts. He was convicted and fined $250, but when the City Attorney's office unaccountably failed to contest his appeal, the conviction was vacated. Owen assumed that the "thief" in Hopkins' purported statement referred to the shoplifting incident.

In preparing for the trial, the defense team had assembled a hefty background file on the plaintiff. He was born Oliver Brindley Owen on April 13, 1913, in Ashland, Ohio, the son of a Baptist minister who subsequently migrated to California. In his youth Owen took to the boxing ring, and by the early 1930s was a sparring partner—"a punching bag," as he puts it—for Max Baer, who became heavyweight champion in 1934. The amiable behemoth paid Owen $100 a week and took him around the country. "If not for him, I'd be pickin' cotton in Bakersfield," Owen once wise-cracked to a reporter. Baer gave his protégé a diamond initial ring with an inscription inside: "To Curly from Max Baer."†

During this period "Curly" Owen was a Hollywood fringe character, playing bit roles in such movies as Mae West's *Diamond Lil* and *Prison Cell Break* with George Raft. He enjoyed rubbing elbows with celebrities, and according to several persons who knew

---

* Defendant's Exhibit #132, filed for identification in Los Angeles County Superior Court on October 10, 1974. (In another interrogatory, Owen's handwritten responses read that he had been falsely accused of being "a T shirt steeler [*sic*], a theif [*sic*], [a] church burnner [*sic*], Hypocrite and Impostor, Involved with assination [*sic*] of Kennedy.")

† Ely (Nevada) *Times* (April 26, 1974).

him, dropped names like Humphrey Bogart, Loretta Young and Bob Hope.* After Baer lost his crown to Jimmy Braddock in 1935, Owen enrolled at the University of Southern California to play freshman football.

But his budding gridiron career ended in 1937 when, in a flash of inspiration, he became "acquainted with a man named Jesus." As his own promotional brochure described it, Owen "found a prayer room by a little church, and for the next seven days he didn't leave this little room, but read the Bible through from Genesis to Revelation, without eating, drinking or shaving. It was as though he were spellbound by the majesty of the scriptures as they opened up to him for the first time in his life! He read-read-read until sleep blurred his vision. He did not speak to anyone, but just read the Bible through." Miraculously, Owen found that he had total recall of the Bible and "the verses tumbled out for him to read to the people." Ordaining himself, he embarked on an evangelistic career.

Soon thereafter, Owen's name began appearing on police blotters from coast to coast. In 1939 he was hauled into court in San Francisco to answer grand-theft charges brought by an elderly member of his congregation who complained he had bilked her out of $2,700. "He told me that God had directed him to come to me in his hour of need," she testified. "I gave him the money. He said, 'This is between the Almighty God and you and me. Above all, don't tell your husband.'" As a newspaper account described the scene: "The packed courtroom was sympathetic when the Rev. Mr. Owen's 20-year-old wife, Beverly, nearing motherhood, cried and was led from the courtroom. But at other times in the hearing some of the spectators were openly hostile to the evangelist. Those, he proclaimed, were former sheep who had been turned against him by rival preachers jealous of the growth of his Gospel Center."†

On February 17, 1945, Owen was arrested by the Portland, Oregon, police vice squad in a downtown hotel and charged with "disorderly conduct involving morals." Said Owen of the woman in the case: "She has been just like a sister to me. She's a good kid and has gotten off on the wrong foot. When I got off the train she

---

* In his "Walking Bible" brochure—sent on request to KCOP viewers— Owen features himself in a publicity photo with Baer and Hope.

† San Francisco *Examiner* (May 17, 1939).

told me she was in trouble and wanted me to go to her hotel room and wait until her boyfriend could come so I could talk it over with them."

"You don't expect us to believe that, do you?" the judge rejoined, leveling a sentence of a $50 fine and thirty days in jail (Owen posted an appeal bond and the case was continued indefinitely). Again he blamed his predicament on rival preachers out to defame him.*

In 1945 a Los Angeles woman filed a complaint seeking support of a minor child and to establish that he was the father, but it was never brought to trial.† In 1947 a girl whom he had met four years earlier when he ran his "Open Door Church" in Des Moines, Iowa, followed suit. According to a police report, "The child was born in November, 1947, and Owen forwarded $420 for hospital expenses. [The girl] later received word that Owen . . . would not be able to marry her."‡

A glimpse of the flamboyant preacher in action was given in a Terre Haute newspaper when he pitched his tent in Indiana in 1948. As two thousand people packed the tent and spotlights bathed the platform, "A big man, well over six feet, tall and of athletic build, wearing a sporty-looking gray suit, a rather flashy four-in-hand tie and bareheaded (his curly hair was cut rather short) appeared at the side of the platform. An excited hum swept the tent. 'That's him . . . that's Jerry Owen,' those who knew him whispered to those who had come for the first time." As ushers hawked programs for fifty cents, Owen bounded onto the platform and began an intimate monologue with the sky: " 'Bless these good people, Dear Jee-sus, and return their offering two-fold in your blessing. Oh, here's a sweet little girl. I bet she's got a great big kiss for old Jerry. Why don't some of you older girls come on down with your $10 and give the preacher man a kiss?' "

As the reporter described the event, Owen shouted, " 'Well, let's get going. The spirit is on me tonight.' " He did a jitterbug

---

* Portland *Oregonian* (February 18, 1945).

† Los Angeles Superior Court Docket No. D282986, May 29, 1945.

‡ Notarized Los Angeles police report obtained from Los Angeles County Clerk's office, July 7, 1969.

and grabbed the microphone to reel off Bible verses. "Text after text would be shouted, screamed at the audience," the reporter marveled. "The man was wearing himself into a hysterical frenzy that communicated itself to the audience." After scoring the evils of alcohol and tobacco, the preacher told of a faith healing he had accomplished. "Save me Jerry, save me Jerry!" Owen quoted a man on the brink of death as imploring. "I don't want to die!" Owen held his hand and prayed with him for five hours, and the crisis passed. "Isn't he wonderful!" the newspaper reporter overheard an elderly woman say as she daubed at her eyes. "I'll be back again tomorrow."*

In March 1950 Owen got into another scrape with his pray-for-pay competition while holding revival meetings in a Baltimore theater. With a contingent of followers he broke up a service being conducted across town by one Reverend C. Stanley Cook because of "a misstatement made by Brother Cook about me and another man's wife." Owen was convicted of disorderly conduct and fined $55. The newspapers had a field day quoting Max Baer, who happened to be visiting Baltimore, as being surprised that his erstwhile ring mate had turned to preaching. "The first time I heard you quoting from the Bible," Baer twitted Owen in front of reporters, "I couldn't believe it. I didn't think you could memorize 'The Village Blacksmith'—you'd leave him standing under the tree."†

Scarcely two months later the Indianapolis *News* headlined: EVANGELIST FACES CHARGES OF "SEX AND SALVATION" TOUR. The local prosecutor had filed charges against Owen for taking a sixteen-year-old delinquent schoolgirl on a six-state junket, helping her assume aliases to escape authorities and being intimate with her on at least two occasions. However, the federal authorities declined to prosecute under the White Slave Traffic Act because there had been no commercialization, and the state charges were dropped when the girl changed her mind and refused to testify. The girl, an accomplished pianist, disclosed that Owen had her play hymns "in a different manner" at the church services he conducted so that the

* Terre Haute *Standard* (August 15, 1948).
† Baltimore *Sun* (March 8, 1950).

emotions of the worshipers would be aroused. "I believe he was very sincere in his religion and believed in what he preached," she said, "because he wouldn't let me drink or smoke."*

Smoke? Owen's rap sheet under FBI Number 4 261 906 revealed that on March 22, 1964, a warrant was issued in Tucson, Arizona, charging him with "Arson in the first degree with intent to defraud Insurer and Conspiracy" in connection with the 1962 burning of his church building. Although Owen alibied that he was out of town at the time, a witness at his trial, Samuel Butler, testified that the preacher had offered him $1,000 to torch the church. Owen was convicted of arson conspiracy and sentenced to eight to nineteen years in prison, but the conviction was reversed on June 27, 1966, after Butler recanted his testimony in a deathbed statement.

The Tucson church was not the first of Owen's premises to go up in smoke. Los Angeles police records list similar incidents in Castro Valley, California, in 1939; Crystal Lake Park, Oregon, in 1945; Dallas, Texas, in 1946; Mount Washington, Kentucky, in 1947; and Ellicott City, Maryland, in 1951. Owen collected insurance settlements in several of the fires, but in the Maryland blaze his $16,000 claim was rejected because of alleged fraud. "A witness observed Owen moving personal effects out of the house prior to the fire and then return them," the police records state. But the persistent preacher appealed and was eventually awarded $6,500.

BY 1968 OWEN WAS LIVING IN SANTA ANA, THIRTY MILES SOUTH of Los Angeles in Orange County. He styled himself the "Shepherd of the Hills," and circulated around shopping centers giving free pony rides to children who promised to memorize a Bible verse and attend church on Sunday. He traded horses on the side. And he owned a piece of a club fighter named "Irish Rip" O'Reilly.

It was the horses and the boxing game, Owen testified in the KCOP trial, that brought about his chance association with Sirhan Sirhan. On the afternoon of June 3, 1968, the eve of the California primary election, he said that he was driving his pickup truck

* Indianapolis *News* (May 18, 1950).

through downtown Los Angeles on his way to purchase some boxing gear for O'Reilly. At a red light he let two hitchhikers climb into the back of the truck. After a dozen or so blocks they got off at another red light and appeared to converse with a man and woman standing on the corner. As Owen got ready to pull away, one of the hitchhikers got in the cab with him and struck up a conversation. Owen described him as a diminutive young man of foreign extraction who remarked that he worked as an exercise boy at a race track. When Owen mentioned that he traded horses as a sideline to his ministry, the young man said that he was in the market for a lead pony (used to walk horses around the track before and after races). After some haggling, he agreed to buy a palomino from Owen for $300.

The young man asked Owen to stop for a few minutes at the rear entrance to the Ambassador Hotel so that he could run in and "see a friend in the kitchen." Owen obliged. When he returned, the young man told Owen that he would meet him that night with the money for the horse. But at the appointed time and place the young man, accompanied by the same two men and the woman he had been seen with that afternoon, said he hadn't been able to raise all of the money. He produced a single $100 bill. The upshot of this intricate story was that Owen was asked to deliver the horse to the same rear entrance to the hotel the following night at eleven, at which time the full amount would be paid. But Owen couldn't make it because he was due to preach a sermon in Oxnard, seventy miles northwest of Los Angeles.

When Owen returned to Los Angeles on the morning after the election, he recognized Sirhan's picture on television as the hitchhiker who was going to buy his horse. At the urging of some friends he went straight to the police and told his story "like a good citizen." He felt that he nearly had been duped into becoming part of a bizarre getaway scheme after Kennedy was shot at the Ambassador Hotel the previous night.

For the first thirteen days of the trial the question of Owen's strange story about picking up Sirhan had been muted as the plaintiff's lawyers completed their case and the defense began its preliminary arguments.

Then, on July 29, KCOP trial attorney Vincent T. Bugliosi

stood and prepared to call his star witness. In 1970 Bugliosi had gained fame as the chief prosecutor of Charles Manson and his killer cult. Leaving the District Attorney's office a year later, he entered private practice and wrote *Helter Skelter*, a best-selling account of the Manson case. Trim and fastidious, the forty-one-year-old Bugliosi was wearing the midnight-blue pin-striped suit and vest with red tie that had become his trademark during the Manson Family trial, one of the longest and most intricate in the annals of American jurisprudence.

The brilliant criminal lawyer had (as we shall see) been summoned to enter the trial at virtually "one minute to midnight."

Bugliosi hooked a thumb to his vest. "The defense calls Mr. Bill Powers," he sang out.

A lanky cowboy strode to the witness stand. Jerry Owen thrust his head forward from powerful shoulders and glared at the surprise witness.

When Owen told his story, he apparently had no inkling that Bill Powers would appear for the defense. In fact, Bugliosi had located the cowboy only two days before, and it was not until the last minute that he had been able to persuade him to testify. What he had to say clashed head-on with Owen's account of the chance encounter with Sirhan.

William Lee Powers was a cowboy straight out of the Marlboro ads, raw-boned with a weather-beaten face cross-hatched with scars from endless wrangles with wild mustangs and sharp-horned steers. He spoke in the drawling, idiom-laced argot of the range. By 1968 he had settled down to running Wild Bill's Stables on the banks of the Santa Ana River in Santa Ana. "I had horses for hire, I boarded horses, and also trained horses and gave riding lessons," he testified after being sworn in.

Yes, he knew Jerry Owen back then, he said. Owen had a place "three or four blocks down the river," and used to come by Wild Bill's Stables quite often. "Did you have many conversations with this Reverend Owen?" Bugliosi asked.

A. Numerous conversations. He come around periodically. I kept some horses for him before. One time I boarded some ponies for him and then I had two horses in there that he wanted broke.

Q. During these conversations you had with him, did he ever talk about his political philosophy?

A. Yes, he talked about—

The answer was cut off by one of Owen's attorneys, Arthur Evry, who leaped to his feet and shouted, "Your Honor! I will object! What is the relevancy of his political philosophy in this action for slander?"

"We are trying to show this man has a possible involvement in the assassination of Senator Kennedy," Bugliosi replied. "If that doesn't have relevancy, I don't know what has!"

Owen alleged in his complaint that he had been libeled and slandered by KCOP officials when they allegedly claimed that he had been involved in the RFK assassination.

Bugliosi was asserting a defense to the charge of libel and slander—that the statements were in fact true. Judge Crickard, however, seemed dumfounded at this sudden escalation of the trial from alleged civil wrongs to the murder of a presidential candidate. Before he could recover, Bugliosi continued on the offensive, "Let's assume for the sake of argument, your Honor, that this Jerry Owen was a right-wing reactionary type, who had a dislike for Senator Kennedy. Is counsel saying this wouldn't have any relevancy to this case?"

"I imagine you could find 15,000,000 people who might fit that same bill," Evry argued. "I don't think that in itself has any relevance to this case."

Bugliosi thought differently. "Mr. Owen, your Honor, by the pleadings, has said that the allegation he was 'involved' in the assassination of Senator Kennedy was untruthful. We are trying to show Owen's background—and counsel is objecting!"

Evry responded that he was only objecting to questions about Owen's "political beliefs and political motives," in effect saying that the question of motive did not bear on the crime. And the judge sustained him. Actually, a hint as to Owen's political leanings was already in the trial record: in his testimony earlier Owen had pedantically commented that "we have to be on the lookout for communists that want all religious programs off television and radio."

Bugliosi turned back to his witness and asked, "Did Mr. Owen ever mention President Kennedy or Senator Kennedy?" Evry objected again, but Crickard overruled him. Powers replied that Owen had in fact talked about the Kennedys at different times. But when Bugliosi asked, "What did he say?," it was Crickard who cut in, questioning the relevancy. Bugliosi argued that he was trying to establish the origins of Owen's involvement in the assassination. "It's not relevant," the judge ruled. "I am sure there are millions of people who talked about the Kennedys and still do, and about the government of the United States. It doesn't seem pertinent to this lawsuit."

It was difficult for Bugliosi to understand why Owen's frame of mind about the Kennedys was not pertinent. Shaking his head in frustration, he walked slowly back to his place at the far end of the counsel table and flipped through some papers. Now he would have to go straight to the point.

"DID YOU EVER HEAR JERRY OWEN USE THE NAME SIRHAN?" Bugliosi asked Powers.

Yes, Powers replied. He had employed a stablehand named Johnny Beckley who was breaking in horses belonging to Owen. "Well, he didn't like the way Johnny was handling the horses and was cowboying around," Powers recounted, "and he said he had other people at the [race] track and stuff that could handle horses in the right manner, and the name Sirhan was mentioned."

Q. By whom?
A. By Mr. Owen.
Q. Are you positive about this? [Bugliosi asked.]
A. I am *very* positive.

How could he be so certain? "Well, because it was an unusual name," Powers replied, "and then shortly after the assassination I heard Sirhan's name again. And Mr. Sirhan was a horseman, too, and that's why I remember."

The preacher and his lawyers stirred in their chairs. Owen's contention that the first time he had met Sirhan before the assassination, entirely by chance, had just been rebutted by a witness testifying under oath in a court of law. This would be the first in a series of dramatic breakthroughs in the case.

Powers testified that Owen began coming to the stables between sixty and ninety days before the assassination. Then, in the month of May, Powers sold Owen a 1951 Chevrolet pickup truck for approximately $350. But the preacher put down only about $50 and never did pay the balance. One afternoon "a very short time" before the assassination—it might have been election eve—Owen rolled up to the stables in a late-model Lincoln Continental and said he'd pay what he owed on the truck. The preacher offered him a $1,000 bill, but Powers didn't have the $700 change. The cowboy was duly impressed, testifying in answer to Bugliosi's question, that in the past, Owen "kind of never had any money" and sometimes had to borrow bales of hay to feed his horses. All at once he was flashing a roll consisting of what Powers estimated to be between twenty-five and thirty $1,000 bills and driving an expensive car in place of his battered family station wagon or the old pickup he had bought from Powers.

Q. Then I take it that it wasn't one of these "Montana bankrolls" with one $1,000 bill on top and one-dollar bills below?
A. No. Being in the horse business, that is what I carry. No, it wasn't one of those.
Q. It is your testimony, then, that there were many $1,000 bills?
A. There was a lot of serious money there, yes.

Powers recalled that there were two other men in the Lincoln that day. In the front passenger seat was "a large colored man" who talked about his days as a boxer. And in the rear was a dark-complexioned young man whom Powers believed he had seen before "in the backyard" of Owen's home. "He was a slender, small person," he said.

Sirhan Sirhan is approximately five feet four inches, 140 pounds, of slender build, with dark complexion. Bugliosi produced an official photograph of Sirhan Sirhan, entered it as an exhibit and displayed it to Powers.

Q. The gentleman seated in the back seat of Owen's Lincoln, did he resemble this man?
A. There is a resemblance, yes. I am not going to say this is him, but there is a likely resemblance, yes.
Q. When you say "a likely resemblance," are you talking about the face or physique, or both?
A. Just overall.

Bugliosi was satisfied with the answer, since an unqualified identification of a person seen only fleetingly would indicate a witness too eager to please.

Q. At the time of this $1,000 incident, was anyone with you?
A. Johnny Beckley and a man by the name of Jack Brundage.

Powers had told Bugliosi, when they conferred prior to the court session, that Beckley, Brundage and a third stablehand, named Denny Jackson, were present when Owen drove up in the Lincoln. Brundage had repaired a taillight on the old pickup for Owen a day or so before. According to Powers, after the assassination all three were fairly certain that it was Sirhan in the back seat. In fact, Beckley was absolutely sure: he even mentioned that he had seen Owen and Sirhan riding horseback together on the levees of the Santa Ana River in the weeks before the assassination. Powers had lost track of Brundage and Jackson,* but he was still in touch with Beckley, who was living in Los Alamitos. The previous day, at Bugliosi's urging, he had phoned his former stablehand to ask him to consider testifying. Instead Beckley left town. "This ain't like Johnny to run off," Powers told Bugliosi. "Maybe he knows more'n he ever told me."†

The plaintiff's lawyers were repeatedly objecting that Powers' testimony was not relevant. In overcoming one such objection,

---

* A year after the trial, Powers located Denny Jackson and arranged for author Christian to talk to him. Jackson confirmed the Sirhan sighting in Owen's Lincoln. "Yeah, I saw that roll of thousand-dollar bills and those strangers in that Lincoln that day," he acknowledged. "I thought it looked kind of funny, him with all that money, fannin' it out like that, showin' off."

† Powers located Beckley three months later—in the most rural part of Missouri. The ex-cowhand said he feared for his life.

Bugliosi argued, "Well, your Honor, we are alleging, in defense, that Mr. Owen possibly was involved in the assassination of Senator Kennedy. Now, if just prior to the assassination he was walking around with $30,000 and he was not the gunman, I don't see how the court can say that is not relevant. We have an eyewitness testifying that this man had about $30,000 on his person and he never had been seen with large amounts of money before. Right before the assassination he is with someone who looks like Sirhan and he is carrying $25,000 or $30,000. It couldn't possibly be more relevant circumstantial evidence."

After some parrying back and forth, Crickard allowed Bugliosi to "go directly to that particular incident." The attorney asked Powers about Owen's late-model Lincoln again, making certain that the record reflected Owen's sudden and unexplained wealth at a crucial time. Then he elicited a more thorough description of the young man in the back seat of the Lincoln. Powers said that he was a "Spanish-type fellow . . . I would say in his twenties, early twenties." Nationality? "Well, I wouldn't think he was American." Did he speak with an accent? "I don't remember that."*

When Evry objected again, the judge sustained him. With that, Bugliosi had to give up his attempt to draw a clear picture of Sirhan in the back seat of Owen's Lincoln on or just before June 3, 1968. And when he tried to get a fuller description of the roll of bills, Crickard himself interrupted, saying, "We have to get to something that bears on this case."

Bugliosi looked exasperated. "Well, we are talking about some things that are pretty important, your Honor, not just to this lawsuit, but to Senator Kennedy's assassination."

"They have to be relevant to this lawsuit or this isn't the place to take them up," Crickard retorted, invoking the undue consumption of time rule. When Bugliosi asked to be heard on the point, the judge curtly responded, "Let's go on to the next point."

But Bugliosi persisted, trying to break out of Crickard's confinement of the issues. He suggested that there was a link between Owen's carrying a large roll of $1,000 bills and the assassination,

---

* A native of Palestine, Sirhan was often mistaken for a Mexican. He spoke English without an accent.

one that would become clearer when tied in with other areas of testimony. "There is no foundational proof for it," Crickard countered. Bugliosi said that he intended to bridge the testimonial gap. "Well, the tie-in will be when I call Mr. Owen back to the witness stand and I ask him where he got the money. Conspiracies are not hatched down in Pershing Square with a megaphone.* These conspiracies are hatched in the shadows. The court is demanding that I put on evidence, either a tape-recorded conversation or a film, showing Mr. Owen saying, 'Let's get Kennedy!' Anything short of this apparently is not admissible in this courtroom."

Crickard seemed irritated and embarrassed. "You are setting up your own standards that are different than the court's," he remonstrated. He repeated his criteria of relevancy and foundational proof.

Bugliosi kept up the challenge: "I can just say in deference to the court, that I personally have handled many murder cases, your Honor, and I am not walking into this courtroom having just been sworn in across the street by the State Bar. I have never in all my experience as a trial lawyer, in handling criminal cases, been told by any court—or seen any opinion by any appellate court— that for someone who allegedly is involved in a murder, his having large sums of money in his possession around the time of the murder has no legal relevance."

Crickard insisted that there had to be an evidentiary tie-in between the money and the other events. "Just the fact that they can exist separately for a million other causes is just as possible, and we don't have the time to go down the million other causes," he said.

It annoyed Bugliosi that the judge was providing an argument for the other side. "We are not 'going down' a million other causes," he protested. "Now, if Mr. Owen wants to get on the witness stand and testify that he got this $30,000 through the stock market, swell; but I think we have the right to put this evidence on. As the world knows, Sirhan was at the assassination scene. The question is: was anyone behind him?"

* Pershing Square is the Los Angeles counterpart to London's Hyde Park where "soap-box orators" hold forth.

Evry and his client whispered at their table as Bugliosi continued, "We have someone who is close to Sirhan with a large sum of money. If he can explain how he got that money, fine. But to preclude us from showing that Owen had $30,000, while *with* Sirhan, right before the assassination, on the grounds it is not relevant—the only thing I can say is—what do we have to put on in this court to show it has relevance?"

Evry stood up to offer a concession. "We will offer a stipulation to the fact that Mr. Owen had $30,000. Apparently he is trying to confirm that the plaintiff in this case was, during 1968, raising very substantial sums of money. I am willing to stipulate to that extent." Evry said that he was making the offer to "save a good deal of the court's time."

What Bugliosi did not know (he had just been brought into the case) was that in a deposition taken some time before, Owen had declared that in 1968 he "lived off my wife's tax-free inheritance," having earned only $1,000 from a three-week preaching engagement. But Bugliosi sensed that Evry's concession was no more than a ploy to dispose of the sudden-wealth issue before it could be fully explored, and insisted that the stipulation include a time frame "within a couple of days prior to the assassination." Evry refused, saying Owen had the money "long before the assassination." Bugliosi declined to accept the stipulation.

Q. Have you testified to the truth on the witness stand today, sir?
A. Yes, I have. I have told it just the way it is [Powers answered].
Q. Do you have any hesitancy about your statement being examined by anyone?
A. No, I would take one of those lie detector tests if necessary. What I told is just the way it is.

As we'll see later on, Bugliosi's key witness would have further damaging testimony to offer at this unusual trial.

The judge declared a recess. Owen's lawyers huddled to assess the sudden and dramatic turn in the course of the trial.

The following morning the story in the Los Angeles *Times* was headed: BUGLIOSI CLAIMS CONSPIRACY IN ROBERT KENNEDY SLAYING.

"Choosing the unlikely forum of a civil slander suit," the story began, "veteran prosecutor Vincent T. Bugliosi sought this week to reopen the investigation into possible conspiracy in the June 5, 1968 assassination of Sen. Robert F. Kennedy." The account contained highlights of Powers' testimony, pointing out that it contradicted Owen's story that he had first met Sirhan hitchhiking in Los Angeles the day before the election.

AS JUDGE CRICKARD WOULD OBSERVE TOWARD THE END OF THE trial, Jonn Christian was the "proximate cause" of the Owen versus KCOP litigation. Shortly after the RFK assassination we had by chance come upon Owen's hitchhiker story and learned that Owen had recited it to the Los Angeles police nine hours after the shooting. For reasons that we will explain later, we decided that the story was spurious and began to probe behind it. In 1969 Christian briefed the KCOP management on the curious background of Owen when *The Walking Bible* program went on the air. Hoping to find out where Owen was getting the substantial amounts of money required to pay for the program, Christian urged KCOP not to cancel it.

But KCOP did cancel, and the lawsuit ensued. It was not until virtually the end of the 1975 trial that the station's legal counsel, fearing that Crickard was leaning toward the plaintiff, decided to mount a vigorous "affirmative defense" by attempting to prove that the allegedly slanderous statements attributed to KCOP representatives about Owen's involvement in the assassination were in fact true statements. At this point we arranged for Vince Bugliosi to join the KCOP defense and bring his formidable forensic skills into play.

We had not learned about Bill Powers and what he had witnessed until several months after KCOP terminated *The Walking Bible* program. Powers told us that the police had interviewed him several times shortly after the assassination, but had dealt with him harshly and warned him not to repeat to anyone what he had seen. This was no surprise, since we had found that the Los Angeles police had systematically browbeaten witnesses whose accounts conflicted with the official verdict that there had been no conspiracy.

As the *Times* observed, a civil trial was an unlikely forum to press for the reopening of a political murder case, but by 1975 the unlikely was becoming commonplace. Watergate had jarred Americans into the realization that no dirty trick was impossible, and rekindled skepticism about the assassinations of John and Robert Kennedy and Martin Luther King, Jr.

It was through a mutual interest in reopening the investigation of the death of President Kennedy that the authors first met in 1968. We decided that since assassination was, by definition, a political crime, we would make a political issue of it by running for Congress. And in part because of that campaign, we were eventually introduced to the enigmatic Jerry Owen, "The Walking Bible."

2

Campaign '68

WITH JONN CHRISTIAN AS HIS CAMPAIGN MANAGER, BILL Turner ran in the Democratic primary in what was then the 6th Congressional District of California, comprising a diagonal half of San Francisco and practically all of Marin County to the north across the Golden Gate Bridge. It was the same Democratic primary that Eugene McCarthy and Robert Kennedy were hotly contesting at the presidential level. And this was the first time that the JFK assassination issue, which had been raised in a plethora of books and articles, became the principal plank in a campaign for national office.

In January, Turner had appeared on a San Francisco television program to discuss his own lengthy investigation into the Dallas tragedy, focusing on elements connected to intelligence agencies, anti-Castro Cuban exiles and organized-crime figures (this was long before the CIA-Mafia alliance to assassinate Fidel Castro was exposed). Christian was in the studio audience, and after the program he introduced himself. Turner's initial impression was that the stocky, bearded man came on too strong and should be kept at arm's length. What the investigation didn't need, he thought, was another "researcher" whose theories were based on guesswork rather than evidence.

But as it turned out, Christian's approach was hardly bluster. He carried solid credentials, having been a radio and television newsman from 1956 to 1966. Born thirty-five years earlier in a farm town not far from Sacramento, Christian first went on the air with a CBS affiliate in his home area. Gravitating to San Francisco, he did free-lance stints before winding up as assignment editor at KGO-TV, the local ABC outlet. His specialty was rooting out "political crooks," which amounted to pioneering in those pre-Watergate days of television news. His first major target was Oakland Mayor John O'Houllihan, suspected of embezzling funds belonging to a client in his private law practice. With camera crews and reporters, Christian chased the elusive mayor across the country. He got his story, and O'Houllihan was soon out of office and in jail. Christian next zeroed in on the tax assessors for San Francisco and Alameda counties, and they ended up convicted of accepting "campaign contributions" that were actually graft. But when he turned to those who had given the bribes and demanded a grand jury investigation, his cameras were shut off by the station management.

Christian's friend and mentor through his investigative-reporting career was one of the legends of the print media, Paul C. Smith, former editor of the San Francisco *Chronicle*. Personal secretary to President Herbert Hoover, confidant of FDR, press secretary to Wendell Willkie and journalistic godfather of Pierre Salinger, Smith had been close to John and Robert Kennedy from the inception of their political careers. After the President was struck down and the Warren Commission blamed Oswald alone, Smith intuitively felt that the truth had not been revealed. "Something's really wrong," he told Christian. "I can't put my finger on it, but this country is going in the wrong direction."*

Christian had reason to recall Smith's disquiet when he became a special consultant to an association of service-station operators who had filed an antitrust suit against a giant trading-stamp company, charging fraud, price manipulation and conspiracy. Although close to $100 million in damages was sought, the case was eventually compromised and settled out of court for less than one percent of that amount. Christian viewed the token settlement as the consequence of a power play begun several years before. Robert Kennedy's Justice Department had filed an antitrust action against the company—Justice attorneys drew on Christian's store of knowledge in the field of corporate buccaneering—but after the President's assassination, Lyndon Johnson's new team at Justice quietly dropped the prosecution. This severely compromised the service-station operators, who were forced to enter their civil suit playing a much weaker hand. If large corporate interests could benefit so decisively from an abrupt change in administration, Christian wondered, could not some cabal among them somehow have arranged for the President's death?

The notion was hardly dispelled by a set of events that began on a quiet Sunday afternoon in April 1967. An erstwhile broadcast colleague named Harv Morgan, who was doing a radio talk show on San Francisco's KCBS station, phoned Christian and asked him to come down to the studio and sit in on an interview with Harold Weisberg, author of a series of self-published books called *Whitewash* that were critical of the Warren Report. Weisberg lived in rural Maryland, so the interview was held via long-distance phone. The show was scheduled for one hour but ran on for four, with listeners calling in such numbers that the switchboard was jammed.

After reading the books, Christian called Weisberg in Maryland to discuss references to FBI bungling and cover-up in its investigation of the assassination. Several days later Christian was contacted by an FBI agent who had worked tangentially on the trading-stamp-

---

* Smith's autobiography, *Personal File*, is required reading in many journalism classes. Smith died in 1976.

company case. "Meet me at Roland's," the agent said, referring to a saloon where the two had occasionally met for drinks.

"Who do you know in Maryland that might be of extreme interest to certain people within the FBI?" the agent whispered.

"Harold Weisberg," Christian answered. "He's the only one I know in Maryland."

The agent confided that he had heard an "inside rumor" that a phone tap had intercepted Christian's conversation with Weisberg a few days before, and hinted that an order had been issued for Christian's line to be monitored from then on.

At first Christian was stunned, then angered. "To hell with the taps," he fumed. "If the FBI is that concerned about the critics, there must be something to the criticism!"

It was against this backdrop that Christian met Turner. Tall and sandy-haired, forty-one-year-old Turner came across as a nice enough guy but hardly the type of push-and-shove journalist that Christian was accustomed to. But Christian noted that he had a capacity for collecting and storing data. His investigative approach was disarmingly low-key, but it seemed to work.

Turner was a Navy veteran of World War II and a Canisius College graduate whose ice-hockey career had been interrupted by appointment as an FBI special agent in 1951. He participated in a number of well-known FBI cases, including the 1959 kidnap-murder of Colorado brewery magnate Adolph Coors, Jr., and as an inspector's aide he reviewed the Los Angeles division's program against organized crime. He was also specially trained in wire-tapping, bugging and burglary—a "black-bag job" on the Japanese consulate in Seattle was one assignment—and did counterespionage work. He received three personal letters of commendation from J. Edgar Hoover.

But by 1961 Turner's doubts about the aging Director's policies had grown to the point where he poked the tiger from inside the cage by seeking a congressional investigation of the FBI. He urged them to look into the Bureau's questionable tactics, softness on organized crime and the stultifying personality cult surrounding Hoover. At the time, Hoover was at the peak of his power, and he was able to discharge Turner as a "disruptive influence" with hardly a murmur of dissent from members of Congress.

Taking up journalism, Turner wrote for magazines ranging from *Playboy* to *The Nation* and wrote a number of police science articles for the legal press. In 1968 his first books, *The Police Establishment* and *Invisible Witness: The Use and Abuse of the New Technology of Crime Investigation*, were published, and he began work on *Hoover's FBI*.

Turner's involvement with the investigation of John Kennedy's assassination had begun immediately after the shooting when he flew to Dallas on assignment for a national magazine to look into the breakdown in security. As the Warren Commission inquiry progressed, stories appeared in the press that witnesses heard all the shots come from the building where Lee Harvey Oswald was employed. Turner wrote to the Commission, pointing out how deceptive the sounds of gunfire could be. On August 8, 1964, general counsel J. Lee Rankin replied that the Commission had "concluded its deliberations and was in the process of preparing its final report." When the hurried report was issued in time for the fall elections, Turner read it through and decided it was heavily flawed. He turned from skeptic to critic.

THE DECISION THAT TURNER WOULD RUN FOR CONGRESS STEMMED from a February 1968 "ways and means" meeting that Christian arranged at the Pacific Heights mansion of a friend, Fremont Bodine Hitchcock, Jr. "Peter" Hitchcock was a millionaire many times over, a member of the polo-playing Hitchcock family that moved in the most select society circles. He was hardly a Kennedy man (during the 1964 Republican National Convention in San Francisco, the Barry Goldwaters stayed at his home, and in 1968 he contributed substantially to the U.S. Senate campaign of the reactionary Max Rafferty) but he had gone to Harvard with John Kennedy and harbored a kind of perverse admiration for him. The sentiment survived the fact that before their marriage his wife, Joan, carried on an affair with Kennedy, whom she had met through Peter Lawford.*

* In 1975, when JFK's extracurricular romances were being dragged through the press, Joan Hitchcock could not resist going public with her

Hitchcock was skeptical about the conclusions of the Warren Report, and invited to the gathering Amory J. "Jack" Cooke, a vice president of the Hearst Corporation married to Phoebe Hearst; newscaster Harv Morgan, now with KGO; and Hitchcock lawyer George T. Davis. Turner presented his findings from Dallas and New Orleans, where he had assisted District Attorney Jim Garrison in his probe. There was unanimous agreement that the Warren Commission had fumbled its assignment.

What to do about it was another problem. Although Jack Cooke thought that the Hearst press might be open-minded, we were dubious. Editor in chief William Randolph Hearst, Jr., possessed an unshakable faith in the institutions of government, whether they concerned the Vietnam war or the Warren Report. Hearst feature writers Jim Bishop and Bob Considine had endorsed the Warren Report virtually before the ink was dry.

When someone suggested that the issue belonged in the hands of Congress, the idea of a political campaign was born. For the first time in his life Peter Hitchcock agreed to contribute to a Democrat, at least to the extent of paying the filing fee. So we sat down and composed a brochure for the Turner campaign.

THE ASSASSINATION OF PRESIDENT KENNEDY BROUGHT IMMEDIATE AND DRASTIC CHANGES IN THE FOREIGN AND DOMESTIC POLICIES OF THIS COUNTRY. WE MUST SOLVE THE PROBLEMS THESE CHANGES CREATED.

The polls show that an overwhelming majority of Americans don't believe the Warren Report. After investigating the case for over three years, I am convinced that the President was the victim of a domestic extremist plot. Whether to allow his murder to remain an unsolved homicide on the books of the Dallas Police Department is the silent issue of this campaign. I intend to bring it into the open by seeking a joint Senate-House investigation.

To do less not only is indecent but might cost us the life of a future President of John Kennedy's instincts.

---

memoirs. See, for example, the San Francisco *Chronicle* (December 27, 1975).

It was California's master politician Jesse Unruh who said "money is the mother's milk of politics," and it quickly became apparent that we were in for a difficult weaning. Due to our late start we lost out on funds that had been committed elsewhere. Besides, interest seemed to be fixed almost exclusively on the close contest between McCarthy and Kennedy. We received a few contributions from persons who were concerned by the assassination issue, most notably Sally Stanford, the legendary ex-madam of San Francisco. "I want to contribute to your campaign," she said after we dropped by to talk about it, "but first I have to go to my vault." With that, she reached down into her ample bosom and withdrew five $100 bills. We immediately named her "vice chairlady" of the campaign.*

But the Democratic regulars whose nods could loosen purse strings were resolutely opposed to reopening the Kennedy case. For one thing, the Warren Commission had been set up by a Democratic President, and Earl Warren was a liberal hero. For another, the Kennedy family themselves were on record as opposing further inquiry. Throughout the campaign we would be braced with the questions "What about the Kennedys? If there was a conspiracy, don't you think that Bobby Kennedy would do something about it?"

"Certainly," we'd reply, "but only if he could positively prove it." When the Warren Report was released, Robert Kennedy had acquiesced in its findings, although adding the enigmatic comment, "I have not read the Report and do not intend to." In fact, RFK had suspicions about his brother's death from the moment it happened. He instinctively felt that his archenemy Jimmy Hoffa might somehow have been responsible, and that members of the Secret Service had been bribed because the protection broke down so badly. He assigned Daniel P. Moynihan, then Assistant Secretary of Labor and a trusted member of the Kennedy inner circle, to investigate. Although Moynihan's report exonerated the Teamsters boss and the Secret Service of any complicity, Kennedy remained

---

* In 1976 Ms. Stanford was finally elected mayor of suburban Sausalito after being frustrated for years by the city's bluenoses. When the election results were in, the city manager commented, "She'll be the most interesting mayor in the state." But her enemies were ungracious, saying she was just out to upgrade her image. Sneered Sally: "Prestige, my ass!"

curious. In 1967 he sent his former press secretary Edwin O. Guthman, then a Los Angeles *Times* editor, to New Orleans to meet with Jim Garrison, and during the 1968 primary campaign he disappeared for several hours in Oxnard, California, to check privately on a report that a telephone call warning of the assassination originated there on the morning of November 22, 1963.*

When RFK announced that he was going to run for President, we considered it important that he be briefed on the evidence of conspiracy in his brother's death, for his own life might now be in danger. The most promising channel to the candidate was Jesse Unruh, speaker of the California Assembly and Kennedy's campaign chairman in the state, who happened to be a friend of Christian's. At first Unruh resisted any involvement, but Christian persisted into early 1968. Eventually he became receptive to the idea that lightning might strike twice and suggested that Christian be brought into the press relations section of the campaign, where he would have access to Kennedy. In late May Christian received notice to stand by for a summons to Washington headquarters— after RFK was nominated at the convention in July.

Yet in public RFK deflected questions on the assassination or, if pushed, paid lip service to the Warren Report. For example, on the campus of San Fernando Valley State College on March 25 he tried to brush off students' questions on the subject and became visibly annoyed when they persisted. "Your manners overwhelm me," he finally yielded. "Go ahead, go ahead, ask your questions."

"Will you open the archives if elected?" a student shouted in reference to the more than two hundred documents Lyndon Johnson had authorized to be sealed until the year 2039.

"Nobody is more interested than I in knowing who is responsible for the death of President Kennedy," he responded. "I would not reopen the Warren Commission Report. I have seen everything that's in there. I stand by the Warren Commission."†

* Curiously enough, Oxnard, then a small town off the beaten track, also figured in Owen's hitchhiker story. As we have seen, he said that he could not meet Sirhan at the Ambassador Hotel on election night because he had to preach in Oxnard.

† London *Times* (March 26, 1968).

Such statements were highly pragmatic, for it would have been damaging to his campaign to publicly express doubts—anything less than absolute proof would have left him open to accusations of irresponsibility and rumor mongering. The practical course to discovering more about the assassination was to control the Justice Department with its vast investigative resources. And the only way to control the Justice Department was to gain the presidency.

ON THE EARLY EVENING OF APRIL 4 A BULLETIN OUT OF MEMPHIS reported that Dr. Martin Luther King, Jr., had been shot and killed by a sniper. The next morning we received a call from George Davis, the attorney we had met at Peter Hitchcock's, asking us to come to his office for a conference. We had high hopes that Davis might be able to get our campaign off dead center. A peppery sixty-two-year-old with flowing silver hair and a staccato manner of speech, Davis was a widely known trial lawyer in California.

After some discussion about the King assassination, Davis pointed to his bookcase and remarked almost casually, "You know, I am the leading authority on hypnosis and the law." Then he dropped a bombshell. The lawyers for Clay L. Shaw, then under indictment in New Orleans for conspiracy in the JFK assassination as a result of DA Jim Garrison's investigation, had asked him to associate in the case. "The main witness against Shaw was hypnotized by the prosecution to help him recall details," Davis explained. The witness, Perry Russo, later testified that he had been present in September 1963 when Shaw and Lee Harvey Oswald talked about a plan to kill the President.

Davis proposed that Turner, who was close to Jim Garrison, arrange a private meeting between himself and Garrison at which the DA would lay out his entire case against Shaw. "If I can be more convinced than I am now about Garrison's case," he said, "I might be of a mind to move into the case and, you know, help him out."

We exchanged glances. The only way Davis could help Garrison by joining the Shaw defense would be to feed back information, which would be a serious breach of the canon of ethics. Whatever he was trying to propose, it didn't sound helpful and we let it pass.* Davis capped the meeting by offering to become our campaign chairman, which we gratefully accepted, since he thought he could raise enough money to get us through the election. But as it turned out, he generated no contributions at all.

Practically bereft of funds for advertising, we sought some way to pull off a press coup. The opportunity came on the languid Sunday of May 5. Sundays are usually slow news days, and this one was no exception. By chance the city editor's desk at the San Francisco *Chronicle* was being manned over the weekend by an old sidekick of Turner's, Charlie Howe. A hard-bitten combat veteran of the Korean War who specialized in military-affairs reporting, Howe possessed an independent streak the newspaper's editors found difficult to manage. Turner dropped in on Howe and took him out for a quick drink. He laid out some photographs on the bar.

Charlie Howe knew he was eying a grabby picture story. The photographs, taken by press photographers at Dealey Plaza within minutes of the JFK shooting, showed three men being led away by shotgun-toting Dallas policemen. They had been picked up behind the celebrated Grassy Knoll, but the Warren Commission had evinced no interest in who they were, why they were detained or what became of them. The scowling man leading the trio had a thin face, jutting jaw, wide mouth, thin lips, a triangular nose and squinty eyes. In juxaposition to him Turner had placed an artist's sketch of the suspect in the Martin Luther King slaying. The sketch bore no resemblance to James Earl Ray, then being sought by the FBI as the "lone gunman" in the King case, but it did appear strikingly similar to the Dealey Plaza suspect.

"I'll run it," Charlie Howe said. "Should be able to give it good play."

The slow-news day helped. On the front page of the *Chronicle* when it hit the streets that evening were a report of scattered

* As far as we know, Davis never did join the Shaw defense. Shaw was acquitted in a 1969 trial. According to Victor Marchetti, at the time an assistant to CIA Director Richard Helms, Shaw had collaborated with the Agency and Helms reciprocated by instructing that every possible aid be given to his defense. Shaw died in 1975.

fighting on the outskirts of Saigon, word that telephone workers had ratified a new contract, and an item out of Washington that the House Un-American Activities Committee advocated the restoration of detention camps to confine black militants. There was also a filler story that Robert Kennedy was optimistic on the eve of the Indiana primary.

But the headline read: STARTLING THEORY: KING KILLER "DOUBLE"! Centered on the front page were the two pictures with the caption "Strange Parallel." The story said: "A former FBI agent yesterday raised the spectre of a link between the assassinations of President Kennedy and Dr. Martin Luther King" with evidence strong enough to "warrant a Congressional investigation." It said that Turner noted that in both assassinations a rifle with telescopic sight "was conveniently left at the crime scene," and that in both there was an abundance of similar physical evidence, including city maps with significant points circled. " 'As you know,' " Turner was quoted, " 'the police use modus operandi files in any crime. Criminals tend to repeat certain things, have certain habits.' "

The story was a shot in the arm for the campaign, and for several days the city was abuzz with "strange parallels" talk. But the coup turned out to be a final lunge. The war chest, which had contained only a paltry $2,000, was empty. Although a private poll showed us neck and neck with our opponent, he doubled his previous expenditure of $17,000 and put on a media blitz. When the votes were tallied on the night of June 4, he had about 41,000 to Turner's 32,000. It was not a bad showing under the circumstances, and certainly indicated that people were responsive to the assassination issue.

Then came the electrifying news from Los Angeles. We stared mutely at the final line of our campaign brochure: " might cost us the life of a future President of John Kennedy's instincts . . ."

3

"The Walking Bible" Talks

ON MONDAY MORNING, JULY I, LESS THAN A MONTH AFTER the RFK assassination, George Davis phoned Jonn Christian. "Well, I suppose by now you've read the newspapers," he began. "I've cracked the Kennedy assassination wide open, and I need your help and Bill's."

Christian was perplexed. We had both been out of town over the weekend and hadn't read the papers. "Read yesterday's *Examiner*," the attorney urged with a note of excitement in his voice, "then get down here as soon as you can."

The story was headed: MINISTER HIDING IN S.F., CLAIMS R.F.K. CLUE. Credited to the Associated Press, it opened:

A clergyman from Southern California is hiding for his life in the San Francisco area today, claiming that he met the killer of

Sen. Robert F. Kennedy before the assassination, that he has evidence of possible conspirators he saw with him, and that his life and the lives of his entire family have been threatened.

The minister—whose name cannot be revealed at this time for his own security—used San Francisco attorney George T. Davis as his spokesman.

There followed a brief account of how the unnamed clergyman happened to pick up a young hitchhiker in Los Angeles on the day before the assassination whom he later identified as Sirhan. He immediately reported the incident to the Los Angeles police, and shortly thereafter received a telephoned threat. "Keep your mouth shut if you know what's good for you and your family," the anonymous caller warned. A week later the threat was repeated. The clergyman contacted Davis, who appealed unsuccessfully to the Los Angeles police for protection.

According to the article, Davis believed that the clergyman's life was actually in danger and that the police were negligent. "Los Angeles authorities," Davis charged, "have taken the position that there is no conspiracy in this case, so this man's story is not important."

We hurried to Davis' office. He said that the clergyman was one Jerry Owen, who was not only a client but a friend of thirty years' standing. Owen had called him on Friday evening after arriving in the Bay Area, and when Davis couldn't reach us he called the Associated Press because he thought something had to be done without delay. The AP had dispatched reporter Jim White to Davis' ranch near Napa Valley, where Davis had Owen sequestered. The attorney had tried unavailingly to get help from Los Angeles Police Chief Tom Reddin, and had been unable to reach either Attorney General Thomas Lynch or Jesse Unruh.*

Davis thought Owen's story strongly suggested that Sirhan had accomplices—the three men and a girl who had offered Owen

---

* Reporter White, who happened to be a neighbor of Turner's in suburban Mill Valley, later gave us a copy of the tape recording he made at the Davis ranch. In the background Davis can be heard placing calls to the police and the Attorney General's office.

$100 as down payment on the horse Sirhan was going to buy, and who had instructed him to deliver the animal to the rear of the Ambassador Hotel at eleven o'clock on election night. If the police would not guard Owen, Davis said, there was only one insurance policy: "Break this story wide open all across the country!"

Relying on Davis' judgment, we agreed to help. Christian would offer an exclusive national story to his ex-colleagues at ABC, while Turner would act as investigative adviser on any follow-up to the story. We were not discouraged by the fact that the AP story, which had gone out on the national wire Saturday night, had not been widely picked up. Owen had insisted that his name not be used, which detracted from the story's credibility. And the Los Angeles press had been put off by the police labeling the clergyman as a "nut." By producing Owen in the flesh on nationwide television, the story should pack a wallop. And once it was out, anyone who tried to silence Owen would only be adding credibility to his story.

Davis promised to bring Owen before the cameras at ten-thirty the following morning. When Christian outlined the story to the radio and television people, they reacted enthusiastically. It was important that the interview come off on time in order to feed the network in New York, which was three hours ahead of the West Coast.

BY TEN-THIRTY IN THE MORNING THE ABC CREWS HAD THEIR equipment set up in the reception room of Davis' office suite. The room was shut off from the outside but brightened by a large picture window framing an interior garden of subtropical flora. As the clock ticked, the room became enveloped in small talk. And speculation. Who were the other persons? What kind of conspiracy was there?

Finally, at eleven-twenty, Davis appeared and the crews switched on their floodlights. Davis introduced the two men with him as bodyguards for Owen. Apologizing for the delay, he explained that only minutes before, the Los Angeles authorities had called advising that they were flying to San Francisco to "take charge." Davis said that he had finally made contact with Attorney General Lynch, who had personally phoned Chief Reddin in Los Angeles. The police had personally warned Davis that there was a judge's gag order outstanding that prohibited witnesses from making public statements. There could be no interview.

The broadcast crews complained bitterly, and Christian angrily remonstrated with Davis that the public interest demanded that Sirhan's accomplices be exposed. The authorities had no right to misuse a court order to squelch versions of the case conflicting with their own, he argued. Davis said that he was sorry, but there was nothing he could do. "Anyway, I've already sent Mr. Owen back to my ranch to wait until the authorities arrive tomorrow," he said.

As Christian and the ABC contingent trooped out the door, Davis beckoned to Turner to follow him. "Bill, see what you make of all this," he said as they rode the private elevator up to Davis' inner sanctum. The attorney led the way into a large conference room where, standing at the end of the table, was the object of all the fuss. "Bill, meet Jerry Owen," Davis said. At sixty-two Owen still exuded physical strength. He stood well over six feet and weighed close to 250 pounds, a beefy, florid man with a roundish face dominated by a bulbous nose and darting blue eyes. His hair was graying-dark and kinky, which long ago had given rise to the nickname "Curly." He was dressed in a brown business suit, and he wore wing-tip oxfords. His hands were like hams, and his handshake was crushing. Owen looked every inch the aging prizefighter, which he was.

After Davis left the room to make some phone calls, Owen raised the question of John Kennedy's assassination. Obviously Davis had briefed him on Turner's participation in the Jim Garrison investigation. As Turner spread a number of photographs from his attaché case on the table, Owen looked them over. His finger came to rest on one of Edgar Eugene Bradley of North Hollywood, who six months before had been indicted by a New Orleans grand jury for conspiracy in the JFK assassination (the charges were later dismissed). Bradley was the West Coast representative of Dr. Carl McIntire, the fundamentalist minister who founded the American Council of Christian Churches in opposition to the "modernist" National Council of Churches.

"Do you know Bradley?" Turner asked.

"Yes," said Owen. He explained that he had casually met him a couple of times in Los Angeles, the last in 1964. "I was affiliated with McIntire's church in the late fifties," Owen said, "but got out because those people were too radical for me."

The mention of the right-wing McIntire church, which had roundly condemned Roman Catholicism in general and the Kennedys in particular, prompted Turner to ask Owen to tell his story on tape. The preacher complied. Clutching the microphone in his hands, his eyebrows knitted in concentration, he began a minutely detailed rendition. Noting his intensity, Turner didn't interrupt during the fifty-seven-minute soliloquy. In condensed form, this is what Owen said occurred:

On Monday afternoon, June 3, Owen left his Santa Ana home in his old Chevy pickup truck with a conspicuous chrome horse ornament on the hood. He was dressed in Levi's, cowboy boots and a plaid shirt. He was on his way to Oxnard, where a friend boarded a dozen Shetland ponies and a palomino horse for him. He had a buyer for a Shetland, and he was going to bring one back.

Owen stopped at a Los Angeles sporting-goods store to pick up a robe, shoes and trunks for a heavyweight boxer named O'Reilly who he had an interest in. He was going to drop off the shoes and robe in Hollywood for decorating with shamrocks.

While he stopped at a red light at 7th and Grand, two young men asked if he was going out Wilshire Boulevard toward Hollywood, and without waiting for an answer hopped in the back of the truck. "I looked in the mirror and noticed that the one was kind of a bushy, dark-haired fella and the other was of the same complexion and I thought that they were Mexicans or Hindus or something, kind of on the hippie style."

At a stoplight at Wilshire and Vermont, the pair got out and the taller one began talking to a well-dressed man, about thirty-five and a "dirty blonde" girl, who looked about twenty-one, who were standing on the corner. The pair was wearing "occult" medallions on chains around their necks. The smaller man returned to the truck and asked, "Do you mind if I ride with you on out?"

Turner noticed that Owen was talking very deliberately, and that his tone was turning very confidential.

> The horse ornament prompted a discussion of horses. The hitchhiker said "he was an exercise boy at a race track, and talked about how he loved horses, and quickly wanted to know if I had a ranch where he could get a job." As they proceeded out Wilshire, the hitchhiker pointed to Catalina Street and asked, "Would it be all right if we stopped? I have a friend in the kitchen."
>
> Owen swung left on Catalina and stopped in a cul-de-sac at the rear entrance to the Ambassador Hotel. The hitchhiker mentioned that he wanted to buy a lead pony to use at the race track, and "I told him I had a dandy up in Oxnard." After some ten minutes went by, Owen started to leave, thinking the hitchhiker would not return, when "he came on a run. I noticed his tennis shoes on, a sweatshirt."
>
> As they headed toward Hollywood, Owen asked the young man if he was Mexican, and he said no, he was born in Jordan. "Well, that struck up a little conversation because my wife and I are planning to go to Jerusalem."
>
> Owen parked in front of the Hollywood Ranch Market and delivered the boxing paraphernalia to a shop across the street. Upon his return to the truck the hitchhiker "told me that if I could meet him at eleven o'clock on Sunset Boulevard, he would be able to purchase this horse for the sum of three hundred dollars. There was a little talk of two hundred fifty dollars or something, but I told him that I would let it go for three hundred. I'd guarantee the horse, if it didn't work out I would take it back because the horse is a ten-year-old comin' on eleven, and he had been used as a pickup horse and as a pony horse and well broke, but he's a one man's horse."*

---

* The references to "pickup" and "pony" horse indicated that the Owen animal had been used at thoroughbred race tracks.

Owen made it clear that he needed money, and that the $300 would help him pay some pressing debts.

It was now close to six o'clock. The hitchhiker directed Owen to a bowling alley on Sunset Boulevard and said, "At eleven o'clock tonight I'll meet you here and I'll have the money to pay for the horse." Owen mentioned that he might kill some time by going to the Saints and Sinners Club on Fairfax, which caused the hitchhiker to ask if he was Jewish. "No, I'm not Jewish, I'm Welsh," Owen replied. "Well, I have no use for the Hebes!" the hitchhiker sneered. Owen smiled, "I'll be there at eleven."

Owen went to the Plaza Hotel, where his old friend "Slapsie Maxie" Rosenbloom [an ex-fighter] lived. "Curly," Maxie said, "you gotta be at the Saints and Sinners tonight, it's the last night at Billy Gray's Band Box—they're closin'. This'll be the greatest meeting of all and, with you and Henry Armstrong being the charter members, come on and be there!" Owen balked, "I can't go, Max. I'm dressed like a hayseed." Rosenbloom insisted, "Ah, what's the difference, Curly?" He looked at the truck and horse and laughed at Owen driving that rig right in the heart of Hollywood.

"And I went to Saints and Sinners, and I had O'Reilly the boxer with me, and they introduced him that night." At eleven, Owen pulled up to the bowling alley. Across the street was an older-model off-white Chevy sedan. In the streetlight Owen could see a man resembling the man he had seen that afternoon on the corner of Wilshire and Vermont, and there "was the girl, from the looks of her hair and that." The hitchhiker got out from the car and said, "I am very sorry. Here's a hundred-dollar bill, and I was supposed to have the rest of the money but I don't. But if you'll meet me in the morning about eight o'clock, I assure you that I'll take the horse definitely."

"Well, now look," Owen said, "I've waited and I should be up in Oxnard. But I'll tell you what I'll do if you really mean business and want the horse. I'll stay in this hotel right across the street."

Owen registered in a $4 room with phone but no bath. At close to eight the next morning the telephone rang and a voice he had never heard before wanted to know if he was the man with the truck in the parking lot. Owen went down to the lobby. The man was wearing an "expensive-looking late-style suit. He had on a turtleneck sweater that was kind of an orangish-yellow color with a chain around his neck and a big, round thing that you see 'em all wearing now, and as I looked at him, he had on what appeared to be an expensive pair of alligator shoes. He had a manicure. He had one of those cat's-eye rings on his little finger." The stranger said, "Joe couldn't make it. Take this hundred dollars if you can be down on the street where you left him out yesterday afternoon.* At 11 o'clock tonight. If you can be there with the horse and trailer, he'll definitely take the horse." Joe was the hitchhiker.

Owen peered into the man's car outside and recognized the same girl. "Look," Owen said, "I've waited overnight, I stayed in the hotel and I was told that we would have it definitely at eleven this morning. I have to be in Oxnard tonight to speak at the Calvary Baptist Church there, and I got some business there, and I cannot be down on the street tonight at eleven."

Owen handed the man his card with the legend "SHEPHERD OF THE HILLS, Free Pony Rides For Boys and Girls Who Go To The Church Of Their Choice, Learn a Bible Verse, and Mind Their Parents." On it was his unlisted telephone number at his Santa Ana home. Owen said that he would deliver the horse wherever they wanted when they had the money. He left for Oxnard, where he preached a sermon at the Calvary Baptist Church. He stayed overnight with unnamed parishioners.

The following morning Owen hooked his two-horse trailer to the pickup truck and loaded it with a brown-and-white-spotted mare, a little white stallion and a black gelding. The last two were extras he hoped to sell because he "needed a little extra finances." He drove back to Los Angeles en route home. He had not seen television or heard a radio, and knew nothing about RFK having been shot.

Arriving in Los Angeles around noon, he stopped on the spur of the moment at the Coliseum Hotel to see if an old-time

---

* The cul-de-sac at the rear of the Ambassador Hotel.

fight manager named Bert Morse still ran the coffee shop there. He was going to talk to Morse about the fight game. "But coming through the bar there is a television. I heard something about the rigmarole, and about the eight shots being fired, but being a minister, I just went through the bar and into the counter area and set down and ordered a lunch."

While eating, Owen got his first word of the RFK shooting. He heard a radio report that the suspect had black, bushy hair and wore tennis shoes. Bert Morse arrived and started talking about his horses, Diamond Dip and Hemet Miss, which raced on local tracks, and about boxing. Then Owen repeated to Morse his story about picking up "a couple of hippies." He said, "Isn't it funny, a guy shows you a hundred-dollar bill?"

All of a sudden a picture flashed on television and Owen thought, Hey, that's the guy that was in my truck!

Then a waitress handed him a copy of the Hollywood *Citizen-News* and there he was. "That's the kid!" So the waitress and Morse and boxing trainer Doug Lewis urged him to report his experience to the police. Owen balked, saying, "It's no use, they've caught him single-handed." And Morse spoke up, "I know, but have you been following this Garrison investigation of the other Kennedy?" Owen retorted, "Naw, I'm in church work and a minister. I don't want to be bothered with it." But the waitress said, "Well, I'll tell you what I'd do if I was you," and everyone agreed with her that Owen should report his story.

Owen drove over to the nearby University Station of the Los Angeles police. The minute the police heard his story they had him "drive in and leave the pickup and trailer in the back, and I heard them say something about taking fingerprints." Owen recited his story with a tape recorder going and a stenographer taking notes. One cop came in the room and said, "He sure knows what he's talking about because it was just released that they found four-hundred dollars in bills on the suspect, and there was nothing about any money on him until then." After telling his story, Owen was allowed to leave. "I went outside and it looked like on the doors and on the side of the truck that there'd been some kind of powder or something.

I didn't see them take any fingerprints, but I heard the detectives say they would."

That was the basic hitchhiker story.* Owen said that about two o'clock the next afternoon he received the first threatening call on his unlisted number at home. "Are you the Shepherd?" the anonymous voice growled. "The man with the horses? Keep your motherfucking mouth shut about this horse deal—or else!"

On Wednesday, June 19, the police called and invited Owen to come down to their Parker Center headquarters. Owen called a retired Methodist minister and old friend named Jonothan Perkins, and asked him to come along. "Perk, come on, let's go down to the police station. I want you to be with me when I go in there, I don't want to go in alone." The aged minister obliged. "Now look, Perk," Owen said as they entered Parker Center, "you believe in prayer. You pray because I've just had a threat."

Owen was ushered into the offices of Special Unit Senator (SUS), a group set up especially to investigate the assassination. He was shown an assortment of mug shots, and picked out one as being the hitchhiker. The detective said he was "not at liberty" to reveal whether it was Sirhan.

That afternoon Owen headed for Phoenix, Arizona, on unexplained business. Two days later he drove through the night to arrive in Santa Ana by early morning. He was asleep when the phone rang with a second threat. "We told you to keep your motherfucking mouth shut," the caller rasped, slamming down the receiver without another word.

On June 26 Owen received another call from SUS asking him to come right down to Parker Center. He begged off, however, insisting that he had to leave for a speaking engagement in Oxnard, after which he was going straight to the San Francisco area. A man identifying himself as Sergeant Sandlin came on the line, saying that he, too, was going to the Bay Area and would like to meet with him there. Owen gave Sandlin the name of George Davis as his contact.

* The complete Owen-Turner interview appears as the first section of the Appendix.

On Friday, June 29, Owen called home from Oakland and was told by his wife that Sandlin was at the Hyatt House in Palo Alto and wanted to get together with him. The preacher made a note of the hotel's number and stuck it in his pocket. Then an old pal, Ben Hardister, a private detective who had volunteered to act as his bodyguard, took him to the Athens Club, where he picked up a newspaper to pass the time. It contained a story headed "Witnesses Disappear" about the Martin Luther King case. "And the report stated that the two witnesses in this case mysteriously disappeared," Owen said. "The woman that owned the rooming house, and one of the tenants there that saw suspect James Earl Ray and could identify him with the gun, or goin' into the bathroom or somethin'." Seeing Ray's picture, Owen said his mind "drifted back to Jack Ruby goin' in and shootin' the fella. Then I have occasionally heard flashes about Jim Garrison and witnesses dyin' or mysteriously disappearing or somethin' happening all of a sudden." Owen's voice seemed to reflect genuine concern.

Owen said that he heard about threats made to prosecuting attorneys in the Sirhan case, and now he, too, was worried about his own predicament. The detectives at the University Station had assured him that his name wouldn't get in the newspapers, but still he wondered. When he had told Ben Hardister about a Sergeant Sandlin wanting to see him, Hardister rumbled, "You mean you're going to go over there and see somebody you don't even know? I'm not going to let you!"

Hardister rushed Owen to the office of Wesley Gardner in Napa, telling Owen that Gardner had FBI training and had solved a number of murders when he was with the sheriff's department. After listening to the story, Gardner offered the same counsel: "You couldn't identify him and you're going to walk over there with two threats? No sir!"

Hardister and Gardner, who was also now serving as a volunteer bodyguard, decided that Owen should stay at the Hardister ranch, which happened to be adjacent to George Davis'. The next morning Owen and Hardister drove over to the Davis ranch, interrupting the lawyer's breakfast. After hearing the story, Davis took charge. He phoned the Hyatt House but was told no Sergeant Sandlin was registered. Owen was glad he had taken the advice of

Hardister and Gardner. "Man, I could have walked in there and got plugged," he said, "or a fellow come along and pose as an officer and got me in a car and said, 'Well, let's go in and see the sheriff or the policemen here,' and dumped me in the bay or something.

" 'Maybe this is just the hand of God!' " Owen quoted Hardister.

Davis began a flurry of telephone calls. The Los Angeles Police Department (LAPD) confirmed that a Sergeant Lyle Sandlin had scheduled the trip, but they had decided to interview Owen when he returned to the Los Angeles area. But the officer with whom Davis talked didn't take the threats against Owen and his family seriously. "Oh, I'm sure they'll be all right," he said soothingly. "Just a misunderstanding."

This was when Davis tried to reach us, then called the Associated Press.

But the melodrama was not over. On Monday morning Owen rode into San Francisco with Davis. As he alighted from the car, Owen said, a Cadillac pulled up "with a heavy-set Italian-looking man with a cigar in his mouth and a hat on, and he pulled over and said, 'Say, was that George T. Davis who's car you just got out of?' " Owen muttered "Who's car?" and scurried inside the nearest building. And later that day when he was driving with Hardister on a country road, a car kept pulling in front of them and slowing down, and the man in the passenger seat kept looking back. When Owen tried to jot down the license number, the car sped away.

Owen's convoluted narrative finally was at an end. Turner posed some preliminary questions. "They wanted to meet you at eleven o'clock that night? Election night?" Owen nodded affirmatively. "And where did they want you to meet them?" Off of Catalina Street, Owen explained, "at the same place that I let the little fellow out the day before to see somebody that worked in a kitchen." For some reason Owen was reluctant to name the Ambassador Hotel. Turner elicited that the spot was in fact the rear entrance closest to the Embassy Room, where RFK was shot.

"Were they very insistent that you try and make it that night?" Turner asked.

"Yes, yes. That's when I was offered the hundred-dollar bill.

Give 'em a receipt and they'd have the balance of the money if I would be there and have the horse in the horse trailer, see?"

"At eleven o'clock?"

"At eleven o'clock with the horse. And then I was to pick up my money and take the horse where he wanted it."

Sirhan *did* have four $100 bills on him when arrested, Turner remembered. "In other words, the hundred dollars was an enticement for you to break your engagement in Oxnard?"

"Yeah, that's right. It looked like it. I feel that it was a come-on now. I do in the bottom of my heart."

Turner sensed that Owen was becoming a bit peeved at the persistent questioning, and he signed off the tape. It was three-fifteen in the afternoon. The LAPD had called Davis to advise that they would be delayed until the following morning, so Hardister took Owen back up to his ranch for safekeeping.

Turner entered Davis' office and closed the door. "George," he said, "there's an incredible chain of coincidence here. You call me in. Owen knows Eugene Bradley, who was indicted by Garrison. I have worked with Garrison . . ." Davis cocked his head as Turner posed the obvious question: "How well do you know Owen?"

"I've known him for thirty years," Davis said. "And I'm inclined to believe what he says."

THE LOS ANGELES LAW ENFORCEMENT CONTINGENT ARRIVED ON schedule the following morning, and Davis and Turner took them up on the private elevator to the conference room where Owen was waiting. Lieutenant Manuel Pena of the LAPD had the blocky build of a football guard, Turner thought, while Sergeant Enrique Hernandez resembled a tackle. They dwarfed a third man, Deputy District Attorney David M. Fitts, who soon would be named Sirhan's co-prosecutor.

The trio questioned Owen alone, but after two hours, during which they tried to break down his story, he held fast. The slender, youngish Fitts then instructed Pena and Hernandez to take Owen over to the San Francisco Police Department and use their polygraph instrument. Hernandez was a qualified operator.

In his polygraph report (which we did not see until much later), Hernandez stated that Owen "resisted the control test," but his responses indicated that he was "a suitable subject for testing." Hernandez was predisposed to try to prove that Owen was fabricating the story, while Owen vehemently insisted that it was true. The detective flatly told Owen that he had flunked the test, moralizing, "You're a preacher, a man of God supposedly. What does the Bible say about lying?"*

"Psalms, 120 and 2. 'Deliver my soul from deceitful lips and a lying tongue,' " the preacher responded by rote.

Hernandez lectured Owen on quoting from the Bible on the one hand and lying to the police on the other. Owen stuck to his story. The detective countered, "You failed to identify Sirhan in ten photos," shoving a mug shot at Owen that he allegedly had selected at SUS headquarters two weeks before. "That's not Sirhan."

"I—listen, I might be wrong. It might not be the guy. Maybe I picked up someone else. I don't know . . . If I saw him face to face, or heard his voice or something, then I'd come out and make a definite statement. I don't know. It looks like him to me."

But Hernandez persisted, telling Owen that he had lied when he said he had no arrest record. The preacher rose to his feet and raised his arms skyward imploringly. "Get me out of here, please, God! God, please! Please, God, listen! Please, God!"

"Try to calm yourself."

"O God, help me!" Owen cried out. "God help me. I'm not goin' to do it. I'm goin' to have a nervous breakdown, pret' near."

Hernandez handled Owen as a teacher handles an unruly child. Did Owen want to tell George Davis that he was lying or did he want Hernandez to do it? Owen sputtered incoherently. "Just wait here," the detective said, leaving the room. He phoned Davis and told him that his client had abused the truth so badly that he "blew the box." Owen had concocted the story, he said, and that was the end of it as far as the police were concerned.

While Hernandez was on the phone Owen soliloquized, "No! I'll tell you, George, what you ought to do. You're not going to

* Robert Blair Kaiser, "*R.F.K. Must Die!*" (New York: Dutton & Co., 1970), pp. 156–57.

get away with anything like this, George. Come on, George! No! No! I won't, George! They're doing everything to break me. No!" The hidden tape recorder in the polygraph room kept recording as Owen's voice trailed off to a mutter.

On his return to Davis' office Owen indignantly recounted the polygraph interrogation to Hardister, Gardner and Turner. Contrary to the taped version, he claimed that Hernandez had confided to him that the instrument indicated that he was being truthful. But then the detective would later report that Owen couldn't have picked up Sirhan on June 3 because "we've accounted for his activities for days beforehand." Hernandez insisted that there had been no conspiracy, citing the fact that the police "went through eighteen witnesses on the polka-dot-dress girl" who reportedly had been seen with Sirhan at the hotel as proof of how exhaustive the investigation had been.* The detective even disclosed that the police had dusted Owen's truck for fingerprints, but he neglected to say what the results were.

Owen said that Hernandez had accused him of "quibbling over questions" and not giving straight yes or no answers. The detective contended that the fact that Sirhan had been in the United States for thirteen years—which Owen quoted the hitchhiker as mentioning—was in the newspapers, implying that Owen had pieced together scraps of published material to manufacture his story.

At the end Hernandez tried to mollify Owen by conceding he might have made an "honest mistake" in identifying Sirhan, but warned him not to say anything on the subject to anyone because there was a court order that witnesses must remain silent. He advised Owen not even to talk to the FBI because "it wasn't necessary."

But the preacher saw no saving grace in his police inquisitors. "They walked in there [San Francisco police headquarters] and you'd think they were from Cuba," he said. "They looked like they were Al Capone's henchmen. I hear them down the hall. They're phonin' around for dates and phonin' the topless places, and phonin' the best places to eat and tryin' to get some guy to get dates

---

* A number of witnesses at the Ambassador Hotel reported seeing Sirhan with a girl wearing a polka-dot dress prior to the shooting.

for 'em. Yes, out for a fling and a good time, and they let me set there for an extree forty-five minutes 'til they got their reservation and was assured there would be some gals for 'em, and they'd see some of the new topless places. Yeah, they were up on their expense accounts."

PENA AND HERNANDEZ BEGAN MOPPING UP THE ANNOYING LOOSE ends of the Owen story on Friday, July 5, by reinterviewing Mrs. Mary Sirhan, mother of the accused assassin. They had first talked to her on Tuesday, which presumably was why they delayed their trip to San Francisco. One of the problems with writing off Owen's account was the fact that when arrested, Sirhan had, in addition to $6 and some change, four $100 bills in his pocket. Where did the long-unemployed young man get that amount of hard cash? And why was he carrying it? The policemen must have recognized one possible answer: that $300 of it was to pay Owen for the horse when he delivered it to the Ambassador Hotel.

A 21-page SUS summary report titled JERRY OWEN INVESTIGA-TION, which we obtained some time later,* revealed that in the initial interview Pena and Hernandez asked Mrs. Sirhan about a $2,000 insurance settlement that Sirhan had received a few weeks before the assassination. According to the report, she "recalled that Sirhan asked for $300 a day or two before the shooting. She said that she believed that Sirhan had spent most of the remainder from the $1000 he gave her from the insurance settlement. She thought that he had given some of the money to Adel [a brother]. Adel Sirhan was present during the interview, and he stated at one point, 'I think Sirhan wanted the $300 to buy a horse with.' "

Adel Sirhan's unsolicited information squared perfectly with the part of Owen's story that Sirhan had agreed to buy his horse for

* The SUS report was released to Christian by the Los Angeles County Clerk's office shortly after Sirhan's 1969 trial. Most of the court exhibits and investigative material had been routinely placed with the Clerk's office for storage. Although the SUS report was not supposed to be available to the public, the office of LAPD Detective Chief Robert Houghton apparently got its wires crossed and authorized release of a copy to Christian. (See Appendix.)

$300. Pena and Hernandez were armed with this when they grilled Owen in San Francisco, yet they acted as if they didn't believe a word of his story. It was not something that Owen could have picked out of the newspapers, but the policemen never asked a single question.

Pena and Hernandez seemed to have this nagging little problem very much in mind when they revisited Mary Sirhan. Where had her son been on June 3? As best as she could recall, he drove her to work at eight o'clock, but he was not at home when she returned at one. "However, there was evidence that he had just taken a shower and there was a warm cup of coffee," the SUS men reported in the best tradition of detective fiction. "Sirhan was gone most of the afternoon, but she noticed that he was watching television at 4:30 P.M." He did not leave the house again that day, Mrs. Sirhan said. "At least from the time of 4:30 P.M.," the report concluded, "Mrs. Sirhan's statement contradict's Owen's statement."

This was an overly simplistic conclusion, and SUS should have known better. What mother can recall what her son did on an uneventful day a month previously? Pena and Hernandez, perhaps with this in mind, prevailed upon Mrs. Sirhan to question her son about that day when she visited him in jail. She reported back that he said "he did not know Owen, had never seen him nor had he ever ridden in his pickup truck. He also denied that he had attempted to purchase a palomino horse."

The SUS report contained several contradictions and inconsistencies in Owen's story. For example, when he reported to the University Division of the LAPD on June 5, Owen said that on June 3 he "left his residence in Santa Ana en route to the Coliseum Hotel," where he "spoke with the manager of the coffee shop, John Bert Morris [sic], and Rip O'Reilly, a heavyweight boxer. Morris and Owen discussed the purchase of some boxing equipment from the United Sporting Goods Store." But in the version he later told Turner in San Francisco (a copy of which was subsequently furnished to SUS), he said that he was about to go directly to Oxnard when the phone rang and he was notified that boxing equipment he had ordered at United was ready. As a result he detoured through Los Angeles to pick it up. And he claimed that he had not contacted Bert Morse, an "oldtime fight manager who had Baby Armendez back in the '30s," until on his way home from Oxnard on June 5.

Perhaps the most glaring discrepancy stemmed from an SUS interview of "Rip" O'Reilly. The boxer advised that "on June 3, 1968 Owen called him at about 10:30 A.M. and invited him to attend a Saints and Sinners Club that night. At 6:30 P.M. Owen picked up O'Reilly at the Coliseum Hotel, and they drove to the meeting on Fairfax Avenue. Owen was driving a dark-colored pickup truck with a horse trailer attached. A horse was in the trailer. They remained at the meeting until 11:30 P.M., and Owen took O'Reilly back to the hotel." This statement contradicted Owen's story that he decided to remain in Los Angeles and attend the Saints and Sinners affair to kill time only after picking up Sirhan that afternoon and making a deal on the horse. And it clashed with Owen's version that he fetched a trailer and three ponies from Oxnard on June 5.

Apparently SUS didn't take seriously the implications of O'Reilly's account—that Owen had brought the trailer and horse with him to Los Angeles, that he never went to Oxnard the night of the RFK shooting, and might have been outside the Ambassador Hotel when the Senator was shot.

"TAKE THIS HOME AND PLAY IT," TURNER TOLD CHRISTIAN, HANDing him the tape recording of Owen telling his story. "Make notes as you go along."

By the time Turner got over to Christian's apartment that evening he had already found a number of discrepancies in the Owen story, which he noted on a yellow legal pad. First of all, Owen said that he was ready to leave his Santa Ana home on June 3 for Oxnard, but the speaking engagement was not until the night of June 4 and Oxnard was less than a hundred miles away. Then there was the incident in which the two men who had climbed onto his truck jumped off at a stoplight and began talking familiarly with a man and girl on the corner—the same couple who were with Sirhan at the Sunset Boulevard rendezvous that night and appeared to be a part of the implicit conspiracy. But Christian noted that Sirhan couldn't possibly have known what route Owen would take or that the light would be red when he arrived at the stoplight. And Owen said that he was going to Oxnard to pick up the horse and trailer, but slipped when he mentioned that Maxie Rosenbloom "looked at the truck and horse and laughed at Owen driving that rig right in the heart of Hollywood."

The list went on and on. Turner agreed that Owen had spun a web of fiction around elements of the truth—such as somehow being acquainted with Sirhan. But why? Owen obviously had a bent for self-promotion, but in this case he had shied away from publicity. He had quietly reported the story to the police, seeking and getting an assurance of anonymity. Instead of trying to capitalize on the polka-dot-dress-girl (conspiracy) angle that was getting heavy play in the media—the "dirty blonde" girl of his story certainly fit her description—he ran to his attorney looking for protection. It was Davis' idea to break the story in the Associated Press to provide that protection, but even then Owen insisted that his name not be used. As a result, we ruled out the possibility of a publicity stunt.

After wrestling with the problem for several days, we tried to reach George Davis to find out if he had any ideas. His secretary said that he had abruptly canceled his entire appointment schedule to go to his ranch to "meet with some business associates," among whom were Owen, Hardister and Gardner. The urgent conference stretched into five days. When Davis failed to call us back, Christian asked Peter Hitchcock to intervene. "I guess they want to talk to you about the Owen thing," Hitchcock told Davis after locating him at the ranch. "Well, you know some things take precedence and other things come later," Davis asserted, "and that's a subject that comes later as far as I'm concerned. You know, I'm not really lying awake nights worrying about whether Owen gets shot. That's basically his problem."

It was clear that Davis was ducking any further discussion of the situation. Did he now, after being closeted with Owen for five days, know more about what was behind the hitchhiker story than when he was frantically dialing the state's top law enforcement officers seeking protection? We had felt that Owen's concern for his safety was genuine, but we now began to wonder.

Owen might have been telling the essential truth despite the flaws in his story and his failure to pass the polygraph test. In his excitement he could have inadvertently garbled details, and we knew that the outcome of the polygraph test depended more on the objectivity and skill of the operator than on the instrument itself. Hernandez seemingly had arrived in San Francisco with his mind made up.

At this point we knew little about Owen's curious background —only that George Davis had vouched for him as a friend of thirty years' standing. And we were unaware that the LAPD's cavalier dismissal of the hitchhiker story as a publicity stunt was part of a pattern that had begun the moment RFK was shot.

4

Tinting Sirhan Red

WITHIN HOURS OF THE SHOOTING, A CAMPAIGN WAS UNDER way to paint Sirhan a deep Red. The chief brush-wielder was Sam Yorty, the cocky bantam-rooster mayor of Los Angeles. Yorty had a reputation for sounding off on practically every issue. During the height of the Vietnam war he made two "inspection trips" to Saigon and returned with hawkish pronouncements on the necessity to increase the American military commitment. Wags dubbed Los Angeles the only city with its own foreign policy.

The Kennedy brothers had long been near the top of Yorty's enemies list. In 1960, despite his nominal Democratic affiliation, Yorty had endorsed Richard Nixon over JFK, and in 1965 he had clashed with RFK during a Senate hearing. In 1968 he was again in Nixon's corner.

Ironically, Christian had been a kind of unofficial campaign adviser to Yorty in 1966, called in by a former colleague of friend Paul Smith. Christian didn't know that Yorty was such a hard-line right-winger when he agreed to advise him; however, he soon found out how deep ran the waters of political intrigue when he learned that the so-called Maverick Mayor had a double strategy. He intended to win, if he could, in the Democratic primary against incumbent Edmund G. "Pat" Brown, father of Jerry Brown. But in case he didn't win, he was mounting a mud-slinging and Red-baiting campaign that he hoped would alienate conservative Democrats from Brown during the November election. In fact, Yorty held five secret strategy meetings with the Republican standard-bearer, Ronald Reagan, to divide the Democrats from within. The plan worked. After Brown barely disposed of Yorty in the primary, he was battered by a vicious assault from the right in the general election and was handily beaten by Reagan.*

During the midmorning of June 5, 1968, as Robert Kennedy lay comatose in the hospital, Yorty appeared before network television cameras with Chief of Police Thomas Reddin, resplendent in his gold-braided uniform, sitting solemnly by his side and nodding in approbation. He revealed that according to a "reliable police informant," a car traceable to suspect Sirhan had been seen several times parked in front of the W. E. B. DuBois Clubs, a leftist young-people's group. The implication was that the man responsible for Kennedy's shooting was a left-wing radical.

What Yorty neglected to point out was that the DuBois Clubs were moribund and had vacated that address over a year before. One of Sirhan's brothers owned the car and played in the band at an Arabian night club a couple of doors away. Sirhan used the car frequently because his beat-up De Soto was forever breaking

---

* In 1972 Yorty announced that he was a candidate for President and campaigned in New Hampshire. He even garnered the endorsement of publisher William Loeb, noted for his radical right leanings. But Yorty was so soundly thrashed he must have wondered if anyone outside of Los Angeles had heard of him. Shortly thereafter, Yorty denounced the Democratic party, turned Republican, and (again) backed Richard Nixon.

down, and visited his brother at the Hollywood Boulevard location on many occasions.

Following the television appearance, Yorty showed up at the field command post set up in the LAPD's Rampart Division, not far from the Ambassador Hotel. The mayor began sorting through material the police had just brought in from a warrantless search of Sirhan's room in the family residence in Pasadena. His attention centered on some Rosicrucian literature—Sirhan had recently applied for membership in that mystical society—and a pair of spiral notebooks filled with repetitive and often disjointed handwriting that indicated strong occult affinities.

As Yorty left the police station he was cornered by several members of the press. "What can you tell us about Sirhan Sirhan?" one asked.

"Well," the mayor replied, "he was a member of numerous Communist organizations, including the Rosicrucians."

"The Rosicrucians aren't a Communist organization," a newsman corrected. In fact, it would turn out that Sirhan had never been affiliated with any Communist-oriented group.

"It appears," Yorty amended, "that Sirhan Sirhan was a sort of loner who harbored Communist inclinations, favored Communists of all types. He said the U.S. must fall. Indicated that RFK must be assassinated before June 5, 1968." Yorty had excerpted passages from the spiral notebooks, but at this point no one had verified that they were actually written by the man in custody. (There would remain a question of their authorship even after Sirhan was tried and convicted in 1969.)

Evidential niceties didn't faze the lawyer-mayor. Returning before the television cameras, Yorty brandished the notebooks and flipped though pages, reading off entries that he thought sounded Communistic. "He does a lot of writing, pro-Communist and anti-capitalist, anti-United States," he commented.* No one in the vast television audience could fail to get the message that Sirhan had been inspired to his deed by his Communist sympathies and occult dabblings.

State Attorney General Thomas C. Lynch phoned Yorty to

* San Francisco *Examiner* (June 6, 1968).

register concern that his televised statements "referred to evidence that would have to be ruled upon by the court," and prominent local lawyers upbraided him for, as one put it, "your lack of understanding of the fundamentals of American justice." But the irrepressible Yorty would not be muzzled. He held another press conference, at which he dwelt at length on the notebooks and their "timetable" to kill Kennedy. Sirhan, he said, was "inflamed by contacts with the Communist Party and contacts with Communist-dominated or infiltrated organizations."*

Both Yorty and Reddin went to great pains to convey that RFK's assassination had virtually been his own fault. Why? Because, they insisted, the presidential aspirant had allegedly told the LAPD that he wanted no police protection during his visits to Los Angeles. Thus, they said, no members of the LAPD had been present at the Ambassador Hotel at the time of the shooting.

Apparently none of the newsmen present gave any thought to the laws pertaining to the LAPD's responsibility for "public safety" and "crowd control" that should have applied to the gathering that night. (The hotel housed no fewer than three major political candidates, RFK, Senator Alan Cranston and Max Rafferty; their supporters covered the spectrum from extreme left to far right— the makings of potential spontaneous turmoil and violence.) It was also strange that no one in the RFK campaign entourage could recall anyone, RFK included, having called off LAPD protection. But no one stepped forth to challenge the contentions of the Yorty-Reddin press conference. The impression that prevailed was that RFK had somehow managed to orally sign his own death warrant.

Watching Yorty in action, Christian nodded knowingly at his display of demagoguery. "He may shoot from the lip," Christian said, "but there is *always* a motive behind it." That was one thing Christian knew from the 1966 campaign.

WHILE YORTY WAS HOLDING FORTH DOWNTOWN ON THE MORNING of June 5, a group calling itself American United called a press conference in Westwood, near the UCLA campus. American

* Associated Press (June 7, 1968).

United was the two-man show of John Steinbacher, a John Birch Society propagandist and part-time reporter for the Anaheim *Bulletin* in Orange County, and Anthony J. Hilder, a firebrand activist. Both were protégés of the well-known anti-Semite Myron J. Fagan, a leader of the Hollywood blacklisting clique during the McCarthy era.*

In fact, Hilder and a gaggle of followers had been at the Ambassador Hotel the previous night trying to race-bait RFK by handing out buttons and pamphlets depicting him and black Congressman Adam Clayton Powell, Jr., of New York on the same ticket. After the shooting the Hilder group created considerable confusion by alleging that the assailant was a Eugene McCarthy supporter.

Steinbacher and Hilder had prepared a press kit crammed with their prolific output of ultraright polemics. The year before, Steinbacher had published a turgid volume called *It Comes Up Murder†* that expounded the conspiracy theory of history. According to the theory, a vast international plot to control the world began in Bavaria in 1776 when Professor Adam Weishaupt organized, in Steinbacher's words, "the secret and evil cult of the Illuminati in order to wage Satan's war against Christian civilization." Weishaupt's acorn grew into a mighty oak of conspiracy, its branches numbering the Rothschild international banking family, the Rockefellers, Freemasonry, the Zionist movement and mystical societies such as the Rosicrucians and Theosophists. Through an alchemy of the most diabolical sort, the theory went, the elements of the Illuminati coalesced into the modern "international Communist conspiracy," which also manifested itself in such power centers as the United Nations, the Council on Foreign Relations and the Rockefeller Foundation, and such influential leaders as Franklin D. Roosevelt, Joseph Stalin, Charles de Gaulle and J. William Fulbright.‡

---

* Authors' interview with Anthony J. Hilder, 1970.

† Los Angeles: Impact Publishers, 1967.

‡ This list was recently expanded to include the Trilateral Commission— whose membership includes former Secretary of State Henry Kissinger and President Jimmy Carter.

"The success of the Illuminati," Steinbacher wrote, "lay in enlisting the services of dupes, and by encouraging the fantasies of honest visionaries or the schemes of fanatics, by flattering the vanity of the ambitious, and by playing upon the passion for wealth and power. It was in this way that the Illuminati were able to secure the services of countless thousands."

In *It Comes Up Murder* Steinbacher contended that "assassinations within the borders of the United States are carried out by the conspirators," and prophesied: "We can look forward to more strange deaths." (One grisly album cover depicted Nelson Rockefeller at the moment of his own assassination, as bullets shatter his skull and a look of terror comes on his face.) *

In early April the American United group sent a large contingent of congressmen a packet of anti-Semitic propaganda in the form of a long-playing album tagged "The ILLUMINATI-CFR (Council on Foreign Relations) . . . the MOST SHOCKING . . . REVELATORY EXPOSE of the 'IN CROWD' which has, UNTIL NOW, controlled the course of the MODERN WORLD . . . and is now attempting to bring about WORLD CURRENCY, WORLD GOVERNMENT, and WORLD CONTROL . . . The POLICIES of THIS GOVERNMENT have reached the point of INSANITY." The covering letter included the notation that records had been sent to every senator "except Morse, Fulbright, Church, Hartke, and the Brothers Kennedy . . . and the Brothers Rockefeller." The slogan emblazoned on the American United stationery warned:

---

* During a taped telephone interview on May 3, 1970, Hilder told Christian: "I *predicted* Bobby Kennedy would be shot . . . then he was shot. I *predicted* [Dr. Martin Luther] King would be shot . . . and *he* was shot! . . . Right now they have to have another killing . . . preferably a so-called Conservative . . . maybe Nixon . . . But it would be wonderful to have one-two-three [Kennedy] brothers."

Christian interviewed Steinbacher via phone on the same day. His words were equally disconcerting: "JFK was on to the thing [the alleged "Illuminati Conspiracy"], and he was about to blow the whistle [just before the President was killed. Sirhan was a lot like Oswald, *very* much so, *very* similar. They *definitely* were just patsies . . .] Ted Kennedy better not run. He would be next."

"OUR COUNTRY CAN NEVER GO RIGHT BY GOING LEFT!"* Thus, the main political leaders in America had been alerted to the "ILLUMINATI" threat to the survival of the nation. It was a name that would surface again—soon.

With RFK struck down, Steinbacher and Hilder were ready to claim that their timely prophecy had been fulfilled—that the senator was yet another victim of the "Illuminati-Communist conspiracy," which this time used Sirhan as a pawn. It just so happened that the Sirhan notebooks, which Sam Yorty was at that very moment inspecting (and which would remain out of the public domain until after the trial), contained repeated references to "Illuminati," as well as the entry "Master Kuthumi" (an apparently phonetic spelling of "Master Koot Hoomi"), a Tibetan mystic from whom Madame Helena Petrovna Blavatsky, the founder of the Theosophical Society, was said to receive ethereal guidance.

Not one member of the press showed up. Most were acquainted with the far-out ideology of Steinbacher and Hilder, and besides, were chasing down the main story and covering Yorty's press conferences. Undaunted, the pair appeared on talk shows to spread the word that the Illuminati were behind the shooting.† In jail, Sirhan added fuel to the fire by requesting *The Secret Doctrine*, by

---

* Letter signed by Anthony J. Hilder, April 7, 1968; mailed from 1141 North Highland Avenue, Hollywood, Calif. 90038.

Foundation researcher Walter Carrithers informed us in 1971 that American United once used the address P.O. Box 285, Woodland Hills, Calif. on some of its ILLUMINATI record albums. This is the same address on the letterhead of EUGENE BRADLEY DEFENSE FUND, an ad hoc group of right-wing preachers raising money to defend him against the charges levied by DA Jim Garrison in the JFK assassination case. One of the signators of a fund-raising letter sent out in July, 1968, was Orange County evangelist Dr. Bob Wells. In his 1968 interview with Jerry Owen, Turner asked if the preacher knew Wells: "Very well. He don't live far from me. Know him well." Did Owen know of the Bradley-Wells tie-in? "I think Bradley was to speak for him once."

† One appearance was on KHJ-TV's *Tempo* program, with right-winger Robert K. Dornan hosting (June 19, 1968). In 1976 Dornan was elected to Congress in the most costly congressional campaign in history. His main political target: the Trilateral Commission and its alleged "liberal" policies.

Madame Blavatsky, and *Talks at the Feet of the Master*, by C. W. Leadbeater, a theosophy follower, from his home library. Coupled with Yorty's disclosure of Sirhan's membership in the Rosicrucians, the pieces of an "Illuminati Conspiracy" were falling into place. "This is an Illuminist killing!" Steinbacher declaimed.

The Illuminati theme was soon picked up in the national media. Supplied with Steinbacher-Hilder "expertise," Walter Winchell devoted a column to it, and *Time* magazine ran a photograph of the late Madame Blavatsky with its story. Truman Capote, appearing on the *Tonight* show on NBC, ventured that Sirhan might have been hypnoprogrammed, and that Madame Blavatsky had shown "how you could undermine the morale of a country and create a vacuum for revolution by systematically assassinating a series of prominent leaders."

Capote was repeating a gross canard, originated by Steinbacher and Hilder, that Madame Blavatsky had authored a "secret manual" for assassination. Actually, she had pointed out in her writings how evil-minded men could employ assassination to subvert a nation. She was no Dragon Lady, but a pioneer in what is now called ESP, and her followers are the gentlest of people. They believe that God is present in all things, and advance the universal brotherhood of man. But to the radical right, such philosophies are occult-bred heresies.*

AT SEVEN-FIFTEEN ON THE EVENING AFTER THE RFK SHOOTING, a compact man with goggle eyeglasses marched into LAPD headquarters with four companions. He gave his name as Major Jose Antonio Duarte, and said he and his men were "freedom fighters against Fidel Castro." A Cuban exile, Duarte reported that on May 21 he had attended a leftist meeting because he knew that support for Castro was on the agenda. When he rose to speak out, he said, a small olive-skinned young man angrily accused him of

---

* For a convincing, thorough refutation of charges against Madame Blavatsky and the Theosophists, see *The Hall of Magic Mirrors*, by Victor A. Endersby (Fresno: The Blavatsky Foundation, 1969).

being a CIA agent, and they got into a shoving match. The young man was Sirhan Sirhan.

Duarte tried to unload his story on the news media, but it was ignored. Then, on June 11, the Anaheim *Bulletin* headlined: PRO-CASTRO LINK TO RFK SLAYING. The article, written by Duarte's political associate John Steinbacher, recounted the Cuban's putative encounter with Sirhan. Steinbacher arranged radio appearances for Duarte,* and in an instant paperback book, *Senator Robert Francis Kennedy: The Man, the Mysticism, the Murder,†* summed up: "Mayor Sam Yorty of Los Angeles has already brought out the pro-Communist inclinations of Sirhan, but it was left to Major Jose Duarte, the Cuban anti-Communist, to link Sirhan with the riots and unrest in our nation, today."

In time the LAPD discredited Duarte's identification of Sirhan by producing a look-alike Iranian student who had been at the leftist meeting and recalled being involved in the altercation. However, the entire scenario struck us as all too familiar. In August 1963 Lee Harvey Oswald was accosted by an anti-Castro exile while handing out pro-Castro literature on the streets of New Orleans. Shortly after the scuffle Oswald was invited to participate in a radio debate on the subject. In the evening of the day John Kennedy was shot, taped excerpts were broadcast nationally and Oswald was heard by millions proclaiming, "I am a Marxist!"

Both the debate and the assassination-evening airing of the excerpts were arranged by Edward S. Butler, who headed a right-wing propaganda outfit in New Orleans called the Information Council of the Americas. By 1968 Butler had moved to Los Angeles, where he carried on with financial aid from Patrick J. Frawley, Jr., chief executive officer of the Schick Safety Razor Company. For years Frawley generously supported hard-line conservatives such as Ronald Reagan, Barry Goldwater and Sam Yorty. Frawley and Yorty belonged to the American Security Council, an embodiment of the military-industrial complex that lobbied for a bigger military establishment and ran a political blacklist service

* Authors' interviews with Steinbacher and Hilder, spring 1970.
† Los Angeles: Impact Publishers, July 1968.

for its large corporation clients. Anthony Hilder also claimed to have the backing of Frawley.* And Butler was present when Steinbacher and Hilder held their unattended press conference.

Thus a right-wing clique colored the facts and conjured up visions of a sinister occult cabal to depict Sirhan as the pawn of an international plot. As the Anaheim *Bulletin* rhetorically asked in an editorial: "Are foreign influences at work to conquer this country? Is a hidden plot progressing to eliminate the Liberal leadership of the country and throw the movement completely into control of Communist agents?"

It was a bit mind-boggling to think of liberal leaders being knocked off by the radical left rather than the radical right, but the general theme that Sirhan had somehow been influenced by Communism stuck in the public mind. One effect of this popular impression was to permit the LAPD to suppress evidence leading in the opposite direction.†

* Hilder also claimed the backing of well-known conservative funder Henry Salvatori, in a telephone call to attorney Barbara Warner Blehr on July 27, 1971. (Salvatori was one of the principal financiers of both Sam Yorty and Ronald Reagan.)

† The LAPD is more blatantly right-wing than any other major force in the country. At the time of the RFK shooting the Fire and Police Research Association, dominated by and openly affiliated with ultraconservative groups, waged effective propaganda and lobbying campaigns. John Rousselot, then the national public relations director of the John Birch Society, claimed that some two thousand Los Angeles County law enforcement officers, including not only the LAPD but the District Attorney's staff and Sheriff's Department, were members of the Birch Society. Alan Cranston, now the senior U.S. Senator from California, found it hard "to suppress a shudder" when he heard the claim. "Whether two thousand or two hundred," Cranston said, "that frankly disturbs me more than all the reports of Minutemen training in the hills with rifles and bazookas."

5
The Cover-up

BUT THE ALLEGATIONS LEVELED BY YORTY AND STEINBACHER
and Hilder also presented the LAPD with a major headache.
As Chief of Detectives Robert A. Houghton, who was in
overall charge of SUS, has observed in his book *Special Unit
Senator*, the widespread belief that Sirhan had Communist
connections and acted with premeditation raised the specter
of conspiracy. So did the reports of a polka-dot-dress girl
with Sirhan, and rumors that he was tied in with an Arab
extremist group contemplating the assassination.*

* Houghton is alluding to a report received by SUS that an affiliate
of the Arab terrorist organization El Fatah had Sirhan under control.
According to Houghton, SUS learned that El Fatah had not become
active in the United States until three months after the RFK shooting.

"We were faced with a crime that would be examined everywhere in the world," Houghton wrote. "There had never been one like it in Los Angeles history. Already it was under the public magnifying glass." Houghton could envision Kennedy haters and lovers, skeptical Americans, police critics and partisans of the FBI wanting to seize upon the LAPD's slightest miscalculation. Most of all he seemed haunted by a fear that the assassination "buffs" were lurking in ambush. "There were the clever people, as usual," he went on, "standing by to profit by the cry of conspiracy, hooking their theories to journalistic wagons before the Arlington soil was tamped. Sooner or later—sooner, probably—they would all come running from everywhere to demand, 'What really happened?' "*

Houghton's disparagement of those with differing views as crass opportunists was singularly inappropriate, since he himself contracted for a book exploiting his inside position while on the public payroll. But the bitterness of his attack on the critics as journalistic ghouls raises the question of how he, in the very early stages of the RFK investigation, could be so sure there was no conspiracy.

For SUS, from the inception of its probe, seemed to direct its energies at quashing evidence indicating a conspiracy while accepting uncritically information which pointed to Sirhan as a lone assassin. Because homicide is a violation of state laws, the LAPD assumed primary jurisdiction over the investigation. The FBI possessed a parallel jurisdiction under the civil rights statutes and federal legislation enacted after Dallas regarding violence against the President or a candidate for federal office. But from the start the LAPD made it clear that the FBI would be playing second fiddle. "They elbowed us out of it right away," Roger J. LaJeunesse, the senior FBI agent on the case, has said.†

Upon arriving at his office on the morning of the shooting, LaJeunesse was told that President Johnson had ordered the Bureau into the investigation and that he was to take charge. He left immediately for the "Glass House," the LAPD's Parker Center headquarters, arriving by nine-thirty at the office of Chief Houghton. Houghton appeared somewhat surprised that LaJeunesse was there,

* *Special Unit Senator* (New York: Random House, 1970), pp. 95–96.
† Authors' interviews with Roger LaJeunesse.

since he had talked to local FBI chief Wesley G. Grapp earlier, before the President's order arrived, and was assured that the FBI would not become involved.

Houghton expressed keen interest in the projected scope and nature of the Bureau's inquiry. He even proposed that two of his top men accompany the FBI agents on their rounds because, he said, he was planning on writing a manual about what local departments could learn from the FBI, and this would be a model case. The chief repeatedly insisted that the investigation was a "local matter" and that his men could handle it without day-to-day assistance from the FBI. LaJeunesse was somewhat disquieted by Houghton's uncharacteristic possessiveness. In his long experience with the LAPD, there had never been a "withholding" problem.*

LaJeunesse paid a visit to a special squad of detectives, isolated on the top floor of Parker Center, who were setting up an investigation office. It was later to become SUS. He noticed that an old acquaintance from his days on the bank-robbery detail, Lieutenant Manny Pena, was very much in charge.

Within days the LAPD announced that the elite squad called Special Unit Senator had been formed to handle the investigation. According to Houghton, it was entirely his idea to create SUS, "a unit completely detached from any other organizational branch of the Los Angeles Police Department." He tapped Chief of Homicide Detectives Hugh Brown, with whom he had worked for fifteen years, to head SUS, telling Brown that if there was a "great conspiracy" linking the RFK murder with those of JFK and Martin Luther King, Jr., it had better be unveiled because their work would be subject to "much fine-comb study."†

Houghton assertedly gave Brown free rein in electing the personnel for SUS—with one exception. He specifically designated Manny Pena, who was put in a position to control the daily flow and direction of the investigation. And his decision on *all* matters

* LaJeunesse, who had known Houghton previously, is certain that this meeting took place on the morning of June 5. However, Houghton stated in *Special Unit Senator* that he was camping in Yosemite Park at the time of the shooting and did not return to Los Angeles until two days later.

† Houghton, *op. cit.*, pp. 101–2.

was final. Working under Pena on what was called the Background/ Conspiracy team assigned to dig into Sirhan's past and the possibility of conspiracy was Sergeant Enrique "Hank" Hernandez. As a polygraph operator, Hernandez questioned the witnesses whose accounts indicated a plot. In each instance, as we have seen with Jerry Owen, Hernandez would get them to alter their stories, or if they refused, shredded their credibility with his polygraph interpretations.

The choice of Lieutenant Manuel Pena for the key slot in SUS was a curious one. Among members of the force and the Mexican-American community, Pena was a living legend—reputedly he had killed eleven suspects "in the line of duty," more than any other officer in the history of the department. In *Special Unit Senator* Houghton described him as a "stocky, intense, proud man of Mexican-American descent" with twenty-two years of experience under his belt at the time. Houghton boasted that Pena had commanded detective divisions, supervised a bank-robbery squad, and "spoke French and Spanish, and had connections with various intelligence agencies in several countries."*

What we did not know at the time that Pena and Hernandez interrogated Jerry Owen was that both had long-standing connections with the CIA. Our first clue about Pena came months later when a faded newspaper article came to our attention. On November 13, 1967, more than six months before the RFK slaying, the San Fernando Valley *Times* had reported Pena's formal retirement from the LAPD. A surprise testimonial dinner was held in his honor at the Sportsmen's Lodge, with LAPD Chief Thomas Reddin prominent among the law enforcement fraternity in attendance. It was "a rousing and emotion packed" affair, the article said, and then quoted Reddin: " 'I have known Manny for many years. I would not have missed being here for anything.' "

The article revealed: "Pena retired from the police force to advance his career. He has accepted a position with the Agency for International Development Office of the State Department. As a public safety advisor, he will train and advise foreign police forces in investigative and administrative matters. After nine weeks

---

* *Ibid.*, pp. 102–3.

of training and orientation, he will be assigned to his post, possibly a Latin American country, judging by the fact that he speaks Spanish fluently."

It is an open secret that the Office of Public Safety of the Agency for International Development (AID) has long served as a cover for the CIA's clandestine program of supplying advisers and instructors for national police and intelligence services in Southeast Asia and Latin America engaged in anti-Communist operations. In 1968 California Chief Deputy Attorney General Charles A. O'Brien informed us that this ultrasecret CIA unit was known to insiders as the "Department of Dirty Tricks," and that one of its specialties was teaching foreign "intelligence apparats" the techniques of assassination.

FBI agent Roger LaJeunesse, whom Turner had known years before in the Bureau, confided that Pena had left the LAPD for a "special training unit" at a CIA base in Virginia. In fact, said LaJeunesse, Pena's departure in November 1967 had not been a one-shot deal—the detective had done CIA special assignments for a decade, mostly under AID cover. On some of these assignments, in Central and South America, he worked with CIA operative Dan A. Mitrione, a former Indiana chief of police.* Further confirmation of Pena's CIA role came from his brother, a high school teacher, who casually mentioned to television newsman Stan Bohrman how proud Manny was of his services for the CIA over the years.

Reporter Fernando Faura, whose by-line appeared on the newspaper story of the farewell banquet, recounted that in April

---

* In the summer of 1970 Mitrione and an AID associate named Claude L. Fly were abducted by Uruguayan Tupamaros guerrillas. Press reports identified Mitrione as a "U.S. police advisor" to the military junta ruling Uruguay; his assignment was said to be the "special training" of militia personnel in "counterrevolutionary" tactics. The Tupamaros were more pejorative in their version of Mitrione's expertise: in a note pinned to his body after they shot and killed him, they accused him of being a "CIA killer" and "teacher of horrible tortures" whose atrocities against the revolutionaries could not remain unpublished. Fly was released unharmed. The affair was made into a 1972 motion picture, *State of Siege*, featuring Yves Montand as Mitrione.

1968, only five months after Pena's departure, he was sauntering along a corridor in Parker Center when he spotted a vaguely familiar figure. The square face and fireplug frame seemed to belong to Manny Pena, but now he sported an expensive dark-blue suit, a black handlebar mustache and heavy horn-rimmed glasses.

"Manny?" Faura probed.

The figure stopped and looked sheepish as the reporter approached with hand extended.

"Hey, Manny, I damn near didn't recognize you with that disguise!"

The detective was not amused. Faura asked what he was doing back in Los Angeles. Pena explained that the AID job wasn't quite what he had expected, so he quit and resumed his duties with the LAPD.

Pena's stints with the CIA were hardly unique. For example, Hugh C. McDonald, who was Chief of Detectives for the Los Angeles County Sheriff's Department before retiring in 1967, recently revealed in a book* that for many years he had gone on detached duty with the CIA as a contract agent, primarily in operations in conjunction with White Russian émigré elements in Europe. And according to Morton Kondracke of the Chicago Sun-Times, "a high-ranking former official of the spy agency said in an interview that he remembered some Chicago policemen attending training sessions at the CIA's super-secret facility at Camp Peary, near Williamsburg, Va., either in late 1967 or early 1968." The Agency itself conceded that "briefings" were given to "less than 50" policemen from "about a dozen departments."†

And we learned much later that Pena's SUS sidekick, Sergeant Hank Hernandez, who was promoted to lieutenant in recognition of his status in the special unit, also had CIA connections. Now retired from the force, he boasts in a résumé offering his services as a private investigator that in 1963 he played a key role in "Unified Police Command" training for the CIA in Latin America. He functioned under the usual cover of AID's Office of Public

---

* *Appointment in Dallas* (New York: Hugh C. McDonald Publishing Corp., 1975). McDonald talks about his CIA role throughout the book.

† Chicago *Sun-Times* (February 8, 1973).

Safety, and even received a medal from the Venezuelan government, then concerned with Fidel Castro's "exportation" of the Cuban revolution.

In retrospect it seems odd that two policemen who doubled as CIA agents occupied key positions in SUS, where they were able to seal off avenues that led in the direction of conspiracy. One of those avenues was the trail of "the girl in the polka-dot dress."

VETERAN LAPD SERGEANT PAUL SHARAGA WAS CRUISING IN THE vicinity of the Ambassador Hotel at 12:23 A.M. on June 5 when an "ambulance shooting" call crackled over his radio. In half a minute he wheeled his patrol car into the large parking lot at the rear of the hotel. People were running in all directions. An older couple hurried up to Sharaga. As he recalled it, "They related that they were outside one of the doors to the Embassy Room when a young couple in their early twenties came rushing out. This couple seemed to be in a state of glee, shouting 'We shot him! We shot him! We killed him!' The woman stated that she asked the young lady, 'Who did you shoot?' or 'Who was shot?,' and the young lady replied, 'Kennedy! We shot him. We killed him!'

"The only description I could get from this older couple was that the suspects were in their early twenties. The woman was wearing a polka-dot dress. Neither of the couple could furnish any additional information—they were quite hysterical and it was difficult for them to talk."

Sharaga said he jotted down the information on his note pad—he thinks the couple might have been named Bernstein—and immediately radioed a Code One (emergency) from his car. "I informed communications that I was setting up a command post in the area, and requested that they broadcast the description of the suspects as given to me." An All Points Bulletin went on the air at once advising all units to be on the lookout for the "two suspects."*

This was the debut of the famous polka-dot-dress girl. Although

* Art Kevin's taped interview with Sharaga, KMPC radio, Los Angeles, December 20, 1974.

the LAPD would later claim that she never existed, there were a number of others who reported sighting her that night.

The first was Sirhan himself. In a post-conviction interview in early 1969, Sirhan told NBC correspondent Jack Perkins that the girl materialized in mid-evening at the Ambassador Hotel as he was looking for a cup of coffee. He found a coffee urn, and a pretty girl was there. Perkins asked, "All right, after you poured coffee for the girl, then what happened?" Sirhan replied, "Then, ah . . . I don't remember much what happened after that."*

Possibly the first person to spot them together that evening was Lonny L. Worthey, who had come to the hotel with his wife and a friend for the anticipated Kennedy victory celebration. Unable to get into the Embassy Room, they went to another room on the ground floor that had been set up for campaign workers. An FBI interview report states:

At about 10:00 P.M., when going to the bar to get a Coke for his wife, [Worthey] accidentally bumped into an individual at the end of this bar. After seeing newspaper photographs of SIRHAN SIRHAN, he believes the individual he bumped into was SIRHAN SIRHAN. WORTHEY apologized for bumping into this person to which this individual made no reply. A few minutes later WORTHEY observed a female standing along side this individual, but he did not observe them talking to each other.†

Kennedy supporter Booker Griffin, head of the Los Angeles chapter of the Negro Industrial and Economic Union, arrived at the hotel about ten-fifteen and found that he could not get into the Embassy Room without a pass. So he, like Worthey, contented himself with waiting in the other room. There he saw the small, shabbily dressed man he later identified as Sirhan. With him was a slightly taller girl with an upswept hairdo and a white dress that had designs of another color, possibly polka dots. Griffin told police

* Aired on NBC May 22, 1969.

† Interview June 7, 1968: unpaginated in FBI Summary Report by Special Agent Amedee O. Richards, Jr., August 1, 1969. Many of the interviews in this report, including Worthey's, remained classified until 1976, when they were released as the result of a Freedom of Information Act request.

that he thought "the two people seemed out of place . . . because everyone else but these two were celebrating the apparent Kennedy victory."

Upon obtaining a press pass from Kennedy aide Pierre Salinger, whom he knew, Griffin went to the temporary press headquarters in the Colonial Room, which was adjacent to the Embassy Room, where RFK was due to speak. It was now after eleven. Griffin noticed Sirhan and the girl standing in the corridor between the two rooms that led to the pantry where Kennedy subsequently was shot. With them was a casually dressed man, muscular and taller than six feet. Shortly before the shooting, Griffin saw Sirhan again and remarked to a friend, "There's a guy I've been seeing all evening and for some reason we don't seem to take to each other."

When the shots rang out, Griffin saw the same girl and the tall man dash out of the pantry and down the corridor. Griffin shouted, "They're getting away." Then he ran into the pantry and helped overpower Sirhan. Still bothered by the girl's escape, he ran out into the rear parking lot to try to find her, but she had vanished.*

Just before Kennedy entered the Embassy Room for his speech, campaign worker Susanne Locke noticed a girl "wearing a white shift with blue polka dots" standing between the stage and the main door. According to an FBI report, Locke "observed that the girl was not wearing a yellow press badge and thought this to be very unusual, since it was necessary to have such a badge to gain entry into the Embassy Room." As Locke recalled, "The girl was expressionless and seemed somewhat out of place where she was standing. She was a Caucasian in her early twenties, well proportioned, with long brown hair pulled back and tied behind her head. Her hair appeared to be dried out, similar in appearance to the hair of a girl who does a lot of swimming."†

Cathy Sue Fulmer, who had come to the hotel with a boyfriend and "gate crashed" the Embassy Room, advised the FBI that as Kennedy began his speech she was close to the stage and

---

* Interview at the LAPD Rampart Division, June 5, 1968, by Officers W. M. Rathburn and R. R. Phillips.

† Interview June 7, 1968; pp. 404–5 in FBI Summary Report, *op. cit.*

"standing near her was an individual she described as short male Mexican, about 20 years of age, whom she recognized from newspaper photographs as SIRHAN SIRHAN."*

How Sirhan and the polka-dot-dress girl gained entry to the restricted Embassy Room is answered by the testimony of twenty-year-old Sandra Serrano, a "Youth for Kennedy" volunteer. At about eleven-thirty Serrano bought a vodka and orange juice at a temporary bar set up in the southwest corner of the room. It was hot and crowded inside, so she stepped out a door that led onto a platform with metal steps leading to the ground—an emergency exit. She sat on a step about halfway down and sipped the drink. In two or three minutes a woman and two men climbed the stairs and brushed past her. "Excuse us," the woman said. As Serrano afterward described her to the FBI, the woman was

a white female, 23 to 27 years of age, 5'6" tall, medium build, 125 pounds. She had dark brown hair, ear length (bouffant style) and wore a white voile cloth dress with black quarter inch polka dots. The dots were about 1½ to 2" apart. This dress had three-quarter length sleeves, a bib collar with a small black bow and was A-lined. (SERRANO said she took special note of the dress, since she had a friend with one just like it.) This woman wore black shoes and no purse SERRANO said this woman did not wear glasses and had a "funny nose" which she described as a "BOB HOPE" type. [One of the men was] white male (Latin extraction), 5'5" tall, 21 to 23 years, olive complexion, black hair, long—straight, hanging over his forehead and needed a haircut. He wore dark pants, light shirt, and a gold or yellow cardigan type sweater and had nothing in his hands. [The other was] white male (Mexican-American), about 23 years of age, 5'3" tall, curly, bushy hair and wore light colored clothes. She said after seeing the picture of SIRHAN SIRHAN in the newspaper, she felt certain this was the same person she saw go up the stairs with this woman.†

Kennedy field worker Darnell Johnson spotted a girl answering the same description in the pantry off the Embassy Room only moments before the shooting. Johnson told the FBI that after RFK

* Interview June 8, 1968; unpaginated, *ibid.*
† Interview June 8, 1978; *ibid.*, pp. 464–67.

finished his speech and walked off the rear of the stage platform, he "walked around the platform to the narrow space in the serving area where the shooting took place and got there before KENNEDY." Sirhan was already there, among a group of four others that included a

white female wearing a white dress, with 25¢ size polka dots; the dress was fitted, not a miniskirt but was above the knees; was not a loose shift but was fashionable for the time. She was 23–25 years of age, tall, 5'8", medium build, well built, 145 pounds, long light brown hair, carrying an all white sweater or jacket, pretty full face, stubby heel shoes in the fashion of the time.

The others in the group were men, one over six feet tall in a light-blue washable sports coat and tie with "blond hair parted over on the left side with the right side long and hanging toward his face like a surfer haircut, outdoor type." The remaining two were neatly dressed in jackets and ties. Johnson could not tell whether any or all of these people knew each other or just happened to be together."*

A teen-age Kennedy fan who hoped to get close to her idol by slipping through the pantry recalled this group in vaguer terms. Robin Karen Casden told the FBI that instants before the shooting she saw someone who might have been Sirhan, as well as "several men in suits in the kitchen area [sic] and one or two women."†

Part-time waiter and college student Thomas Vincent DiPierro, the son of an Ambassador maître d', shook hands with Kennedy as he entered the pantry. DiPierro said he stopped by the ice machine to the right of Kennedy's path in the narrow pantry and "noticed there was a girl and the accused person standing on what is—what we call a tray stacker, where we had all the trays." Testifying on June 7, 1968, before the grand jury that indicted Sirhan, he explained that the tray stacker was just beyond the ice machine, to the right of Kennedy's path to the temporary press room. The

* Interview June 7, 1968; *ibid.*, pp. 406–9.
† Interview June 8, 1968; *ibid.*, pp. 432–34.

darkly handsome DiPierro said that the only reason he noticed Sirhan was that "there was a very good-looking girl next to him. That was the only reason I looked over there. I looked at the girl and I noticed him." Sirhan was "grabbing onto the tray stacker with his left hand."

"I could not see his right hand," DiPierro added. "He looked as though he was clutching his stomach, as though somebody had elbowed him." DiPierro had cause to remember the polka-dot-dress girl:

I would never forget what she looked like because she had a very good looking figure—and the dress was kind of lousy. . . . it looked like it was a white dress and it had either black or dark-purple polka dots on it. It kind of had—I don't know what they call it, but it's like a bib in the front, kind of went around like that [describing a scoop neck].

The girl had a peculiar-looking nose, and brown hair, he added. As the girl and Sirhan stood together by the tray stacker, DiPierro testified, Sirhan

looked as though he either talked to her or flirted with her, because she smiled. Together they were both smiling. As he got down, he was smiling. In fact, the minute the first two shots were fired, he still had a very sick-looking smile on his face. That's one thing—I can never forget that.

Kennedy campaign worker George Green also saw the polka-dot-dress girl. He told the FBI that he was just entering the pantry when the firing broke out, and that

once inside the kitchen door, he noticed a woman in her 20's with long blond free flowing hair in a polka dot dress and a light colored sweater and a man 5'11", thin build, black hair and in his 20's. GREEN stated that this man and woman were running with their backs toward him and they were attempting to get out of the kitchen area. GREEN stated that the reason he noticed them was that they were the only ones who seemed to be trying to get out of the kitchen area while everyone else seemed to be trying to get into the kitchen area.

Green's account was reinforced by Evan P. Freed, a press photographer, although in less explicit terms. Freed said that right after the shooting a girl and a man ran from the pantry. He thought that the girl was wearing a polka-dot dress but could not describe her further. The man was tall, thin and dark.*

The statements of Green and Freed back up Booker Griffin's report of seeing a girl and man rush from the pantry—the same girl he had seen with Sirhan on two occasions earlier.

Meanwhile Sandy Serrano was still sitting on the stairway from the emergency exit at the far side of the Embassy Room, the emptied glass in her hand. Some thirty seconds after she heard what sounded like automobile backfires,

this same woman who had gone up the stairs came running down the stairs toward her, followed by one of the men who had gone up the stairs with her. Miss SERRANO stated that as this woman ran down the stairs toward her, the woman shouted, "We shot him—we shot him!" Miss SERRANO said, "Who did you shoot?" to which this woman replied, "Senator KENNEDY!"†

Serrano's account is confirmed by the frantic report of the "Bernstein" couple to Sergeant Paul Sharaga, even to the precise language, "We shot him! We shot him!" The "Bernsteins" were within a hundred feet of the stairway where the young Kennedy volunteer was sitting.

Thus far we have traced the flight of the polka-dot-dress girl and her male companion from the pantry, diagonally across the Embassy Room, out the emergency exit, down the stairs past Serrano, past the "Bernsteins," and down a service driveway leading past the parking lot, where Sharaga would arrive in a matter of minutes.

Certainly the "dirty blonde" girl of Jerry Owen's story, as well as the three young men who appeared in his narrative, at least loosely fit the descriptions of the polka-dot-dress girl and her companions on the night of the shooting. But as Sergeant Hernandez

* Interview June 7, 1968; unpaginated, *ibid.*
† FBI interview with Serrano, *ibid.*

told Owen, in illustrating the supposed thoroughness of the investigation that determined there was no conspiracy, the police "went through eighteen witnesses on the polka dot dress girl."

AFTER PUTTING OUT THE APB FOR THE POLKA-DOT-DRESS GIRL and her male companion, Sergeant Paul Sharaga continued to man his parking-lot command post. Suddenly there was a police-radio blackout. "The thing that still has me confused," Sharaga later reflected, "—and as a police officer it shouldn't affect me that way but it sends cold chills down my spine—is that for a fifteen- or twenty-minute period we lost all radio communication. I've got it recorded in my log. There was that period when I could not communicate with another car, I could not communicate with the monitor, and I could not communicate with Communications, either on the main frequency or on Tac 1 or Tac 2 [tactical channels]."*

When the blackout ended, as inexplicably as it had begun, Communications kept broadcasting the APB at fifteen-minute intervals. At about two-thirty Detective Inspector John Powers came by the command post. "You'd never forget Powers," Sharaga said. "He had a reputation for carrying more than one gun. I think at one time he carried three or four guns." Powers wanted to know, "Who's responsible for this description of the two suspects that's going on the air?" Sharaga said that he was, and briefed Powers on the report of the "Bernstein" couple. "Let's cancel that description," Powers instructed. "We don't want to make a federal case out of it. We've got the suspect in custody."

Sharaga agreed to cancel the APB on the male suspect, since in the confusion of the moment he thought it possible that the "Bernsteins" had seen the man taken into custody, even though the description did not match. But he continued in force the APB on the polka-dot-dress girl in defiance of Powers' wishes. "He didn't

* Authors' taped telephone interview with Sharaga, May 21, 1976. In 1977 the Los Angeles District Attorney John Van de Kamp announced that there was no blackout—because the LAPD radio logs didn't show one.

have any choice," Sharaga explained. "It was either that or relieve me of my post." Nevertheless Powers had the last word, contacting Communications directly and ordering the APB discontinued.

Although the APB had not resulted in anyone's being stopped and questioned, there was no way the lid could be kept on the story. Within an hour of the shooting Sandy Serrano had been corralled by NBC newsman Sander Vanocur and thrust on live national television to tell about the girl in the polka-dot dress with a "funny nose." And Vincent DiPierro, a prime witness to the shooting, mentioned her in his testimony before the grand jury that indicted Sirhan a few days later, which was duly reported in the newspapers. It was, of course, impossible for the press to resist the angle of a well-endowed mystery woman.

THE LAPD'S CONCERN OVER THE GIRL IN THE POLKA-DOT DRESS manifested itself during an urgent meeting on Sunday morning, June 9, in Robert Houghton's office. "What have you found out so far?" Houghton asked Lieutenant Charles Hughes, head of the Rampart Division detectives who had carried the initial burden of the investigation. Hughes ticked off several aspects to the case, then brought up the polka-dot-dress girl. "Do you know about her?" he queried Houghton, who purportedly had just returned from a vacation in Yosemite National Park.

"I read it in the papers," the chief replied, "but what's the story?"

Hughes summarized Sandy Serrano's account, adding, "She's a long way from the kitchen, and she calls her mother in Iowa or some place before she tells anybody about the polka-dot-dress girl. Incidentally, she didn't tell her mother, either. She was grabbed by some TV guy, and tells her story to the world."

Hughes shook his head. "Maybe? But it looks pretty thin so far."

Inspector K. J. McCauley chimed in, "Except that one of the waiters who shook hands with Kennedy says he saw a gal in a polka-dot dress there in the kitchen. How about that?"

"Yeah, I know." Hughes shrugged. "The waiter's name is DiPierro. He places Sirhan in the kitchen, and says a pretty girl in a polka-dot dress is standing next to him. I know it. That's what's convincing the Bureau [FBI]."

Thus at least some of the police brass were skeptical about the polka-dot-dress-girl sightings from the start, even though the FBI was keeping an open mind. However, the entire police investigation was tailored to the conclusion that the girl didn't exist, beginning with the suppression of the report of Sergeant Sharaga. Sharaga told the authors that he shut down his command post shortly after noon on June 5, but not before sending a detail of officers to guard the floor of the hotel on which the Kennedy family was housed. He drove directly to the Rampart Division and dictated to the secretary of Captain Floyd Phillips a report of everything that had happened, with special emphasis on the "Bernsteins' " sighting of the polka-dot-dress girl and her companion.

When SUS was officially created about five days later, Sharaga was instructed to prepare a second report covering his command-post activities "from beginning to end." He complied, in even more thorough fashion. "I personally delivered the report to SUS one night," he said. "There was a deadline on it." Sharaga recalled a brief conversation about it with Manny Pena, whom he knew, but SUS was tight-lipped about the case. "That was a locked-door type of operation," he said. "You didn't get in there."

The meticulous Sharaga had made three copies of his report "in the event additional copies were needed." He put one in the Watch Commander's drawer at Rampart, and another in the mail box in the Sergeant's Report Room. Because he had spent so much time at home drafting the report, he kept a third copy for himself. As it turned out, this minor deviation from procedure was fortuitous.

"About two weeks later," Sharaga said, "there was something I wanted to refer to in the report, and I found the copies gone." He asked his superior, Lieutenant William C. Jordan, what happened to them, but Jordan professed not to know. "I inquired from SUS if there was some reason why they came to Rampart and disposed of the copies," he continued, "and their attitude was that they didn't even know what I was talking about." At the time Sharaga thought nothing of it, but when Houghton's book was published in 1970 and there was no mention of the command post, including the report of the "Bernsteins" about the polka-dot-dress girl, "the first questions started to form in my mind."*

Sharaga's report on the polka-dot-dress girl was vitally important, for it provided independent corroboration for Sandy Serrano's story. With the report buried, Serrano was on her own and vulnerable to persuasion. On June 10 officers from the LAPD, FBI and DA's staff took her to the Ambassador Hotel and asked her to re-create the events of election night. She was treated not as a cooperative witness but as a threat to the lone-assassin theory. FBI agent Richard C. Burris, who apparently agreed with the LAPD's position, marched her from the pantry across the Embassy Room to the stairway where she had sat, pointed out that the distance was some 170 feet, and rhetorically demanded "if she still felt she had heard the shots." The young lady stood her ground, saying "she had never heard a gunshot in her life and never claimed she had heard gunshots, but had described what she heard as six backfires, four or five of which were close together."†

Burris then confronted her with the fact that when she called her mother in Ohio after learning that Kennedy had been shot, she didn't mention seeing anyone she "felt was connected with the shooting." Serrano explained that "she always had difficulty communicating with her mother and was not able to talk to her to explain anything." Referring to the Sander Vanocur television interview over NBC, the FBI agent asked why "she had not said anything about seeing this woman and the two men go up the stairs, but only told about the woman and the man coming back down. It was pointed out to her the fact she claimed one of the men going up the stairs was SIRHAN SIRHAN was the most significant part of the incident described by her."

Burris may have been trying to influence Serrano, for at the time of the NBC interview she had not seen who had been taken into custody in the pantry. It was not until the following day, when she saw published pictures of Sirhan, that she recognized him as the third person sneaking into the Embassy Room. Serrano became

* Art Kevin's interview with Sharaga, *op. cit.*

† Interview June 10, 1968; FBI Summary Report, pp. 540–42.

angry, and according to Burris' report, "accused those present of lying to her and trying to trick her." She became so distraught that she had to be taken home.

The Sandy Serrano problem remained high on the SUS priority list. On June 20 Manny Pena dispatched LAPD criminalist De-Wayne Wolfer to the hotel to "prove" scientifically that she could not have heard the gunfire from the pantry. Mounting a sound-level meter on the stairway where she had sat, Wolfer had assistants fire test shots in the pantry. His meter supposedly registered no higher than one half a decibel, below the minimum that a person with sharp hearing might pick up. In his book, Robert Houghton dismissed Serrano as the victim of her own imagination:

> She obviously thought, in the furor of the moment, that she heard and saw certain things which were not physically possible or did not actually occur. It happens every day, in petty cases as well as in major crimes. People are positive they see someone who later turns out to have been miles away. They hear something which can barely be detected by the most sensitive electronic device.*

Houghton's was a specious argument, avoiding the fact that she did not claim to hear gunfire and did not identify someone who was "miles away." In an ordinary case SUS might have been able to close the book on Sandy Serrano. But as Houghton observed, this was no ordinary case:

> . . . Manny Pena knew that as long as Miss Serrano stuck to her story, no amount of independent evidence would, in itself, serve to dispel the "polka-dot-dress girl" fever, which had by now, in the press and public mind, reached a high point on the thermometer of intrigue. She alone could put that spotted ghost to rest.†

So Serrano was singled out for the special attention of Hank Hernandez. As Houghton told it, Pena asked Hernandez "what he was doing for dinner that night, and suggested he might like to take Sandra Serrano out for a SUS-bought steak." Hernandez got the message. He wined and dined the young lady but was unable to break her story. So he took her to Parker Center for a polygraph

---

* Houghton, *op. cit.*, p. 119.
† *Ibid.*, pp. 119–20.

test at the unseemly hour of 10:15 P.M. The polygraph is a forbidding instrument, and it must have been especially so to the twenty-year-old young lady. It shares the aura of invincibility attached to scientific gadgetry, and polygraph operators rarely miss the chance to intimidate their subjects by exaggerated claims of accuracy. Yet half a century after its invention, the instrument has yet to be accepted as meeting evidentiary standards by the courts of the land. Much depends upon the operator, not only as to his competence in interpreting the graph readings, but his independence and objectivity. Some authorities believe that the principal usefulness of the polygraph is not its ability to detect lies, but to aid the interrogator to break down his subject.

Hernandez opened his interrogation of Serrano by asking about the vodka and orange juice she had consumed, thus implying that the alcohol might have affected her faculties. The burly detective warmed up to his task. "Okay, now, we have statements here that obviously are incorrect," he declared. Having confronted Serrano with a conclusion, he gave her a way out by suggesting "you heard the kid—some kid mention something about a white dress and dots." The "kid" was Vincent DiPierro, who had given the graphic account of seeing the polka-dot-dress girl next to Sirhan in the pantry. It would have been physically impossible for Serrano to have picked up the story from DiPierro, for she had never met him until after the NBC interview. "She had on a white dress with polka dots," Serrano said on NBC, "she was light-skinned, dark hair, she had black shoes on, she has a funny nose, it was . . . I thought it was really funny, my friends tell me I'm so observant." But now, under pressure from Hernandez, Serrano was beginning to doubt her own eyes. "I don't know," she said, confused.

According to Houghton, "Miss Serrano's monitored autonomic responses to key questions indicated deception: the dress she saw had merely been white, not white with black polka dots, and as the girl ran past she had not shouted, 'We shot Senator Kennedy,' but rather, 'He shot Kennedy,' or 'They shot Kennedy.' "*

* *Ibid.*, p. 122.

HAVING GOTTEN SERRANO TO MODIFY HER STORY, HERNANDEZ moved in to try and destroy it completely. He labeled it a "pack of mistruths," and asked her when it had gotten out of hand. At the Rampart Station, she responded. "I was sitting there hearing descriptions and descriptions of these people, of these people, of these people. Oh God, no, maybe that's what I'm supposed to have seen. It messed me up, that's all; and I figured, well, they must know what they're doing."

Serrano was whipped. She was conceding the impossible, since she had told the story on television *before* being taken to Rampart with scores of other witnesses. But Hernandez interpreted her concession as mission accomplished. "Of course, we're going to have to cancel all these reports," he said. "You know that."

"I know that," the defeated young lady responded.*

The detective was overreaching—all he had proved was that he had confused Serrano badly. She hadn't recanted seeing a girl hurrying down the stairway yelling, "We shot him!," which Sergeant Sharaga's suppressed report of the "Bernsteins" tended to support. She simply had consented to say that her description of the girl was adjusted to fit that of DiPierro, an idea Hernandez first proposed.

APPARENTLY CONVINCED THAT IT HAD MANAGED TO DISCREDIT Sandy Serrano's story, SUS then turned its attention to Vincent DiPierro, the only other publicly known prime witness to the polka-dot-dress girl. On July 1, eleven days after the polygraph interrogation of Serrano, Hernandez summoned DiPierro to Parker Center for a similar session. The detective again got what he wanted.

"As a matter of fact," Hernandez summed up, "you have told me now that there was no lady that you saw standing next to Sirhan."

"That's correct."

"Okay. Now, I can appreciate what you would have been or could have been going through on that evening—"

"Yes."

* Kaiser, *op. cit.*, pp. 143–45.

"—but I think what you have told me is that you probably got this idea about a girl in a black-and-white polka-dot dress after you talked to Miss Sandra Serrano."*

Hernandez was having it both ways—Serrano got it from DiPierro, DiPierro got it from Serrano. But DiPierro's credibility had to remain intact, not only because he had testified before the grand jury but because the DA's office intended to use him as a witness at Sirhan's trial. Hernandez asked if anything else he had reported was not the truth.

"No, nothing," the young man said. "Only about the girl."

"Only about the girl?"

"Yes, sir. That good enough?" DiPierro knew what the police wanted him to say.†

However, it would be harmful if Sirhan's attorneys brought out that the girl was pure invention on cross-examination. Hernandez told DiPierro that he had described the polka-dot-dress girl "so well that in my experience I believe you were describing someone that you had seen during the night." Hernandez had a "someone" in mind—Valerie Schulte, a pretty "Kennedy Girl" from the University of California at Santa Barbara who had tagged along after the Kennedy party as they headed into the pantry. Reading about the mysterious polka-dot-dress girl, she had presented herself to the police on the possibility that someone had mistaken her.

Valerie Schulte had worn a polka-dot dress, all right, but it was bright-green with yellow polka dots. Pinned to it was a big red Kennedy button. Her hair was silky blond and her nose was not "funny" but nicely shaped. Moreover, she was hobbled by a huge leg cast from her ankle to her waist, the result of a skiing accident. And she was in back of Kennedy, not in front, as was the girl seen by DiPierro. The police had already shown her to Booker Griffin, but he took one look and said no.

But all of that didn't deter Hernandez. "When did you decide to interpose or inject [sic] this girl [Valerie Schulte] that you have described to me as being the girl that was in the kitchen?" he asked DiPierro. "It's possible that when I did that I could—I don't re-

* Houghton, op. cit., p. 124.
† Kaiser, op. cit., pp. 154–55.

member exactly, it could have been I saw her right after the shooting in that area," he answered. "I may have done that, too. I am not sure. There was so much confusion that night."

Actually, Hernandez had planted much of the confusion with both DiPierro and Serrano. But with that, Houghton wrote: "SUS closed the vexing case of the polka-dot-dress girl."*

SANDY SERRANO QUIT HER JOB AS A KEYPUNCH OPERATOR WITH A large insurance firm and fled back to her parents' home in Ohio, reportedly to escape further police harassment. Vincent DiPierro appeared as scheduled at the Sirhan trial, where he readily identified Valerie Schulte as the girl he had seen. The defense attorneys, themselves committed to the no-conspiracy theory, made no attempt to impeach this testimony by showing how it clashed with his grand jury testimony.

Young DiPierro evidently regretted his about-face, for on April 20, 1969, he wrote a congratulatory letter to Art Kevin, then a reporter with radio station KHJ, on a series Kevin was broadcasting on the unanswered questions in the RFK assassination. Before the series was aired, LAPD Inspector John Powers had visited Kevin and put pressure on him not to raise the question of the polka-dot-dress girl, but Kevin declined. In his letter DiPierro termed that segment "the first 'real, true' report" and lauded Kevin "on the extensive research and brilliant job of reporting a factual story." DiPierro said that since the question of the polka-dot-dress girl "concerned my character personally, I was deeply interested in hearing the facts straight for a change." He offered his assistance on "this controversial issue."

Due to the pressure of work, it was several days before Kevin could drive out to the DiPierro residence. The doorbell was answered by the senior DiPierro, a maître d' at the Ambassador Hotel, while Vincent stood in the background. Kevin thought that they "looked all shook up." The father said that the FBI had come by and explained how painstakingly the police and the FBI had reconstructed events in the pantry. Almost pleadingly, he told

* Houghton, *op. cit.*, p. 126.

Kevin to forget it, that his son's life might be in danger. When Kevin pressed on, the father blurted out, "I know who you are. You run around with those kooks Bill Turner and Mark Lane."* He shoved the door shut.

In the short interval since his polka-dot-dress girl broadcast, the FBI or someone purporting to be from the Bureau had probably gotten to the DiPierros, not only giving them a hard sell on the no-conspiracy theory but libeling the two critics Kevin happened to know. Kevin recalled that one of his colleagues, Tom Browne, had overheard FBI agents and LAPD officers discussing Turner in bitter terms. And Kevin learned that after he put the polka-dot-dress girl segment on the air despite Inspector Powers' intercession, high-level elements of the LAPD tried unsuccessfully to "get" his job.†

Art Kevin's experience was not unique among the press people who tried to force the polka-dot-dress-girl issue into the open. Reporter Fernando Faura was commissioned by *Life* bureau chief Jordan Bonfante to pursue it. He interviewed DiPierro and Sandy Serrano, and had an artist draw a composite sketch of the girl they had seen. Then Faura interviewed other witnesses, prevailing upon them to submit to polygraph tests by an operator not linked to the police. All passed. At this juncture, SUS contacted Bonfante.

After a six-hour conversation with the police, Bonfante refused to call off the investigation. But within a week, Bonfante was told by *Life* editors that the story would never see the light of print. Someone had gone over his head.

Thus the LAPD buried the girl in the polka-dot dress with a blank tombstone. On the eighth floor of Parker Center, in the old sound stage that served as SUS headquarters, there was no mourning.

---

* Long-time Warren Commission critic and author of *Rush to Judgment*.

† Authors' interview with Art Kevin, May 12, 1969. When Kevin aired the interview with ex-LAPD Sergeant Paul Sharaga on KMPC Radio in December 1974, Powers stormed into the studio and once again threatened to "get" the newsman's job. However, KMPC management backed Kevin completely—and the LAPD chieftain backed off.

6

Investigative File

ALTHOUGH DISAPPOINTED IN THE WAY MANNY PENA AND
Hank Hernandez summarily dropped the Jerry Owen angle,
we considered that it might have been a rather typical bureaucratic reaction rather than a systematic cover-up. In this case,
Sirhan Sirhan was it from ground zero, and the LAPD
apparently was not budging from that position, even though
this conclusion was wholly premature.

When we decided to launch our own investigation, we
saw no reason that we could not cooperate with SUS provided they would reciprocate. If nothing else, we wanted to
compare our tape of Owen's story with the police recording
of what he had told them at the University Station. Calling

the LAPD, we were shuffled from one office to another, then told that no one would speak with us. Christian decided to go over the heads of the police. He phoned a senior aide to Mayor Sam Yorty, Jack Brown, whom he had known well during Yorty's 1966 campaign for governor. Brown was a former Hearst political editor. He said that SUS and the DA's office had shut the door on newsmen, opening it only to hand out self-serving statements. He would ask Yorty, without going into any details, to instruct the police to get in touch with us.

Within twenty minutes Sergeant Manuel "Chick" Gutierrez of SUS was on the line. When Christian mentioned Turner's taped interview with Owen, Gutierrez asked to be furnished a copy immediately. Christian obliged. But in a phone conversation several days later, Christian proposed to Gutierrez that we work closely ("undercover") with his unit on the Owen angle. We would abide by any legitimate restrictions on the release of the story, but we wanted the journalistic inside track. There was nothing precedent-shattering in the proposal—law enforcement agencies frequently open their files to friendly journalists in return for cooperation. But Gutierrez's superiors rejected the proposal out of hand. "We've already checked that out, and Owen was not involved," Gutierrez said.

It baffled us that SUS, which had been so anxious to obtain our tape, had dismissed the Owen story as merely a publicity stunt. We decided to go one step higher. In California the Attorney General is empowered to step in when local law enforcement is lax or malfeasant. In approaching the AG's office we were in luck. The Chief Deputy Attorney General was Charles A. "Charlie" O'Brien. O'Brien was a graduate of Harvard Law School, and like a number of Harvard men, he had close political ties to the Kennedy brothers over the years. After migrating to San Francisco and opening a law practice, he soon became bored and joined the AG's staff in 1958. He rose swiftly to the chief deputy's position, although some of his colleagues felt he was too active for the job. In 1964, for example, he used karate chops learned in the Army to fend off a Hell's Angel motorcycle thug intent upon maiming a young girl participating in an antiwar demonstration. Ironically,

O'Brien had been high on Robert Kennedy's list of prospects for U.S. Attorney General after he became President.

On August 13, 1968, Christian called O'Brien at his main office in the State Building in San Francisco. The chief deputy listened to his brief presentation, then invited us over. Charlie O'Brien had a bulldog Irish face, thinning hair, an ever-present pipe and a manner of cool assurance. He let the Owen tape run non-stop through its hour-and-six minutes' duration. He listened intently, cocking his head at significant points, making notes on a legal pad. When it was over, he stared at his personal shorthand, then looked up with a wry grin. He agreed that Owen was no clown performing an ego act. He handed the tape to his secretary and asked her to make a copy and type a transcript as quickly as possible. He would run all the mentioned names and pseudonyms through the files of the California Bureau of Criminal Investigation & Identification, which was under the AG's jurisdiction, and get back to us shortly. The whole case was funny, he said. His office had made numerous attempts to monitor SUS progress on the investigation, but had been thwarted at every turn. In fact, his was the *only* law enforcement agency not invited to review the case.

About a week later O'Brien called us, his voice deadly serious. "Look out for this joker," he warned of Owen. "He's got a rap sheet that runs wall to wall. He's a dangerous man." O'Brien didn't elaborate, but we got the message. It was now more important than ever to try to find out why "The Walking Bible" talked.*

A SIGN ON THE LAWN OF THE CALVARY BAPTIST CHURCH IN Oxnard read: *A truly independent Baptist Church.* The stucco building was only slightly larger than the well-kept homes lining the residential street. It was the only church of that name listed

---

* At that same time O'Brien had just finished reviewing the extradition request by Louisiana law enforcement authorities for Edgar Eugene Bradley, who had been indicted for conspiracy in the assassination of John F. Kennedy. O'Brien recommended to Governor Ronald Reagan that the extradition be granted. Reagan waited until after Richard Nixon's election to the White House—then turned down the request without comment.

in the directories of this farming community nestled close to the Pacific Ocean about seventy miles northwest of Los Angeles.

Jim Rose pulled up in his gray van. We had met Rose earlier when he volunteered to help in the investigation of the John Kennedy assassination. Rose was not our man's real name; Turner and he had decided upon it when they had their first meeting at midnight in the parking lot of the Rose Bowl in Pasadena (when they began working together on the JFK assassination case for DA Jim Garrison). A one-time contract employee of the CIA—as a combat and reconnaissance pilot—the man who also sported such names as Dawes, McLeish and McNabb is somewhat of a "living legend" within intelligence circles. When we asked him to take the lead for us in the "Walking Bible" angle, he'd just landed his World War II B-26 attack bomber after having made a well-publicized bombing run on the palace of Haiti's fascistic dictator, "Papa Doc" Duvalier.

We decided early on that Rose could fill our needs perfectly, and managed to scrape together enough money to send him to Southern California to retrace Owen's steps in his hitchhiker story. Rose was checking on Owen's claim that he was unable to show up at the Ambassador Hotel with the horse on election night because he had to speak at the Calvary Baptist Church in Oxnard.

Tall, blue-eyed and clean-cut, Rose was posing as a recently discharged serviceman with strong anti-Communist convictions. As he entered the church he noticed literature of the American Council of Christian Churches, the organization Owen said he was once affiliated with. Rose talked with the pastor, a Reverend Medcalf, who said that he had only taken over the church in mid-July. For the previous six months, Medcalf said, the church was closed because his predecessor had not made a financial go of it. No, the name of the Reverend Jerry Owen rang no bell.

It appeared that if Owen had in fact gone to Oxnard that night, it wasn't to preach at the Calvary Baptist Church.

In Hollywood, Rose found other discrepancies in Owen's story. Billy Gray's Band Box on Fairfax Avenue, the night club where the preacher purportedly attended a Saints and Sinners meeting on Monday evening, had for some time been remodeled into

Temple Catering. And the "bowling alley" on Sunset Boulevard where the preacher said he met with Sirhan and his companions later that night had long since given way to the offices and studios of Golden West Broadcasters.

But "right across the street," as Owen had put it, there was a hotel called the St. Moritz. This was where Owen said he spent the night after Sirhan failed to produce the $300 for the horse on the night of June 3. The registration records confirmed that one J. C. [sic] Owen, giving the correct address for the preacher in Santa Ana, checked into Room 203 at midnight. It was a bathless $4 room, just as Owen had said, and there was a telephone in it, so that he could have received a call the next morning.

Finally, Rose filmed and photographed the layout of the Ambassador Hotel, whose sprawling grounds occupy a large city block. The front looks north to Wilshire Boulevard across a broad expanse of lawn. At the southwest quandrant is the rear parking lot toward which the polka-dot-dress girl and her companion were seen fleeing, and where Sergeant Sharaga set up his command post. And on the eastern side is the 7th Street cul-de-sac off Catalina Street, where Owen said he dropped off Sirhan to see "a friend in the kitchen" on Monday afternoon—the spot where he asserted he was to deliver the horse on election night.*

Rose's photographs and film revealed that the cul-de-sac was an ideal place for an escape vehicle to wait. It was dimly lit, and there was virtually no traffic at night. To reach it from the Embassy Room pantry was only a short dash through a lobby and out the doors of the Palm Court, then down a palm-fringed walk to the cul-de-sac. The total distance is approximately 240 yards.

WHILE ROSE WAS IN SOUTHERN CALIFORNIA, JERRY OWEN SURfaced in Sonoma, about forty-five miles north of San Francisco,

---

* Curiously enough, we later obtained a taped interview made by Los Angeles radio newsman John Goodman with George T. Davis, wherein the lawyer insisted that Owen had been seen at the Ambassador Hotel, *with Sirhan in his company*, on the afternoon of June 3, and that the name of that witness had been turned over to the LAPD. We could find no such police report later on.

where he was staging a nightly Bible crusade.* The engagement provided an opportunity for Rose to look over Owen's residence in Santa Ana. It turned out to be a rambling ranch-style home on the outskirts of the growing city. A decrepit barn and small corral stood in the large yard, which backed onto the dry Santa Ana River. Suddenly a girl in her late teens came out of the house and asked what he was doing.

"I'm a free-lance reporter from San Francisco," Rose improvised. "I've heard about Reverend Owen's story and . . ."

The girl smiled. "Why don't you come in and ask him yourself? He's out in his office."

Concealing his surprise, Rose accepted, wondering why the preacher had flown back from Sonoma when he was due to speak again that night. Owen exuded cordiality. He said he was sorry that he could not be quoted on the Sirhan story because of a court gag order, but nevertheless launched into a fragmented account

* The Sonoma crusade demonstrated again that Owen sought publicity for his ministry—but shunned it in connection with the assassination. We decided to hire NBC cameraman Ron Everslage to film the preacher in action after we heard him touting the crusade over a San Francisco radio station. Everslage told Owen that he was doing a television documentary on religion in California. Owen told his audience how television viewers would see "how God put 31,173 Bible verses in this preacher's heart." He put on a banner performance, alternating between a dulcet love motif and a thundering warning that America was going to hell in a hurry because she had forgotten God. A few days later Ben Hardister, the private detective who had helped guard Owen and was involved with the crusade, called Everslage and wanted to know when the documentary would be aired. Failing to get a satisfactory answer, Hardister hopped a plane to Los Angeles to confront personnel at the television station Everslage had named in his cover story. They, of course, knew nothing. Twice Hardister contacted Everslage again, grilling him in a manner indicating that he suspected the RFK assassination inquiry was behind it. Everslage taped Hardister's thinly veiled threats, and we gave a copy to Chief Deputy Attorney General Charles O'Brien. According to one of O'Brien's aides, the AG's office had come across Hardister's name in the course of an investigation of the paramilitary right in California two years before. Hardister left one item behind at the Everslage household, however, that intrigued us the most: it was his "personal card" not as a private dick, but as "President, The California Appaloosa Horse Racing Association." Again, the smell of horse droppings and gunpowder pointed in the direction of Sirhan.

that corresponded closely with the one he had given Turner two and a half months before.

Then, with an air of confidentiality, he identified Sirhan's hitch-hiking companion as Crispin Curiel Gonzalez, a seventeen-year-old Mexican youth whose story, with photographs, had recently appeared in the press.

It was a bizarre account. On June 17 Gonzalez had stopped at a soft-drink stand in Juarez, across the Rio Grande River opposite El Paso, Texas. The woman behind the counter bought a yellow legal pad from him for one peso. Later an El Paso man was idly leafing through the pad when he noticed an entry dated June 4 that said:

I will have to try to erase completely from my memory—before the world learns about me—that I was in on the plot to kill Robert F. Kennedy. That crazy Arab has a tremendous hate for all the Kennedys . . . easy enough to get him to take some of the money and do the job. The whole world knows it was a grand plot but, unfortunately, they do not know the whole truth.

I never knew who organized the assassination but that's not important. I know the world will never know all about it. I'll probably die soon in some part of Mexico.

The El Paso man notified Mexican police, who picked up Gonzalez for questioning. "You wait and see," the youth warned the police. "The next will be Edward Kennedy. All they have to do is wait—wait—wait for the best time. They told me the Kennedys wanted to be dictators of the United States." But Gonzalez was unwilling or unable to disclose who "they" were. He claimed that he knew Sirhan, and several days before the assassination had met with him in a library in Santa Monica to plan RFK's death.

In checking out the story, Juarez police determined that on election day Gonzalez had been in the custody of the FBI in El Paso, having been brought there from Los Angeles by immigration officials uncertain of his nationality.* Although this seemed to rule out Owen's identification of him as one of the hitchhikers, it

* *Alerta*, Mexico City (July 6, 1968); *Alarma*, Mexico City (July 17, 1968).

did not eliminate the possibility of a link to Owen and Sirhan. Juarez Deputy Police Chief Jose Regufio Ruvalcava was quoted in the press as saying, "There were so many factors connecting Curiel with Los Angeles that when we arrested him we decided he should be investigated thoroughly. We checked with your FBI and a spokesman there told us definitely that Curiel knew Sirhan—was a friend of his. There is no doubt that Curiel knew Sirhan—they had met a number of times at the Santa Monica library and elsewhere and had usually discussed politics." (FBI agent Roger LaJeunesse later confirmed that the two were somehow linked.) Ruvalcava added that his prisoner was intelligent and politically sophisticated, and had in fact talked about forming a political party "to replace the socialistic structure of Mexico."

On July 4 Gonzalez was found dead in his isolation cell in the Juarez jail. Ruvalcava announced that he had fashioned a noose from strips of a mattress cover, tied it to a window bar, and let himself sag and strangle. The suicide verdict was greeted with skepticism by many, considering the circumstances. The father, Crispin Curiel Gonzalez, Sr., was certain it was murder. "In the last letter we had from him," the elder Gonzalez revealed, "he hinted at a promise of big money for him—but that it was very dangerous."*

Not long afterward Robert Kaiser, a journalist acting as a defense investigator, showed Sirhan a news clip with Gonzalez's picture. "Ever see this kid before?" he asked. "No," Sirhan replied. "Who is he?" But when Kaiser mentioned that he was dead, a flicker of dismay crossed Sirhan's face. A week later Sirhan implied that he had known Gonzalez. "That kid didn't have to die. He didn't do anything," Sirhan told Kaiser. "Who would have wanted to get him out of the way?" the journalist asked. Sirhan thought for a moment, then smiled. Then he changed the subject.†

Was Gonzalez merely a tortured psychotic who had written about Kennedy's death *after* the assassination in an attempt to identify himself with the crime? Or was his legal pad the same kind of "notebook" Sirhan had kept, with its mandate that "R.F.K.

---

* *Ibid.*
† Kaiser, *op. cit.*, pp. 238 and 239n.

must die!" and its mention of large sums of money? Apparently Gonzalez had been taken into federal custody shortly before the assassination, and could not have been the youthful Mexican-looking companion of the polka-dot-dress girl. But he had been in Los Angeles, and the authorities connected him to Sirhan. And now Jerry Owen was pegging him as one of Sirhan's companions.

We felt that somewhere in the assassination jigsaw puzzle, the pathetic figure of Crispin Curiel Gonzalez was a perfect fit.

AS SEPTEMBER DREW TO AN END IT BECAME OBVIOUS THAT IF we were to pursue our investigation, one of us would have to move to Los Angeles. SUS and the FBI were trying to wind up their investigations in the face of a Sirhan trial date originally set for December 14, then postponed until after the first of the year.

Christian volunteered to make the move. Before leaving, he checked out with Charlie O'Brien. The chief deputy was unhappy at the way the LAPD was still by-passing his office and mis-representing facts. "Something or someone is manipulating that goddamn investigation," he grumbled. "We're not getting any information, and I'm going to find out why!" O'Brien disclosed that SUS and the Los Angeles DA's office had already "marked" us, and admonished Christian not to "spook" his contacts within those agencies by revealing our close link with his office.

In Los Angeles a mutual friend, Dick Livingston,* offered to arrange a meeting between Christian and Deputy DA David Fitts, who had participated with Pena and Hernandez in the San Francisco interrogation of Owen. "He's a bright, nice, open-minded guy," Livingston said. To his surprise, however, Fitts declared that he already knew Christian was in town. No, he would not meet him personally, but he would talk on the phone. The conversation was chilly. Fitts told Christian that he had carried the brunt of the questioning of Owen, and that in his opinion the preacher was "a

* Richard Kinkaid Livingston was the first person Christian met in Los Angeles. He was one of Kennedy brother-in-law Peter Lawford's closest friends and as a consequence had known the brothers Kennedy. Ironically, Livingston was also a good friend of another (soon-to-be) "famous" man in politics—Robert Haldeman, Richard Nixon's "chief of staff."

self-serving son-of-a-bitch" who conjured up the story for publicity's sake. Fitts said he wasn't interested in seeing or hearing anything further about Owen—that chapter was closed.

Christian phoned Jack Brown, the Yorty aide who had arranged the initial contact with SUS, on the possibility that the mayor might intervene once again. Brown set up a meeting in his office with Ronald Ellensohn, the mayor's liaison with the LAPD, sitting in. Christian played the Turner interview with Owen, and ran through some of the follow-up material. Brown and Ellensohn agreed that SUS had missed some vital clues, which could lead to severe embarrassment for the Yorty administration. They concluded that an immediate liaison between us and SUS should be negotiated, and it was left that Ellensohn would contact SUS and report back to Brown. Brown would prepare a letter of recommendation for Yorty to act upon.

It took a month for Ellensohn to complete his talks with a balky SUS, and Brown was finally able to compose the memorandum:

On October 13, Ron Ellensohn and I had a lengthy conference with Jonn Christian, a free-lance investigative reporter from San Francisco. You may recall I previously memoed you about Christian and his belief that the murder of Robert Kennedy was a conspiracy. Christian played for us a taped interview with Oliver "Jerry" Owen, an evangelist and horse trader with homes in both Orange County and the Oxnard area [sic].

The memo synopsized the hitchhiker story, mentioning that Owen had reported it to the LAPD. It continued:

Apparently acting on my previous memo to you, police contacted Christian in San Francisco and he offered to turn over his tape and other material to them. But he heard nothing further from the officers. Ellensohn checked police and learned they had spent 100 manhours investigating Christian's allegations that the assassination was an ultra right-wing plot. . . . Police dismissed Owen's statement as one of the many false stories arising around the assassination. Christian was also said by the police to be an associate of Jim Garrison, District Attorney of New Orleans, which I suppose discredited him. [Actually, it was Turner, not Christian, who had been associated with Garrison. Back in 1968, critics of the Warren Report were looked upon with disdain in establishment circles.]

Brown's memorandum concluded with the news that Christian had just "called me to say that Charles O'Brien, Chief Deputy Attorney General, has taken direct interest in the Owen case." Brown advised that if the LAPD wanted "to look any further into this matter, they can now reach Christian in the Los Angeles area." The memo was tagged with Christian's temporary address and telephone number in Beverly Hills.

Brown told Christian that he was certain that the memo, especially the part about O'Brien's interest, would prompt Yorty to pick up the phone and reopen the Owen file at SUS headquarters. But the mayor did nothing; he did not even acknowledge the memo in the usual way by initialing and returning it to Brown.

It would be eight months before we found out why.

ONE DAY EARLY IN DECEMBER WHEN TURNER VISITED LOS Angeles, we had lunch with Robert Kaiser, who had spent ten years in a Jesuit seminary, then become a *Time* correspondent covering the ecumenical conferences in Rome in the early 1960s. We had met Kaiser four months earlier when *Look* magazine, for whom he was a stringer, expressed an interest in pursuing our story. Kaiser had been assigned by *Look* to evaluate our material, and submitted such a negative report that the magazine backed off.

We didn't know at the time that Kaiser had a sharp conflict of interest. He was already busy talking to Sirhan's attorneys to obtain exclusive rights to Sirhan's own story, hoping to crack the conspiracy from inside, for Kaiser instinctively felt that the enigmatic little Palestinian was not alone. He finally negotiated a deal with chief defense attorney Grant Cooper which gave him official status as a defense investigator to boot. Thus he had exclusive access not only to Sirhan but presumably to police data as well. It was a journalist's dream for Kaiser, but it had made him a competitor of ours.

Nevertheless, we decided that we should keep in touch with him. We were anxious to find out what his marathon sessions might have extracted from Sirhan in the way of a tie to Owen.

Nothing, Kaiser said, absolutely nothing. Sirhan flatly denied knowing Owen or anything about a horse transaction. But Kaiser sensed that Sirhan might have lied to him on this score. "I've caught him lying about things that he said and did before the assassination," Kaiser said, "things that can be proven conclusively, and this tends to make me believe he might be lying about being with Jerry Owen, too. He's a smart little bastard, you know. He's been playing games with me from the very start of our sessions. I can feel it down deep. I know he's concealing the actual facts— the identities of those who put him up to it."

Kaiser sounded frustrated. Here he had the man who apparently had killed Robert Kennedy and he couldn't crack him. What did Sirhan have to gain by keeping silent, by feigning ignorance, by lying? Kaiser had argued with him that if he agreed to open up, he would not only escape the death penalty but might get off with a lighter sentence for his cooperation. And if Kaiser got the exclusive inside story, they both would end up wealthy from sales to media around the world. It was a powerful argument, but Sirhan only blinked and went on with evasive word games.

Did Sirhan fear another kind of death penalty if he talked? Or was it just possible that his mind *was* a blank? "What about hypnosis," Christian offered, having read a book or two on the subject. "You know they can screw up a guy's mind with hypnosis —blow his memory—just like they can stop you from smoking." For the rest of the luncheon we talked animatedly (if not too expertly) on the possibility that Sirhan had been hypnoprogrammed to kill—and to forget.

A FEW BLOCKS FROM THE LOS ANGELES MEMORIAL COLISEUM, built for the 1932 Olympic Games, the Coliseum Hotel stands as a fading landmark in an area that has seen better days. The high-ceilinged grill—GOOD FOOD it says simply on the window—is cooled on muggy summer days by a fan mounted on a stand.

The fan must have been whirring on the morning of June 5, 1968, as Jerry Owen parked his pickup truck and horse trailer in the rear parking lot and walked inside. He had been on his way back to Santa Ana from Oxnard, he said, when he felt hungry and decided to drop in on his old pal Bert Morse, who ran the grill. As Owen told it, Morse and a waitress, Mabel Jacobs, were present when he saw Sirhan's picture on television and the front page of the Hollywood *Citizen-News* and recognized him as the hitchhiker of two days previously. So was a fight trainer named Doug Lewis, but Owen's story downplayed his presence.

The Coliseum grill was clearly the crossroads of Owen's story, where fact and fiction met. As the New Year of 1969 began, Christian resolved to interview both Lewis and Morse.

Douglas T. Lewis was an affable, rotund black man then in his early sixties. He said that he had known Owen for years through the fight game, and recalled him arriving at the Coliseum grill before noon on the morning after the shooting and "telling us that he picked up this young man on the freeway, and he brought the young man in town." The hitchhiker was on his way to the race track, and Owen said, "Well, I'm going that way and I'll drop you off at the hotel." The hotel, Lewis clarified, was the one "where the catastrophe happened." When the waitress brought over an *EXTRA!* edition newspaper, Owen immediately recognized Sirhan's picture.

What Lewis had to say contradicted Owen in one other important respect. Owen had said that his decision to stop at the Coliseum grill was impromptu, but Lewis was insistent that he and Owen's boxer, "Irish Rip" O'Reilly, were supposed to meet Owen at the grill that morning. "Yeah, I met him over there every day to take this boy to the gymnasium," he said. The time frame encompassed the entire week before the assassination. O'Reilly was staying at the Coliseum Hotel, and as we also later discovered, was present when Owen arrived as expected.

If Lewis was correct, Owen was meeting his trainer and boxer daily at the grill before going over to the gym nearby. This would mean that he went there Monday, in contrast to his version that he only detoured through Los Angeles to pick up boxing gear at a sporting-goods store. It would mean that he went there Tuesday, in contrast to his version that after checking out of the St. Moritz Hotel in Hollywood he went directly to Oxnard. That Owen had even gone to Oxnard, much less preached at the Calvary Baptist Church, was beginning to look more and more dubious.

What Bert Morse told Christian tended to back up Lewis. Morse said that Owen had come to the grill because he had a "big clown" of a boxer staying in the Coliseum Hotel. But Morse nervously denied being present when Owen recognized Sirhan, and in fact sought to minimize his relationship with the preacher. "Oh, years ago I used to see him around the fight racket," Morse conceded. "I think he was handling fighters or around fight racketeers years ago." Was he a legitimate preacher? "All those preachers are legitimate when the dollar's there," he scoffed.

We learned later that Morse was more than a fight manager turned restaurant and saloon proprietor. In Hemet in Riverside County he owned the Morse Stock Farm, where he raised thoroughbred horses and raced them at Santa Anita, Hollywood Park and other tracks throughout the state. Two of his horses, Hemet Miss and Diamond Dip, were winning their share of purses.

Owen's own connection with the race-track crowd provided a possible answer to the enigma of how he might have met so unlikely a person as Sirhan, assuming that it wasn't as a hitchhiker. In 1965 and 1966 Sirhan, aspiring to become a jockey, had worked as an exercise boy at the Santa Anita and Hollywood Park tracks, and later in 1966 was employed as a groom at a thoroughbred ranch in Corona, not far from Hemet. It was not difficult to imagine him crossing paths with Owen somewhere among the horse fanciers.

The Reverend Jonothan Perkins, the elderly minister who Owen said accompanied him for the interview at SUS headquarters, did not appear at first glance to be a promising witness. He was a long-time friend of Owen, and for over twenty years had been personal secretary to the late Gerald L. K. Smith, the virulent anti-Semite who founded the Christian Nationalist Crusade. Perkins conducted his own ministry at the Embassy Auditorium in downtown Los Angeles, a favorite meeting place for right-wing fundamentalists. The Christian Nationalist Crusade held meetings there, as did the racist Church of Jesus Christ-Christian.* And occasionally Jerry Owen staged revival meetings there.

---

* The Church of Jesus Christ-Christian figured prominently in the previously mentioned investigation by the California Attorney General's office into right-wing paramilitary groups. It was led by the Reverend Wesley A. Swift

As it turned out, however, the white-maned Perkins was a gold mine of information. He related that on the morning of June 5 Owen telephoned him and asked if he could come right over to his apartment in the hotel adjacent to the Embassy Auditorium. When he arrived a few minutes later, Owen was visibly shaken. "I'm about to get mixed up in that thing," Owen said in reference to the RFK shooting. "And I don't want to get mixed up in another scandal like that."

It was the second visit from Owen in two days. Perkins revealed that on election day, June 4, Owen had dropped by and mentioned that a former exercise boy at a race track was going to buy one of his horses. Owen said that he met the young man hitchhiking the day before, and he thought that a price of $400 had been reached. The only reason that Owen was hanging around Los Angeles was to complete the sale. He had the horse trailer with him and was to meet the young man and some of his friends the same night.

"You mean he was supposed to meet Sirhan at the Ambassador the night of the election?" Christian asked.

"Oh yes, the night Kennedy was shot," Perkins confirmed.

"He was out there with his horse and trailer?"

"Well, he was here in town. He came up here. I knew about that. I wasn't with him. I talked with him the next day or so."

Christian reiterated his question about whether Owen was actually at the Ambassador Hotel on election night. As Perkins recalled it, Owen said that on election night he "went down there to meet him and to pick up this other three hundred dollars—that was the night of the assassination. He waited around there, and

---

of Lancaster, on the fringe of the Mojave Desert. According to the Attorney General's 1965 report, Swift was "a former Ku Klux Klan rifle-team instructor" and legal representative of Gerald L. K. Smith. It said that he "has purchased over a hundred concealable firearms in the past few years. Moreover, he maintains a firing range on his Kern County ranch, as well as a reported secret arsenal." The church had a paramilitary arm called the Christian Defense League. In 1976, after Swift's death, a huge buried arsenal (including ground-to-air missiles) was discovered on lands that had belonged to Swift, touching off an investigation leading to the arrest and conviction of an East Los Angeles man linked to extremist causes.

when Sirhan didn't show up, he went to a hotel here. Thought he'd stay all night, that Sirhan would very likely show up in the morning because he was very much interested in the horse. If I remember correctly, he went to some little motel in Hollywood so he wouldn't have to drive back and haul this horse trailer to Santa Ana."

Perkins said that when Owen came by about ten in the morning on June 5 he seemed genuinely frightened at the asserted chance encounter with Sirhan. "Listen," he told Perkins, "that's the fella that was gonna buy my horse. I brought the horse in here to deliver it. The other man didn't show up and so forth. I waited for him. Man alive, they was just gonna use me as a getaway, as a scapegoat. They could have gone four or five miles and shot me in a vacant lot."*

What Perkins had to say seemed enormously important, for here for the first time was a witness to whom Owen had related the hitchhiker story *before* the shooting. It was a significantly different version from what he had told Turner about going to Oxnard on election day. Owen gave Perkins the impression that he was in Los Angeles with the horse and trailer from at least late Monday through Tuesday—and that he had been waiting outside the Ambassador Hotel for Sirhan when the shooting happened.

ON JANUARY 21, 1969, CHRISTIAN PAID HIS FIRST VISIT TO THE LAPD "Glass House" at the invitation of Lieutenant Roy Keene, a polite, low-keyed man who oversaw SUS's administrative paperwork. In discussions over the phone, Keene had expressed an authentic interest in Reverend Perkins' disclosure that his fellow cleric had in fact been in the company of Sirhan on election day. Christian thought he had struck a bargain with Keene: he would let SUS listen to the taped interview of Perkins in return for being allowed a dubbed copy of the original interview of Owen at the University Station. "I can't see any reason why that can't be arranged," Keene had said.

Keene ushered Christian into the office of Captain Hugh Brown, commander of Homicide Detectives, who was serving as operational

---

* Taped interview with Jonothan Perkins, January 8, 1969. Perkins died in 1974.

chief of SUS. Brown, a chunky, red-faced man, wasted no time on cordialities. "Look, we've spent hundreds of hours checking out that lying bastard's phony story," he boomed in reference to Owen. "There's nothing to it, absolutely nothing!"

"Well, if that's the case, why didn't you arrest him for filing a false police report?" Christian replied.

Brown softened his tone. He said that a couple of his men had gone over to the Embassy Hotel and questioned Perkins. "He is an old man," the captain argued. "His mind is fuzzy. He's senile. He got all his dates mixed up. Anyway, he admitted to us that Owen wasn't in town on June fourth. It was June fifth or sometime after that."

Christian reached into his briefcase, withdrew the Perkins tape cassette and inserted it into his Sony recorder. The minister's steady voice filled the office, reciting how Owen had visited him twice, how Owen said he was with Sirhan both days. In no way did he sound like an addled old man. As Christian ticked off examples of Perkins' keenness of mind, Brown said, "He's just not telling the truth, that's all!"

Christian caught a glimpse of Lieutenant Manny Pena, who had been standing in an adjacent room. Brown peered into Christian's briefcase and saw two dozen other cassettes. "What're those of?" he demanded.

"You'd be surprised how many witnesses we've dug up, Captain," Christian said, "and some of their statements make Owen appear more than just your 'liar.' Now, how about letting me listen to Owen's initial statement?"

Brown was angry. "We want those tapes, now!" he ordered as he rose from his chair and started toward the briefcase. Christian felt a surge of panic—several of the tapes hadn't yet been dubbed for safekeeping. He knew Brown could seize the lot and later deny it. Snapping the briefcase shut, Christian bluffed, "Sorry, Captain, but I'm on my way to an appointment with Charlie O'Brien, and he's waiting to hear all of these tapes."

The policeman stopped in his tracks. "O'Brien? Which Charlie O'Brien?" There was only *one* Charlie O'Brien in California law enforcement, and Brown knew it. "What's he want that stuff for?" he asked.

"When your people told us to get lost last year, we had the choice of backing off or going to someone in authority who would listen," Christian explained. "And O'Brien listened."

"Well, why doesn't he call us if he's so damn curious?" Brown said.

Christian replied that the AG's people had tried to get information from SUS but had received no cooperation.

"That's a lie!" Brown exploded. "We've cooperated with every law enforcement agency on this thing from the beginning!" The captain stood up and pointed a finger menacingly at his visitor. "You know, you guys are messing around with official police business. You could find yourselves in trouble, big trouble, if you don't watch it. Just remember that, eh?" The knot in Christian's stomach mutely affirmed that he took the captain at his word.*

Roy Keene seemed embarrassed as he walked Christian to the elevator. "The captain doesn't like civilians messing around with his thing," he said. "But he does mean business, you know." Keene handed Christian his card. "Keep in touch," he suggested.

With a feeling of relief Christian walked past the uniformed policemen on duty in the "Glass House" lobby and out into the bright sunlight. He had the feeling that Keene wanted to be helpful, but Keene obviously wasn't running the show. A couple of months later Keene took early retirement to become chief of a small police department in Oregon. Christian and he had a parting phone conversation. "It's a good thing you guys can't get your hands on some of our files," Keene said. "You'd go wild!"

CHARLIE O'BRIEN WAS FURIOUS WITH CHRISTIAN WHEN WE MET with him a week later in his office in the Old State Building in Los Angeles. "Goddammit!" he yelled. "I told you not to mention

---

* Behind Brown on the top of a file drawer was a framed photograph of a group of persons astride some handsome horses. He could just make out the word "Appaloosa," but couldn't read the club or association identification that followed. He instantly wondered if this had anything to do with the organization headed by Owen's long time friend and paramilitary "bodyguard, Ben Hardister"—The California Appaloosa Horse Racing Association President.

anything about our arrangement in this thing! I was set for a meeting the next morning with Chief Reddin at ten o'clock sharp and you go and tell Brown about my interest in this thing. Well, I got a call from Reddin's office a half-hour before our meeting, calling it off. Then I check with my contact at the LAPD and find out you'd been over there popping off!"

Christian tried to explain how harrowing the session with Brown had been, and that his witness tapes might have been gone forever. O'Brien's displeasure seemed to stem as much from embarrassment that he'd been caught by the police playing games with "civilians" as with the cancellation of the meeting. Christian wasn't exactly happy with O'Brien, either. Why was he letting the LAPD put him off? If the police were cooperating, as Brown insisted, he should get all the information he wanted, Christian's visit notwithstanding. And if they weren't, he should make an issue of it.

And why was he keeping our relationship in the closet? It would not have been unprecedented for O'Brien to accredit us officially. He did it for Bill Davidson, a veteran journalist who wrote a book called *Indict and Convict* that chronicled O'Brien and his staff in action. "For six months I worked out of a desk in their office," Davidson said in the book. "I had complete access to their files and memoranda, and I personally accompanied them into the courtroom and into the field—even, on one occasion, as a 'Special Assistant to the Attorney General.' "

But there was of course an obvious difference: Davidson hadn't been bucking the official police position.

SEVERAL WEEKS LATER CHRISTIAN AGAIN CALLED THE REVEREND Perkins, who said that the police had questioned him for a second time a few days after Christian's visit with Captain Brown. Christian was just a phony and would cause him and Owen nothing but trouble, they said, warning him that he should not talk to any member of the press because witnesses were under a blanket court order to remain silent. Perkins complained that the police had tried to get him to change his story, but he had refused.

It was beginning to sound as if Captain Brown was getting

worried. If he was so sure that Owen fabricated his story, why was he sending his men around to discredit Christian and threaten an old man with a nonexistent gag order? Neither the prosecution nor the defense had any intention of calling Perkins or Owen as a witness at the trial.

7

The Quiet Trial
of Sirhan Sirhan

CAPTAIN BROWNE'S EDGINESS OVER THE PERKINS DISCLOSURES may have been heightened by the fact that the trial of Sirhan Sirhan had begun on January 13 with both sides resolved not even to hint at a conspiracy. During pre-trial hearings, the prosecution had been instructed to turn over, under discovery rules, any evidence in its possession that the defense might require. At an October 14, 1968, hearing, co-prosecutor David Fitts plunked down a tall pile of documents on the table in front of Sirhan attorney Russell Parsons. Among them were the interviews of sixty-seven persons who had seen Sirhan at the hotel, as well as fifteen who had spotted him on election morning while practice-shooting at the San Gabriel Valley

Gun Club. Although the defense had specifically requested it at the insistence of Bob Kaiser, the LAPD's file on Jerry Owen was missing. It remained squirreled away at SUS, its contents flagged in an anonymous handwriting, "No discovery."

At a press conference following the hearing, Parsons had gone along with the prosecution. "We have seen no evidence of a conspiracy," he said. The next morning the Los Angeles *Times* banner read: BOTH SIDES AGREE SIRHAN WAS ALONE.

In the interval before the trial began, Kaiser had tried to open the minds of the defense lawyers to the indications of a conspiracy but had run up against a stone wall. "Parsons simply would not talk about the evidence, let alone pursue it," Kaiser said. "We should have demanded their file on Jerry Owen." The main stumbling block apparently was entries in Sirhan's notebooks such as "Robert F. Kennedy must be assassinated before 5 June '68" and "Please pay to the order of Sirhan the amount of . . . 8000000" which, by any literal interpretation, clearly implied that Sirhan had been a hired assassin. Looking at it that way, Kaiser agreed, the lawyers were right. "What kind of a defense would it be," he rhetorically asked Christian, "to claim that your client was some kind of paid killer?"

A PROTRACTED PERIOD OF JURY EMPANELMENT WAS PUT TO USE by the defense psychiatric team to conduct additional testing of Sirhan. Its leader, Dr. Bernard Diamond of the University of California at Berkeley, had first interviewed the defendant on December 23, after the trial was originally scheduled to start. Diamond had recently won acquittal for an Air Force officer accused of mailing a bomb, by putting him under hypnosis and enabling him to recall details that he had forgotten in his normal state. He used the same tactic on Sirhan. Because the hypnotic state is one of magnified concentration—not sleep, as is commonly thought—it can be used to dredge up thoughts impossible to recollect by any other means. But hypnosis does not necessarily bring out the truth, because the subject is prone to tell the same lies and evasions he would in the normal state.

On January 11 Diamond hypnotized Sirhan, then asked a series of questions drawn up by chief defense attorney Grant Cooper. Cooper was concerned about the entries in the notebooks that suggested not only premeditation, a requisite for first-degree murder, but a contract killing. Diamond asked, "Sirhan, did anybody pay you to shoot Kennedy? Did anybody pay you to shoot Kennedy, Sirhan? Yes or no." Sirhan sighed but didn't answer. "I can't hear you," the doctor prodded.

A. No.

Q. No? No one paid you to shoot Kennedy. Did anyone know ahead of time that you were going to do it, Sirhan?

A. No.

Q. No. Did anybody from the Arabs tell you to shoot Kennedy? Any of your Arab friends? [Cooper and Diamond supported the prosecution's belief that the young Palestinian was passionately attached to the Arab cause, and theorized that he might have been motivated by Kennedy's support for Israel. No evidence exists that Sirhan belonged to any revolutionary Arab faction.]

A. No.

Q. Did the Arab government have anything to do with it, Sirhan?

A. No.

Q. Did you think this up all by yourself?

There was a five-second pause.

A. Yes.

Q. Yes. You thought this up all by yourself. Did you consult with anybody else, Sirhan?"

Another pause.

A. No.

Q. Are you the only person involved in Kennedy's shooting?

A three-second pause.

A. Yes.

Q. Yes. Nobody involved at all. Why did you shoot Kennedy?

No response. When Diamond pressed for an answer, Sirhan mumbled something about "the bombers," which the doctor interpreted as the war planes Robert Kennedy had promised to send to Israel. Diamond snapped him out of the trance, and Sirhan noticed blood trickling down his hand. "Jesus Christ!" he yelled. "What's that?" Diamond had pricked him with a safety pin after hypnotizing him and he hadn't felt it. Diamond had instructed him not to feel the pain.

Diamond apparently assigned no particular significance to the three pauses following questions about the involvement of others. But the pauses strongly pointed to what experts call "blocking," which occurs when a subject has been hypnoprogrammed to forget certain details, a process known as "artificial amnesia."

The climactic session was on February 8, when Diamond realized that Sirhan was highly susceptible to hypnotic suggestions that ran counter to his natural instincts. After "putting him under," Diamond suggested that he climb the bars of his cell and act like a monkey. Sirhan complied, even swinging upside down ape-style. Afterward Diamond played back a tape of the session.

"Ohhh, it frightens me, Doc." Sirhan shivered. "But goddamn it, sir, killing people is different than climbing up bars."

"There's this difference, Sirhan," Diamond explained. "I couldn't force you to do something you were opposed to. But if you wanted to do it, you could do it under hypnosis. Do you know, Sirhan, if five men had wanted to stop you from climbing those bars, they couldn't have done it?"

But Diamond didn't propose that Sirhan might have been a Manchurian Candidate hypnoprogrammed to kill—that was a "crazy, crackpot theory." "I think you did it to yourself," he said, meaning that Sirhan had hypnoprogrammed himself by thinking hostile thoughts about Kennedy while in self-induced trances.*

THE PROSECUTION CASE WAS DAMNINGLY SIMPLE. A PARADE OF witnesses testified that Sirhan was caught with a smoking gun in his hand, and as the scrawlings in the notebooks attested, he committed the crime with considerable malice aforethought and premeditation. Over Cooper's objection, eight pages of the notebooks were admitted into evidence. (The most damaging page read: "May 18 9.45AM—68 My determination to eliminate R.F.K. is be-

---

* Kaiser, *op. cit.*, pp. 302–4.

coming more the more of an unshakable obsession . . . RFK must die.")

On Monday, March 3, Cooper called Sirhan to the stand. An attempt had to be made to rebut the mute testimony of the notebook pages, and Cooper's line of questioning was designed to set the stage for later psychiatric testimony.

Q. Have you heard these notebooks read?
A. Yes, sir.
Q. And you wrote these notebooks? [A prosecution handwriting examiner had already testified that Sirhan was the author.]
A. Yes, sir.
Q. And you don't deny it?
A. I don't deny it.
Q. You bought the gun?
A. Yes, sir, I did.
Q. Did you have in mind going to the Ambassador Hotel for the purpose of killing Robert F. Kennedy?
A. No, sir, I did not. That was completely forgotten from my mind. That emotion was good as long as I was writing it. Something for a time only.
Q. And did you kill him?
A. Yes, sir.

Although Sirhan had all along insisted that he had an amnesia block over the span of the shooting—he awkwardly called it "completely forgotten from my mind"—Cooper didn't pursue the point. Instead, he skipped to the question of conspiracy:

Q. Were you hired to kill Senator Kennedy?
A. No.
Q. Did any government hire you?
A. No.

With this perfunctory exploration out of the way, Cooper moved on to Sirhan's state of mind at the time.

Q. Had you been going to the races?
A. For two weeks before—almost every day.
Q. Were you betting?

A. Yes.

Q. You didn't do too good, did you? [Cooper was planting the idea that Sirhan was depressed because of consistent losses.]

A. Good and bad. I lost more than I won. I had been losing all the time before that.

The chief prosecutor was Lynn D. "Buck" Compton, the top aide to District Attorney Evelle Younger. He took over on cross-examination.

Q. What about your notebooks? You don't remember when these were written?

A. No, sir, I don't.

Q. You had a habit of doodling? [It was as if the automatic writing were no more than graffiti on a men's room wall. As we shall see, this type of writing can be indicative of a trance condition.]

A. No, sir, I don't.

Q. You had a habit of writing words or even sentences of things that were on your mind?

A. I don't know, sir. I didn't sit there and doodle intentionally.

Q. These were the things that interested you? Race horses? Girls, now and then? Poems? Sometimes you liked to write in Arabic? Jockeys' names? [Compton apparently was driving at the idea that the entries were what Sirhan might jot down in a conscious state.]

A. Yes, sir.

Q. It doesn't surprise you to find these things in your notebooks?

A. No, sir, it doesn't.

Q. Did you ever look at your notebooks at the things you wrote?

A. I guess, sir. I don't remember.

Q. You don't remember looking and thinking, "Gee whiz! Here I wrote that Kennedy must be assassinated!" and wonder why? Don't you remember that?

A. No, sir, I don't.

Q. On this envelope, see that writing? "RFK must be disposed of like his brother." Did you write that?" [Compton waved an envelope retrieved from a trash can at the Sirhan residence in Pasadena.]

A. It was my handwriting.

Q. You have no memory of ever writing that?

A. No, sir, I haven't.

Sirhan had not convinced his own defense team that he was not feigning the amnesia block, much less the prosecution and jury. On

March 21 Diamond took the stand to try to make the best of a bad situation. He testified that in his opinion Sirhan was in a trance state at the time of the shooting, citing the fact that his subject was easily hypnotizable and appeared to have been hypnotized many times in the past. Sirhan admitted, Diamond said, that he had on occasion put himself into trances by staring in a mirror. The notebooks, Diamond theorized, were the product of a series of self-induced trances in which Sirhan wrote "like a robot." On the night of the slaying, he posited, circumstances combined into a remarkable coincidence: Sirhan took the gun from his car "because he didn't want the Jews to steal it"; he met a girl and had coffee with her; he was dazed and confused by the lights, mirrors and crush of people in the hotel; he stared at a teletype machine; and people rushed at him. Involuntarily, he slipped into a psychotic, dissociated state. He cried out, "You son of a bitch!" and shot Kennedy.

Diamond was describing a surrealistic binge that he conceded sounded "absurd and preposterous." Nonetheless, he gamely summed up: "I see Sirhan as small and helpless, pitifully ill, with a demented, psychotic range, out of control of his own consciousness and his own actions, subject to bizarre, dissociated trances in some of which he programmed himself to be the instrument of assassination, and then, in an almost accidentally inducted twilight state, he actually executed the crime, knowing next to nothing as to what was happening."

In other words, Sirhan was some sort of automatic assassin, a hypnotic time bomb which could go off at any time. The next day's edition of the Los Angeles *Times* headlined: SIRHAN IN TRANCE ON ASSASSINATION NIGHT, PSYCHIATRIST INSISTS.

In his final arguments, Lynn Compton derided Diamond's testimony. "Nobody knew what happened until Dr. Diamond descended on the scene. [Sirhan] did it with mirrors."

The jury deliberated for sixteen hours and forty-two minutes before returning a verdict of guilty in the first degree.

WHILE THE TRIAL WAS STILL IN PROGRESS, CHRISTIAN COMPARED notes with Bob Kaiser, who had the advantage of being inside the defense team. Kaiser was becoming increasingly addicted to the conspiracy idea. "That's the hell of it," he complained on the evening of March 23 after Diamond had testified. "It's irrelevant to both the defense and the prosecution."*

In May, after the trial was over, Christian arranged a sit-down session with Kaiser, who was now busy organizing his book "*R.F.K. Must Die!*" After about two hundred hours of interviewing Sirhan, Kaiser had not been able to extract any solid evidence of a conspiracy, but he did not see this as either an indication of no plot or as Sirhan's fault. "I'm convinced he really is suffering from some kind of amnesia in regard to some of the critical evidence against him," Kaiser said.

When Kaiser first broached the subject of Jerry Owen a couple of months before, Sirhan had flatly denied ever hearing of him, he confided. Lately, however, Sirhan had retreated a bit from that position. It came about when Kaiser threw out the possibility that on the occasions when Sirhan sat down in front of a mirror, hypnotized himself and scribbled in the notebooks, he might have been "a tool used by others." Sirhan didn't reject the notion—he simply couldn't remember anyone using hypnosis on him, let alone writing the incriminating passages. Kaiser suggested to Sirhan that he might have met someone somewhere who wanted Kennedy dead, and he ticked off the names of several known acquaintances of Sirhan. No reaction. Then he mentioned Jerry Owen. "Sirhan didn't say he didn't know Owen," Kaiser remarked. "He said that he was home on Monday, June third—raked the leaves, slept quite a bit, read the papers, and went to Corona that night."

Corona, of course, was where Sirhan had been employed in 1966 as a groom on a thoroughbred horse ranch. But this conflicted with what Mary Sirhan had told SUS: that her son was gone when she returned from work in the early afternoon of June 3, but was back watching television around four-thirty and remained home that night. However, Mrs. Sirhan had no particular reason to

---

* Christian called co-prosecutor John Howard right after the Sirhan diaries were read off in court, asking the Assistant DA if he didn't concur with our interpretation of Sirhan's having been a "programmed killer for hire." Howard indicated that there was a considerable dispute going on about this in the DA's office—although none of this difference in opinion ever surfaced in court.

remember that day and could easily have been mistaken, and Sirhan himself could have been in error or lying. As far as Kaiser was concerned, Sirhan's movements on that Monday had yet to be accounted for.

According to Kaiser, Sirhan himself had brought up the fact that Owen had failed a lie-detector test. (His mother or brothers must have passed along this LAPD contention.) "Yeah," Kaiser retorted, "but he knew more about you in that first interview with the police on June fifth than he should have."

"Bob," Sirhan replied pedantically, "I know that a person doesn't have to meet you to know all about you."

"But he had more details than he should have," Kaiser insisted.

"Well, I was home Monday."

"But later you went to Corona [some fifty miles away]?"

"Yeah," Sirhan said. "I drove out there." He had just contradicted his mother, who told SUS that she thought he had been home all evening. But he evaded saying why he went or whom he saw.

Sirhan parroted the police explanation that maybe Owen had made up the story for publicity. But then he had another thought: "Maybe he could lead to someone who was playing with my mind."

Winding him up like a toy soldier and sending him out to kill? Since he first broached the idea to Kaiser months before, Christian had become more and more persuaded that this was exactly what had happened. In his next meeting with Kaiser, Christian proposed that if Sirhan had been hypnoprogrammed, he might be deprogrammed. "When Sirhan expressed an interest, 'Do you think I could have been hypnotized?,' was he willing to discuss it at great length?" Christian asked.

"He didn't know," Kaiser replied. "We talked a couple of hours about it. He was bugged by the thought. He'd squinch up his eyes, and shake his head, and shudder and say, 'Geez! That really scares me!' "

"He could remember no circumstances whatsoever where he might have been hypnotized?" Christian asked.

"I'm not sure about that. If he was hypnotized by another, he was not willing to say who the other was, because he wouldn't want to get that person in trouble."

Christian raised the possibility that Sirhan might want to co-operate with an expert to try to unlock his mind.

"I'm kind of doubtful he wants to be deprogrammed," Kaiser offered. "He'd rather go to the gas chamber as an Arab hero than anything else. It's more noble, you see, than to have been an un-witting tool of some people who got inside his mind." But Christian discounted the "Arab hero" rationale, since Sirhan had no known involvement in Arab activism.

It was not until a meeting some months later that Kaiser con-fided to Christian that Sirhan had never trusted him because of warnings from other members of the defense team that any revela-tions about any conspiracy might wipe out what little defense he had. Of all the defense lawyers, only Emile Zola "Zeke" Berman shared Kaiser's suspicions about a conspiracy. "He knew what those diaries were saying just like I did," Kaiser said. "He tried to get his colleagues to consider the implications, but they wanted no part of it. He finally gave up."

ON MAY 16, 1969, SHORTLY AFTER THE END OF THE TRIAL, A highly irregular meeting took place in the chambers of Assistant Presiding Judge Charles A. Loring. Its purpose was to devise meth-ods to keep "cranks" away from the LAPD's investigative files that according to procedures were supposed to be deposited with the Clerk of the Court's Office in the same manner that the Warren Commission's documents were lodged in the National Archives. Participating were trial judge Herbert V. Walker, co-prosecutor David Fitts, SUS Chief Robert Houghton, and two officials from the Clerk's office. The defense lawyers had deliberately been excluded.

Houghton expressed concern about the availability to the public of files such as Owen's "which were not subject to testimony." Fitts brought up the fact that Sirhan's lawyers had asked to see the Owen file. "Most of that stuff was ordered delivered on discovery and, in one way or another, they had a lot of specific names, so they got that stuff, and let me assure you here and now that what was delivered on discovery and what was filed with the court was scaled to this extent." As Fitts explained it, the defense lawyers got only what they specifically asked for and nothing more. (That claim is disputed by the members of the defense team, who say that they asked for the LAPD file on Jerry Owen but didn't get it.) "They asked for interviews and interviews they got, but," Fitts continued, "I abstracted from the file" parts dealing with police conclusions. As for the rest of it, he said, "let it stay in the record."

But Houghton wanted to suppress it. "We had a meeting, so all of you will know," he said, "with Buck Compton and John Howard [another deputy DA] and Dave Fitts and my staff." They had discussed such "red herrings" in the case as the anti-Castro Cuban, Jose Duarte, and the preacher, Jerry Owen. Some of the material obtained by the defense on discovery was returned without reaching the press, Houghton reported, and "nobody knew it except us, the District Attorney and the FBI."

Houghton argued that the material should only be used to rebut contentions about "the conspiracy or anything." His investigators' conclusions, he said, "are not put very tactfully as they call people liars and things like that." There was also the matter of arrest records. "As far as I'm concerned we are not going to release any of that. When we find someone has a criminal record, that is confidential information and I don't think we ought to disclose that. I don't know what you have."

Fitts did. "I am not too sure there might not be a kick-back sheet on Jerry Owen," he said.*

ON MAY 28 DISTRICT ATTORNEY EVELLE YOUNGER HANDED OUT a thirteen-page press release reviewing the Sirhan case. He disclosed that Captain Hugh Brown of SUS and his forty-seven investigators had interviewed "well in excess of 4,000 possible witnesses and others pretending to some knowledge of events." In this mass of material, the DA went on, "are the assertions of a number of individuals who have attracted the attention of the news media with respect to the possibility of a conspiracy to effect the death of Senator Kennedy."

Assuring that the allegations had been "investigated in depth"

* Transcript of official reporter Vesta Mennick.

and "discredited," Younger briefly mentioned several of the more prominent ones. There was the polka-dot-dress-girl angle, which the DA dismissed by saying that Sandy Serrano and Vincent DiPierro had changed their stories. There was the episode involving the anti-Castro Cuban Jose Duarte, which Younger said was resolved when Duarte flunked a polygraph test. There was an incident in which Sirhan's brother, Saidallah Sirhan, was shot at as he drove on the Pasadena Freeway on the early morning of July 3, but although police could not close the case, neither could they connect it with the assassination. And then there was Jerry Owen and his hitch-hiker story.

Younger synopsized the story, then commented, "Although Mr. Owen professes to be a preacher of the gospel, there are a number of instances of his past conduct on the police blotters of several states that indicate a less than saintly reluctance to grasp certain opportunities which have been afforded him. The investigators have concluded that Mr. Owen concocted a bizarre tale in the expectation of some advantage from the attendant publicity."

Later that day Art Kevin gained a private interview with Younger during which he pressed for a fuller explanation of the Owen angle. "Are we to gather from the substance of your comments today that obviously the man was untruthful for whatever personal reasons he had?" Kevin prodded. Younger fidgeted with his press release, repeating excerpts from it. The two stared silently at each other.

When Kevin aired his series on the unanswered questions in the RFK case over KHJ, which had the largest listener rating of any station in the Los Angeles basin, he opened one segment by asking, "Whatever happened to the minister who claimed Sirhan and two other persons tried to dupe him into being the getaway driver after the murder?" Kevin retold the hitchhiker story, then criticized Younger and his office for their attitude and closed with a comment about the grand jury: "Even the grand jury refused to hear the minister. Grand jury foreman L. E. McKee was quoted as saying that he'd received no communication from the minister or his attorney, and furthermore that the grand jury had at that point heard as much of the Sirhan case as it intended."

Younger, apparently incensed, lifted Kevin's press privileges, but when KHJ management moved to challenge him in public, he quietly backed down.

On the same day that Younger held his press conference, the LAPD took its turn. Flanked by Hugh Brown and Acting Chief Roger Murdock (Tom Reddin had just retired to join KTLA-TV as news anchorman at $100,000 a year), Robert Houghton insisted that "there was no conspiracy whatsoever." Like Younger, Houghton ran down the major possibilities and eliminated them. "At the beginning of the investigation we did have much information from hundreds of sources," he said, "much of it highly imaginative, some of it from people with serious psychotic problems."

TOP POLICE FIND NO SIRHAN PLOT, the Los Angeles *Herald-Examiner* headlined. As Christian read the article he thought back to the angry meeting with Hugh Brown at Parker Center. What was it Brown had blurted out in a moment of frustration? Something about their having to make sure there was no conspiracy so that Younger's chances for eventually becoming governor wouldn't be jeopardized.*

---

* Younger's ascension toward the California governor's mansion began in earnest in 1970 when he was elected Attorney General. One of his first appointments was a new head of the Criminal Intelligence and Investigation bureau under his aegis. His choice: Robert A. Houghton.

Houghton retired as CII chief in 1976—and was appointed as a member of the 1976–77 Los Angeles County Grand Jury, at a time when the RFK case began hitting the headlines again. The grand jury refused to convene on the case during this period.

In 1978 Younger made his formal announcement about running for governor.

8

"The Walking Bible" on Television

ALTHOUGH IT SEEMED AN EXCHANGE IN FUTILITY, CHRISTIAN decided to make one last appeal to Younger and Yorty. In his letter to the DA, he sought to "sit down and compare notes" with his staff, and posed several nagging questions. "If Owen was merely seeking publicity," Christian reasoned, "as many other 'kooks' were, why didn't he approach the news media directly, as many other 'kooks' did, rather than go directly to the police, where he requested and was assured total anonymity?"

Younger wrote back that the "highly-skilled and experienced investigators" from his office, the LAPD and the FBI had failed to uncover "any credible evidence" of a conspiracy.

"There appears to be no need for any comparison between our notes and yours," he declared, but at the same time he implored Christian to turn over whatever information he had. Failure to do so, Younger sarcastically noted, would force him to conclude that "you in fact have nothing except pure speculation and a fanciful hypotheses [*sic*] upon which you seek to capitalize for monetary advantage."

Christian also wrote directly to Sam Yorty outlining the overall situation and asking for "a personal gettogether with you in total privacy, after which you can make the kind of judgment that is required in so serious a matter." A copy went to Jack Brown, the mayor's aide, who responded: "Received your communication today, and memoed my recommendation to the Mayor regarding your request for appointment. Keep the faith, baby."

But Christian heard nothing from Yorty, and Brown later said that he tried unsuccessfully to see his boss on the matter. Then, on June 11, Brown was summoned to the office of Vice Mayor Eleanor Chambers and given an ultimatum to resign or be fired. She gave no explanation.

But one came four days later on a sultry Sunday afternoon as Christian was flipping channels on his television set. Suddenly, on Channel 13, a station break faded and Mayor Yorty came on. "How do you do, ladies and gentlemen," he began. "It's a great privilege to present to you my friend, evangelist Jerry Owen, 'The Walking Bible.' Glad to see you, Jerry."

Christian watched stupefied as Owen strode into camera range and slipped a thick arm around Yorty's shoulder. "Thank you, Mayor Yorty, and I'm glad to have you here," Owen beamed. "Mayor, I know of several thousands of God-fearing people that prayed you would be elected, and I believe God answers prayer, don't you, Mayor?"

Yorty grinned sheepishly. He had just won re-election against black City Councilman Thomas Bradley after mounting a campaign that appealed to white prejudices.* "Well, I certainly do," Yorty finally agreed. "Of course, I was doing a little of that praying

---

* For example, Yorty claimed that Chief Tom Reddin had resigned because he was afraid that Bradley might win and the city would have an anti-police mayor.

myself, you know, along with thousands." He emitted a strained chuckle.

A grinning Owen kept up the patter. "And I'd like to ask you another question, Mayor. Don't you believe that America, the world, needs to put their faith and trust in the God of Abraham, Isaac and Jacob like never before?"

Yorty, not used to the role of straight man, hemmed and hawed. "Well, Jerry," he said, "I think that this is one of the, er, missing links that's causing so much disturbance and turmoil today, especially of young people. I think they've sort of lost their moorings, and, ah, too many have gotten away from, ah, belief, a real belief in a supreme being and a . . . a direction . . . to all the affairs of human beings."

Christian was bewildered. What was the one-time congressman, three-time mayor of Los Angeles, twice a candidate for governor of California, doing fumbling around with Owen? The question answered itself. Eight months before, Yorty had not even acknowledged Jack Brown's memorandum concerning Owen. Four days previously, Brown had been ousted when he again recommended that the Owen angle be looked into. Yorty hadn't just walked in on the television debut of *The Walking Bible*. Somehow, he and Owen were old friends.*

"Except the Lord build the house, they labor in vain that build it, and except the Lord keep the city, they waketh but in vain." Owen was now in full oratorical flush, portraying Yorty as the City of Angels' ordained guardian. The preacher clutched the "bantam mayor" around the shoulders. "How grrreat is our God," Owen warbled. "How great is His name." As he approached the end of the ancient hymn, he tailored the verse: "He rolled back the water of the mighty Red Sea, and He said, 'Mayor Yorty, keep your faith in me!' "

The camera panned to Yorty as Owen's voice clung to the last

* In his subsequent lawsuit against KCOP, Channel 13, Owen submitted several photographic exhibits showing him and Yorty in the mayor's office posing with such personages as boxer Henry Armstrong. Other exhibits contain references to Yorty's authorizing the loan to Owen of horse trailers and other city property. We were unable to determine either the duration or origins of their relationship.

note. The mayor looked a trifle embarrassed. But Owen was not through. "Do you know that fella out there?" he asked.

Yorty squinted under the bright lights in the direction Owen was gesturing. "Oh, he's an old friend of mine!"

Owen chortled. "That's 'Slapsie Maxie' Rosenbloom!" On cue, the aging fighter shuffled on stage. And there they stood, the odd couple-plus-one, gawking uneasily at one another while Christian stared incredulous at his television set.

Christian sat back to try to sort out this startling new twist. If Owen knew Yorty this well, why hadn't he simply called the mayor when he supposedly received death threats as the result of agreeing to sell Sirhan a horse? Yorty could easily have picked up the phone and instructed the LAPD to provide protection. And if Owen was having so much trouble making ends meet in June 1968 that he needed Sirhan's $400, as he himself had said, where was he now getting the kind of money an unsponsored television show cost? Most crucial of all, however—what was the mayor of the nation's third largest city doing by appearing in such a blatantly public fashion with a man his own top aide had confided was being investigated by the California Attorney General's office for possible criminal involvement in Robert Kennedy's assassination? Perhaps the strained expression on Yorty's face throughout the obvious ordeal offered an explanation of sorts: he surely didn't like being there.

A WEEK AFTER THE INAUGURAL TELECAST OF THE WALKING BIBLE show, Jonn Christian called KCOP program director Gary Waller and requested a confidential meeting with the station management. "There's someone on the air at KCOP who was involved in the Robert Kennedy assassination," Christian confided. "I'd like to come in and talk about it with your top people—in strict privacy." After a brief discussion, Waller invited his caller to come in.

Located in a modest studio at 915 North LaBrea on the south fringe of Hollywood, KCOP was the kind of chipped-paint operation common to independents struggling in the shadow of the big three networks. It was a subsidiary of Chris-Craft Industries, the pleasure-boat manufacturer that had followed the conglomerate trend of the 1960s.

Christian was ushered into an office that seemed a relative haven of luxury. It belonged to station president John Hopkins, a ruddy-faced, silver-haired man pushing sixty who spoke in nervous bursts. Waller was present at the meeting, as were two other executives and the company's general counsel, Victor F. Yacullo. There was an air of uneasiness, undoubtedly generated by the fact that the Federal Communications Commission played God over the broadcast industry, exercising the power to suspend, revoke or transfer a license should the rigid FCC codes and laws be transgressed.

Yacullo, a slight, wispy man in his mid-thirties, put on his horn-rimmed glasses and began the session by giving every indication that he would briskly dispose of the business at hand. But his summary attitude vanished as soon as the unknown visitor presented his credentials. Pulling out letters and documents from a bulging briefcase to support his statements, Christian named as local references Jesse Unruh, speaker of the California Assembly, and Unruh's political lieutenant, attorney Frank J. Burns, Jr. As a "character reference," Christian gave Charlie O'Brien.

Stressing that the information he was about to present must be held in the utmost confidence, Christian began by playing Turner's taped interview with Owen. Then he played the tape of Art Kevin's recent interview with DA Evelle Younger, commenting that Younger's "publicity stunt" explanation was hardly reasonable. Christian pointed out that there had been no publicity, and that the preacher had in fact shied away from it. So the question remained: Why would a man with a voluminous police record come forward with such a story to the police?

Christian continued that we had undertaken our own investigation to try to provide answers to that enigma and others that had cropped up. He urged the executives to keep Owen on the air in the hope that his source of funds to pay for the program could be discovered. Not long before, Christian said, Owen reportedly had complained that unspecified repercussions from the hitchhiker incident had put him in debt "more than eighteen hundred dollars." How much was he laying out for the program? Waller roughly estimated that each weekly program cost upward of $1,350, on top of which were Owen's own production and advertising costs, including display ads in *TV Guide*, television spots and newspaper ads.*

Christian quickly calculated that the preacher was committed to more than $113,000 a year, not much by Oral Roberts and Billy Graham standards but apparently far more than he previously had been able to pull out of his pocket.

The show did generate a modicum of revenues. During the premiere broadcast Owen held up a record album featuring a religious singing group that had just performed: "Everyone that will write in this week and send a free-will donation of five dollars or more to help purchase this time, we're going to send them one of these albums."

On the second broadcast Owen said, "Now Roberta, my partner, my wife, I want her to read some letters. We got so many wonderful letters and some of 'em just made tears come in our eyes. Honey, would you read this wonderful letter to our viewers right now?" Sitting at the organ console, Roberta Owen read a letter from a "sister in Christ" in Pomona who enclosed $5 and wanted Owen to send "the story of your life."

The Walking Bible would have to have taken in sufficient "love offerings," as Owen styled his appeal, to paper the walls of Winchester Cathedral to break even, and we seriously doubted that donations were pouring in at that rate. Although we didn't know it at the time, the preacher was actively planning to go national with the program with an air time budget approaching a million dollars, not including production and promotion costs. What we also didn't know at the time was that there was limited and quiet police curiosity about Owen's source of money. In the 1975 trial, KCOP president John Hopkins would testify that shortly after Christian's visit to the station, an Officer Reed of the Hollywood Station bunco-vice squad contacted him and asked if *The Walking Bible* "was a paid political program." Reed revealed that Owen's "activities were being watched" to try "to determine where the money was coming from."

* Case file *Owen* vs. *KCOP*, Plaintiff's Exhibit 18.

Hopkins inferred from what Reed said that he suspected it came from a tainted source.*

Upon leaving the meeting at KCOP, Christian wrote letters to Hopkins and counsel Yacullo reiterating his opposition to terminating the program, warning that such a move might lead to a lawsuit as well as "sever a valuable line of investigative pursuit." But Yacullo would testify in 1975 that "after we had concluded the meeting with Mr. Christian the intent to cancel the program and my advice to do so and the general concurrence along those lines took place that same day."

Before acting, however, Yacullo wanted to verify Owen's brushes with the law. "We were in a position," he testified, "where we would have an individual on television as a man of God, a man of the cloth, who would be portraying himself as a person of the absolute highest ethical and moral character, that under those circumstances it might be considered as being a deception of the public if, in fact, he did have a police record much less was involved in all of the various allegations which Mr. Christian at some length went through that day."

Yacullo set up a meeting with Robert Houghton, the former SUS chief, who said "that Mr. Owen did have a police record, that he was—he said—I think the words he used were 'had been involved peripherally' " in the RFK case. Houghton claimed there was a code section on privileged information that prevented him from saying more, but suggested that Yacullo contact Sirhan prosecutor Lynn Compton. Compton produced what looked like an investigative file on Owen, and although he would not let Yacullo inspect it, read off a number of items that confirmed Owen's police record.

Yacullo's meeting with Compton took place on the morning of

---

* In an interrogatory filed March 26, 1974, in his suit against KCOP, Owen maintained that he put $12,000 from the sale of the Santa Ana home, which was part of his wife's inheritance, toward the program, and "borrowed $10,000 from church friends in Northern California for additional television time." If this was true, it was still far short of his projected costs versus income. By his own count, for example, he sold only twenty-six of the record albums, for a net profit of $55.90.

July 10, 1969. That afternoon John Hopkins dictated the letter notifying Owen that his program was being canceled. Owen responded by mailing letters to his contributing viewers seeking their support.

S.O.S. EMERGENCY!! This is a hurried note to let you know we have been FORCED OFF OF TV for the time being! Just when we have begun to win many souls, and are hearing of thrilling results! Many enemies of the gospel such as atheists and communists are fighting this program, we know.

We believe we will be back on TV very soon!

Meanwhile Owen showed up at the KCOP studios attempting to buy his way back on the air. At this point he apparently assumed that the sole reason for the termination was the shoplifting arrest at Orhbach's department store, which had made him late for a scheduled taping. One of Owen's long-time sidekicks, John L. Gray, would later give testimony that when Owen confronted John Hopkins, he whipped out a roll of seven $1,000 bills and demanded, "Why won't you accept my money? What are you doing canceling my program?"

"We don't want any phony preachers on the station," Hopkins is said to have replied.

"Do you mean 'The Walking Bible' is a phony?"

Hopkins supposedly responded by not only citing the shoplifting rap but accusing Owen of burning churches and being "tied up" with the Kennedy assassination.

Hopkins' alleged accusations, coupled with purported statements made by KCOP personnel to viewers who called in to the station in response to the "S.O.S." letter gave Owen sufficient grounds to file suit, claiming that the station "published" defamations. There would be five years of preliminary sparring and delays before the case finally came to trial. In that interval we would learn much more about "The Walking Bible."

9
The Weatherly Report

WE FIRST GOT WIND OF "THE WEATHERLY REPORT," AS WE came to call it, from Peter Noyes, then television news producer at KNXT, the Los Angeles outlet for CBS. We had been friendly with Noyes, who shared our views on the JFK and RFK assassinations, for some time, and he called regularly to compare notes. "Have you guys ever run into any reports about Sirhan being seen hanging around a horse stable in Orange County, in Santa Ana to be exact?" he asked during a conversation in late July 1969. No, Christian said, but Santa Ana was where Jerry Owen had lived in 1968. "Have you ever heard the name Powers, Bill Powers, from Santa Ana?" No again. "How close have you guys been working with Bob

Kaiser?" Noyes wanted to know. Close enough, Christian replied. Noyes obviously felt he was walking a tightrope. "Why don't you call Kaiser and ask him if he knows anything about the name Bill Powers?" he urged. "But don't tell I'm your source."

At first Kaiser acted as if the name didn't register, but when he realized we had a solid tip he opened up. While reviewing some files obtained from the LAPD by court order, he said, he came upon a confidential memorandum that had inadvertently been stuck between the pages of a report on another subject. That memorandum was so potentially explosive that he had approached Pete Noyes on the idea of having CBS fund an independent investigation. But the network had declined with only a cursory evaluation of the report's ramifications. Yes, it did concern Jerry Owen, although not by name. Kaiser guessed that Noyes had tipped us off because of our interest in the Owen angle.

Christian proposed that we conduct a joint investigation, but Kaiser said that he was so tied up with his book manuscript that he had no time to help in the interviews. We could have the contents of the memorandum, and follow it up ourselves. It was about a couple of cowboys named Bill Powers and Johnny Beckley, and a teen-ager in trouble with the law named John Chris Weatherly. Don't get too excited, he cautioned, because in the interim he had checked it out with the LAPD. At first they stalled, then told him that the follow-up reports to the memorandum were confidential and not available to outsiders. But forget it, they said, Powers and Beckley and Weatherly were not worth worrying about.

ON NEW YEAR'S EVE 1968, SEVENTEEN-YEAR-OLD JOHN CHRIS Weatherly was arrested by Los Angeles County sheriff's deputies for auto theft and forgery of a gasoline credit card. Weatherly had tried to use the card at a service station in Lakewood, a small town near the Orange County border. It was strictly a routine police case in that Lotusland of souped-up, wide-track cars where auto thievery is as common as oil derricks on the landscape.

Routine, that is, until young Weatherly suddenly switched the topic of his interrogation in the sheriff's substation from mag wheels and racing stripes to what he described as a plain Chevrolet one-ton truck that was used to transport horses. In an evident attempt to bargain his way out of trouble, Weatherly linked that truck to the Robert Kennedy assassination.

As immediately written up by Deputy F. G. Fimbres, the sheriff's report stated that Weatherly

> was told by a Bill Powers m/w/37 . . . that a preacher (name unknown) that preaches in a church in Santa Ana and Sirhan Sirhan had come to Bill Powers' house at the A-Bar-T Ranch in Santa Ana and borrowed his 1967 Chevrolet 1-ton truck, blue in color, with a body used for transporting horses, to take a horse to Los Angeles for sale the day of the Kennedy murder; that when the preacher returned Sirhan was not with him, but he still had the horse, said he couldn't sell it in LA.

Weatherly told the deputies that not only Powers but a cowboy named John Beckley "said that this was true." The report continued:

> Preacher and Sirhan Sirhan were seen numerous times riding horses at the A-Bar-T Stables. Subject claims that Powers will exaggerate on many things, but in this case he was certain in his own mind that Powers was not exaggerating; that the reason Powers would not give him any additional information was because he was afraid of the preacher and stated if the preacher found out they had given the press any information he had enough money to "waste" both of them.
>
> Subject stated in his opinion he felt that the preacher wanted Senator Kennedy killed because the Senator wanted the war stopped. He felt the preacher's reasoning was that if the war was stopped the North Vietnamese would come to this country via Honolulu or Hawaii and God would get angry and cause a tidal wave.
>
> Lt. O'Keefe and W. J. Glidden, Lakewood Station, feel that subject is sane, all points in his story regarding the theft of the credit card which he claims he stole in Buena Park and forged four or five times, check out and other parts of his story appear to be true.
>
> Inspector Humphreys notified L. White, Homicide Bureau, who contacted LAPD, Sgt. Manuel Gutierrez of the SUS Kennedy Investigation Team; he stated they would come to Lakewood Station at 5:30 PM this date and talk to subject.

Manuel "Chick" Gutierrez was the SUS operative who had contacted us in August 1968 in response to Christian's initial overture to Yorty's office, and subsequently dismissed Owen as a crackpot. When he received the news from Lakewood, he called his SUS partner, Sergeant Dudley Varney, at home. Together they hurried to the Lakewood sheriff's substation, where they quizzed Weatherly for three hours. Gutierrez had no difficulty in identifying the preacher in Weatherly's account as Jerry Owen. The SUS pair began a follow-up investigation that was treated as a military secret; not even the FBI, which was supposed to be kept apprised of developments, knew about it.

We tracked down Weatherly on October 2, 1969, at his parents' home in Chino, a Riverside County town thirty miles east of Los Angeles. He turned out to be a soft-spoken young man raised in ranch country who had naturally gravitated to stables. His information was hearsay, he said, from Bill Powers and Johnny Beckley. At first he declined to talk. "I've been asked not to say anything by Sergeant Varney and Sergeant Gutierrez," he apologized. "They just said I shouldn't speak to anyone. The judge was, ah—that any publicity would be against the law, that I couldn't even tell anyone."

Once again SUS had tried to silence a witness. The judge's order had applied to potential trial witnesses only, and the trial had been over for six months. Weatherly's name was never on the list anyway. When we explained to Weatherly that the court order never did apply to him, he loosened up.

Johnny Beckley, he said, knew Owen "pretty well." About a week after the assassination, Beckley confided to him that he had seen Owen and Sirhan "ride up and down the Santa Ana River together quite often." (The river is bone-dry in the summer and is used as a bridle trail.) "That morning that Kennedy was assassinated, they came out and borrowed Bill's truck." Weatherly evidently didn't know that Powers had sold the truck to Owen sometime before.

Weatherly told several friends what Beckley had divulged. They suggested that he and Beckley cash in on the story by going to the press. But when he broached the idea to Beckley, the older man apparently realized the jeopardy involved and "didn't want no part of it." So, around November, Weatherly phoned the Los Angeles *Times* himself. "They thought it was a joke," he recounted. "I didn't talk to the reporter for more than two minutes." He made no further overtures to the press.

After Weatherly spilled the story to the sheriff's deputies, Beckley gave him a dressing down. "The reason John didn't want to say anything," Weatherly explained, "was because he felt this preacher had enough money to get us all knocked off." Powers, too, was upset. "Bill told Beckley that he was gonna twist my head off," Weatherly said, "but I seen Bill and he never said nothin' to me."

Gutierrez and Varney traced Beckley through an outstanding traffic warrant and hassled him roughly. "He got frustrated," Weatherly said. "They had him handcuffed at his mother's house, and they was gonna take him in." But Beckley didn't talk—he just said, "Bill Powers knows all about it. Go talk to him!"

We intended to talk to Bill Powers ourselves, but we had one final question for Weatherly: how had he fared on the stolen-car and credit-card rap?

"I wasn't even charged with a misdemeanor," he chuckled.

It would be the last time he found the situation even faintly amusing.

BEFORE WORLD WAR II, SANTA ANA WAS THE SOMNAMBULANT seat of Orange County. But the postwar boom saw bulldozers swarming like locusts, leveling acre after acre of citrus groves to make way for housing tracts and industrial parks. Space-age industries sprang up, and Disneyland, and freeways. Lured by the balmy climate and coastal beaches, immigrants flocked in from east of the Rockies and the nation's Southern tier. Despite its phenomenal growth, Orange County was hardly a melting pot—even by the mid-1960s the Jewish and black populations both amounted to less than one percent. It was an ultraconservative stronghold, a place where the John Birch Society flourished and the Santa Ana *Register* advocated private ownership of schools and the police department. "Orange County is radical in its conservatism," Republican Governor Goodwin Knight once remarked.

In early 1968 Bill Powers sold his interest in the A-Bar-T

Stables and moved a couple of miles downstream to set up his Wild Bill's Stables. Weatherly apparently had the two stables confused when he reported to the deputy sheriffs.

When Christian interviewed him on October 12, 1969, Powers initially exhibited the cowboy's characteristic suspicion of strangers. But the suspicion soon melted, and he began talking about Jerry Owen in his easy drawl. He had known Owen, who lived within walking distance up the river, for some four years through their mutual interest in horses. The preacher kept a small private stable himself, selling and trading on occasion, and often bought or borrowed bundles of hay from Powers. Powers was awed by the shifts in Owen's moods. The preacher might be a roistering good fellow one minute, then lapse into "little spells when he'd want to tell you how tough he was."

Powers thought that there was a bit of Elmer Gantry in Owen. Once when he went to the preacher's home to talk about a horse trade, he found him locked in an outhouse in the backyard. "He couldn't talk to nobody," Powers recounted. "His wife said he couldn't be bothered. He was meditatin'. And a few days later he come by my place and, boy, he was all cleaned up and really shaven and he said he fasted for three days and nights and meditated, and he said the Lord told him how to do it. And I said, 'What's that, Jerry? Make a little money?,' and he said, 'Yeah!' "

On a couple of occasions Owen hinted that Powers was sharp enough to get away with something illegal. "He told me that I was smart enough that I didn't have to fool with them horses," the cowboy recalled, "that I could do something else." Once Owen talked vaguely about a deal in which Powers would help in transporting horses around the first week in June 1968—up in the Oxnard area, he thought the preacher said. But Powers never rose to the bait.

Powers corrected Weatherly's impression that Owen and Sirhan had borrowed his late-model Chevrolet truck on election day to drive into Los Angeles. When he bought this vehicle, he sold Owen his old 1951 Chevrolet pickup that Owen had previously borrowed to haul hay. "So then a few weeks before the assassination he came down and bought the truck," Powers explained. The price was either $300 or $350, and Owen made a $50 down payment. Powers hung on to the "pink slip" proving ownership until the balance would be paid.

It never was. On or about Monday, June 3, Powers related, Owen drove into Wild Bill's Stables at the wheel of a late-model Lincoln Continental four-door sedan. When Powers brought up the money due, the preacher nodded and said he had to go to the bank. Upon returning, he fished in his pocket and pulled out a roll of $1,000 bills. "I don't know how many of them there was," the cowboy marveled, "but there was a big handful of them."

"I'll pay you for that truck," Owen said, peeling off a $1,000 bill.

"Jerry, I don't have no change for *that*," Powers replied.

"Well, I'll have to go to the bank and get one cashed and bring you back the money for the truck."

Owen drove off in his luxury car, but didn't return. "The assassination was the next day, I guess," Powers said. "I never did figure him," he continued. "He often had to borrow a bundle of hay. I don't know where he got his money, but it sure wasn't in the horse business." Could Owen have flashed a "Montana bankroll"? Christian asked, referring to a roll of $1 bills covered with a $1,000 note that con men use to impress their victims. "No, no, no," Powers insisted—he knew a Montana bankroll when he saw one. "Oh, no! I'd say there was probably twenty-five, maybe thirty of them, at least. They filled one pocket, and there were money orders, traveler's checks, something like that in the other pocket. He showed me that roll of bills a couple of times. He showed 'em to all of us there." The sight of Owen in his flashy new car had attracted several of the stable hands. Johnny Beckley was one of them.

If Powers was correct, "The Walking Bible" was walking around with a cool $25,000 to $30,000 in cash. But if he had any fear of being mugged, he wasn't relying on the Lord for his only protection. With him that afternoon were two other men, one a bulky and powerful-looking black man and the other young, small and "Mexican-lookin'." How did Owen introduce him? Christian asked. "Can't remember what his name was," Powers replied. "He said a friend of a partner, or an associate. I shook hands with . . . ah . . . him, and the nigger both." The cowboy commented on the black man's appearance: "He just shined like a diamond in a goat's ass!"

"Was Sirhan with him when he had the roll of thousand-dollar bills?"

"Ah, yeah." Powers was slightly hesitant, perhaps feeling himself slipping into deep waters. He backed off a bit by saying, "There was two guys with him."

"Did the kid get out of the pickup and walk around?" It was a rigged question, but the cowboy wasn't trapped.

"No, he was in the car," he corrected. "He just raised forward there and I shook hands with him."

Shortly after the assassination, Bill Powers told Christian, he returned from a brief trip trying to round up wild mustangs to be broken and trained when his stablehands told him, "The FBI's been looking for you." Two men identifying themselves as Bureau agents had come by in an unmarked beige Chevrolet. Concerned, Powers dialed the FBI resident agency in Riverside but was informed that there was no record there or in Los Angeles that he was being sought.

A day or so later two plain-clothes men showed up, but they said they were from the LAPD. It was a routine interview, apparently prompted by the fact that Powers was still listed as the legal owner of the pickup truck Owen had driven. The policemen mentioned that the truck had been dusted for fingerprints, and that Sirhan's had in fact been found on the glove compartment and rear window.

Then, about a week later, the first pair of detectives reappeared, driving the same Chevrolet. They announced themselves as "FBI" and flashed credentials. They told Powers that the old pickup truck had been recovered abandoned in Barstow, some 130 miles northeast of Los Angeles on the route to Las Vegas, and had been brought back to the FBI crime lab in Los Angeles for fingerprint testing. In a menacing manner they demanded to know what Powers knew about Owen and Sirhan and the RFK case. "They tried to scare me," Powers recounted. "They tried to give me a bunch of bullshit at first. They wanted to make sure I knew who they were, and that they weren't fooling around. All I told them is what they asked me. I didn't make no statements, no nothin'."

Powers said that the putative FBI men handed him a card "and told me that if anybody tried to arrest me or pick me up to phone them before I went with them, that I wasn't to get in no cars or anything like that. They told me it was for my own protection—'they' might bump me off." The cowboy was specifically instructed not even to speak to other law enforcement officers. Turning nastier, the pair intimated that they had been watching Powers, knew of his dalliance with a girl of "jailbait" age, and might have to "bust" him if he didn't "cooperate."

The "FBI agents" returned three times in the next few months. "They asked me something and I'd tell 'em if I wanted to. And if I didn't, I didn't say nothin'.

"I figured it was none of their business if that was Sirhan with Owen in the car," Powers declared. "I mean, I don't care who it was, you know. There's no use gettin' involved. Why should I care who it was, you know. There's no use gettin' involved. Why should I get involved? The only thing it might do is get me killed or something. I'll tell you the truth, I'm kinda scared."

It was the preacher who frightened Powers. "He can have you bumped off. He wouldn't just think about it—he'd do it.

"And then he'd say a little prayer."

After the assassination, Powers told Christian, Owen never returned to Wild Bill's Stables. But five months later, in November 1968, they encountered each other at the Hilton Hay Company in Santa Ana. Owen either knew or guessed that Powers had been questioned by the police, and pumped him on what he told them about "that day" at the stables. "They asked me a lot of questions," Powers replied. "But I didn't say nothin' at all."

Apparently satisfied, Owen pulled Powers off to the side and whispered confidentially about his innocence in the case. As Powers remembered it, the preacher said "well, he guessed he'd kinda got mixed up in the deal. He didn't know anything about it, but he thought they was gonna have him take Sirhan out of the country in that little truck with the horse in back. They'd never look for him back there with the horses."

IT APPEARED TO US THAT THE HILTON HAY COMPANY INCIDENT was an attempt by Owen to quell what suspicion Powers might have of him as anyone other than a victim of circumstances. Once he had established that Powers had not divulged what he saw and heard "that day" at the stables, he probably felt he owed the cowboy some kind of explanation for the roll of $1,000 bills, Sirhan's presence in the Lincoln and Sirhan's fingerprints on the pickup truck.

Had Sirhan's lawyers known about Bill Powers, the whole complexion of the trial might have changed. Powers impressed us as a straight shooter, and we didn't doubt that what he recounted was accurate to the best of his recollection. This raised the question of the supposed FBI agents who had intimidated Powers into silence. They had shown up even before the legitimate LAPD plain-clothes men checking on the ownership of the truck, and had returned several times over the months. It seemed obvious to us that the pair was determined that neither the prosecution nor defense would learn that Powers even existed.

We doubted that they were actually from the FBI. For one thing, the FBI did not have a crime lab in Los Angeles. For another, the Bureau knew nothing about the Jerry Owen angle until a month after the assassination, when George Davis contacted the San Francisco office. At that juncture the FBI, relying on the representations of SUS that the Owen story was spurious, promptly lost interest in it. We had discussed the Owen matter with Roger LaJeunesse, the FBI's top agent on the RFK case, back in May 1969; he said that Captain Brown and Manny Pena had assured him that the hitchhiker story had been gone over with a fine-tooth comb. LaJeunesse had read the SUS summary report on Owen, and while he found it too opinionated by FBI standards, he did not quarrel with its conclusions.

But at the time LaJeunesse had not mentioned Bill Powers and the incident at Wild Bill's Stables, and we now wondered if he knew about them. Christian arranged a meeting and played the tape of his interview with Powers. The agent's pugnacious face writhed in displeasure as he heard Powers' voice spill out of the recorder. SUS had never mentioned Powers or the cowboys despite an agreement for the complete exchange of information. LaJeunesse doubted that anyone from the FBI had ever interviewed Powers and Beckley. Just to make sure, he promised to check the master case index when he got back to the office.

LaJeunesse called back to report that the FBI's index was in fact negative on the cowboys. Moreover, he had phoned the Riverside resident agency and received confirmation from agent Sanford L. Blanton that Powers had called in shortly after the assassination inquiring as to who from the FBI was looking for him. LaJeunesse at first speculated that Powers and the stablehands might mistakenly have assumed that the detectives were from the FBI when they were actually from the LAPD. In fact, the description of the detective who had shoved Powers into the back seat of the beige Chevrolet and gruffly warned him of the danger of talking was very close to that of Manny Pena. But if it was the LAPD, what became of their reports? LaJeunesse conceded that it was highly peculiar that there was not even an allusion to Powers or Beckley or Weatherly in the SUS final report.

ELEVEN DAYS AFTER HE INTERVIEWED POWERS, CHRISTIAN CALLED Chick Gutierrez at the LAPD. After striking out with Johnny Beckley, Gutierrez and his SUS partner Dudley Varney had questioned Bill Powers, but the cowboy, still intimidated by the "FBI agents" and a fear of Owen, had responded only grudgingly and equivocally.

"Did you ever get any reports at all on Sirhan being seen down in Orange County with Jerry Owen?" Christian probed. The former SUS man* sounded surprised that we had gotten wind of the Weatherly Report. Although the Sirhan trial was over, the LAPD remained concerned that Charlie O'Brien might step in and reopen the case on the basis of new evidence. "I think there was some guy that said something about he'd heard of him down there," Gutierrez hedged. "Weatherly said he saw them riding down there, but we followed that up and it turned out to be nothing."

"Another crank?" Christian prodded.

"No, I think the kid just wanted some help—he was incarcerated

---

* Special Unit Senator was officially disbanded on July 25, 1969. This would be our last contact with Gutierrez. In 1972 the forty-year-old physical-fitness buff was stricken with a fatal heart attack. It was said that he had privately voiced doubts about the police conclusion.

on some other thing. He'd heard this other guy talk about Jerry Owen, so I guess he made up the story." But Gutierrez admittedly had no proof that Weatherly was lying. "How are you going to disprove his story unless you put him on a polygraph?" he said. "He was half high on weed and all that. We made a real good follow-up and there was nothing to it."

Funny, Christian thought, the sheriff's deputies who arrested Weatherly made no mention of marijuana in their report, and in fact described him as normal and lucid. But SUS had a habit of slurring witnesses whose accounts did not square with the police version. Like Sandy Serrano. And Vincent DiPierro. And now Dianne Lake, late of the Manson Family. At the time of Christian's call, Gutierrez was working on the yet-unsolved Tate-LaBianca murders that had taken place the previous August. Although there was no evidence that the sixteen-year-old Lake, a fringe member of the Family, was implicated in the murders, Gutierrez tried to coerce her. "I don't know how tight you are with the Family," he asserted. "You're probably real tight with them, but somebody's going to go down the tubes, and somebody's going to get the pill in the gas chamber for a whole bunch of murders which you are a part of, or so some other people have indicated." Then Gutierrez tossed her a life preserver: "I'm prepared to give you complete immunity, which means that if you are straight with me, right down the line, I'll be straight with you, and I'll guarantee that you will walk out of that jail a free woman . . ."*

Gutierrez had absolutely no authority to guarantee immunity— that was a decision for the DA's office, subject to ratification by the court. In any event, Dianne Lake told Gutierrez nothing. She was later interviewed by Inyo County sheriff's deputies, without the threats and false promises, and they secured her cooperation to the point where she became one of the prosecution's most valuable witnesses. As Vincent Bugliosi commented after listening to a tape of Gutierrez's blustering tactics, "I couldn't believe what I was hearing."†

---

* *Helter Skelter*, by Vincent Bugliosi with Curt Gentry (New York: Bantam edition, 1975), p. 204.

† *Ibid.*, p. 203.

FOUR DAYS AFTER TALKING TO GUTIERREZ, CHRISTIAN REACHED Captain Hugh Brown and repeated the question he had put to Gutierrez: Had Brown heard of reports that Owen and Sirhan had been seen together down in Orange County? "There was some kind of report," Brown answered, "where they were supposed to have been seen at some riding stable—which we checked out and was proven erroneous. In other words, the people couldn't identify Owen's picture or Sirhan's picture." Brown was either ignorant of the facts or dissembling: Powers and Beckley were well acquainted with Owen, and could identify him without photographs.

But Brown volunteered a fresh bit of information. Somewhere in the El Monte area (east of Los Angeles, not far from Sirhan's home) Sirhan reportedly rode horses regularly, not with Owen but with somebody else. And there was another stable where Sirhan and Owen were spotted, although not necessarily together. Brown was frustratingly vague, but in his view it didn't really matter. "Every one of those reports that came in was thoroughly checked through," he said, "and none of them proved that these guys were together any place."

ON NOVEMBER 3 CHRISTIAN PHONED CHIEF ROBERT HOUGHTON and charged that Pena and Hernandez never asked Owen, when they interrogated him in San Francisco, whether he had any kind of conspiratorial arrangement with Sirhan. "Oh yes, they did too!" he retorted. "I read the manuscript [sic]. They asked him if he ever knew, if he ever saw him. And that's certainly very pertinent!" Actually, Hernandez had simply asked Owen if the man who shot Kennedy ever offered to buy his horse, which caused the polygraph to give a strong indication of deception. But Christian pointed out that this question stayed within the framework of the hitchhiker story—which no one believed—and consequently was useless in determining if a different relationship had existed.

"Well, I think we basically agree the guy's a liar," Houghton conceded in exasperation. "Our problem was finding concrete proof leading to conspiracy. We couldn't find any."

Christian didn't bring up the Weatherly Report, for Houghton seemed intractable. In two months his book, *Special Unit Senator*, would be out, and it systematically rejected conspiracy theories, including the Jerry Owen angle.*

ON NOVEMBER 11 CHRISTIAN COMPLETED HIS TELEPHONIC ROUNDS of former SUS men by calling Sergeant Dudley Varney, Gutierrez's partner in the Weatherly Report investigation. Asked about Bill Powers, Varney was curious how we knew about the "rumor," which he contended was cooked up by a bunch of cowboys who wanted to sell it to the Los Angeles *Times* at a big price. "You understand cowboys?" he asked. "Well, they're a breed all to themselves. They talk their own language, they have their own humor. The humor will throw you. You can't understand them. They're wild!"

Varney downplayed events at Wild Bill's Stables, saying simply that the police had a report that Owen had rented a stable before the assassination for a horse he was going to sell to Sirhan. SUS uncovered no information that the report was accurate, "so it came to a dead end right there."

Christian was incredulous: "You mean if Owen hadn't rented a stall for a horse for Sirhan at that stable, then—"

"—then I wouldn't have to pursue it further, would I?"

Varney obviously had no inkling of how much we knew, or he wouldn't have expected to put off Christian with that gambit. When Christian kept plugging, Varney revealed that the source of their information was a James Clark, the "other owner" with Powers of the A-Bar-T Stables. Clark told them that he was aware of a rumor that Owen had something to do with Sirhan, but that there had been no arrangement for Sirhan to keep a horse there. Varney said

* Houghton, *op. cit.*, p. 148. Houghton described our theory: "The clergyman, the two journalists argued, feared he would be uncovered, now that Sirhan had been captured alive. So he had come to the police with his 'discrepancy-ridden' alibi, one designed to establish his 'innocent' contact with Sirhan. . . . Actually, they alleged, he was part of the 'get-away' plan, and should have been waiting with his truck and horse at the side exit of the hotel the night of June 4–5."

this indicated that Powers either was lying or was "honestly mistaken."

Could the SUS duo have been that confused? Christian wondered. It had been Weatherly who was mistaken in naming the A-Bar-T in place of Wild Bill's Stables. Apparently sensing that we knew more than he had thought at first, Varney pulled out his files, and flipping through the pages, gave a brief rundown of their interview of Powers. The cowboy said that he sold the pickup truck to Owen in May 1968, at which time the preacher was accompanied by a large Negro. Owen had at least one $1,000 bill covering what might have been a Montana bankroll, and when Powers couldn't change it, Owen gave him $100 as down payment. Nothing was recorded about Powers' mentioning a third man being in the preacher's company.

This version was a far cry from what Powers had told us. A few basic elements were there, but they were telescoped in time so that they all took place on the day Owen bought the truck. It was a Montana bankroll, not the real thing, as Powers had insisted to us. And there was no Lincoln Continental, and no "skinny man in the back seat." Of course, Powers might not have been forthcoming with Gutierrez and Varney because of their heavy-handed approach.

Varney claimed that Powers had made some conflicting statements, and that SUS had requested him to come in to headquarters to clear them up. But they canceled the request after finally locating Johnny Beckley. The way Varney told it, Beckley denied ever seeing Sirhan. Yes, he had seen Owen riding along the Santa Ana River bed many times, but not with Sirhan or anyone who resembled him.

For SUS, that perfunctory denial was sufficient to mark the Weatherly Report "closed."

10

Flying Bullets

OUR INVESTIGATION REMAINED OPEN. WE WERE STILL STUMPED as to the identity of the bulky black ex-fighter who had been in the front seat of Owen's Lincoln. Whoever he was, he was a prime witness.

Doug Lewis, the trainer of "Irish Rip" O'Reilly, had provided a possible clue when Christian interviewed him about Owen's appearances at the Coliseum Hotel. Lewis had said that he was filling in for one Johnny Gray, O'Reilly's regular trainer who supposedly was working temporarily with another boxer. From Lewis' description, Gray might be our man. But we had no idea of his current whereabouts, even though we'd been trying to locate him on general principle for several months. Anyone who knew Owen was worth talking to, we believed from the very outset.

On a hunch Christian called Owen's younger brother, Richard Owen, an instructor at Los Angeles Trade Tech College. He didn't know Gray, but he was familiar with a man named Edward E. Glenn who had claimed he was O'Reilly's co-manager with his brother and footed the bills for the fighter's stay at the Coliseum Hotel. Perhaps Glenn would know where Gray was. Glenn was president of the Midland Oil Company of Wyoming, which purportedly was exploring for oil in that state. Glenn had sold stock in the company to Richard Owen and several other instructors. When he became uneasy about his investment, Owen said, Glenn assigned him "stock" in O'Reilly as a good-faith gesture. Glenn left Los Angeles immediately after the assassination and Richard Owen had not heard from him since.

A check with Dun & Bradstreet disclosed that Midland Oil had been headquartered in Littleton, Colorado, in 1968 but had disappeared, abandoning a single wildcat well in Lusk, Wyoming. The dry-hole venture was under investigation by the Attorney General of Wyoming for possible violation of state securities laws regarding the sale of unregistered stock and fraud.*

Since Glenn appeared to have been a fast-buck operator in several states, we threw his name at FBI agent Roger LaJeunesse. "How did you get on to him?" LaJeunesse asked with an astonished look on his face. Yes, he said, the mysterious Mr. Glenn had come to the attention of the Bureau. Glenn moved in circles known to have right-wing views and underworld ties. His headquarters had been in Littleton, all right, but he frequently ranged to Los Angeles, San Diego, Phoenix, Albuquerque, Dallas, Miami, New Orleans and Chicago as well as Central and South America. His line? "Oil-equipment salesman."

"You guys know Jim Braden?" LaJeunesse asked, knowing the answer full well. "He and Glenn pal around together on occasion— from Miami to San Diego—with stops in between like Dallas and New Orleans."

---

* Christian telephone conversation with the Wyoming Attorney General's Office, November 1969.

Jim Braden had been detained by Dallas sheriff's deputies minutes after the assassination of John Kennedy after being found on the third floor of the Dal-Tex Building on Dealey Plaza, across the street from the building from which Lee Harvey Oswald allegedly fired at the President. Braden told the deputies that he was an "independent oil dealer" from Los Angeles and that he had walked in off the street to try to find a telephone. He was released.*

However, Turner had suspected that there was more to Jim Braden than met the eye, so in 1967, while visiting Los Angeles, he tried in vain to find him at the two addresses given on the Dallas sheriff's report. However, the report had Braden's California driver's license number scrawled on it, which led Turner to a posh Beverly Hills office building whose directory listed Braden under the Empire Oil Company. But the receptionist said that Braden traveled most of the time and only stopped by to pick up his mail.

Turner handed over his findings to Peter Noyes, the CBS producer who had excellent sources in the Los Angeles area. Noyes obtained a three-page rap sheet under FBI Number 799 431 showing that Jim Braden was one of several aliases for Eugene Hale Brading. LAPD intelligence files revealed that Brading had hung around with Mafia heavies, among them Jimmy "The Weasel" Fratiano, described as "the executioner for the Mafia on the West Coast," and the Smaldone brothers of Denver. In 1956 the LAPD tied Brading in with two California syndicate men operating the Sunbeam Oil Company in Miami, characterizing Sunbeam as "a pure front for con men schemes." Noyes found out that Brading's Empire Oil Company also had an office in New Orleans, and that Brading was in Dallas on the day of the JFK shooting with the permission of his parole officer, who reported that Brading "planned to see Lamar Hunt and other speculators while there." On the day before the assassination, Brading did see Lamar Hunt and his brother Nelson Bunker Hunt, executives of the Hunt Oil Company. The patriarch of the family, H. L. Hunt, was noted for his ultra-right activism, and Nelson Bunker Hunt helped pay for the full-page ad in the Dallas *Morning News* of November 22, 1963, that

---

* Warren Commission, Decker Exhibit No. 5323, Vol. 19, p. 469.

showed a picture of John Kennedy with the legend "WANTED FOR TREASON."

From what Noyes was able to learn from his law enforcement sources, Brading was a syndicate courier transporting large amounts of cash around the United States and to Europe. His home base was the luxurious La Costa Country Club north of San Diego, built with Teamsters loans and run by the Las Vegas syndicate of Moe Dalitz. Following the Robert Kennedy assassination, Noyes tipped off Robert Houghton about Brading's curious background, and Houghton dispatched "Chick" Gutierrez to La Costa to question him. Brading admitted that he had been in Los Angeles the night RFK was shot, but claimed he was at the Century Plaza Hotel, a half-hour drive from the Ambassador.* SUS was apparently satisfied with the alibi, for Houghton chalked up the matter to "historical coincidence." In *Special Unit Senator* the chief alluded to Brading by saying: "In addition to his Mafia and oil contacts, he was friendly with 'far-right' industrialists and political leaders of that [the Texas] area."†

After LaJeunesse's startling revelation, Christian put in a call to Edward Glenn's home in Colorado. Mrs. Glenn answered. "This is the Attorney General's Office," he bluffed in his most official voice. It worked. Mrs. Glenn said her husband was out of the country, probably in South America. She related that on the day Robert Kennedy was shot her husband had called from Los Angeles and told her how his new partner, Jerry Owen, had had a "brush with history" by picking up Sirhan. Several months before, Mrs. Glenn said, Owen had wanted her husband to play some role in his projected television series, but he had declined for reasons unknown to her.

Yes, she had heard of Johnny Gray. In fact, he had called frantically only a few weeks before and told her husband about a shooting scrape he and Owen had just been in. Mrs. Glenn read off Gray's unlisted number in Los Angeles. Then she volunteered

---

* Peter Noyes, *Legacy of Doubt* (New York: Pinnacle Books, 1973), pp. 37–38.

† Houghton, *op. cit.*, p. 158.

that Owen frightened her, especially when he went off on his religious tangents, and that she had been suspicious of his story about Sirhan from the moment she heard it.

"My husband isn't in any trouble, is he?" she asked plaintively. Without answering, Christian thanked her for her help.

WHEN CHRISTIAN MADE A PRETEXT CALL TO THE HOLLYWOOD DI-vision of the LAPD, an officer in the records section obligingly read off the report of the shooting incident involving Owen and Gray.* It stated in part that on August 14, 1969, "Owen was northbound on Vermont Canyon Road from the Griffith Park Observatory, in Owen's '65 Continental being driven by a friend. [Note that Johnny Gray's name is omitted here—a highly unlikely oversight, as we'll soon see.] They were going downhill on Vermont Canyon Road about 25 miles an hour. Suspects' vehicle approached from the opposite direction. The vehicle passed Owen's vehicle and made a U-turn and swung in behind his car. They pulled up alongside of Owen's car. Suspect #1 pointed an unknown type rifle at his moving vehicle and fired two rounds. He states there were no hits on the vehicle. The suspects car was described as a '67 or '68 Mustang, dark blue." Complainant Owen described the man who fired as being in his late twenties, tall, with a "hippie haircut." The driver was a black man with a heavy build and long hair.

The shooting incident gave Christian a handle for contacting Johnny Gray. He reached Gray on his unlisted number on November 20, 1969, again posing as an "Attorney General" deputy. Gray said that in mid-August he was standing by while Owen was making a phone call from a booth outside the Carolina Pines restaurant in Hollywood when a dark-blue Mustang with two occupants pulled up to the curb. One of them yelled, "You son of a bitch! You better keep your motherfuckin' mouth closed!" The car sped off. Gray wasn't sure whom they were yelling at or why, but he was frightened.

He and Owen hopped into Owen's Lincoln Continental and

* Report No. DR 69-589-101, written by Officer Howard Moses, August 14, 1969.

hurried to the preacher's apartment on Gramercy Place in Holly-wood that he had moved into after selling the home in Santa Ana. As they were pulling into a parking space Owen cried out, "That looks like the same car that those guys were in!" The suspect car wheeled into a U-turn, and Owen yelled, "Yes, it is!" and dashed for his apartment building. The two men got out and started after him. Soon they returned to their car and sped away. Owen then returned to the Lincoln and slipped into the back seat.

Gray began to stammer at this point, and complained about having high blood pressure. Christian prompted him, "What next, Gray?"

Gray related that after a while Owen decided, "Well, take me for a ride. I gotta get all this worry and pressure off me!" Gray drove the Lincoln while Owen slumped in the back seat. At the preacher's direction he drove past the crowd entering the Holly-wood Greek Theater and up into Griffith Park near the observatory. It was dusk. Suddenly the same Mustang came out from a hillside tunnel and pulled abreast of them. One of the men raised some-thing. "I figured it was a rifle," Gray recounted. "I says, 'Duck, Reverend! I think they got a rifle!' And just about that time they passed by. *Whing! Whing!* They fired two shots right straight through the car." Only moments before, Owen had instructed Gray to "switch open" the windows, and Gray assumed the bullets went right through.

The story had an even more bizarre ending. Owen ordered Gray to rush to the Hollywood Station. Gray said that as they were sitting in a room reporting the shooting, "two shots went off by the window there. And the officers said, 'Well, it's just a couple of the boys, ah, you know, havin' some fun.' But it wasn't no fun to us, you know. This was right in the police station. Down in Holly-wood! *Bang! Bang!*, you know, two bullet shots. Well, we hit the deck and I didn't know what the hell was goin' on."

Christian made a mental note of the fact that the police report had mentioned nothing about any gunshots at the station. Gray doubted that the two shooting episodes had been an innocent joke. In fact, he sensed that the entire evening's events might have been staged by the police—that the occupants of the Mustang "might have been two police officers, a colored and a white officer." Gray said he was so frightened that his blood pressure shot up to the danger level, and he had to be rushed to the hospital.

Christian broached the subject of Wild Bill's Stables in Santa Ana, and Gray remembered being there with Owen. "Were you with him there just before the assassination of Senator Kennedy, the day before?" Christian asked.

"Yeh, uh-huh," Gray acknowledged, apparently not suspecting what Christian was leading up to.

"You and Owen there in the Lincoln?"

"Yeh."

"Our report says there was a colored fellow in the front seat with him." Christian pretended that he was reading from an official report.

"That was—that was me," Gray said, his voice beginning to waver.

The boxing trainer recalled vaguely that Owen had driven down there to find out about "a trailer or horses or something." Gray was introduced to the owner of the stables but remained in the car while the business was being discussed.

"Did Owen have a big wad of money with him when you were down at the stables that day?" Christian wanted to know.

"Every time I've seen him he's got a wad," Gray said evasively.

"Where does he get that money?"

"I don't know."

"Preaching?"

"I don't know. It might have been from preachin'. Maybe he had other things, I don't know. He can be broke when he wants to be broke." Gray gave a forced laugh.

Christian sprung the loaded question: "Was there a skinny Mexican kid or anything with you that day?"

Gray haltingly said he couldn't remember; then said no.

"Are you *sure* there was nobody with you?" Christian asked with a tone of skepticism.

"I can't remember exactly," Gray said. "There might have been, but you know, I'm just sitting there, and I been to the hospital twice." He lapsed into his high-blood-pressure complaint.

After hanging up, Christian analyzed the situation. Gray had talked fairly freely about the shooting incident, but once the topic shifted to the stables he became extremely nervous and flustered. The "You son of a bitch! You better keep your motherfuckin' mouth closed!" threat hurled at Owen and Gray from the Mustang had an altogether familiar ring. It was virtually word for word the threat Owen claimed he had received twice over the phone shortly after the assassination. Gray was apparently being truthful as far as he went, but there were sensitive areas he was obviously terrified to get into.

Christian decided to make another run at him, calling on Thanksgiving Day with the excuse that he had developed new information. "Did Owen introduce you to the young man in the back seat?" Christian asked.

"No," Gray muttered. "The only one I was introduced to was the man at the stables. He didn't introduce me to the other fella." Christian permitted himself a slight smile—Gray had now let slip that there was an "other fella" in the back seat.

Well, Christian went on, the man in the back seat had been identified by other witnesses as Sirhan Sirhan. "Is that right?" Gray responded. "Well, it could have been . . . I really can't say." Gray allowed as to how Owen picked up an awful lot of different people. "I don't remember if he was Sirhan or who he was," Gray said, " 'cause I've met a lot of people with him."

Christian kept his questioning on the positive side by asking, "Did Sirhan leave the house with you and Owen that day?"

There was a pause, followed by raspy coughing. Gray moaned about another siege of high blood pressure coming on.* Christian left him to his holiday, thankful for the bountiful information.

---

* The high-blood-pressure aspect seemed to fit into the theme that either the Griffith Park attackers had deliberately missed their target(s) or fired blanks. If Gray's blood pressure was dangerously high in the first place, the sudden shock of gunfire might cause a fatal stroke or heart attack, both of which could be classified as "natural causes." The gun explosion at the Hollywood Station makes this all the more a distinct possibility—that Gray had been a witness to things that neither Owen nor the police wanted him capable of repeating. (And remember: Gray's name did *not* appear on the LAPD interview.) All this took place shortly after Christian had begun to inquire around the local boxing emporiums about the background and location of Johnny Gray (early July 1969). We knew he'd been close with Owen for some years.

SINCE THE UNEXPECTED WAS NOW BECOMING COMMONPLACE, WE took the next bit of news in stride. On August 16, two days after the shooting scene in Griffith Park, Owen reported to the Hollywood Division that his Gramercy Place apartment had been burglarized and all his records taken. This meant, he said, that he could not account for his "love offerings" income for the year 1968. The police report filed by Owen noted that the burglar had scrawled *"Remember S. S."* on the bottom of the toilet seat, which the preacher took to mean Sirhan Sirhan. When Christian relayed the news to Turner, the ex-FBI man asked, "Was the seat up or down?"

"Up," Christian replied.

"Ah ha," Turner deduced, "we have a male suspect."

Owen evidently found no humor in the latest developments. On the day after Christian's second "Attorney General" interview with Gray, Owen precipitously moved out of the Gramercy Place apartment and headed for a remote spot high up in the Sierra Nevadas. But he left behind yet another bizarre episode that we would not learn about for several months. On January 8, 1970, Christian finally reached Captain Hugh Brown after repeated attempts and asked him if he knew that Owen had been shot at. "I don't think that ever got to us," Brown replied. "I'm sure it didn't happen, or I would have known about it." Christian didn't argue.

The two renewed their argument over the police position that Owen had told the hitchhiker story to reap publicity. To try and bolster his point, Brown suddenly revealed that the preacher had also injected himself into the Tate-LaBianca murder case. He reported to the Hollywood Division that the day before the killings he picked up a hitchhiker named William Garretson—the nineteen-year-old caretaker of the Tate estate whom the police held for several days as a suspect before releasing him. Owen said that Garretson was looking for extra work as a dishwasher, and he took the young man to the Carolina Pines restaurant to introduce him to the management. (The Carolina Pines was the origin point of the Griffith Park shooting incident, which occurred five days after the Tate-LaBianca murders.)

However, Brown said the police had dismissed this latest episode as simply another publicity stunt by Owen. "He just wanted to get himself involved," Brown said. "Anything that gets a little publicity he wants to get involved with, apparently."

But Christian was not so sure. He asked Brown to name a newspaper or broadcast facility approached by Owen. He couldn't recall any names. Christian then checked every media outlet in the Los Angeles area for the pertinent period, with negative results. Once again, Owen's purpose in involving himself in still another major murder case did not seem to be "publicity."*

DURING HIS DAYS AS KHJ'S ACE NEWSCASTER, BAXTER WARD HAD a reputation not only for courage and tenacity, but an occasional touch of impulsiveness. For this reason Christian blocked out the names on the Weatherly Report and our follow-up investigation when he handed Ward a copy in the spring of 1971. Ward could be a valuable ally, but Christian didn't want a story put on the air that might jeopardize Weatherly and the cowboys.

But as fate would have it, Bob Kaiser had just joined Ward's news staff and he was able to fill in the names and details so that Ward could pick up the story and run with it. Ward began by querying the LAPD, which summarily dismissed Weatherly's story. This only made him more suspicious, so he went ahead and talked to Weatherly at his parents' home in Chino. Ward was so impressed with the young man's evident sincerity and the consistency of his story that he decided to put it on the air. He paraphrased the script, changing names and places and altering events to protect the witnesses. Afterward, Ward told us that he had hoped his "bombshell" story would force an official review of the case.

Ward broadcast the story in early August 1971. A few days

---

* In late 1975 we informed Vince Bugliosi about Owen's "involvement" in the Manson case. His reaction was instant: "I personally examined every single LAPD report in that case, including those dealing with publicity freaks and the nuts. Owen's name never appeared anywhere. If it had—especially after his involvement in the Kennedy case—you can bet I'd have found out why, fast!"

later, at approximately three o'clock in the morning on August 11, Weatherly pulled into the driveway of his parents' home. Two teen-age companions were with him, both slumped in their seats, dozing. A shot from a high-powered rifle pierced the night air. The bullet smashed through the rear window of Weatherly's 1957 sedan, exploding it into shards of flying glass. The missile narrowly missed Weatherly's head. His foot hit the accelerator, and the car crashed into a tree next to the house, its horn stuck and one headlight smashed. The three young men lay frozen, terrified that the unseen gunman would approach the car and fire again.

A shaken Baxter Ward went on the air that same evening to report the attempt on the life of a crucial witness in the RFK case. Still disguising Weatherly's identity and whereabouts, he reconstructed the incident with diagrams and photographs of the damaged vehicle. He ruled out the idea of a "scare shot"—the bullet had come too close. He pointed out that the target was "part of a small, very small group, who claim to have some knowledge of Sirhan prior to the Kennedy assassination. They knew him. That group had members who say they saw Sirhan several times with a man later identified as a possible co-conspirator. They say that co-conspirator was with Sirhan prior to the assassination."

The newsman pleaded that the shooting merited an immediate and thorough official investigation. "We would be relieved if there were nothing to it," he closed. "But we would be shocked if it were true that the links do exist, and that a man was marked for murder because he knew of the links."

Ward conveyed his concern to U.S. Attorney Robert L. Meyer, who promised to look into the matter. Meyer called in the FBI. But the Bureau subsequently phoned Ward's office with the message that it had no interest in a purely "local matter."

11

Bucking City Hall

WE HAD NOW GONE ABOUT AS FAR AS WE COULD WITH OUR own investigation. To sum up, no fewer than three cowboys were able to put Owen's relationship with Sirhan in a context different from Samaritan and hitchhiker. They had seen the two riding horses together along the Santa Ana River bed, and believed that it was Sirhan in the Lincoln on the day Owen was flaunting the thick roll of $1,000 bills. Johnny Gray had grudgingly confirmed this sighting, and obviously knew much more than he cared to admit. There were other witnesses, such as the Reverend Jonothan Perkins, who had much to tell, and other leads, such as Owen's connection with Edward Glenn, that needed exploring.

The investigation was at the stage where it should pass into the hands of a special prosecutor or grand jury with the power to subpoena witnesses and suspects, grant immunity and send its own investigative staff into the field.

We were in a quandary as to where to turn. The LAPD was stonewalling the case. The FBI door had been shut by J. Edgar Hoover himself, who took the unprecedented step, according to LaJeunesse, of ordering all the files shipped back to Washington. Not only had Sam Yorty ignored us, he turned out to be an old pal of Jerry Owen's. District Attorney Evelle Younger had made it abundantly clear that he would resist any attempt to reopen the investigation. The cover-up had become institutionalized on a national scale.

At this point W. Matthew Byrne, the U.S. Attorney in Los Angeles, entered the picture. Handsome Matt Byrne was one of the ambitious young Kennedy New Frontiersmen who would continue to rise in succeeding Administrations. In the late summer of 1969 Frank Burns, Jesse Unruh's lieutenant, had discussed the case privately with him. Byrne was interested in what we had found out, and Burns suggested that we give him a call.

"Cops?" Byrne exclaimed after Christian gave him a rundown that included the intimidation of Bill Powers by FBI imposters. He apparently sensed the same thing that Charlie O'Brien had complained about—manipulation of the investigation at a high level of the LAPD. Byrne asked for copies of what material we had that might fall under federal purview—as, for example, impersonating an agent of the FBI. He called Christian back shortly after receiving the package. He was impressed with what he had seen, he said, and wanted to arrange a meeting with us and Bob Kaiser. "But I'm not sure what I can do about it," he remarked, referring to the array of political power lined up against any reopening.

The meeting never came off. At the last minute Kaiser had to fly back to New York to meet with his editor, and time ran out on a rescheduling. President Nixon appointed Byrne to the Scranton Commission on campus violence, and, later, to the federal bench.*

---

* In 1973 Matt Byrne was the presiding judge in the Daniel Ellsberg trial. It was during the trial that he took his celebrated strolls with John

Nixon named Robert L. Meyer, a conservative Republican from a staid Los Angeles law firm, to succeed Byrne as U.S. Attorney. On the face of it, it did not look very likely that Meyer would buck the establishment by reviewing the RFK case. But through a mutual friend we put out feelers, and the feedback was positive. A discreet meeting was proposed at a residence in Beverly Hills which Charlie O'Brien would also attend. At the last minute, however, Meyer called it off, saying he was busy with other matters and would reschedule it. It never happened.

Meyer, it turned out, had already started marching to a different drumbeat from Nixon and his Attorney General, John Mitchell. The rift came to a head in 1971 when Meyer stepped in to prosecute three Los Angeles policemen involved in the fatal "mistake" shooting of two Mexican nationals after local authorities, most prominently Evelle Younger, had turned the other way. According to the Los Angeles *Times*, LAPD Chief Edward M. Davis told the Justice Department in Washington that Meyer had been overheard to say that "prosecution of cops was good for President Nixon's political future." The remark was reported to Davis by Manny Pena, by now the LAPD's liaison with Sam Yorty's City Hall.* Caught in a squeeze play by Yorty and the LAPD, Meyer was forced to resign.†

OUR LAST HOPE FOR INTERVENTION RESTED WITH THE CALIFORNIA Attorney General's office and Charlie O'Brien. In the summer of 1970 O'Brien marched into the office of his boss, Thomas C. Lynch, to announce that he had something important to discuss about the RFK assassination. Lynch, a lugubrious Irishman who had been elected to the post after years as San Francisco's DA, was the only

---

Ehrlichman during which the possibility of his being named FBI director was brought up. Byrne dismissed the charges against Ellsberg on the basis that he had been illegally wiretapped.

* Los Angeles *Times* (January 19, 1972).

† On November 14, 1972, Meyer was found dead at the wheel of his car in the parking lot of the Orange County Court House. The *Times* reported: "Friends were surprised at word of his death; they knew of no history of heart trouble."

Democrat left holding statewide office after Reagan's Republican sweep of 1966. Sixty-five and ailing, Lynch was on the verge of retirement. He had long since let it be known that he would not run again, and he had hand-picked O'Brien to run as his successor.

This morning Lynch looked more doleful than usual. He had known for some time that his chief deputy suspected malfeasance in the Kennedy case, and he had ducked a showdown in the hope the issue would fade away. Now he knew it wouldn't.

We had been keeping O'Brien posted on developments in our investigation, and he had reciprocated by telling us what he knew through his law enforcement contacts. O'Brien gave Lynch a brief status report and reminded him that the AG had the responsibility of taking over when local law enforcement is inadequate or obstructing justice. Earlier he had sent Lynch a memorandum outlining the case against the Los Angeles authorities.

"Tom," O'Brien told Lynch, "I think we should go for a special prosecutor to investigate the Kennedy case."

"Charlie," Lynch replied, "you can do anything you want after you're elected. But as long as I'm attorney general of this state, we'll make no such move."

O'Brien strenuously argued that the case should be pre-empted without delay, but Lynch was adamant. The discussion ended on an acrimonious note, with O'Brien hinting he might "go public" with the issue, and an ashen, trembling Lynch shouting that if he did, he would revoke his endorsement.*

Lynch's determination to leave office without fuss did not enhance O'Brien's election chances. O'Brien was pitted against Evelle Younger, and although it was not a motivating factor in his desire to reopen the case, he realized that it could tip the scales. If a grand jury was merely convened, it would be politically embarrassing to Younger because of his role in prosecuting Sirhan and shutting down the conspiracy angle. And if a grand jury returned indictments, Younger's whole political future—he intended to run for governor eventually—could go up in smoke.

But to simply make a campaign issue out of the assassination was a different matter, and O'Brien's brain trust counseled against

* Authors' interview with O'Brien, August 1971.

it. What baffled us, however, was O'Brien's reticence to exploit another whiff of scandal that had been hanging over Younger's head for some time. The central figure was a high-powered Beverly Hills attorney named Jerome Weber whose clientele numbered celebrities such as Desi Arnaz and crime-syndicate kingpins such as Frank M. "Big Frank" Matranga of San Diego. Interestingly, Weber was a past president of the Saints and Sinners Club, whose meeting Jerry Owen purportedly attended as he waited to sell Sirhan the horse. And Weber was Owen's first attorney in the suit against KCOP television.

The potential scandal revolved around Thomas E. Devins, a former parking-lot attendant who had talked a wealthy widow out of a large chunk of money and then taken her to Europe, where she disappeared (her remains were later found in the Swiss Alps). An indictment for murder was pending against Devins. Weber told him that he could quash the case through his "influence" inside the DA's office. According to grand jury testimony, Weber's asking price was $35,000, of which $25,000 would go to two top DA investigators. To demonstrate his "control" of the situation, the attorney said he would have a pesky DA investigator transferred so that his "two top investigators" could take charge. The transfer went through. Then Weber told Devins that he had arranged for senior investigator George Murphy to accompany the investigator to "control" an out-of-town interview. We considered this of more than passing interest, since Murphy and chief investigator George Stoner had been Younger's two top men on the RFK case, and had put down Owen as nothing more than an unfunny clown.

Devins paid part of the money, but then, perhaps sensing a double cross, went to the AG's office and complained of being blackmailed. O'Brien's agents hid a transmitter in his clothing and sent him in to bargain further with Weber. The attorney produced a confidential report from the DA's office to prove his connections. Devins expressed skepticism: "Have they ever failed to come through—that is, have they ever taken any bread and then that's it?" "No, no, no," Weber replied. "Never in a million years."

Weber was convicted of bribery and eventually disbarred. When he appealed the conviction, none other than Jerry Owen supplied an affidavit on his behalf. Owen claimed that he was introduced to

Devins by Weber, who said, "Curly, this is Mr. Devins. Mr. Devins, this is Curly Owen; he is a minister." Several months later Owen and Devins met on the Sunset Strip and Devins tried to get Owen to say he overheard Weber solicit the bribe "to give to somebody downtown to take care of the thing." Owen said he answered, "No, I didn't hear that." The California Supreme Court, in denying Weber's appeal, opined that "Owen's testimony was incredible" and full of "discrepancies and suspicious statements."*

The Weber case was potential dynamite, since Younger had made no move to clean house by singling out the corrupt investigators and prosecuting them. But O'Brien never detonated it, electing instead to try to outgun Younger on his strong point of law and order. A major general in the Air Force reserve, Younger was firmly identified with the Nixon Administration's hard line that was in vogue before Watergate. O'Brien lost in a photo finish—by less than one third of 1 percent of the total votes.

For the time being, at least, we had no place to turn. But in the meantime, a controversy was shaping up that would cast extreme doubt on the police position that Sirhan, and Sirhan alone, gunned down Robert F. Kennedy.

* Decision June 20, 1974, California Supreme Court, Case No. Cr. 16157.

12
Too Many Guns– Too Many Bullets

ONE MORNING IN AUGUST 1971, VETERAN CRIMINALIST WILliam W. Harper pulled out of the driveway of his Pasadena home on a quiet, tree-lined street within punting distance of the Rose Bowl. As he headed downtown to pick up his wife he noticed that a blue Buick seemed to be following him. He made several evasive turns, but the car kept on his tail. He could see two men in it, both wearing workmen's caps pulled down over their foreheads. Harper floored the accelerator pedal and put the family car through its paces. His pursuers gave chase. As he spun back and forth in the maze of residential streets, his car hit a deep dip. Coming out of it with the rear end bouncing high, he heard a muffled explosion from the rear and the familiar slap of a bullet striking metal.

Eluding the other car, Harper drove straight to the home of another prominent criminalist, Raymond Pinker, the retired founder of the LAPD crime lab. They examined the dent in the rear bumper and agreed that it had been caused by a slug from a high-powered gun—possibly a .45 or a .357 Magnum. Harper shuddered to think what might have happened had he not hit the dip at that moment. If the car had been running level, the shot could have gone through the rear window and struck him in the head.

The attempt on Harper's life came within days of the sniper attack on John Chris Weatherly in Chino. As in the case of Weatherly, the timing was too exquisite to ignore: Harper was scheduled to testify the next day before a grand jury investigating the handling of firearms evidence in the RFK case. Harper had set in motion the train of events leading to the grand jury probe by fathering, in 1970, what has become known as the "second gun" theory.

In over three decades as a qualified criminalist, Harper had conducted thousands of examinations for both prosecution and defense, and testified as a firearms expert in more than three hundred criminal trials around the nation. For seven years he had been a forensic science consultant to the Pasadena Police Department. His crime lab is in a detached structure in the backyard of his old brown-shingle home. It is a warren of scientific instruments, weapons mounted on the walls, blown-up photographs of footprints, tire treads and expended bullets, and shelves of criminalistics texts. A crusty septuagenarian with a dry sense of humor, Bill Harper labors under a green celluloid eyeshade like those worn by old-time city editors.

Initially, Harper had no special interest in the RFK case, but he belongs to a dwindling breed of criminalists who jealously guard the integrity of their profession. For some time he had been double-checking the work of LAPD laboratory examiner DeWayne Wolfer. Harper was skeptical about the quality of Wolfer's work. This doubt first cropped up in the 1967 trial of Jack Kirschke, a former Los Angeles deputy DA charged with the love triangle murders of his wife and another man. The cocksure Wolfer displayed blown-up photographs of bullets to the jury and declared, "No other gun in the world other than Jack Kirschke's could have killed his wife and her lover." Then he disposed of a sticky problem with an inventive explanation. A reconstruction of the crime scene conclusively showed that the victims were lying on their backs in bed when shot, but when discovered, the man's body was on the floor. Wolfer said that a post-mortem settling of body fluids caused the center of gravity to drop, rolling the body onto the floor.

It was a crucial point, for the time element involved tended to discredit alibi witnesses that placed Kirschke halfway to Las Vegas. Called by the defense, Harper and a pathologist disputed the "rolling body" theory—the pathologist sarcastically observed that the only way the body could roll off the bed was if "there was a major earthquake." Both testified that the body had to have been moved by someone after rigor mortis set in. After Kirschke was convicted, an appellate judge agreed that Wolfer had been wrong but ruled that "just as error is not the equivalent of perjury, neither is ignorance."*

Before the Sirhan trial began, Harper warned chief defense attorney Grant Cooper not to accept Wolfer's testimony at face value, but Cooper, as we have seen, adopted a strategy of not contesting the state's contention that Sirhan had acted alone. Harper even approached District Attorney Evelle Younger, an old friend and one-time Pasadena neighbor, cautioning him to "watch out" for Wolfer's handling of the evidence. But during the trial Wolfer's testimony went unchallenged—he did not even bring blown-up photographs to show the jury how he made his bullet comparisons.

After the trial and appeals, Harper decided to make his own review of Wolfer's findings. Late in 1970 he obtained permission from Sirhan's attorney to examine the evidence bullets that were stored in the County Clerk's office. Since they could not be taken out, Harper took along a portable Balliscan camera that he had helped develop. The camera takes a series of photographs of a

* Opinion of Judge George W. Dell, Los Angeles Superior Court, filed November 1, 1973, in response to habeas corpus petition.

cylindrical object rotated in front of its lens; the photographs are later blown up and used for comparison purposes.

Harper focused on two bullets that were relatively unmutilated, one from the body of Senator Kennedy and the other from injured ABC newsman William Weisel. "I can find no individual characteristics in common between these two bullets," he concluded, although warning that his findings should not be regarded as complete and definitive. Harper also compared the bullets with ones Wolfer said he had test-fired from Sirhan's gun. Again, there was no match. Harper's conclusions clashed head-on with Wolfer's trial testimony that the bullets from the victims were fired from Sirhan's gun "to the exclusion of all other weapons in the world."*

Coincidentally with Harper's findings, Wolfer was promoted to chief forensic chemist in charge of the crime lab. Appalled, Harper tried to block the promotion in the Civil Service Commission. He retained attorney Barbara Warner Blehr, who submitted a request for a hearing on Wolfer's competency by setting forth six universally accepted precepts of firearms identification and alleging that in one case (Kirschke) Wolfer violated two, and in the Sirhan case four. For example, Blehr charged that Wolfer apparently did not compare bullets from the victims with bullets test-fired from Sirhan's gun (Serial No. H53725), but with bullets from a similar but unrelated weapon (Serial No. H18602), which was destroyed a month after the testing. This "glaring error," Blehr asserted, led like a chain reaction to the four precept violations.†

Blehr's charges, which could have paved the way for a reversal of Sirhan's conviction, stunned Los Angeles officialdom. District

---

* A bullet is impressed with two types of markings and indentations by the barrel of the gun from which it is fired. One type is distinctive to the make and model of gun. The other, consisting of wear marks, scratches and other imperfections, is distinctive to the individual gun. If sufficient imperfections are present, the bullet can be positively mated to the gun.

† To prove the immutability of the precepts, Blehr attached declarations from three unimpeachable experts: Raymond H. Pinker, who founded the LAPD crime lab in 1929; Dr. LeMoyne Snyder of Paradise, California, a medical doctor and lawyer who wrote the landmark text *Homicide Investigation*; and W. Jack Cadman, chief criminalist for the Orange County crime lab. Implicit in their declarations was a deep concern over Wolfer's competence.

Attorney Joseph P. Busch, Evelle Younger's hand-picked successor, announced that his office would look into the matter and report in three weeks, but his probe actually was strung out for half a year. Police Chief Edward M. Davis immediately created an internal board of inquiry, composed of two deputy chiefs and a commander, but this was widely interpreted as no more than a public relations gesture. Any doubt about Davis' intent was dispelled shortly thereafter when he branded the allegations a vendetta and hailed Wolfer as "the top expert in the country."*

IN ADDITION TO THE FIREARMS EVIDENCE, THERE WAS EYEWITNESS testimony of the most compelling sort to reinforce the theory that more than one gun was fired.

Donald Schulman, a CBS News employee who was behind Kennedy in the pantry and whose line of vision included both Sirhan and a uniformed security guard, told radio reporter Jeff Brant moments after the shooting: "A Caucasian gentleman stepped out and fired three times, the security guard hit Kennedy all three times. Mr. Kennedy slumped to the floor. They carried him away. The security guard fired back."

Brant said, "I heard about six or seven shots in succession. Is this the security guard firing back?"

"Yes, the man who stepped out fired three times at Kennedy,

* Davis is noted for his verbal intemperance, and one of his favorite forums is John Birch Society meetings. He has contended that the city's "swimming-pool Communists" pose a serious threat to law and order, and resisted the hiring of minorities and gays with the crack, "I could envision myself standing on the stage on graduation day and giving a diploma to a 4-foot-11-inch transvestite moron who would kiss me instead of saluting."

A far more qualified evaluator of Wolfer than Davis was of an opposite mind. He was Marshall W. Houts, a former FBI agent, law professor, medico-legal expert and author of *Where Death Delights*, an account of the New York City Medical Examiner's office. Houts was a conservative Republican and Establishment-oriented. Yet he felt obligated to write his friend Evelle Younger a letter, dated June 26, 1971, over "blunders" committed by Wolfer. The purpose of the letter was to warn Younger, who aspired to succeed Ronald Reagan as governor, not to get "burned" by siding with Wolfer.

hit him all three times, and the security guard then fired back . . . hitting him . . ." Schulman apparently thought that the guard fired at Sirhan but accidentally hit Kennedy.

Contemporaneous accounts such as Schulman's are in legal circles considered to be the most reliable, since they are uncontaminated by other witnesses' versions and attempts by police questioners to lead the witness. Although Schulman's language is somewhat cloudy, due no doubt to the trauma of the moment, he clearly stated that both Sirhan and the uniformed guard fired multiple shots. At the time, Schulman was interviewed extensively by the LAPD, but his name was not put on the witness list. They had insisted that he was mistaken in what he saw.

But Schulman's account was consonant with other testimony before the 1968 grand jury that indicted Sirhan. Eyewitnesses uniformly recounted that Sirhan accosted Kennedy from the front, and never got closer than two to three feet from the senator before he was grabbed and wrestled to the floor.

Yet County Coroner Dr. Thomas T. Noguchi, who performed the autopsy, declared that all three of the bullets striking Kennedy entered from the *rear*, in a flight path from down to up, right to left. Moreover, powder burns around the entry wound indicated that the fatal bullet was fired at less than one inch from the head and no more than two to three inches behind the right ear.

Thus it would have been physically impossible for Sirhan to have fired the shots that struck Kennedy. Even allowing for the remote possibility that Kennedy twisted completely around—which is contrary to witnesses' accounts that he threw his arms in front of his face in a protective reaction and sagged backwards—there remained the point-blank shot. Noguchi later revealed that before he entered the grand jury room he was approached by an unnamed deputy DA who solicited him to revise the distance "from one to three inches" to one to three feet.* The coroner bravely refused to "cooperate" with this blatant attempt to suborn perjury.

Instead, an apparently suspicious Noguchi would attempt to set off an independent investigation of his own (coroner's offices call them "inquests"). Alerting Dr. Vincent P. Guinn that he would be

* Los Angeles *Herald-Examiner* (May 13, 1974).

needed to conduct Neutron Activation Analysis tests on the various victim bullets, the LA coroner immediately asked for access to these items of evidence; and he was immediately given the old shell-game treatment by both the LAPD and the DA's office, neither of which would allow Noguchi access to anything.

As the summer of 1968 wore on, not only did the LA coroner find his attempts to subject the official firearms conclusions to formal scientific review rebuffed at every turn, but suddenly he found himself the target of an insidious attack on his competency and character. The crux of these "rumors" centered on Noguchi's handling of the RFK autopsy. Word being passed around (and out) of his office was that he had "bungled" the examination of RFK's body because of his alleged propensity to "take drugs," with resultant "erratic behavior."* And before 1968 ended, Noguchi had found himself suspended from his position as Coroner of Los Angeles County, a suspension he would appeal.

In early 1969 an ex-LAPD officer, Ronnie Nathans, told Christian that he had come in contact with a government official with proof that "[DA] Evelle Younger suppressed evidence" in the RFK case. Naturally intrigued by this information, Christian made contact with the source of the alleged facts, one Dr. Donald Angus Stuart, a deputy coroner in Noguchi's office. During a subsequent session with Stuart (in early February 1969, in the middle of the Sirhan trial), Christian listened as the thick-accented (Australian) medical man implored him to act as a "cover" for "solid information" he wished to pass along to Christian's numerous news-media contacts. The "suppressed evidence" turned out to be verbalized details about Dr. Noguchi's alleged mishandling of the RFK autopsy —which, Stuart insisted, DA Younger was keeping from the public. Did it involve the concealing of anything relating to conspiracy in the case? a puzzled Christian asked. No, just the botching of the official autopsy, Stuart insisted, without saying either how it had been done or why. We dropped the subject and kept our eyes glued on the Sirhan trial.

When Noguchi was summoned to testify at the trial, his actual findings never saw the light of day. The DA's questioning of the

* Los Angeles *Times* (May 27, 1969).

coroner kept away from any conflict whatever with their shaky account of the assassination, and Sirhan's lawyer didn't help when he cut short Noguchi's answers, claiming it was "not necessary" for the coroner to go into "gory detail" about the nature and location of RFK's various wounds.

Noguchi was reinstated after the trial when, during a public hearing on the issue, his lawyer, Godfrey Isaac, pressed for a complete review of the RFK autopsy. A visibly nervous Deputy County Counsel Wartin Weekes shouted, "This is a terribly serious matter!" He strongly urged that no further discussion of the RFK case take place in public because it might trigger off "an international incident." Weekes didn't elaborate. Instead, he sheepishly stipulated that Noguchi's autopsy had been "superior,"* and the hearing was called to a close.

CORONER'S AIDE SEIZED ON PERJURY CHARGE read the headline in the Los Angeles *Herald-Examiner* on February 12, 1972. The story that followed outlined how one Donald Angus Stuart had been arrested that day and charged with perjury "stemming from testimony he gave regarding Dr. Thomas T. Noguchi." It seemed that Dr. Stuart had been discovered not to be a medical doctor at all; he'd been an impostor who had falsified all of his medical-background credentials, including his physician's license, No. 11279, "which had been assigned to a Harry Mathew Edward Lowell in 1914, according to the Illinois State Department of Registration." Suddenly our interest in "Dr." Stuart was rekindled. By this time we'd met criminalist Bill Harper and come to understand his discoveries about the "second gun" aspects of the case, and how Dr. Noguchi's findings fitted in to a T. However, it wasn't until April 15, 1976, that we got our chance to question Dr. Noguchi about the earlier events. Accompanying Dr. Robert J. Joling to the coroner's office at the close of day, Christian (posing as "Jack Cross," a Joling assistant) asked Noguchi two questions:

Q. Do you now believe that Stuart was some kind of "agent-provocateur" sent into your office to destroy you, and the RFK autopsy findings in the process?†

---

* *Ibid.*
† Stuart had arrived on the scene in the spring of 1968.

A. I can't be positive . . . but anything is possible.

Q. Well, do you now believe that the attempt to run you out of office in 1968–69 was directly related to your challenge of the official lone-assassin theory?

A. [Long pause, deep sigh] . . . . Yes.

One other thing: even though found guilty on all counts, Stuart never served a minute in jail or paid a fine—on the recommendations of Younger and his successor, DA Joseph Busch. Even so, the central issue lived on.

WHEN THE "SECOND GUN" CONTROVERSY SHOWED NO SIGN OF DYING, the authorities apparently felt they had to take steps not to get caught short. On July 14, 1971, investigators from the DA's office and Sergeants Phil Sartuche and Chuck Collins, formerly of SUS, secretly questioned a private security guard who had been at Kennedy's elbow when he was shot. The guard, Thane Eugene Cesar, was employed on the day shift at the Lockheed Aircraft plant in Burbank, and was moonlighting for the Ace Guard Service. The sallow-faced, black-haired security man was the only person in the crowded pantry other than Sirhan assumed to have drawn a gun (although witness Donald Schulman said he'd spotted two other revolvers, both of which he insisted had been fired).* Cesar told the DA and LAPD investigators that when he saw Sirhan fire the first shot, "I immediately ducked, and I immediately got knocked down." As he got up, he drew his gun. "Did you ever fire a shot?" he was asked. "No," he replied.

Cesar identified the gun he was carrying as a Rohm .38 caliber revolver that he had purchased especially for his guard duties. Asked if he owned any other handguns—the recovered bullets were .22 caliber—he said that he had had a .22 H & R pistol but sold it to a friend at Lockheed who retired in February 1968 and moved to Arkansas. Cesar mentioned that he had told a police sergeant about this gun when he was interviewed after the assassina-

* In late 1975, testimony and statements would be introduced at official hearings in Los Angeles Superior Court that would confirm three weapons having been drawn (and sighted) at the assassination scene.

tion. "In fact," he said, "I don't remember if I showed it to him, but I did mention that I had a gun similar to the one that was used that night."

The investigators picked up on this contradiction in Cesar's earlier statement that he had sold the gun three months *before* the assassination. Their initial concern was whether he had told any outsider about it, and Cesar said he couldn't be sure. He then backtracked, saying he couldn't have shown it to the sergeant because he had already sold it. That seemed to satisfy the investigators, who told Cesar that it wouldn't be necessary for him to take a lie-detector test.*

It didn't satisfy us, however, and on October 13, 1972, Christian reached the man to whom Cesar had sold the .22 revolver, Jim Yoder, who was living in Blue Mountain, Arkansas. Yoder said that he had been an engineer at Lockheed before retiring in the fall of 1968, and that he knew Cesar casually from the plant. Yoder was uncertain of what Cesar's specific job was, saying that he had "floating" assignments and often worked in an off-limits area which only special personnel had access to. (This was, said Yoder, the CIA-controlled U-2 spy-plane facility.) Yoder related that about a month after the assassination, Cesar showed him the revolver and he offered to buy it to use in the Ozarks after his retirement. At Yoder's request, Cesar later wrote out a receipt that read: "On the day of Sept. 6, 1968 I received $15.00 from Jim Yolder [*sic*]. The item involved is a H & R pistol 9 shot serial No. Y 13332. Thane E. Cesar."

Here was documentary evidence that Cesar sold the gun three months *after* the assassination.

Yoder remembered that during their post-assassination meeting, Cesar dragged out his security guard uniform, the H & R .22 and his .38 pistol, but didn't mention the RFK assassination. But Cesar "looked a little worried and he said something about going to the assistance of an officer and firing his gun. He said there might be a little problem over that."

* Statement of Thane Eugene Cesar, reporter's transcript, Room 113, Bureau of Investigation, DA's Office, 524 North Spring Street, Los Angeles, July 14, 1971, 7:30 P.M., pp. 47–48.

Had Yoder ever been interviewed by the LAPD? Yoder said that the Los Angeles police had called him approximately a year earlier (or shortly after Cesar was questioned), and he gave them essentially the same information. He specifically recalled telling the police about the receipt for the gun dated three months after the assassination. But he no longer had the gun. Around the time that the police called, his home was burglarized and the gun taken.

Once again the LAPD and DA's office had squelched information that might have pointed to a conspiracy. They knew that Cesar sold the gun after the assassination, not before, as he had contended. They knew that if Cesar had been situated to Kennedy's immediate right and rear, as he himself stated, the entry angle of the three bullets striking Kennedy was consistent with that position. They also must have known that Kennedy apparently clutched Cesar's snap-on bow tie from his neck. In the famous news photo showing the senator lying on his back on the floor, his head in a pool of blood, the shiny black tie appears next to his right hand. Cesar conceded that the tie was his and that he returned to the pantry to retrieve it. But no one ever asked him how it had been ripped from his neck.

In early 1976 Allard Lowenstein retrieved a series of assassination broadcast tapes from the Kennedy family and sent them on to West Coast researchers for review. One of those tapes (discovered by Lillian Castellano and Floyd Nelson) involved an interview made by KFWB reporter John Marshall within minutes following the shooting in the kitchen pantry of the Ambassador Hotel:

MARSHALL: I have just talked with an officer who tells me that he was at the senator's side when the shots occurred . . . Officer, can you confirm that the senator has been shot?

OFFICER: Yes, I was there holding his arm when they shot him.

Q. What happened?

A. I dunno. Gentleman standing by the lunch counter there and as he walked up the guy pulled a gun and shot at him.

Q. Was it just one man?

A. No, yeah, one man.

Q. And what sort of wound did the senator receive?

A. Well, from where I could see, it looked like he was shot in the head and the chest and the shoulder.

Q. How many shots did you hear?
A. Four.
Q. You heard four shots. Did you see anyone else hit at that time?
A. Nope.
Q. What is your name, Officer?
A. Gene Cesar.

In Cesar's 1971 interview by Los Angeles law enforcement officials, he (1) denied ever seeing Sirhan himself, only his gun-wielding hand, and (2) stated that he got knocked down and didn't see the actual shooting events after the initial shot was fired. Yet right after the shooting he tells reporter Marshall details that conflict severely with his later version. It is also curious that Cesar's contemporaneous account locates the exact number and placement of shots and wounds in RFK's body—inflicted from the rear, his own conceded position—when no such identifications were possible until doctors examined the senator at a nearby hospital some twenty minutes later.

We find two more of the interview answers equally intriguing: Cesar's reference that "they shot him" and his response "No, yeah, one man" shot RFK. This same information was available or known to Los Angeles officials from the outset.

But instead of focusing on Thane Cesar, District Attorney Joe Busch would swing the beams of his 1971 conspiracy probe onto Bill Harper and Jonn Christian.

IN EARLY AUGUST, BUSCH ANNOUNCED THAT HIS GRAND JURY IN-vestigation had yielded no evidence of a conspiracy to kill RFK, but that the probe would continue in a new direction. Busch said that "serious questions" had surfaced about the handling of the exhibits in the County Clerk's office. He intimated that the bullets Harper had examined had been "tampered with" sometime after the close of the Sirhan trial, and that employees of the Clerk's office might have been derelict in allowing "unauthorized persons" access to the exhibits which had resulted in "altered" and possibly even "switched" evidence. Although he didn't name names, it would soon become clear that his targets were Harper and Christian.

Christian received his first hint of this ominous turn when he got a tip that Bob Kaiser had been put on the DA's payroll as the house "expert" on the investigation. One of Kaiser's duties was to monitor the activities of the "buffs," as the journalist referred to critics of the official position. Coincidentally, a group of the critics held a meeting a few days before Busch's surprise announcement. Christian was there, and so was Kaiser. The discussion centered on the forthcoming testimony of Bill Harper before the grand jury. Kaiser took the position that if the bullets didn't match as Harper claimed, then they probably had been tampered with or possibly even switched by unauthorized persons. It was almost verbatim the line that Busch would soon make public.

"We all know how easy it would be to get hold of that evidence, don't we, Jonn?" Kaiser teased.

Kaiser's seemingly offhand remark took on serious significance a few days later when DA investigators William R. Burnett, Jr., and DeWitt Lightner interviewed Christian. Burnett produced a half-dozen or so slips that Christian had filled out in the County Clerk's office more than two years before when (due to crossed wires in Chief Houghton's office) he was given SUS material on Jerry Owen and copies of pages from Sirhan's notebooks. Christian, noticing that several of the slips had exhibit request numbers added (the numbers not only were in someone else's handwriting but were written with a different style pen), emphatically pronounced the additions crude forgeries. The investigators said nothing.

Christian thought back to a visit Kaiser had paid him just after he obtained the material from the County Clerk. Kaiser had seemed miffed that Christian had the documents, and wanted to know, "How'd you get your hands on those?" Putting on a conspiratorial smile, Christian replied, "I have friends on the inside, too!" Now the flippant remark was coming back to haunt him.

A week later Burnett notified Christian that a subpoena would be issued for him to testify before the grand jury. Fearful of a frame-up, Christian went into hiding and called Charlie O'Brien, who was now in private law practice in San Francisco. O'Brien instructed Christian to sit tight until he could fly down for a conference. When they met O'Brien said he had learned in the interim that the DA intended to charge Christian with stealing the original

Sirhan notebooks. It was obviously an absurd and malicious charge, because not only did Christian have the receipts for the copies he had obtained but the originals were in the custody of the California Supreme Court as it considered a Sirhan appeal. O'Brien was puzzled. "There's something else they're going to try and pin on you," he said. "Something big—but I can't find out what it is."

The nature of the "something big" gradually emerged as the grand jury's closed-door probe progressed. Once Christian had been set up for having obtained the notebook pages "illegally," he would be vulnerable to additional charges that he had bribed or duped employees of the Clerk's Office into allowing him to enter the restricted vault where the Sirhan exhibits were kept, and proceeded to "fondle" or "mutilate" or even "switch" the evidence bullets. The scenario was obviously designed to strike at the heart of the "second gun" theory. DA Busch could claim that the bullets Harper recently examined were not the same bullets or not in the same condition as the bullets examined by the LAPD's DeWayne Wolfer back in 1968.

With Christian missing, Bob Kaiser was called before the grand jury and questioned by hard-nosed Deputy DA Richard W. Hecht. Kaiser repeated Christian's remark about having "friends on the inside" who purportedly helped him gain access to the notebooks. But when Hecht leaned on the journalist, trying to get him to testify that Christian admitted stealing the pages, he balked. "As far as I'm concerned," Kaiser said to Hecht's dismay, "Christian's just a great big bullshitter!"*

Busch's shabby plot was collapsing, and Bill Harper, who appeared despite having been shot at the previous day, finished it off. The straight-talking criminalist stuck by his conclusion that the bullets didn't match, and steadfastly denied any tampering with them. When the DA was unwilling to produce the supposedly altered bullets for inspection, the grand jury had no other recourse than to refuse to return indictments. But it did save face for Busch by issuing a nitpicking criticism of the Chief Clerk's handling of

---

* From his hideout, Christian wrote the grand jury foreman a letter suggesting that O'Brien be called in his stead, which was calculated to panic the DA's office. However, no summons was issued.

the evidence.* Several months later, however, both the Superior Court and the County Chief Administrative Officer decided that the criticism was unwarranted, and scolded the grand jury and Busch for leveling it. But by this time the matter of the "second gun" was in limbo.

IT WAS NEARLY TWO YEARS AFTER BUSCH'S ABORTIVE GRAND JURY probe that former newsman Baxter Ward, who had been elected a county supervisor, called for a new investigation into the "unanswered questions" about whether the fatal bullet came from Sirhan's gun. "Someone is protecting a position or person," Ward charged. "People in authority in Los Angeles County have conspired to prevent the re-examination."†

In May 1974 Ward convened a hearing to present the "second gun" debate in a public forum for the first time. Harper was ailing and could not appear. DeWayne Wolfer refused to appear on orders from Chief Davis, and DA Busch declined on grounds that it was an "improper forum." But Coroner Thomas Noguchi testified as to the entry wounds in Kennedy's back, and the point-blank range from which the fatal bullet had been fired. And two independent firearms experts, Herbert MacDonnell, a New York professor of criminalistics, and Lowell Bradford, a well-known veteran of the California state crime lab, concurred with Harper that the Kennedy and Weisel bullets could "not be identified as coming from the same gun."

MacDonnell and Bradford proposed a straightforward resolution to the bullet controversy: set up a panel of experts to refire the Sirhan weapon, and compare the test bullets with those removed from the victims. The proposal and similar ones had been made before, but Busch and the LAPD had consistently opposed them. But now new forces were coming into play. Former Congressman

---

* At the urging of the DA's office, the grand jury allowed the transcript of the highly suspect and questionable testimony against Christian and Harper to be released to the press—an abject violation of both the legal requisites and the rights of both men. (Unless indictments are issued, grand juries never release such unverified information.)

† Associated Press story datelined Sacramento, April 4, 1974.

Allard K. Lowenstein, an RFK intimate who had led the "Dump LBJ" movement in 1968, had interviewed Busch and police officials about the evidence and come away appalled at the stonewalling and deceit he encountered;* he was stumping the country trying to get the case reopened. And the prestigious American Academy of Forensic Science, composed of the leading firearms, ballistics and pathology experts in the country, accepted the recommendation of its own panel that had studied the bullet evidence and requested that the case be reopened. As then-President of the Academy Dr. Robert J. Joling put it, "Only an independent, non-governmentally controlled body of experts can really be relied upon to let the arrows of truth come to rest wherever that may be."

Although the DA and LAPD continued to insist that only "assassination freaks" were raising questions about the shooting, Baxter Ward finally garnered enough votes from his fellow supervisors to officially request that the Superior Court order a reexamination of the firearms evidence. On September 18, 1975, Presiding Judge Robert A. Wenke complied. A seven-man panel of firearms experts was named.†

No sooner had the panel begun work than it was confronted with several baffling questions. For one, the LAPD unaccountably

* Lowenstein was introduced to us in mid-1973 by mutual friend Robert Vaughn (*The Man from U.N.C.L.E.*), another of RFK's closer friends. In the interview with Busch on January 8, 1974, Lowenstein was accompanied by Mayor Thomas Bradley, himself a former LAPD policeman. Lowenstein has confided to us that Busch overreacted emotionally, suggesting that he was terrified of the repeated challenges to the official stance. If that position was so unassailable, Lowenstein reasoned, why the refusal to open up the LAPD's files?

† Technically, Wenke acted on a civil suit brought by former union official Paul Schrade, who was wounded while in the pantry standing immediately behind RFK. The judge ruled that Schrade had a right to discover if others were responsible for his injuries. CBS Television News joined in the suit, which was supported by the City Council as well as the Board of Supervisors. Interestingly, the DA's office selected as its expert on the panel Alfred Biasotti of the state crime lab, who was on record as backing DeWayne Wolfer in the Jack Kirschke–case ballistics controversy. And Attorney General Evelle Younger picked Cortland Cunningham of the FBI crime lab, who had been the focal point of scientific dispute in the John Kennedy case.

could not produce the laboratory records supporting its claim that in 1968 it test-fired eight bullets from Sirhan's gun. For another, the gun's bore was heavily coated with lead, yet copper-jacketed bullets such as Sirhan allegedly fired leave a lead-free bore. The panel simply noted the leaded condition—two copper-jacketed bullets were fired to clean out the lead so that the testing could go ahead—and did not speculate on how it happened.

On election day (June 4) Sirhan had practiced rapid-shooting for about seven hours on a San Gabriel range, using unjacketed "wad cutter" target bullets which deposit lead in the bore. If this was the source of the extreme leading, he could not have fired copper-jacketed bullets of the type recovered from the victims and supposedly matched to his gun by Wolfer, for they would have cleaned out the lead. And Wolfer could not have test-fired bullets of that type to make the match, for they, too, would have had a cleaning effect.

A third mystery revolved around the Kennedy and Weisel bullets. After test-firing Sirhan's gun, the experts were startled to observe that the test bullets did not bear the microscopic indentations that appeared on the Kennedy and Weisel bullets as well as on a bullet Wolfer had introduced at the trial of Sirhan as having been test-fired from Sirhan's gun. Nor did the indentations appear on photographs that Bill Harper took with the Balliscan camera for his 1971 comparisons. But they were visible on photographs taken for Baxter Ward's 1974 hearing. The indentations could have been made with any sharp object, including the tip of a pencil. They coincided on each bullet, so that they could have been mistaken for matching marks. Whoever made them was obviously hoping to reinforce the single-assassin position.

The tampering must have been done sometime after Bill Harper's examination, which concluded that the bullets did not match.* By the time Harper made public his findings and the "second gun" controversy erupted, the bullets were in the custody of the

---

* The LAPD photograph of the bullet removed from RFK's back was located and subpoenaed. The 1968 photo revealed that this exhibit was in the identical condition as depicted in Harper's 1970 photos—meaning positive proof that no "tampering" or "mutilation" or "switching" had ever taken place in the County Clerk's office, as contended by DA Busch in 1971.

California Supreme Court in San Francisco. We learned from a clerk in the Exhibit Section of the Supreme Court that in July 1971 —about the time Joe Busch was announcing that he would look into the firearms discrepancies—a contingent from the DA's office, the LAPD and Attorney General Younger's office visited the Supreme Court offices and spent several hours alone examining the Sirhan gun and the evidence bullets.

The panel created by Judge Wenke found that three bullets— those from Kennedy, Weisel and a third victim, Ira Goldstein— were sufficiently undamaged by impact to permit comparison. It was determined that all came from the same model gun, an Iver Johnson like the one confiscated from Sirhan. But the model was a popular one. Judge Wenke had specifically asked the panel to determine whether a second gun was involved, and the panel's report on October 6, 1975, responded: "There is no substantive or demonstrable *evidence* that more than one gun was used to fire any of the bullets examined."

But when Wenke opened the sealed report on October 6, 1975, before a packed courtroom and read it aloud, the impact was entirely different. Somehow, the report was composed so that the sentence about the lack of "evidence to indicate that more than one gun was used" came first, and before the judge even completed reading it, reporters were dashing for the telephones. The erroneous impression that it was necessarily Sirhan's gun was flashed to the world. A typical story was headed: PANEL SAYS ONLY ONE GUN.*

Because of the erroneous reporting of the panel's true findings— especially by the Los Angeles *Times'* John Kendall—most of those who had believed that a second gun had been involved in RFK's assassination jumped off the bandwagon. In effect, the distorted

---

* Ironically, CBS, which had been a party to the suit, was one of the worst offenders in jumping the gun. When Lowell Bradford, the CBS expert on the panel, viewed the Walter Cronkite news that evening he was outraged. He stormed over to the Los Angeles news center and demanded that the record be set straight or he would "go public" with a press conference charging the network with intentional distortion. The next evening Cronkite apologized, and in a rare correction of a major news story, clarified the situation.

report of the seven experts had sounded the death knell for the reinvestigation into the assassination of RFK. But Allard Lowenstein, Paul Schrade's lawyer, was able to keep the inquiry alive. He petitioned Judge Wenke to allow cross-examination of the experts in a court of law on their findings, and the judge granted the petition.

It was all-important that the experts' findings be placed in their true *legal* perspective. Lowenstein reached Vince Bugliosi at the Ambassador Hotel in Chicago (he was in the Windy City on business) and importuned him to return to Los Angeles (earlier than scheduled) to conduct the crucially sensitive cross-examination. The former prosecutor had two reservations: (1) The firearms cross-examination was extremely complex and would require an enormous amount of time for preparation. There were literally hundreds of pages of documents to be reviewed by the cross-examiner, and because of other commitments, Bugliosi was concerned that he wouldn't be able to find the time; and (2) he felt that his involvement in the case might be misconstrued by the Establishment press in Los Angeles (especially the Los Angeles *Times*) as an attempt on his part to thrust himself into the spotlight of another major case. (The details of this political dilemma are covered in the Epilogue.)

Lowenstein responded with the truism that the assassination of a candidate for President of the United States, with its incalculable implications, was far more important than any concern Bugliosi might have about being accused of self-seeking. (Ironically, this was not unlike the argument Bugliosi had earlier used on witness Bill Powers.) The former congressman from New York had impressed the former prosecutor with the simple logic of his cause: the future of this nation is everyone's responsibility, if not the Establishment press, too.

Bugliosi resolved his first reservation himself: in the few days remaining, he would prepare his cross-examination in hotel rooms and airplanes as he crisscrossed the country attending to other commitments. By the time mid-November arrived, Bugliosi was ready, and then some.

Because Bugliosi's cross-examination of the experts involves sophisticated and highly complicated firearms testimony, which consumed several hundreds of pages of court transcript, we must necessarily condense the points he established as follows:

1. Although five of the seven experts testified under oath that it was their "belief" that three of the seven bullets recovered from the victims (one from RFK) came from Sirhan's gun, *not one* of the experts was willing to make a *positive* identification. (Positive ID is very common in criminal trials.) In a case of this magnitude, the *lack* of a positive identification is of monumental significance. (Note: This testimony literally destroyed the LAPD's DeWayne Wolfer's grand jury and trial testimony that he was "100% sure" that all seven bullets *positively* came from Sirhan's gun "to the exclusion of all other weapons in the world.")

2. All seven experts testified that it was *not* their conclusion that there was no second gun involved at the assassination scene. Their testimony was merely that based on the exhibits they had been furnished (and they never saw some that they should have), they could find no *evidence* of a second gun. (As Bugliosi would argue: "There's more than a semantic distinction involved here. In fact, there's all the difference in the world between *no evidence* of a second gun and a flat statement that *there was no second gun*! It would be like my walking down the street and saying I saw no avocados on the street. That doesn't mean that there *weren't* any avocados, only that I didn't *see* any avocados!")

3. Five of the seven experts recommended that further scientific tests (ballistics, spectrographic, etc.) be conducted. As Bugliosi pointed out to the court: "As the court knows, there is a tremendous controversy in this case as to which bullet struck which victim and, based on the uncontested position of Sirhan (at the assassination scene) whether it was physically possible for him to have fired all the recovered bullets. If *any* case ever cried out for a thorough, in depth independent ballistics examination, *this* case is it!" (A ballistics test attempts to determine the flight path a bullet follows from the moment it leaves the gun muzzle to its ultimate point of rest.)

4. Five out of the seven experts testified that they did reach a positive conclusion that three of the victim bullets had been fired from the "same gun," but they were *not* able to positively identify

Sirhan's gun as being the weapon from which the subject bullets were fired.

5. The experts *did* acknowledge that there were some "significant differences" between the striations (markings) on several of the victim bullets and those on the bullets test-fired by the panel from Sirhan's gun.

6. All seven experts testified that they were unable to determine the *number* of bullets fired at the assassination scene.

7. *All* seven experts testified that they *did not* rule out the possibility of a second gun.

Here, fortunately now memorialized in a courtroom under oath, were the true findings of the seven experts, not the flat "No Second Gun" reportings of an ill-informed press. The previous written findings of these panelists, which had been misinterpreted by the news media (with the sole exception of CBS reporter Bill Stout), and which appeared to slam the door tight forever on further inquiry, had, due to Bugliosi's deft cross-examination, been reduced to their proper import and accurate legal dimensions. Unfortunately, however, Bugliosi's effort came three months too late to eradicate the impression that had been embossed in the public's mind by a mostly unthinking mass media.

"CAN'T ANYONE ON THAT PANEL COUNT?" BILL HARPER FUMED. "They have just finished examining the ninth and tenth bullets and don't even know it!" Sirhan's revolver had held only eight bullets.

The two extra bullets that Harper was referring to in his phone call to Jonn Christian were labeled Court Exhibit 38 from the Sirhan trial: two expended slugs that the police had found on the front seat of Sirhan's old DeSoto sedan parked several blocks from the Ambassador Hotel. It had always been a source of curiosity as to why Sirhan would have retrieved the useless slugs and left them in his car. It was even doubtful that they had been fired from his gun, since they were so mutilated from impact that they could not be compared with test bullets.

Actually, the panel had discovered a clue as to the origins of the extra bullets. On their worksheets they had notated: "wood in nose" and "wood in nose & base." Wood? From where?

In the official LAPD ballistics report dated July 8, 1968, DeWayne Wolfer had stated that all eight shots in Sirhan's revolver had been fired, and all eight bullets were accounted for. Seven had physically been recovered from the bodies of six of the victims (two from Senator Kennedy, and five from the five victims who survived) at nearby hospitals, and the eighth "was lost somewhere in the ceiling interspace."

In other words, the official LAPD position was that *no bullets were found at the assassination scene*, and other than an entry and exit hole in the ceiling caused by the lost bullet, *there were no bullet holes on any of the doors or walls of the pantry.*

Therefore, if any bullet holes or bullets were observed *in addition* to those accounted for in the LAPD report, they would constitute almost unassailable evidence of a second gun having been fired, since no one claimed Sirhan fired more than eight bullets.

Yet there was evidence that more than eight bullets had been fired in the pantry. Only hours after the shooting, the Associated Press disseminated a wirephoto that was captioned "Bullet found near Kennedy shooting scene." (See official LAPD photo exhibit p. 10 depicting same scene.) It showed two LAPD officers inspecting an object imbedded in a doorjamb behind the Embassy Room stage, from which Kennedy had spoken. The door was in a direct line from the pantry. The ceiling panels, pierced by the bullet entering the interspace, had been removed by the LAPD, booked into its property division as evidence, and later destroyed by the LAPD. On August 22, 1975, Deputy Chief Daryl Gates advised during an interview on the NBC network, "The ceiling panels were destroyed, pursuant to the same destruction order that was issued for the destruction of the doorjambs, June 27, 1969." The destruction was highly premature, and completely improper, for Sirhan's attorneys had scarcely filed their appeal.*

---

* In a declaration and cover letter November 3, 1972, Sirhan's chief trial attorney, Grant B. Cooper, stated that although he had been "warned prior to the trial by Bill Harper that Wolfer could not be relied upon," he nevertheless took into consideration the eyewitness testimony and "proceeded under the assumption that Sirhan alone fired the shot or shots that killed Senator Kennedy." Cooper said that had he known then what he knew now, "my approach to his defense would have been materially altered."

One of the principal problems in attempting to re-open the investigation, although not an insurmountable one, was that the LAPD had engaged in almost wholesale destruction of the physical evidence in the case. In addition to the ceiling panels having been removed by the LAPD, booked into evidence, and destroyed, the center divider between the swinging doors, and the doorjamb on the left side received like treatment. (This is *not* the Rozzi-Wright doorjamb.)

The LAPD also destroyed the gun that they used for decibel sound tests in the Sandra Serrano affair. Also curiously missing are the left sleeves on RFK's coat and shirt.

Most suspicious of all, however, all-important LAPD scientific reports in this case were, per the LAPD spokespeople, "either lost or destroyed." These included the spectrographic report on all the victim bullets. The purpose of a spectrographic test is to determine the metallic and chemical constituency of the recovered bullet. Boxes of ammo have code numbers which refer to the origin of the bullets therein; by furnishing this code number to the manufacturer of the bullets, they can ascertain the metallic and chemical constituency (makeup) of the "batch" of lead from which the ammo came. If, for instance, a bullet recovered from a crime scene contains, among other elements, antimony, but a companion bullet from that same crime scene does not, a powerful inference can be drawn that the two bullets were not fired from the same gun.

Since the LAPD contended that all eight expended cartridges in the Sirhan gun came from the same box of ammo which was discovered in the Sirhan car, the spectrographic report could have supported their scientific case. Conversely, however, it could also have refuted it.

Commenting on the wanton destruction of evidence, Bugliosi said: "The destruction of the evidence may have been completely innocent, but it *looks* bad! And it is totally inexcusable! You do *not* destroy evidence in *any* case, particularly a case of this magnitude, which conceivably could have altered the course of American history."

With the jambs destroyed, the only alternative was to talk to the two policemen in the AP wirephoto. For seven years, the LAPD had refused to divulge the identity of the two uniformed officers.

In fact, no LAPD report ever mentioned their names. Who these two officers were became a talked-about mystery. In 1974 Allard Lowenstein had asked DA Busch who they were, but Busch put him off with the excuse that the policemen had never said that a bullet was in the hole, and the caption was in error. When Lowenstein showed Bugliosi the AP photo, which Bugliosi had never seen before, he told Lowenstein it would be an easy matter to ascertain the identity of the officers. "How?" Lowenstein asked, totally perplexed. "These two officers almost undoubtedly either came from Rampart Division, which has jurisdiction over the Ambassador Hotel, or from an immediately adjacent one—Wilshire or Metro," said Bugliosi. With the wirephoto in hand, Bugliosi made the rounds of the LAPD stations inquiring if anyone knew who the officers were. (Bugliosi is admired and respected by most workaday cops in Los Angeles.) On November 15, 1975, he hit paydirt at the Wilshire Division. A sergeant there identified them as Sergeants Robert Rozzi, at present with the Hollywood Division, and Charles Wright, at present out of the West Los Angeles Division. Both worked out of the Wilshire Division at the time of the assassination.

Bugliosi went straight to the Hollywood Division and showed Rozzi the photo. Rozzi readily identified himself as the officer aiming a flashlight at the hole in the doorjamb. Lodged in the hole, Rozzi said, in a signed statement he gave Bugliosi (see Exhibit 1), was "the base of what appeared to be a small-caliber bullet." Any doubt that the LAPD knew it was a bullet hole was dispelled by official police photograph A-94-cc (see photo insert p.10), in which Rozzi was pointing his pen at the hole while Wright was holding a crime-lab ruler showing it to be approximately eleven inches off the floor. Rozzi said that he himself did not remove the bullet, but was "pretty sure" someone else did.*

Bugliosi had some difficulty in reaching Sergeant Wright, but

---

* Because of the location of the "object" in the doorjamb, and the exit hole caused by the "lost" bullet in the ceiling interspace, it could not have been the lost bullet. Even the LAPD, which would benefit from the possibility that the object was the lost bullet, concedes that it was not.

finally talked with him by telephone the following evening. Wright unequivocally declared that a bullet had been in the hole. When Bugliosi mentioned that Rozzi was pretty sure someone had removed it, Wright replied, "There is no 'pretty sure' about it. It definitely was removed from the hole, but I do not know who did it." Wright agreed to meet Bugliosi the following evening to furnish another signed statement.

The next day Bugliosi appeared in Judge Wenke's courtroom to cross-examine firearms expert Stanton Berg. He showed Berg the wirephoto, and Berg agreed that a ballistics test should be done on the questioned bullets if this was indeed a bullet in the hole. Even though Rozzi's name had *not* been mentioned in court, when court adjourned, Bugliosi was approached by Sergeant Phil Sartuche, an SUS veteran who was monitoring the proceedings for Chief Ed Davis, and who had worked with Bugliosi as an investigating officer in the Manson case. "Vince, do you have Rozzi's statement?" Sartuche asked. When Bugliosi said yes, Sartuche wanted to see it, but the lawyer said he didn't have it with him. Sartuche dashed out the nearest exit in such a rush that his service revolver was jostled loose and fell clattering onto the floor.

The race was on. Bugliosi hurried to the West Los Angeles Division to try to get a statement from Sergeant Wright before the LAPD could get to him. "I was not quick enough," Bugliosi recounted. "When I arrived I was told Wright was on the phone. Ten minutes later he appeared holding a yellow paper in his hand. The name 'Sartuche' was written on it."

"Old Phil really works fast, doesn't he?" Bugliosi said with a smile to the uneasy officer. Wright admitted that Sartuche had just called, as had Deputy City Attorney Larry Nagen, who instructed him not to give a statement. The sergeant retreated from his positive position of the evening before, now saying that the object only looked like a bullet but since it was so long ago, he was not at all sure and he could have been mistaken. Moreover, he had merely assumed that someone had extracted the bullet.

The LAPD's obstructive tactics only heightened Bugliosi's determination. If, in fact, there was a bullet in the doorjamb, it constituted a *ninth* bullet and hence, a second gun. On December 1,

1975, he took a signed statement from Coroner Thomas Noguchi (see Exhibit 2), who had gone to the Ambassador Hotel as soon as he got word of the Kennedy shooting. Previous attempts by other interested parties to get the County Coroner to comment (let alone give a signed statement) about his observations at the crime scene had been futile. Noguchi told Bugliosi that he asked DeWayne Wolfer about any *bullet holes* at the scene, and the lab man pointed "to one hole in a ceiling panel above, and an indentation in the cement ceiling. He also pointed to several holes in the door frames of the swinging doors leading into the pantry." Noguchi continued, "I directed that photographs be taken of me pointing to these holes. I got the impression that a drill had been placed through the holes. I do not know whether or not these were bullet holes, *but I got the distinct impression from him that he suspected that the holes may have been caused by bullets.*"

One of a number of photographs of Noguchi taken that night shows him holding a ruler under two circled holes in one of the swinging-door jambs (see photo section p. 11). The holes had been circled and initialed by an LAPD officer. They are only a few inches apart, and chest-high. But the jambs were destroyed by the LAPD along with the ceiling panels, and the Rozzi-Wright jamb one year later.

Between the swinging doors was a center divider post that also had been sawed off and carted away by the LAPD, and like the ceiling panels, subsequently destroyed. Bugliosi sought out hotel personnel who might have been around the pantry as the police conducted their crime-scene search. One, the former maître d', Angelo DiPierro, had spotted a bullet in the divider post. In a signed statement he gave Bugliosi on December 1, 1975, DiPierro recounted that "many people, including the police and myself, started to look over the entire pantry area to piece together what had happened. That same morning, while we were still looking around, I observed a small-caliber bullet lodged about a quarter of an inch into the wood on the center divider of the two swinging doors. Several police officers also observed the bullet. The bullet was approximately 5 feet 8 or 9 inches from the ground. The reason I specifically recall the approximate height of the bullet location is because I remember thinking at the time that if I had entered the pantry just before the shooting, the bullet may have struck me in the forehead, because I am approximately 5 feet 11½ inches tall." If DiPierro's observation was correct, it would constitute a *tenth* bullet.

Bugliosi then located one of the waiters who was present at the assassination scene, Martin Patrusky. Patrusky had since changed jobs several times. He gave Bugliosi a signed statement on December 12, 1975, that four or five days after the assassination he and others who had been in the pantry at the time were summoned by the LAPD to appear for a video-taped reconstruction of the crime. "There were four or five plain-clothes officers present," he recalled. "The reconstruction incident took about an hour or so. Sometime during the incident, one of the officers pointed to two circled holes on the center divider of the swinging doors and told us that they had dug *two bullets* out of the center divider."*

If Patrusky was correct, it would constitute *eleven* bullets (one of the two bullets dug out of the divider most probably being the bullet DiPierro observed).

The LAPD explained away the holes in the center divider as "dents caused by food carts." Bugliosi went to the Ambassador Hotel. The general manager of the hotel told Bugliosi the food carts were still in use and had not been replaced. The lawyer went down to the pantry. He observed that there were absolutely no protrusions on the carts—they were flat on all sides—to cause the holes. Moreover, he joked, "Even if there were protrusions, which there are not, those food carts would have had to have been travel-

---

* The observations of Patrusky, DiPierro and Noguchi are validated by two independent photographers, William Meyer and R. Carleton Wilson, who arrived at the pantry at eleven o'clock in the morning on June 5. Surprised at finding no one guarding the pantry, they proceeded to take photographs. Meyer placed Xs on the doorjamb locations marked by the LAPD. Curious about the circled holes in the divider post, he pulled off the one-inch-thick facing, exposing two dents on the face of the inner stud that looked as if they had been caused by bullets impacting. The dents lined up perfectly with the holes.

ing at a speed of a hundred and fifty to two hundred miles an hour to have caused the deep holes in that center divider."

The new evidence, Bugliosi argued to Judge Wenke, justified an extension of the probe to study the number of shots fired and their flight path.

DA special counsel Thomas Kranz responded that it would be fruitless to continue the probe because most of the evidence had been destroyed. Bugliosi told Judge Wenke that since it was the police who had destroyed the evidence, Kranz's argument reminded him of "the story of the young man who murdered his father and mother and then begged the court for mercy because he was an orphan."

Moreover, Bugliosi pointed out that fortunately there still were close-up photos of the relevant bullet holes, and eyewitnesses like Rozzi and Wright were available to give sworn testimony and be cross-examined. He asked the judge to take judicial notice of the overwhelming concern of Americans about unresolved questions in all of the assassinations. "They want to know if there is a pernicious force alive in this land," he intoned, "which is threatening to destroy our representative form of government by systematically orchestrating the cutting down of those Presidents or candidates for President who espouse political philosophies antithetical to theirs."

Kranz had been commissioned by the Board of Supervisors to conduct an *independent* investigation to see if the LAPD and the DA's office were correct in their conclusions on the RFK case. Yet Kranz actually became part of the DA's office and was on their payroll. Furthermore, he and Dinko Bozanich, another deputy district attorney assigned to assist Kranz, were taking orders from their boss, District Attorney John Van De Kamp. And Van De Kamp was doing what he has proven to be very adept at—talk to different audiences different ways on the same subject. To the news media he proclaimed that he wanted to "get to the bottom of the RFK case," but in the courtroom, where it counted, his own deputies, Kranz and Bozanich, were fighting tooth and nail, at Van De Kamp's insistence, to discourage Judge Wenke from continuing the inquiry.

Kranz, not to be deterred by Bugliosi's last argument, countered to Judge Wenke that any further inquiry and testing would stretch costs beyond the $100,000 already expended. It was on this note of penury, a drop in the bucket compared with the cost of cracking the Watergate cover-up, that the proceedings ground to a halt with Judge Wenke refusing to broaden their scope. Wenke stated that he did not have "jurisdiction" to continue the hearing.

Bugliosi told Wenke that he had never been able to understand how the court had any jurisdiction to conduct this hearing in the first place. Since he had not been the Sirhan trial judge, and because Sirhan's conviction had long since been affirmed on appeal all the way up to the Supreme Court of the United States, any further inquiry or investigation would have to be by law enforcement, not a court such as his. However, Bugliosi reasoned, under the prevailing circumstances, and as the Presiding Judge of the Superior Court, Wenke already *had* assumed jurisdiction of the matter. Why terminate it at this crucial point when important evidence had been "uncovered," Bugliosi argued.

But Wenke reiterated that he simply had no power to continue the inquiry. And with that he closed the curtain on what might have been the first ray of light and hope in the case for legitimate judicial review.

On April 5, 1977, Kranz completed his "report" on the RFK case. Predictably, he found no evidence of a second gun.

Although for seven and a half years there had been considerable speculation as to the existence of extra bullets, prior to the signed statements obtained by Bugliosi there had been no substantive available evidence to support these suspicions. In the remarkable period of a few short days, the indefatigable and resourceful lawyer had come up with evidence which pointed to the existence of more than eight bullets and, therefore, a multiple-gun shooting.

Bugliosi, who is hardly a "conspiracy buff" and who is very conservative when it comes to the opinions he reaches in such serious matters, later told us: "I have no way of knowing for sure whether or not more than one gun was fired at the assassination scene. And I have formed no opinion at this point. What I will say is this: the signed statements given me perhaps can be explained away; but in the absence of a logical explanation, these statements, by simple arithmetic, add up to too many bullets and therefore, the *probability* of a second gun."*

In the spring of 1976 Bugliosi's findings as to extra bullets were starkly confirmed by documents released by the FBI under the Freedom of Information Act. They reveal that shortly after the LAPD had completed its crime-scene examination within hours of the shooting, the Ambassador Hotel's assistant manager, Franz Stalpers, led an FBI special agent and his photographer into the pantry area. The Bureau men proceeded to cover the same ground as had the LAPD. The results of their examination are contained in a report entitled "CHARTS AND PHOTOGRAPHS SHOWING LAYOUT OF AMBASSADOR HOTEL AREA WHERE SHOOTING OCCURRED," the pertinent section of which contains what the FBI designated as an "E" series of photographs (see photo insert p. 12):

E-1 View taken inside kitchen serving area [the pantry] showing doorway area leading into kitchen from the stage area. In lower right corner the photo shows two bullet holes which we circled. The portion of the panel missing also reportedly contained a bullet.
E-2 A close up view of the two bullet holes of area described above.

The corresponding photographs unmistakably show the same two holes that Dr. Noguchi was pointing to on the jamb. The FBI notation that the "portion of the panel missing also reportedly contained a bullet" obviously refers to a triangular piece of the adjoining wall panel that the LAPD already had torn off. This piece was about eighteen inches above the two bullet holes. The FBI report continues:

E-3 Close up view of the two bullet holes which is [*sic*] located in center door frame inside kitchen serving area and looking towards direction of back of stage area.

This photograph is of the center divider post of the swinging doors, where, Angelo DiPierro stated, he saw a bullet imbedded and from which Martin Patrusky was told by a police officer two bullets

* Interview with the authors, January 14, 1978.

were removed. The photograph shows the two circles drawn around the holes, just as depicted in the Noguchi and LAPD photographs. These were the holes that the DA's spokesman dismissed as gouges from food service carts. Finally the FBI report asserts:

E-4   Close up view of upper hinge on door leading into kitchen area from back of stage area. View shows reported location of another bullet mark which struck hinge.*

With the release of the FBI documents, the box score of extra bullets now reads:

Definite
    2 in a jamb of the swinging doors
    2 in the center divider post of the swinging doors
    1 in a jamb of the stage door (the Rozzi-Wright bullet)
    TOTAL: 5

Probable
    1 in the triangular piece of panel referred to in the FBI report
    1 that struck the hinge
    TOTAL: 2

This makes a total of between thirteen and fifteen bullets that were fired that night—five to seven more than the capacity of Sirhan's revolver, or those shots accounted for by the LAPD. Now we realized why many witnesses compared the sound to a string of firecrackers going off.

One was Los Angeles *Times* photographer Boris Yaro. "My first thought was some jerk has thrown firecrackers in here," he said. Another was RFK political lieutenant Frank Burns: "I heard a noise sounding like a string of firecrackers going off." Waiter Martin Patrusky agreed: "I immediately heard a sound like that of a firecracker. A second later I heard a series of sounds like firecrackers." Erwin Stroll, who was wounded, and Kennedy supporter

---

* An RFK supporter named Roger Katz told Christian that he saw sparks from a bullet striking this hinge. Katz immediately reported it to the LAPD. No report of that interview can be found.

Suzanne Locke—among a good many other witnesses—used the firecracker analogy to describe what they heard: a rapid, erratic series of explosions. The badly wounded Paul Schrade likened the sound to the uneven crackling of "electrical discharge."*

One gun being fired as rapidly as possible would have produced distinct, evenly spaced shots, which is how the witnesses described Sirhan's firing pattern. But two or more guns would have given the "firecrackers" effect. We conducted a simple experiment to illustrate the point. First, we test-fired eight shots as rapidly as possible from the same model Iver Johnson .22 revolver as Sirhan's. Then we set off a string of thirteen firecrackers, again recording the sounds. Here are the results in graph form:

TIMESPAN/3 SECONDS:

0————————————————— 1————————————— 2—————————————3

.22 REVOLVER:

1———— 2———— 3———— 4———— 5———— 6———— 7————8

FIRECRACKERS

1——— 2——— 3— 4— 5—— 6— 7——— 8— 9— 10————— 11— 12————13

As the reader can see, the effect of a single revolver being rapid-fired does not at all resemble that of a string of firecrackers.

The question that arises about the multiple-gun theory is that witnesses, with one exception, did not report seeing anyone else fire a gun. (The exception was CBS News employee Donald Schulman, who, as we have seen, said "the security guard then fired back . . . hitting him.") This can be explained, however, in terms of people's normal reaction to a sudden, surprising event taking place before their eyes. The witnesses' attention would automatically have been riveted on Sirhan (according to one witness, he shouted, "Kennedy! You son of a bitch!"—then fired off a first shot). Some froze in their tracks, mesmerized by the sight. Others ducked for cover as Sirhan unloaded the chamber of his revolver with seven more shots while maître d' Karl Uecker, Frank Burns (and others) struggled to overpower him.

* FBI Summary Report, *op. cit.*, unpaginated.

In this mass confusion other gunmen could have fired unnoticed.

This leads us back to the autopsy report. All three of the bullets that hit Kennedy, including the point-blank fatal head shot, entered from the rear. Yet Sirhan was at Kennedy's front. It is possible that he completely missed his target. Witnesses said that he managed to fire no more than two shots at the oncoming senator before being pounced upon and thrown off target.

But there is an alternative explanation for this seeming inaccuracy, a clue to which lies in an object taken from Sirhan's pocket after the shooting. It was an unfired .22 bullet which, according to investigating officers, had been manually removed from a live cartridge. We had long theorized about this unexplained object of evidence and as to what significance this bullet might have. Then the 1975 hearings before Judge Wenke produced astounding physical evidence that tended to confirm our own earlier speculation that *three* guns, not one or two, had been fired at the assassination scene. Moreover, we can now logically contend that Sirhan never actually fired any bullets at all.

A VISIBLY NERVOUS DEPUTY DA DINKO BOZANICH FIRST BROUGHT up a matter relating to the unfired bullet in arguing against the granting of further scientific tests in the "second gun" theory before Judge Wenke. It was the heavily leaded condition of the bore of Sirhan's gun which posed a dilemma that opposing counsel, Vincent Bugliosi, was sure to raise. The seven firearms panelists had noticed that the bore was in such a "severely, extremely" leaded condition that they could not conduct their examination without first cleaning it out, which they did by firing two copper-jacketed "minimag" bullets through it—standard procedure in such instances. The first bullet removed the excessive lead, they noted, while the second cleaned out all traces.*

How had the leading been caused? Sirhan had spent a good part of election day at a San Gabriel Valley shooting range, rapid-firing

---

* One of the firearms experts later postulated that the leading might have "grown" within the gun barrel (like algae)—a theory completely beyond the comprehension of scientists in the field of metallurgy, we discovered.

hundreds of rounds of ammunition. The range master said he had used "wad cutters," an unjacketed lead bullet designed especially for target practice. Although cheaper and making a neater hole, wad cutters leave lead deposits.

Deputy DA Bozanich was stuck with the problem of why the copper-jacketed "minimag" bullets Sirhan allegedly fired in the pantry, and those purportedly "test-fired" in the Sirhan weapon by Wolfer, had not cleaned out the deposits, just as the firearms experts later cleaned them out by firing two rounds. *None* of the Wolfer-originated test-fired minimag slugs could be matched to the Sirhan weapon by *any* of the experts, raising the distinct possibility that they had been fired through a *different* weapon— possibly the one identified by Bill Harper—a gun that resided in the LAPD property room at the time of the assassination, the gun that the LAPD prematurely destroyed (HI8602) in July 1968. Bozanich had no pat answer, so he resurrected the 1971 ruse that someone had gained access to Sirhan's gun while it was in the County Clerk's office—then hand-pounded bullets through the bore.*

There is a plausible explanation, however, and it is bolstered by the presence of the bullet in Sirhan's pocket. It proposes that a hypnoprogrammed "robot of another" arrived at the crime scene firing *slugless* cartridges which served as hand-made "blanks." Witnesses who saw Sirhan fire the first shot uniformly attest that a tongue of flame was emitted from the gun's muzzle—a tongue they variously described as six inches to more than a foot in length. Firearms experts say that a regular "minimag" load (with a bullet) gives off a tongue of only an inch or so, and that one as long as the witnesses saw is characteristic of a slugless cartridge.

We can think of only one logical reason for Sirhan to fire a weapon loaded with slugless cartridges: to attract attention while at the same time not hitting the intended (actual) killer-gunman immediately behind Kennedy who administered the fatal

* The DA's steadfast refusal to allow the re-examination of the Sirhan weapon during the 1970–75 period suggests that the authorities were aware of the "problem" with the leading all along, and why the DA went to such extremes in trying to frame Christian and Bill Harper on the trumped-up "tampering" charges.

shot. In other words—and there are scientific tests available to verify or refute this—an unseen *"coup de grace."**

If this is what actually happened, it almost certainly follows that Sirhan was cast in the double role of decoy and fall guy—a "patsy"—which is the heart of our "Manchurian Candidate" theory. While this may sound like a plot straight out of detective fiction, the overwhelming evidence at hand indicates that it was actually acted out in real life.†

Taken as a whole, the firearms evidence alone virtually shouts conspiracy and is reason enough to reopen the investigation. As Vincent Bugliosi half jokingly chided newsmen at a press conference after the statements he received kept adding up: "Gentlemen, the time for us to keep on looking for additional bullets in this case has passed. The time has come for us to start looking for the members of the firing squad that night." The press then asked Bugliosi, "Does all this mean that Sirhan is not guilty?" Bugliosi responded, "No, not at all. Sirhan is as guilty as sin, and his conviction was a proper one. But just because Sirhan is guilty does not automatically exclude the possibility that more than one gun was fired at the assassination scene."

---

* In 1976 we advised Supervisor Baxter Ward that neutron activation analysis could be employed to establish the crux of our theory: that if slugless cartridges were fired through the Sirhan weapon at the crime scene, the lead deposits from the "wad-cutter" firings through the gun at the San Gabriel firing range earlier in the day would contain elements of both scorched and unfired gunpowder. Conversely, no such deposits would be present if the gun was fired as contended by the DA. (As of early 1978, no such tests were either conducted or proposed.)

† We presented our discoveries in the form of a White Paper to the American Academy of Forensic Sciences convention in Chicago on February 18–21, 1975. The treatise was titled *The RFK Assassination: An Evidential/Theoretical Analysis of the Murder Scene.* However, scheduling difficulties kept it off the expert-panel agenda.

13

The Manchurian Candidate

ON A FOGGY DAY THE PALE-YELLOW WALLS OF SAN QUENTIN
Prison seem to rise out of the waters of San Francisco Bay like
a medieval fortress. On the morning of September 10, 1972,
Turner visited the aged institution with the latest in Sirhan's
series of attorneys, Roger S. Hanson of Beverly Hills. Hanson
was drawing up a fresh appeal to the California Supreme Court
based on William Harper's recent finding that the bullet that
fatally wounded Robert Kennedy could not be matched to
Sirhan's gun. Hanson had retained Harper, Christian and
Turner as unpaid "investigative consultants" in what would
turn out to be a futile attempt to gain a new trial.

At the gatehouse Hanson presented his attorney's identification while Turner displayed his California private investigator's license. After being searched, they were cleared into the visitors' waiting area, a high-ceilinged room with oaken benches reminiscent of an old-time railroad depot. A guard escorted the pair through a large adjacent room where prisoners in blue dungarees and denim shirts were conferring with their visitors and attorneys, then up several steps and into a screened-in cubicle. The guard shut the door behind them. Facing them was a grille, through which they could see into a similar cubicle on the other side.

Two heavily armed guards brought Sirhan into the opposite cubicle, shut the door and hovered outside. The prisoner's handcuffs were chained to a wide black leather belt. His face was ashen, due no doubt to long confinement under strict security measures. But it was unmistakably the face that had appeared in hundreds of newspapers and magazines, the face that had so dominated our efforts for the past four years. The eyes were soft and doe-brown, set under arched, bushy eyebrows.

As Sirhan began talking with Hanson about his appeal, Turner observed that he was bright, articulate and personable, not at all the cardboard cut-out that had emerged from the news coverage years before. But then, he had gone to college for a year and a half, and according to his brother Munir spoke fluent German and Russian in addition to Arabic and English. He had come to the United States intent upon majoring in political science, but somehow got the idea that he wanted to be a jockey.

When Turner asked about that night at the Ambassador Hotel, Sirhan's face took on a vague look. He remembered going to the hotel, he said, but not necessarily because Kennedy would be there. The night was still a jumble of twisted images. There was the meeting with the girl in the polka-dot dress whose name he never knew. "I met the girl and had coffee with her," he recounted. "She wanted heavy on the cream and sugar. After that I don't remember a thing until they pounced on me in that pantry."

That was it. Sirhan claimed to have no memory of any other detail that might provide a clue as to why he was there or what happened. The name Jerry Owen rang no bell, he insisted; he could remember no preacher of that description, no horse deal. And he could shed no light on the "Pay to the order of . . ." entries in the notebooks. The guards opened the door and announced that time was up. Sirhan was led away, shuffling under the restraint of the heavy chains.

As he walked out of San Quentin, Turner was more convinced than ever that Sirhan had been hypnoprogrammed to act out his role in RFK's death. He recalled a remark Sirhan had made when interviewed by NBC's Jack Perkins shortly before being whisked off to San Quentin. To Perkins' baiting, "You were planning to kill Senator Kennedy?," Sirhan replied, "Only in my mind. I did it, but I was not aware of it."

EARLY ON WE HAD TOYED WITH THE THEORY THAT SIRHAN WAS A real-life version of the automated killer in Richard Condon's novel *The Manchurian Candidate*. Truth may be stranger than fiction, but it is also sometimes more difficult to accept. This is especially the case when delving into the mysteries of the mind.

Yet we had entertained the possibility virtually from the moment RFK was shot. Christian recalled a night in the fall of 1966 when he was rummaging through the basement law library of Melvin Belli's Gold Rush era office building in San Francisco doing research on bank monopolies. He tripped over a thick, dust-covered legal packet that had carelessly been left on the floor. The hand-lettered name on it caught his eye: "Ruby, Jack."

Jack Ruby was perhaps Belli's most infamous client. His shooting of Lee Harvey Oswald in plain view of millions of television watchers (eliminating any chance that the prisoner might talk) made it an open-and-shut case—just like Sirhan's capture in the pantry. Belli put forth a defense of "psychomotor epilepsy," a form of insanity. But Ruby was convicted, and died in prison of galloping cancer.*

* Within hours of the shooting one of Belli's partners, Seymour Ellison, received a phone call from a senior partner in a Las Vegas law firm where he had previously worked. The firm was connected with organized-crime figures who had been stripped of their gambling casinos in Cuba by Castro and relocated in Nevada. "Sy," the Las Vegas attorney said, "one of our guys

Thumbing through the packet, Christian noticed a letter to Belli from a New York attorney named Leonard L. Steinman on the subject of hypnosis. It was dated January 21, 1964, not long before Ruby's trial began. Steinman noted that since his previous contact with Belli, he had done exhaustive research on case histories and concluded that everyone was

virtually on all fours with the picture presented not only by your client, but Oswald as well. I have an absolute and earnest conviction in me— that Jack Ruby was in fact hypno-conditioned.

You have probably never heard of "locking suggestions," Mel. This is the problem Ruby is up against—and the tragedy is that Ruby doesn't even know it.

Referring to the fact that the defense psychiatrists had attributed Ruby's "fugue or dissociated state" to psychosis, Steinman elucidated:

. . . the brain damage picture is not the result of previous concussion and physical trauma, but of hypno-conditioning, of induction by suggestion through deep hypnosis of an artificial psychosis. Unlocking of this psychosis, of establishing the identity of the hypno-conditioner, requires a dedicated hypno-therapist with an exhaustive knowledge not only of Freudian but of Pavlovian principles.

You must understand, that the question of hypnotic induction of criminal acts and behavior is one which has a long history. . . . I am thoroughly convinced of Ruby's innocence, that he was a robot of another. . . . The criminal who makes use of hypnotism has unrivaled opportunities of wiping out all traces of his action and, moreover, avoiding discovery.

I tell you, Mel, this case is insidious. The theory isn't really a second-line defense. It's what actually happened.

---

just bumped off that son of a bitch that gunned down the President. We can't move in to handle it, but there's a million bucks net for Mel if he'll take it." The lawyer stressed that his clients wanted their relationship with Ruby kept strictly confidential. Before long the lawyer called Ellison back and told him that the deal was off because they had just found out that Ruby had been in with another powerful element and his clients didn't want to get involved in any way. Belli eventually took the case on his own initiative, but he took a financial bath of staggering proportions.

The Steinman letter was very much on Christian's mind after RFK was shot. That Sirhan might have been programmed through hypnosis sounded like science fiction, but the symptoms began to crop up. CBS cameraman James D. Wilson, who was at the Ambassador when Kennedy was shot, told Turner that he and his colleagues covering the court case had observed that Sirhan seemed permanently depressed "with his mind working on the basis of separate compartments."

"I know this sounds silly," Wilson said, "but I still find no explanation for Sirhan as satisfactory as the hypothesis that he has been acting and talking under hypnosis or in posthypnotic suggestion."

Later Bob Kaiser also reserved the possibility that Sirhan was under the influence of hypnosis. In private discussions he said that he believed Sirhan's amnesia block, which could have been hypnotically induced, was genuine, and in his book he stated that although he didn't know who the programmer might have been, he "still had a feeling that somewhere in Sirhan's recent past there was a shadowy someone." And he quoted Roger LaJeunesse as saying, "The case is still open. I'm not rejecting the Manchurian Candidate aspect of it."*

The symptoms of hypnoconditioning are not easy to describe, but as our knowledge of the subject expanded we thought that we perceived them in abundance. In tracing Sirhan's movements after he arrived at the Ambassador Hotel during the early evening of June 4, 1968,† we came upon a number of indicators of the trance state. At first Sirhan roamed the cavernous hotel in a talkative and assertive mood, possibly emboldened by a Tom Collins or two. Around nine he dropped into the Venetian Room, where a celebration for Republican Senate candidate Max Rafferty was in progress—Sirhan had known the candidate's daughter in high school—and when a waiter balked at serving him a drink because of his scruffy attire, he contemptuously tossed a $20 bill at him.

Stalking out of the Rafferty affair, Sirhan engaged in a conver-

* Kaiser, *op. cit.,* p. 536.
† This reconstruction is made from FBI and LAPD interviews of witnesses.

sation with a stranger named Enrique Rabago, a Kennedy fan. "Are we going to win?" Rabago asked. "I think we are going to win," Sirhan replied. When Rabago remarked that Senator Eugene McCarthy was still slightly ahead in the count, Sirhan growled, "Don't worry if Senator Kennedy doesn't win. That son of a bitch is a millionaire. Even if he wins, he won't do anything for you or me or the poor people." Rabago's companion, Humphrey Cordero, didn't think Sirhan was on drugs or alcohol but merely disgusted with the social scene at the hotel.

In the ensuing hour, however, Sirhan underwent the kind of dramatic personality change that hypnosis can cause. At about ten-thirty, he was staring mutely at the clattering teletype machine in the makeshift press headquarters next to the Embassy Room. When Western Union operator Mary Grohs asked him what he wanted, he just looked blank. "I'll never forget his eyes," she said later.

His eyes were similarly striking to two men who helped overpower him in the pantry after the shooting. George Plimpton called them "dark brown and enormously peaceful," and Joseph Lahaiv thought that Sirhan looked "very tranquil" during the furious struggle. This seeming paradox can be explained by the hypnotic trance: the outwardly tranquil appearance belies a fierce inner concentration. Sirhan's determination to carry out posthypnotic commands was consistent with the fact that it took a half-dozen strong men several minutes to subdue him. As an encyclopedia describes the condition: "Supernormal feats cause no fatigue."

What puzzled us, however, was Sirhan's behavior after being taken into custody. Taken to the Rampart station, he verbally sparred for hours with his captors over such a foregone matter as his identity, and he had left his wallet containing identifying documents in his car parked three blocks from the Ambassador. He refused to discuss the shooting at all, acting as if it had never happened. Lieutenant William C. Jordan thought he might be stalling to allow confederates to get away.

What Sirhan did talk about, practically in a stream of consciousness, was the Jack Kirschke murder case. A former deputy DA, Kirschke had recently been convicted of the love triangle murder of his wife and another man. "I was hoping you'd clue me in on it," Sirhan told a deputy DA who interviewed him. "You know, brief me on it, you might say." Sirhan's preoccupation with the Kirschke case was leaked to the press, prompting Kirschke's lawyer to file a legal motion contending that his client's rights had been violated because the conviction was under appeal. Curiously enough, the lawyer had called for permission to employ hypnosis in the case, which the court summarily denied. The lawyer was none other than our former campaign chairman, George Davis.

We could only guess as to what was behind the leak. But its effect was to complete the picture begun by Yorty. Now he was a murder-minded Communist sympathizer occultist.

After being transferred to the county jail later in the morning, Sirhan was visited by the medical director, Dr. Marcus Crahan. The prisoner suddenly hunched his shoulders and shivered violently. "It's chilly!" he stammered, his face contorted.

"You're cold?" Crahan was puzzled, because the room was warm.

"Not cold," Sirhan replied.

"Not cold, what do you mean?"

"No comment."

"You mean you're having a chill?"

Still trembling, Sirhan conceded, "I have a very mild one, yes."

Here was a clue of withdrawal from the hypnotic state. It was illustrated again when Dr. Diamond, the defense psychiatrist, put Sirhan into a deep trance to try to fathom a motive. But his subject slipped into an even deeper trance, sobbing and causing the doctor considerable alarm. As Diamond snapped him out of it Sirhan began trembling, and goose bumps surfaced on his arms. "Doc, it's cold," he complained.

Sirhan also stubbornly insisted that temporary amnesias had blotted out any memory of writing the notebooks and committing the crime. Such a claim was obviously self-serving, but Sirhan continues to cling to it long after all appeals have been exhausted and such obstinance no longer serves any purpose. Dr. Diamond believed that the blackouts were real. "To a considerable degree," he had explained to the trial jury, "when a resistance is overcome through the use of hypnosis and an individual talks about something he was unable to talk about when awake, this is clinical evidence that the resistance against bringing it up in a conscious state was unconscious in itself and not an intentional withholding or an intentional lie."

But Diamond didn't attribute the amnesia blocks to locking suggestions implanted by a programmer—suggestions that would make Sirhan forget that he had been programmed and by whom. The doctor was, after all, functioning within the defense parameters that did not admit of a conspiracy. Instead Diamond postulated that Sirhan was the victim of his own self-hypnosis habit coupled with a chronic paranoid schizophrenia. The dazzling lights and mirrors and the confusion had somehow combined to throw him into a trance, one that he had inadvertently programmed himself as the notebooks with the anti-Kennedy scrawlings attest.

So Sirhan, in Diamond's opinion, was a kind of automatic assassin, dissociated, a dual personality acting on both the conscious and subconscious levels, the subconscious being in control when he fired. In his summary to the jury, Diamond said it was "an astonishing instance of mail-order hypnosis, dissociated trances and the mystical occultism of Rosicrucian mind power and black magic." But even Diamond conceded that his theory of "primitive, psychotic, voodoo thinking" having triggered Kennedy's death was "the ultimate in preposterous absurdity, too illogical even for a theater of the absurd."

AFTER HE WAS PLACED ON SAN QUENTIN'S DEATH ROW IN THE spring of 1969, Sirhan was thoroughly examined by Dr. Eduard Simson-Kallas, chief of the prison's psychological testing program. After spending a total of thirty-five hours with his subject, Simson was convinced that Sirhan was indeed a Manchurian Candidate. "He was easily influenced, had no real roots and was looking for a cause," Simson said to Christian during our first contact with him in late 1972. "The Arab-Israeli conflict could easily have been used to motivate him."

Simson didn't believe that Sirhan was sufficiently devious or mentally unbalanced to have planned the assassination on his own. "He was prepared by someone," the doctor maintained. "He was hypnotized by someone."

Simson disclosed the results of his examinations of Sirhan in a later interview with Turner on August 14, 1975, in his home in Monterey. Simson is now in the private practice of psychology and teaches abnormal psychology in the state universities at Santa Cruz and San Jose. On the walls of his study are such mementos as a gold-braided Heidelberg University fraternity cap and Haitian voodoo masks, as well as a bevy of diplomas from Stanford, Heidelberg (Ph.D. cum laude) and other prestigious universities. Staggered among them are plaques attesting to professional honors, including a fellowship in the British Royal Society of Health and the American Society for Clinical Hypnosis.

When he began examining Sirhan, Simson noted that his subject was not the ordinary murderer who spoke with great expression and detail about his crime. Although Sirhan was resigned to having shot Kennedy, he spoke as though he was "reciting from a book" and baffled Simson by his lack of details. "A psychologist always looks for details," he said. "If a person is involved in a real situation, there are details."

As he grew to trust Simson, Sirhan confided, "I don't really know what happened. I know I was there. They tell me I killed Kennedy. I don't remember exactly what I did but I know I wasn't myself. I remember there was a girl who wanted coffee. She wanted coffee with lots of cream and sugar." Pouring the coffee was the last act Sirhan could remember before being choked and pummeled by the crowd in the pantry.

If Sirhan was hypnoprogrammed, Simson pointed out, the girl might have been, by prearrangement, the triggering mechanism. "You can be programmed that if you meet a certain person or see something specific, then you go into a trance."

Sirhan himself tossed out the possibility that he might have been hypnotized. "Sometimes I go in a very deep trance so I can't even speak," he told Simson. "I do not remember what I do under hypnosis. I had to be in a trance when I shot Kennedy, as I don't remember having shot him. I *had* to be hypnotized! Christ!" Sirhan was exhibiting a common symptom of persons who have been hypnotized and programmed: they have no recollection of having been put in a trance without their cooperation.

Sirhan suggested that Simson hypnotize him to help him remember what happened. The doctor agreed, feeling he had achieved the high degree of rapport with his subject that deprogramming required. "He was extremely eager to talk to me," Simson related. "He himself wanted to find out. If I had been allowed to spend as much time with him as necessary, I would have found out something."

But Associate Warden James W. L. Park intervened, on the curious ground that Simson "appears to be making a career out of Sirhan." Park instructed the doctor to curtail his visits to conform with "the services offered other condemned prisoners."* Simson, who had worked in the prison for six years and had never been cut off before, handed in his resignation. "A medical doctor spends as much time with a patient as the disease demands," he said. "So does a psychologist."

Simson displayed equal indignation when he talked about the testimony of Dr. Diamond and other psychiatrists at the Sirhan trial, which he labeled the "psychiatric blunder of the century." He scoffed at Diamond's self-induction theory, pointing out that it is utterly impossible for a person to place himself in such a deep trance that he suffers an amnesia block. Simson allowed that insanity could cause a memory loss, but stressed that there is no such thing as "temporary insanity" and that Sirhan was perfectly sane when he arrived at the prison. "Nowhere in Sirhan's test responses was I able to find evidence that he is a 'paranoid schizophrenic' or 'psychotic' as testified to by the doctors at the trial. My findings were substantiated by the observations of the chief psychiatrist at San Quentin, Dr. D. G. Schmidt."

It was Simson's belief that Diamond and his colleagues erred by judging Sirhan under preconceptions that he was both guilty and deranged, prompting Sirhan, who resented the insanity inference, to turn distrustful and uncooperative in their examinations of him. "Sirhan told me he deliberately misled these doctors," Simson stated. "They were not in a position to unlock his mind. This could only be done by a doctor Sirhan fully trusted."

As Simson saw it, Sirhan was "the center of a drama that un-

* Memorandum from Park to Dr. D. G. Schmidt, chief psychiatrist, San Quentin Prison, September 24, 1969.

folded slowly, discrediting and embarrassing psychology and psychiatry as a profession. The drama's true center still lies very much concealed and unknown to the general public. Was Sirhan merely a double, a stand-in, sent there to attract attention? Was he at the scene to replace someone else? Did he actually kill Robert Kennedy?

"Whatever the full truth of the Robert F. Kennedy assassination, it still remains locked in Sirhan's other, still anonymous mind."*

FOR SIRHAN TO HAVE BEEN THE "ROBOT OF ANOTHER," HE WOULD have to be highly susceptible to hypnosis. Some people's psychological make-up renders them totally unresponsive to hypnotic induction, while others can be "put under" but only with difficulty. Noted Hollywood hypnotist Gil Boyne told us that hypnoprogramming is possible, provided that the programmer is highly skilled and the subject's psychological profile ideal. What was Sirhan's profile? Dr. Diamond had reported that he succumbed to hypnosis practically at a snap of the fingers, but we wanted to explore this crucial area further.

In 1971 Christian talked to Richard St. Charles, a practicing hypnotherapist who also performed on stage. In 1966 St. Charles was booked into the Bahama Inn, a Pasadena night club within walking distance of the Sirhan home. It was his habit to compile a mailing list by leaving slips of paper on the tables and urging customers to "Join the Richard St. Charles Fan Club" by writing down their names and addresses. After the performances he marked the slips of those customers who had volunteered to be hypnotized on stage.

Following the assassination St. Charles felt that Sirhan's name was vaguely familiar. He searched his file and found the name with the Pasadena address on a slip of paper made out in late 1966. "The notes that I had were that he was a very good subject," St. Charles said. "I would say from my notes that Sirhan had very definitely been hypnotized prior to the time that I hypnotized him. That is a matter of a professional being able to detect just from watching

* Affidavit by Dr. Simson-Kallas, March 9, 1973. The authors provided him with data from the investigative files, as did criminalist William Harper.

the subjects go under on the stage whether they have or have not been in a state of hypnosis previously."*

Corroboration of this evaluation came from Dr. Herbert Spiegel, a professor at the Columbia University College of Physicians and Surgeons in New York who ranks in the top echelon of American psychiatry and is a pre-eminent authority on hypnosis. Spiegel is a pioneer in the field of hypnotic susceptibility. He spent years developing and refining his Hypnotic Induction Profile, which grades persons from 0 to 5 by recognizing their "clinically identifiable configuration of personality traits."† Spiegel was first exposed to our file data on the "Manchurian Candidate" aspects of the RFK case in late 1973. The psychiatrist flew out to the West Coast and met privately with Jonn Christian, who gave him a thorough presentation on how we thought the hypnosis evidence fitted into the overall modus operandi.

Spiegel returned to New York and immediately went to his lawyer's office and executed an affidavit attesting to what he'd seen and heard from Christian, asking his personal counsel to lock the document away in the safe. It was to be released to the Rockefeller family—he is an intimate friend of both Nelson and David—if or when anything should happen to him.

One of the documents provided to Spiegel was the album cover from *It Comes Up Murder* that had been sent to congressmen and senators by American United's Anthony Hilder just before RFK's

---

* St. Charles mentioned that a friend of his, LAPD Sergeant Michael Nielsen, had been a member of SUS and had seen a manuscript by an unnamed author who established a convincing "direct connection between Sirhan Sirhan, Lee Harvey Oswald, Clay Shaw, James Earl Ray—and directly back to the preacher in Los Angeles." Ray had consulted a hypnotist during his stay in Los Angeles before he killed Dr. Martin Luther King, Jr., and a text on the subject was found in a Toronto rooming house where he resided briefly before fleeing to Europe. In 1977 Nielsen was named to head a new division within the LAPD that specializes in the use of hypnosis as "an investigative tool" for witnesses and suspects alike. Several lawyer groups and legislators protested the use of hypnosis by the LAPD in this pioneering effort by a law enforcement agency.

† Herbert Spiegel, M.D., "The Grade 5 Syndrome: The Highly Hypnotizable Person," *International Journal of Clinical and Experimental Hypnosis*, Vol. XXII, No. 4 (1974), pp. 303–19.

assassination. (This is the artist's depiction of Nelson Rockefeller at the moment an assassin's bullet is shattering his skull.) On August 28, 1974, Christian notified Spiegel that there were new signs that the Hilder-Steinbacher elements of the John Birch Society were making "familiar" noises again, and in the direction of Vice President Rockefeller too. He instantly forwarded it to the Rockefeller brothers, then wrote Christian: "After many months of reflection and tidbits of new information, your hypothesis still makes sense to me."*

The renewed warning to the Rockefellers went unheeded, however. Then, on the 4th of July, 1976, an attempt was made on Vice President Rockefeller's life by a man openly belonging to the Birch Society. The would-be assassin was tried and convicted as "a lone and unassisted assailant."

Turner visited Spiegel on March 17, 1976, at his uptown Manhattan office. The doctor had not personally examined Sirhan, but he had studied Dr. Diamond's testimony and the psychiatric reports on Sirhan, much as a physician would analyze X-rays without seeing the patient. Spiegel unequivocally designated Sirhan a Grade 5, placing him in the 5 to 10 percent of the general population who are the most susceptible to being hypnotized.

Spiegel emphatically rejected Diamond's diagnosis of Sirhan as a paranoid schizophrenic that was indispensable to his theory of automatic induction. A Grade 5 rarely becomes schizophrenic, the doctor said, and what Diamond misdiagnosed as schizophrenia was actually gross symptoms of hysteria under duress, a relatively new discovery. "It is a transient, mixed state, often of frightening appearance—even mistakenly thought to be a psychosis," Spiegel explained, noting that the back wards of mental hospitals are filled with misdiagnosed patients.

Spiegel offered to show Turner graphic evidence of how easily a Grade 5 could be hypnoprogrammed. In 1967 he had been retained by NBC television news to assist in a documentary special that was sharply critical of New Orleans District Attorney Jim Garrison's probe into the John Kennedy assassination. Garrison had

* Letter dated September 3, 1974.

used hypnosis on a star witness, Perry Russo, to try to expand his recollection of a meeting during which Oswald, anti-Castro pilot David Ferrie and the defendant in the case, Clay Shaw, purportedly discussed a plan to assassinate the President. NBC was attempting to demonstrate that Garrison had misused hypnosis to implant a conspiracy fiction in Russo's mind. The network had no proof, but wanted to show how it could be done.

Spiegel arranged an unrehearsed video-taped session in which the subject was a forty-year-old New York businessman of liberal political views who once, for example, had marched in a Bayard Rustin civil rights demonstration. Spiegel had predetermined that the subject was a Grade 5. The segment was narrated by NBC anchorman Frank McGee. But the network cut the segment out of the documentary before it was aired. "I suppose it was too graphic," Spiegel told Turner. "It might have frightened a lot of people."

Spiegel screened it for Turner. After a brief warm-up with the subject, Spiegel is seen achieving a quick induction. "Try to open your eyes, you can't," he tells the subject, whose eyelids quiver but remain shut. The doctor confides that there exists a Communist plot aimed at controlling television and paving the way for a takeover. "You will alert the networks to it," he instructs. Then he shifts the subject from the formal or deep trance to the posthypnotic condition where his eyes open and he appears normal.

At this point Spiegel explains to McGee that the subject is in the grip of what he terms the "compulsive triad": (1) he has no memory of having been under hypnosis; (2) he feels a compulsive need to conform to the signal given under hypnosis; and (3) he resorts to rationalizations to conform to the instructions of this signal.

Glaring accusingly at McGee, the subject launches into an "exposé" of the Communist threat to the networks. He talks about dupes in the media and how they are brainwashing the entire nation. "I have a friend in the media," he says, "but friendship should stop when the nation is in peril." Spiegel suggests the name Jack Harris at random, and the subject readily adopts the name as that of his duped friend. The rationalization has set in. McGee hands him a blank pad on which he says three names are written. The subject nods. Yes, those are the men who were at a Communist cell meeting in a theater loft over a restaurant.

Spiegel snaps his fingers 1-2-3, reinstating the formal trance. With his eyes closed the subject persists in the same argument* about Communist penetration of the media. He names Harris as a ringleader. McGee argues against the subject, and as he increases the pressure of his rebuttal the subject slips into a deepening paranoiac depression.

Spiegel snaps him out of the trance. The subject can't remember a thing. Later, when the videotape is run for him, his face mirrors disbelief as he hears and sees himself sloganeering in Birch Society rhetoric. "I can't conceive of myself saying those things," he protests, "because I don't think that way."

When the video tape ended and Spiegel switched on the lights, Turner had to agree that it was all too graphic. "Tell me," Turner asked, "if you had stuck a gun in the subject's hand and instructed him to shoot McGee, what would he have done?"

"Ah," the doctor said, "the ultimate question. I'm afraid he might have shot him."

IN RICHARD CONDON'S NOVEL THE MANCHURIAN CANDIDATE, ANTI-hero Raymond Shaw's captors in North Korea brainwash him and program him through hypnosis to act as a "hit man," using an ordinary deck of playing cards as his remote control. Back in the United States, when he hears the key phrase "Why don't you pass the time by playing a little solitaire?" he goes into a deep trance and starts laying out the cards until he comes to the queen of diamonds, which is "the second key" that will clear his mechanism for any assignments. Then, upon receiving instructions, he kills without any later remembrance of having done so.

Some authorities maintain that *The Manchurian Candidate* could never be more than fiction because, they claim, a person cannot be hypnoprogrammed to commit a crime he would not normally even think of committing. In *Hypnotism Comes of Age*,* Bernard Wolfe and Raymond Rosenthal contend that "the hypnotized per-

* Bobbs-Merrill (Indianapolis, 1948).

son will perform only those acts which are compatible with his ego, his total personality. And this applies to crime as well as any other form of human activity." The late Dr. William Joseph Bryan, Jr., who had a hypnotherapy practice in Hollywood and was technical adviser on the filming of *The Manchurian Candidate*, declared in his book *Legal Aspects of Hypnosis*: "It is impossible by means of hypnosis to force a subject to commit an act which violates his basic moral code."*

Accordingly, Dr. Spiegel's law-abiding businessman would not have shot Frank McGee, and Sirhan, with no background as a killer, could not have been hypnoprogrammed to attack RFK. But as the annals of crime attest, a person's inherent reluctance to commit a crime can be overridden by conditioning him to believe that the act he is performing is in the interest of a high moral purpose. A civilian conscript who has never harmed a fly will kill the enemy in wartime in the interest of protecting his country and family, and hypnotic subjects can be inculcated with the same type of lofty imperative.

A classic case occurred in Denmark in 1952. Bjorn S. Nielsen and Palle Hardrup became intimate friends in a Danish prison. After their release the dominant Nielsen continued to forge the malleable Hardrup into a robot who would go into a trance at the sight or sound of a simple key—the letter *X*, representing a guardian spirit—and do Nielsen's bidding. How Nielsen gradually developed control over Hardrup was learned when Hardrup was being deprogrammed and related under hypnosis: "There is another room next door where Nielsen and I can go and talk on our own. It is there my guardian spirit usually comes and talks to me. Nielsen says that X has a task for me. I get uncomfortable at the thought because I know that the tasks he sets for me are usually unpleasant. He expects a lot of me." One of the first tasks was for Hardrup to arrange for his girl friend to submit to sexual intercourse with Nielsen.

Subsequently Nielsen directed Hardrup to rob banks in order to raise money for a new political party that would achieve the unification of all Scandinavia. In his hypnotized condition, Hardrup saw

* Charles C. Thomas Co. (Springfield, Ill., 1958).

the order as coming from the guardian spirit X and obeyed. The first robbery was successful and he turned over the loot to Nielsen. But during a second attempt he fatally shot a teller and bank officer in Copenhagen and was apprehended by the police. After being convicted and returned to prison, Hardrup was examined by Dr. Paul J. Reiter, chief of the psychiatric department of the Copenhagen Municipal Hospital. Reiter observed amnesia symptoms of a kind that led him to suspect hypnoconditioning. In Europe especially, the recognition of hypnosis became widespread after World War I, and Reiter explored the possibility that Hardrup had been subjected to programming. After nineteen tedious months, Reiter "unlocked" Hardrup's mind. As a result of his work the court absolved Hardrup, and on July 17, 1954, Bjorn Nielsen was convicted and sentenced to life imprisonment for "having planned and instigated by influence of various kinds, including suggestions of a hypnotic nature," the commission of robbery and murder by another man.*

In the Copenhagen case the overriding moral purpose was the unification of all Scandinavia, a goal Hardrup subscribed to. It was sufficient to make a murderer out of an innocuous petty criminal.

It is Dr. Spiegel's opinion that Sirhan may have acceded to participating in the RFK assassination through a suspension of his critical judgment. His psyche may have been altered to the point where Kennedy became a malevolent figure, to be feared and violently hated. "It's possible to distort and change someone's mind through hypnotic conditioning," Spiegel asserted. "It can be described as brainwashing because the mind is cleared of its old values and emotions, which are replaced by implanting other suggestions. Highly hypnotizable persons, when under the control of unscrupulous persons, are the most vulnerable."

There was virtually nothing in Sirhan's background to indicate that he normally viewed Robert Kennedy as a malevolent figure. (He was a Palestinian merely by birth, not by political conviction.) On the contrary, he had every reason to favor Kennedy. Sirhan was an immigrant, a member of a minority group and of meager means,

---

* Paul J. Reiter, *Antisocial or Criminal Acts and Hypnosis* (Springfield, Ill.: Charles C. Thomas Co., 1958).

1. Senator Robert F. Kennedy, 1967, with friends Marlon Brando (*left*) and Robert Vaughn at campaign fund-raising event.

2. Robert Kennedy with wife Ethel (*left*) and campaign chief Jesse Unruh (*right*) after victory speech, June 5, 1968.

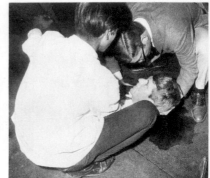

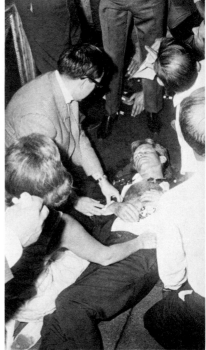

1. Gunfire erupts in the kitchen pantry. Rosey Grier (*left*) and hotel maître d' Karl Uecker (*right*) grab apparent assassin, Sirhan Bishara Sirhan.

2. Sirhan Sirhan is taken into custody by armed officers of the Los Angeles Police Department.

3. Robert Kennedy after the shooting.

4. RFK is attended by a doctor and his wife comforts him as he whispers to her, "Am I going to die?"

5. Thane Eugene Cesar (*right*) with fellow Ace Security guards moments after the shooting. Note his missing clip-on tie.

6. Robert Kennedy lies dying on the floor of the kitchen pantry of the Ambassador Hotel. Note clip-on tie near his right hand.

EXTRA

LOS ANGELES EVENING AND SUNDAY

HERALD EXAMINER

CLASSIFIED ADVERTISING Richmond 8-4111
All Other Calls Richmond 8-1212 or Richmond 8-4141

VOL. XCVIII   NO. 72   THURSDAY, JUNE 6, 1968   8★R   TEN CENTS

8 STAR
LATEST SPORTS

TODAY'S
COMPLETE NEW YORK
AND AMERICAN STOCKS

RFK IS DEAD

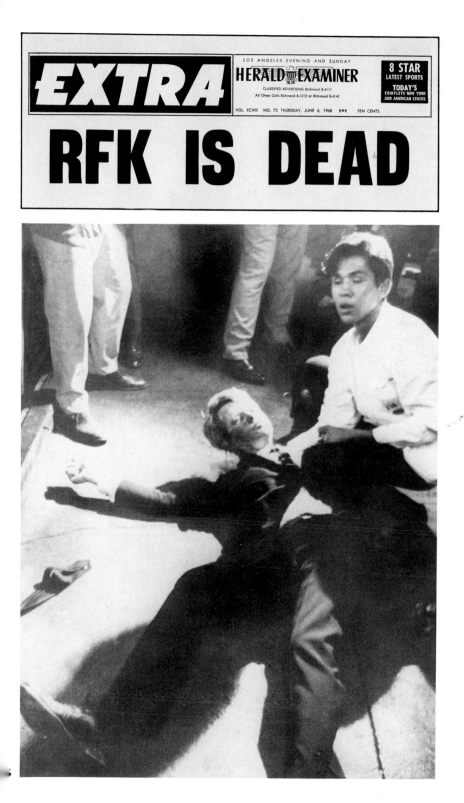

Amazing Bible Crusade

FOR ALL FAITHS AND ALL CHURCHES
(NON-DENOMINATIONAL)

Featuring

Reverend
OWEN

"THE WALKING BIBLE"

SPEAKING NIGHTLY

Sept. 5
thru
Sept. 15,
1968

7:30 P.M. EVERY EVENING

War Memorial Building

FIRST STREET WEST, SONOMA, CALIFORNIA

ALL SEATS *free* — COME EARLY TO HEAR
REVEREND OWEN WHO HAS SOLVED THOUSANDS OF
PERSONAL HUMAN PROBLEMS THROUGH HIS AMAZING
BIBLE PREACHING.

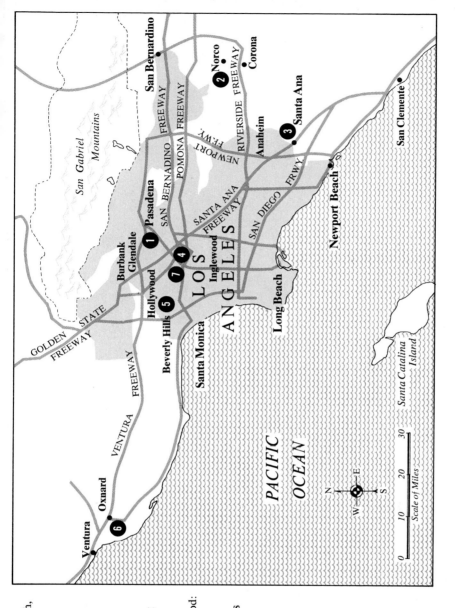

1. Sirhan home: Pasadena.

2. Granja Vista del Rio Ranch, Norco: Sirhan worked/lived here in 1966 and continued to visit area until June 1968.

3. Home of Oliver Brindley Owen, Santa Ana; near Sirhan-Owen sighting on June 3, 1968, and several times in weeks before.

4. Alleged accidental meeting between Owen and Sirhan on June 3, 1968.

5. St. Moritz Hotel, Hollywood: Owen registers for the night of June 3—4, 1968.

6. Alleged Owen whereabouts from 9 A.M., June 4, to noon on June 5, 1968.

7. Ambassador Hotel, Los Angeles: RFK murdered on June 5, 1968.

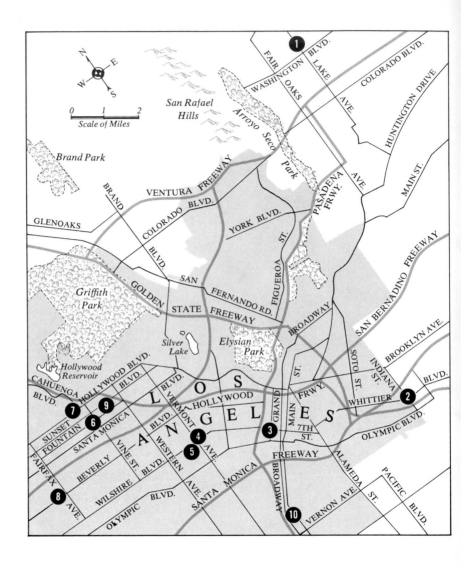

1. Sirhan family home at 696 E. Howard Street, Pasadena.

2. Beginning of Owen's alleged route through Los Angeles in his pickup truck on June 3.

3. Picks up Sirhan and friend at 7th and Grand.

4. Drops off friend with other associates at stoplight at Wilshire and Western.

5. Stops at the Ambassador Hotel at Sirhan's request "to visit a friend in the kitchen."

6. Proceeds to shoe-repair shop at Vine and Fountain in Hollywood.

7. Leaves Sirhan around 6 P.M. and goes to the Hollywood Plaza Hotel to visit "Slapsie Maxie" Rosenbloom.

8. Goes to Saints & Sinners meeting in Hollywood.

9. Meets Sirhan and associates again, then checks into the St. Moritz Hotel at midnight; meets Sirhan's associates in the early morning; then leaves for Oxnard.

10. Arrives at the Coliseum Hotel around noontime on June 5: reports to LAPD University Station to tell story at 2 P.M.

1. The corner of 7th Street and Grand Avenue, Los Angeles, where Owen allegedly first ran into Sirhan and one of his associates on June 3, 1968.
CREDIT: JIM ROSE

2. Cul-de-sac at the east entrance to the Ambassador Hotel—where Jerry Owen said that Sirhan's associates wanted him to appear with his horse and trailer at the moment of the assassination.
CREDIT: JIM ROSE

3. St. Moritz Hotel in Hollywood. Owen stayed here on the night of June 3–4 while negotiating to sell his horse to Sirhan. CREDIT: JIM ROSE

1, 2. Wild Bill's Stables, Santa Ana. Owner Bill Powers reported that Owen and Sirhan were together there just before the assassination. CREDIT: JONN CHRISTIAN

3. Stables and corrals at Owen's residence in Santa Ana, California. CREDIT: JONN CHRISTIAN

4, 5. Apparently in early 1968, Sirhan Bishara Sirhan wrote these entries in his spiral notebooks, which would later be classified by law enforcement authorities as "diaries."

6. Sirhan's final diary entries, written sixteen days before the assassination.

May 18 9.45 AM - 68

my determination to ~~eliminate~~ eliminate R.F.K. is becoming more the more of an unshakable obsession

Please pay to the order

port wine :   port wine   port wine

R.F.K must die - RFK must be killed Robert F. Kennedy must be assassinated R.F.K must be assassinated R.F.K. must be assassinated R.F.K must be assassinated R.F.K, must be assassinated R.F.K must be assassinated R.F.K. Must be assassinated assassinated ~~the~~ Robert F. Kennedy Robert F. Kennedy Robert F. Kennedy must be assassinated assassinated Robert F. Kennedy must be assassinated assassinated assassinated assassinated Robert F. Kennedy must be assassinated Robert F. Kennedy must be assassinated before 5 June 68 Robert F. Kennedy must be assassinated I have never heard please pay to the order of of of of of of of of of of of this or that   HL

0 0   0 0   0   0

Please pay to the order of

6

⑨

1

2

3

1. Unidentified LAPD investigators apparently pointing to bullet holes at the crime scene, June 5, 1968. OFFICIAL LAPD PHOTO

2. LAPD criminalist Wolfer pointing toward bullet ricochet mark. OFFICIAL LAPD PHOTO

3. LAPD officers Rozzi and Wright inspect a bullet hole discovered in a door frame in a kitchen corridor of the Ambassador Hotel in Los Angeles near where Robert Kennedy was shot. Bullet is still in the wood. CREDIT: AP WIREPHOTO

4, 5. Criminalist Wolfer attempts to demonstrate to Los Angeles County Coroner Thomas Noguchi the flight paths of bullets through RFK's jacket and body, June 8, 1968. OFFICIAL LAPD PHOTO

4

1. Coroner Noguchi measures area near two bullet holes (circled and initialed by LAPD officers, but unaccounted for later on), June 5, 1968. CREDIT: LOS ANGELES COUNTY CORONER'S OFFICE

2. Coroner Noguchi conducts his independent investigation. CREDIT: LOS ANGELES COUNTY CORONER'S OFFICE

1

1. (E 1): View taken inside kitchen serving area showing doorway leading into kitchen from the stage area. The lower right corner of the photo shows two bullet holes, which are circled. The missing portion of the panel also reportedly contained a bullet.

2. (E 2): A close-up view of the two bullet holes of the area described above.

3. (E 3): Close-up view of two bullet holes located in center door frame inside kitchen serving area, and looking in the direction of back of stage area.

4. (E 4): Close-up view of upper hinge on door leading into kitchen area from back of stage area. View shows reported mark of another bullet which struck hinge.

Note: All of the above are Official FBI Photos, taken under the supervision of Special Agent Al Grenier, and verified by Special Agent William Bailey.

1. Sirhan diary: "Di Salvo."

2, 3, 4. Three faces of William J. Bryan, Jr., who was billed "America's Most Famous Medical Hypnotist."

1. "Concerned Citizens for Bugliosi" meeting, April 1976: Paul Le Mat (*second from left*), Jonn Christian (*fourth from left*), Vincent Bugliosi, Robert Vaughn and Joseph Gellman. Seated are Lorraine Y. S. Cradock and Jocelyn Brando. This adjunct campaign support group designed a brochure detailing Bugliosi's position on the RFK case. CREDIT: MEG GLEASON

2. Press conference conducted in Los Angeles in October 1975 by (*left to right*) Dr. Robert J. Joling, Vincent Bugliosi, Paul Schrade and Allard K. Lowenstein. New evidence of a "second gun" in the RFK case was presented. CREDIT: PAUL LE MAT

3. Authors Turner and Christian with William W. Harper in his Pasadena crime lab, June 1976. CREDIT: LORRAINE Y. S. CRADOCK

1. Vincent Bugliosi with authors Christian and Turner, August 1975, Beverly Hills.
CREDIT: DIANNE HULL

2. Paul Le Mat as "Big John Milner" in *American Graffiti* (1972). CREDIT: UNIVERSAL STUDIOS

3. Dianne Hull with co-star Paul Le Mat in a scene from *Aloha, Bobby and Rose* (1975). CREDIT: CINE ARTISTS, COLUMBIA PICTURES

1. Rosalynn Carter with Dianne Hull during Wisconsin campaign of April 1976. CREDIT: GREG WALLING, ATLANTA, GEORGIA

2. Dianne Hull with Governor Jimmy Carter in Green Bay during Wisconsin primary tour. CREDIT: GREG WALLING, ATLANTA, GEORGIA

thus representing causes the senator championed. In his postconviction interview, NBC's Jack Perkins asked Sirhan what wish he might want granted. "I wish"—Sirhan's eyes glistened and his voice cracked—"I wish that Senator Kennedy were still alive." His hands reached up to cover a stream of tears.

Yet the Sirhan who went to the Ambassador Hotel on election night snarled that Kennedy was a millionaire who didn't give a damn for the poor. And the "automatic writing" in the notebooks reveal a Sirhan whose growing antipathy toward Kennedy culminated in a determination to get rid of him. But logic suggests that Sirhan was conditioned by someone else while in these trances. Sirhan himself had no reason to single out Kennedy from the other candidates—McCarthy, Hubert Humphrey and Richard Nixon— who also were openly in favor of aid to Israel. Yet his murderous intent was fixed on Kennedy long before the pre-election weekend when the warplanes issue arose in a debate.

Both Dr. Simson and Dr. Spiegel believe that Sirhan's latent Arab nationalism—what Spiegel terms, in his Grade 5 specifications, a personality core containing "a dynamism so fixed that it is subject to neither negotiation nor change"—was exploited to turn Sirhan against Kennedy. Once Sirhan accepted the idea that Kennedy was anti-Arab because he was pro-Israel, he would be freed from the bonds of inhibition that normally prevented him from killing. He would possess the high moral purpose that would justify eliminating Kennedy, just as Palle Hardrup had not scrupled to kill while under hypnosis in order to achieve "the unification of all Scandinavia."

FINALLY, WE TURN TO THE AMNESIA BLOCKS SIRHAN ASSERTEDLY continues to experience concerning his writing the notebooks and assaulting Robert Kennedy. Dr. Diamond thought that they were genuine, but caused by schizophrenia. However, after thorough examination of Sirhan, Dr. Simson concluded that he was not psychotic, and Dr. Spiegel agreed, contending that what appeared to be schizophrenic symptoms were actually manifestations of hysteria under duress. If Sirhan's trances were self-induced, as Dr.

Diamond felt, he should have been able to remember them. If they were induced by another, and a locking mechanism implanted, he would have no memory of them.

So the crucial question is whether Sirhan is telling the truth when he says he cannot remember, as he did most recently when Los Angeles Supervisors Baxter Ward and Kenneth Hahn visited him in prison in May 1977. In fact, the equivalent of a lie detector has concluded that he is telling the truth. The test was conducted by means of a technique called Psychological Stress Evaluation. PSE has gained wide acceptance as a substitute for the polygraph, although the manufacturers of the PSE instrument prefer to call it a truth detector because it can determine more positively whether a subject is being truthful than if he is lying. They maintain that the instrument, by "using electronic filtering and frequency discrimination techniques, detects, measures and graphically displays on a moving strip chart certain stress-related components of the human voice," and that the stress, "induced by fear, anxiety, guilt or conflict facilitates detection of attempted deception."*

The unique feature of the PSE instrument is that the subject does not have to be present or even know that he is being tested— it can analyze pre-recorded tapes. Recently the *National Enquirer* commissioned PSE expert Charles McQuiston, a former Army intelligence officer who helped develop the technique, to analyze the tape recording of Jack Perkins' interview of Sirhan. The key portions are:

SIRHAN: To me, sir, he [Kennedy] is still alive . . . I still don't believe what has happened . . . I don't believe that he is dead. I have no realization still that I killed him, that he is in the grave.

Analysis: Sirhan's stress level is relatively low, showing that he's telling the truth. He actually believes RFK is alive and this can only be explained by the fact that Sirhan was under some kind of hypnotic influence.

SIRHAN: There was no American dream for me. I tried, I sincerely tried to find a job. I had nothing, no identity, no hope.

* The PSE instrument is made by Dektor Counterintelligence and Security, Inc., Springfield, Virginia. It is used regularly by some 1,500 law enforcement agencies in the United States and is admitted as evidence in the courts of at least five states.

Analysis: His phrases are very indicative of hypnosis. From my days in Army intelligence, I know the words are those a skilled hypnotist would use to beat a man down, to change his thinking, to reshape his mind.

SIRHAN: I thought he was heir apparent to President Kennedy and I wish to hell he could have made it. I loved him.

Analysis: There is genuine sincerity in his statements. When Sirhan says he wished RFK could have made it, this shows me that Sirhan didn't know what he was doing—that hypnosis was governing his actions.

SIRHAN: There was a girl there.

Analysis: He's not lying. There was a girl, and, judging from the stress in his voice, he's trying to block her out of his mind. This indicates she may have played a role in the assassination. [Here again was the specter of the girl in the polka-dot dress.]

SIRHAN: I don't have the guts to do anything like that.

Analysis: He's telling the truth. There must have been some outside guiding force—hypnosis—that was responsible for him pulling the trigger.

McQuiston summed up: "Everything tells me that someone else was involved in the assassination."

Dr. John W. Heisse, Jr., president of the International Society of Stress Analysis, who has used PSE to study hundreds of persons under hypnosis, concurred with McQuiston after reviewing the PSE chart. "Sirhan kept repeating certain phrases," Heisse elaborated. "This clearly revealed he had been programmed to put himself into a trance. This is something he couldn't have learned by himself. Someone had to show him and teach him how. I believe Sirhan was brainwashed under hypnosis by the constant repetition of words like, 'You are nobody, you're nothing, the American dream is gone,' until he actually believed them. At that stage, someone implanted an idea, kill RFK, and under hypnosis the brainwashed Sirhan accepted it."*

* *National Enquirer*; also San Francisco *Examiner* (June 19, 1977).

14

Tracing the Programmer

IF SIRHAN WAS A MANCHURIAN CANDIDATE, THERE IS LOCKED within his mind the secret of who hypnoprogrammed him and how. It can be unlocked, but only by an expert on hypnosis after painstaking search and probing. As Dr. Heinz E. Hammerschlag observed in his *Hypnotism and Crime*,* the programmer assumes that "because of his very cunning precautionary measures, his deed will not be discovered."

As we have seen in the Copenhagen case, it took Dr. Reiter nineteen months to ferret out the secrets locked in Hardrup's mind—that X was the triggering signal and that

* Published by E. Reinhardt (Munich, 1954).

there were several locking mechanisms. For example, Nielsen would instruct Hardrup under hypnosis: "As soon as I give my date of birth in court, that is, the figure 10/12/1901, you will no longer know what happened to you." Or, "As soon as I raise my hand, blow my nose, turn my head to left or right, or as soon as your name is called out you will become completely confused, you will feel faint, you will begin to shout or sing out loud, or you will say that up to now you have been lying."

Dr. Hammerschlag has described a case in Bavaria in 1934 that took even longer to unravel. A husband complained that a man had swindled his wife by posing as a doctor and giving her hypnotherapy for imagined ailments. He then pushed her into prostitution and, later, programmed her to put a gun to her husband's head and pull the trigger. Fortunately, the gun had been unloaded. The woman's mind was a blank—she had no memory of turning tricks or attempting to murder her husband. As Hammerschlag put it, "In uncovering a crime committed under hypnosis, account must be taken of the fact that the culprit has tried to suggest to his hypnotized subject loss of memory in relation to all details in the deed and the preparation for it."

The deprogrammer, after attaining a high degree of rapport with the woman, put her into deep hypnosis and had her repeat everything that came into her mind. From the spasmodic outpouring of words—similar to the automatic writing in Sirhan's notebooks—there emerged two clues: "Auto—6071" and "19-3." The former turned out to be the license number of the fake doctor's automobile, and the latter "a suggestion word for producing complete blockage of memory." The "doctor" had threatened her that "she would fall dead if she would cross the boundaries which he had set to her memory." The deprogramming took two years, but the culprit was convicted and sentenced to ten years in prison.

A more recent case occurred in 1967 in the Philippines, although it ended unsuccessfully. The National Bureau of Investigation (NBI) suspected that a man they had in custody had been hypnoprogrammed to assassinate President Ferdinand Marcos. The NBI called in a hypnotist to try to deprogram him. In his report, the hypnotist asserted that while "it is firmly accepted that a properly hypnotized subject can be made to set out a posthypnotic instruction during his normal, waking state with the use of pre-arranged key words or devices . . . the remarkable character of the zombie state in our subject is its deeply ingrained and systematic presentation, indicating a certain disturbing degree of conditioning." The subject exhibited a "deep-seated resistance due to the presence of a posthypnotic block," but the hypnotist did draw out of him that he used the name Luis Castillo and had been trained by the CIA for activities against Fidel Castro. After six months the deprogramming was discontinued for political reasons and the subject deported to the United States.*

During the Napoleonic Wars, French couriers were hypnotized and given messages preceded by key words. Once they were safely through enemy lines, their contacts on the other side would repeat the key words, enabling the courier to repeat the messages. But if captured by the enemy, the hapless couriers could not remember the messages even under torture. The late Dr. G. D. Estabrooks, a pioneer in the military use of hypnosis, recounted an experiment after World War II in which a message was locked into the mind of an Army captain in Tokyo with the phrase "The moon is clear." When the unwitting captain arrived in Washington, Dr. Estabrooks spoke the phrase and the captain delivered the message he could not have remembered moments before.

There exists no clinical reason why Sirhan could not be deprogrammed at this late date. In one case a woman who was put under hypnosis recalled everything she experienced in a trance thirteen years previously, although in the intervening years she had remembered nothing. To regress Sirhan hypnotically to try to find clues to the locking of his mind would require a hypnotist with whom he had attained a high degree of rapport. Dr. Simson said that he had reached such a stage and was about to begin hypnotic deprogramming sessions when he was halted by the prison administration. From his study of the case, Dr. Spiegel is convinced that he could achieve significant results in as little as three days.

But any such attempts hinge on the cooperation of the California authorities, and thus far it has not been forthcoming. In

* Report of Victor R. Sanchez, September 1, 1967; copy in possession of the authors.

September 1977, for example, a Los Angeles judge turned down Sirhan's request to be allowed to return to the Ambassador Hotel in the hope that his memory might be jogged. "There is no indication—psychological, medical, astrological or otherwise—that this man's memory can be refreshed." The judge, William Hogaboom, had the unfortunate luck of being put in juxtaposition, in many newspapers, with news of the CIA's MK-Ultra Mind-Control Program.* The program included a study called Operation Artichoke to determine if a person could be induced to involuntarily commit an assassination.

Returning Sirhan to the scene of the crime, however, would not have jarred a return of his capacity to recall crucial events, not if the experts are right. This still requires intensive deprogramming by medical men with the requisite training and understanding of the evidential side of the RFK assassination case.

Curiously enough, though, Sirhan's own latest lawyer, Godfrey Isaac of Beverly Hills, resisted any kind of medically supervised probing into the area of amnesia, on the grounds that too much pressure in this case might somehow jeopardize his client's parole status—which had already been set by the parole authorities in California to be 1984. How merely attempting to find out if Sirhan had been a helpless pawn in the RFK case would have been compromised by such a petition to the court was never explained by Isaac.

Then, again, neither was the strange rationale once offered by another of Sirhan's string of barristers. In early 1971 Bill Harper showed noted Hollywood lawyer Luke McKissack the evidence pointing toward an assassin other than his client. The lawyer refused to incorporate the criminalist's findings in his appeals case for Sirhan, then later insisted to newsmen that if there had been a "second gun" fired at the assassination scene, it would have been someone without any connection with Sirhan or his actions "who seized on the impulse of the moment" to fire a bullet into RFK's brain. (No newsman challenged that gem either.)

* See, for example, the San Francisco *Examiner* (September 2, 1977).

SPURRED BY BOB KAISER'S FEELING THAT SOMETHING IN SIRHAN'S recent past there was "a shadowy someone," we combed through our background file on Sirhan for clues. From the case histories, it appeared that the programmer would have to have had prolonged access to Sirhan in order to condition him. Even the LAPD had conceded that it was possible. In his book Chief Houghton wrote: "SUS explored the hypnotic-programming contention and was advised that it would take a series of sessions between the hypnotist and Sirhan, if, in fact, it was workable at all. No evidence of such sessions could be found; no hypnotist could be produced."*

Sirhan Sirhan had spent his early childhood in a Palestine torn by the Arab-Israeli conflict of 1948. His family belonged to a Lutheran congregation but in 1956 switched to the Greek Orthodox Church, and soon thereafter was able to migrate to America. Their immigration sponsors were a socially prominent Pasadena couple active in the Republican Party and, in time, the Nixon campaigns. (The couple had known Richard Nixon at Whittier College.)

In 1965 Sirhan took the first step toward becoming a jockey by signing on as an apprentice groom at the Hollywood Park and Santa Anita race tracks. He became friendly with a fellow groom, forty-one-year-old Walter Thomas Rathke. Rathke's main interests seem to have been fundamentalist Christianity and, paradoxically, the occult. "We had many discussions on the occult—reincarnation, karma, clairvoyance, astral projection, the human aura," Sirhan wrote us about his relationship with the older man. "But I don't remember that we ever discussed politics."

Apparently Rathke's politics corresponded with his fundamentalist beliefs. A man who knew him advised us that Rathke was "far right politically and has the general 'don't argue with 'em, knock 'em on their ass' attitude toward kid-raising, liberals and malcontents in general."†

Rathke seemingly exerted a profound influence over Sirhan. The two experimented with meditative exercises, a mild form of

* Houghton, *op. cit.*, pp. 149–50.
† Letters from Victor Endersby to the authors, May 28, and July 11, 1970.

hypnosis. In 1967, after Rathke moved north to the Livermore Valley near San Francisco to work at the Pleasanton Race Stables, they kept in touch. Rathke remained very much on Sirhan's mind, for in the "automatic writing" in the notebooks there appears: "Hello tom perhaps you could use the enclosed $ Sol [Sirhan's nickname at the racetracks] . . . 11 o'clock Sirhan Livermore Sirhan Sirhan Pleasanton . . . Hello Tom racetrack perhaps you could use the enclosed $ . . . Tom—Eleven Dollars—would like to come up for several days—meet me at the airport."

According to a friend of the Sirhan family, Lynne Massey Mangan, Rathke visited Sirhan in Pasadena in December 1967 and again in March 1968, on which occasion he had dinner with the family. After the assassination Mary Sirhan found a letter from Rathke that she hid from the police. "He wrote Sirhan telling him that he should stop practicing his self-hypnosis rituals with the mirror and the candles and the likes," Lynne Mangan told us, "or if he didn't he might lose control of himself and do something terrible."*

Rathke expressed this concern himself to the Theosophists in early 1968, after he had begun attending their meetings. According to Theosophist elder Victor Endersby, Rathke told a local meeting of the society shortly after the assassination that "Sirhan had been studying a course in meditation which might have had a bad effect on his psyche." When Endersby learned that Rathke was actually an "evangelistic type" who "runs some sort of spiritualistic church himself," he became suspicious of his abrupt appearance in the Theosophists' midst. The society was hardly Christian evangelist, and the spiritualists were its hereditary enemies.

Rathke came to the attention of the LAPD in early 1969 after one of Sirhan's attorneys, in his opening statements at the trial, contended that his client was in a dissociated state at the time of the shooting. The statement evidently prompted police to look for rebuttal evidence. They were curious about Sirhan's notebook entries concerning Rathke, which were followed by the exhortation "Let us do it" repeated four times. In juxaposition to these jottings appeared "Al Hilal," "Master Kuthumi," "Illuminati" and "North-

* Authors' interview with Mrs. Mangan, October 1972.

ern Valley." Al Hilal was an occult sect originating in England at the turn of the century, while Master Koot Hoomi was the Tibetan mystic from whom Madame Blavatsky, founder of the Theosophist movement, received ethereal guidance. Illuminati, of course, was the gigantic "one-world conspiracy" that was the nightmare of the ultraright. As we have seen, John Steinbacher and Anthony Hilder pointedly named the Theosophists, Rosicrucians, *et al.*, as part of the "Illuminati conspiracy" they held responsible for the JFK and RFK assassinations. "Northern Valley" was an enigma, but it was possible that it meant the Livermore Valley.

The LAPD was evidently concerned that the defense might convince the jury that Sirhan's occult practices had inadvertently compelled him to shoot Kennedy. On February 21, while the trial was in progress, SUS Sergeant Phil Sartuche flew north to the Livermore Valley and interviewed Tom Rathke. (What he learned, if anything, was not in any SUS document we were able to obtain.) While in the area, he also talked to Victor Endersby, wanting to know what connection might exist between the Theosophists and the Rosicrucians, as alleged by Steinbacher and Hilder. There was none, Endersby said. Sartuche also asked whether there were any Theosophist or Rosicrucian "meditation" or "development" practices that might have put Sirhan into a hypnotic condition. None, said Endersby. The sergeant showed Endersby a "rogues' gallery" of photographs, but none was even faintly familiar. Almost as an afterthought, Sartuche inquired about Rathke, but when Endersby offered to put him in touch with persons who could give first-hand information about Rathke's infiltration of the Theosophists, he dropped the subject.

Sartuche's line of questioning convinced Endersby that the LAPD suspected someone had tampered with Sirhan's mind, and he was equally certain that someone had set up the Theosophists to absorb the blame. We agreed. We decided to ask Sirhan himself about the "Illuminati" and "Kuthumi" entries in his notebooks. Surprisingly, he replied that he did not know "anything about the Illuminati, unless the word is attached to the name of the organization headed by Manly Palmer Hall" (it is not), and that Kuthumi "sounds familiar in occult literature." No student of Theosophy would fail to recognize Master Koot Hoomi, much less fail to spell his name correctly. Thus it seemed to us as if someone had verbally implanted these words in Sirhan's trance-susceptible mind, which produced the phonetic spelling.

In his hitchhiker story, Jerry Owen had intimated that several of Sirhan's possible co-conspirators, a swarthy man and a blond girl who negotiated for the purchase of the horse, were involved in the occult. "He had on a turtleneck sweater that was kind of an orangish-yellow color with a chain around his neck and a big, round thing that you see 'em all wearing now, even men on television," the preacher had said. "And I noticed a chain hanging around her neck with a round ornament on." Owen was clumsily describing an occult amulet with the ankh symbol, but John Steinbacher was more articulate in his book, claiming that the Illuminati were behind the RFK assassination. "Within the so-called 'peace movement' in America runs this same cabalistic and occult strain," Steinbacher wrote, "with its ANKH symbol around the necks of such celebrities as TV personality Les Crane."*

We had no direct information that Owen knew Steinbacher and Hilder, or, for that matter, that Steinbacher and Hilder had ever laid eyes on Sirhan.† But we did learn that Hilder, who had been at the Ambassador Hotel on election night passing out anti-Kennedy handbills, had acquired more than a passing interest in hypnosis. In discussing the possibility that his programmer might have discovered Sirhan at a hypnosis school or demonstration, Hollywood hypnotist Gil Boyne mentioned to Christian that he himself held a "Self-Help Institute" using hypnosis in the fall of 1967 that attracted several political extremists who might have seen some potential in Sirhan. One that Boyne named was Anthony Hilder.

Hilder signed up for instructions for himself and a girl friend, explaining that he wanted to find out the nature and effect of hypnosis on the individual. After attending several classes, they dropped out. Then, in December 1967, he came to see Boyne,

---

* Steinbacher, *op. cit.*, p. 19.

† There was a distant linkage of personages that trailed back to Owen, however. The admited closeness of Owen to preacher Bob Wells, his mutual link to Edgar Eugene Bradley's "Defense Fund" in the JFK conspiracy case in New Orleans, and the address of the Steinbacher-Hilder American United being used therein.

wild-eyed and agitated, muttering about something "political." He whipped out a .38 police special and two boxes of shells and offered them to the frightened Boyne as payment for arrears tuition. Hilder confided that Boyne would soon have "great need" for the weapons because an event would occur that would touch off race riots around the country. But Hilder had been quite insistent that he not be placed under hypnosis himself. He knew "big things," he said, and he didn't want them to come out.

IN THE SPRING OF 1966 SIRHAN QUIT HIS JOB AT THE RACE TRACKS because he felt he wasn't getting anywhere. Shortly thereafter he scribbled in his notebook: "I have secured a position as assistant to the manager of Corona Breeding Farm—(Dezi [sic] Arnaz's) Res Sirhan $600 per month." The farm was actually the Granja Vista del Rio Ranch near Corona, owned by a group that included Desi Arnaz, the former husband of Lucille Ball. The ranch bred and trained racing horses.

Sirhan purportedly secured the job through a Frank Donneroummas, whom he had known at the Santa Anita track and who reputedly was a relative of the ranch manager, Bert C. Altfillisch. Donneroummas' true name was Henry R. Ramistella, but he had employed the alias to hide a long rap sheet acquired in New York and Miami. Donneroummas was Sirhan's boss at the ranch, and according to co-workers, the two became quite friendly.* In one of Sirhan's notebooks was the passage: "happiness hppiness Dona Donaruma Donaruma Frank Donaruma pl please ple please pay to 5 please pay to the order of Sirhan Sirhan the amount of 5..."

After the assassination the FBI interviewed one of Sirhan's co-workers, Terry Welch, who "listed Desi Arnaz, Buddy Ebsen and Dale Robertson, prominent television personalities, as horse owners who were well-acquainted with Sirhan." All three actors were prominent in Hollywood's more conservative political circles. Desi Arnaz came from a wealthy Cuban family and was a fervent opponent of Fidel Castro.

* LAPD report I-1931.

Welch pegged Sirhan as a staunch anti-Communist. "In conversations with fellow employees who were refugees from Communist countries, such as Cuba and Hungary, Sirhan always gave Welch the impression that he was very much opposed to Communism," the FBI report stated. "He indicated a strong liking for the United States and never exhibited any particular loyalty or feeling toward the country of his birth." Welch said that "the Reverend Leo Hill, Circle City Baptist Church, Ninth and Sheridan, Corona, would possibly know Sirhan inasmuch as Sirhan gave Welch a card for this church and suggested that he see Rev. Hill when he was having personal problems."* Hill's church subsequently merged with the large Riverside Baptist Church, a pillar of the fundamentalist right, and we located him there. "Sirhan attended services a couple of times," the reverend recalled. "But as far as coming to me personally, he never did that."†

It is not difficult to envision how Corona, with its mix of the horse crowd, Hollywood actors, fundamentalist religionists and political conservatives, might have been the locus where Owen's and Sirhan's paths first crossed.‡ Even though Sirhan left the ranch in December 1966—he spent the ensuing year unemployed and frequenting the Santa Anita track with Tom Rathke—Corona seems to have remained a focal point. Bob Kaiser asked him about his whereabouts on Monday, June 3. "He first denied that he was anywhere. Then, later on, he admitted that he'd gone to Corona late in the day—4 or 5 o'clock. Then, still later on, he admitted that on that occasion and other occasions he really wasn't in Corona—that Corona was on the outer periphery of his travels."

Still, it was Sirhan who had brought up Corona, which was only twenty miles upstream on the Santa Ana River from Owen's home, and the previous Saturday he had shown up at a Corona

* FBI report June 6, 1968, at Southfield, Michigan.

† Authors' interview with the Reverend Leo Hill, November 8, 1969. The Riverside Baptist Temple is listed in the "First National Directory of 'Rightist' Groups, Publications and Some Individuals in the United States," sixth edition, published by the Alert Americans Association of Los Angeles.

‡ A possible linkage might have been: Owen's close ties to Jerome Weber, the lawyer for Desi Arnaz, and Sirhan's claim to having been employed at the actor's thoroughbred-horse ranch.

pistol range. This came out at the trial when Sirhan was asked, "On June 1, do you remember you went to the range at Corona, signing in?" At first Sirhan claimed he could not remember, then acknowledged, "Yes, sir, I do. A policeman was there teaching some people, and the way he taught them to fire guns, that was the way I was taught, too." Neither prosecutor nor his defense lawyers asked the who and why behind this curious answer.

Earlier on that Saturday he was tentatively identified as a young man target-shooting in a secluded part of the Santa Ana Mountains south of Corona. A two-sentence LAPD report advised that Santa Ana insurance executive Dean Pack, who was hiking in the area with his teen-age son, "was exhibited a photograph of Sirhan" which he said "strongly resembled" the shooter, but the police dropped the matter when Pack said he "was not positive of this identification."

In an interview on December 12, 1969, Pack told Christian that the LAPD had talked to him only by telephone and thus could not have shown him a picture. But Pack related that after the assassination he thought he recognized news photos of Sirhan as the young man accompanied by another man who was six feet tall and ruddy-complexioned, with sandy hair, and a girl in her early twenties with long brunet hair.

"The main thing that struck me was how unfriendly they were," Pack recounted. "The person who looked like Sirhan didn't say a word. He just stood there and glared at me. The other fellow was the only one who would talk." They were shooting at cans set up on a hillside. "Sirhan was shooting a pistol," Pack said. "As I walked away from them, you know, you get the funny sensation that it would be possible for them to put a bullet in your back. I was relieved to get out of their sight."

Dean Pack said that he offered to take the FBI to the spot so that they could recover the bullets and shell casings and look for fingerprints on the bottles and cans the trio had handled, but the Bureau was uninterested. "I got the attitude that they had their man so why spin wheels about anything else," Pack remarked.

ALTHOUGH SIRHAN NEVER KNEW IT, HE BECAME THE STAR—AND sole actor—in a motion picture filmed after his return to the family residence in Pasadena in 1967. The 16mm color film clearly shows him roaming the streets of Pasadena, but the purpose for which it was taken remains an enigma.

The existence of the film came to light in 1969 when the manager of a Los Angeles office building was cleaning out premises vacated by private detective Earl LaFoon and found a canister labeled "Sirhan B. Sirhan—1967" that contained a reel of film. Curious, the manager ran the film on a projector, then turned it over to the FBI.* In 1975 a copy turned up in the hands of Los Angeles CBS television correspondent Bill Stout, who aired it with comments about its "strange" implications.

Shortly thereafter Jonn Christian located Earl LaFoon and found him evasive about the film. First he said it had been stolen from him, then denied having done the filming, and finally abruptly terminated the conversation by saying, "You'll have to ask the Argonaut Insurance Company about this. That's all I have to say."

The Argonaut Insurance Company was the firm that had paid Sirhan $1,705 in settlement of a workmen's compensation claim for injuries received in a fall from a horse while employed at the Corona ranch. On occasion insurance companies hire private investigators to secretly film claimants in the hope of documenting, for example, a person pretending to have a severe back injury lifting a heavy object or even playing golf. But Sirhan's injuries had been minor, and he did not claim to be disabled. There was nothing to prove by motion-picture surveillance, which undoubtedly would not have been ordered in any case because of the relatively small amount involved.

Christian decided to check with the Argonaut Insurance Company. A spokesman denied knowing anything about the film. We called on private detective Al Newman to use his inside contacts at Argonaut to see what had happened. He reported back that

* Authors' interview with United Press International photographer Michael Ellard, Los Angeles, 1976.

"their file has been destroyed."* Another trail had ended on a familiar note.

IN LATE 1967 SIRHAN INEXPLICABLY DROPPED FROM SIGHT. A VET-eran LAPD officer (who wishes to remain anonymous) told us that SUS, in tracing Sirhan's activities during the year preceding the assassination, wound up with a three-month gap in his where-abouts. A neighbor of the Sirhan family advised the FBI that Mary Sirhan became "extremely worried" when her son left home "and she did not know his whereabouts for quite some time."†

When he returned, Sirhan's interest in the occult had deepened. He haunted a Pasadena bookstore specializing in occult subjects. In March 1968 he reportedly appeared at a Theosophical Society meeting in Pasadena, although he curtly refused to identify him-self. He mailed in a membership application to the Rosicrucian Order, paying $4 dues, and in late May attended a meeting of the Pasadena lodge. These wholly tentative links with the Theosophists and Rosicrucians set the stage for the propaganda theatrics immedi-ately following the shooting, in which Mayor Sam Yorty branded the Rosicrucians a "Communist organization," and Steinbacher and Hilder implied that the Theosophists had exerted a sinister in-fluence over Sirhan. Conveniently omitted was the fact that a police search of Sirhan's car yielded a volume entitled *Healing: The Divine Art*, by Manly Palmer Hall, founder of the Philosophical Research Society (the book mysteriously disappeared from the grand jury exhibits). Hall, a man with penetrating eyes, chiseled features and a Buddha-like figure, was a master hypnotist with a practice in hypnotherapy. Some time ago he had gained consider-able publicity from hypnotic antics, on one occasion "putting under" a movie actor and convincing him he was suffocating, with the result that the actor tore apart a movie set in his frantic search for "air."

We queried Sirhan in San Quentin about Hall and his society.

* Memo to the authors dated October 15, 1975.
† FBI Summary Report, *op. cit.*, pp. 859–60.

He wrote back that he remembered paying several visits to the headquarters, an alabaster temple near Griffith Park. "The secretary there had a distinct foreign accent," he said (Hall's wife is German-born), "and I had to ask her to unlock the book cases for me to get the books I wanted to read in the library. I remember seeing Manly Hall himself there." Sirhan's dabbling with the occult society is, by itself, innocuous, but there is a certain irony in the fact that he was drinking from the same mystical fountain as Sam Yorty. For some two decades, the mayor had been a student of Hall, whom he regarded as his guru.

OUR QUEST FOR SIRHAN'S PROGRAMMER HAD BEEN NO MORE SUC-cessful than the search for Amelia Earhart until Dr. Herbert Spiegel gave us a lead. Anything mentioned in the presence of a subject under hypnosis is automatically etched into his mind, especially if it comes from the hypnotist. And it might flow out at any time.

This brought us back to the notebooks containing Sirhan's "automatic writing." Could he have scrawled something during a trance regression that the hypnotist had mentioned while programming him? There was a passage that stood out because it was unlike the others, having nothing to do with horses, politics, money or past acquaintances. It read: "God help me . . . please help me. Salvo Di Di Salvo Dic S Salvo." The reference apparently was to Albert Di Salvo, the notorious Boston Strangler. That case had been cracked by the use of hypnotism, and the hypnotist was Dr. William Joseph Bryan, Jr., of Los Angeles. Bryan billed himself as "probably the leading expert in the world" on the use of hypnosis in criminal law, and often boasted about being called into baffling cases by law enforcement agencies, including the LAPD. The Boston Strangler case was his tour de force, and he was incessantly mentioning it.

An imposing man with a wrestler's girth, Bryan claimed he was once drummer with the Tommy Dorsey band and a commercial airplane pilot. During the Korean War he had put his hypnotic skills to use as, in his words, "chief of all medical survival training for the United States Air Force, which meant the brainwashing section."* After the war he reportedly became a CIA consultant in the Agency's experimentation with mind control and behavior modification.

Refused membership in all traditional medical societies, Bryan set up a medical and hypnotherapy practice on the Sunset Strip in Hollywood which he named the American Institute of Hypnosis. He used it as an aegis for wide-ranging symposiums on such topics as "Successful Treatments of Sexual Disorders." "I enjoy variety and I like to get to know people on a deep emotional level," he once told a magazine interviewer. "One way of getting to know people is through intercourse." In 1969 the California Board of Medical Examiners found him guilty of unprofessional conduct for sexually molesting four women patients who submitted under hypnosis.†

Despite his advocacy of sexual freedom, Bryan was a Bible-quoting fundamentalist who belonged to a fire-and-brimstone sect called the Old Roman Catholic Church, which broke away from the Vatican over a century ago.‡ Bryan claimed to be a descendant of the fiery orator William Jennings Bryan, who opposed the teaching of evolution in the celebrated Scopes "monkey trial," and he frequently was a guest preacher at fundamentalist churches in Southern California.

Only hours after the RFK shooting and before Sirhan had been identified, Bryan appeared on the Los Angeles radio program of Ray Briem (KABC) and offhandedly commented that the suspect probably acted under posthypnotic suggestion. Two years later, when Bryan appeared on another local radio program, Christian called in and asked him about his prescient analysis on the Briem show. At first Bryan hedged, then declared that he had no professional opinion because he had not personally examined Sirhan. He quickly switched the subject to the Hollywood Strangler case in which a Henry Bush was executed for murder. "He utilized self-

* Interview on KNX-FM, Los Angeles, February 12, 1972.

† Bryan was given five years' probation on the condition that he have an adult woman present whenever treating female patients.

‡ Curiously, David W. Ferrie, a prime suspect in New Orleans DA Jim Garrison's 1967 probe into the John Kennedy assassination, also belonged to this small sect. Ferrie was found dead on February 22, 1967, shortly after being interrogated.

hypnosis," Bryan asserted, noting that Bush once tried to burn off his own arm with cigarettes under self-hypnosis "to get rid of the offending part—just like the old thing in the Bible, you know: 'If the left hand offend thee, cut it off!' "

When we asked Sirhan about the Di Salvo entry in his notebook, he replied that the name was entirely foreign to him. Was it possible that Bryan had placed Sirhan in a trance state and, given his propensity to boast constantly about the Boston Strangler case, repeated Di Salvo's name over and over—thus etching it into Sirhan's subconscious? In any case, Sirhan would not remember either the circumstances of his exposure to the name or who mentioned it.

Since Bryan's ego seemed boundless, it was possible that an interview with him would produce the unexpected. It did. On June 18, 1974 Betsy Langman, a disarmingly attractive New York writer with whom we had been comparing notes, talked to Bryan in his Sunset Strip office suite on the pretext of doing a general article on hypnosis. The doctor went on at length about his standing in the field of hypnosis ("I am probably the leading expert in the world") and abilities ("I can hypnotize everybody in this office in less than five minutes"), detailed his successes with Henry Bush and Albert Di Salvo, and ventured opinions on various aspects of hypnosis. But when Langman, who had been researching the possibility of assassination through mind control, asked, "Do you feel that Sirhan could have been self-hypnotized?," his expansiveness vanished. "I'm not going to comment on that case," Bryan said curtly, "because I didn't hypnotize him." When Langman explained that she simply wanted his opinion, Bryan exploded. "You are going around trying to find some more ammunition to put out that same old crap," he said, "that people can be hypnotized into doing all these weird things." He charged out of his office, snapping, "This interview is over!"

Shaken by the angry outburst, Langman went across the street for coffee accompanied by a sympathetic secretary. Langman was in for another shock. According to the secretary, Bryan had received an emergency call from Laurel, Maryland, only minutes after George Wallace was shot. The call somehow concerned the shooting. (Governor Wallace was shot and badly injured on May 15, 1972, at

Laurel while campaigning for the presidency; his assailant was Arthur Bremer.)

In the spring of 1977 Bryan was found dead in a Las Vegas motel room, "from natural causes," the coroner said. (Curiously, this word was issued *before* the official autopsy.) Shortly thereafter we were put in contact with two Beverly Hills call girls who claim to have known Bryan intimately. They had been "servicing" him on an average of twice a week for four years, they said, and usually were present at the same time. During the last year of his life, he was deeply depressed because his paramour had run off with another man. He became strung out on drugs, and his groin and thighs were pocked with bruises from hypodermic needles. (No mention of these marks appeared on the coroner's report.)

The girls said that to relieve Bryan's depression they repeatedly titillated his enormous ego by getting him to "talk about all the famous people you've hypnotized." As if by rote Bryan would begin with his role of deprogramming Albert Di Salvo in the Boston Strangler case for F. Lee Bailey, then boast that he had hypnotized Sirhan Sirhan. The girls didn't sense anything unusual in the Sirhan angle, for Bryan had told them many times that he "worked with the LAPD" on murder cases, and they didn't know that he had absolutely no contact with Sirhan following the assassination. One of the girls thought that Bryan had mentioned James Earl Ray once, but wasn't sure. But both girls were certain of the name Sirhan Sirhan.*

The call girls also linked Bryan to the CIA. At the outset of their relationship with him, he instructed them to call an unlisted phone number at his office. If someone else answered, they were to say they were with "the Company" (an insider's term for the CIA) and they would be put through to him. According to the girls, Bryan repeatedly confided that he was not only a CIA agent but involved in "top secret projects." However, when he began

---

* In October 1977 the LAPD was awarded a $10,000 grant from the American Express Company for "pioneer work in developing hypnosis as an investigative technique." It has been established that Ray, while residing in Los Angeles immediately prior to the King assassination, did consult with a hypnotist named Xavier von Koss.

bragging about such escapades as crawling over rooftops at night in Europe, they were a bit skeptical. "We couldn't see Doc doing that kind of thing—not all three hundred pounds of him, we couldn't," one of the girls said, laughing.

Upon Bryan's death his offices were sealed off to newsmen by his estate's probate lawyer, John Miner (who had also helped prosecute Sirhan as a deputy DA). There remains the question of Bryan's claimed hypnotist-subject relationship with Sirhan, and what role his connection with the CIA might have played in it.

15

The Trial

THE LOS ANGELES SUPERIOR COURTS BUILDING PERCHES ON a slope on North Hill Street in the heart of the Civic Center complex. On the fourth floor is Judge Jack A. Crickard's courtroom. Its walls are paneled with oak squares, and a large frosted-glass ceiling panel diffuses artificial light with the effect of a skylight. The room is comfortably intimate, seating only thirty-six spectators.

Judge Crickard is one of the more anonymous components of the judicial machinery. Born in a small town in Ohio in 1920, he obtained a law degree from the University of Southern California and became a partner in a staid Glendale firm specializing in water law. In 1970 Governor Ronald Reagan appointed him to the bench. His bland, pinkish face rarely shows expression, and on the infrequent occasions when he does smile, it seems that only one side of his wide, thin-lipped mouth curls up, as if not to commit him fully to levity.

The trial of Jerry Owen versus television station KCOP began before Crickard on the late afternoon of July 2, 1975, only twenty minutes before the five-year statute of limitations governing pursuit of a lawsuit would have expired. In fact, KCOP's lawyers had been fairly certain there would be no trial—for one thing, Owen was listed as his own attorney, although it was apparent he had outside legal assistance, and for another, they could not conceive that he would want his dirty linen hung out in public.* But as the trial deadline neared and it began to look as if Owen would go through with it, KCOP offered him an out-of-court settlement of $50,000 to spare the tremendous cost of a trial. But to the station's surprise, the preacher haughtily countered with a demand for $650,000 cash plus an equal amount of free air time on KCOP. The reason for his confidence surfaced only days before the trial opened when a battery of seven lawyers from five law firms from as far away as Utah and Arizona stepped up beside him.

KCOP's trial lawyer was Michael Wayland, a short, tow-headed man whose office is lined with trophies earned in figure-skating competition with his pretty wife as a partner. Wayland's law firm (Robert Brimberry Associates), representing KCOP's insurance carrier, had assigned Wayland as an observer during the preceding three year period. He took complete charge when it began to look like a trial was imminent, some two weeks before it actually convened. At first Wayland insisted on his right to a jury, but changed his mind when he looked over the list of prospective jurors and decided that they might be susceptible to "The Walking Bible's" glib, God-invoking tongue and might not grasp the intricacies of the

---

* When Owen filed his original lawsuit on July 7, 1970, no reference whatever was made to the RFK assassination. The pleading read "Breach of Contract and Conspiracy," and it merely referred to the "starting and spreading of rumors" by the defendants. It wasn't until the lawsuit developed depositions on both sides that the RFK case became as issue—even though court records indicate that Owen knew about the alleged slander at the very outset (July 1969).

assassination issue. The attorney expected that the trial judge would be Charles Older, who had performed capably at the complex trial of the Manson Family. But at the last minute a malpractice case Crickard was scheduled to hear was settled out of court and he drew the assignment.

Neither of us were present at the trial, although both sides wanted us as witnesses. Owen had prepared subpoenas—we guessed that he wanted to question us about the material we had furnished KCOP—but Turner lived well outside the 150-mile radius that compelled his appearance. Prior to the trial Owen had offered $500 to a young assassination buff named Rusty Rhodes, who was acquainted with Christian, to serve the subpoena on him, and Rhodes had obliged. But Christian wrote the presiding judge of the Superior Courts explaining that the service was faulty and that our "file data on Owen . . . is of such a nature that it hardly belongs in any civil action." We doubted that Owen had any idea of the breadth of our knowledge about his activities, and we did not feel that a civil courtroom was the appropriate place to air them. We had seen enough intimidation, violence and disappearance of evidence over the years to justify reserving our investigative file.

For his part Mike Wayland wanted us to testify to help demonstrate that Owen himself, not KCOP, was responsible for making the hitchhiker story a public issue open to conjecture. Christian met with Wayland only four days before the trial opened, presenting him with the reasons we did not feel free to testify. He did agree, however, to assist Wayland from behind the scenes. He gave the attorney a copy of the transcript of Turner's interview with Owen in 1968 and briefed him—strictly for background—on the events at Wild Bill's Stables, the subsequent attempt on John Chris Weatherly's life and the general content of our file. After the trial began, Wayland called Christian practically every night and read pertinent portions of the "dailies"—the court reporters' hurriedly typed transcripts of the day's proceedings—to get his reaction and guidance.

The trial opened with Owen's lawyers trying to show that their client had been in the evangelistic big league until his career was ruined by the slanderous actions of the KCOP and Ohrbach's management. To this end they even subpoenaed Kathryn Kuhlman, a superstar on the Bible circuit whom Owen claimed as a close friend and co-equal in the "business," but Kuhlman's attorney successfully fought her appearance.* The first reference to the RFK assassination came when KCOP president John Hopkins was questioned by Owen attorney Arthur Evry about the June 1969 meeting between Christian and the station management.

Q. Was there a discussion of an alleged involvement of Reverend Owen in that assassination?
A. Yes.
Q. Did you understand that involvement to be criminal in the assassination?
A. Yes.

Mike Wayland objected, but Crickard overruled the objection.

An uncomfortable-looking Victor Yacullo, the KCOP counsel who had participated in the 1969 meeting, was the next witness summoned by Owen. Evry questioned him about our suspicions that *The Walking Bible* program might have been used to disguise payoff monies as contributions from a legion of viewers. "Other than Mr. Christian's allegations," Evry asked, "was there any other evidence which came to your attention to indicate that the show was being used as a method of obtaining a payoff for the Reverend Owen as a result of his being involved in the assassination of Robert Kennedy?" Yacullo shook his head; he had studiously avoided exploring the assassination aspect.

Next Owen's side put on a parade of character witnesses attesting to his ministerial goodness. Conspicuously absent was Sam Yorty, the ex-mayor who had engaged in a back-slapping session with Owen on *The Walking Bible* show. But Owen sidekick Johnny Gray took the stand, describing himself as a "boxing trainer and technical adviser" to professional fighters, among them ex-heavyweight champion George Foreman. On cross-examination during the fourth day of the trial, Wayland, armed with notes from Christian's 1969 interviews with Gray, pried an admission from Gray that for some thirty years he had been a "commissioned special officer" who performed bodyguard services for Owen around

* Ms. Kuhlman was dying of cancer at the time.

the country, which removed Gray from the "objective witness" category and raised the question of why the preacher required an armed companion. Next, Wayland brought up the 1969 shooting incident in Griffith Park.

"I don't specifically recall it," Gray mumbled, but when Wayland consulted his notes as if they were an official document, Gray's memory suddenly revived. Despite emphatic hand signals and body language from Owen, he laconically told of the two men in the blue Mustang who shot at them near the observatory, but instead of the black and white men described to Christian earlier, the assailants were "just American white boys."

After getting Gray to recount the gunfire episode at the police station, Wayland asked, "And based on that, you think that the police were trying to do away with Mr. Owen?"

"I don't know," Gray replied. "That remains open to this day. I don't know what they were doing!"

"Mr. Gray, what was your profession during the time Mr. Owen came in contact with Sirhan?" Wayland asked. Gray's mouth went sand-dry. "You wish a drink of water, sir?" the attorney inquired politely, noting that his witness seemed hypersensitive about the RFK case. He then established that Gray was living not far from the Coliseum Hotel at the time.

Q. Did you ever see Mr. Owen with Sirhan?
A. No . . . not to my recollection.
Q. Did Mr. Owen tell you what transpired on the Monday and Tuesday before Kennedy was shot?
A. Something—he told me something pertaining to that deal. He—he had a big . . . [The words hung in the air.]
Q. You had contact with him that Monday and Tuesday, is that correct?
A. Possibly.
Q. It would be very probable you did, inasmuch as you were training his fighter and living up the street from him!
A. Right. That is what I say. It is a possibility we were conferring together at that time. I can't recall explicitly.
Q. Tell me what you recall that Mr. Owen told you regarding those two days. [Owen waved his arm, but the judge ignored this attempt to coach the witness.]
A. I recall that he had a fighter by the name of Rip Reilly [sic] living

at that big hotel . . . and that he was going there and coming there or something, and he met a hitchhiker, and he gave the hitchhiker a ride.

Q. Did Mr. Owen ever identify this hitchhiker to you as Sirhan Sirhan?
A. No, he said it might have been. That is all the information I can have of that. [Gray obviously wanted to get away from this unexpected line of questioning.]
Q. That is what he told you that Monday or Tuesday *before* the assassination, is that right?
A. Yeah, right.
Q. Is that right? [the attorney wanted to make sure Gray knew what he was saying.]
A. Yes.

So the thrust of Gray's testimony was that Owen had related the hitchhiker story, including mentioning Sirhan's name, *before* the assassination. This squared with what the Reverend Perkins had told Christian, and buttressed what Bill Powers and the cowboys had reported about: a prior relationship between Owen and Sirhan. Although it was evident that Gray had been very much a part of the events of the days immediately preceding the assassination, Owen had avoided mentioning him in the versions of his story given to Turner and the LAPD. This could have been because Gray had accompanied him and Sirhan to Wild Bill's Stables.

The LAPD had learned about Gray and his close relationship with Owen, and in fact detectives had driven Gray to the Apple Valley area, on the fringe of the Mojave Desert, shortly after the assassination in a fruitless attempt to find a ranch where the preacher was said to keep horses. Gray had mentioned this to Christian in 1969, and Christian had told Wayland. Now Wayland made a tactical error. Without laying a testimonial foundation, he braced Gray with the Apple Valley trip. Evry objected, and Crickard made Wayland explain what he was driving at. Wayland said that he was engaged in a defense that Owen was somehow "involved" with the assassination, and that while he didn't want "to lay out all my cards at this point," it could be that Gray had "told something to the police which directly implicates Mr. Owen."

Crickard was seething. "Sustain the objection!" he cried. "It is not relevant!"

But Wayland forged on, asking Gray, "Have you ever been advised or admonished by any law enforcement agency not to talk about Owen's involvement in the RFK incident?"

Crickard was beside himself. "That's not relevant either!" he injected. "Sustain the objection!"

There hadn't been an objection, which gave Wayland the impression the judge was beginning to take sides. Gray was allowed to step down. But if he thought his testimonial ordeal was over, it was just beginning.

WAYLAND'S PLANNED STRATEGY WAS TO DEMONSTRATE THAT THE KCOP management, once they verified Owen's arrest record, had acted responsibly and in accordance with federal guidelines by terminating *The Walking Bible* program. But that strategy was becoming more and more snagged on the RFK assassination issue. Owen brought a parade of witnesses into court to testify that when they called the station to find out why the program had been canceled, they were told, among other things, that Owen was "involved" in the assassination.

As it turned out, Owen had solicited most if not all of these viewers to phone the station. But he hadn't stopped there, as became evident when an aging lady evangelist calling herself the Reverend Olga Graves took the stand. She produced a poor Xerox copy of a KCOP internal memorandum from counsel Yacullo to president Hopkins that summarized Christian's allegations about Owen's criminal record and connection with the assassination; crudely grafted to the bottom of it was Christian's signature over our typewritten names obviously reproduced from correspondence previously introduced. Graves testified that she had received the document in the mail approximately two weeks beforehand, and that Jonn Christian's name and address were typed on the envelope. But when asked by Wayland if she had mentioned receiving it to Owen, she said, "I did not. He asked me!"

Crickard allowed the hybrid document to be entered as a legitimate exhibit, even though the defense protested vigorously.

Grace M. Holder, the wife of a retired postal worker who had set up his own ministry, was an old friend of Owen brought in to testify about his travails at the hands of KCOP. On cross-examination it turned out that Owen had confided a great deal about Sirhan and his companions who wanted Owen to deliver a horse to the Ambassador Hotel.

Q. Mr. Owen told you that he knew who all these people were?
A. Oh, I don't know if he knew who they were.
Q. He told you that he also continues to know to this day who these people were?
A. As far as I know he said he thought he could identify them when he went and told the police about it, that it was a conspiracy, and at that time he said he thought he could identify the men if he were shown pictures or something.
Q. Mr. Owen involved himself in the Robert F. Kennedy murder by going to the police, didn't he?
A. Yes, he did.
Q. He told you he went to the police on the *night of the assassination*, didn't he? [Wayland was looking at his notes. Mrs. Holder glanced at Owen, who was vigorously shaking his head in the negative.]
A. No, wait a minute. It was that night as I recall that he was sitting in a hotel, and he saw it on television . . .

Trying to straighten her out, Wayland held up a deposition Mrs. Holder had given the previous year and read from it: " 'He went to the police and told them that at the night [*sic*] there was somebody else with him. He didn't go down to the police that night.' "

Visibly nervous, Holder explained, "The court reporter should have had in there 'at that night there was somebody else with Sirhan.' "

Q. And Mr. Owen knew who that person was?
A. Yes.
Q. Mr. Owen, in fact, continually affirmed to you that there was a conspiracy to kill Robert F. Kennedy, and has continued to affirm that to you over the years, isn't that true?
A. Yes.

Appearing on Owen's behalf, Jerome Weber was a shadow of the dapper attorney who had originally represented Owen in his suit against KCOP. "He picked up some rider, as I recall," was his vague recollection of Owen's hitchhiker story. But he did acknowledge to Wayland that he had discussed Owen's "involvement" in the Kennedy case with DA investigators George Murphy and George Stoner (the two men he had admitted bribing in the Devins murder case). "Yes, I may have," he said, "I recall I was busy with Stoner and Murphy at that time." This reinforced our suspicions that Owen had had help inside the DA's office with his "story" problems.

ON THE EIGHTH DAY OF THE TRIAL OWEN TOOK THE STAND TO testify. One of his attorneys, Walter Faber of Salt Lake City, held up Plaintiff's Exhibit 36-B, the hybrid KCOP-Christian document, and asked, "Where did you first see that document?" Owen answered that he had first seen it in a church in Modesto, California, and subsequently in churches in a host of towns around the state. Yes, he had been cut off from further preaching at the churches that received the document. Faber asked how long this "harassment" by Jonn Christian had been going on. From July 1969 to the present, the preacher replied. (This confirmed Owen's awareness of the RFK aspects prior to the original filing of his lawsuit in July 1970.)

It had caused him great mental anguish and loss of income, Owen complained. Practically sobbing, he said, "I have been shamed. I have walked in to visit at a church and set down and watched people turn around and look at me. . . . I have been to the doctor. I can bring the doctor in here. Excuse me, could I have a couple of aspirin, your Honor?"

No sooner had Owen finished this theatrical testimony than his attorneys approached the bench and demanded that Christian be brought into court—by force if necessary—to answer their questions. The matter was put off until the following morning so that college student Barbara Jean Grimes, whom Rusty Rhodes had co-opted to serve Christian with the subpoena, could appear to testify. On cross-examination Wayland got her to admit that Christian had neither acknowledged his identity nor even touched the subpoena ("I think it hit his feet," she said), raising a distinct question of whether the service was legal and proper. But Crickard ordered that a "body attachment" be issued for Christian with bail fixed at $500. "Issue that as promptly as possible," he instructed his bailiff, "and see if we can get Mr. Christian in here forthwith!"

Since the previous evening was one of the few on which he had not talked with Wayland, Christian was unaware that a warrant, highly unusual in a civil case, had been issued for his arrest. But he had already made preparations to pull up stakes because he felt a menace hanging over the trial.* On the day that it had begun, the phone rang in his apartment in the Brentwood district. It was answered by his then ladyfriend, Lorrie Cradock, a teacher at the nearby Westlake School for Girls. The caller was Jerry Owen, demanding to talk to Christian. Told that he was out, Owen turned nasty. "I know who you are," he said. "You're Christian's mistress. You work in a nursery." The blonde retorted, "Oh, yes, the flowers are lovely." Owen hung up.

When he heard about the intimidating call, Christian called Supervisor Baxter Ward and City Attorney Burt Pines to plead for protection, but both were out. He dropped a note to Ward saying: "As we both know from experience, Owen's threats have a most profound way of manifesting themselves into violence." Then he called Charlie O'Brien in San Francisco, who promised to try to contact Pines the next morning. "Why don't you pull out of that place?" O'Brien advised.

Christian took the advice, moving our files and his belongings to the home of a close friend, actor Paul Le Mat. (Le Mat of *American Graffiti* fame and his co-star in *Aloha, Bobby and Rose*, Dianne Hull, had become deeply interested in the RFK case and were attending the trial daily.) To prevent any harm to his ladyfriend, Christian put her on a plane to England to stay at her parents' home on the Isle of Wight.

One hour after Crickard had ordered the body attachment, an

---

* By this time Christian had been instrumental in getting subpoenas issued for a sizable number of police officials and their submerged documents on the Owen aspects of the case. He knew it was just a matter of time before the police figured out that it was our investigative file that was being used by the defense—and that the earlier warnings might turn into harsher reaction.

unmarked beige sedan pulled up at the Brentwood apartment that Christian had selected because it was outside the jurisdiction of the LAPD. One occupant remained at the wheel while a beefy man in a tacky sports coat and a hefty woman in a tight khaki skirt got out and asked the landlady for Jonn Christian. "Who's looking for Mr. Christian?" Marie Reno inquired. "Oh, we're just some friends," the woman lied.

Christian had returned to pick up the last of his belongings and was at that moment in a storage area, oblivious to what was going on. Apparently disbelieving the landlady's protest that Christian had moved, the man and woman went directly to his vacant apartment and searched it. "Wait a minute!" Mrs. Reno challenged. "Who are you people?" "Police!" the woman snarled, but when the landlady demanded to see their identification they ignored her. Not finding Christian in the apartment, the pair proceeded to shove open doors and peek into windows. Mrs. Reno slipped off and warned Christian, who hid as best he could. For an hour he heard the sounds of voices and tromping feet as the pair shook down every one of the twenty-four units in the building. Meanwhile two patrol cars roared up to the Westlake School for Girls, and uniformed officers searched the grounds, forced open the classroom door and riffled through the desk of his departed lady friend. They ordered the caretaker to help locate her—even though no warrant had been issued or applied to her.

Christian heard a loud and persistent banging on the locked door of his refuge, then silence. Fifteen minutes later there was the sound of rattling keys. The door opened slowly—and in slipped Paul Le Mat, Dianne Hull and Mrs. Reno, who had alerted them to what was going on. Concerned that the "police" might have begun a "stakeout," Le Mat and Christian improvised some serious theatrics of their own. Le Mat left with a plumber's helper in hand as if he had been called in to fix a plugged toilet. Then, after making sure he hadn't picked up a tail, he doubled back to the apartment and began a slow pass down the back alleyway. Christian dashed out of his lair, shuffled down the pathway like an old man, and then suddenly leaped into the moving car. Le Mat accelerated to safety as Christian took off the towel he had wrapped around his head to conceal his beard, removed the threadbare bathrobe, and rolled down his pants legs.

Christian first learned that sheriff's deputies had been authorized to bring him in when he called Wayland that night from the sanctuary of Le Mat's West Hollywood home. Wayland said that he had tried to prevent the issuance of the body attachment, but no one in the office of Presiding Judge Robert Wenke knew anything about the hand-delivered (by Paul Le Mat) letter Christian had written spelling out why he wouldn't testify. As for the trial, it was not going well and high-powered help was needed. "Do you think Vince Bugliosi would be interested in stepping in?" Wayland asked.

"You better hope so," Christian replied. "He's the only guy in the country who *might* be able to handle it."

Christian called Bugliosi and set up an appointment with him in the lawyer's Beverly Hills office on July 24, 1975. (The trial had been in progress since July 2.) Christian had met the former prosecutor for the first time in late 1972, when they had a brief chance to discuss the RFK case in mostly theoretical terms. The lawyer had no knowledge of either "The Walking Bible" or the current lawsuit aspects when the July 24th meeting (also attended by Mike Wayland) took place.

It was a pressure situation, all right. The lawsuit was scheduled to terminate by Judge Crickard's edict the following Monday, just two court days later. Christian realized that he was asking Bugliosi to undertake a "Mission Impossible," where the odds were as stacked against him as was the attitude of the court against the RFK issue. The counsel was merely being asked to assume the responsibility of establishing "The Walking Bible's" "involvement" in the assassination of Robert Kennedy, the crux of KCOP's hastily prepared defense.

Christian ended the session by giving Bugliosi a rundown on the day's events, including the heavy scene in Brentwood. "Something's very wrong here," Bugliosi said. "I never heard of a mere witness being pursued in a civil case like this. You are not a defendant, and that's the only justification for any court to turn on this kind of heat." The lawyer had heard enough of the strange events in and out of the courtroom to be intrigued with the prospect of entering the case. He would meet with Wayland the following day.

While the formalities for Bugliosi's association with the defense were being worked out, Mike Wayland got a chance to cross-examine Jerry Owen. Using the transcript of Turner's 1968 interview with Owen as a kind of road map, he led the preacher through the twists and turns of his own hitchhiker story, eliciting a number of variations on the original theme. For instance, Owen now claimed that Sirhan "showed me a hundred-dollar bill" after returning from seeing his "friend in the kitchen" of the hotel, which conflicted with his original statement that it was not until that midnight that Sirhan first tendered the $100 down payment. And the transcript showed Owen saying that Sirhan "told me that he was an exercise boy at a race track, and talked how he loved horses, and he quickly wanted to know if I had a ranch where he could get a job," but when Wayland posed these exact words to him, Owen, unaware that the lawyer was reading from a transcript, objected that they were only partially correct. "He didn't have a job at a race track," the preacher amended. "He had a job at a ranch in Corona. He needed a pickup horse where he could get a good job." It was some time before Owen realized he was being trapped by his own words, a revealing lapse for a man who claimed to recall the entire Bible. "Could I see it?" he asked, pointing at the transcript. "Not at this time," Crickard ruled.

During the cross-examination Wayland, frustrated by the judge's repeated interference on grounds of "undue consumption of time," breached his understanding with Christian by moving into the forbidden area of Bill Powers and the cowboys. He began innocuously enough, asking Owen if he had bought the pickup truck from a "Bill Parker," which the preacher readily acknowledged despite the variation on the name. But then the attorney pressed his advantage: "In truth and fact, sir, on the Monday before the assassination, on Monday the 3rd of June 1968, you were together with Mr. Sirhan at a place called Wild Bill's Stables in Santa Ana?"

"That is an untruth!" The preacher was almost shouting.

"Wild Bill's Stables in Santa Ana is just down the Santa Ana River from your more-or-less Santa Ana mini-ranch?"

"I don't know where Wild Bill's Stable is, I never heard of it before." Owen was obviously alarmed that this sensitive area had been broached.

When Wayland read the dailies to Christian over the phone that night he heard a low whistle at the other end of the line followed by a burst of expletives. The cat was out of the bag. Weatherly had already been shot at. Now Powers and the other cowboys could be in danger. Shaken by the implications of his misstep, Wayland gave Christian blanket authority to hire a bodyguard for the men.

By the next day the details of Bugliosi's entrance into the case had been settled. In his formal letter of acceptance the ex-prosecutor declared that he was aware of the "enormous implications of the case," and that when he had run for DA in 1972* "it was common knowledge that had I been elected, I intended to reopen the investigation of the Kennedy assassination. I am still of the same frame of mind." Bugliosi had taken that position after having spoken to criminalist Bill Harper.

Vincent T. Bugliosi was born August 18, 1934, in the northern Minnesota town of Hibbing, the son of Italian immigrants. His father owned a grocery store and later became a railroad conductor. In a land that wags quip has only two seasons, winter and the Fourth of July, young Bugliosi took up tennis. He edged up the ladder to become state champion, whereupon his proud father took him to Los Angeles, where the competition was hotter and the season endless. There the quick, slender youngster proved himself by winning the area high school championship, and he went off to the University of Miami on a tennis scholarship. He returned to Los Angeles and the UCLA law school, graduating in 1964 as class president.

Hired out of law school as a deputy district attorney, he wasted little time in becoming the top trial lawyer in the staff of 450. Out

---

* In that race Bugliosi, outspent nearly four to one, taking on an incumbent, Joseph Busch, who had the support of very nearly the entire "Establishment" of Los Angeles County, had nonetheless polled just over 50 percent of the vote on the day of the election and was overcome on absentee ballots which had been submitted two weeks earlier. Out of close to 3 million votes, Bugliosi lost by one quarter of one percent. There were those who suspected fraud in the tabulation of the absentee ballots.

of 106 felony jury trials he lost only one, which is believed to be the highest conviction rate in the history of the DA's office. The feat earned him selection as the model prosecutor in a TV series produced by Jack Webb in which he was portrayed by Robert Conrad while he served as technical adviser. Yet he was just as satisfied with those cases in which he moved for dismissal after going out into the field and digging up evidence favorable to the accused. "For far too many years the stereotyped image of the prosecutor has been either that of a right-wing, law-and-order type intent on winning convictions at any cost," he wrote in *Helter Skelter*, "or a stumbling bumbling Hamilton Burger [the fictional DA in the *Perry Mason* series], forever trying innocent people, who, fortunately, are saved at the last possible moment by the foxy maneuverings of a Perry Mason."

Harry Weiss, who has the largest criminal law practice in Los Angeles, told *Los Angeles Magazine* in November of 1972: "I've seen all the great trial lawyers of the last thirty years. None of them are in Vince's class."

Former Governor Edmund G. "Pat" Brown (the current governor's father) recommended Bugliosi as the Watergate Special Prosecutor, saying, "There is no finer and fairer prosecutor in the land than Vince Bugliosi."

However, Bugliosi's skill as trial lawyer is not limited to that of a prosecutor. Since he entered private practice, his record shows that if a defendant is fortunate enough to get him interested in his case, he is almost assured of an acquittal.

As Jonn Christian briefed Bugliosi on the contents of our investigative file, Bugliosi shaped his plan of attack. "He's the guy we have to find and get to testify," he said of Bill Powers. The same was true for Powers' former stablehands, Johnny Beckley and Chris Weatherly, whose potential testimony would tend to corroborate Powers, and perhaps plow new ground. Concurrently, Bugliosi subpoenaed LAPD records and personnel to back up the cowboys' testimony and, we hoped, shed additional light on the case.

We calculated that if the cowboys could be persuaded to testify and the police veil of secrecy ripped away, the trial might be forced to a sudden and explosive halt. Faced with probable cause to believe that a conspiracy had in fact taken place, Judge Crickard would be compelled to refer the matter to a criminal grand jury or federal prosecutive authorities.

Private detective Dan Prop located Weatherly in Chino and served him with a subpoena, but the young man promptly disappeared for the duration of the trial in the apparent belief that one brush with a bullet was more than enough. Bugliosi decided that he himself should make the overture to Powers and try to talk him into appearing voluntarily. We learned that after closing Wild Bill's Stables, Powers had moved to the tiny town of Murietta in the remote Santa Ana Mountains. Christian, Jim Rose and Paul Le Mat accompanied Bugliosi on the two-hour pre-dawn drive the next day, Saturday, playing the tapes of our 1969 interviews with the cowboy to acquaint Bugliosi with his potential testimony.

Powers wasn't home. Bugliosi was due to make his courtroom debut in the case on Monday. Unable to wait any longer, he decided to return to Beverly Hills to begin his trial preparation in what little time was left. The next day Bugliosi finally reached Powers by telephone and explained the situation.

Powers was opposed to testifying, but Bugliosi managed to convince him to come in and at least "talk it over." Punctually at seven o'clock on Monday morning Powers appeared at the attorney's office, showing the effects of a sleepless night. Bugliosi broke the ice by handing him a subpoena and telling him to tear it up if he wished. Powers responded to this candor. "My lady thinks you're a great man, and I want to help you, I really do," he said. Together they phoned Johnny Beckley at his residence in Los Alamitos and it seemed to be settled: Powers would drive down and bring his former employee back for a talk. Still, as far as his own testimony was concerned, he would have to think it over. It was nine o'clock and Bugliosi had to leave for court. He autographed a copy of *Helter Skelter* for the Powers family. The cowboy left for Murietta and some hard thinking.

16

Vincent Bugliosi's Affirmative Defense

INTRODUCED BY MIKE WAYLAND AS KCOP'S NEW ASSOCIATE counsel, Vince Bugliosi rose to address the court. "Your Honor," he led off, "as I understand it—I am just new on the case—one of the allegations by the plaintiff is that Mr. Hopkins accused Mr. Owen of somehow being involved in Senator Kennedy's assassination."

Bugliosi thought Judge Crickard looked surprised and curious that he was taking part in the trial.

"I believe then that it is an affirmative defense on our part," Bugliosi went on, "to prove the truthfulness of that charge."

The lawyer told Crickard that he had just located a "key witness" who might be able to offer relevant testimony on the issue of Owen's possible involvement in the RFK case. He asked the judge not to conclude the lawsuit that afternoon (as previously threatened) —but to put it over until the following day. The judge reluctantly consented to Bugliosi's request.

Owen and his attorneys looked stunned. Arthur Evry stammered, "Your Honor, as your Honor knows, we are caught somewhat by surprise. This is the first I have heard of any indication that there was some truth in defendant's case to the allegation that he was"—Evry paused, seemingly unable to utter the word "assassination"—"Mr. Owen was criminally involved."

Bugliosi noted the reaction of Crickard, before whom he was appearing for the first time. The judge was frowning, obviously displeased that the assassination was being made a full-blown issue in his courtroom. He was an establishment judge, Bugliosi estimated, who starts off with the idea that anything bearing the stamp of government is ipso facto valid.

That estimation was immediately put to the test. Included in the batch of subpoenas issued by the defense was one calling on the LAPD to produce all records, documents and tape recordings concerning their Owen investigation. In response, Officer Ronald L. Schaffer of the Records Identification Division showed up. After being sworn in, Schaffer declined to produce any material, saying that his superior had instructed him to invoke Section 1040 of the California Evidence Code that declares certain police records "to be considered confidential information unless ordered released to the parties by a magistrate of this state."

Wayland argued that the LAPD material was highly relevant to the defense because "an issue has been drawn" as to Owen's criminal implication in the assassination. Skirting the point, Crickard asked rhetorically, "Well, if Mr. Owen was charged with some public crime, that would be a matter of public record that is easily available to any citizen, isn't that correct? . . . So, Mr. Wayland, if you want to find out if Mr. Owen has been charged with a public crime in the State of California, all you have to do is walk over there a couple or three blocks."

The judge was sarcastically alluding to the County Clerk's office, where records of criminal filings are maintained. Bugliosi's suspicion of Crickard's blind faith in agencies of government was now confirmed.

Bugliosi observed that the LAPD claim of privilege should not be allowed unless, in the language of the code, "it would be against the public interest because there is a necessity for preserving the confidentiality of the information that outweighs the necessity for disclosure in the interests of justice." He argued that the public interest far outweighed any need for secrecy. "I think the court can take judicial notice," he said, "that the whole tone, the whole tenor in this country at this particular moment is that there is a tremendous distrust, there is a tremendous suspicion, there is a tremendous skepticism about whether or not people like Oswald and Sirhan acted alone, and many, many people, many substantial people—I am not talking about conspiracy buffs who see a conspiracy behind every tree—many, many substantial people feel that Sirhan did not act alone, that he did act in concert."

Crickard remained impassive. Bugliosi pressed on, saying that the defense was in a position to offer circumstantial evidence "which would be extremely incriminating to Mr. Owen. . . . No one is going to say that they saw Mr. Owen pull the trigger and shoot Senator Kennedy. We intend to offer evidence from which a very strong inference could be drawn that possibly Mr. Owen was a co-conspirator in this case." Bugliosi pointed out that Owen had voluntarily injected himself into the investigation by reporting the hitchhiker story to the police. "Now, all we want to do is take a look at these [LAPD] reports. Just because the LAPD concluded that Mr. Owen was not involved in the Kennedy assassination doesn't mean anything to me personally, and it shouldn't mean anything to the court. The LAPD is not the trier of fact."

Why were the police so determined to keep secret records they had deemed to be meaningless? "I have to say," Bugliosi commented, "as a prosecutor for eight years I find it extremely strange that the LAPD would not want this information at this point to be public. I find it very strange indeed. If Owen was not involved, as LAPD, I assume, has concluded, there is no conceivable reason under the moon why they shouldn't permit us to look at those records." Officer Schaffer was ordered by Crickard to fetch them immediately.

Bugliosi was understandably leery of police conclusions. As a deputy DA he had worked closely with the LAPD on major cases and was keenly aware of how inept this self-promoting agency could be. The Manson Family case, which like the Kennedy case called for a sophisticated investigation, provided numerous illustrations of police bumbling. In *Helter Skelter* Bugliosi described how a gun later determined to have been used by Manson's followers in the Tate murders was found three weeks after the crime by a citizen living not far from the scene, but the patrolman who responded to his call handled the weapon with both hands, obliterating any chance for developing fingerprints. Then the gun was filed away and forgotten in the property room of the Valley Services Division of the LAPD while headquarters carried out a nationwide search for it. It was three and a half months before the police connected the languishing gun with the case. This embarrassment was compounded by the fact that a television crew, following the same clues the police had, found bloodied clothing discarded by the killers.*

In *Helter Skelter* Bugliosi described how complacent LAPD detectives dragged their feet in the Manson case. Even after three months of police investigation the prosecution case was so evidentially weak that Bugliosi had to take charge personally; he gave the detectives a long list of overlooked leads to pursue. Hearing nothing for three more weeks, he summoned the detectives and found, to his utter dismay, that only one of the leads had been covered.† To make matters worse, there was internal rivalry between the unimaginative senior detectives assigned to the Tate investigation and their ambitious younger colleagues handling the LaBianca murders, and for a long time this intramural friction prevented the LAPD from linking the two cases. The police even failed to recognize that the inscription "Pigs" scrawled in gore at

---

* Bugliosi, *op. cit.*, pp. 96–97, 265, 740.
† *Ibid.*, p. 257.

both murder scenes was part of the link. And they failed to perceive Charles Manson's far-out philosophy* as a motive for what on the surface was senseless random killings. As one LAPD sleuth scoffed when a witness divulged Manson's designs, "Ah, Charlie's a madman; we're not interested in all that."†

To cap this flawed performance, Chief Edward M. Davis staged a press conference in response to public pressures to announce that the Tate-LaBianca murders were solved.‡ But there was not nearly enough backup evidence at the time to take the case to court, and the chief's premature grandstanding almost cost a successful prosecution. Yet Bugliosi sensed that Judge Crickard believed the fictional image of LAPD efficiency as portrayed in *Dragnet, Adam-12* and *The New Centurions.*

When Officer Schaffer returned with an LAPD file marked OWEN, JERRY, Judge Crickard decided that he himself would examine the investigative report to determine whether it was relevant. After a recess for this purpose he ruled that "there would be no relevant information disclosed by making the record public." Bugliosi said he was "shocked by the court's ruling on this. I am almost at a loss for words, which doesn't happen too often to me. To say that the public interest is against disclosure—"

The judge interrupted to repeat his opinion that the report was irrelevant. After further verbal sparring, the attorney began to suspect that what Crickard had read was not what the subpoena called for. Bugliosi asked to look at the index, which revealed that the report was not about Owen and the RFK case, after all.

Reading from the subpoena served on the department, Bugliosi

---

* "Helter Skelter" was Manson's term for his prediction that the blacks would rise and take over America, and practically the only whites who would survive would be those with the foresight to set up enclaves in remote areas. Manson tried to set this apocalypse in motion by killing monied whites and scrawling the word "Pigs" at the scene to suggest falsely that blacks were responsible. By his racist reckoning, the Manson Family would afterward be needed by the inferior blacks to lead the way out of chaos into a new order.

† *Ibid.,* p. 335.

‡ Davis was acting Chief of Police on the night of the RFK assassination. Headquartered at Rampart Station as "Watch Commander," he was still on duty after midnight—an unusually lengthy period for such a high-level LAPD official.

stressed that Schaffer was supposed to have brought the "entire file on plaintiff, that is, Mr. Owen, including the original tape recording and transcript of Owen's June 5, 1968, story of the Los Angeles Police Department University Station officers and including the tapes and transcripts of all other interviews made with Owen up to and including the July 3, 1968, one in San Francisco at the George T. Davis office, together with polygraph tests." That was certainly specific, but Schaffer's excuse was that he "never had the birth date of Mr. Owen."

It was as if the FBI couldn't find its Lindbergh kidnap file because it didn't have the baby's birth date. Crickard instructed Schaffer to return to headquarters with Owen's vital statistics and search for the specified material. When it was located, he was to bring it to court at once.

THAT NIGHT BUGLIOSI CALLED BILL POWERS, TRYING TO CONVINCE him to testify. But Powers was still uncertain and not at all encouraged by the fact that Johnny Beckley had vanished. Powers had gone to Beckley's residence that day as had been arranged, but found only an abandoned girl friend, who ruefully explained, "He don't want to talk about nothing." But Powers agreed once again to meet Bugliosi the first thing in the morning.

Again he showed up at seven, bleary-eyed from another restless night. For over two hours Bugliosi reasoned and cajoled, pointing out that once his testimony was in the record, any purpose in silencing him or harming his family would be gone. But it was not until the attorney waved the flag—"Don't do it for me, do it for the good of the country!"—that Powers yielded. As they were about to enter the courtroom Powers grabbed Bugliosi's arm and exacted a promise: "Be my lawyer for my estate if anything happens to me. Just make sure no shyster lawyers take everything I've put away for my son."

Powers was not put on the stand immediately, however, for Officer Schaffer had returned from his quest for the Owen material. Putting him on the stand, Bugliosi half-smiled and inquired, "You were successful?"

"No, sir, I wasn't," the policeman answered. "We looked

through all the records we could possibly go through all afternoon and we were unable to locate any such records, documents or tapes . . ."

"It is your testimony that you could find no records at the LAPD pertaining to one Jerry Owen?"

"No, sir, unless I had a DR number or something. More information possibly, like I say a DR number, an arrest booking number or something to go on."

Bugliosi frowned in disgust. Crickard said nothing. The witness was excused.

Now Bill Powers was called to the stand. Bugliosi led him through the scenes at Wild Bill's Stables: how in early 1968 Owen boarded two of his horses there; how Owen objected to Johnny Beckley's handling of his horses and threatened to bring in someone from a race track named "Sirhan" to handle them properly; how Owen, hitherto short of funds, drove up in a Lincoln Continental a day or so before the RFK shooting and flashed a thick roll of $1,000 bills; and how Powers was introduced to a young man in the back seat who bore a "likely resemblance" to Sirhan. This was Powers' skeletal story, and Bugliosi now began to expand on it to the court.

Q. This gentleman, this young gentleman who was in the back seat of Mr. Owen's Lincoln shortly before the assassination, who you testified resembled Sirhan, did you ever see that man prior to that time in Mr. Owen's home?

A. There is a possibility that I seen him there once before or maybe twice before when I was there, yes.

Q. When was that?

A. It was approximately, I would guess, ninety days before the assassination. Mr. Owen had his home for sale or wanted to sell it. Some people had a Western store there and was interested in it, and I was going to show them the home, and that's when I seen this man at Mr. Owen's house.

Q. Where was he in the house?

A. He was in the backyard.

Q. And he looked like the same individual whom you saw in the back seat of Mr. Owen's car during the thousand-dollar-bills incident?

A. That's correct.

Powers' testimony appeared to heighten Crickard's displeasure that the assassination issue had been dragged into his court, and he began to bridle at Bugliosi with increasing frequency. When the attorney asked Powers if he had ever seen the preacher with a $1,000 bill before (the answer was no), the judge interposed, "Mr. Bugliosi, we have to get to something here that bears on this case. I am going to exclude this line of questioning under Evidence Code 352, undue consumption of time." The attorney could hardly believe his ears.

BUGLIOSI: May I be heard on that?
THE COURT: Let's go to the next point.
BUGLIOSI: Well, we are talking about some things that are pretty important, your Honor, not just to this lawsuit but to Senator Kennedy's assassination.
THE COURT: They have to be relevant to this lawsuit or this isn't the place to take them up.
BUGLIOSI: May I be heard on this, your Honor? I have to state why I think it is very relevant.
THE COURT: Let's go on to the next point.

With questions about Owen's sudden prosperity cut off, Bugliosi asked Powers about the law enforcement officers who visited him following the assassination. Arthur Evry objected on grounds of relevancy, and Bugliosi asked to make an "offer of proof." Crickard hesitated, then assented, sending the witness from the courtroom.

"There is some evidence in this case," Bugliosi began, "and we will put the evidence on, which smacks of a possible cover-up. And I am not using the word cover-up because it's a word that's fashionable right now, but there are some strange things that happened in this case, and I will mention just a few of them to you.

"The most obvious thing is something that happened in this very courtroom about thirty minutes ago. An officer from the LAPD took the witness stand and testified that he could find no records on Jerry Owen over at the Los Angeles Police Department in response to a subpoena duces tecum. It is a matter of common knowledge, your Honor, that Jerry Owen was investigated by the LAPD. If the court will give us time we will present documentary evidence that he was investigated by the LAPD. A book was

254 | THE ASSASSINATION OF ROBERT F. KENNEDY

written by the chief detective in this case, I think the name of the book was *Special Unit Senator*, in which pages upon pages are devoted to Jerry Owen. And yet we have an officer from the LAPD taking the witness stand and searching for the records for an entire day and coming up with nothing on Jerry Owen. That's the first point."

The second point was the visit paid to Powers a day or two after the assassination by officers quizzing him about the truck he sold the preacher. It would be the first of a half-dozen interviews the police had with Powers. "They told him that it was his truck Owen was driving when he allegedly picked up Sirhan, and that Sirhan's fingerprints were found on the glove compartment and the rear window of his truck." Also, already in the trial record, Bugliosi pointed out, was Owen's testimony that when he reported his story to the University Station, the police "fingerprinted the truck and thanked me for cooperating with them." But the LAPD had never let on that fingerprints had been lifted from Owen's truck and trailer rig, let alone that they were Sirhan's. In fact, it publicly took the contradictory position that Sirhan had never been in the truck and Owen was nothing more than a "publicity seeker."

Concerning Powers, Bugliosi continued, "Now, this gentleman lives in Murietta, California, close to 100 miles from L.A., and he is a fringe witness. He did not testify before the grand jury. He did not testify at the trial. And yet law enforcement was so concerned about this man that they interrogated him six times. And the first officers that came out to see him, the ones that told him about the fingerprints, he never saw those officers again. As for the officers who came later, Bugliosi said that they told Powers they "did not want him to talk to anyone else about this case no matter who it was and to call them if anyone else came out to see him."

Bugliosi was making the point that this conduct was highly suspicious, that from his own experience he knew that law enforcement agencies ordinarily don't pay that much attention even to the star witness, much less a fringe witness. And yet here were officers going back time after time to warn Powers to keep his mouth shut. "If there was a cover-up, it's implicit in the cover-up that somebody else was involved," the attorney concluded. "And if somebody else was involved we are trying to show that maybe"—Bugliosi turned to face Owen—"maybe the gentleman seated at the counsel table now with a smile on his face, maybe it was Jerry Owen."

Bugliosi laid out the legal points establishing why Powers' testimony about the police was relevant, but Crickard would not go along with cover-up allegations. "If law enforcement people had thought that Mr. Owen was involved in any criminal activity in this connection," he admonished, "there certainly would have been some kind of prosecution within the seven years that have elapsed since that time, so—"

Bugliosi, looking incredulously at Crickard, cut in. He noted that FBI statistics showed that a substantial percentage of crimes never result in a prosecution. "The court is saying the LAPD was above board in this case and if Owen was involved he would have been prosecuted," the attorney remonstrated. Although Bugliosi had often said publicly that the LAPD was one of the least corrupt police departments in the country, he told Judge Crickard he still didn't see "how the court, sitting on the bench without the taking of *any* evidence, can categorically say that the LAPD was 100 percent above board in this case."

"I have no problem about that, Mr. Bugliosi, because that is not my job," Crickard retorted. "All I am concerned with is the civil suit of Mr. Owen against KCOP. The evidence has shown, which already has been introduced, that Mr. Compton, who was the district attorney in charge of the Sirhan investigation, knew of Mr. Owen, had checked out the story, and so far as your offer of proof in having this Mr. Powers testify to the things which you have just outlined, the objections to those things are sustained."

Crickard was referring to former Chief Deputy DA Lynn Compton, who led the prosecution of Sirhan. But Compton had not personally investigated the Owen angle—he had relied on the LAPD reports which, as we have seen, were doctored. It was a Catch-22 dilemma for Bugliosi, but Crickard's mind was made up. The question of police malfeasance was out.

Bill Powers was brought back into the courtroom. "How many times did you speak to law enforcement in this case?" Bugliosi asked him in defiance of the court's ruling. Crickard broke in,

"Mr. Bugliosi, that is exactly what we have talked about. We are not going to get into this area." With his major avenues of inquiry blocked by the judge, Bugliosi was forced to end his examination of Powers.

Arthur Evry's cross-examination was short and tame. He tested Powers' memory of some of the details of Owen's appearance at the stables driving the Lincoln, and only got him to repeat that he was not absolutely positive that it was Sirhan in the back seat.

Bugliosi asked Judge Crickard if he could cross-examine Owen. Crickard responded that he could not, because Owen had already been cross-examined by Wayland. Bugliosi said he would be satisfied to ask just "a few questions," and Crickard grudgingly consented. Bugliosi asked Owen whether he was a self-ordained minister or officially ordained.

A. I am God-ordained.
Q. Are you also called "The Walking Bible"?
A. Yes.
Q. Is that because of your memory? [The attorney was setting up a line of questioning which would show that the man with the phenomenal memory couldn't tell his hitchhiker story two times in a row without contradicting himself. But Owen would have none of it.]
A. No, not memory. It's because of the anointing of the Holy Spirit. God has given me a gift to quote the entire Bible, 31,173 verses, verbatim without looking at the Bible.
Q. . . . You have quite a memory to memorize the whole Bible, is that correct?
A. No. I flunked sandpile in kindergarten. It is a God-given gift. It is not a memory.
Q. Well, you have a gift—
A. A gift from God.
Q. Of memory?
A. Have you ever read the Bible, sir? I feel he is being sacrilegious or something. [The preacher pouted to the judge].

Bugliosi had Owen repeat his alibi for election night. No, he said, he was not at the rear entrance to the Ambassador Hotel as Sirhan had requested because he was presiding over a prayer meeting at the Calvary Baptist Church in Oxnard. The engagement had been booked several months in advance, he claimed, after he had appeared in neighboring Ventura with Maxie Rosenbloom, a former light-heavyweight champion who had embraced fundamentalist religion after retiring from the ring.* "Slapsie Maxie" Rosenbloom, who figured in one version of the hitchhiker story as the man who had enticed Owen into attending the Saints and Sinners meeting on election eve, was typical of the preacher's ecumenical choice of friends. Owen was also an old acquaintance of Paul J. "Frankie" Carbo, convicted in 1960 of an organized crime boxing extortion in Los Angeles, according to another strange exhibit Owen had entered in the suit. The exhibit was a letter from Carbo in the Marion, Illinois, federal penitentiary referring to a recent visit between the two. (Owen's choice of exhibits often seemed to be damaging to his case.)

Bugliosi, feeling very circumscribed by Crickard's imposed limitation of just a "few questions," nevertheless began a line of questioning that had been seven years too long in coming in a judicial setting:

Q. Mr. Owen, is it your belief that the man you picked up on the after-noon of June the 3rd in 1968 at 7th and Grand in downtown Los Angeles was Sirhan Sirhan; do you believe that?
A. I don't know. I don't know.
Q. Didn't you tell the police at the University Station on June the 5th, 1968, that the man you had picked up was Sirhan?
A. He looked like the picture of the man that I had in the truck, or the boy that was in the truck.

Now to "The Walking Bible's" allegedly "immaculate" memory:

Q. On the evening of June the 4th, 1968, [the night of the assassination] you spoke at the Calvary Baptist Church in Oxnard, is that correct?
A. Yes, sir.

* Rosenbloom retired from the ring in 1939 suffering permanent brain damage from the poundings he had taken. Like Owen, he played bit parts in movies and was type-cast as a punch-drunk fighter. In 1969 he was a partner of Owen in the R & O Boxing Stable, but shortly thereafter he entered a nursing home and died in 1976.

Q. Who invited you?

A. Mr. Compton.

Q. What's his first name?

A. *I forget.* He is the oldest delivery boy, and he is a deacon of the church. My wife has the name. She is seated outside. *I can't remember* his first name. Might be Paul. Paul Compton.

(Note: There was no Paul Compton listed in any Oxnard phone directory in 1968.)

Q. How long have you known this gentleman?

A. I only had met him about in March, I think, of 1968.

Q. Where did you meet him?

A. At a prayer meeting.

Q. In Oxnard?

A. In Oxnard.

Q. When did he invite you to this prayer meeting on the evening of June the 4th?

A. *I can't remember.* I think it was sometime in March.

Q. When did this prayer meeting start? What time in the evening?

A. 7:00 o'clock. [Owen then says both his wife and daughter were there too.]

Q. Can you give me the names of the people who were at the prayer meeting with you other than your family?

A. I can recall Mr. and Mrs. Compton, perhaps their family, and I can recall Mr. and Mrs. Rose from Ventura.

Q. Do you have a first name for the Roses?

A. I don't—*I can't recall* the first name, sir. There is others [*sic*] but *I can't recall* the others.

Q. How many people were at that prayer meeting, approximately?

A. Oh, just a handful.

Q. When you say handful, you mean five or ten?

A. No, that's an expression. There could be between—it is maybe between 5 and 18 people.

Bugliosi went for the heart of Owen's fading alibi with the kind of interrogation he was noted for:

Q. Isn't it a fact, sir, that on the evening of June the 4th, 1968, that church was shut down and hadn't been open for the previous several months?

A. That is not a fact. That's a *different* Calvary Church you are talking about.

Q. The church that *you* are talking about, can you give me an *exact* location on it?

A. *No*, but I will even take you up there and introduce you to the people.

(The court:) Can you give him an exact location?

A. I can't, your Honor. I travel so much.

(The court:) Okay.

Q. How long were the services?

A. The prayer meeting, oh, it wouldn't be over an hour.

Q. Where did you go after that?

A. I went to the home, I stayed at some people's house. *I can't recall* their name.

Q. How did you end up in their home?

A. They are friends. As an evangelist, people invite you to their home to stay. They cook for you, they give you food.

Q. You stayed at their home on the evening of June the 4th, you slept at their home?

A. Slept at their home, and from their home phoned my wife that night.

Q. You can't give me any names for these people?

A. You want to call my wife in? She will tell you.

(The court:) You don't know?

A. I can't remember thousands and thousands of people's names.

(The court:) Thank you.

Q. Do you know where the gentleman at whose home you stayed works?

A. His—*no, I don't.* I think he works for the city, and I think his wife works for one of the department stores. We'll bring my wife in, and she has them all, the names written down.

Q. Was he at the prayer meeting that night?

A. . . . *I can't remember exactly.*

Q. Could this church be located at 601 South F Street?

A. *I don't know*, sir.

Q. Does that ring a bell?

A. *I don't know*, sir.

Q. Was this church, the Calvary Baptist Church, affiliated with the American Council of Christian Churches?

A. No, it wasn't. It was independent, sir. [The sign out front of the F
   Street church read: "A Truly Independent Baptist Church."]
Q. Was it affiliated with the 20th Century Reformation Hour Church?
A. No, that's McIntire. No.
Q. Do you know Carl McIntire?
A. Oh, yes. I have known him for years, sir. I have held meetings in
his church back here.*

Dr. Carl McIntire was the founder of the ACCC, a New Jersey
preacher who feuded with the National Council of Christian
Churches, the mainstream group, because of its supposed drift into
liberalism. McIntire, a forceful speaker, built his rival ACCC into
one of the most potent components of the religious right. His 20th
Century Reformation Hour broadcast over a network of 636 small
stations, and pulled in an annual gross of $3 million. McIntire
zeroed in on the Roman Catholic Church, once branding it "the
harlot church and bride of the anti-Christ," and when John Kennedy
and Billy Graham played golf together, McIntire criticized the
evangelist for associating with "persons whose fidelity to something
other than the scriptures is evident."

By 1968 McIntire was embroiled in a bitter dispute with his
own ACCC hierarchy, who wished to divorce themselves from his
increasingly radical politics.

Q. Do you know a Reverend Medcalf?
A. No.
Q. Have you heard that name?
A. No, not to my knowledge. If I see the gentleman, I might know him.

Moving on to the incident at Wild Bill's Stables—Owen now
acknowledged that he had been there, though earlier he said that he
had never heard of the stables—Bugliosi got Owen to admit that
he did in fact have a roll of $1,000 bills on him that day, albeit a
smaller one than Powers had described.

* In early 1977, Christian interviewed McIntire employee Edgar Eugene
Bradley, who said that neither he nor McIntire had ever known Owen under
any circumstances. He also denied that the Calvary Baptist Church in
Oxnard was ever associated with the ACCC.

Q. These $1,000 bills, how many did you have?
A. I think maybe at that time I had eleven or twelve because I just come back from up north with some good donations, getting ready to build up to go on television.
Q. You say donations. People gave you $1,000 bills?
A. Yes, many times, sir. I have had ten thousand dollars given to me at one time by people.
Q. In $1,000 bills?
A. I had ten $1,000 bills given to me, sir.

Bugliosi couldn't imagine bills of that denomination, which were uncommon, being dropped in the collection box of an itinerant preacher. "Do you know who these people were that gave you $1,000 bills?" he challenged. Owen seemed to sense that he was being led into a trap, and switched his story. The northern windfall had been reaped in smaller-denomination bills, and he had taken them to a bank and turned them in for ten, eleven or twelve $1,000 bills. Owen testified that he converted the smaller bills into $1,000 bills at "a Chinese bank in San Francisco."

Q. Do you have any documentary evidence to support this? Did you sign your name or anything?
A. *I don't remember.*

When Bugliosi asked him why he carried around $1,000 bills, Owen said that it expedited things. "When you go into a city to rent big auditoriums and buy television time," he explained, "they don't want out-of-state checks, but if you have the cash there you can deal." When Bugliosi raised the point that it might be more practical to deal in $100 bills, Crickard cut off the questioning as "undue consumption of time."

But Bugliosi did not let the story of a donations bonanza just before the assassination go unchallenged. Fifteen months earlier Owen had answered a compulsory interrogatory submitted by KCOP's lawyers that asked about his income. In 1965, he said, he had no income and borrowed from his wife's inheritance in the amount of $5,000. In 1966 he gave free pony rides to kids in Huntington Beach and had "No salary or income." Ditto 1967. In 1968 he "Lived off wife's tax free inheritance. Preached three weeks at Embassy Auditorium for Wings of Healing." The stint earned him $1,000 he said, not enough to file a tax return. This jibed with Powers' observation that Owen appeared chronically broke, even borrowing hay, until the sudden affluence just prior to the assassination.

Referring to the large roll of $1,000 bills that Owen admittedly displayed at the stables, Bugliosi demanded, "How come this was not declared on your income tax?"

Owen replied, "Gifts, sir. Gifts for the Lord."

Bugliosi next brought up Owen's encounter with Powers at the Hilton Hay Company in Santa Ana five months after the assassination. Owen said he vaguely remembered it. He remembered commenting about Sirhan, "Of all the thousands of millions of people in Southern California, a guy like that would have to jump in my pickup truck." But he denied having mentioned Sirhan to Powers before the assassination.

Q. Did you ever ask Mr. Powers if the police had asked him about Sirhan?
A. No, because I'm the one that told the police when they questioned me and I gave all the information.
Q. So your testimony is that you did not ask Mr. Powers?
A. I don't believe. I might have later on when I came to move when we sold the house. I might have bumped into him—yes, because he came one day and I told him if his friend bought the house I would give him a thousand dollars extra commission, and he came to the house, and I believe at my house . . . he told me the police had been there and I said—that's right, because I had to give every place I had been, names of people and so forth. I believe I did there, yes, but at my home, not at the hay place. [Owen had at least confirmed the conversations with Bill Powers.]

Bugliosi probed the threats Owen said he received because of his putative horse deal with Sirhan. As he had told the story, he had given his calling card to Sirhan's emissary in the purchase. The card was imprinted with "Shepherd of the Hills"—another of his religious trade names—and unlisted telephone number.

Q. What type of threats were these? What did the people say?

A. Whoever was phoning just said, "Are you the Shepherd of the Hills? Keep your mouth shut about the horse deal!" That's all. Hang up. Another threat was, "You want your head blown off, your family, your children? Don't go to the police."*

Q. You still have a bodyguard?

A. No. Yes, I have. God's my bodyguard, the greatest. He takes care of me. Proverbs 18 and 10, "The name of the Lord is a strong—" [Crickard interrupted, ruling the answer unresponsive.]

Under Bugliosi's questioning Owen did not deny the events Powers had testified to, but he tried to explain them away. His appearance at the stables in the Lincoln Continental was not a day or two before the assassination, but the previous March. The luxurious automobile was a gift from one of his religious flock. And the youth in the back seat was not Sirhan but Johnny Gray's son, Jackie Gray. Gray, the black ex-boxer who was sitting in the front passenger seat, had a number of sons. "He has some boys that look like they're mulattos or Creoles," Owen said. This was how Jackie Gray could have been mistaken for Sirhan.

Owen was now shifting gears so fast that he confused himself. When Bugliosi asked if he was aware that the police at the University Station "dusted the inside of the truck for fingerprints," he blurted out, "No!" One of his attorneys, David Lloyd, caught the *faux pas* and interrupted, "Objection! Asked and answered." Several days before under questioning by Wayland, Owen had testified that the police had not only dusted the truck for fingerprints but even got black powder on the horse in the trailer.

As if dictated by a seasoned Hollywood scriptwriter, the scenario was much in need of a little comic relief at this point, and Mike Wayland produced same when he called Oral K. "Buck" Weaver to the stand. Like Jerry Owen, Weaver had been a friend of heavyweight champion Max Baer for a good many years; in fact, the bearish Weaver had fought Baer in Oakland in 1929, then become good friends with him ever since 1932. Wayland asked Weaver about an incident that took place in Los Angeles in 1958,

---

* Owen's wife confirmed these calls.

when Baer had come into town from his home in Sacramento and Owen was with him.* Weaver recalled one aspect of the initial meeting with Owen as follows: "I am not a religious man, but Owen made a remark to me that I never forgot: 'When I get broke I hold a couple of meetings a night and I take a couple of hundred dollars off the suckers.' "

Owen looked as if he wanted to jump into the ring with Weaver. When his lawyers put him on the stand to rebut this testimony, he managed to make matters worse, and slightly hilarious; lawyer David Lloyd asked, "Do you recall who was present during the conversation [with Weaver]?" (Which took place at the Kipling Hotel in Los Angeles.)

A. Yes.
Q. Who?
A. Primo Carnera, Max Baer, I believe Humphrey Bogart and George Raft.
Q. Do you recall a comment made about evangelists taking money from suckers being made [sic]?
A. Yes.
Q. Would you relate to the court that conversation?
A. Yes, Buck Weaver came in and said that he had just seen a movie and wanted to know if I knew Elmer Gantry [sic], and I said, "That was before my time, Buck! What's it all about?"

He said, "I just saw a picture and he's attending a meeting with a lady evangelist, and Elmer Gantry was getting drunk, and this girl was trying to convert him, and they would go behind the platform and he would say, 'Now it's my turn to go out and get a few hundred dollars from those suckers out there! Watch me go get it!' "

And Buck Weaver said to me, "I'm of a different religion, Curly." And he said, "Do *you* do that?!"

And I says, "No, the only ones that do that, Buck, would be men that are not called of God. A *real* Christian wouldn't do a thing like that!"

The reality here was that Humphrey Bogart had died the year before (1957) and the Academy Award-winning motion picture

---

* Ironically, Christian had known Baer in 1956 when they co-hosted a broadcast that originated from the newly built Sacramento Inn.

Elmer Gantry (starring Jean Simmons and Burt Lancaster) wouldn't even be made until two years hence (1960).

"DO YOU KNOW ARTHUR BREMER'S SISTER?" BUGLIOSI ASKED OWEN. Arthur Bremer was the young man who had gunned down Alabama Governor George C. Wallace in Maryland on May 15, 1972, thus effectively removing him from the presidential race.* In fact, Bremer's elder sister had been standing by to testify for Owen —until Mike Wayland told the court that he intended to ask questions about this relationship. She was flown out of town that same night. Her name was Gail Aiken, and she had previously furnished a signed statement saying that she happened to be shopping in Ohrbach's department store when the shoplifting incident occurred. "There was a small colored lady standing near me," Aiken said, "and she stated, 'I know that man, he's "The Walking Bible" and he is on TV every Sunday, Channel 13, at 12:30.' I was curious and watched the program. . . . It astounded me how this man could quote the Bible and it was a very good program. . . . I sent in a donation for one of the records of the Gospel Lads." When the program was canceled, Aiken received one of Owen's "S.O.S." letters asking viewers to protest to KCOP. When she called the station, she reputedly was told "that Jerry Owen was a thief, an arsonist, and involved in the Sirhan Sirhan matter."

Actually, we'd discovered that Gail Aiken had known Owen for some time and undoubtedly accompanied him to the store. She had been a secretary to his college-instructor brother since 1966, and was one of his most devoted religious followers. Immediately following the Wallace shooting, Owen somehow felt compelled to report his association with Aiken in an innocent context, just as he had with Sirhan, and, again, he didn't go to the news media. However, instead of going to the police this time, he phoned newsman Baxter Ward's campaign headquarters (Ward was then running

* At the time of the shooting, the polls showed that Wallace, if he ran in the November election as an independent or third-party candidate, would siphon off enough votes from Richard Nixon to enable any top Democratic candidate to pose a serious threat.

for his supervisorial post) and excitedly insisted upon meeting with the candidate. An appointment was set for the next day, but Owen failed to show up.

Due to some five years of contact with us, Owen's name was familiar to Ward. We had informed him of the Weatherly Report and our follow-up investigation, and he had interviewed Weatherly with violent results. Quite naturally, Ward wondered what Owen wanted, but his curiosity went unsatisfied for two years. Then, on May 20, 1974, one week after his "second gun" hearing before the Board of Supervisors, Owen called again. He said he had "new evidence" in the RFK case. Ward invited him to come right over, and to the supervisor's surprise, this time he showed.

Owen settled into a padded chair in Ward's wood-paneled office in the county Administration Hall—and okayed the tape recording of this belated get-together. He was wearing a full beard —for a role in a Biblical movie, he explained.* After first insisting to Ward that he hadn't called right after the Wallace shooting, he leaned forward sheepishly and in a low voice confided, "Do you realize that the girl who worked for my brother at Trade Tech College was the sister to the fella who shot Wallace?"

"No!" Ward gasped.

". . . and she just came to me, and I helped her get an airplane ticket to go to Florida. They've been drivin' her crazy! Poor little thing. She was my brother's secretary at Trade Tech for eight years." The police and FBI had hounded her, Owen said, and she came to him "as a minister" for help. But he quickly revealed that there was more to it when he mentioned her promised return from her home in Miami to testify at his trial against KCOP and Ohrbach's.

"Unbelievable!" Ward had commented when he informed Christian about Owen's disclosure. "Owen showing up in the back-ground of the Wallace shooting is just too much to ask of coincidence!"

Now, with Bugliosi asking him if he knew Arthur Bremer's sister, Owen suddenly tried to disown Aiken as thoroughly as he dared. "I know a Gail Aiken," he conceded. "I was told that is

---

* Owen claimed he was about to co-star in a feature motion picture with Robert Mitchum about the life of Moses—which, he said, was to be filmed in South Africa.

his sister, but I don't know Arthur Bremer and I didn't know a sister by the name of Bremer, but I know Gail Aiken who I was informed when this trial started that she had a brother that was three years old when she left him and hasn't seen him since." Owen's sworn testimony clashed with what he had told Ward—on tape.

Owen had presumably brought Aiken from Miami in the expectation that no one would identify her as Bremer's sister. But why was that connection now an embarrassment when he had volunteered it to Ward the year before? All we knew was that coincidence was being stretched to the breaking point. Two months before Owen's meeting with Ward, Bill Turner had interviewed the patriarch of the Bremer family in Milwaukee. William Bremer, Sr., was a blue-collar worker who favored Hubert Humphrey, and he seemed completely baffled by his son's act. He said that his elder daughter Gail had left home at a fairly early age, as had her brother William Bremer, Jr., who after service in the Army paratroops had settled in the Miami area.*

When Owen stepped down from the stand, he understandably looked shaken.†

---

* On August 25, 1973, William Bremer, Jr., was sentenced to eighteen months in jail and ordered to make restitution in a weight-reducing swindle in which he took $36,000 in advance fees. Bremer was represented by attorney Ellis Rubin, who had long represented CIA-sponsored anti-Castro activists and was attorney for the Miami Four (Frank Sturgis, Bernard Barker, Eugenio Martinez and Virgilio Gonzalez) in the Watergate break-in.

† In the October 1972 edition of the John Birch Society's *American Opinion*, in an article (by Arnold Stang) titled "The Communist Plot to Kill George Wallace," it was related that the FBI had interviewed Earl S. Nunnery, "boss of the Milwaukee station of Chesapeake & Ohio Ferry" where Arthur Bremer was (according to Nunnery) seen with a mystery man just before he shot Governor Wallace. The description intrigued us instantly: "With him was an older man over six feet tall . . . He was well-dressed, and he seemed to be the boss of whatever he and Bremer were involved in. Nunnery characterized the mystery man as a 'former athlete and political science teacher, who flopped at both.' " The Bircher identified a left-winger named Dennis Kushman as the mystery man, who had been found murdered in Canada under mysterious circumstances shortly after the alleged encounter with Arthur Bremer.

During the pretrial depositions, whenever Owen would mention Ms. Aiken's name he would stay away from the Bremer tie-in completely. But

There was one other exchange between Owen and Ward at that curious 1974 session that bears repeating here. It dealt with Sirhan's alleged intentions vis-à-vis the attempt to get Owen to appear with trailered horse outside the Ambassador Hotel just before the shooting began. "Was it his hope to get out in the horse van?" probed the supervisor. Owen's response was intriguing indeed:

I don't know! Wh-why would he want a horse there at eleven? I don't know. And all I know from what I've had people tell me that . . . Mr. Kennedy was s'posed to make his appearance at eleven [true], and he was late and he didn't make it until after midnight. Now . . . if I take you out and show you where he . . . wanted me to park . . . See, you come out of the kitchen and out by [a parking lot]. He could jump right in a horse trailer and tell me to drive. . . . Who's gonna stop an old farmer with a horse trailer?

Ward played Owen's game and whispered an encouraging "Yeah" as the peripatetic preacher opened up further.

I have a walk-in trailer. He could open the door and walk in. He could jump right in these beside a horse . . . and maybe have me deliver it out in the country—and BOOM! Put a bullet in me, and there they'd find the horses in the trailer. . . .

Bugliosi recalled Bill Powers to rebut portions of Owen's testimony. The first point was Owen's contention that the incident in which he flashed the roll of $1,000 bills took place in March, not June.

Q. Are you sure it was June of '68 or could it have been March?
A. There is no way at all that it could have been March because I know for a fact, I was going to Big Bear [a mountain resort northeast of Los Angeles] with horses when school got out and school gets out sometime in there, and I was going to take horses up there when

---

he did say that he had once contacted her at the Milwaukee YWCA in 1969, which meant she had gone "home" after leaving "at an early age." Was it possible that she failed to make contact with *anyone* in her family?

this happened, and so I know it wasn't in March. I mean I know for a fact that it definitely was not.

Q. Is there any other reason you feel it took place very shortly before the assassination?

A. I bought a new Chevrolet truck from Guarantee Chevrolet, and that was one reason I got rid of this other truck [that was sold to Owen]. And I remember at the time I was putting the stock rack on the truck to start transporting horses to Big Bear, so I know it was right in that time. It wasn't March, definitely not, and I can say that and be positive.*

Now Bugliosi attacked Owen's testimony that the person in his car during the $1,000-bill incident was not Sirhan, but the son of Johnny Gray, a black man.

Q. This young man in the back seat of Mr. Owen's Lincoln whom you testified earlier resembled Sirhan, did he have any Negroid features whatsoever?

A. No.

Q. Do you feel positive about that?

A. I feel very positive about it, yes.

Q. Could he have been part black?

A. I would say no, definitely not.

When Bugliosi asked, "The roll of $1,000 bills, could they have been as few as 10 or 11 or 12?" Powers replied, "No. I would guess there would be maybe twice that many."

After a mild cross-examination by Owen's lawyers that broke no new ground, Powers was dismissed. Bugliosi was pleased with Powers' testimony. He had sized up his witness as a plainly honest, retiring man who had no wish to insert himself into the limelight, and was sure this impression had come across on the stand.

BUGLIOSI'S NEXT WITNESS WAS LAPD COMMANDER FRANK J. Beeson, a cool-eyed detective who might have stepped out of the

---

* Powers annually supplied riding horses for the Big Bear resort in the San Gabriel Mountains. The season did not begin until the public schools closed for vacation—the first week in June.

Dragnet series. Bugliosi had subpoenaed Beeson because he reportedly was the officer who interviewed Owen at the University Station on June 5, 1968. But when the attorney talked to him during a recess, Beeson denied any recollection of Owen, his hitchhiker story or even any incident connected with the assassination, adding that there was another Officer Beeson at the LAPD. "Okay, if you don't know anything I guess I have the wrong guy," Bugliosi said. "But I want you to know I'm going to check this out further because my records show that you took Owen's statement."*

When court had resumed, Bugliosi informed the judge of Beeson's denial. But a few minutes later Wayland tapped him on the shoulder and whispered, "Beeson's outside again. Now he remembers interviewing Owen."

On the stand, Beeson's memory continued to be foggy, an impairment he blamed on the lapse of time. Yes, he had been a lieutenant in charge of the University Division detectives on June 5, 1968, when Owen walked in with the hitchhiker story.

Q. To the best of your recollection, officer, what did Mr. Owen tell you about his involvement, if any, in the Kennedy case?
A. That he had picked up Sirhan in his truck and driven him certain places, talked to him, and specifically I don't recall at this point what the conversation was, but I—I will end it there. [The detective shrugged, as if there was nothing more to tell.]
Q. Was your conversation with him tape-recorded? [Bugliosi knew there was much more.]
A. Yes, it was.

Beeson recalled that he had seen Owen's pickup truck, although he said he couldn't remember whether a horse trailer was attached.

Q. Do you know of any effort that was made to ascertain whether Sirhan's fingerprints were found inside that truck? [It was a key question, for a positive answer would solidify an Owen-Sirhan link.]
A. I can't recall.

Beeson said that after the initial interview a follow-up session was decided upon. This in itself indicated LAPD interest in the story.

* Authors' interview with Bugliosi, October 28, 1975.

Was Owen's story corroborated by the police investigation? Bugliosi asked.

A. His story was not corroborated. In fact, in my judgment at that time, his story was fictitious.

Q. So your judgment as a lieutenant, a detective for LAPD, is that Mr. Owen had given you a false story?

A. That is true.

Q. And you reached that conclusion based on your conversations with him and the investigation you had ordered?

A. Yes.

Knowingly furnishing false information to a law enforcement agency is a violation of the California penal code, and Owen's story had cost hundreds of hours of investigative time. Yet Beeson offered no explanation as to why Owen wasn't prosecuted.

Under cross-examination by Evry, Beeson explained why the police concluded Owen's story was "fictitious." "As I recall, it was impossible for Mr. Owen to be in two places at the same time, and if you believed his story he had to be . . . The investigation would tend to indicate that if he was here, then he couldn't have been here." Beeson demonstrated by pointing in different directions.

Where? With whom? Doing what? Had the LAPD placed him at Wild Bill's Stables that day? These are questions Evry seemed afraid to ask, realizing they might only get his client in deeper trouble.

As Beeson stepped down, Bugliosi asked for a court order compelling Beeson to return the following morning with four items of evidence: the tape recording of his interview of Owen; the transcript of the interview; all information pertaining to a fingerprint examination of the truck; and the LAPD's complete report on the Owen affair. Crickard made the order when he saw that Bugliosi was not only well within his judicial rights, but fully intended to battle him to the floor on this issue.

The unexpected developments in the courtroom that day apparently had put Owen in a foul mood. When Paul Le Mat snapped his picture in the corridor during recess, Owen pounced on him and yelled, "Give me that camera! Get the sheriff!" Dragging Le Mat into the courtroom, Owen howled at the bailiff to arrest him for taking the picture. "Now, just sit down, Mr. Owen," the bailiff directed. "There's been no harm done here. There's been no violation of the court's rules." At this point Rusty Rhodes summoned Owen and his attorneys into a huddle, identified Le Mat as a friend of Christian's, and proposed that he be called to the stand and forced to tell where Christian was hiding. But Owen broke from the huddle and grabbed Le Mat, shaking him by the shoulders. "Hold this man under arrest!" he shouted. "He knows where Christian is! He's hiding him!"

Le Mat was sorely tempted to punch it out with Owen right there, and it might have been over with quickly. Despite his mild manner and steel-rimmed glasses, Le Mat was a former AAU welterweight boxing champion with lightning fists. But he restrained himself, aware of the approaching bailiff and the .38 Cobra revolver tucked in his belt for his role as a bodyguard to Bill Powers. Bugliosi was absent, but Wayland realized the danger. "Get out of here," he whispered to Le Mat. "And get Christian out of my office, now!" Le Mat complied.

FORMER SUS LEADER MANNY PENA ARRIVED AT THE COURTHOUSE after being subpoenaed by Bugliosi. We had briefed Bugliosi on his clandestine connection with the CIA, and the attorney agreed that the question of why this detective, of all the detectives on the LAPD, was picked for the key SUS position demanded an answer. Was he selected because of his CIA affiliation? What control might the CIA have exerted through him? What did SUS know about Bill Powers and the cowboys? Was it SUS that had intimidated Powers into silence? Was there a cover-up? Pena was a vital witness—if he could be opened up.

Bugliosi approached Pena in the corridor and got an idea of what to expect. "I'll be asking you on the witness stand if you've ever been associated in any fashion with the CIA," he said.

"No, I've never been associated with them," Pena asserted. "Where'd you get the idea I was?"

"Your brother told Stan Bohrman that you were proud of what you did for the CIA over the years."

"Did my brother say that?" Pena said, frowning. "He doesn't know what he's talking about."

Bugliosi decided that in view of this bit of "plausible deniability," to borrow the CIA's parlance, a little strategy was in order. Unless the judge allowed him to bear down on Pena, he would not get the answers he was seeking. Owen's lawyers had echoed their client's belief that there had been a conspiracy in the RFK case, although not one criminally involving Owen. Bugliosi called their hand. "If that's what you believe I don't want you to object to the CIA question being posed to Pena," he told the Owen lawyers before court resumed. "So let's go back in chambers and talk to the judge."

Back they trooped, informing Crickard of their agreement. "Well, I have an objection," he grumbled. "It's not relevant."

"It's extremely relevant," Bugliosi argued. "They're obviously not covering up Sirhan's involvement, so what are they covering up?"

Crickard was adamant, falling back on his "undue consumption of time" plaint.

Bugliosi flared, "Well, we're spending all this time in your chambers arguing about it when we could settle it in court."

But Crickard had the last word. "It's not relevant and I'm not going to let you go on it."

Court resumed with Manuel S. Pena raising his right hand to be sworn in. Lulling the judge, Bugliosi began with routine questions about his police career. Then he got to the "retirement" banquet in 1967, which Pena confirmed.

Q. But you continued to work at LAPD? [The bait was out.]
A. No, I went with the U.S. State Department. I went to Washington, D.C. [Bugliosi smiled indulgently. Manny Pena, diplomat.]
Q. Is that the first time you had ever been associated with the State Department?
A. Correct.
Q. Were you trained back there at the State Department at all?
A. I attended the Foreign Service Institute while I was back there. [The game of semantical dodgeball was on.]
Q. Did you ever go on assignment for the State Department?
A. Not at this time.
Q. At a later time?

A. In I believe the latter part of '69 and first part of '70, I took a trip
to South America.

Crickard finally caught on to Bugliosi's ploy and instructed him
to move on to a "relevant" area. "This is his background," the
attorney insisted. "I want to know about his training and education."

Q. Why did you go to South America?
THE COURT: That is not relevant!
Q. Well, were you on assignment by the State Department in South
America?
THE COURT: That is not relevant either. Let's get to this case.
BUGLIOSI: I want to know whether it was a vacation or anything to
do—

He never got out the word "CIA." Crickard cut in again,
directing Bugliosi to the Jerry Owen inquiry that the witness had
supervised.

Q. Was that truck ever checked for fingerprints to ascertain whether
Sirhan's prints were inside?
A. I couldn't say without going back to the files. I can't at this moment.
Q. That would have been the normal thing to do, right?
A. Normal, routine. But I can't tell you that it was without going back
through the files.

According to Pena's testimony, SUS concluded that Owen was
neither with Sirhan in the truck nor implicated in the assassination.
But details eluded him, due, he said, to the passage of time.
Bugliosi took one more stab at pinning down his covert CIA
activities, asking, "Mr. Pena, throughout your law enforcement
career have you ever worked directly or indirectly for the CIA?"
Pena sat in stony silence. Crickard, so angered that his gavel hand
trembled, loudly interjected, "That's—you don't have to answer
that. That's not relevant in this case. The court discussed that with
you in chambers, Mr. Bugliosi, and told you not to inquire into
that area."

After a brief exchange with the judge, Bugliosi tried another
tack. "You indicated earlier that you worked for the State Depart-

ment," he addressed Pena. "Was this on a paid basis or was it—" Crickard burst in again, "That's not relevant, either. You don't have to answer that question."

The door was closed. Insofar as the court record was concerned, Manny Pena wore striped pants and a homburg instead of a cloak and dagger. But Bugliosi had already gotten in the back door a good portion of what Crickard had forbidden him to elicit directly. Why was an LAPD officer attending the Foreign Service Institute (a CIA Cover-Front Outfit), and on assignment to South America for "the State Department"?*

BUGLIOSI CALLED GLADYS ROBERTA OWEN, THE PLAINTIFF'S WIFE, to the stand. His purpose was to explore a new wrinkle Owen had brought into his hitchhiker story when he testified earlier: that on the night of the RFK shooting, his wife had accompanied him on the overnight preaching trip to Oxnard. He had not mentioned this in his interview with Turner, nor, so far as we could tell, to the LAPD. Putting her on the stand was a calculated risk. If she swore that she went with him to Oxnard, it would strengthen his alibi for the night of the assassination. On the other hand, it didn't seem likely that she would claim to have been with him when he supposedly picked up Sirhan and spent the night before election day in Los Angeles. The records of the St. Moritz Hotel had showed him registered as single. It was possible

---

* "CIA Link to L.A. Police Reported" read the headline in the January 12, 1976, edition of the Los Angeles *Herald-Examiner*. "Documents released by the Central Intelligence Agency show the Los Angeles Police Department received training by CIA personnel" during the late 1960s, the story read. "(LAPD) Chief Edward M. Davis, in a statement issued through police department spokesman Cmdr. Peter Hagen, denied any connection between the LAPD and the CIA . . . Hagen said there would be no further elaboration."

Shortly after this story appeared, Davis appeared on *The Sam Yorty Show* (on KCOP, Los Angeles) and offered, "Heck, I don't think I've ever met anyone in the CIA," again denying the LAPD-CIA link.

After retiring in January 1978, Davis announced his candidacy for governor of California.

that he had backtracked to Santa Ana to pick her up on election day before heading for Oxnard, but not very probable.

Roberta Owen, as she preferred to be called, was a matronly grayish-blond woman with a pleasant if bland personality. Bugliosi inquired politely, "You are aware that your husband has testified that on the evening of June 4th you and he were up at Oxnard?"

A. *I don't recall any particular dates, sir.* I know we spent some time in Oxnard.
Q. Was it around the time of the assassination?
A. Yes. [Owen was nodding from his coaching box.]
Q. Do you recall a prayer meeting at a church up there called the Calvary Baptist Church?
A. Yes.
Q. Do you recall where you stayed that night? [Jerry Owen had stated that it was with lay people whose name his wife might remember.]
A. Which night, sir?
Q. The night of the prayer meeting.
A. Well, we had several prayer meetings at Oxnard and several meetings over quite a period of time.
Q. You were not with your husband when he supposedly picked up a man in downtown Los Angeles who he thinks is Sirhan?
A. No, sir, I was not.
Q. Were you with him the following day, which would be June the 4th?
A. Let's see. Yes, I think so.
Q. Where did you join him? [There was a pause. Roberta Owen was in a blind alley, and she was forced to double back.]
A. No, no, he had gone up to Oxnard and returned, which would have been probably two days before I saw him.
Q. *So he went up to Oxnard by himself?*
A. *Yes.*

Roberta Owen had just put an enormous dent in her husband's shaky alibi. There was no cross-examination. Court was adjourned for the day.

COMMANDER FRANK BEESON WAS WAITING NERVOUSLY WHEN court resumed in the morning, and Bugliosi put him right on the stand. Running down the inventory of material on the Owen investigation that Crickard had instructed him to bring, Bugliosi asked, "Were you successful in getting those documents?" The policeman said no. In his search for the material he "learned that there is deployed another task force relating to the Sirhan Sirhan investigation—"

"You say another task force?" Bugliosi interrupted. "Is this another investigative task force?"

"It's probably more of a coordination task force in that there are efforts presently under way to reopen the Sirhan investigation," Beeson replied, "and that's the purpose of this task force."

Considering the LAPD's intransigence on the matter, Bugliosi posed a perfectly logical question: "Is the purpose of the task force to resist, as far as you know, the reopening of the investigation, or go along with it?" But Crickard intervened, ruling the question immaterial. Bugliosi was left to ask Beeson to produce the material he had been ordered to bring. The policeman declined. After consulting with members of the new task force, he said, he spoke with Deputy City Attorney Ward McConnell, whose office counseled the police on legal matters.

Q. What was the position given to you by the deputy city attorney, Mr. McConnell? [Bugliosi asked.]

A. That any of the files—or any information contained in those files— the divulging of that information would be strongly resisted by the city.

Q. So you were flat-out told that you would not be given these records which you were seeking?

A. That is true.

Q. Let me ask you this: Did you ascertain yesterday afternoon whether in fact these records exist?

A. I determined there is a file, and there is a file specifically on Mr. Owen.

Q. And you have been advised by counsel, the City Attorney's office, which is the counsel for the LAPD, that this file would not be turned over voluntarily in this court?

A. That is true.

Even though Beeson had defied his order, Crickard dismissed him and thanked him for coming. On that politely ludicrous note the judge allowed the LAPD's charade to pass. It had begun with Schaffer's supposed inability to find the files, continued with Pena's circumlocutions, and ended with Beeson's flat refusal to produce the files Schaffer couldn't find. Bugliosi shook his head. What did the police have to do to affront Crickard?

17

The Trances

WHEN JERRY OWEN TESTIFIED THAT THE YOUNG MAN IN THE back seat of his Lincoln was Johnny Gray's son, he set off a game of musical chairs that had his lawyers in a tizzy. At first, David Lloyd promised to bring Jackie Gray into the courtroom that afternoon. Then, after a luncheon conference, he announced that it was not Jackie Gray, after all, but someone named Charles Butler. However, when the promised witness had not been produced by the end of the day and Bugliosi raised the issue, Arthur Evry disclosed that during lunch Johnny Gray "indicated to us the person in the car was not his son, but he will testify in our rebuttal testimony as to who that person was and it was not Sirhan Sirhan."

The next morning Johnny Gray was back in the courtroom. Bugliosi and Wayland watched expectantly as Evry cautiously questioned Gray, evoking his memory of the visit to Wild Bill's Stables.

Q. Do you recall if Reverend Owen had any amount of money with him that day?
A. Well, he had a roll. That's all I can say. I didn't count it.
Q. Do you recall seeing that roll?
A. Yes.
Q. Who was present in the car with you?
A. Well, we first had Charlie Butler. He lived close by that place over there where they had the horses at.
Q. Anyone else?
A. We went by and dropped him off. And my son was with us, Jackie Gray.

Back to Jackie Gray! Bugliosi and Wayland looked at each other, incredulous. Only the previous afternoon Evry had declared that Johnny Gray would testify that it was not his son, and overnight the signals had changed.

Evry completed his brief questioning by making sure that he and Gray were talking about the same incident. Yes, Gray said, they were in Owen's Lincoln Continental. Yes, Owen "met some tall white fellow there that run the stables"—Bill Powers, No, it was not Sirhan seated behind him, it was his son Jackie. No further questions.

In beginning his cross examination, Bugliosi couldn't resist needling Gray. "Do people ever come up to your son in your presence and say, 'Gee, you are a spitting image of Sirhan Sirhan'?" Crickard interceded, ruling the question irrelevant. Bugliosi showed a picture of Sirhan to Gray and asked whether his son "resembled the man in the photograph in any fashion whatsoever." Gray said that he did "in some respects." Then Bugliosi established the fact that in 1968 Jackie Gray was only thirteen, while Sirhan was twenty-three.

Bugliosi asked, "At the age of thirteen he looked just like the man in this picture, is that what you are saying?"

"That's right, that's right." Gray seemed unnerved.

"Are you having trouble seeing that photograph?" Bugliosi's tone was sarcastic.*

The next line of questioning concerned Owen's roll of bills, which prompted Crickard to cut in again to rule that it was repetitious and unduly consumptive of time, and that in any case the passing of the money was "an extremely collateral matter." This touched off a sharp exchange:

BUGLIOSI: How is it collateral if it happens that Mr. Owen is lying about this incident? How is it collateral if Mr. Powers is to be believed that within a couple of days of the assassination, the assassin, Sirhan, is with Owen, and Owen is in possession of 25 to 30 $1,000 bills? If that is collateral, then I have to go back to law school.

THE COURT: I am not telling you to do anything.

BUGLIOSI: In effect you are. [The attorney was exasperated with Crickard's wave-of-the-hand dismissal of the heart of the defense case, but his ridicule might have provoked some judges to threaten him with contempt.]

THE COURT: You can draw any conclusion that you want.

Bugliosi was convinced that the judge thoroughly resented the assassination issue being dragged into his court. There was nothing left to pursue with Johnny Gray. He was excused.

That afternoon Christian used a private detective contact (Dan Prop) to try and obtain copies of Johnny Gray's phone records during the time he lived just down the street from the Coliseum Hotel, June 1968. The report came back short and succinct: "Pulled—cops!"

Crickard's diminution of the Sirhan connection as an "extremely collateral matter" clearly signaled to both sides that his mind was made up. There was actually no need for the plaintiff's attorneys to attempt to rebut Bill Powers' testimony further; for all intents and purposes this issue was already decided in their favor.

---

* Dianne Hull (with Paul Le Mat) had been our eyes and ears at the trial. When she conveyed this exchange, we sent her off to scour the myriad of grade and junior high schools young Gray had attended during the 1967–69 period. She found lots of school records on him, but none had accompanying photographs. School officials could not account for the loss.

But they knew that Bugliosi intended to call Jackie Gray to the stand if they did not. "At the risk of belaboring this one point, I would like to call Jackie Gray to the stand for just a few questions," plaintiff's attorney, David Lloyd, announced.

Jackie Gray, age twenty, was a somber, mentally deficient, mulatto-appearing young man with kinky black hair; his resemblance to Sirhan seemed superficial at best. He spoke softly, almost inaudibly, in awkward phrases, and seemed extremely uncomfortable in his role as center of attraction. Under sympathetic questioning by Lloyd, he said that he had been to the Reverend Owen's home in Santa Ana many times, often as a houseguest. Yes, he recalled accompanying his father and Owen to a nearby stables in 1967 or 1968. On this occasion he sat "in the back seat on the corner" of Owen's car.

Lloyd had called Gray for the sole and limited purpose of establishing that it was he, not Sirhan, in that back seat. No further questions.

On cross-examination Bugliosi handled Jackie Gray gently in deference to his obvious slow-wittedness. The young man remembered that Owen was buying a red truck from the cowboy at the stables, but thought it was a 1967 model. (Powers' old pickup was blue.)

Q. . . . During this incident when Reverend Owen was going to buy this 1967 truck, where were you seated in Mr. Owen's car?

A. The front seat. [He had testified during direct examination that he was seated in the back seat.]

Q. Where was your father?

A. Like, he is sitting like this [indicating to his right] and I am sitting in the middle.

Q. You both are seated in the front seat?

A. Right. [Jackie was sandwiched between Owen and his father in the front seat of the Lincoln.]

Q. Was there anyone seated in the back seat?

A. No.

Q. This white cowboy from whom Mr. Owen was going to buy the truck, was he with anyone?

A. Well, only thing I know is he had on Levi's and boots.

Q. But was he with anyone?

A. He was with a lady standing outside.

Q. Did Reverend Owen have any money in his hands, any $1,000 bills?

A. Yeah. He had them rolled up.

Q. Were they $1,000 bills?

A. Number 50's.

Q. They were $50 bills?

A. Fifties and hundreds.

Q. Not thousands?

A. Not thousands.

Q. Did Reverend Owen tell you where he got this roll of money?

A. No, he did not.

Q. Did he actually buy the truck from this man?

A. Yes.

Q. The man took the money?

A. Took the money.

Q. Do you know how much he took?

A. No.

Q. Where was the truck at this time, this red truck?

A. Sitting in a lot like this, sitting like this.

Q. Was it right next to the car?

A. Yes.

It all added up. The late-model red truck parked at the stables, a lady present rather than the stablehands, Owen carrying only $50 and $100 bills, Bill Powers accepting some cash. Jackie Gray wasn't describing the incident which occurred just before the assassination when Owen was flaunting $1,000 bills and Powers couldn't make change for the balance owed on the old pickup. He most likely was talking about the day about four weeks before when Owen first bought the pickup and handed Powers $50 or so as part payment. In fact, the elder Gray had said that he was at the stables with Owen "one other time." So Jackie Gray's visit to Wild Bill's Stables was not on the day Sirhan reportedly was there.

Intuitively, Bugliosi sought to capitalize on Jackie Gray's lack of guile, asking, "Have you ever heard the name Sirhan Sirhan?" Gray nodded affirmatively at the mention of the well-known name. Then the attorney took a shot in the dark.

Q. Did you ever hear your father mention that name?

A. Yes.

Q. When?

A. Every time I ride with him he just say it.

Q. Pardon? [Bugliosi could hardly believe what he was hearing.]

A. He just mention it. It comes out of his mouth. He mentions it. He mentions it every time. Every time it comes out of his mouth, he mentions it when he riding.

Q. You say your father talks about Sirhan all the time?

A. Uh-huh. [Again the affirmative nod.]

This was incredibly heavy testimony, and Bugliosi sensed that possibly, just possibly, the disingenuous youth on the stand could blow the lid off the case. Not wishing to alert the witness to the enormity of his testimony, Bugliosi very casually asked him to explain in more detail what his father would say about Sirhan.

A. He tells me he always look like me, and say things like me and talk like me and say good things, do good things and nice things and want to do good things and want to do excellent things and stuff like that. [The words sounded as if Gray had been told that he was practically interchangeable with Sirhan.]

Q. He told you that he knows Sirhan very well, is that correct?

A. Yes.

Q. Did he tell you where he first met Sirhan?

A. Yes.

Q. Where did he tell you he first met him?

A. He tells me he meets him—

Q. Pardon?

A. He meets him through . . . [Gray hesitated. His eyes rolled in the direction of Jerry Owen, and Bugliosi didn't have to turn around to know it.]

Q. Through Mr. Owen?

A. Through Mr. Owen.

Owen blanched while his lawyers seemed stunned. Evry started to object, but Bugliosi drove on:

Q. When is the first time that your father told you he met Sirhan through Reverend Owen?

A. First time?

Q. Yes.

A. In '67.

Q. Are you sure about that?

A. Sure.

Q. Pardon? [Gray was speaking softly, matter-of-factly. Bugliosi was encouraging him to speak up.]

A. Sure. Yes. [The emphasis was picking up.]

Q. Did your father tell you where this incident took place—where Mr. Owen—

A. Yes.

Q. —introduced him to Sirhan? [There was the hum of low voices at the plaintiff's counsel table.]

A. Yes.

Q. Where?

Lloyd rose to his feet. "Your Honor," he said, "I am going to object to the rest of the testimony and impeach my own witness. I have been informed by Mr. Gray that his son is not competent to testify and would like to talk to the court in private about this."

An air of crisis hung over the courtroom. Lloyd was impeaching his *own* witness! Presumably, an attorney has done his home-work and is satisfied with the competency of his witness before putting him on the stand; and he certainly knows the risks of cross-examination. "This is so much hogwash," Bugliosi said. "I can't believe this. This is their witness, called to the witness stand for a particular point. When he is blowing the lid off the case, they say he is incompetent!"

Crickard granted Lloyd's request for a conference in chambers. Reluctant to leave young Gray unattended, Bugliosi requested that since "the testimony of this witness is exceedingly incriminating to Mr. Owen, I would like to have this witness in protective custody for his own safety." Crickard instructed his bailiff to watch over Jackie Gray while they were out of the courtroom.

Up to this juncture Owen had been his usual ebullient self, back-slapping his coterie of associates in attendance and coaching his witnesses with motions of his head and hands to such an extent that Crickard had to scold him on several occasions. But now, as Bugliosi passed his table, Owen snarled, "You're in big trouble!"

Bugliosi had the court record reflect that Owen made "some type of threat to me."

Following the conference, Lloyd made a motion in open court that all of Jackie Gray's testimony be stricken and he be dismissed on grounds of incompetency. He was under a mental physician's care, Lloyd argued, was unemployed, was receiving disability compensation and was unable to recollect events accurately. Evry chimed in that he had "mental problems through the use of drugs, particularly hallucinogenic drugs," and quoted the senior Gray as saying his son's drug use had begun as early as 1968.

Crickard decided that he himself would question the witness on the point, using as a guide *Judge Jefferson's Evidence Book*, which sets forth certain criteria of mental competency. Jackie Gray told the judge that he was a ninth child, divided his time between his separated parents and had held only one job. He said he was seeing a psychiatrist who "gets me on the right track," but flatly denied using drugs.

After Crickard's quiz had gone on for half an hour, Bugliosi interposed that although young Gray was "a little slow-witted," it was evident that under the law he was capable of testifying. "If this witness is telling the truth," he told the judge, "as I tend to believe that he is, I am very, very concerned about his safety." Bugliosi noted that the noon break was coming up, and again petitioned Crickard to place Gray in protective custody "not just for himself but for this country. We have to find out what he knows." Although Evry resented the implication that "this kid is in danger," Crickard directed his bailiff to accompany the witness to lunch.

When court resumed in the afternoon, Crickard ruled that Jackie Gray was competent to testify.

Bugliosi picked up where he had left off—the place where Owen had introduced Sirhan to Johnny Gray. It was at Owen's Santa Ana home, young Gray said. He remembered because he "was leaning on the seat and [Sirhan] was giving me a quarter." Twenty-five cents to a thirteen-year-old black from Watts was something to remember.

As Bugliosi warmed up to his questioning, Lloyd interrupted to say that young Gray's psychiatrist had arrived and "will testify that the witness has a schizoid, paranoid, psychotic personality." Lloyd wanted the opportunity to throw this whole aberration book at his prodigal witness right away rather than after Bugliosi finished. Bugliosi objected on the basis that the court had already ruled as to competency, a question a psychiatrist could not legally determine. "Now if they want to put this psychiatrist on to rehabilitate the position they are now in, that is a different story," he argued. "But to try to prevent other words from coming out of this witness's mouth—"

Evry broke in, objecting to "the inference we are trying to take anything out of this witness's mouth and have it not said." All they wanted, he insisted, was to put on the psychiatrist so he could return to his own practice. Bugliosi estimated he would finish with Jackie Gray about two-thirty, but Crickard, trying to compromise, said the doctor could come on a bit earlier.

Returning to Jackie Gray, Bugliosi asked, "Did you hear Reverend Owen talk about Sirhan many times?"

A. Yes, many times. [Owen was clutching the table edges, straining to hear what the sotto voce young man would say next.]
Q. What did you hear your father say about Sirhan?
A. Good things like schooling and going to school and stuff like that. Buying clothes, stuff like that. Going to school.*
Q. Who was buying clothes?
A. He, for him. For him.
Q. Who was buying clothing? Who was doing the buying?
A. The Reverend.
Q. Reverend Owen was buying clothing for Sirhan?
A. Yes.
Q. . . . What were the good things that Reverend Owen said about Sirhan?
A. Like giving him money, you know to do something for hisself and stuff like that. [Jackie Gray glanced at Owen, apparently unaware of the significance of what he was saying.]

* In a 1972 interview with Christian, Mrs. Mary Sirhan and her sons Adel and Munir said that in late 1967 and early 1968 Sirhan Sirhan talked about going back to college, and how he needed new clothes and a new car to return with dignity.

Q. Reverend Owen used to give Sirhan money?
A. Yes.*

At this point Bugliosi flashed onto something he recalled from skimming through our raw manuscript—the theory that Sirhan was a real-life version of the Manchurian Candidate, hypnoprogrammed to kill. The attorney had been impressed with our research, but not entirely convinced. Now he thought of the queen of diamonds that had been used to plunge the novel's antihero into a trance, and decided to draw to an inside straight.

Q. Do you know what the word trance means?
A. Yes.
Q. Did you ever hear your father or Reverend Owen say anything about Sirhan being in a trance?
A. Yes. [The answer came matter-of-factly.]
Q. What did you hear them say?
A. This is in a room to hisself, in a room that he always been in, in a room that some of the things he is doing is wrong.

The language of the man-child. Bugliosi patiently sought to clarify it, remembering that Sirhan had closeted himself in a room when he put himself into a trance and did the "automatic writing."

Q. Talking about Sirhan?
A. Yes. I don't know what it is.
Q. You heard your father and Reverend Owen saying that Sirhan used to be in a room all by himself?
A. Right.
Q. Did the word "trance" come up?
A. Right.
Q. Did you ever hear them say that sometimes Sirhan would do things and not know that he did them?
A. Right.
Q. Have you ever heard of the word "hypnosis"?

* Throughout Sirhan's notebooks containing the "automatic writing" indicative of the trance state, there are such entries as "Jeeerry," expectations of large sums of money from unspecified sources and the promise of "a new Mustang" automobile.

A. Yes.

Q. Did you ever hear Reverend Owen or your father saying anything about Sirhan being under hypnosis?

A. No.

Q. But you did hear them saying that sometimes he would be in a trance?

A. Right.

Q. Did you ever hear your father or Reverend Owen say that Sirhan was involved with other people in killing Senator Kennedy?

A. No.

The talk was mostly about Sirhan in a trance. "That's all I ever heard," Jackie Gray volunteered.

Crickard suspended Gray's testimony so that the hastily summoned psychiatrist could take the stand for the plaintiff. He was Henry Gene Robinson, a former Army psychiatrist in Vietnam, now director of the Kendrin Community Mental Health Center in Los Angeles. Dr. Robinson said that young Gray was a regular patient at the clinic. The gist of his testimony was that Gray suffered from a degree of psychotic disorder and schizophrenia, displayed hostility toward those closest to him and tended to fantasize. On cross-examination Bugliosi asked Robinson what percentage of the general population of the United States was schizophrenic to some degree. His answer: Up to 25 percent. Did Gray ever say anything that had been proven to be fantasy? No, the doctor conceded, thus neutralizing his earlier testimony. Robinson's testimony was so undamaging that Bugliosi wondered if he had been told the nature of the emergency that demanded his appearance.

Upon resuming with Jackie Gray, Bugliosi administered an impromptu test of his own. Would Jackie Gray, by his answers, *adopt* whatever was contained in a question, or was he capable of independent answers?

Q. Mr. Gray, you say that your father and Reverend Owen spoke a lot of times about Sirhan, is that correct?

A. Yes.

Q. Did they talk a lot about Joe DiMaggio?

A. Yes. They mentioned him *one time*.

Q. So you heard Joe DiMaggio's name mentioned one time, is that correct?

A. Yes.

Q. Did you ever hear them talk about Marilyn Monroe?

A. No.

Q. Did you ever hear them talk about Michael Crulowitz?

A. No.

The last name was pure invention. Bugliosi was satisfied that Gray had the ability to discriminate and sort out fact from fancy.

Jackie Gray thought that Owen had mentioned Sirhan having "a good wife," but the Palestinian immigrant had never been married.

Q. You said Reverend Owen was always talking about how Sirhan was in a trance?

A. It was a trance when he would be in his room, he would sit back and think about something to do that he liked to do all the time. [Unwittingly, Gray was describing the intense concentration preparatory to slipping into a trance.]

Q. Do you know where this room was?

A. Like a room of his own.

Q. You don't know whether that was at Reverend Owen's house or someone else's house?

A. No.

Gray said that his father and Owen talked about the fact that Sirhan had been convicted of the murder of Senator Kennedy. "What did they say?" Bugliosi wanted to know.

"A few words that he was just convicted of a crime or something and he never done that before or something like that, and that's all," Gray responded.

"Did they say anything about Sirhan being in a trance at the time he killed Senator Kennedy?" the attorney asked. The answer never came. Crickard again charged "undue consumption of time." Somewhat surprised that the judge had let him go as far as he did, Bugliosi put up only a token argument.

"Well, you have had your chance to examine him, Mr. Bugliosi."

"I have, and I am very satisfied with the answers, your Honor."

But David Lloyd was distinctly displeased with the answers, and he vehemently insisted on being allowed to cross-examine Jackie Gray as an adverse witness. He launched into a pitiless exploitation of the young man's vulnerability to leading questions. "How long had the Reverend Owen been training as a boxer?" he asked.

Gray, who never said he had, responded, "A good while."

"They were boxing in Phoenix, too, weren't they?" the attorney suggested.

Bugliosi objected to the blatantly leading questions, and Crickard sustained him. But once the words had been put in his mouth, Gray swallowed them. "Have you had occasion to spar or fight with Sirhan in Phoenix?" Lloyd asked. Yes, young Gray replied, in the summer of 1972. This was not merely fantasizing, since he had often tagged along with his father, and occasionally Owen, as they worked in various gyms with various fighters. But in his eagerness to please, he seemed to be garbling people, places and times. It was like playing with word blocks, trying to make sentences out of them.

Lloyd recalled the father to the stand. It was Johnny Gray who had said it was his son in the back seat of the Lincoln, but putting Jackie Gray on the stand to verify it had backfired badly. Now the hapless father was to be used to try to destroy his son as a witness.

No sooner had Johnny Gray mounted the stand than Bugliosi protested that information about his son's testimony had been relayed to him outside the courtroom. "We have an exclusion of witnesses order here," he reminded Crickard, "and I have received word that Reverend Owen has been kind of an errand boy, running out of the courtroom telling the witness what his son was testifying to." This might have been cause for a contempt citation or mistrial, but the matter was defused when Lloyd agreed to ask only questions about the son's mental state, not his testimony. Gray stated that in the past his son had described events that turned out to be fantasies—he couldn't think of a specific example—and had used the drug LSD.*

Bugliosi's counterquestions were succinct and direct:

---

* Jackie Gray testified that he never used LSD—and no evidence was ever produced to support this contention.

Q. You are a very close personal friend of Reverend Owen?
A. Yes, I am.
Q. Have you been talking to Reverend Owen about this case?
A. Sure I have talked with him about the case.
Q. Has he ever given you any money?

Gray squirmed and glanced quickly at a glaring Owen. "Beg pardon?" he stalled. When the question was repeated, Gray mumbled, "Well, he has given me money for sometimes different transactions."

WHILE THE TRIAL WAS TAKING ITS DRAMATIC TURN, CHRISTIAN was experiencing enough drama of his own to last a lifetime. He and Paul Le Mat had stopped at Cine Artists, a motion picture production company in the Playboy Building on the Sunset Strip that had produced *Aloha, Bobby and Rose.* Christian took the opportunity to make a phone call to our then motion picture attorney Jack Schwartzman. Schwartzman was on another line, said an unusually nervous secretary. At her suggestion, Christian left his name and the Cine Artists number.

Five minutes later the phone rang. "This is the West Los Angeles Sheriff's Department calling," the caller informed the Cine Artists secretary. "We have word that there is a man named Jonn Christian in that office. We want him. Keep him there until we arrive—we're on our way up there right now."

The secretary was well aware of Christian's "fugitive" status and said there was no employee by that name, but she would check around. Putting the caller on hold, she alerted Christian to what was going on.

Christian had no intention of being taken into custody by any Los Angeles law enforcement officers. The whole case, beginning with the heavy-handed silencing of Bill Powers and ending with the roughhouse search in Brentwood a couple of days before, had been filled with lawless law enforcement. Los Angeles cops were noted for their hair-trigger guns,* and Christian could even envision

* In the preceding eighteen months, Los Angeles cops had killed seventy-five civilians. In many of those cases, the use of deadly force had been

himself being shot "trying to escape." Here he was, merely a potential witness in a civil suit, and the cops were hunting him with twenty-four-hour stakeouts and wiretaps as if he were one of the FBI's Ten Most Wanted men. Why?

Expecting cops to pour out of the elevators, Le Mat and Christian started down separate stairwells, but when he heard the metallic clang of footsteps above, Christian ducked into a fourth-floor office suite. It was Playboy Productions, and it so happened that one of the executives, Eddie Rissien, had talked with Christian on the phone a couple of times about a motion picture version of this book. (Le Mat managed to escape in time.)

"Don't ask too many questions right now, Eddie," Christian implored as he shook hands with Rissien, "because there are some cops in this building trying to arrest me on bullshit charges having to do with a phony subpoena in the RFK case." Rissien blinked in astonishment, but pointed to a vacant office that could be locked from the inside and out.

Christian called Wayland's office and instructed a secretary to deliver a message personally to Bugliosi at the courthouse. "Tell him that I'm trapped in Playboy's offices—they're some cops after me—and that I need him to get over here right away or call!" She called the court instead—and passed the message through Crickard's bailiff. Christian glanced out the window and saw a sheriff's patrol car come roaring up the hill to the rear of the building and slam to a halt at the rear exit. One of the two uniformed deputies that leaped out of the car and ran into the underground garage area had his service revolver in hand. Suddenly Captain Hugh Brown's warning about Christian getting into "big trouble" for "messing around" with the Homicide Commander's "thing" hit home with full impact. Bugliosi returned Christian's call about twenty minutes later. "Vince, I'm in Eddie Rissien's office at Playboy and I—" Christian's words were clipped off in mid-sentence as Bugliosi imparted his own excitement.

"Have you heard the news? We may have blown the lid off the case!"

---

criticized by the community as unwarranted, often racist and in some instances plain murder.

"*Vince!*" howled Christian futilely.

"They put Johnny Gray's kid on the stand to try and make him into a surrogate Sirhan, and he starts talking about Sirhan being at Owen's *home* clear back in '67, and about Sirhan being in *trances* and—"

"*Goddammit*, Bugliosi!" Christian screamed, "there are cops going through this joint with drawn guns . . . and I need your *help!*"

"What?!" said Bugliosi.

"What's ass! There are cops on their way up inside this goddam building, and they are *not* planning on bringing me back alive! Do you understand what I'm saying?!" Christian's voice was trembling slightly, a sign Bugliosi quickly identified as flat-out fear.

A hasty discussion of Christian's severe plight made it clear to both that Bugliosi's dispatch to the Playboy Building, some fifteen miles away, would not accomplish anything anyway. He wasn't a DA anymore, and he'd likely arrive too late to forestall whatever might have been in store for the entrapped "fugitive." Both agreed there was a more practical solution.

Christian quickly placed calls to Supervisor Baxter Ward and City Attorney Burt Pines, government officials with the power to intervene. But to no avail. Ward's deputy Robert Pratt advised him that he'd be interfering with "due process" (i.e., the warrant that had been questionably served on Christian), and Pines refused his call.

When court resumed, Crickard called the attorneys into chambers and said that it had been brought to his attention that Bugliosi had received a message from Christian. Bugliosi readily acknowledged talking on the phone with him, saying that Christian had expressed a fear for his life at the hands of the police.

Crickard seemed so dead set on having Christian brought in that Bugliosi felt compelled to give a brief lecture. "This man apparently has devoted the last several years to finding the co-conspirators, if there are any, with Sirhan," he said, "and it is not far-fetched that more than one person was involved. And if other persons are ever found and traced up the ladder, I think the guy that will be commended ultimately in Congress is a guy by the name of Jonn Christian. I think he has done a brilliant job of investigation, and his fears, I don't know whether they are justified or not, but in view of the crazy things happening in this case, they may be justified. His life is more important to him than a court subpoena. . . . He is a very elusive guy, but understandably so. We are dealing with a case where there are a lot of bullets flying around."

As offices began closing for the day in the Playboy Building, Eddie Rissien informed Christian that the patrol cars had left in a hurry (it turned out that they were mistakenly dispatched to the Playboy Club in Century City to look for Christian). However, Rissien's security officer had just told him that two plain-clothes men posing as building inspectors were still combing the building. Rissien proposed that Christian try to get out of the building while there were still witnesses around for his possible protection. The two improvised a plan of action. Rissien would play himself and escort Christian out as if he were another Playboy producer. When the elevator automatically stopped and the doors opened at the lobby, Rissien berated Christian, "I don't care what your problems are, goddammit! We've got five days to get that film finished or you will be in big—" The guard gave Rissien a cool wink as the doors slid shut and the elevator sank to the basement level. Rissien checked for cops first. The coast was clear, and Christian slipped out the exit that earlier had been blocked by the patrol car.

Christian met up with Le Mat (by prearrangement) later that night at the seaside home of Russ O'Hara, one of the better-known radio personalities in Southern California. After midnight they sidestreeted their way out of Los Angeles, staying overnight (under assumed names) at the one place they were sure no police would think to look for them: Disneyland. An hour before dawn they began their circuitous trek northward, into the backroads of the Mojave Desert. By midday the thermal temperature had passed the 120° mark. Somehow, though, Los Angeles had seemed hotter for these two "fugitives."

They hid out for several days in a small fishing village (Cayucos) some 350 miles north of Los Angeles at the earthy pad of Christian's godson, Jack De Witt. Calling in to LA from a phone booth in nearby Morro Bay, Christian was told that the trial was over, that Crickard had lifted the ominous body attachment. He didn't have to ask who had won.

Intuition told them to tarry awhile longer, and to slip into Los Angeles like a pair of Rio Grande wetbacks. Their instincts weren't wrong either. Even though Crickard's order was immediately forwarded by his bailiff to the police, Christian and Le Mat remained on their still-wanted list for five more days—hardly an oversight. (We discovered this in the trial record when it was released for public view by Crickard a year later.)

18

This Conspiracy Might Ultimately Make Watergate Look Like a One-Roach Marijuana Bust

THE DEFENSE WAS UNABLE TO PUT ON ALL OF THE WITNESSES it wanted. Process servers had been unable to find a trace of the Reverend Medcalf, the ex-pastor of the Calvary Baptist Church in Oxnard who in 1968 had told our investigator Jim Rose that the church was shuttered the night Owen claimed to have preached there. Johnny Beckley and John Chris Weatherly, both of whom might have shed considerable light on the nature and extent of Owen's association with Sirhan, had fled in fright. Bill Powers still couldn't find his former stablehands Jack Brundage and Dennis Jackson, who had been present during the $1,000 bills incident at the stables. When the LAPD refused to produce its records, the defense team had subpoenaed the Weatherly Report from the sheriff's office but were told it never existed. So they had issued subpoenas for the two sheriff's deputies whose names appeared on the report as having interrogated Weatherly, but they were not locatable.

Despite the vanishing witnesses, no time for trial preparation, and law enforcement stonewalling, Bugliosi had, in four days, accomplished what a team of lawyers and investigators working for a full year could well be very proud of, establishing what we believe to be probable cause to conclude that a conspiracy and cover-up took place. In fact, Bugliosi's final argument on the morning of July 31 was more that of criminal prosecutor than civil lawyer. Bugliosi began by referring to Owen's hitchhiker story.

It is a very strange, bizarre story. It's not a likely story. Sirhan is someone determined and hell bent on murdering Senator Kennedy, yet he is roaming around the streets of Los Angeles jumping on pickup trucks, and has this Mr. Owen drop him off at the Ambassador Hotel, and tells him he is going to go visit a friend in the kitchen, where the assassination later took place.

It is just not a believable story, it just does not have the ring of truth to it, and apparently every time Mr. Owen tells the story it overflows with contradictions and inconsistencies. He can't tell the same story the same way twice, and this is the man who has this incredible memory!

Even the police said that Mr. Owen was not telling the truth, they didn't buy his story at all. . . . Assuming that he lied—and I tend to think, based on the evidence, that Reverend Owen did lie, that he did make up this story because it's not a credible story at all and the investigators did not think it was credible—the question that of course presents itself is, Why should he lie? Why would he lie?

Now, I can imagine one could argue that maybe he was just seeking publicity, and I guess you could write it off at that. That happens many, many times. I recall a very famous murder case called the Black Dahlia murder case back in the '40s, I think, in Los Angeles. And if I recall correctly, about 250 people came forward and confessed to murdering the Black Dahlia, all of whom were hopeful that their name would be on the front page of the Los Angeles *Times*.

So you could write it off if—I say *if*—Owen never knew Sirhan. You could say that he was seeking publicity, it's a phony story. But you could write it off only if Owen never knew Sirhan.

The problem is that we have testimony from the witness stand under oath that prior to the assassination, prior even to June the 3rd, 1968, Owen may very well have known Sirhan Sirhan.

Johnny Gray's son, Jackie. We'll stipulate that he is a mental defective, that he is easily confused, that he contradicts himself, that he makes outrageous statements. . . . I will stipulate to that.

But the fact remains, and we simply cannot erase this fact from the record, that he did say he heard Reverend Owen and his father talking about Sirhan many times, that Owen bought clothing for Sirhan, gave Sirhan money, and that his father frequently said that he wanted Jackie to be just like Sirhan.

And it would be nice to say, "Well, this kid's a nut, forget about it." But sometimes nuts can say things that have much more validity than some person with an I.Q. of 200.

When Jackie said Sirhan, the obvious question is: did he mean someone else? And just because he is a mental defective, we can't automatically say he meant someone else. I don't think there is any evidence or indication that Jackie Gray confuses the names of people.

I asked him if his father and Owen had talked about Joe DiMaggio, and he testified he heard them mention his name once.

I asked, "Did you ever hear them talk about Michael Crulowitz?" And he responded, "No." He never heard them talk about Michael Crulowitz. So I wasn't putting a bib on him and spoon-feeding him and having him adopt everything I said. He was able to distinguish names.

And he was *certain* about Sirhan. I would like to read just a few excerpts from his testimony.

Page 1632 of the transcript:

Q. Jackie, you say that 1967 was the first time that Reverend Owen introduced Sirhan to your father?
A. Yes.
Q. Were you present at this time?
A. Yes.
Q. Where did this take place?
A. At his place.
Q. At whose place?
A. Reverend.

Q. And where was that located.
A. Santa Ana.

In Santa Ana. He didn't say in Madagascar, he said in Santa Ana. Where did he get this notion that he met Sirhan in Santa Ana? It just happens that Owen happened to live in Santa Ana in 1967.

If someone is a nut, and they come up with a fantasy, the likelihood that this fantasy would correspond with reality is probably one out of a million. Yet we have this young boy saying things that just happen to be accurate.

Turning to page 1640:

Q. What did you hear your father say about Sirhan?
A. Good things like schooling and going to school and stuff like that, buying clothes.
Q. Who was buying clothes?
A. He, for him. For him.
Q. Who was buying clothing? Who was doing the buying?
A. The Reverend.

I'm not putting words in his mouth.

A. *The Reverend!*

Page 1642—again, we have to ascertain whether this boy just adopts and accepts anything that's put out to him, and I don't think that's the case:

Q. Did you ever hear Reverend Owen talk about Senator Kennedy? [Senator Kennedy's name is as well-known as is Sirhan's. So if he is going to adopt names he would adopt that too.]
A. No. [Why does he say no to that?]
Q. Did you ever hear your father talk about Senator Kennedy?
A. No.
[I said, "Have you ever heard of the word hypnosis?" Answer: "Yes."]
Q. Did you ever hear Reverend Owen or your father say anything about Sirhan being under hypnosis?
A. No.

What I am trying to say is that the boy *can* distinguish, he knows names, he knows events. So he is *not* a hopeless, mental basket case, although I will concede that unfortunately the lad is obviously not too bright. I would say that of all the things that the boy said on the witness stand there is one area, your Honor, I would ask the court to focus on. One area that from my experience as a trial lawyer stands out above everything else, because it had that unmistakeable ring of truth to it.

Jackie was a person who was easily led on the witness stand. His answers were flat. They were apathetic. But in this area, his responses were different.

I want the court to ask itself whether this sounds like someone who is fantasizing, because I am convinced that it's *not* a fantasy:

Page 1599.
Q. Have you ever heard the name Sirhan Sirhan?
A. Yes.
Q. Did you ever hear your father mention that name?
A. Yes.
Q. When?
A. Every time I ride with him he just say it.
Q. Pardon?
A. He just mentions it. It comes out his mouth. He mentions it. He mentions it every time. Every time it comes out his mouth. He mentions it when he riding.

It doesn't sound like fantasy. I didn't even ask him how many times he heard about Sirhan, and he volunteers the emphasis, not a flat, phlegmatic answer; he says, "All the time. My father talks about it all the time." [Bugliosi snapped his fingers to illustrate the spontaneity of the response.]

I can say from my experience as a trial lawyer, having hundreds upon hundreds of witnesses on that witness stand, that the answer, "That's all I ever heard," that Jackie Gray volunteered, and the aspect about his father mentioning Sirhan all the time, "He talks about it all the time. It is always coming out of his mouth," just the way those answers came out, sounded to me like he is telling the truth.

I will stipulate that Jackie Gray was certainly not the best witness in the world; and if we had to rely on his testimony as being "the star witness for the prosecution," we would be in rather sad shape.

The only problem for the plaintiff is that there happened to be another individual who was *not* a mental defective, a pretty straight-shooter, a cowboy, just as sensible and rational as the day is long, Bill Powers.

Bill Powers said some rather incriminating things about Reverend Owen. Plaintiff's counsel just glossed over his testimony like it was worthless, but there are a couple of things he said that obviously are extremely important.

He testified that a month or so before the assassination, a young lad by the name of Johnny Beckley was exercising Owen's horses, and Bill Powers and Reverend Owen were present, and Reverend Owen said something to the effect, "You're not doing a good job. And I know quite a few young boys at the track, including a kid by the name of *Sirhan Sirhan*, who I might bring in here."

That man Powers, it was obvious on that witness stand, when he didn't know something he said so. Many times he said, "I believe, I think," but he said he was *absolutely positive* that Reverend Owen used the name Sirhan!

"How can you remember?" I asked him.

He said, "Number one, it was an unusual name, and number two, shortly thereafter I heard the name again in connection with the RFK assassination."

Then we have the curious incident a day or two, or maybe a week or two, before the assassination. Reverend Owen, who prior thereto, at least in Bill Powers' mind, was not a man of substantial means—he used to drive around in an old clunker worth $50 or so—all of a sudden presents himself in a Lincoln Continental, a brand new car, and he has a roll of $1,000 bills, 25 to 30 $1,000 bills; and Powers testified that there was a black man in the front seat, and it turns out that this black man actually does exist and is a friend of Reverend Owen; and he is Johnny Gray.

So we *know* that the incident at Wild Bill's Stables was not fabricated by Powers—if the court had any notions about that.

And in the back seat there was an individual who *looks* like Sirhan. Now, Powers is not trying to frame Jerry Owen. He says the young man in the back seat of Owen's Lincoln *resembled* Sirhan. If this is a guy who was coming in here just seeking publicity, he would have said, "*Unquestionably*, it *was* Sirhan!" He would have said, "Reverend Owen *told* me it was Sirhan!" But he said, "I don't know; he *resembled* Sirhan."

Then there is this other related event where Reverend Owen takes out a thousand dollar bill and offers it to Bill Powers in payment for that pickup truck. Owen says, with respect to the thousand dollar bills, that he got them up North through his ministry, apparently talking to his flock, or his sheep, or what have you, and they gave him five or ten dollar bills, and he goes to some Chinese bank in San Francisco and has them converted into $1,000 bills. I think the court can take judicial notice that you have to sign your name when you secure $1,000 bills at a bank. "Did you sign your name?" I asked him, and he said, "I don't remember."

I say that this is a cockamamy story. Anybody who would believe a story like that would believe someone who said they heard a cow speaking the Spanish language. It is *not* a believable story!

Reverend Owen got the money someplace *other* than from the anonymous Chinese bank in San Francisco!

Jackie Gray in the back seat? Bugliosi conceded that there was a vague resemblance between Jackie and Sirhan, but the problem was that "Johnny Gray's son at the time of this incident would have been 13 years old and Bill Powers said the boy in the back seat was in his 20's." That would be difficult to mistake, he said, and so would the fact that the junior Gray "certainly has some Negroid features."

Then there was the encounter at the hay company during which Owen wanted to know whether the police had asked Powers about Sirhan. "If Owen did not know that Powers had seen him with Sirhan," Bugliosi pointed out, "he would have had no reason under the moon to ask Powers that question." As Bugliosi saw it, the issue was whether Owen or Powers was to be believed.

Well, if Owen was involved, he has every reason in the world to lie. Bill Powers, your Honor, I submit has no reason at all to lie. This man is in fear of his life. He doesn't want to get involved in this case. He wants to fade into the woodwork.

Moving to a legal point, Bugliosi argued that Owen's "cockamamy story" about picking up Sirhan hitchhiking was circumstantial evidence of a "consciousness of guilt." Citing the California code, he declared that "the jury is instructed that if a defendant lies about something or gives inconsistent statements, et cetera, it is circumstantial evidence of a consciousness of guilt." The attorney wanted to make sure the judge considered Owen in the context of a defendant who makes false statements to cover his participation in a crime.

Bugliosi went on to say that not too long ago, anyone who uttered "conspiracy" or "CIA" was chalked off as a "conspiracy buff."

But recent revelations, your Honor, have indicated that there is a little more credibility to the word "conspiracy." If there is a conspiracy here—[he paused for emphasis] it could possibly involve people in the highest levels of our government, or people out of the government who had substantial political interests inimicable to Senator Kennedy. And if it was a conspiracy, it most likely was a conspiracy of considerable magnitude, and someone like Owen would have been a lowly operative.

It was a quantum leap from horse trailers, boxing rings and sawdust evangelism to the corridors of power and executive suites, Bugliosi granted, but Watergate began as a "third-rate burglary" confined to low-level operatives. The attorney continued:

I will say this: if we are talking about a major conspiracy, the 25 to 30 $1,000 bills that Reverend Owen suddenly and mysteriously had in his possession just prior to the assassination is really a small amount of money, because if there was a conspiracy here, we are not talking about bugging one's opposition, which basically, when we separate the wheat from the chaff, is what Watergate is all about; we are talking about a conspiracy to commit murder, a conspiracy to assassinate someone who was a major candidate for the Presidency of the United States, a conspiracy the prodigious dimensions of which would make Watergate look like a one-roach marijuana case.

Bugliosi reiterated that the case was a circumstantial one, and that it was not necessary to present

a tape recorded conversation between Owen and Sirhan in which Owen is saying, "I want you to bump off Kennedy for me." Conspiracies are proven bit by bit, speck by speck, brick by brick, until all of a sudden you have a mosaic. They are proven by circumstantial evidence. Conspiracies are conceived in shadowy recesses. They are not hatched on television in front of 5,000,000 witnesses.

In deference to the position Crickard had taken during the trial, Bugliosi agreed that the civil trial was "an inappropriate forum to get at this issue." But he argued that Owen himself had perhaps inadvertently raised it by bringing the slander charge, and that the defense had merely attempted to prove the truth of the charge. Bugliosi closed by calling attention to the pall of fear hanging over the trial.

If Owen's story is just a silly Alice In Wonderland concoction to focus some cheap attention on himself, your Honor, and Powers lied on that witness stand, how come everyone is in fear in this case? Owen, I believe, testified that people are making death threats against him, which would be compatible with the notion that he was a lowly operative in the conspiracy, and people up above are the ones making the threats.

This young lad, Johnny Beckley, flees for his life. Bill Powers has to be brought into court with a crane. Jonn Christian, no one can find him. I don't think this is typical. I have handled many murder cases, but I have never seen a case where so many people are frightened. Are these things all meaningless? Are these people all cuckoo birds? [The deadly serious expression on Bugliosi's face answered these rhetorical questions.]

Declaring that the defense had "certainly put on just as much or more evidence that Owen was involved in the assassination of RFK than that he was not involved," Bugliosi asked the court to find for the defense in the RFK aspect of the civil defamation counts. The word "involved" (KCOP had said Owen had been "involved" in Senator Robert F. Kennedy's death) didn't necessarily mean that Owen was a witting part of a criminal conspiracy—many witnesses to crimes "don't want to get involved." But there was no escaping that he was up to his ears in the case. "If going to the police on the very same day of the assassination and telling them that you picked up the assassin the previous day and drove him to the scene of the assassination—if that's not being involved in the whole assassination episode, I don't know what in the world would be."

MIKE WAYLAND'S CLOSING REMARKS MIGHT HAVE BEEN KEPT TO himself, even though his contentions were both sound and valid:

neither KCOP nor any of its employees had, in any legal sense, done anything to libel Jerry Owen; and certainly "The Walking Bible" had presented no real evidence to prove that they had.

Wayland was to be made the victim of his secret relationship with Jonn Christian, however, once it was discovered by Judge Crickard that they had been rubbing shoulders when the suspect subpoena ("body attachment") had been issued on him. In what has to be the most questionable bit of judicial exercise ever to occur in Los Angeles Superior Court annals, Crickard virtually made Wayland throw away his clients' case, by ordering him to stipulate to one item of evidence put forth by Owen: the Yacullo-to-Hopkins memorandum that carried Christian's superimposed signature and our mailing address at the bottom, which the preacher's lady evangelist pal, Olga Graves, had densely admitted (in effect) had been sent to her by Owen, not Jonn Christian, as per the return address on the envelope.

Incredibly, Crickard instructed Wayland to make amends with the plaintiff's lawyers, who instantly demanded that he concede that his client, John Hopkins, had sent this otherwise innocuous document to Christian, with the full knowledge that he would then begin circulating it through the mails and having it attached to cars parked in lots belonging to the myriad of churches Owen insisted had shunned him. Once this Kafka-like move was effected, Crickard ruled it as valid evidence that malice had been involved by defendant Hopkins; then came his ultimate *non sequitur*, his comments on the RFK aspects of the trial:

> . . . The court feels that the phraseology that we spent so much time on, that plaintiff was involved in the killing of Robert Kennedy, that the use of that phrase and the reference to the word "involved" certainly had reference to the plaintiff being criminally involved, and as such was slander against the plaintiff. . . .
>
> The memorandum from Mr. Yacullo clearly explained to the people at KCOP [sic] that plaintiff's contact with the RFK assassination was not believed by the police, and we have to remember that the slander took place a year after the Kennedy assassination—the Robert F. Kennedy assassination—and so KCOP had a memorandum from its attorney, Mr. Yacullo, saying that plaintiff was not involved as far as the RFK assasination was concerned. . . .

The testimony—we have certainly spent quite a bit of time on during the trial [*sic*]—shows that plaintiff was not involved and that his only relationship to the assassination was that he may or may not have picked up Sirhan on the day before the assassination, but it certainly is not—does not make a person criminally involved in the killing of Robert Kennedy the next day.

The frown of puzzlement and extreme concern on Vince Bugliosi's brow rivaled anything displayed during the toughest moments of the Manson Family trial as Crickard banged down his gavel for the last time.

TV Official Found Guilty of Slander
Said Evangelist Was Involved
in Sen. Kennedy's Killing

The accompanying story in the Los Angeles *Times* read:

KCOP television executive John Hopkins slandered Oliver B. (Jerry) Owen, known as "The Walking Bible," when he said Owen was involved in the killing of Robert Kennedy, Superior Court Judge Jack A. Crickard ruled Thursday [after the trial ended].

Crickard, who will decide later how much KCOP must pay Owen in damages, ruled at the end of the month-long trial in which veteran prosecutor Vincent Bugliosi again raised the legal specter of a conspiracy in the June 5, 1968, slaying of Sen. Kennedy here. . . .

Bugliosi said his interest in reopening the investigation would not end with the civil trial. . . . He said he believes a special prosecutor should be named to take the case again to an "independent body," perhaps the grand jury here. . . .

A few days later Crickard fixed the award at $35,000, a token amount compared with what Owen was seeking. Moreover, the judge, who had dismissed Ohrbach's as a defendant, ordered Owen to pay the store $5,000 in court costs. Obviously the preacher considered the award a judicial slap in the face, if his behavior at an August hearing before Crickard to set counsel fees and expenses is any gauge. Arthur Evry and Mike Wayland came to an agreement, but Owen protested vehemently that he should receive

$10,000 for acting as his own attorney in pre-trial proceedings, not the mere $2,000 Crickard allowed. The preacher went so far as to tell the judge that if he would award the higher amount, the difference would be donated to his favorite charity. Wayland angrily called it a "flat-out bribery attempt," but Crickard acted as if he hadn't heard it. Later, outside the courtroom, Owen and Wayland tangled again—the ex-boxer invited the slender attorney outside to fight—before Evry and two bailiffs could separate them.

SEVERAL WEEKS LATER BUGLIOSI, CHRISTIAN AND TURNER WERE reviewing the trial in the lawyer's Beverly Hills office. As far as our own investigation was concerned, the outcome of Owen versus KCOP was not all that important—the stakes were merely monetary. For seven years we had tried to get the RFK case reopened in an appropriate criminal tribunal, for there was much more to it than could be presented within the confines of a libel and slander suit. Nevertheless, the trial had been a testing ground for important parts of our investigative file and the generating of sworn testimony from some key witnesses we had discovered. And the give-and-take questioning had convinced us more than ever that we were on target. This unprecedented trial had also produced a wealth of new information that had made the conspiracy "mosaic" Bugliosi talked of become much sharper in detail. And the cover-up was laid absolutely bare.

Bugliosi was in a reflective mood on this mid-August afternoon. He was somewhat chagrined that he had had no time to prepare for the *Owen* vs. *KCOP* trial. Nonetheless, his one-minute-to-midnight entrance into the affair had produced a near-miracle.

"Who knows where we might have been able to take this case if things had been different?" he contemplated. "But there's one thing I'm absolutely sure of now: this case has to be reopened and re-examined, from top to bottom—and not by those law enforcement officials who gave us the original conclusions either."

Epilogue

"The important thing to know about assassinations is not who fired the gun, but who paid for the bullets."

—Turkish police inspector in
Eric Ambler's *A Coffin for Dimitrios*

THE GEORGETOWN DISTRICT OF WASHINGTON IS NOTED FOR ITS lively dinner parties where high government officials and celebrities mix, discussing affairs of state as casually as the weather. But in August, 1975, shortly after the *Owen* vs. *KCOP* trial, a small circle of guests at the home of attorney Lester Hyman took bites of a forbidden conversational fruit along with dessert and coffee. The subject was the evidence of conspiracy in the assassination of Robert F. Kennedy.

The touchy point was raised by Dianne Hull and Paul Le Mat, in town to attend the premiere of their latest motion picture together, *Aloha, Bobby and Rose*. Their host, a former Democratic chairman of Massachusetts, friend of all three Kennedy brothers, and chairman of the American Jewish Committee, was well aware of Hull and Le Mat's interest in the RFK case. He knew that they were close to Jonn Christian, whom he had met two years earlier at the wedding of another friend of Robert Kennedy's, actor Robert Vaughn. And he knew that while in Washington they had buttonholed members of Congress and appeared in the media to press for a reopening of the RFK investigation.

What Hyman wasn't sure of was the reaction of his other guests that evening: Senator Walter Mondale and his wife Joan. Hyman had managed Mondale's brief campaign for the 1976 Democratic

310

310

presidential nomination, but the question of assassination conspiracy never came up, as it almost never did in Washington political circles.

The Mondales listened intently as Hull and Le Mat gave their presentation. "If what you say is true," the senator remarked somewhat skeptically, "this would involve a cover-up of incredible dimensions." Hyman assured him that the stonewalling facts spoke for themselves. Joan Mondale chided her husband, reminding him that neither of them believed that Lee Harvey Oswald alone had shot John Kennedy. From what Hull and Le Mat had said, there was no reason to put stock in the official verdict in the death of Robert Kennedy.

Ironically, all of those at the table that night would figure prominently in the campaign of a then-obscure candidate for the presidency, Jimmy Carter. Senator Mondale, of course, was selected by Carter as his running mate and became Vice President. Lester Hyman introduced Carter to former Israeli Prime Minister Golda Meir and Jewish leaders in Beverly Hills, which both helped melt the instinctive distrust American Jews felt for a "born again" Christian from the South and generate vital campaign backing. And Dianne Hull and Paul Le Mat were among Carter's earliest supporters, drumming up interest in his candidacy in the Hollywood movie colony. After Hull had introduced him at a Green Bay, Wisconsin, primary rally, Carter hugged and kissed her and told the crowd, "I have had many introductions in the last few years, but that was the finest, most moving one yet."

When Jimmy Carter won we felt that there might now be an attentive ear in the White House. We recalled that in the early stages of his presidential bid, in an appearance on the Los Angeles television show of satirist Mort Sahl, he had expressed a belief that the John Kennedy case should be re-examined, if only by unlocking the National Archives and reviewing the many classified documents sequestered there. But it is virtually axiomatic that political action is contingent upon public opinion being brought to bear, particularly in controversial areas. In the JFK case the polls had long shown that an overwhelming majority of Americans disbelieved the conclusions of the Warren Report, but this was largely the result of scores of books and articles published over the years demonstrating why Oswald could not have acted alone and illuminating shadowy areas. There is no comparable body of literature in the Robert Kennedy assassination, and in fact this is the first major book.

So we were heartened several years ago when the Washington *Post* decided that the RFK story should be pursued. Of all newspapers it was the least likely to reject the idea of conspiracy and cover-up in high places. Through its penetrative reporting on the Watergate affair, the *Post* was instrumental in convincing the American public of what really happened—and sending Richard Nixon to his political doom. The newspaper emerged as the paragon of what journalism was all about, and raised investigative reporting to a level of esteem it hadn't enjoyed in some time. The *Post* was the place where a new look into the RFK case should start.

IN LATE 1974 LESTER HYMAN CALLED HIS FRIEND BEN BRADLEE, the *Post* editor whose perspicacity and encouragement enabled reporters Bob Woodward and Carl Bernstein to persevere in trying to pierce the Watergate cover-up. Hyman told Bradlee about us and the elements of our investigative file. He also mentioned the "second gun" controversy that was then shaping up. The editor agreed that the *Post* should look into it. He assigned the story to veteran investigative reporter Ronald Kessler.

Before leaving for Los Angeles, Kessler phoned Turner, whom he previously had consulted on a number of stories. The reporter said that he was starting from scratch, and wanted to know whom to see and what to look for.

"Do you have the green light like on the bugging series, Ron?" Turner asked. The *Post* editors had indulged Kessler almost six months of digging on that one.

"Yes," Kessler affirmed. "I'll probably have to make several trips to Los Angeles."

"Okay," Turner said, "if you want to know what didn't happen, talk to Bill Harper, the criminalist. He can tell you why the official version is wrong—why there was more than one gun. Then if you want to know what did happen, about the conspiracy, talk to Jonn Christian." Kessler took down their phone numbers as well as the names of others Turner thought he should see to get going.

We later learned, however, that Kessler spent his first few days interviewing Los Angeles law-enforcement and FBI officials, and Bob Kaiser, who by this time had become a vehement critic of the "second gun" theory. Finally he showed up at Bill Harper's Pasadena home, but the criminalist considered his questions so uneducated that he offered Kessler a copy of his affidavit in the case, which is a kind of *McGuffey's Reader* of the "second gun" hypothesis. Kessler politely declined, saying he'd be back in several days. "There'll be plenty of time for me to read it then," he said.

Kessler never interviewed Christian or examined our files. When Christian tracked him down at his hotel, wondering what had happened, he was writing away. But he could not spare the time to talk, he said, because he was about to fly back to Washington. "How much time has Bradlee allowed to develop the story?" Christian asked, now somewhat concerned. "No deadline on this one," Kessler replied. "I'll be back next week and we can go from there."

So it was with utter disbelief that we read Kessler's by-lined story, run three days later on the *Post* front page, that was head-lined: "Ballistics Expert Discounts RFK 2d-Gun Theory." Date-lined Pasadena December 18, it began: "The nationally recognized ballistics expert whose claim gave rise to a theory that Robert F. Kennedy was not killed by Sirhan Bishara Sirhan this week admitted that there is no evidence to support his contention." The story was picked up by practically every major news outlet in the country.

Bill Harper was outraged when a distressed Lester Hyman called from Washington to find out about the story. Kessler must have distorted what he said, twisted the facts. There had been more than one gun, he was sure of it, and he had hardly "admitted" there was "no evidence" to support his position. But when Hyman called Ben Bradlee to complain, he received no satisfaction. Kessler had filed his story, and that was the end of it. The *Post* was not pursuing it further. Despite persistent requests, Bradlee refused to print a correction, retraction or Harper's version.

But the newspaper whose reporting was so exemplary in the Watergate scandal was not about to go unjudged by its peers in this one. In its September 1976 issue, the prestigious *Columbia Review of Journalism* rebuked: "The *Post*'s contentious and dilatory handling of the affair is a lesson in how *not* to accomplish [fair and accurate reporting]."

FOR THE LOS ANGELES TIMES, WHOSE RULING CHANDLER FAMILY wield enormous power in Los Angeles through their paper, the assassination of Robert F. Kennedy struck close to home. The candidate had been fatally shot in one of the city's landmark hotels, the case had been investigated by the LAPD, and Sirhan had been tried and convicted by Los Angeles prosecutors. As the *Times* saw it, the local institutions of government had performed well, unlike the shambles of Dallas. So when Vince Bugliosi declared himself a candidate for district attorney in August, 1975, only weeks after the *Owen* vs. *KCOP* trial, the *Times* raised its editorial voice in opposition to the prodigal son who wanted to reopen the RFK case.

The DA vacancy was created when Joe Busch had died suddenly a month earlier, and the County Board of Supervisors was considering a list of eleven candidates for the interim appointment. In his turn before the supervisors, Bugliosi stated that if selected he would launch a tough program against organized crime, try to get vicious criminals off the streets while preventing police harassment of those exercising First Amendment rights, and prosecute industrial polluters and corporations engaged in consumer fraud (the DA's office had always trod softly in those areas because members of the very Establishment controlling Los Angeles politics were implicated).

Bugliosi also promised to take steps to get at the actual facts in the RFK case. He said that he would name a blue-ribbon scientific task force to re-examine the evidence from top to bottom. He would assemble a team of top investigators and prosecutors in the DA's office to "examine and analyze the entire investigative files" of the LAPD, and issue a public invitation for all persons having information, including law enforcement officers, to come forward under a cloak of anonymity. He would ask the supervisors to help convene a special grand jury to hear the testimony of witnesses whose evidence contradicted the lone-assassin conclusion. He would cooperate with congressional committees that might look into the case, and open a "positive line of communication" with the citizenry after the years of secrecy.

Five years earlier, one of the *Times'* front-line reporters, Dave Smith, had recommended that the newspaper commit limited resources and backing to help our investigation progress. Contact with the *Times* had been made by our original benefactor, Peter Hitchcock of San Francisco, who interceded with his close friend Otis Chandler, the publisher. Editor Bill Thomas assigned Smith to vet our files and submit a recommendation. But after Smith urged a go-ahead, nothing happened. When he persisted he was at first ignored, then belittled, and finally shunted to a minor slot.

On August 20, 1975, the *Times* editorialized: "One interpretation of all this [Bugliosi's pronouncements on the RFK case] is that Bugliosi believes he has an emotional issue that he can exploit next summer in the election for a full-term district attorney." Bugliosi fired back an indignant letter that read in part: "For you to insinuate that my personal commitment to help resolve this controversy is selfish and politically motivated, is an affront to my professional integrity. . . . It is truly unfortunate that on the Robert F. Kennedy assassination, the editors at the *Times* are apparently out of touch with this community's attitude about this issue, and totally unaware of the concerned mood of the entire country. . . ."

It was no surprise when the supervisors passed over Bugliosi and settled on a compromise candidate, bakery heir John Van De Kamp. Although he had never even prosecuted a rape or murder case, Van De Kamp had more important credentials—his family were close to the Chandler family of the *Times*. When Bugliosi contested Van De Kamp in the 1976 election, he had a high degree of name recognition through *Helter Skelter*, which had eclipsed *In Cold Blood* as the best-selling crime book of all time. But that was about all. The Establishment saw him as someone they could not control, and closed ranks behind Van De Kamp, whose war chest brimmed with money. Even Attorney General Evelle Younger, who as a Republican might have been expected to stay out of a fight among Democrats, was so anxious to keep the lid on the RFK case that he endorsed Van De Kamp.

The Establishment's fear of Bugliosi was so great that they even succeeded in pressuring CBS into blacking out the entire Los Angeles area for the airing of the TV movie based on Bugliosi's book *Helter Skelter*.

The *Times* naturally favored Van De Kamp but exceeded the bounds of fair play by not reporting Bugliosi's press announcements and publishing critical attacks on him instead. When actor Robert Vaughn and Jocelyn Brando, Marlon's sister, wrote a letter protesting the manner in which the *Times* "has been using its editorial pages and reporters to attack our friend and candidate with a brand of journalism that is below the dignity of this community," the newspaper refused to publish it. So Vaughn, remembered from *The Man from U.N.C.L.E.* and the recent television special *Washington Behind Closed Doors*, was left to make his point to a thousand people at a fund-raising dinner at the Hollywood Palladium. "Vince Bugliosi alone," Vaughn told his audience in an emotional speech, "has committed himself to resolve the very serious and disturbing questions that have arisen about the death of my good friend, Robert Kennedy, whose murder eight years ago in this very city surely changed the course of American history."

Van De Kamp's public position was that he was not intractable but would have to see proof. Six weeks before the election, veteran CBS correspondent Bill Stout plunked down on his desk a set of FBI photographs with captions—the same photographs that showed extra bullet holes in the hotel pantry. The DA stared at them, unwilling or unable to answer Stout's rhetorical questions about their significance, then called FBI Director Clarence Kelley in Washington. Kelley said he didn't know anything about the photographs but would check. He called back to say that the FBI had not conducted any ballistics investigation in the case, which was a semantical dodge. Van De Kamp assured Stout that he would look into it and let him know. Stout is still waiting.

Bugliosi predictably lost the election, but he has lost none of his determination to resolve the RFK case. In the fall of 1976 Bugliosi, one of the most-sought-after campus speakers in the country, appeared before a packed house at Glassboro State College in New Jersey to talk on the Manson Family case. By this time, however, he had been the subject of a *Penthouse* magazine interview in which he discussed the "extra bullets" aspect of the Kennedy assassination, and invariably someone would ask about it. When he finished that evening, a well-dressed man approached and politely asked, "May I have a word with you in private, Mr. Bugliosi?"

He introduced himself as William A. Bailey, an assistant professor of police science at a nearby college. He said that in 1968 he was an FBI special agent assigned to the Los Angeles office, and that some four hours after the Kennedy shooting he was instructed to meticulously examine the pantry to try to reconstruct the crime. "At one point during these observations," Bailey declared in a signed statement he wrote out for Bugliosi, "I [and several other agents] noted at least two [2] small caliber bullet holes in the center post of the two doors leading from the preparation room [pantry]. There was no question in any of our minds as to the fact that these were bullet holes & were not caused by food carts or other equipment in the preparation room."

Bugliosi now had in his pocket unimpeachable evidence that the holes had been caused by extra bullets, not food carts, as the Los Angeles authorities had tried to portray. Subsequently Bugliosi and Christian have posed a number of questions to Bailey by letter, and his answers cast further doubt on the integrity of the official investigation. Among other things, the ex-FBI agent recalled seeing bullet holes in the ceiling panels (which were destroyed by the LAPD) and discussing his observations with LAPD investigators on the scene, but there was no formal exchange between the two agencies attempting to reconcile the number and location of bullets. "I recall some discussion of FBI-LAPD discrepancies in ballistics findings by agents in the L.A. Office," he said, but he could not recall the details. Bailey said that he and his fellow agents had never bought the LAPD story that the last-minute change in routing RFK into the pantry was a "fluke" of fate. And he revealed that several agents who worked on the polka-dot-dress-girl angle "personally were not satisfied that they had found 'the right' woman," but their superiors ordered the matter closed.

As for the Jerry Owen investigation, Bailey commented: "First and foremost, to 'kiss off' OWEN's story as a 'publicity stunt' is investigative suicide considering the magnitude of the R.F.K. case and the information contained in [OWEN's] interview. One does not have to be a Sherlock Holmes to deduce that if OWEN was seeking publicity he sure 'screwed up' the chance of a lifetime." In Bailey's opinion, there were "Too many stones left unturned, too many coincidences!"*

BY THE LATE SUMMER OF 1976, WORD WAS CIRCULATING THAT the U.S. House of Representatives was seriously considering re-opening the John Kennedy and Martin Luther King, Jr., cases. The congressional black caucus had been profoundly disturbed by the account of a former Memphis police officer who had been assigned to watch over King during his visit in April 1968. The officer, Detective Ed Redditt, who is black, said that he had been pulled off the assignment only hours before the civil rights leader was slain. He was summoned to headquarters, Redditt related, and informed by Chief Frank Holloman, "Ed, there's a contract out on you." Holloman introduced him to a man identified as a Secret Service agent who had learned about the "contract" and flown down from Washington. Redditt thought the whole thing sounded fishy. Why would anyone want to pay to have him killed? Why would a Secret Service agent fly down when there was a local office that could have advised him? Holloman insisted that he not return to duty, and he was taken home in a police car to be placed under guard. Just as he was stepping out of the car, the radio blared the news that King had been shot.†

* The Bailey affidavit is dated November 14, 1976. His answers to the Bugliosi/Christian interrogatories are dated February 4 and June 17, 1977.

† According to Memphis *Press-Scimitar* reporter Wayne Chastain, Redditt subsequently told him about a Memphis undercover policeman who had played a part in the "security stripping" of King: "He left the police department shortly after, and the word was that he went to Washington, D.C. Then a couple of years after the King slaying I ran face to face with him in downtown Memphis. He was wearing a disguise. He acted very mysterious, saying that he was now with the Central Intelligence Agency, and begged me not to blow his cover." (San Francisco *Examiner*, October 10, 1976)

Shortly after Redditt told his story, a strikingly parallel story bobbed to the surface in Los Angeles. DID RFK's ORDER SEAL HIS DEATH? the *Herald-Examiner* bannered a front-page story on August 29, 1976. "In an angry outburst eight hours before his 1968 assassination," it began, "Robert F. Kennedy ordered Los Angeles Police Department bodyguards to stop protecting him and barred them from his presence—thereby possibly sealing his death warrant, according to sources here."

The principal source was retired LAPD security specialist Marion D. Hoover, who was quoted as saying that the LAPD had assigned a "Hot-Squad" of a dozen men from a headquarters "intelligence group" to guard Kennedy. Had the senator not ordered them off, Hoover contended, "we would have had three trained men on either side of him and one out front. And, although some of us might have been shot, we could have made all the difference in the world. . . ."

This was the first we heard that the police on their own initiative had attached an intelligence "Hot-Squad" to Kennedy (RFK intimates such as Jesse Unruh and Frank Burns knew nothing about it). But Hoover had another surprise. "Parker Center veterans don't bother to conceal their disgust over a presidential candidate entering a strange room," the story said, adding a direct quote from Hoover, "with only a few sports stars and what Secret Service could get through the mob to cover him.' " The story was doubly explicit on the matter of Secret Service protection. It asserted: "The Secret Service, traveling in two cars, advised LAPD commanders that they were 'walking on eggs' and that they were worried about their man's constant exposure from point to point." And it quoted LAPD press spokesman Commander Peter Hagan as saying of Hoover's abrupt dismissal by Kennedy: "That was one of our first indications that [Kennedy] intended to waste our usefulness and depend upon his small Secret Service contingent."

At the time that RFK was shot, the Secret Service was not authorized to protect presidential candidates—it was restricted to guarding the President and Vice President and their families. It was only as a result of the RFK assassination that the law was changed to include candidates.

From what Christian could find out from *Herald-Examiner*

City Editor Jack Brown, it appeared that the story had been planted on reporter Al Stump by the police. Braced about it by Lillian Castellano, a housewife and long-time assassination-conspiracy investigator, Commander Hagan disavowed the story completely. "He's no different than most of the others in the news media," Hagan said of Stump. But Stump, who had close law enforcement contacts, stuck by his story. "I trust the police! The police wouldn't lie!" he protested to Castellano.

Castellano brought the allegations about the Secret Service to the attention of Robert E. Powis, the agent in charge in Los Angeles. Special Agent Powis replied: "Be advised that the Secret Service was not guarding Robert F. Kennedy prior to the time of the shooting. We did not have agents with him at any time during his campaigning as a Presidential candidate." Powis said that he had written the *Herald-Examiner* asking that his letter be published or a retraction made.

A few weeks later the tabloid *National Enquirer*, in its issue of October 26, 1976, ran a feature story on Marion Hoover, who was billed as "a fantastic marksman who shot to death nine criminals in his 26-year, story-book career as a cop." Hoover repeated the claim that Kennedy had canceled the police protection, and this time was backed up by former Police Chief Thomas Reddin, who was quoted: "The indisputable fact is that he told us to get lost— and he paid for that order with his life." But this time not a word was mentioned about the Secret Service.

It was a baffling episode. While it was conceivable that the LAPD floated Hoover's story to forestall charges that it had been asleep at the switch at the time of the assassination, there is no accounting for the canard that the Secret Service guarded RFK. From the strange Secret Service man who told a Memphis detective he was under a death threat to the phantom Secret Service squad at Los Angeles, it was simply a riddle piled upon an enigma.

IT HAS BEEN A DECADE NOW SINCE ROBERT F. KENNEDY WAS MURdered, yet developments continue to unfold like a newsreel: The House of Representatives forms a Select Committee on Assassinations, but, initially at least, confines it to the John Kennedy and

Martin Luther King, Jr., cases. According to an FBI report filed by Bill Bailey, two men claiming to be police officers and wearing KENNEDY signs on chains around their necks had approached Ambassador Hotel busboy Juan Romero *the day before the assassination* to obtain kitchen workers' white jackets. An FBI document is released, disclosing that a wealthy Southern California rancher who had ties to the ultraright Minutemen and detested RFK because of his support of Cesar Chavez reportedly pledged $2,000 toward a $500,000 to $750,000 Mafia contract to kill the senator "in the event it appeared he could receive the Democratic nomination" for President. It is revealed that in 1954 the CIA began Project Artichoke, a secret study to determine whether a person could unwittingly be induced to commit an assassination against his will. It is learned that in 1963, following the John Kennedy assassination, the CIA undertook a study of the assassination applications of RHIC-EDOM (Radio-Hypnotic Intracerebral Control—Electronic Dissolution of Memory), scientific jargon for creating a Manchurian Candidate. Sirhan's lawyer, Godfrey Isaac, vacillates on whether he would allow his client to submit to a deprogramming effort, thinking it might somehow jeopardize a future release on parole.

Considering the hostility and intransigence of the Los Angeles Establishment, it is clear that the RFK case will have to be reopened at the federal level, either within the Justice Department or by a special prosecutor named by the President. With this in mind Dr. Robert Joling, who wrote the introduction to this book, sent a letter to President Jimmy Carter on May 17, 1977, advising him of the obstructionist tactics by Los Angeles law enforcement officials. "For too long now," Joling wrote, speaking of the Kennedy, King and Kennedy assassinations, "the uncertainties, half-truths, and blatant falsehoods about these events have led to widespread frustration and a disrespect for and a lack of faith in our governmental institutions."

A belated answer came from Albert L. Hartman, chief of the General Crimes Section of the Justice Department, who by letter dated October 18, 1977, maintained that while discrepancies in the case did exist, "the evidence that Sirhan Sirhan acted alone in the assassination remains compelling."

We hope that this book will shed enough light on the conspiracy and cover-up to persuade the Carter Administration and others in a position to act that the investigation must be reopened without further delay. Accordingly, we have asked Lester Hyman to deliver two sets of the bound galley proofs to Vice President Mondale, one for himself and one for President Carter.* To discover the truth is not simply an exercise in nostalgia, it is an insurance policy for the future. As we wrote in our 1968 congressional campaign brochure in calling for a reopening of the John Kennedy case, "To do less not only is indecent but might cost us the life of a future President of John Kennedy's instincts."

It did.

And it might again.

* In addition, we arranged for sets to be delivered to Governors Jerry Brown of California and George Wallace of Alabama; Leo McCarthy, speaker of the California Assembly; Senator James Mills, president pro tem of the California Senate; Los Angeles Mayor Thomas Bradley; Yvonne Brathwaite Burke, member of the House Select Committee on Assassinations and as of this writing a 1978 candidate for California Attorney General; U.S. Attorney Andrea Ordin, Los Angeles; and Mrs. Dorothy Courtney, foreperson of the 1977–78 Los Angeles County Grand Jury.

Appendix

The following unedited transcript is from William Turner's interview with Jerry Owen, tape-recorded on July 2, 1968; the interview took place at the law offices of Owen's personal attorney, George T. Davis, at 745 Market Street in San Francisco:

JERRY OWEN: I'm not going into full details, but I am going to give the highlights of a . . . incidents that happened . . . on a Monday afternoon . . . on June the 3rd . . . in downtown Los Angeles. I have a 19 . . . 48 Chevvy pickup truck . . . half-ton . . . and on the hood . . . I have a large . . . chrome horse that stands out that . . . everybody that is a horse-lover is attracted to it/whether driving, passing on the freeway or parked . . . and I left . . . my home in Santy Ana . . . California, headed for Oxnard to bring back . . . a Shetland pony that I had . . . sold to a schoolteacher from Huntington Beach for his two little children. . . . At Oxnard I had . . . 12 Shetland ponies and a Palomina saddle horse that I was leaving a man up there ride that works on the newspaper in . . . Oxnard.

And, I received a phone call that a robe was ready for a heavy-weight boxer . . . by the name of O'Reilly . . . and I went down Los Angeles, with the truck, dressed in my old clothes . . . with Levis on . . . cowboy shoes and a plaid shirt . . . and . . . parked in the parking lot, went in and picked up the boxing shoes and picked up the robe and the trunks . . . and headed for Hollywood . . . to a friend that I know that is a sh-colored shoe man, to have him put some green shamrocks on the boxing shoes and his wife, who has her place of business joining his, who . . . is one of the leading . . . sewers, to sew the name and the decorations of shamrocks on the boxing trunks . . . and her husband put the shamrocks on his shoes.

So as I came down Hill Street, I cut over and ended up over on 7th Street . . . and was stopping at the light on 7th Street and Grand, knowing that if I made a right turn I could come in to the beginning of . . . Wilshire Boulevard, which ends on Grand.

And, as I was at the light, I noticed-eh two men . . . one of them was standing on my truck, about to crawl into the backend . . . and the other put his head in the door and asked if we were/I was going towards Hollywood out Wilshire . . . and . . . without practically sayin' . . . yes or no . . . the one boy jumped in and he said "We will ride in the back." . . . so I saw no harm in that . . . and they both crawled in the back and sat in the open pickup with their backs against the back of the cab. I looked in the mirror, occasionally, and noticed the one was kind of a bushy, dark-haired fella . . . and the other'n . . . was . . . of the same complexion and I thought that they were . . . Mexicans or . . . Hindus or something . . . and . . . got the impression that they were . . . kind of on the hippy-style and . . . as we . . . stopped at lights and went out Wilshire, out to MacArthur Park, and . . . made the stop at-eh . . . I believe its-eh . . . Wilshire . . . Place, and then maybe one more light or two—it's close to Vermont and Wilshire . . . and there, as I stopped at the light, I . . . noticed the one stand up and get out and they both got out . . . the taller one . . . and talked to someone standing there/there's a bank . . . and there is some seats . . . and they were talking to someone and quickly as I glanced, I noticed one was a well-dressed fellow that wasn't a young man, he seemed to be . . . past 30, maybe 35, in that neighborhood . . . and I noticed a girl who looked like she could have been around 19, 20, 21—dressed in slacks and-eh . . . kind of straight-like hair and kind of . . . what I would call a dirty blonde.

And . . . as . . . the light was getting ready, I was wa-watching my light to turn, the smaller of the two . . . put his head in the cab and had the door handle and he started to open the door, and said "Do you mind if I ride with you on out?"

So he got in and as we crossed, he talked about the horse . . . and he told me . . . that he was an exercise boy at a racetrack, and talked how he loved horses/quickly wanted to know if I had a ranch where he could get a job . . . and . . . talking, I . . . can't remember the exact little conversation back and forth, but something to that effect . . . and

. . . he turned to me and he said "Would it be all right if I stopped . . . I have a friend in the kitchen?" . . . and as . . . pointed to the street. . . . I made a left turn off Wilshire and, if my memory is right, I believe the street is Catalina 'r Santa Catalina or something like that . . . and there was a new-like building, a white place—Texaco—a parking place, parking lot or garage-like. He left, I waited and 10 minutes had gone by . . . I . . . felt that that was the last that I was going to see him, but he did say something about he would like to buy a lead pony . . . so he could go to work at the racetrack, and I told him I had a dandy up in Oxnard, a Palomina and so forth. And I gave up of him coming back and so I started the truck up, and I was going to make a U-turn at a little intersection, whip back and hit Wilshire and go on out to Wilshire and cut across . . . into Vine Street and Hollywood.

And he came on a run . . . I noticed his tennis shoes on . . . noticed his dress—a sweatshirt. He got in and he . . . kind of, he was sorry he was a little late, and we talked about different things going out, and I asked him if he was Mexican and . . . said "No"—and-eh . . . he informed me that he was born in Jordan. Well, that struck up a little conversation because my wife and I are planning to go to . . . Jerusalem and-eh . . . take a visit there . . . and-eh . . . we talked back and forth, and it seems to me he that he said that he had been over here for 13 years or was 13 years old when he left. Spoke good English . . . and-eh . . . seemed alright. And I just thought he was a young kid in his early 20's and so forth, and. . . .

As we turned and I stopped . . . at the Hollywood Ranch Market, where I had to park . . . and I went across the street . . . took my robe in, took the shoes in . . . came back and in the conversation he told me that if I could meet him at 11 o'clock . . . on Sunset Boulevard, that he would be able to purchase this horse . . . for the sum of $300 . . . there was a little talk of 250 or something, but I told him that I would let it go for $300, I'd guarantee the horse/if it didn't work I would take it back . . . because the horse . . . is a 10 year old, comin' 11, and he has been used as a pickup horse and as a pony horse and well-broke but he's a one-man's horse.

So, by this time, now, I would say it was . . . late in the afternoon, it was before 6 o'clock . . . and-eh I only went a few blocks up to Sunset, turned right, went a few blocks, and there . . . by the old . . . I believe back in '29 or '31 or 2 it was a Warner Brothers Studio Park, and then it was turned into a skatin' rink, and now it's a bowlin' alley . . . just before you get to the bowlin' alley on the corner is a bar, and then there is another business or somethin', and then there is a sign that says-eh . . . "Topless"—and I pulled there on that side and . . . he said "At 11 o'clock tonight I'll meet you here and I'll have the money to pay for the horse." . . . and . . . then somewhere along there in the conversation I said I could kill some time by going out to Saints and Sinners on Fairfax, and the minute I said Saints and Sinners he says kind of . . . like-startled, he wanted to know if I was a Jewish, and I said No, I'm not Jewish, I'm Welsh." . . . and he said "Well, I have no use for the . . . Hebes!" . . . and-eh . . . I kind of smiled and laughed and I said "I'll be here at 11."

So, I left, and I 'mediately went up to the Plaza Hotel and . . . put the car in the parking lot, right next to the Plaza Hotel, the truck, where Slapsie Maxie, my old friend for many years, and . . . we talked, and he said "Look" he said-eh . . . to me . . . calling me by name, "Curly, you gotta be at Saints and Sinners tonight, it's the last night, we've been there for years—Billy Gray's Bandbox—they're closin', next Monday night it's going to be out at the Friar's on Beverly, and . . . this'll be the greatest meeting in all and . . . with you and Henry Armstrong being the chartered members. . . . Come on and be there!" So . . . Max come out and he says-eh-I said "I can't go, Max. I'm dressed like a hayseed."— "Ah, what's the difference, Curly?" and he looked at the truck and the horse and he laughed, he said-eh . . . seeing me drive the old '48 truck right in the heart of Hollywood.

And . . . I went to Saints and Sinners, and I had O'Reilly . . . the boxer with me, and they introduced him that night . . . and at 11 o'clock—at little after 11, in that neighborhood—I went to the appointed place . . . down by the bowling alley . . . and as I pulled over to the right . . . plenty of places to park, and as I looked I didn't see anybody, but across the street . . . was a white . . . either 1948 or 1949 . . . Chivvy, off-colored white, and it looked like it could stand a wash job . . . and-eh . . . in the front . . . was a man . . . sittin' . . . and from the lights . . . he resembled the man . . . that I has seen, in the afternoon . . . down on Vermont and Wilshire . . . and there was the girl, from the looks of her hair and that, it looked like her, and on the other side was another person that I couldn't see . . . and this little fella . . . came across the street, come up, put his head in and said "I am very sorry" he said "Here's a hundred dollar bill . . . and I was supposed to have the rest of my money . . . but I don't have it, but if you'll meet me in the morning about 8 o'clock, I'll assure you that I'll take the horse definitely." . . . So, I didn't know . . . at first, I said "Well, now, look.

I've waited and I should be up in Oxnard . . . but I'll tell you what I'll do if you really mean business and want the horse . . . I'll . . . stay in this hotel right across the street" . . . where I registered . . . and I believe when I registers it was-it-it's have to be between 11:30 and 12:15 . . . that I registered there, in the hotel . . . and I said "I'll meet you at 8 o'clock and my truck will be in the parking lot right next to it." So, I went into a bar right next to the hotel and got a sanrich, a heated sanrich, and a cup of black coffee . . . 'cause I hadn't eaten . . . and went to bed . . . and got up and . . . I was shavin' . . . because I had a little cheap room, with . . . no shower, toilet—it was $4 for the room, plus tax . . . and the telephone rang, and a fellow . . . this-eh/I/a voice . . . that I had never heard before . . . wanted to know if I was the man that had the truck in the parking lot . . . and I said "Yes." . . . and . . . I . . . came down . . . and it was close to 8 o'clock, and all I had with me was my shavin' kit, dressed in my cowboy boots, my old clothes. I went out to the truck, which was parked right close to the street. Standing at the truck was a very well-dressed man . . . with . . . a expensive-looking late-style suit. He had on . . . a turtleneck sweater that was kind of an orangish-yellow color . . . with a . . . chain around his neck and a big, round thing that you see 'em all wearing now, even, many on television and that . . . and as I looked at him, he had . . . on what seemed to be an expensive pair of alligator shoes. He had a manicure. He had-eh . . . one of those cat's eye . . . ring on his little finger . . . and he said to me, he said . . . "Joe . . . couldn't make it." he said "Take this hundred dollars . . ." and he said "If you can be tonight . . . down, on the street . . . where you left him out this afternoon—at 11 o'clock tonight— if you can be there with the horse and a trailer . . . he'll definitely take the horse!" See? And he said "Take the hundred now, and just give us/ me a receipt . . ." and in my talkin', I look over and here set the car and I recognized the girl . . . because the car was parked close to me/ the night before the car was on the opposite side of the street, and I could just see the driver and the girl, but this time . . . the fella sittin' next to the girl, and the girl was in the car, and this man . . . was the driver, because the driver's seat was empty . . . and-eh . . . we talked back and forth and I said "Look" I said "Now, I've waited tonight . . . I stayed in the hotel . . . and I was told that we would have it definitely at 11, told we'd have it this morning. I have to be in Oxnard tonight to speak at the Calvary Baptist Church . . . and I got some . . . business there . . . and I cannot be . . . down . . . on that street" . . . which is S-S . . . Catalina 'r Santa Catalina Street . . . "tonight at 11!" . . . and finally I left, and before I left, I pulled a card out of my pocket and on the card it says:

SHEPHERD OF THE HILLS

Free Pony Rides For Boys
and Girls Who Go To The
Church Of Their Choice,
Learn A Bible Verse, And
Mind Their Parents.

. . . with my . . . unlisted phone number on it . . . and my address . . . in Santy Ana. And I said "Now, if he really means business" I said "It's not much from 11 til 8 in the morning . . ." I said "I can be there, and I'll deliver the horse where he wants it delivered . . ." and with that . . . I left, see . . . and . . . went on up to Oxnard, took care of my business, and in the morning . . . I . . . went out . . . I went down and got, I think, 5 bales of hay . . . to leave for some ponies that I have there. I have a church man that feeds them . . . and got in my truck . . . hooked on my two-horse trailer, loaded in a brown and white . . . spotted mare, and I roaded/loaded in . . . a little white stallion and a black gelding, two extrees, to see . . . if I could have Orie Tucker sell them for me . . . and I needed a little extree finances. . . .

And I drove into Los Angeles—it was around noon time, it might . . . I can't be exact. I know I was hungry and I had nothin' to eat, I didn't have any breakfast, so . . . eh-I stopped at the Coliseum Hotel, which is just off the Harbor Freeway . . . on . . . Exhibition. There . . . is a man by the name of . . . Bert Morris [Morse] who is an oldtime fight . . . manager, who had Baby Aremendez-eh . . . back in the '30s . . . and I knew that he had this restaurant and sanrich bar there by the University of Southern California and the Coliseum . . . and I thought I would go in and talk to him . . . and especially about this boxer, heavy-weight boxer, and a few things. So, I pulled off the freeway and just circled the corner, went right into the parking lot behind the hotel, and there was an entrance in . . . through his bar, into his restaurant. And . . . coming through the bar, there is a television/I heard something about the rigamarole, and people watching, and about the . . . 8 shots being fired and such, but I . . . being a minister, I just went/cut through the bar and went on into the counter/set down and ordered . . . a lunch. And . . . there was the . . . girl, the hostess and cashier, and I asked for Bert and [she] said "He will be here in just a moment." . . . So, I'm listening to television blast, and I believe there was a radio or something saying that . . . "Suspect has not spoken—can't get nothin' from him . . . but fast work by the police department/they have traced the gun . . . found out the gun was sold to a lady . . . in Pasadena . . . Lady didn't want it around"—and the lady, I think, either sold it or gave it to a neighbor or someone . . . and it came along about the name, some funny name . . . and what have you, and then as I'm listening, why I hear something sayin' . . . as a . . . commentator . . . on the boy . . . liked race horses, he was an exercise boy . . . and dressed in tennis shoes and different things . . . black, bushy hair. And, I'm not paying too much of it because . . . Bert. I'm waitin' for Bert, and Bert comes along, and I'm tellin' him, he's talkin' about his horses. He has a horse called Diamond Dip, and he has one called Hemet Mis . . . talkin' about boxing and now how . . . well he is doin' with his horses and so forth . . . and I told him, I said "You oughtta come back in back" and I said "I got some . . . nice little pony stallion back here." "Boy" he said "I got a little black one out on the ranch is a teaser, is a dandy." And, we're just talkin' old times and so forth.

"And, I-ya . . . you know, I had a funny thing happen. I-(laugh) I'm gonna have to get goin' pretty quick, my wife is 'spectin' me. I started out Monday and picked up a couple of hippies, I guess, or kids, and isn't it funny, a guy shows you a hundred dollar bill, wants the horse'n stalls you in a wait-over." and blah-you just as a matter of conversation. And all of a sudden . . . a picture was flashed . . . on the television. And doin' my talkin', I'm listening to him and thinking and . . . and as I jus/sai . . . (whisper) "Hey . . . that's the guy . . . was in my truck . . ." And then the . . . "Yeah, that's the fella was in my truck!!!"

And then the waitress and the cashier, she handed me the Hollywood Citizen News, who had a picture of him in this extree on the front page. I looked at it, and I said "That's the kid . . . That's him!!" So . . . Doug Lewis, another old trainer, has some boys who train up at Jake's (Shugrue) Gym, was there . . . and I went over the whole st-ah—said "Can you beat that. That rascal" and so forth, and we got to discussing and one of 'em said "Well, man . . . maybe they wanted you there at 11 o'clock so that if this thing went the way it should have, they could have jumped in and rode away with the horse, with you, or something." I said "Well, that could be . . . I wonder . . ." . . . just talkin' back and forth . . . so . . . Doug spoke up and said "You oughtta do the right thing and take this to the police." . . . I said-eh . . . "Ah, it's no use. They've caught him single-handed. Listen, they're fayi-sayin' that after this . . . athlete has grabbed him and they got the gun, they don't need no more." And then . . . Bert spoke up and he says "I know, but have you been following this-eh Garrison investigation of other stuff and so forth? You never can tell, maybe Kennedy'll die" . . . See at this time he was unconscious. . . .

And they . . . must have talked to me for 15 minutes, and I said "Naw, I don't want to forget it. I'm a/in church work and a minister. I don't want to be bothered with it." and so forth . . . "just a coincidence." I said-eh "He sure looks like the fella." I said "I'd have to really hear his voice/I'd ner/and I'm sure if I could hear his voice I'd know definitely." Then the waitress came over, the hostess, and she said "Well" she said "I'd tell you what I'd do if I 'as you. I'd be a good citizen. I think it's your duty." . . . and all of them together. . . .

So, the next thing you know . . . the University police station is just a little ways from there . . . and I played Freshman Football at the University of Southern California . . . and the station used to be right on the campus, but they moved up on Exhibition on there between Vermont and Western. So . . . I end up going/driving the . . . trailer down there and the car . . . my ponies on the back . . . go in and talk to the men, and . . . the minute they hear it, they . . . have me drive in and leave the car in the back, and I heard them say something about taking fingerprints. They took me inside and . . . I phoned my wife and told my wife I would be detained for a while, and-eh . . . they took a recording of . . . what I am saying here . . . and . . . also had a stenographer there, who took it all . . . in shorthand. . . . And, as I . . . told them about seeing the $100, well, one of them . . . must have been listening in the other room, because the machine wasn't there, and I think the machine was behind the desk into the relay room, and one of them came in and said . . . "He sure . . . knows what he's talkin' about 'cause it was just released now that they found $400 bills . . . on this man . . . and there was nothin' about any money on him until then . . . " and I had already told them about . . . this in the early part that I was in there before they took the recording. . . . So the detectives talked about "What shall we do? Well, it's assigned downtown . . ." . . . so I left, and I—they had me there from in the afternoon, and it was about 6:30, quarter to 7 when they were finished with everything . . . and . . . I went outside and it looked like on the doors and on the side that there'd been some kind of powder or something—I didn't see them take any fingerprints, but I heard the detectives say that they should. . . .

I got in my truck and went home. And-eh, of course my wife was-eh wanted to know, and I told my wife and my daughter about what I thought . . . had happened, that this was the fella . . . that was in the truck. And, the next afternoon . . . now the police assured me, the detectives assured me, at the University Station, that . . . my name wouldn't be mentioned and nothin'd be in the paper, 'cause I told them. I said "Look what's happened to this . . . Ruby shootin' a fella and all this stuff that's goin' on. And . . . if this is/they are together, they've got my card and my telephone number, why, anything could happen." So they said this is going to be one of the most secret things/nothin's going to happen in this case like it happened in Dallas.

So, the next afternoon . . . I don't know exactly what time but it was . . . I am sure after 2 o'clock . . . eh-telephone rang and . . . somebody answered it at—home and no answer. It rang again and no answer. It was either my wife or my daughter, and . . . wasn't too long 'til it rang again and I picked the phone up and it said—eh "Are you the Shepherd? . . . the man with the horses? . . . Keep your mother-blankety-blank mouth shut about this . . . horse deal . . . or else!" I don't know wha/by that time I was startled . . . and I remember that much of it, and I remember the phone . . . hittin' fast, like they just banged it. I went out in the back . . . where the horses were and looked at the-these . . . horses, petted the dog, and I got to thinking, and I . . . I didn't want to say nothing to my wife about it . . . and that night, she told me, she said "Well, honey, they/why did you give them the card/our phone number, unlisted?" I said "Well, you know, honey, we need some money, and . . . it'll help on the . . . payment." And I said "Three hundred bucks isn't bad, and the fella shows me a hundred dollars and says that they'd have it . . ." and I said "Well, look, I can't be there at 11 o'clock tonight, but if he . . . wants the horse and he's got the money, why . . . 8 o'clock Wednesday morning, I'll deliver the horse." So she said "Well, at least, anyhow, they know where you are." and I passed it off and didn't say anything. . . .

So, that week went by . . . next weeks/well, I-I-they've got it on record. I-I can't remember the day . . . exactly on this, but they ca-I got a call fr-to come to the detective agency downtown and whoever called me said "Look you know where the place is . . ." I said "I know where the building is/I've never been in it." He says "Come to the 3rd floor, that's the detective . . . information, you stand there and . . . you be there at such and such a time and a man'll come down and just say 'Are you Owen?' and you go from there." . . .

So, as I went downtown, I got hold of Reverend Perkins—a man that's almost 80 years old—a retired Methodist minister, a very dear friend of mine. I said "Perk, come on. Come on, let's do down to the police station" and I briefed him, I said "I want you to be with me when I go in there, don't wanna go in alone. . . ." So, he went along with me and, of course, I told him, I said "Now look" I said "Perk, you believe in prayer" I said "You pray because . . ." I said to Perk "I've had one threat, I haven't told Roberta or the kids about it . . ." . . . So . . . we walked up to the 3rd floor, and a man came up . . . at the . . . time that my appointment was made, took me to the 8th floor . . . I don't remember the room number, but . . . as you walk in a large room . . . first is a-eh small narrow . . . place, about this long, maybe 20 feet long, and it's all glass, and here's a wooden counter, and as I look through I saw 5 or 6 . . . typewriters goin' and . . . saw a bunch of men around. Found out it was a special room handling this case and everything was on this case, I guess, in there—the girls and all the detectives with their stuff. And while I'm watchin' this little door, like a cupboard I thought it was, opened up and a man came out and he said "Are you-eh . . . Jerry Owen?" "Yes." He said "Well, the man that you had the 'pointment with is called away . . . and could you wait for an hour?" and I said "Well, I tell ya, I'm leavin' for Phoenix, it's important I go to Phoenix. I want to drive straight through . . . and I want to get a little sleep tonight because I got business early." Now this is in the afternoon . . . so . . . he said "Well, just a minute." I said "I'd 'preciate if we could do it right now." So, finally, he went through the door . . . and two or three minutes elapsed, another man came out . . . and handed me . . . a stack of pictures . . . with the white, like this, facing me, but they were a little narrow and longer . . . and I believe, if I remembers right, there was . . . a picture on each side, see . . . I think it was divided in the middle and the same fellow, one with a front view and the one with the side view, all had numbers on the front of 'em, see? Ah . . . so he said "You look through here and see if you can find . . . anyone that was riding . . . in your truck." So I took them, like this . . . and turned each one of them over and put it down, covered it up and I don't know how many pictures they were, they were several . . . and after going through a few, I said "This is one of the fellows . . . right here." and I laid it down and I went on through and I said "This is all I see . . ." but I says "Let's make sure now." See? So, then I . . . turn/I ask him "I-can I turn the pictures over?" and I laid them all down on this long thing on the windows and went through them and I said "This is him." See? So, he took the picture . . . and had a piece of a report sheet, like this, with a snap on it . . . and s-took this/the picture, like this, behind them, like that . . . then he said "Now" he said "I haven't had time to read the report from the University Station . . . and-eh is there anything, anything that you can remember that you didn't put in?" See? And-eh, I said to him "Ah, yes . . . I had a threat . . . the day Kennedy died . . . in the afternoon." And then

Mr. Perkins said to him, he said "Is that Sirhan Sirhan's picture that he needs?" He wouldn't say a word, see? I don't know if that's the way they do it. He said that he wouldn't comment. He said "I don't know. I'm not at liberty, I don't know." And it was covered up, see, behind. . . .

So, now we leave. Now I go to Phoenix and drive all night and return home early in the morning—my wife and I sleep until about noon . . . and . . . she goes . . . out in the back . . . to fool with the . . . we got a big backyard and an orchard and then the corrals. And she was watering the philanth-roses or somethin'. . . . The phone rings, I answer it, right by the bed. "We told you to keep your Mother 'F' mouth shut." Again, another threat-like . . . hung up fast . . . and-eh, my wife came in and-eh "Who was that?" . . . and I said "Oh, honey, just . . . somebody callin'," . . . brushed it off. . . . Now, that's on Saturday. Sunday I go to Oxnard, with my family. I come home . . . Monday goes by . . . Tuesday goes by . . . Wednesday afternoon . . . between 3:30 and 5 . . . the phone rings . . . my wife answers, calls me to the phone. "Hello, is this-eh Jerry Owen?" "Yes." "This is Sergeant . . . somebody." Now, I don't remember the name . . . this was a sergeant. "I'd like to talk to you about this case. Could you come right down?" . . . "Well" I said "you caught me . . . at the wrong time." I said "It's 106 miles to Oxnard and I . . . speak there tonight . . . and the freeway traffic is terrible, and if I leave at 5 o'clock I'm lucky to get there at-at 7:30, 2 hours and a half going-eh all the freeway practically all the way up there to Oxnard." "Ah . . . What are you doing after your s-s-speaking tonight?" "Well" I said "I'm leaving, I'm packed. I'm leavin' for the Bay, Oakland. I got 'mportant business." . . . "When will you be back from Oakland?" I said "I don't suppose I'll be back until Monday . . . 'cause I'm goin' to speak in Hayward . . . over Sunday . . ." . . . "Just a minute . . ." . . . Now a man . . . someone comes to the phone and . . . gives the name . . . of Sandlin . . . "And it happens to be that I'm going to be in the Bay District . . . Saturday. I'd 'preciate it very much if I could see you about this and have time to sit down and go over it."—"Well" I said . . . "certainly" I said "Officer Sandlin." . . . Then he turned to me and he said to me "Are you Owens . . . was an athlete around here? . . . Did you go to high school?" I said "I went to Manual Arts." He said "That's where it rings a bell." he said "I see that you are the same age as me when you were at Manual Arts . . . I was at Jefferson." So he said "I guess we played football against each other." So we reminisced a little. Now, I never saw the man. I'm just talkin' on the phone. . . .

I leave . . . go on to Oxnard . . . drive all night. I arrive Thursday morning on this . . . last week . . . which would be about the 26th or

27th, I arrive up here, and I check in a motel on Telegraph . . . I phone . . . Ben Hardister, who is an investigator-friend that I had been at his ranch and rode horses 'n went deer huntin' and . . . been over to George Davis' place, and . . . first met him when he was about 16 or 17 years old . . . which goes back to 30 or 30/maybe 30 years ago, or maybe 28 years ago, whatever it was. And-eh I phoned him, and I said "I drove all night." He said "Well, pardner" he said "I'll pick you up around 1:00, maybe 12:30, 1:00, 1:30." So he came over and we got in the car and I went with him out to Richmond where he had to put some-eh guards on a garbage place that had been threatened by the strike, and another few things to do. And then we drove down into Richmond and . . . saw the windows . . . that had been broke out, and saw the furniture store that had been fired and . . . all . . . nothin' left but the . . . debree. . . . And I said "Ben, I am so tired. I know you are busy and I don't want to interfere. Take me back and I'm going to bed 'cause I . . . haven't had any sleep, and I lost sleep when I went to Phoenix, over and back . . . I'll catch up . . . I'll go to sleep now, and I'll sleep until noon tomorry. You come at 12." So, I went right in and . . . went to bed early in the afternoon, maybe 5 o'clock or somethin' . . . and slept through until 10 o'clock Friday. . . . Got up . . . and . . . what I forgot to put in there . . . was the officer . . . that I talked to . . . this Sandlin, he told me . . . wanta know where he could contact me up in the Bay District and I gave him "George T. Davis, 724 Market Street" I stated that "I don't have the phone number here, but information will give it to you . . . but here's my brother's telephone number in San Bruno." And if I recall, the man that I talked to said "Well, I'm going to be in Palo Alto." I said "Well, that's not too far from San Bruno . . . and . . . sure I'll come and see you. Let me know." Now this is Wednesday afternoon. I hear no more until I phone my wife on Friday. My wife tells me that . . . "Mr. Sandlin will be . . . at the . . . Tower . . . of Hyatt . . . House in Palo Alto . . ." And that he was insured, she insured him that I'd certainly be there at . . . Saturday before noon. So, on the phone, the girl there at the switchboard just scribbled, I told her I didn't have a pencil . . . "Would you please write this for me?" and she wrote, I think "The Hyatt House . . ." and the message was "Be in there Friday night—and stay Saturday and leave Sunday morning." See? So I stuck the message in my pocket, thought no more of it . . . and went with Ben. And then, about 4 o'clock, 3:35 or 3:30, I think we stopped at the Athens Club, went in and sat down . . . and Ben says "Now, I'm going to be busy from 4 to 5."—it was about quarter 'til 4 then ". . . and-eh, do you want a paper?" And he went over and purchased a paper. And

. . . we sat down there, and he took/he gave me the front half, he took the other half. And we read it back and forth and kicked it around a little. And I didn't read the one part of it. I looked at the Sports Page and the front and Ben left. So, I picked up the paper again and . . . the second or third page I see . . . "Witnesses Disappear. . . ." I look at the fella's picture first and see his name. Then I look and see that it's the Ray thing. The fella that's over in England. And the report there in the paper states that the two witnesses in this case mysteriously disappear, the woman that owned the rooming house, or the landlady, and one of the tenants there that saw Ray . . . there and could 'dentify him with the gun, or goin' into the bathroom or somethin'—had mysteriously disappeared. Nobody knows what happened to 'em—no information from the police . . . unless to the effect that they were under protective custody. But nobody knew anything about it. . . . Then as I looked there at his picture, I got to thinkin', I said "Isn't it a funny thing? . . ." My mind drifted back to Ruby goin' in and shootin' the fella. Then I have occasionally-eh heard flashes about Garrison and witnesses dyin' or disappearin' mysteriously or somethin' happening all of a sudden. Then I really got to thinking about it. I said "Now, what? . . . If this is so. . . ." And then there was another flash, another section, a little tiny bit. If you remember, if you get that Oakland paper, it stated that the attorney on the case now had received two threats. One of them stating there was 250,000 . . . Arabians over here, se? And-eh, that he had received . . . a phone call and a written thing, see? And I said "Well, just think. They want to go after the attorney . . . wants to prosecute a man." Then I started to thinking seriously for the first time. Now I had told ̤ . . . I was told . . . by the University Division, I don't know which one, of course, when I cam in there, I believe every detective left his desk and came around, when I was standing there telling about it, see? On Wednesday, they were all bubbling over there. The head fellows, assistants and all of 'em. And I was told not to . . . say anything, not to worry, that my name wouldn't be put in the papers or anything else. Then I got to thinkin' again about giving them the card and the two phone calls . . . and I wasn't going to tell Ben Hardister a thing about it . . . and Ben came back a little after 5 and he says "Well, let's go to the ranch for the weekend." He says "Let's go up and get your car . . . park your car in the parking lot here at the Athens . . . lock'er up and come with me. . . ." So I got to thinkin' "Well, I'd better come back and tell Ben." "Ben, I'll be at your ranch tomorrow afternoon . . ." 'cause I knew about this appointment with this supposed-to-be-man Sandlin. And I got in the car with Ben. And, if Ben remembers—he's seated right here—I said "Ben I'm gonna tell tell you somethin' . . . it's like a pipe/like a pipedream or a mystery, see? It's hard to believe, but here's what happened." So I started tellin' Ben, see? I said "Ben" I said "I'm to meet a detective tomorrow over in . . . Palo Alto. . . ." Well, I saw Ben startle a little bit. He says "Now, what is it now, pardner?"—He has an expression of sayin' "pardner."—I said "Ben, now listen to this. Of all the people in the world, and the millions of people . . . that I would be drivin' . . ." I went around the bush at first. I told him "I'm drivin' an old truck, with my old clothes on, and the horse. . . ." And I tell Ben about it, give him a rundown, tell him about the two threats, tell him about this phone call. Ben's drivin', and he says "Do you know this man?" I says "Never saw him before in my life." "You can't identify him?" Ben says "You mean to tell me you are going to go over there now and see somebody you don't know who it is?" He says "I'm not gonna let ya!" That's what he said "You're not going without me!" He says "No. sir! You got (an) appointment in the morning" he says "we'll go to the ranch and we'll think this over." So, 3 or 4 times he shook his head and he said "Just think of all the millions of people. . . ." You remember this, don't you, Ben? ". . . in California, that you have to be at that time, with that truck?" But he says "I guess" he says "I guess there's a reason for everything. I don't know what it is." and he just seemed to be startled, as he shook his head, and then he told me, he says "We'll stop in Napa." he said "I got a friend here named Wes Parker . . ." I mean Wes Gardner, I'm sorry. . . . "who has been to . . . the FBI school or something about the FBI, and he's been the under-Sheriff or next to the Sheriff and a lot of experience and solved a lot of—murders and different things. Let's go just . . . get his viewpoint on it. Let's talk to him." So, we drove into the Boy's Club, where he happened to be . . . in his own office back there, and we told him the story and he told me "No, that's the worst thing you can do. You mean to tell me you don't know who Sandlin is? You never met him? You couldn't identify him . . . and you're gonna walk over there . . . with two threats? Maybe that's just the way that they're settin' it up. No sir." and Wes says "Well, I'll tell you what we'll do" he says "We'll see if the FBI agents herein town that I knew . . ."—found out that he wasn't, that he was gone. So, then, finally, he phoned the Sheriff, and I guess the Sheriff didn't know of any FBI numbers there. The next thing, we finally got, somehow, we got hold of an FBI agent in . . . Vallejo, said "All we want you to do is find out if there is a L. L. Sandlin . . . and if he is at the Hyatt House." See? "And if this is authentic. We want to know." Well, now, that was approximately between 8 and 9 o'clock . . . on . . . Friday night, we heard no word back. They knew where to contact Ben's home number . . . the information. We get up in the morning . . . and we decide to go over and see George T. Davis, who I've known since 1937, who has a ranch . . . just a little ways from Ben's ranch, in Pope Valley. George and his wife is havin' breakfast, and we sit down and laugh a little bit. Then . . . I talkin' over old times . . . I says "George" I says "Here's a funny thing happened." So I tell George . . . and I said "George, what should I do?" He says "Why, certainly" he says "Let me/we'll solve it." He went to the phone. He picked up the phone. Now here it is between 11 and 12 o'clock noon. He puts the call through to the Hyatt House for an L. L. Sandlin, in Palo Alto. We're listenin' to him there. The answer is "There is no L.L. Sandlin registered. No reservation." They know nothing about it. So I get to thinkin' "Friday night he's supposed to be there, the man tells me Saturday. Maybe it's a good thing I did tell Ben about this. Maybe it's a good thing. Man, I could have walked in there and got plugged or . . . a fellow come along and pose [as] an officer and got me in a car and said 'Well, let's go in and see the Sheriff or the policeman here . . .' and dumped me in the Bay or something." I said "Maybe this is just the hand of God!!!"

So, then George says "Alright, the next move will be I'll phone the District Attorney's office and find out who's in charge." George ran up against a stone wall. Nobody was there Saturday. They knew nothin' . . . couldn't get through to nothin' . . . and just seemed like they were stalling. So George says "I'll get hold of . . . someone else." I don't know if it was Unruh, Jessie Unruh, or something. Now, he put another call through to the Sheriff, couldn't get the/she couldn't get the Sheriff. Then, after the D.A.—no answer. Then he got Unruh . . . and we sat in George's house.

And now it's-eh now it's pushing 1 o'clock and then the next thing, the phones start ringing back and forth. He gets the-eh ("Chief of Police") Chief of Police, phones him down there. Chief of Police says "We'll check on things . . ." this and that . . . "Phone you back." Back 'nd forth it went. So, finally, in the afternoon, maybe 3 o'clock or 3:30, the Chief of Police confirms there is an L. L. Sandlin that's a Sergeant. Nobody, I guess . . . so that's that. So we find out that much. Now, in the meantime, we've heard not a thing from the F-FBI department. ("You don't know whether Sandlin was up here?") No, sir. Now, I'm g-gonna go a little farther. No, sir, we didn't know, we didn't find a thing out. They knew nothin' about it . . . 'proximately 5:30, I was watchin' the clock . . . off and on, because they was a reporters, a cameraman there waitin' 'n come in on the thing . . . and-eh at about

5:30 the phone rings and George talks and it's another policeman in the investigation department . . . that's talkin' to George and verinfyin' that L. L. Sandlin and so forth, and they want to talk to me, so George puts me on, see? And he said "Mr. Owen" he said "I can verify that you talked to L. L. Sandlin . . . Wednesday afternoon." Now Sandlin told this man it was Thursday morning he talked to me, but it wasn't, 'cause I was up here Thursday, see? "You had a conversation with him today?" So . . . I verified "Yes, you talked to him, but we decided after he made the appointment . . . that it was the wrong thing to talk to you up in Palo Alto, see? . . . that we should talk to you here." I said "Well, then, whyyy . . . din't you notify my brother, my wife, or George T. Davis?" Well, he didn't have an answer, see? I said "You phoned me to make the appointment . . ." and I says . . . hummed and hawed around, and I said "You know I've got some threats." and he says "I've read the report."

And-eh . . . I hadn't had time, I hadn't seen him, I only told him about the first threat. I haven't told him about the second threat. That morning, Saturday, after I came back from Phoenix, but I was going to tell Sandlin when I met him . . . my next interview with him, see? And I said "I've had two threats" and so forth . . . I said "I got a wife down there, two children and a grandson. How about now?" "Oh" he says "I'm sure they will be alright. Just a misunderstanding." Yes, he should have, but something, and he tried to . . . apple-polish the thing and do something to it in someway.

And, in the meantime, I didn't know that the 'sociated Repre-Press was listening on an extension in George's front room—he heard this, see?—conversation to verify I had the appointment. So, finally he said "Well, how do you feel now?" I said "Well, I'll feel a whole lot better when I find out this was Sandlin and was/wasn't somebody else." "Well" he says "I'm sure it'll be alright. Just let things go as they were . . . before . . . When you came back in town, when you come in Monday or Tuesday, come on in and see us." and so forth. And, then, the last thing he said . . . he said "Say Owen" he said "The report's here some place, ah, could I have your telephone number and your address again?" See? And with that, then George took the phone and the 'sociated press fellow, boy, that got him, he said "Boy, what kind of a . . . police force is this? Wantin' to know your telephone number . . . what/how are they handlin' things?"

So, that is the situation and from now on, why . . . eh, that's as far as I can tell you. That's it. And if Wes wants to say something or-eh if-eh Mr. Hardister wants to say anything . . . they can both confirm . . . my part here . . . of bein' in Oakland and so forth . . . and him telling me . . . not to go over and see him and takin' me . . . to-eh-his-eh . . . the man he works for, Wes here he's with, see?

("There was the car that almost ran you off the road?") Ah, well, ahmm-eh, I'll tell you this here, what happened. When George . . . I came in with . . . George Davis then, Monday morning, and at 5th and Mission, I got out of George's car to go into the Chronicle . . . and as George pulled away from the curb, there was a . . . 'bout-eh Cadillac, that's maybe a '66 or a '65 or 7 pulled up, with a heavy-set eye-talian-lookin' man with a cigar in his mouth and a hat on, and he just pulled over and said "Say" he says "Was that George T. Davis who-who's car you just got out of?" And, with that I said "Who's car?"—and scrammed inside this building. I don't know who that was. It maybe could of been somebody who wanted George, a reporter or somethin', I don't know.

And, then I'm going to let Ben tell you-eh about the car. He knows the roads and that. We had a car . . . pull up and s-s-almost stop dead in front of us a couple of times and go real slow so we couldn't pass it . . . and put his fist up. And the ki-these/one-the fellow that wasn't driving kept lookin' back, so I took a pencil in a piece of paper and started to/got the license number, and they saw me writing. They . . . disappeared. They sped on it. But, Ben can explain that to you. That was a strange thing.

So-eh, if there's any other questions you'd like to ask me now, I'll answer 'em and maybe Ben wants to say somethin', or maybe Wes does. I don't know. Is there anything else you want to ask me?

("Jerry, you say you know Edgar Eugene Bradley of North Hollywood, that you met him in Dr. (Carl) McIntyre's company?") Yes-eh-yes, I-I met him-eh. I know that-eh he was affiliated with Dr. McIntyre. And I met him at the Embassy Auditorium . . . a place where they give all kinds of lectures . . . and so forth. And I . . . two times. I shook hands with him once, and then I seen him another time.

("Do you know Dr. Bob Wells, down in Orange?") Very well. He don't live too far from me. Yes. He has a big Sunday School and church. Know him well. He started in a . . . little garage or a tent in Orange Grove, and now he's got the largest Sunday School down there. Yes, I know Bob Wells.

("Do you know of his affiliation with Bradley?") Ah . . . no, I . . . don't really. If I remember right, I think Bradley was advertised to speak for him once, or somethin.' I'm not sure. ("Right.") Am-I-na-na-am I wrong? I'm going back to memory. ("Yeah, that's right.") Well, that's it. That's he/that's right.

("Do you know a man by the name of Lorenz? Jack Lorenz or Fred Lorenz?") Ah, Jack or Fred Lorenz? You mean the man from/that's down in Mexico? ("Well, it could be. Originally there's a Fred Lorenz . . . is originally from Germany . . .") Yes, he's another/yes-eh, I . . . ("Drives a car with Texas plates . . .") Yes, yes. I-I don't know him personally, but I'm familiar with those, bein' eh myself a minister and . . . following the-eh papers and handbills. Yes, that name's familiar, but I don't know him personally. ("OK.")

("Is there any question in your mind as to this initial engagement with these two men, that you were just a random choice for them? Is there any possibility that they could have been following you . . . ?") I don't know. It's very strange how . . . that-eh . . . I would be downtown in this truck this day to do this business, and how they would get in the back, and it makes me wonder and think. I believe I've/after thinking much now, I really believe that the man . . . approximately, I would say 35, that I told you was well-dressed, he seemed to be of the same nationality, and my feeling was that . . . he was the brains back of it or something.

("Well, in other words, they hopped on your truck. You didn't invite them?") No, no. I didn't invite them. It happened so fast. As my truck was there, I could/looking at the light at the side and this/If you look at a '48 Chivvy, custom cab, it's got a round window here and a window in the back you can see. And the tallest of the two younger fellows stepped on the running board and had one foot over, and I saw him coming over, and I'm/of course I'm wonderin' what he's doin' . . . but there's nothin' in the back of the truck, see, but some old hay that's laying . . . on the thing . . . and he's half way in, and the other one takes the door, and he's got it part-open with his head. 'Are you goin' towards Hollywood, West?' See? Like this way out Wilshire, see? 'cause I was clear in the right hand turn . . . we had to turn right. My blinker's on, I'm gonna turn right, see. And before I could OK it, see, he said "We'll ride in the back." and just helped themself . . . and they got in the back and sat down . . . and they are not beside me, so nobody can harm my . . . they are in the open, in the back.

("Now, if I understand what you are saying, one of the men that jumped in the back was the same one that offered you the $100 deposit?") No, no, that's a different one. You have three men and a woman, and they was one . . . on the corner, looked like the same nationality that was standing about 4 feet from 'em, looked like he was interested in what they were sayin', but wasn't talkin' to 'em, see?

("Now, was this when the $100 deposit was offered?") No, no. This is the first meeting on a Monday afternoon. That was the first meeting. Yes, sir. ("OK—Alright.")

("Now . . . they wanted to meet you at 11 o'clock at night on Tuesday night, right?") Just wha/I made the appointment with the smallest one. When I left him out on Sunset, he said "I'll meet you here on this corner at 11 o'clock tonight and have the money to pay for your horse." . . . ("Yes, then?") He showed me no money, yet. He said he had money coming, he was going to pick up. ("But then, that was Monday?") That was Monday night. ("Then you met them Monday night at 11?") I met him-eh, just him, the others were parked. Go ahead . . . ("Right . . . and then, the point was, now, the next morning they came around where you were staying . . .") At the hotel. (". . . and they wanted to meet you at 11 o'clock that night?") Again, Tuesday night, they would have wanted to meet me at 11 o'clock. ("And where did they want you to meet them?") That . . . would be down . . . on . . . Catalina Street . . . at the same place . . . that I let the little fellow out . . . the day before the evening to see somebody that worked in a kitchen. That's all. ("Is the Ambassador Hotel at that corner?") Yes, they-no, the-at's the side street that goes down along the side of the Ambassador. ("Yeah.") There is no automobile entrance there, but if you go down about a block you'll see a little street that dead-ends to a fence and a gate that opens up, and you go through that gate that takes you into the back of the Ambassador on the side, see.

("When you said that you had a speaking engagement in Oxnard that night, you couldn't make it, right?") I couldn't make it. That's right. ("Were they very insistent that you try and make it that night?") Yes, yes. That's when I was offered to take the $100 bill, give 'em a receipt and they'd have the balance of the money if I would deliver the/be there and have the horse in the horse trailer, see? ("At 11 o'clock?") At 11 o'clock with the horse. And then I was to . . . pick my money up and take the horse where he wanted it. ("In other words, the $100 was an indicement for you to break your engagement in Oxnard?") Yeah, that's right. It looked like it. I feel that it was a come-on, now. I do, in my/ bottom my heart. ("In other words, you feel that they were striving pretty hard to get you to be there at 11 o'clock?") Yes. They wanted it very, very bad.

("When you made the alternate date of the next morning, they weren't interested?") Ah, well, I-I couldn't say that. I said 'Well, look' I said 'Look, if he wants the horse at 11 o'clock and I can't be there, see, get it? ("Yeah.") 'Here's my card. Phone me tomorrow morning at 8 o'clock . . . at my home' . . . because I always phone my wife, and if they'd a-phoned at 8 and left a message, my wife would have taken the message. Then I could have brought the horse from Oxnard to wherever they wanted it, see? ("Yeah.") So I said 'Here, phone me in the morning if he wants the horse.' I said 'I've wasted . . . yesterday evening and stayed in a motel, cost me $4, see, and nothing happened, see? ("Except that they did offer you the $100?") They offered the $100. The night before the little fellow showed me the hunderd dollars, but didn't offer it to me. He said 'I got a hunderd and I didn't get all my money. I'll have it in the morning at 8 o'clock.' See? ("Yeah—and he still didn't have it?") He didn't show. The other fellow showed. ("The well-dressed fellow?") The well-dressed fellow, and the g-g-girl and another fellow in the car/she . . .

("Can you give a comprehensive description of the well-dressed (man)?") Ah, well, ala, the well-dressed fellow, I would say, hit between 165 to 175 pounds, in there. And-eh he looked of a . . . a . . . a . . . a . . . of a Latin type . . . I mean . . . ("Could he have been from the Near East, from Jordan or somewhere like that?") Yeah, yes. He-he could/he could be either-eh he could either be an Indian or a Hindu or something. He looked of that type. ("Or he could be Mexican or Cuban?") Yes, that's right, that's right. He-he wasn't American. He wasn't . . . ("He was swarthy looking?") That's right. That's right. ("What about his accent? Did he have an accent?") Very good English ("Very good English?") As good as English as the little guy. The little guy that I thought was a Mexican. That's what got me, see. I said 'Are you from Mexico?' 'No' I said 'Well, you sure speak good English.'— 'He says 'No. I'm from Jordan.' ("Yeah, OK. Now what was . . . he was about 5 (feet tall)?") I would say he was 5/for the little fellow, I would say he was around 5' 3" or 4", and weight around maybe 135, 140 pounds. ("But the well-dressed man?") Oh, no, the well-dressed fellow, I would say was about 5' 8" or 9". ("How old?") 30 . . . 'bout/ round 35. Between 30 or 40. He could have/in there. I would say 35. ("Right. What was his hair like?") He had-eh dark hair, see . . . and it was/it wasn't kinky, see? And it wasn't straight. It had kind of a like here. ("Yeah.") He didn't have any beard. He didn't have any long sideburns. I mean he was-ah/it was neatly. ("Did he have any rings or anything that you might [notice]?") Yes. He had-ah-he had a little ring, you call 'em ah-ah . . . What are they? Cat's eye? It's not a pigeon red ruby, what's the other? I been/I can't, for two days I been trying to think of the name of those rings. You know, they're kind of a gray color. Popular ring that you wear. What is the name? I-I . . . for two days I can't think of it. I say Cat's Eye. He had that ring on. That's right, go ahead. ("Shirt and tie?") No. No. He had on a yella . . . ah . . . ah yellowish-eh turtle neck. He had a round—like a chain. Now . . . wasn't a strap. It was like a link chain with a round thing hanging on it, see? ("And you had the impression his suit looked pretty good?") His suit looked like it/well it did. It had the-the late style. In fact, I'd like to have one. It had this here . . . ("Little cuffs on it?") . . . and the pockets are like this now. It's a new style suit. Mani/his nails were manicured. He was immaculate. ("Anything distinctive about him?") No-ah, not too much . . . just . . . the little conversation 'Joe couldn't make it . . . and here's $100.' But he did ask for a receipt for his hunderd, see? Now I don't know if that was to make it legal or what, but he said 'Give me the receipt for the hunderd, be there (with) the horse, you'll have the other two hunderd and that's it, see, 11 o'clock.'

(Wes Gardner: "When he showed you the $100 bill, he mentioned that he had more of these coming, didn't he?") No. This man . . . No, no, this man didn't. The little fellow did the night before. The little fellow said 'I didn't get all my money. I'm gonna have more coming, and I'll have it . . . 8 o'clock in the morning, and I got a hunderd here, but I'll have more of 'em, these. . . .' ("At 8 in the morning?") And he, and he held it, see. He didn't stick it out, but the fellow in the morning at 8 o'clock, he's not standing too far from me, and he said 'Well' he said 'Look' he said 'Ah-take this hunderd and deliver the horse tonight.' And he's/he in a/first he . . . asked 'You got a horse trailer?' See? I said 'Yes, I have a two-horse trailer.' And I told him, I said 'I'm bringing a pony down.' I was only going to bring one pony down, see, and when I come, I brought two more shetlands and they're at Orie Tucker's for sale now, see, to help me out. If he . . . ("Were they rather insistent you bring the trailer to Santa Catalina Avenue?") On that si/on that side street, see? ("At 11 o'clock on Tuesday night?") At 11 o'clock. Tuesday night at 11 o'clock. And-eh/Look, I didn't even know . . . I didn't know that there was any reception there, nothing. Because . . . I re-member . . . wh-when Reegan was up, they most generally hold all their receptions at the Amba/a-at the Biltmore, downtown. That's where Reegan was. I didn't know there was a blow-out there/I didn't know anything was going on/didn't mean a thing to me. In fact, I didn't even know where the kid went when he said 'I got a friend in the kitchen' See? ("Yeah. OK.")

["This tape was cut with Jerry Owen from approximately 2 to 3:15 P.M. on July 2, 1968, in the offices of George T. Davis. Also present during this interview were Wes Gardner and Ben Hardister."]

A cassette recording of the Turner/Owen interview can be obtained by sending $10 in check or money order to: Christian/Turner, 163 Mark Twain Avenue, San Rafael, Calif. 94903.

EXHIBIT 1

Statement of Robert Rozzi given to Vincent Bugliosi on November 15, 1975

On the date June 4, 1968, I was a police officer for the Los Angeles Police Department assigned to Wilshire Division. I was assigned to the morning watch and was riding a patrol car from 2330 hour (11:30 P.M.) on. Shortly after midnight, we heard over our radio that a shooting had occurred at the Ambassador Hotel. Since the hotel is adjacent to the eastern boundary of the Wilshire Division, we drove immediately to the hotel. When we first arrived, my partner (I can't remember his name) and I directed traffic at the main entrance to the parking lot, and we were instructed to write down all the license plate numbers of the vehicles leaving the parking lot. We did this for approximately two hours at which time we proceeded into the hotel and were given the job of maintaining security in the kitchen area. Among other things, we only let authorized people, such as the police and other personnel involved in the investigation, into the crime scene. This I continued to do till approximately 0800 (8 A.M.) hours, June 5, 1968. During the night, one of the investigators for the Los Angeles Police Department suggested that we look for bullets and bullet holes. I don't recall anyone finding any bullets on the floor, et cetera. However, I personally observed some small holes in a partition behind the stage. I have no way of knowing how these small holes were caused.

Sometime during the evening when we were looking for evidence, someone discovered what appeared to be a bullet a foot and a half or so from the bottom of the floor in a door jamb on the door behind the stage. I also personally observed what I believed to be a bullet in the place just mentioned. What I observed was a hole in the door jamb, and the base of what appeared to be a small caliber bullet was lodged in the hole. I was photographed pointing to this object in a Los Angeles Police Department photograph marked A-94-C.C. 68521466, where I signed my name in the upper right-hand corner: Robert Rozzi 11-15-75. In the photograph, I am pointing my pen at the object and LAPD officer Charles Wright, also of the Wilshire Division, is holding a ruler next to the object. I am also shown in a AP Wirephoto marked in the bottom right-hand corner (rhs 40745stf) 1968. In this photo, I am holding a flashlight in my left hand and Officer Wright is pointing at what appears to be the bullet with a penknife. The object which I believed to be a bullet is shown in an LAPD photograph marked

68521466 A-59-C.C. and signed in the upper left hand corner on the reverse side: Robert Rozzi 11-15-75.

I personally never removed the object from the hole, but I'm pretty sure someone else did, although I can't remember who it was.

The above statement is a true statement to the best of my recollection. This statement was given to Mr. Bugliosi by me at Hollywood Station on 11-15-75 2030 hrs.

[signed] ROBERT ROZZI

The above two-page statement was written by me and signed by Sgt. Rozzi in my presence.

[signed] VINCENT T. BUGLIOSI
November 15, 1975

EXHIBIT 2

Statement of Dr. Thomas Noguchi, Coroner of Los Angeles County, given to Vincent Bugliosi on December 1, 1975.

On the date June 11, 1968, I went to the pantry area of the Ambassador Hotel in Los Angeles to make an "at scene" investigation of the scene of the homicide. I had requested that DeWayne Wolfer of the Los Angeles Police Department be present, which he was. I asked Mr. Wolfer where he had found bullet holes at the scene. I forget what he said, but when I asked him this question, he pointed, as I recall, to one hole in a ceiling panel above, and an indentation in the cement ceiling. He also pointed to several holes in the door frames of the swinging doors leading into the pantry. I directed that photographs be taken of me pointing to these holes. I got the impression that a drill had been placed through the holes. I do not know whether or not these were bullet holes, but I got the distinct impression from him that he suspected that the holes may have been caused by bullets.

If there are discrepancies as to the number of bullets fired in the pantry or the number of bullet holes, I would recommend, as I would do in any criminal case, further studies by an impartial panel of experts to resolve this matter. There is a certain urgency in resolving this matter, because if it is not resolved now, I am afraid that there will be a continuing doubt which will be harmful to local government on a matter of national concern.

The above statement was given by me to Mr. Bugliosi freely and voluntarily and everything I have said in this statement is true to the best of my recollection.

[signed] THOMAS NOGUCHI
December 1, 1975

The above statement was written by me and signed by Dr. Thomas Noguchi in my presence at his office on December 1, 1975.

[signed] VINCENT T. BUGLIOSI

EXHIBIT 3

Statement given by Angelo DiPierro to Vincent Bugliosi on December 1, 1975

In June of 1968, I was the maître d' at the Ambassador Hotel in Los Angeles. Just past midnight on the morning of June 5, 1968, I was escorting Mrs. Ethel Kennedy towards the pantry of the hotel. Senator Kennedy was preceding us by 20 or so feet. Five or so paces before we reached the two swinging doors leading into the pantry, I heard the first shot coming from within the pantry. We proceeded towards the two swinging doors and as we reached them, the rapid fire began, so I literally pulled Mrs. Kennedy from the open doorway to take cover behind the closed doorway. (Entering the pantry from the Embassy room, the door on the left was open and the door on the right was closed.) Immediately after the shooting ended, Mrs. Kennedy and I proceeded into the pantry to see what had happened. After Senator Kennedy had been removed from the pantry, many people, including the police and myself, started to look over the entire pantry area to piece together what had happened. That same morning, while we were still looking around, I observed a small caliber bullet lodged about a quarter of an inch into the wood on the center divider of the two swinging doors. Several police officers also observed the bullet. The bullet was approximately 5 feet 8 or 9 inches from the ground. The reason I specifically recall the approximate height of the bullet location is because I remember thinking at the time that if I had entered the pantry just before the shooting, the bullet may have struck me in the forehead, because I am approximately 5 feet 11½ inches tall. It is my belief that the bullet in the hole is the same bullet that struck the forehead of Mrs. Evans who had been standing right in front of the center divider. The reason why I feel that the bullet which struck Mrs. Evans never entered her forehead and instead continued on into the center divider is that if a bullet had entered her forehead, I would have assumed she would have become unconscious, but Mrs. Evans appeared to be coherent and was not unconscious. Her only complaint was that she had been hit.

I am quite familiar with guns and bullets, having been in the Infantry for 3½ years. There is no question in my mind that this was a bullet and not a nail or any other object. The base of the bullet was round and from all indications, it appeared to be a 22 caliber bullet.

A day or so later, the center divider that contained the bullet was removed by the Los Angeles Police Department for examination. I don't know who removed the bullet or what happened to it. The hole that contained the bullet was the only new hole I observed after the shooting. Even prior to the shooting, there were a few holes from nails, et cetera on the two swinging doors.

The above two page statement was given by me to Mr. Bugliosi freely and voluntarily and everything I have said in this statement is true to the best of my recollection.

[signed] ANGELO DiPIERRO

12-1-75

The above statement was written by me and signed by Angelo DiPierro in my presence at his office in the Palladium on December 1, 1975.

[signed] VINCENT T. BUGLIOSI

EXHIBIT 4

Statement given by Martin Patrusky to Vincent Bugliosi on December 12, 1975

On the date June 5, 1968, I was a banquet waiter for the Ambassador Hotel in Los Angeles. About 20 minutes before the assassination in the pantry, I was standing by the steam table in the pantry when this fellow, who looked like a dishwasher from the kitchen, tapped me on the shoulder and asked me if Kennedy was coming back through the kitchen. I said to him "How the hell do I know. I'm not the head waiter." He walked away by the tray rack and I never paid any attention to him, though I think he stayed around the tray rack, which is next to the ice machines in the pantry.

When Senator Kennedy came into the pantry about 20 minutes later, I was standing near the center divider of the two swinging doors. Just after he entered the pantry through the swinging doors, I shook his hand. I was to his left. As Kennedy walked forward through the pantry, I moved forward with him, to his left. I stopped at the alcove which goes into the main kitchen. I stopped and watched Kennedy as he took a few more steps forward. Karl Uecker was to Kennedy's front and was guiding him through the kitchen. The man who had asked me 20 minutes earlier if Kennedy was coming back through the kitchen came out from behind the tray rack, crossed in front of Uecker and was standing against the steam table to Uecker's left. In fact, I saw him pointing his gun over Uecker's left shoulder towards Kennedy. At this time, Kennedy was leaning slightly to the left and shaking somebody's hand or reaching to shake someone's hand. I saw the man, who turned out to be Sirhan, firing at Kennedy. Kennedy's back was not facing Sirhan. Sirhan was slightly to the right front of Kennedy. I would estimate that the closest the muzzle of Sirhan's gun got to Kennedy was approximately 3 feet. After Sirhan fired the first shot, Uecker grabbed Sirhan around the neck with one hand and with his other hand he grabbed Sirhan's right wrist. But Sirhan continued to fire.

After the shooting, I was taken to the Rampart Division of the Los Angeles Police Department with several other employees of the Ambassador. We were supposedly taken there for questioning, but we were not questioned at that time. About 7 or 8 that same morning, they took us back to the Ambassador. I went down to the pantry. The police were there and they didn't want anyone inside the pantry. My boss, Angelo DiPierro, told me I could go home and I didn't have to work the lunch hour that day.

4 or 5 days or maybe a week later, the Los Angeles Police Department tried to reconstruct the scene of the crime and where everybody was standing. I and several other employees of the Hotel were present in the pantry. There were 4 or 5 plainclothes officers present. The reconstruction incident took about an hour or so. Sometime during the incident, one of the officers pointed to two circled holes on the center divider of the swinging doors and told us that they had dug two bullets out of the center divider. The two circled holes are shown in a photograph shown to me by Mr. Bugliosi marked "Exhibit JA" at the top. A man is pointing to the two circled holes. I am absolutely sure that the police told us that two bullets were dug out of these holes. I don't know the officer's name who told us this, but I remember very clearly his telling us this when they were recreating the scene, and I would be willing to testify to this under oath and under penalty of perjury.

I have read the above three page statement which I orally gave to Mr. Bugliosi freely and voluntarily and everything in the statement is true.

[signed] MARTIN PATRUSKY

12-12-75

The above statement was written by me in Martin Patrusky's presence and signed by Mr. Patrusky in my presence in my office.

[signed] VINCENT T. BUGLIOSI

12-12-75

Date 7/10/68

OLIVER B. OWEN, also known as Jerry and Curly, 1113 N. Mar-Les Drive, Santa Ana, California, telephone 839-0123, appeared at the FBI for interview with prior arrangements for the interview having been made through his attorney, GEORGE T. DAVIS. OWEN appeared at the office with BEN HARDISTER, a private detective and WESLEY GARDNER, a former Deputy Sheriff in Napa County. Both of these men were acting as body guards for OWEN. Prior to the interview, GARDNER advised that OWEN had been under sedation and was somewhat tired. OWEN was interviewed out of the presence of HARDISTER and GARDNER.

At the outset of the interview, OWEN was advised that he was being interviewed concerning his knowledge of an individual whom he had identified to his attorney DAVIS and the press as possibly being identical with SIRHAN B. SIRHAN and the fact that he has stated that he had received threatening calls from persons unknown.

OWEN furnished the following information:

On June 3, 1968, he was in downtown Los Angeles on business between 3:30 and 4:00 p.m. He explained that he has part interest in a fighter named RIP O'RILEY. He also is a minister and has been since 1937. He said that he has approximately fifteen ponies which he keeps at his ranch at Santa Ana and takes these horses around to shopping centers to give free rides to children to get them to come to church. He said that his church is located at Oxnard, California, and that he kept some of the ponies at his ranch in Oxnard. His purpose for being in Los Angeles on June 3, 1968 was to pick up some sporting goods for O'RILEY at the United Sporting Goods Store. He picked up a pair of boxing shoes, a white robe, some trunks and other equipment.

He had purchased his merchandise at the sporting goods store and was proceeding on Hill Street. He stopped at a stop light and two individuals approached his truck. He said he was driving a 1942 Chevrolet pick-up truck which had a large palomino horse ornament on the hood. When the two young men approached his truck, the taller of the two asked if he was going out Wilshire Boulevard and when he said that he was, this individual asked if they could ride in the back of the truck, to which OWEN agreed. He described these individuals as follows:

ON 7/8/68 IN San Francisco, California   File # SF 62-5481 & LA 56-156
BY ROBERT W. HERRINGTON and
    H. ERNEST WOODRY / rvn   Date dictated 7/10/68

NUMBER 1

Age	Early twenties
Height	5' 8" to 5' 10"
Build	Slender
Hair	Black, bushy
Complexion	Dark, appearing to be of Latin American origin
Wearing	Sandals, two-tone Mexican type jacket, possibly a vest and a chain around his neck with a medallion thereon.

NUMBER 2

Age	Early twenties
Height	5' 3"
Build	Slender
Hair	Dark, bushy
Complexion	Dark, with Latin American appearance
Wearing	Dark colored khaki levi type pants, dark gray sweatshirt and wearing tennis shoes.

They proceeded west on Wilshire Boulevard. At the intersection of Vermont and Wilshire, OWEN stopped for a traffic light and as he did so, both men got out of the truck. Number one went directly to a bus stop near where the truck stopped and greeted a man and woman. The man was about thirty to forty years of age and dark complected, possibly Mexican. The woman was dressed in slacks with long dirty blond hair, light complexion, possibly a hippie. Number two started to follow Number one but turned around and came back to the truck. He opened the door and asked to ride up front to continue toward Hollywood. When OWEN nodded approval, he climbed in the front seat. They proceeded on leaving Number one at the bus stop.

During the ride, the conversation of horses came up and Number two asked OWEN if he owned horses and he said that he did. Number two remarked that he used to work at a race track and at present needed a horse. OWEN said that he had horses for sale and offered to sell him one for $300. They talked some more about buying and selling a horse and Number two asked OWEN if he could stop for a short time so that he could see a friend who worked in a kitchen nearby where they were at the moment. OWEN said he turned off Wilshire Boulevard onto a side street, the name of which he does not know. He described the street as a deadend street that was several blocks long. He parked the truck and waited while Number two went to see his friend.

After a wait of about ten minutes, OWEN decided that Number two was not going to return so he began to turn the truck around and leave. As he was doing this, he observed Number two come through an opened gate in a fence behind which was a tall building with many rooms. OWEN said that he was later advised by a police officer of the Los Angeles Police Department, University Station, that this building was the Ambassador Hotel.

When Number two got back in the truck, OWEN again began making conversation and asked the man if he was Mexican. He told him that he was not, saying that he was from Jordan having either come from Jordan thirteen years ago or when he was thirteen years old. OWEN could not recall which he said. He said that his name was JOE and gave a surname which OWEN did not understand, but which OWEN believed sounded like ZAHARIAS. OWEN said at about this time, he was arriving at his destination, that is a shoe shop and tailor shop where he was going to leave the boxing shoes and the robe for O'RILEY to have shamrocks put on. He said that he parked the truck in the Hollywood Ranch Market's lot and took the shoes to a bootblack named SMITTY. While he was conducting this business, Number two stayed in the truck. He returned to the truck and drove a few blocks and let Number two out on the corner of Wilshire near a bowling alley and a go-go topless bar. Before he left Number two agreed to meet OWEN at 11:00 p.m. on the same corner at which time he would have the money to buy the horse.

He met the fighter O'RILEY that evening and left him shortly before 11:00 p.m. and arrived back at the agreed meeting place and observed a 1958 or 1959 Chevrolet, off-white in color, in which there were three men and a girl. OWEN believed that one of the men and the girl may have been the same couple that Number one was talking to earlier at the bus stop. He could not get a good look at the second man in the car. Number two came over to the truck and showed him a $100 bill saying he would have the rest of the money the next day early in the morning. OWEN told him he would stay overnight in Los Angeles and pointed out a hotel which was either St. Mark's or St. Martin, which would be where he would stay. He registered at this hotel as J. C. OWEN and requested the clerk give him a call at 8:00 a.m. However, he said that he was up at 7:00 a.m. and just as he was leaving the hotel he received a call from a man asking if he was the man with the pick-up and horse. OWEN acknowledged that he was and said he would meet him in a few minutes at the truck. As he was going to the truck he saw the same white car as before parked at the curb and Number one and the girl whom he saw before, were sitting in the car. The man who had been at the bus stop was standing by the truck and as OWEN approached he said "JOE could not make it." He offered OWEN a $100 bill and asked if he could bring the horse to the same location that night at which time the remainder of the money would be available. OWEN did not take the money and explained that he would not be able to deliver the horse that night because of a prior commitment that he had in Oxnard. He left the man, giving him his business card, which had his home address and an unlisted telephone number and requested that JOE call him if he was interested in the horse. OWEN then proceeded to Oxnard on business and returned to Los Angeles the morning of June 5, 1968.

OWEN said he went to the Coliseum Hotel to see a man, BERT, who owns the restaurant and bar in the hotel. He had, at this time, three ponies in his trailer, which he had obtained in Oxnard. While in the restaurant he learned of the KENNEDY shooting hearing it on television. Someone gave him a copy of the "Hollywood Citizen News," which contained a picture of SIRHAN B. SIRHAN, which he noted looked like the man he knew as JOE. He discussed this with BERT and other of his friends in the restaurant and they suggested that he go to the Los Angeles Police Department, University Station, which was nearby and tell them what had occurred. At first he said that he did not want to do this, but they convinced him that as a good citizen this would be the thing to do. That same day, he went to the Police Department and gave them the same story that he was now relating. He said that he was at the station from about 2:00 p.m. to 7:00 p.m.

On June 6, 1968, several phone calls were received at his residence which were answered by his wife and daughter and on each occasion, the person calling hung up without saying anything. When the phone rang again, OWEN said he answered it and the caller said "Keep your mother blankety blank mouth shut about the horse deal." He believes the caller was a man but his voice was not familiar.

On June 18 or 19, 1968, OWEN received a call from the Los Angeles Police Department requesting that he come downtown to the Detective Bureau on the third floor between 1:30 and 2:30. He took another man named PERKINS with him. When he arrived, the officer on duty asked him to wait, saying that the officer who wanted to interview him was going to be a little bit late. OWEN explained to them that he was on his way to Phoenix and desired to proceed with the interview if possible. After a few minutes wait, the interview proceeded. He said he was handed a number of pictures and asked to pick out the picture of the man who looked like the one who had ridden with him in the truck. He said that after looking through the pictures, he picked out one stating that this man looked similar to the man whom he had given a ride. He recalls that PERKINS asked the officer if the picture was SIRHAN B. SIRHAN and the officer said that he could not answer this question. At the time of this interview, he told the officer that he had received a threatening call and that he would be staying in Phoenix for approximately one week.

On June 22, 1968, OWEN said that he received another call with the caller again using profanities, stating something to the effect "Keep your mother blankedy blank mouth shut or your family may be hurt." OWEN stated that no further calls or threats have been received.

UNITED STATES DEPARTMENT OF JUSTICE
FEDERAL BUREAU OF INVESTIGATION
WASHINGTON 25, D.C.

7-12-68 256 JTN

edgar hoover

DIRECTOR

The following FBI record,   NUMBER 4 261 906   is furnished FOR OFFICIAL USE ONLY

CONTRIBUTION OF FINGERPRINTS	NAME AND NUMBER	ARRESTED OR RECEIVED	CHARGE	DISPOSITION
PD, Long Beach Calif.	Oliver Jerry Owen #9303	3-28-30	investigation Robbery	Released 3-28-30
PD, Portland Oreg.	Oliver Brindley Owen, #22115	2-17-	Dis. Condt.	Hold for Fed. Auth. 2-18-45, $50 fine and 30 days.
SO Santa Ana Calif.	Oliver Brindley Owen #97548	2-19-63	fug Arson & Conspiracy warr BRN 23790	holding for Costa Mesa PD
PD, Tucson Ariz.	Oliver Brindley Owen #31521-M-187727	3-22-63	Warr #23790-Arson in the first deg with intent to defraud Insurer and Conspiracy	
SO Tucson Ariz.	Oliver B. Owen #18701-M	3-22-63	arson	

Civil print from Calif St Bu #S-31697 was identified with this record and returned to contributor 9-24-59.

Civil print from St Athletic Comm Sacramento Calif #17724 was identified with this record and returned to contributor 8-27-62.

DEPARTMENT CORRESPONDENCE

December 31, 1968

TO: Captain Hugh I. Brown
Commander, Homicide Division

FROM: Lieutenant E. Hernandez
S.U.S. Homicide

SUBJECT: Polygraph Examination of Jerry Owen

POLYGRAPH EXAMINATION

Jerry Owen was administered a polygraph examination in the polygraph facilities of the San Francisco Police Department on July 3, 1968. The examiner was Lt. E. Hernandez who utilized a three-channel Stoelting instrumentation.

The purpose of the examination was to determine if Owen was being truthful when he stated that he had picked up Sirhan and an unknown male companion in the downtown area of Los Angeles on Monday, June 3, 1968. Owen stated that he had picked up Sirhan and his companion at 7th and Grand Streets and then drove them to different locations in the Hollywood area.

Owen was advised that the purpose of the examination was to determine whether he honestly believed that he had ever seen or talked with Sirhan Sirhan in person. He was given the opportunity to discuss the matter regarding the polygraph examination with his attorney, George Davis, and to ask questions concerning the testing techniques and the procedures to be followed during the course of the examination. The instrument and its functions were explained to Owen in detail.

During the course of the control test which had been administered to determine whether Owen was a suitable subject capable of being examined instrumentally, the examiner encountered some difficulty. Owen was resisting and being uncooperative. Instead of answering questions with one word, either yes or no as instructed, he was qualifying every answer in narrative form. Owen explained that he had asked the Bible to deliver him from deceitful lips, and he had to explain his answers in detail because he had to give an account to God.

Upon conclusion of the control test, it was determined that although Owen, who is a highly emotional individual, was being uncooperative, he was emitting physiological tracings capable of evaluation.

Owen was asked a total of 25 questions of which 9 were key questions relative to the issues under investigation. His responses to the following relevant questions strongly indicated that Owen was answering untruthfully.

Q. Is everything that you have told me this morning about that hitchhiker true?
A. Yes.
Q. Do you honestly believe that you have talked to the man that is accused of shooting Kennedy?
A. Yes.
Q. When you told George Davis that you had talked to the man that shot Kennedy, were you telling him the truth?
A. Yes.
Q. Did the man that shot Kennedy offer to buy your horse at any time?
A. Yes.

These deceptive responses were also found in his answers to the following questions that had no bearing on the issue under investigation:

Q. Between the ages of 50 and 54, do you remember telling a lie to anyone?
A. No.
Q. During the last three years of your life, do you remember lying to a police officer about something serious?
A. No.
Q. Are you a married man?
A. Yes.

Based on the physiological tracings and his responses at points where crucial questions were asked, it is my opinion that Jerry Owen was being untruthful during the course of the examination. In my opinion he cannot honestly say that he picked up, talked to or saw Sirhan Sirhan on June 3, 1968. Mr. Owen was informed of the results of the examination, and he proceeded to expound in lengthy dissertation saying in essence that maybe he had picked up someone else. He said, "I don't know; I don't know; it may not have been him, but if I had saw him face to face or heard his voice or something, then I would. I'd come out and make a definite statement. I don't know." He said that he had only mentioned that the person to whom he had given a ride looked like the picture of the man he had seen on television and accused of shooting Senator Kennedy. Owen was again informed that due to his responses, it was the opinion of the examiner that he was being untruthful, even to the point that his statements regarding threatening phone calls were contradictory.

The examination was concluded at 3:15 p.m. Subsequent to this exam, George Davis was informed of the results of the test in the presence of Owen.

JERRY OWEN INVESTIGATION

Oliver Brindley Owen, aka Jerry Owen, was an ex-prize fighter turned minister who became involved in an intricate and contradictory series of events which allegedly involved Sirhan and Jerry Owen and the attempted purchase of a horse by Sirhan. The falsehood of Owen's allegation was clearly established through a separate and independent investigation.

Essentially Owen claimed that on Monday, June 3, 1968, at approximately 3:00 p.m., he picked up two hitchhikers in downtown Los Angeles and gave them a ride to the Hollywood-Wilshire area. Owen identified one of the hitchhikers as Sirhan who rode in the cab of his truck during part of the ride. Sirhan allegedly offered to buy a horse from Owen, who had a palomino for sale. The purchase was to be made at 11:00 p.m. that night at a location in Hollywood. Owen and Sirhan then allegedly met at this location at 11:00 p.m., and Sirhan asked Owen if he could wait until the next day when he would have the necessary money. Owen registered at a local hotel for the night.

The next morning, June 4, he was met by a man in a flashy suit and a blond girl who told him that Sirhan did not have the money for the horse but that he wanted Owen to meet him again at 11:00 p.m. that night. The man offered to give him some money as part payment on the horse. The man also told Owen that there was something happening at the Ambassador Hotel that night and that Sirhan would not have the money until then. Owen told the man that he could not meet Sirhan because of an appointment in Oxnard. Owen gave the man a business card and offered to bring the horse to Los Angeles the next day.

Owen allegedly went to Oxnard, California, and remained there the night of June 4. He returned to Los Angeles at approximately 12:30 p.m. on the 5th and learned of the assassination. After allegedly recognizing a picture of Sirhan in a newspaper, he went to University Station where he made his statement to the Department.

During the ensuing months, investigators sought to conclusively

establish the truth regarding Owen's allegation. On the surface his statements were not self-incriminating, and Owen presented himself as a
volunteer witness who was interested in assisting the police. Essentially
investigators needed only to establish the falsity of Owen's statements
to refute his allegation or to verify the truth of his statements and use
Owen as a material witness. All evidence seemed to indicate that Sirhan
was not with Owen on the 3rd. It was necessary, however, for investigators to determine Owen's reasons for fabricating the incident or whether
he was honestly mistaken.

A complication developed early in the investigation when Jerry
Owen became wary about the investigation of his allegation. Owen
allegedly received a threatening phone call on June 6, 1968, telling him
to remain quiet regarding his horse deal with Sirhan. Owen moved to
the San Francisco area where he remained for several months. During
that time his allegation became publicized and Owen engaged an attorney, George T. Davis, to represent him.

A polygraph examination was arranged for Owen on July 3, 1968,
at the San Francisco Police Department. His attorney, Davis, was
present during the test. Owen's responses to key questions indicated that
he was being untruthful. When told of the results of the test, Owen
made a lengthy statement which indicated that he was unsure of his
original statement.

Investigators subsequently interviewed Mrs. Mary Sirhan and Adel
Sirhan, who attempted to assist investigators in determining the truth
of Owen's allegations. After a visit to Sirhan at the Hall of Justice, Mrs.
Sirhan told investigators that Sirhan had denied knowing anything about
Jerry Owen or the purchase of a horse.

At this point in the investigation, there had been three separate
accounts of the occurrence given by Owen. The number of inconsistencies which appeared between the accounts and the results of the polygraph, coupled with Sirhan's denial of knowing Owen, led investigators
to the conclusion that Owen was lying. It remained for investigators to
determine why and to firmly refute Owen's statements with factual information and physical evidence.

In early August 1968, Jonn G. Christian, a magazine writer, and
William Turner, an ex-F.B.I. agent turned free lance writer, entered
into the Owen investigation. Christian contacted this Department offering
his assistance, and he suggested that he would like to be deputized to
work with the Department. Christian had a taped account of Owen's
story. He told investigators that he believed Sirhan and Owen were

together on June 4 and that they conspired to assassinate Kennedy. Christian further alleged that Owen was involved in Sirhan's escape plans and after the aborted escape, Owen was trying to establish an alibi with his horse-selling story.

Christian subsequently wrote a letter to this Department which outlined his reasons for believing that Owen was involved in the assassination. Christian, by enumerating various conflicts in Owen's accounts of the incident, hypothesized that Owen's reasons for lying were that he was involved in the conspiracy and seeking a means to avoid association with Sirhan. Christian subsequently sought to establish a link in Owen's background with Dr. Carl MacIntyre, a minister whose name had been linked through the Garrison investigation with the assassination of President John F. Kennedy.

Investigators, attacking the inconsistencies in Owen's accounts, also concluded that he was lying; however, there was no evidence to indicate that Owen was involved with an extremist group or with Sirhan. The following is an account of the investigation into the allegation of Jerry Owen.

INITIAL STATEMENT OF JERRY OWEN

Jerry Owen went to University Station on June 5, 1968, at approximately 3:00 p.m. He gave the following account regarding a contact that he believed that he had had with Sirhan Sirhan: On June 3, 1968, Owen left his residence in Santa Ana en route to the Coliseum Hotel, 457 West Santa Barbara, Los Angeles. He spoke with the manager of the hotel coffee shop, John Bert Morris, and Rip O'Reilly, a heavyweight boxer. Morris and Owen discussed the purchase of some boxing equipment from the United Sporting Goods Store, 901 South Hill Street, Los Angeles. At approximately 3:00 p.m. Owen purchased one pair of boxing shoes at United Sporting Goods and proceeded to Lester's Shoe Repair, 1263 North Vine Street, to have green shamrocks monogrammed on the shoes.

En route to Hollywood, while stopped at a traffic light at 7th and Grand Streets, two males requested a ride. The two men jumped into the rear of his truck with Owen's permission. Both men were described as Mexican or Latin, in their early twenties, with long hair and wearing old clothing. One hitchhiker was tall and slim and the other three or four inches shorter. At Wilshire and Western the taller man alighted from Owen's truck and greeted four other young adults standing on the corner. One of them was a male in his thirties with a large build wearing a flashy suit; a female Caucasian with dirty blond hair and two other young males were with the older man. The shorter hitchhiker whom Owen subsequently identified as Sirhan asked if he could sit in the cab of the truck.

After moving into the cab, the man asked Owen if he would stop for a few minutes at the "big hotel" while he visited a friend who worked in the kitchen. The hotel was later identified as the Ambassador Hotel. The man returned to Owen's truck ten minutes later and asked if Owen would take him to Hollywood. En route they had a conversation, and the man told Owen that he was an exercise boy at the racetrack. After Owen told him that he had a palomino horse which he was to sell for $250 in Oxnard, the man expressed a desire to buy the horse after receiving some money later that evening. Owen agreed to meet him that night at 11:00 p.m. near a bowling alley on Sunset Boulevard.

The young man remained in Owen's truck while he delivered the shoes to be monogrammed. Owen recalled that the young man also discussed nationalities, and he said that he had been raised in Jordan. He also expressed his opposition to Jews.

At 11:00 p.m. Owen went to the bowling alley and found the young man with the blond female and the well-dressed male he had seen at Wilshire and Western that afternoon. They had a 1957, 1958 or 1959 off-white, hard top Chevrolet. The young man displayed a $100 bill and told Owen he could not pay for the horse at that time. He asked Owen to meet him the next morning, and he mentioned that something was happening at the hotel. Because the deal appeared certain to Owen, he registered at the St. Moritz Hotel, 5849 Sunset Boulevard for the night.

At 8:00 a.m. on the 4th, Owen received a phone call from a man who said he was calling for Joe Sahara. He then went to the parking lot of the St. Moritz Hotel where he was met by the blond woman and the man who was wearing the flashy suit. The man told Owen that the young man could not get the money until that night, and they asked Owen if he could get the young man a job at a ranch. Owen gave them a business card and told them he would be back in Los Angeles the next day. Owen then went to Oxnard where he remained until 12:30 p.m. on the 5th.

When Owen returned to the Coliseum Hotel on June 5 at 3:00 p.m., he recognized a picture of Sirhan in the Hollywood Citizen News as being the young man who offered to purchase the horse from him. He related the incident to a waitress at the hotel coffee shop who suggested that he report it to the police. Owen then went to University Station. Owen subsequently told investigators that he believed that Sirhan was planning to use his truck to escape from the assassination.

INVESTIGATION OF OWEN'S STATEMENT

Owen was reinterviewed on June 18 at Parker Center and added some details to his original account. He said that Sirhan spoke with a slight Mexican accent and that he mentioned that he might sell his home and go to the Holy Land. He told investigators of a telephone conversation which he received approximately a week before. The person sounded like a male Negro and he stated to Owen, "You mother fucker, forget about the horse deal and keep your mouth closed." At this point in the investigation, it was assumed that Owen was being truthful; however, the investigation into the details of Owen's statements had not been completed.

On June 27, Owen was contacted at his home to set up an interview. Owen refused, stating that he was going to San Francisco. When the investigators suggested a meeting in Palo Alto, Owen said, "No," but suggested that they meet at the residence of Owen's brother in San Bruno. On June 29 the scheduled interview was canceled by the Department when investigators decided to wait for Owen to return to Los Angeles. Owen was not told of this decision, and he erroneously became fearful that his life was in danger. Owen's attorney, Davis, reported that Owen had been contacted by someone alleging that he was a Los Angeles policeman.

On July 1, 1968, San Francisco area papers printed an account of Owen's story about Sirhan. The articles reported that Owen was in hiding in the Napa Valley area in fear for his life. George Davis was quoted as saying that he believed that Owen was telling the truth and that he was reliable. Davis further stated that this Department had refused protection for Owen and that he would ask Attorney General Thomas Lynch for a 24-hour guard. Davis gave an account of Owen's allegation.

The article was in many ways the same as Owen's original account, with some notable contradictions and discrepancies. In his first account Owen said that the price to be paid for the horse was $250; in the newspaper account it was $300. Davis also stated that Owen first saw Sirhan's picture on television; contrary to that Owen had said that he had first seen Sirhan's picture in a newspaper. Owen told investigators that he had met one man and a blond woman at 8:00 a.m. on the 4th, but the article said that there were two men and a woman.

On July 2, 1968, Wesley Gardner, owner of the Foremost Protective Agency, notified investigators that he was representing Owen and that future calls to Owen should be channeled through Gardner.

POLYGRAPH EXAMINATION OF OWEN

Owen and Davis were contacted and the canceled interview in San Bruno was explained to their satisfaction. Due to the confusion which was developing in the Owen investigation, investigators arranged for a polygraph to be given by Lt. Hernandez to Jerry Owen at the San Francisco Police Department on July 3, 1968. George Davis was present during the examination, and Owen was explained the purpose of the test and given the opportunity to ask questions concerning the test. Owen resisted the control test; however, his responses indicated that he was a suitable subject for testing.

Owen was asked a total of 25 questions of which 9 were key questions. In response to the following relevant questions, Owen emitted answers which strongly indicated that he was being untruthful.

Q. Is everything that you told me this morning about the hitchhiker true?
A. Yes.
Q. Do you honestly believe that you have talked to the man that is accused of shooting Kennedy?
A. Yes.
Q. When you told George Davis that you had talked to the man that shot Kennedy, were you telling him the truth?
A. Yes.
Q. Did the man who shot Kennedy offer to buy your horse at any time?
A. Yes.

It was the examiner's opinion that Owen could not honestly say that he picked up, talked to or saw Sirhan on June 3, 1968. When informed of the results of the test, he made lengthy rationalizations about the occurrence. At one point he said, "I don't know; I don't know; it may not have been him, but if I had saw him face to face or heard his voice or something, then I would. I'd come out and make a definite statement. I don't know." He said that he had only mentioned that the person to whom he had given a ride looked like the picture of the man he had seen on television and accused of shooting Kennedy.

INVESTIGATION INTO DISCREPANCIES

On July 2, 1968, Mrs. Mary Sirhan was interviewed regarding the money which Sirhan received from the insurance settlement for the fall from the horse. She recalled that Sirhan asked for $300 a day or two before the shooting. She said that she believed that Sirhan had spent most of the remainder from the $1,000 he gave her from the insurance settlement. She thought that he had given some of the money to Adel. Adel Sirhan was present during the interview, and he stated at one point, "I think Sirhan wanted the $300 to buy a horse with." This was the only statement made by either Munir or Adel Sirhan regarding the money Sirhan received from the settlement

On July 5, Mrs. Sirhan was again interviewed, this time regarding Sirhan's activities on June 3, 1968. She stated that Sirhan had driven her to work at 8:00 a.m. but that he was not at home at 1:30 p.m. when she returned. However, there was evidence that he had just taken a shower and there was a warm cup on the kitchen table. Sirhan was gone most of the afternoon, but she noticed that he was watching television at 4:30 p.m. She was certain that he remained home the rest of that night. This information conflicted with Owen's allegation. At least from the time of 4:30 p.m., Mrs. Sirhan's statement contradicts Owen's statement. This would include the conversations at the Sunset Boulevard bowling alley at 4:30 p.m. and 11:00 p.m. and casts additional doubt on the events which preceded 4:30 p.m.

Mrs. Sirhan agreed to speak to Sirhan at the Hall of Justice regarding the Owen allegation. On July 15, after she had spoken to Sirhan, Mrs. Sirhan related his response. Sirhan told her that he did not know Owen, had never seen him nor had he ever ridden in his pickup truck. He also denied that he had attempted to purchase a palomino horse.

The denial by Sirhan, the statements of Mrs. Sirhan and the results of the Owen polygraph caused investigators to conclude that Owen had lied about the incident. Owen's reasons for lying could not be completely determined; however, an intensive examination of Owen's background revealed a history of involvement in questionable and illegal activities. This information tended to cast doubt on Owen's credibility.

Owen's third account of the incident, given when he was administered the polygraph, was compared with the other two accounts. Further discrepancies were noted, some of which indicated that Owen was adding details which he should have given in his first account. In addition he left out details which were in the original account.

He stated that he had purchased a robe and a pair of boxing shoes at United Sporting Goods; this was opposed to his first statement wherein he said he had purchased only a pair of boxing shoes. He also related that during the evening hours between the time he allegedly dropped off Sirhan around 6:00 p.m. and the time he met him again at 11:00 p.m., Owen stated that he had gone to the Plaza Hotel to see a friend, the ex-fighter Slapsy Maxie Rosenbloom. They then went to a Saints and Sinners meeting. This incident did not appear in Owen's first account at University Station. Further, Owen did not mention the stop at the Coliseum Hotel and Teamsters Gymnasium; instead, he said that he went directly from Santa Ana to the United Sporting Goods Store.

When shown a set of mugs, Owen could not identify Sirhan, and he chose a look-alike as the other man who rode in his truck. In addition, Owen changed the time and date on which he received the threatening phone call. The newspaper account had stated that he had received the call the evening of the 5th. During the July 3, 1968, interview Owen said that the call came between 2:00 and 5:00 p.m. on June 6.

Investigation into the alleged activities of Owen on June 3 revealed additional discrepancies in his story. Investigators determined that sales records at the United Sporting Goods Store showed no sale of a boxing robe on June 3. A pair of boxing shoes were sold on that date but not to Owen. The manager of the store, Jack Misrach, stated that he knew most of the boxing people in this area. He does not know Owen or Rip O'Reilly, the boxer. After looking at Owen's picture, Misrach did not recall seeing Owen in his store. Jesse Edwards, the salesman who sold the shoes on that date, thought Owen looked familiar but could not recall the transaction. The transaction for the shoes included several other items including gloves, headgear, shorts, jump rope and other items totaling $39.45.

Lester's Shoe Repair at 1263 North Vine Street was checked to verify Owen's statement that he had taken the shoes for monogramming. Lester Shields, the owner, stated that he had no record of when Owen brought the shoes for monogramming. Shields remembered that Owen came to his shop three times; one time that he remembered seeing Owen's truck, there was no one in it. When he picked up the shoes, two young women were with him and Rip O'Reilly was in the truck.

Dianne Scott, owner of the seamstress shop adjacent to the shoe repair shop, stated that she recalled that Owen brought a robe to be monogrammed on June 10, 1968, not June 3. He picked up the robe on June 26.

Shields estimated the dates of Owen's appearances at his shoe shop as:

Originally brought shoes into the shop	May 23–27, 1968
Picked shoes up the first time	May 25–28, 1968
Brought shoes in second time	May 27–29, 1968
Picked up shoes the final time	June 8, 1968

Investigators interviewed the persons whom Owen stated that he told of the incident who were at the Coliseum Hotel on June 5. Owen allegedly told them of the hitchhiker incident and one of them, Mabel Jacobs, a waitress, told him to tell the police.

Jacobs stated that she spoke to Owen who was in the Coliseum Hotel Coffee Shop with Rip O'Reilly on June 5. Owen pointed to a picture of Sirhan in the newspapers and told her that he was the hitchhiker that he had picked up on June 3. Owen told her that he had taken Sirhan to the Ambassador Hotel and that Sirhan expressed a desire to purchase a horse he was transporting to Oxnard. Bert Morris, the owner, stated that he was not present during Owen's relating of the incident to Jacobs. He did recall that Owen was in the coffee shop on June 5.

Rip O'Reilly, a professional boxer under contract to Owen, was interviewed. He stated that he lives at the Coliseum Hotel and that Owen came there on June 5 to see him. Owen related the incident of the hitchhiker and told him that he believed that the young man resembled Sirhan. O'Reilly, however, provided investigators with information which strongly contradicted Owen's account.

O'Reilly stated that on June 3, 1968, Owen called him at about 10:30 a.m. and invited him to attend a Saints and Sinners Club that night. At 6:30 p.m. Owen picked O'Reilly up at the Coliseum Hotel, and they drove to the meeting on Fairfax Avenue. Owen was driving a dark-colored pickup truck with a horse trailer attached. A horse was in the trailer. They remained at the meeting until 11:30 p.m., and Owen took O'Reilly back to the hotel.

On June 5, Owen came to the hotel and related to O'Reilly that he had picked up a hitchhiker on Wilshire Boulevard on June 3 and that the hitchhiker offered him $400 for his horse. Owen said that he stayed at a hotel the night of the 3rd to complete the transaction the next day. Owen told O'Reilly that he believed that Sirhan was a Mexican. O'Reilly further advised investigators that Owen had purchased the boxing shoes mentioned by Owen prior to June 3, 1968.

Investigators had established sufficient contradiction in Owen's story that they were convinced that he was lying. Owen's uncertainty at the conclusion of his polygraph in San Francisco tended to substantiate that conclusion. The only remaining aspect of the investigation was to establish Owen's reason for fabricating the story.

OWEN'S BACKGROUND

Owen was born on April 13, 1913, in Ashland, Ohio. He attended the University of Southern California where he played varsity football.

For many years he was a sparring partner for ex-heavyweight boxing champion, Max Baer.

Owen had claimed that he had been an ordained minister since 1937 and that he held a credential with the Charles M. Holder Ministry, Inc. on Colton Street in Los Angeles. During his July 3 interview in San Francisco, Owen admitted that he had not been legally ordained. He stated that he had gone into a hotel room for several days during which time he prayed. This constituted his ordainment.

Owen was arrested on suspicion of robbery in 1930 by the Long Beach Police Department but was released the same day. Over the years Owen has been involved in various suspicious and illegal activities. An analysis of the total record of Owen's police record and investigations into his activities reveal that he has been involved in several fire insurance claims involving his personal and church properties, and he has several times been involved in extra-marital and paternity investigations. His religious activities are of the rural evangelistic type with makeshift facilities. Owen has advertised himself as "The Walking Bible" and cites Ripley's "Believe it or Not" as proof that he has complete recall of the Bible. His method is that of a huckster, calling for the believing to listen to his message. Several of those interviewed likened his approach to that of a "confidence man."

His record would tend to support that description. Owen has been involved in six fires beginning in 1939 in Castro Valley, California. On several occasions he collected insurance settlements from these fires. The cases occurred in: (1) Castro Valley, 1939; (2) Crystal Lake Park, Oregon, 1945; (3) Dallas, Texas, 1946; (4) Mount Washington, Kentucy, 1947; (5) Ellicott City, Maryland, 1951; and (6) Tucson, Arizona, 1962.

Owen's $16,000 claim for the fire in Maryland was denied because of fraud. A witness observed Owen moving personal effects out of the house prior to the fire and then return them. Owen subsequently collected $6,500 when the denial was appealed.

In 1963, Owen was arrested in Costa Mesa, California, on a fugitive warrant from Tucson, Arizona, for arson with the intent to defraud an insurance company. A church, Our Little Chapel, which was owned by Owen was destroyed by fire on July 31, 1962, in Tucson. The investigation by the Tucson Police Department revealed that arson was the suspected cause of the fire. Owen was subsequently convicted of three counts of arson and sentenced to serve 8-10 years in prison. The decision was appealed and reversed on June 27, 1966.

In addition to fire claims, Owen has been involved in sex offenses over the years. In 1943, Jacqueline Banks, 16 years of age, joined Owen's gospel camp in Milwaukee, Oregon. She had met Owen when he had his "Open Door Church" in her home town of Des Moines, Iowa. Just prior to Owen obtaining a divorce from his wife in 1947, Banks became pregnant and returned to her home in Des Moines. Owen gave Banks $65 and told her that he would come to Des Moines and marry her. The child was born in November, 1947, and Owen forwarded $420 for hospital expenses. Banks later received word that Owen had gotten drunk, married a prostitute and that he would not be able to marry her. Banks had traveled off and on with Owen's touring churches for approximately seven years. (Owen stated during his polygraph that he had had a paternity suit filed against him at one time.)

On February 17, 1945, Owen was arrested for disorderly conduct in Portland, Oregon. He was found in a motel room with a female, Francis McCarty, both were nude. Owen was fined $50 and given thirty (30) days in jail; however, Owen posted an appeal bond of $250, and the case was continued indefinitely. Intelligence Division reports of Owen's activities reveal that he was reported to have been involved with women a number of times during his evangelistic tours.

Owen's highly suspicious background caused investigators to speculate that he sought to use the story about Sirhan to bring attention upon himself. His involvement in the activities described above were questionable grounds for giving credence to his ministerial goodness, and his suspicious record indicated that he was capable of concocting a story as devious as his alleged encounter with Sirhan. Investigators further speculated that Owen probably did pick up a hitchhiker in the downtown area, though not necessarily on June 3, 1968. Owen then combined a series of events which had occurred on various dates and developed his story. The small discrepancies in his stories would account for some vague familiarity that Owen had with each incident but that he would forget minor details from telling to telling.

INVOLVEMENT OF JONN G. CHRISTIAN

Three telephone calls were received by investigators from Jonn Christian, a magazine writer, one each on August 7, 9 and 11, 1968. Christian indicated that he had a tape of Jerry Owen's account and that he wished to assist the Department in its investigation. He went so far as to suggest that he and an associate, William Turner, be "deputized." Christian sought to listen to the Los Angeles Police Department tape of

Owen's account so that he could note discrepancies. It was Christian's opinion that Owen and Sirhan were together on June 4, 1968, and that Owen was to assist Sirhan with his escape. Because Sirhan had been captured, Christian believed that Owen has concocted his story to establish an innocuous reason for being with Sirhan.

Investigators sought then to establish the validity of Christian's allegation. It was believed that Owen was not involved with Sirhan in a conspiracy or that he had ever seen him. However, Christian's claim had to be disproven completely. Christian himself carried his claim to various governmental bodies to plead for their aid in investigating his allegation. His actions caused investigators deep concern as each time they would feel that the Christian claim had been satisfactorily explained to other interested parties, Christian would successfully enlist the support of another agency.

Christian mailed two extensive confidential letters to the Department outlining his "original, unique and confidential information" regarding the assassination. The material represented Christian's theory regarding the discrepancies in Owen's story. Christian also attempted to establish a link between Owen and Dr. Carl MacIntyre, the minister reportedly connected by New Orleans District Attorney James Garrison with the John F. Kennedy assassination.

Investigators were able to establish that Christian had been contacted by George Davis, Owen's attorney, who told Christian, "I think I'm broken in on the Senator Kennedy conspiracy." Davis asked Christian to handle his press releases.

William Turner, Christian's partner and an ex-F.B.I. agent turned free lance writer, had been previously associated with Davis. Turner had lost a campaign for public office in the June primaries, and Davis had been his campaign manager. In addition, Turner had been associated with the radical publication "Ramparts" and has written a book entitled "The Police Establishment."

It is anticipated that Jonn Christian and William Turner will publish or somehow publicly reveal their theory regarding Jerry Owen and Sirhan. They have consistently attempted to attach credence to their claim by enlisting the support of high ranking government officials for their claim. They will also likely as not show up in conjunction with any attempt to link the two Kennedy assassinations, an event which will definitely occur in one form or another.

On two occasions Christian admitted to investigators that his opinions regarding Owen and Sirhan were only theories. He further admitted that he was investigating the possibility of a conspiracy as a writer and that if a conspiracy did not exist between Sirhan and Owen, he did not have a story.

This investigation has gathered such information as to indicate that Jerry Owen did not know or even meet Sirhan. The remaining pieces to be inserted into the investigation are those which could not physically be obtained. This includes a direct meeting between Sirhan and Owen. Owen himself, on the advice of his attorney, has been reluctant to continue assisting investigators.

EACH SUPERVISOR

July 29, 1975

On July 16th and 18th I wrote memos to Presiding Judge Wenke, advising him that it was my intention to renew my request to the Board of Supervisors that it develop a positive position favoring refiring tests of the Sirhan gun.

I also remarked that any reexamination of the case should deal with the initial proposal by Dr. Noguchi that there be a neutron activation analysis of all of the bullets now in evidence, and that a new spectrograph analysis be taken of these same bullets or numbered fragments, as LAPD ballistics expert De Wayne Wolfer had done in preparation for the trial.

Further, I believe that a comparison microscopic examination should be made of these same materials, which is the process viewed most favorably by law enforcement.

In addition to the continuing obligation of County government to inspect its processes, there is the challenge from one of the nation's most important scientific groups, the American Academy of Forensic Sciences, that government preside over, or at least permit, a re-study of the ballistics evidence. Also, there is the current sidelight to the basic case—the testimony developing during the course of a trial, Reverend Owen vs. KCOP, now being held in Department 32 of the Superior Court. Owen told me over a year ago that he planned to bring the suit, and now it finally is in court, with its direct references to the assassination.

It was Jerry Owen who startled law enforcement authorities the day after the shooting of Senator Kennedy by appearing at a local police station to announce that he had picked up Sirhan the day before the assassination and during the course of a conversation had agreed to sell to Sirhan a horse, which was to be delivered in a trailer to a point outside the kitchen of the Ambassador Hotel at around eleven o'clock the night Senator Kennedy was shot. Owen later was discredited by LAPD and District Attorney authorities, who complained he could not either pass a lie detector test or identify Sirhan by photographs.

In the summer of 1971 as a broadcaster, I attempted unsuccessfully to contact Owen for an interview. In the spring of 1972, while I was campaigning for political office, Jerry Owen left word at my campaign headquarters that he would like to see me the following day. The call was placed only hours after Governor Wallace had been shot. Owen did not keep the appointment the following day.

A short time after the hearing I conducted last May into the Senator Kennedy ballistics evidence, Jerry Owen called again, saying he would like to see me to disclose the full story behind the conspiracy.

He came the following day, and I obtained his permission to tape record his conversation. In my opinion, he provided no information beyond what he had stated in 1968 to the authorities and to the press. However, there was one addition: when I questioned him as to why he did not keep our appointment the day after Governor Wallace had been shot, Owen volunteered that he was personal friends with the sister of Arthur Bremmer (who had shot Governor Wallace). Owen stated that Gale Bremmer was employed by his brother here in Los Angeles for several years and had then just left Los Angeles for Florida because she was continually harrassed by the FBI.

It would be unwise to attempt to read any significance into these associations, but I must advise you now that they and other disclosures are being made during the course of the Owen/KCOP trial.

For example, during the course of a series of broadcasts in 1971, I made reference on the air to a young man who had filed a report with the Sheriff's Department in 1968 asserting that he had information about the Sirhan case. While the information was only hearsay, I was impressed that a day or so after I mentioned that Sheriff's report on the air, the young man's automobile was shot at as he returned to his home in Chino. I reported the incident the following day to the Federal authorities.

This young man's information centered on allegations that Sirhan and Jerry Owen were acquaintances well in advance of the time admitted by Owen in his June, 1968 statements to authorities.

Here again it would be improper to conclude that Jerry Owen was in any way involved in any of the incidents that are being discussed, either before or after the assassination of Senator Kennedy. Indeed, he might be simply a publicity seeker (as has been alleged by law enforcement authorities) or a person who developed associations that might be totally innocent but which troubled him to such a degree that he attempted to explain them away.

However, there is no denying that the trial which he has brought as plaintiff has reintroduced his name into the 1968 controversy.

The longstanding rumors that two key officers (Manuel Pena and Enrique Hernandez) in the LAPD special unit set up to investigate the assassination of Senator Kennedy also had backgrounds that identified them as having had either service or training with elements of the CIA, presumably will be dealt with during the trial.

I do not believe that the Board of Supervisors should attempt to look into most of the aspects in controversy about the Senator Kennedy assassination. The KCOP-TV trial or other formal hearings can bring out the bulk of the points in question.

However, as I stated in my note to Judge Wenke on July 18, the Board does have an interest in the quality of performance by County personnel who were involved in the handling or examination of ballistics materials, etc.

Therefore, I will prepare a motion which I will submit to you for your examination in advance of its presentation, that will call for the reexamination of certain physical elements now at issue in the Senator Kennedy case.

Los Angeles Police Department
EMPLOYEE'S REPORT

SUBJECT
Kennedy - 187 P.C.

DATE & TIME OCCURRED	LOCATION OF OCCURRENCE	DIVISION OF OCCURRENCE
6-5-68	Ambassador Hotel	Rampart Division

TO: (Rank, Name, Assignment, Division)	DATE & TIME REPORTED
Lt. D.W. Mann, O-I-C, Criminalistics Section, S.I.D.	7-8-68

DETAILS:

The weapon used in this case was an Iver Johnson, Cadet Model, .22 caliber, 8 shot revolver (2½" barrel). This weapon had eight expended shell casings in the cylinder at the time of recovery from the suspect. A trajectory study was made of the physical evidence which indicated that eight shots were fired as follows:

#1 - Bullet entered Senator Kennedy's head behind the right ear and was later recovered from the victim's head and booked as evidence.

#2 - Bullet passed through the right shoulder pad of Senator Kennedy's suit coat (never entered his body) and traveled upward striking victim Schrade in the center of his forehead. The bullet was recovered from his head and booked as evidence.

#3 - Bullet entered Senator Kennedy's right rear shoulder approximately seven inches below the top of the shoulder. This bullet was recovered by the Coroner from the 6th cervical vertebrae and booked as evidence.

#4 - Bullet entered Senator Kennedy's right rear back approximately one inch to the right of bullet #3. This bullet traveled upward and forward and exited the victim's body in the right front chest. The bullet passed through the ceiling tile, striking the second plastered ceiling and was lost somewhere in the ceiling interspace.

#5 - Bullet struck victim Goldstein in the left rear buttock. This bullet was recovered from the victim and booked as evidence.

#6 - Bullet passed through victim Goldstein's left pants leg (never entering his body) and struck the cement floor and entered victim Stroll's left leg. The bullet was later recovered and booked as evidence.

#7 - Bullet struck victim Weisel in the left abdomen and was recovered and booked.

#8 - Bullet struck the plaster ceiling and then struck victim Evans in the head. This bullet was recovered from the victim's head and booked as evidence.

A Walker's H-acid test was conducted on Senator Kennedy's suit coat in the area of the entrance wounds. This test indicated that the muzzle of the weapon was held at a distance of between one to six inches from the coat at the time of all firings.

DATE & TIME TYPED	DIVN. RPTG.	CLERK	EMPLOYEE(S) REPORTING	SER. NO.	DIVN.
7-8-68 10 a.m.	S.I.D.	mm	Officer DeWayne A.	#6727	S.I.D.
SUPERVISOR APPROVING		SERIAL NO.	Wolfer		
Lt. D.W. Mann		#2M5			

PROGRESS REPORT - CASE PREP TEAM - CASE PREPARATION FOR TRIAL

TIME OCCURRED 7-5-68/7-18-68	LOCATION OF OCCURRENCE	DIVISION OF OCCURRENCE S.U.S. Homicide
TO: (Rank, Name, Assignment, Division) Lt. M. S. Pena, Supervisor, S.U.S. Unit		DATE & TIME REPORTED 7-18-68 4:30 pm

DETAILS

I. RECONSTRUCTION OF CRIME:

  A. Evidence

Recording - A photograph album containing 8 x 10 photos of
pertinent evidence has been prepared. These photos include
photographs of pertinent autopsy photos (Wounds and angles),
bullets and fragments of money on suspect's person at time of
arrest and ammo boxes. There is also a stand-up color photo of
the suspect at the time of booking and a full face and side
view, black and white, standard mug shot of suspect.

Evaluation - An interview conference was held with DDA Fitts on
7-10-68. At this time DDA Fitts indicated the following items of
evidence would diffently be used at the trial: The gun used by
suspect, the bullets and fragments obtained from victims, the coat
of the late Senator Kennedy and items of evidence removed from
suspect's vehicle. No other items of evidence were discussed at
this meeting.

  B. Lab Work

The Iver Johnson, Cadet Model .22 caliber revolver serial
#H53725, which was taken from Sirhan has been identified as
having fired the following bullets: (1) The bullet from Senator
Kennedy's 6th cervical vertebrae; (2) The bullet removed from
victim Goldstein; (3) The bullet removed from victim Weisel.
The remaining bullets are too badly damaged for comparison
purposes. The following could be determined from the remaining
four damaged bullets. (1) Bullet fragments from Senator Kennedy's
head were fired from a weapon with the same rifling specifications
as the Sirhan weapon and are "minimag" brand ammunition.
(2) Bullet fragments from victim Stroll had the same rifling
specifications as the Sirhan weapon and is "minimag" brand
ammunition. (3) Bullet fragments from victim Evans is "minimag"
brand ammunition. (4) Bullet fragments from victim Schrade is
"minimag" brand ammunition. All eight shots fired at the
Ambassador Hotel have been accounted for and all except one
bullet recovered.

Walker's H-acid tests indicated that the shots entering Senator
Kennedy's suit coat were fired at a muzzle distance of between
one to six inches.

Powder test indicate that the bullet which entered behind Senator
Kennedy's right ear was fired at a muzzle distance of approximately
one inch.

Four hundred-eighty nine (489), .22 caliber shells were examined
and none of the shells were found to have been fired from Sirhan
weapon. These shells had been picked up by Michael Soccoman at
the San Gabriel Valley Gun Club, as he collects brass. He thought
he might have picked up shells that had been fired by Sirhan.

DATE & TIME TYPED 7-18-68 7:30 pm	DIVN. RPTG. SUS Homi.	CLERK bju	EMPLOYEE(S) REPORTING Collins, C.	SER. NO. 6207	DIVN. SUS Homi
SUPERVISOR APPROVING _Spec Exhibit 21_		SERIAL NO.	Patchett, F. Mac Arthur, J.	7872 " 4372 "	" "

AFFIDAVIT

I, WILLIAM W. HARPER, being first duly sworn, depose as follows:

1. I am a resident of the State of California and for approximately thirty-seven years have lived at 615 Prospect Boulevard in Pasadena, California.

2. I am now and for thirty-five years have been engaged in the field of consulting criminalistics.

3. My formal academic background includes studies at Columbia University, University of California at Los Angeles and California Institute of Technology where I spent four years, including studies in physics and mathematics with the major portion devoted to physics research.

4. My practical experience and positions held include seven years as consulting criminalist to the Pasadena Police Department where I was in charge of the Technical Laboratory engaging in the technical phases of police training and all technical field investigations including those involving firearms. I was, during World War II, for three years in charge of technical investigation for Naval Intelligence in the 11th Naval District, located at San Diego, California.

After my release from the Navy, I entered private practice as a consulting criminalist. Extending over a period of 35 years I have handled roughly 300 cases involving firearms in homicides, suicides and accidental shootings. I have testified as a consulting criminalist in both criminal and civil litigations and for both defense and prosecution in both State and Federal Courts. I have qualified as an expert in the courts of California, Washington, Oregon, Texas, Nevada, Arizona and Utah. I am a Fellow of the American Academy of Forensic Sciences.

5. During the past seven months I have made a careful review and study of the physical circumstances of the assassination of Senator Robert F. Kennedy in Los Angeles, California. In this connection I have examined the physical evidence introduced at the trial, including the Sirhan weapon, the bullets and shell cases. I have also studied the autopsy report, the autopsy photographs, and pertinent portions of the trial testimony.

6. Based on my background and training, upon my experience as a consulting criminalist, and my studies, examination and analysis of data related to the Robert F. Kennedy assassination, I have arrived at the following findings and opinions:

A. An analysis of the physical circumstances at the scene of the assassination discloses that Senator Kennedy was fired upon from two distinct firing positions while he was walking through the kitchen pantry at the Ambassador Hotel. *Firing Position A,* the position of Sirhan, was located directly in front of the Senator, with Sirhan face-to-face with the Senator. This position is well established by more than a dozen eyewitnesses. A second firing position, *Firing Position B,* is clearly established by the autopsy report. It was located in close proximity to the Senator, immediately to his right and rear. It was from this position that 4 (four) shots were fired, three of which entered the Senator's body. One of these three shots made a fatal penetration of the Senator's brain. A fourth shot passed through the right shoulder pad of the Senator's coat. These four shots from Firing Position B all produced powder residue patterns, indicating they were fired from a distance of only a few inches. They were closely grouped within a 12 inch circle.

In marked contrast, the shots from *Firing Position A* produced no powder residue patterns on the bodies or clothing of any of the surviving victims, all of whom were walking behind the Senator. These shots were widely dispersed.

Senator Kennedy received no frontal wounds. The three wounds suffered by him were fired from behind and he had entrance wounds in the posterior portions of his body.

B. It is evident that a strong conflict exists between the eyewitness accounts and the autopsy findings. This conflict is totally irreconcilable with the hypothesis that only Sirhan's gun was involved in the assassination. The conflict can be eliminated if we consider that a second gun was being fired from *Firing Position B* concurrently with the firing of the Sirhan gun from *Firing Position A.* It is self-evident that within the brief period of the shooting (roughly 15 seconds) Sirhan could not have been in both firing positions at the same time.

No eyewitness saw Sirhan at any position other than *Firing Position A,* where he was quickly restrained by citizens present at that time and place.

C. It is my opinion that these circumstances, in conjunction with the autopsy report (without for the moment considering additional evidence), firmly establish that two guns were being fired in the kitchen pantry concurrently.

D. There is no reasonable likelihood that the shots from *Firing Position B* could have been fired by a person attempting to stop Sirhan. This is because the person shooting from *Firing Position B* was in almost direct body contact with the Senator. This person could have seen where his shots would strike the Senator, since the fatal shot was fired (muzzle) from one to three inches from the Senator's head. Had Sirhan been the intended target, the person shooting would have extended his arm beyond the Senator and fired directly at Sirhan. Furthermore, two of the shots from *Firing Position B* were steeply upward: one shot actually penetrating the ceiling overhead.

E.   The police appear to have concluded that a total of eight shots were fired with seven bullets accounted for and one bullet unrecovered. This apparent conclusion fails to take into account that their evidence shows that a fourth shot from *Firing Position B* went through the right shoulder pad of the Senator's coat from back to front. This shot was fired from a distance of approximately one inch according to the testimony. It could not have been the shot which struck Victim Paul Schrade in the forehead since Schrade was behind the Senator and traveling in the same direction. The bullet producing this hole in the shoulder pad from back to front could not have returned by ricochet or otherwise to strike Schrade in the forehead. This fourth shot from *Firing Position B* would indicate 9 (nine) shots were fired, with two bullets unrecovered. This indication provides an additional basis for the contention that two guns were involved, since the Sirhan gun could have fired only 8 (eight) shots.

F.   The prosecution testimony attempted to establish that the Sirhan gun, and no other, was involved in the assassination. It is a fact, however, that the only gun actually linked scientifically with the shooting is a second gun, not the Sirhan gun. The serial number of the Sirhan gun is No. H53725. The serial number of the second gun is No. H18602. It is also an Iver Johnson 22 cal. cadet. The expert testimony, based on matching the three test bullets of Exhibit 55 in a comparison microscope to three of the evidence bullets (Exhibit 47 removed from the Senator, Exhibit 52 removed from Goldstein and Exhibit 54 removed from Weisel) concluded that the three evidence bullets were fired from the same gun that fired the three test bullets of Exhibit 55. The physical evidence shows that the gun that fired the three test bullets was gun No. H18602, not the Sirhan gun. Thus, the only gun placed at the scene by scientific evidence is gun No. H18602. Sirhan's gun was taken from him by citizens at the scene. I have no information regarding the background history of gun No. H18602 nor how the police came into possession of it.

G.   No test bullets recovered from the Sirhan gun are in evidence. This gun was never identified scientifically as having fired any of the bullets removed from any of the victims. Other than the apparent self-evident fact that gun No. H53725 was forcibly removed from Sirhan at the scene, it has not been connected by microscopic examinations or other scientific testing to the actual shooting.

H.   The only reasonable conclusion from the evidence developed by the police, in spite of their protestations to the contrary, is that two guns were being fired in the kitchen pantry of the Ambassador Hotel at the time of the shooting of Senator Kennedy.

I. From the general circumstances of the shooting the only reasonable assumption is that the bullet removed from victim Weisel was in fact fired from the Sirhan gun. This bullet is in near perfect condition. I have, therefore, chosen it as a "test" bullet from the Sirhan gun and compared it with the bullet removed from the Senator's neck. The bullet removed from the Senator's neck, Exhibit 47, was one of those fired from *Firing Position B,* while the bullet removed from Weisel, Exhibit 54, was one of those fired from *Firing Position A,* the position of Sirhan. My examinations disclosed no individual characteristics establishing that Exhibit 47 and Exhibit 54 had been fired by the same gun. In fact, my examinations disclosed that bullet Exhibit 47 has a rifling angle approximately 23 minutes (14%) greater than the rifling angle of bullet Exhibit 54. It is, therefore, my opinion that bullets 47 and 54 could not have been fired from the same gun.

The above finding stands as independent proof that two guns were being fired concurrently in the kitchen pantry of the Ambassador Hotel at the time of the shooting.

J. The conclusions I have arrived at based upon my findings are as follows:

1. Two 22 calibre guns were involved in the assassination.

2. Senator Kennedy was killed by one of the shots fired from *Firing Position B,* fired by a second gunman.

3. The five surviving victims were wounded by Sirhan shooting from *Firing Position A.*

4. It is extremely unlikely that any of the bullets fired by the Sirhan gun ever struck the body of Senator Kennedy.

5. It is also unlikely that the shooting of the Senator could have accidentally resulted from an attempt to shoot Sirhan.

Dated: December 28, 1970.
William W. Harper
State of California
County of Los Angeles

On this 28th day of December, 1970, before me appeared, personally, WILLIAM W. HARPER, known to me to be the person whose name is subscribed to the within instrument, and acknowledged that he executed the same.

Notary Public in and for
said County and State

(Seal)

ON OR ABOUT JUNE 5-6, 1968 I, WILLIAM A. Bailey, employed at that time as a special agent of the FBI (Assigned to the Los Angeles office) was present in the preparation room of the Ambassador Hotel approx. 4-6 hours after the attempt on Sen. Robt. F. Kennedy's life. The Pantry was referred to as the preparation Room

At that time I was assigned to interview witnesses present at the time of the shooting. I was also charged with the responsibility of Recreating the circumstances under which same took place. This necessitated a careful examination of the entire room + its contents.

At one point during these observations I (and several other agents) noted at least two (2) small caliber bullet holes in the center post of the two doors leading from the preparation room. There was no question in any of our minds as to the fact that they were bullet holes + were not caused by food carts or other equipment in the preparation Room.

I resigned from the FBI in Jan. 1971 and have been employed as an Assistant Professor of Police science at Gloucester County College, Sewell, New Jersey since that time.

The above statement is in my printing + was furnished freely + voluntarily to Mr. Vincent Bugliosi on Nov. 14, 1976 at Glassboro State College, Glassboro, New Jersey.

William O Bailey
Nov. 14, 1976

The following address was delivered on the night of April 29, 1976, at the Hollywood Palladium by Mr. Robert Vaughn

It is my distinct honor and pleasure to be here tonight, to pay tribute to a man whose election to the office of District Attorney of Los Angeles is more than merely a matter of the right man for that office. It is really an election that could be of the utmost importance to our entire nation—because of the one issue that Vincent Bugliosi, alone, has committed himself to resolve. I speak of the very serious and disturbing questions that have arisen about the death of my good friend, Robert F. Kennedy, whose murder eight years ago in this very city surely changed the course of American history.

For many years I was among those who felt that the questions of conspiracy in either of the Kennedy assassinations came from the minds of the unstable types, who were merely fantasizing when they spoke of mysterious goings on in both these cases. The real truth about myself was, however, that I did not want to believe that these personally painful deaths had been the result of more than single men. However, in mid-1972—in the midst of the many emerging truths about the Watergate affair—my mind and those of a good many other previously disinterested persons were suddenly jolted into the reality that there were things going on within the government of this nation that had no place in a democracy—and the thought of assassination fitting into the mould of these events suddenly was no longer unthinkable. In fact, as the months rolled by and the endless details about Watergate and the "dirty tricks" of the FBI and the CIA began to surface, I became alarmed that such might possibly have been involved in the assassination of the Kennedys, Martin Luther King, and the attempt on the life of Governor George C. Wallace.

I have no doubt that a good many of you here tonight have had this same experience. And I have no doubt at all that the vast majority of our fellow citizens across this country now share this same concern.

At this moment, in the Congress of the United States, there are two legislative measures pending that propose to re-open the investigations into all these cases. These bills are co-sponsored by Republicans and Democrats, Liberals and Conservatives and Independents alike. It is no longer a partisan debate in Washington, D. C. It is serious business by men and women we have elected to represent and protect our interests and rights—the most important of which is the ability for us to freely elect the President of our choice; and the fact of the matter is that since the re-election of Dwight D. Eisenhower in 1956 we have not had a

Presidential election that has not been altered or distorted by the assassination process.

John Kennedy was gunned down in Dallas as he prepared for re-election in 1964—and Robert Kennedy died as he moved into a most viable position in 1968. Then in 1972 Governor George Wallace was felled as he gathered an enormous number of votes—and again, bullets, not ballots, produced a twisted outcome in the Presidential race.

And here we are now in 1976, in the midst of the most turbulent of times for this nation, with no less than eight men running for the office of President. Is there any one amongst us here tonight that has not pondered the thought that maybe—just maybe—another assassination could be upon us at any time?! I think not.

That's why the election of Vincent Bugliosi at this time is an imperative. If there is some kind of sinister force loose in this country that has been systematically cutting down our finest leaders, there is only one man in this country with the proven abilities and courage to seek out the truth and bring about justice; and the Robert Kennedy assassination is where he will begin, the instant he takes the oath of office. He is my good friend, Vince Bugliosi.

Index

ABOUT THE AUTHORS

JONN G. CHRISTIAN, a naval airman during the Korean War, was a broadcast newsman for the American Broadcasting Company until 1966, when he developed an interest in the John F. Kennedy assassination controversy. He soon discovered that the official version (The Warren Commission Report) was untenable and sought out the involvement of high-level political leaders—including Robert F. Kennedy.

WILLIAM W. TURNER, a Navy veteran of World War II, was an FBI special agent from 1951 to 1961 when he turned to journalism. He has written for magazines ranging from *Playboy* to *The Nation* and is the author of *The Police Establishment* and *Hoover's FBI*. He became involved in the assassination investigation of President Kennedy immediately after the shooting when he flew to Dallas on assignment to look into the breakdown in security.

The authors teamed up in early 1968 when Turner ran in a Democratic primary for a U.S. congressional seat on the platform that a joint Senate-House committee should be established to reinvestigate the JFK assassination. His campaign brochure read: "To do less not only is indecent but might cost us the life of a future President of John Kennedy's instincts."